SILICON BURNING

Singularity Rising

Volume 1

To Floz,
Hope this makes for good summer reading! Enjoy the rise of Toko!

Thomas McCaughley

Thomas McCaughley

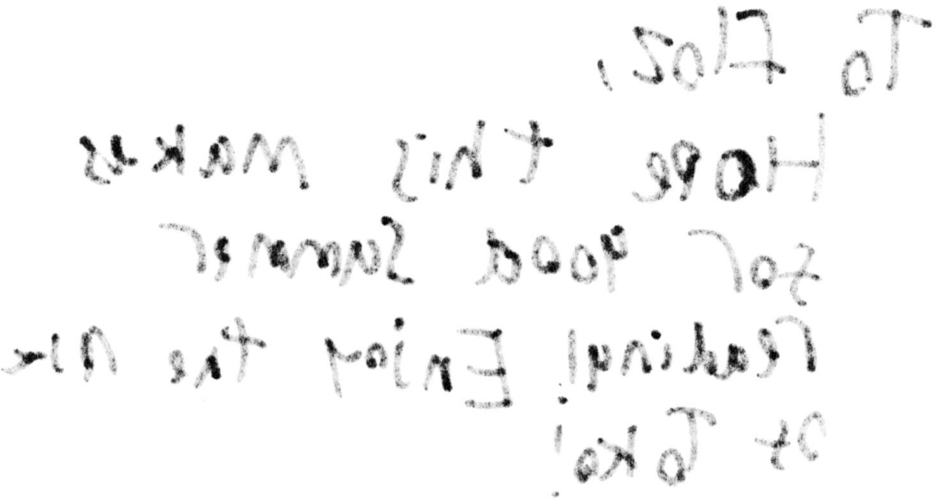

Cover design by Ralph Fajardo

CONTENTS

PROLOGUE

<<8th August 2018>>

<<London Heathrow Terminal 5>>

<<Kenji Awasaki>>

"Oh, come on, Mum, gimme a break!" I pleaded with her down the phone in Japanese, shuffling through the crowd towards the baggage reclaim hall. "Bill Gates dropped out of college! Look where he…"

"You are not Bill Gates!" she cried shrilly back, forcing me to pull the speaker away from my ear. "How could you possibly think…"

"Well, I did just sign a deal with Mark Zuckerberg so…"

"Don't interrupt me!"

I rolled my eyes, taking a heavy breath of the conditioned air, watching the conveyor belt roll endlessly around; surrounded by a hundred eager faces waiting with stereotypical British patience. Having grown up with both cultures, I thought it was safe to say that the Brits have more in common with the Japanese than they realise; but we win in the parental authority category. *We have the better weather too;* I thought miserably as I looked across the runway, watching the planes taking off into the night sky, splattered by constant drizzle.

"You were given a one in a million chance!" she began drilling into me. "How many people get offered a university scholarship at sixteen?!"

How many people could program heuristic learning algorithms at that age? Not that I was expecting her to appreciate that. She still referred to Instagram as 'that brown camera-thing on my phone'. The AI I'd developed had just been a pet project when I was in sixth form. A plug-in program for my World of Warcraft character. A chat-bot capable of passing most Turing tests. It got the attention of IGN and other gaming news sites and spread across social media like wildfire. The internet loved to throw phrases around like '*boy genius*'… followed by a lot of 'likes' and 'shares'. But it certainly caught the attention of the right people, namely *Facebook* executives.

Having become one of the largest AI investors in the world, they were keen to snap up any new talent. They offered to pay my student loans, in exchange for a cushy job lying in wait when. The recruitment officer wanted me to go to either Imperial College or Cambridge at first, but everyone knew MIT was the best place to study Computer Science. I wasn't going to settle for anything less than that. To my amazement, they agreed.

So, I went to the states. To finally be surrounded by like-minded people all the time was a dream come true. You have no idea how frustrating it is to have a list of programmer's jokes as long as your arm that you can never use. The course was challenging, but I was always more keen on advancing my own projects. I founded my own start-up company in my spare time with my three dorm mates: Vinita Narasimhan, Remy Naughton, and Sam Stone. Being the only one with a British background, they couldn't help but snigger every time I called them 'mates'.

Nonetheless, they were founding members of Virtualife Studios, and we went to work on our first project, spending many pizza-fuelled nights developing a massively multi-player online VR game we called Cloudland.

The game was designed to work in conjunction with extension programs we'd developed for the popular web browsers: *Chrome*, *Firefox*, and even *Microsoft Edge*. The game could be interfaced directly with individual websites or social media groups running the HTML plug-in, and provide comprehensive tools for user-created worlds (or virtual hangouts as we called them). Aside from the obvious gaming potential, there was some serious business application as well. For example, you could link your online shop to a Cloudland hangout, and create a virtual department store for your wares and talk to customer avatars in real time. Architects could upload 3D models of their designs, for clients to walk about in. And of course, the word 'conference call' could take on a new meaning. This was just scratching the surface of the potential; who knew what users were going to create. Just click the link to the hangout on the website, slip on your headset and you were good to go. And of course, there was the real beauty of browser extensions; lots of juicy customer data to sell on.

The unique selling points though were the chatbots I'd developed. Highly convincing AIs which could be integrated into non-player characters. We'd even created comprehensive 'personality matrices' for the program. Customisable variables within the software that allowed the user to choose the AI's traits: openness, conscientiousness, extraversion, agreeableness, neuroticism... like the old *Sims* games but way more complex. Creating an in-depth psyche became as easy as sliding bars on a graphical user interface. Eventually, we hoped that we'd be able to create a world filled with both human players and computer-generated characters. We'd run a few of our own Turing tests, and at least seventy percent of the judges couldn't tell if they were talking to the bot or a human

Many companies were developing similar projects using other game engines, and as such, we had prepared the code for future third-party integration. We were planning to beat them all to the punch. Even if our competitors released similar games in the future, we could absorb them into our network *by default.*

The potential implications were staggering. Zuckerberg, in particular, kept a close eye on it. *Facebook* had bought the virtual reality start-up, *Oculus*, in 2014. They released their *Rift* headset in 2016 to commercial success but had still been waiting for a killer app.

That's the gap in the market Cloudland was waiting to fill. The next big MMO. It's precisely what they were looking for. They jumped all over it.

My days were spent on coursework, my nights dedicated to developing Cloudland. I went on like that for six months, living on the brink of exhaustion. I even had a brief love affair with cocaine to sustain it. The source code had gone through twenty-five versions. Countless alpha tests to find all the glitches I could, followed by hours pining over the scripts to see the flaws, culminating in the sudden elation from moments of Eureka when I identified the problem and found a workaround... only to be broken by the daunting crash when the new code created more problems than it solved.

That was the life of the average developer. People said I was a perfectionist. That I spent too much time obsessing over every little detail. After the last few months, I was starting to believe them. My dad made me read *The Art of War* as a kid. *'Let your plans be dark and impenetrable as night, and when you move, fall like a thunderbolt.'* And that's what I did.

I kept the project as secretive as I could, enticing the prospective investors with hints left in Tweets and short *YouTube* clips, advertising Cloudland as *Second Life* on steroids; a cyber-nation waiting to happen. The next big revolution for both gaming and social media.

When I finally gave the official pitch to Zuckerberg, he bought it hook, line and sinker. We drew up a contract; Virtualife would remain my property, but *Facebook* and *Oculus* would be the game's platform. I'd have to pay off my remaining debt on my own, but I was now the CEO of my own business with a client that most people would kill for. Not exactly a problem. With the success of the game's beta version, I had secured a partnership that was going to make me rich. My heart stopped every time I realised that I was going be a millionaire this time next year!

And yet, I was still getting scolded by my mum, my phone vibrating angrily as she nattered on.

I felt a rumble from my *Samsung Gear* watch. I pulled back the black sleeve of my *Final Fantasy* hoodie revealing the screen, projecting a notification from my locator app. I pressed the icon and loaded up a spherical compass, pointing toward the plastic tapestry door at the mouth of the baggage conveyor. Sure enough, my suitcase emerged from it. I'd plastered a 'fragile' sticker on the side. Damn right too; my PC was in there.

The arrow on my watch followed the bag, tracking the RFID chip planted within. More and more products were coming with such devices installed; all sharing data through the so-called 'Internet of Things'. It wouldn't be long before mainstream clothing came with bio-monitor sensors installed as standard.

I heaved the bag off the carousel and wheeled it behind me, heading down the hallway, passing a dozen screens, and even more

CCTV cameras; armed police were never far behind. I ignored them as the shrillness from my phone reached a fever pitch.

"Mum, I don't think you realise…"

"What if it all falls through, huh? What then!?"

"If you saw some of the feedback we're getting I don't think…"

"So, you're going to start reciting statistics at me now?!"

I tried to hide my frustrated sigh; if I couldn't convince her with the raw data, nothing would. Naturally, she picked up on it anyway.

"Don't you take that attitude!" she snapped back.

"You're not giving me a chance to…"

"Here! Speak to your father!"

I stopped on the travellator, gliding past rows of coffee shops and advert screens. I ran my fingers through my wavy, student hair, waiting in anxious anticipation, listening to the phone rustling as she handed me over. I braced myself for a different brand of rage.

"Hi." His gruff voice rumbled from the speaker.

"Uh… hi Dad," I answered cautiously, scratching my head. A tense silence fell. I held my breath.

"You have more potential than anyone in the family," he continued in a calculated tone.

I rolled my eyes to the side as I pondered about how to answer.

"Um… Thank you?"

"Will this be worth it?"' He asked me bluntly. Direct as always.

"I… Yes. Yes, I think so," I said cautiously.

"It had better be," he said firmly, commanding authority without ever raising his voice. "A man finishes what he starts, Kenji. That's all there is to it." He hung up, leaving me feeling somewhat dumbfounded.

He had his ways, I'll give him that. He seemed accepting enough, but that didn't make me any less nervous about what was awaiting me when I got home. I let out a nervous breath and stepped off the travellator into the shopping court. I didn't put the phone away just yet, having noticed a dozen notifications on my home screen; most of them e-mails from Vinita and the others, just double checking the deal hadn't fallen through, and that they weren't all about to wake up to some horrible prank. I chuckled at their eagerness but didn't reply. Today was a me day. No Zuckerberg. No Cloudland. Just me and the family.

I opened my universal social media app to update all my pages at once and started typing an update.

Okay, just a little bit of work.

<<Back in London! Updates to version 1.3 coming soon! #Cloudland>>

I hit the send button and looked around at the last-minute shoppers bustling around. I couldn't help but blush when I noticed the Dixon's electronics shop. A teenage girl was trying a demo of the latest *Oculus* VR headset; the block-shaped goggles hanging in front of her eyes, projecting the simulation. A massive grin lit up on her face as she walked on the spot to move as if in a daze, her movements scanned by an *Xbox Kinect Sensor*, even using her hands to pick up the virtual objects of the game world.

An oversized advertisement for Cloudland was plastered on the wall behind her, an overblown image of my face all over it. My official *Twitter* account was being displayed on a screen mounted beside her; it only took a couple of seconds for the latest post to load up. I pulled my hood up to hide my face and quickly marched away before anyone saw me. I was going to have to do that a lot from now on.

It was starting to sink in. I was a tech-celebrity now; go figure.

I downloaded the airport's map to my smartwatch, and followed the guide to the exit, placing my phone in my pocket while an artificial voice gave me directions through my headphones. My MP3 streaming service played in the background; the latest update to the player's software had a mood-prediction feature, using a deep-learning network. The program had cleverly chosen *'Billionaire'* by Travie McCoy. I headed past a duty-free *Swarovski* jewellery shop, stopping on the spot to admire the gleaming white décor through the glass, mesmerised by the rainbow light glittering from the zircon-encrusted pieces for sale.

My eyes were drawn to one necklace in particular. The more I stared at it, the more I thought about how much Gabrielle would love it, only to cringe at the sight of the £2,000 price tag beneath it. If only I'd come back a week later; the payment from *Facebook's* signing fee would have cleared into my account. Don't get me wrong; I didn't plan to be one of those *MTV* wankers showing off their 'cribs'. A philanthropist. That's what I wanted to be. I had a list of charities I planned on donating to, but seriously; if I couldn't buy nice things for my girlfriend, what was the point of being rich?

I felt a cold rush of excitement just thinking of her, knowing she too was longing for me too. I spun on my heel and headed towards the lobby with a quickened pace, weaving in and out of the human traffic, trying my best not to topple over the travel case or crash it into anyone and generally not trying to draw attention. Aside from wanting to avoid any potential paparazzi, airport security had a way of making me feel safe and terrified at the same time.

I was too young to remember 9/11, but I did remember 7/7, and the mess of Iraq and Afghanistan. The history of the West and Middle-East was just one spectacular blunder after another. First by the British and the French, then the Americans, exploiting the profoundly fragmented region for its resources, supporting dictators to keep the locals in line while they pillaged the continent. Al-Qaeda and the Islamic State that followed were just the logical consequence of that; religious ignorance mixed with political rage; a poisonous cocktail that had consumed the lives of millions since the turn of the century alone. But regardless of how they came into being, they posed a threat. That was one of the reasons I held a somewhat neutral stance towards the Edward Snowden revelations. Nobody likes invasion of privacy, but when Patrick Henry said, 'Give me liberty or give me death,' he didn't have nuclear weapons in mind.

"Turn left here," the app chimed in my ear.

The electronic voice brought my attention back to the real world. My mind did that; getting lost on a train of thought. During campus parties, I'd end up thinking about flowcharts, variable and script arrays… it would take a sledgehammer to get attention at that point.

I checked my watch screen. My destination now less than thirty metres away. My eyes wheeled around the cavernous steel hall, drawn to the automatic doors on the far side.

There she was. Gabrielle Phillips; my girlfriend. She wore darkened *D&G* sunglasses, but there was no hiding that gorgeous, flowing brunette hair dangling around her shoulders, the curves on her lips and cheeks. Her well-fitting blue dress, coupled with the subtle leather belt revealed the meat in all the right places across her otherwise slender body. She saw me and almost began jumping with excitement, waving gleefully with me from across the hall.

I couldn't hold myself back anymore and dashed towards her as fast as-

"Hey, watch it!" someone yelled at me over the sound of my headphones, grabbing my attention. I stopped before I had started, jumping backwards in time to avoid a yellow Sweeper Kart heading right at me; its pair of giant motorised brushes sweeping everything into the vacuum cleaner. I hadn't heard the incessant beeping siren over my headphones. The driver shook his fist violently at me; a silver-haired, wrinkling, skinny, burnt-out wreck, a pack of *Marlboro* cigarettes hanging out from his high-visibility uniform.

"Sorry," I mumbled back.

He shook his head bitterly, grumbling under his breath as the kart whirred away. I couldn't help but feel a little sorry for him. His job would be stolen by a robot in a few years' time. All blue-collar jobs were being taken by the relentless pace of automation. Hell, white-collar jobs were already under threat. Buckminster Fuller had talked about this for years; the rise of the age of fun and education, when machines could do all labour better, faster and safer than people could.

Who knew where it would end? Maybe we were staring down the barrel of the fabled technological singularity that futurists like Ray Kurzweil had predicted for years. An intelligence explosion; the point where AI would be able to advance itself so quickly, that it would become incomprehensible to an ordinary human… unless you *merged your own intelligence with the machines*; becoming godlike.

It sounded utopian, but there needed to be some new economic alternative to traditional employment. A new incentive. All the more reason the world needed VR; software would soon be worth more than physical goods. People were already prepared to pay out hard cash for items in-game. User-generated content was a prominent feature of Cloudland; unleashing the potential of all our creative players, enabling them to create virtual furniture, clothes, or even whole new levels and sell them to other players. The potential for entirely new businesses to grow up inside the game world. A new, fairer, better form of capitalism. I firmly believed that's what Cloudland was going to become; a whole new world of jobs for the users to create for themselves.

An inspirational smile appeared on my face… meanwhile, in the real world, Gabrielle was still waiting for me.

I got off my train of thought and rushed towards her. She sprung towards me, throwing her arms around my neck, giggling gleefully as she squeezed against my chest, the sweet scent of her perfume greeting me. I dumped the travel case and returned the embrace, pulling off her sunglasses in a hurry.

"Really?" I snorted and nudged my head toward the darkness outside.

"Well, I am dating a CEO now," she chuckled back, letting me gaze into her emerald-green eyes. I grinned, thrusting my lips towards hers. We locked passionately as the rush of excitement flooded me.

Now I'm home.

We leaned back, allowing me to softly stroke down her arms while we beamed at each other. We *Skyped* and had virtual meetings in Cloudland every day, but I hadn't seen her in person for over three months. I was in the VR business, but even I was the first one to admit that it would never be a substitute for the real thing... presumably.

"Did I tell you I was proud of you?" She giggled.

"Uh… lemme think," I replied, turning my eyes to the sky in an exaggerated thoughtful manner, making her snigger. "Uh, no. No, I don't think you've ever said that," I lied with a grin. She slapped my shoulder playfully.

"Oh. I'll save it for a special occasion then," she teased.

We took the obligatory selfie together and uploaded it online. Gabrielle had already called an *Uber* cab, so we went through the automatic doors, hand in hand.

"So, how'd it go with your folks?" she enquired as we stepped out into the nippy night air.

"Shoot me now," I replied grimly.

"That bad?"

"Told you it would be."

"Oh, I wouldn't worry about it. I'm sure your little gift will placate them a little."

"Here's hoping," I sighed, crossing my fingers.

I had bought four tickets to the 2020 Tokyo Olympics. Two for my parents, two for us. Their favourite events: the two hundred metre sprint, cycling, and fencing. My dad and I were fans of Noritoshi Kajiyama; not a household name here in the UK, but a celebrity in Japan. The internet called him a modern-day Samurai. He was competing in the fencing competition, but he was famous for his Iaidō skills, the art of drawing the sword. An art he practised with inhuman capability. Not only had he trained under some of the best in the country, but he also possessed reflexes that had to be seen to be believed. He had abilities that were straight out of myths or action movies. Capable of cutting down almost any projectile attack coming towards him.

Tennis balls. Sliced. Arrows? No problem. *BB pellets?* You better believe it. That's right; he could deflect bullets with a sword. Don't buy it? Search the damn *YouTube* video!

Neuroscientists were stunned. They tried studying his meditation rituals with MRI scanners to figure out how he controlled his cerebellum so efficiently. Now I'm *not* a neuroscientist so I can't give you the technical details; but the point is that the results of the project concluded it might be possible to increase the neural transmission rate to stimulate the brains of others, to replicate the *same effects*. How frickin' sweet would that be?

The US Air Force had already developed trans-cranial stimulators to enhance the performance of drone pilots. Magnetic helmets, beaming into regions of the brain to increase the awareness and focus of the subject, allowing them to see the big picture rather than individual objects, similar to how autistic savants view the world. The subjects showed a 40% increase in accuracy with the machines installed, but what was particularly interesting was that the pilots seemed to retain their abilities *even after* the device was removed.

There were some… other side effects that needed work, including a burning sensation in the scalp. We could take our time solving that one before we brought it to market.

In any case, some researchers had speculated that using similar devices, coupled with the right training program, it could be possible for anyone to assimilate any skill within a matter of days or even hours. Virtual Reality was the key to that, I was sure of it, and I was already in talks with the head of the Helmet's manufacturer on *LinkedIn*. Of course, there were the naysayers, the ones who said technological enhancement of the human body was a crime, a sin, a *'violation of the natural order'*. Religious extremists, hippies, or nutters like the Unabomber. It was hard to argue they didn't have a point. Any new technology could give power to the users, in ways never intended by the creators. Some even said cybernetics and genetics had the potential to divide mankind into dozens of metaspecies, and the ultimate extinction of the 'traditional human'.

All valid points. Points that needed to be carefully analysed and monitored for developments. A job I was all too keen to take on.

My smartwatch vibrated to notify me the cab was five minutes away. It was only then I realised I'd been standing in silence with my Gabrielle the entire time.

"You okay?" she asked curiously, looking puzzled.

"Uh-huh."

"Whatcha thinking about?"

"Uh… Transhumanism?"

She scoffed, shaking her head with a grin. "I suppose I shouldn't be surprised." She shrugged with a weary smile.

"Sorry," I apologised, scratching the back of my head.

"That's what I get for falling in love with a genius. Just try not to do that when you're meeting with your investors."

"Duly noted."

Yeah. She was a keeper.

Not to mention I owed so much to her business sense. She'd practically written my pitch to Zuckerberg. I was a developer at heart, not an executive. I had her for that. We'd met at College through the Anime and Gaming Society (nerdy girls for the win). Even then, I looked back on those early days with nostalgia. She had studied at Cambridge while I was in the States, but I came to her for advice almost invariably…and her Dad's funding.

He was a technology investment officer at BAE Systems. A real head-hunter, but he quickly took a shine to me. I wasn't a fan of the military-industrial complex, but *Facebook* didn't put a penny towards the development costs. So, when he offered to give me a loan to start up the company, I set my pride aside and shook his hand. It would've never gotten off the ground without his help. My mates told me she was gold digging. That she'd persuaded her father for the money, purely for the potential *'return on investment'*.

I did my best to ignore it. The taxi arrived; a blacked out, leather seated *Volvo*. I carefully stowed my travel case in the trunk, and we were off, heading into a concrete tunnel, the orange tinge of the lights surrounding us as the traffic hummed on the lanes exiting onto the motorway, guided by the driver's GPS; a Romanian guy with gelled jet-black hair.

The glow of red and white car lights streamed like torrents on the lanes either side of us. I gave a voice command to my watch to get a *Google* traffic report.

"Minimal traffic on route," the AI chimed back.

The scenery changed around us, from dark forests of the green belt, shifting in the suburban area of Sunbury. The spire of an antiquated church stood out over the red brick of the 1930s houses. Our surroundings changed rapidly the closer we got to the city, blazing on the horizon. The outline of skyscrapers in the city centre towered faintly in the overcast clouds, casting shadows across the overpriced Victorian houses, and decrepit council estates.

We sat in silence, holding hands and enjoying the comfortable silence. She kept looking back and forth at me. Like she was expecting me to ask her something but wasn't going to let me know. Realising that it would probably cause more trouble for me later if I didn't say anything, I racked my brain, trying to remember what it could've been. It popped into my head like a Christmas light.

"Oh!" I exclaimed. "How was your stargazing trip?"

She beamed at me to my relief.

Bingo.

BAE Systems had donated several million to the Kielder Observatory in Northumberland to build a new high-powered telescope for public use. Her father had pulled strings and gotten her on the invitation list for the opening ceremony.

"Oh, it was – God, it was like nothing I've ever done before," she said, her voice filled with reverent awe. "Heavenly… is the word that came to mind. I got a clear view of the pillars of creation." She continued, "I've never seen anything so beautiful in my life."

"Wow," I exclaimed, raising my eyebrows. "Those are what…six thousand light-years away?"

"Seven." She grinned.

"Wow… just ten years ago, they would've needed an orbital telescope to see out that far," I said with raised eyebrows.

She scoffed and shook her head with a smile. Obviously disappointed that I wasn't sharing her romantic view.

Astronomy had always been her favourite pastime. Her family had their own telescope in the study of their country house in Charlwood. Spending long, intimate evenings staring through at the craters of the moon. The image is so clear it was like being there. Of course, there were now VR sims using scans taken from lunar probes which could put you right there…but nothing could match what we had in those times.

"Found anyone calling home yet?" I winked at her.

She giggled.

"Still looking," she said coyly.

One of the first films we watched together was *E.T.* One of her childhood favourites. She even had a cuddly toy of him on her bed. Considering myself the 'bigger nerd' in the relationship, she hadn't taken too kindly when I called it good, but still a 'derivative piece of

Christian propaganda'. I tried lending her my copy of *The Star Beast* by Robert A. Heinlein to prove my point. I checked to see if she'd gotten around to reading it yet. Unsurprisingly she hadn't.

We snuggled up while I pulled out my tablet from my man-bag and started flicking through the news. The usual headline: Islamic State on the move again. I shook my head in disgust. It was now just a proxy war between America and Russia, supposedly both against IS, but with every bombing campaign they created more recruits for them.

"Have you been watching the stock market?" Gab asked, waving her phone at me. "There's been a huge run on Saudi oil. Some UN report came out, saying they're two years away from hitting the peak of their reserves. Now everyone wants out."

"Lemme guess…" I said grimly. "We're on course for another recession?"

"Looks like."

"Great."

I remembered the credit crunch plain as day. Tory austerity. The cut in benefits. My parents struggling to pay the bills. They were petrified they would lose the shop; a little bento box café just off the river. There were times when they thought it was all over, but they had a work ethic which had to be seen to be believed. They just soldiered on, somehow making ends meet. They must've seen me as their one chance to amount to anything more. No wonder they lost their shit over me dropping out.

"Gonna be a good time to be rich." I sighed dismissively.

"Has it ever been a good time to not be rich?"

"1789," I retorted quickly.

She raised an eyebrow at me.

"Year of the French Revolution," I answered with a cocky grin.

"Smart ass." She scoffed. "You need to be more up to date on the financial news. You should know it's not enough just to be a techie."

"Yeah, I know, I know," I groaned, knowing she was right. Honestly, interest rates, GDP, PMI, PPI… just thinking about it made me lethargic. All that stock market crap was just a means to end for me… means, that *someone else* could deal with.

"Just get the Forex App," she nagged. "It'll give you all the relevant updates."

"I could…" I admitted, rolling my head from side to side. "But I'll have you by my side, right?"

She gave me an inquisitive stare. "Well, yeah…" she replied slowly.

"I hope it goes without saying, you're going to have a part in Virtualife's future."

She frowned at me as if she'd taken offence. "Look, if this is about my father's contributions…"

"It's not," I said, holding up a reassuring hand. "We make a great team, Gab. I want… I *need* you on the board of directors."

"The board?" She laughed.

"We are a registered company now."

"Being run out of your dorm room."

"Hmmm," I grunted. "I'm looking into upgrading that."

I crossed my fingers discreetly. Even though I was going to be rolling in the dough soon, there was no getting around the crazy housing prices in London.

She was still mulling my offer.

"My dad warned me about mixing business and pleasure," she said cautiously.

"A bit late for that," I chuckled with a shrug.

She rolled her lips and nodded.

"I'm just saying…" I began in a hushed tone, with a sense of serious inspiration. "I believe… I *know* that if we do this, together we could change the world."

I clutched her hand, staring into those deep emerald eyes, her gorgeous face opening into a grin.

"So do I," she answered.

I leaned in once more, our lips brushing and-

SCREEEEEECH!

Without warning, the driver slammed on the brakes, sending us into a jolting, grinding stop. Our embrace was cut short before it had started as we were violently thrown forward before our seatbelts slammed us back again.

The blare of a hundred angry horns began raging around us.

"Hey!" we cried together, rubbing our necks.

"What's the big idea?!" Gab yelled angrily.

"Sorry! Sorry!" the driver apologised loudly, waving his hands and pointing out the windshield. "I don't know what happened! Look, they all just stopped!"

We peered out from behind the front seats. A sea of red lights stretched out before us. The traffic had come to a standstill; a deadlock piling up for a mile in front of us, and even further behind. Red and blue flashes of police lights shone in the distance.

"What happened? A crash?" I asked with concern.

"Not sure…" The driver shrugged. "Hold on."

He reached for the sunglasses holder above his mirror and pulled out a leather case; holstering a pair of elegant binoculars.

"What are those for?" I asked.

"I bird watch," he replied flatly, peering through them.

I hoped that wasn't a euphemism and brought up the traffic report on my watch. The map loaded up. The roads which had previously been nice and green was now plastered with a big fat block of red graphics indicating the congestion. It was a clean cut like something had barricaded the road. I could see on the opposite lane the traffic had grown thicker but was still moving at a steady pace away from the city.

"It's the police all right," the driver announced. "They've got one of those big vans blocking the road into town. Making everyone turn back."

We turned to each other with worried confusion. The roar of an engine whizzed overhead. We peered out the car's skylight and caught a glimpse of a helicopter, its searchlight racing toward the town.

My phone hummed with a text message. Both Gabrielle's and the driver's phone went off at the same time.

"Okay, that's weird," Gab commented with a raised eyebrow. We checked our screens simultaneously, the same message displaying on our home screens:

<< THIS IS AN OFFICIAL MESSAGE FROM THE METROPOLITAN POLICE>>

<<Terrorist incident in progress at Kingston-Upon-Thames. Do not approach! Anyone in the vicinity must evacuate immediately!>>

"Terrorist?" Gabrielle asked, her voice quivering.

"Shit!" I cried, pressing down on my contacts icon in a hurry and searched for my mum's number. I dialled, and waited… and waited…

"Come on, come on!" I growled to the silence, my knee bouncing anxiously, only to be answered by a beeping error message.

"Sorry, but we are currently experiencing network difficulties," the recorded voice spoke, "please try again later."

"Fuck!" I spat angrily and hung up. My parents were right in the danger zone. They should have gotten the same message, but I could only imagine the panic that would be sweeping through the town now. Our phones were going mad, still vibrating furiously with updates from our news apps.

"There's a live TV feed!" Gabrielle cried, pointing to her screen. I huddled over her shoulder as the video from the *BBC* streamed into view. The sound of the helicopter's engine hummed from the phone's speaker, giving us a bird's eye view over the Thames. The camera was moving fast, beaming a spotlight onto the river, following a grimy white boat speeding in a northbound direction. Four men dressed in nondescript black clothes occupied the cabin, their faces covered in balaclavas, brandishing AK-47s.

A pair of sleek blue and green Police Boats were pursuing at top speed; each one had Armed Response Officers stood on the ship's bow. They wore bullet-proof body armour with helmets and goggles and were blasting the terrorist boat with M-15s. Two of the gunmen had taken cover in their boat's cabin, returning fire with blind shots.

Chunks of wood splintered off their boat, but it had been reinforced with armoured panels underneath. The third terrorist was at the helm, jerking the rudder from side to side in a zig-zag pattern trying to evade the line of the fire. A fourth terrorist was squatting beneath a counter in the cabin, working on something just beyond the sight of the camera.

"We still have information coming in," the soft but concerned voice of the female newsreader reported in the feed, "but the Police have confirmed that they received an anonymous tip on a bomb threat earlier today. They did not provide information on the yield of the weapon, so the police have taken every precaution and issued an evacuation order for the entire region. No terrorist organisation has officially taken responsibility, but we have unconfirmed reports that they are members of the Islamic State and… Wait!"

Another police boat came hurtling down the river from the other direction to intercept the terrorists. They swerved hard to the side, blocking their path and boxing them in. The engine of the terrorist boat roared as they tried to ram their way through, but they never got the chance. The barricading boat opened fire; this time with clear shots through the cabin windshield.

RAT-AT-AT-AT-AT!

With a crash, the salvo fire from the police ripped through the glass and slaughtered the crew inside, their arms flailing wildly from the impacts. Blood splattered across the floor and windows in huge messy puddles.

"*Jesus*!" Gab cried, covering her mouth.

The terrorist boat rapidly slowed down, brushing past the police blockade with a splashing thud and came to a standstill, bobbing gently on the surface of the water.

"Uh… the police seem to have… neutralised the crew, and are now moving to board the boat," the newscaster explained.

The officers came storming onto the deck. The roads on both sides of the river banks were now blazing with police lights and the roar of sirens. Multiple armoured vans came to a screeching halt. Gabrielle grabbed my arm, squeezing it tightly as we watched with bated breath.

The helicopter banked to the left and the camera caught something… there was still someone moving inside the boat!

"Hold up!" the caster announced. "There's still one alive… he's moving towards some kind of device! Is… is that the bomb?"

The camera zoomed in on the survivor crawling along the deck, leaving a slimy red trail behind him. He heaved himself over to a machine the size of a suitcase underneath the cabin counter; a tangle of wires and flashing lights with a metal cylinder mounted in the centre.

A triangular yellow sticker was plastered on it. I squinted as I tried to make it out through the fuzzy feed. Then the camera brought it into focus. I recoiled with terror when I recognised it: the Radiation Hazard symbol.

"NUKE!" I yelled. "THEY'VE GOT A FUCKING NUKE!"

Gabrielle screamed. The police would never make it in time. I watched helplessly as his bloodied hand bashed the buttons on the control pad.

A red light began flashing rapidly.

I rapidly unclipped our seatbelts, grabbed Gab, and pulled both of us tumbling down into to the gap between us and the driver's seat, and landed hard on the carpet. I covered our heads in a braced position…

For the briefest of moments, the night turned to day.

An almighty ear-piercing boom reverberated around us.

The blast wave washed over the car with the power of a tsunami.

A storm of broken glass followed as every window surrounding us shattered in an instant.

I held Gabrielle tight while the wind howled, drowning out our screams.

This was it.

Death had come for us.

We waited for the end together.

Silence… Darkness… Haze…

I didn't know how much time had passed… but I was alive. I was reasonably sure of that. My ears were ringing like a poorly tuned TV. My whole body felt like it was spinning on a merry-go-round. I kept my head pressed to the carpet, not daring to open my eyes. Distantly, I could hear a muffled voice.

"Kenji… Kenji!"

I could just about make out Gabrielle; scared and stammering. She shook me violently, snapping me back to consciousness. I opened my eyes to a hundred shards of glass scattered across the carpet, stained with drops of blood I wasn't sure was mine. I whirled round to see the panic on her face, her bloodshot eyes wide open with terror, her hair a mess. A cut on her forehead left a trail of red across her cheek.

"You okay?" I yelled, barely hearing myself, reaching to check her wound. She nodded quickly back at me, examining me as well.

Still, in a daze, I tried looking outside, my view obscured by the seats. My hearing began to clear as the two of us carefully navigated around the glass. We helped each other back up… and my mouth dropped as I looked at the outside world.

"Holy shit…" I breathed.

The sky was ablaze; the night illuminated by a flaming orange. The smell of smoke and burning metal and plastic wafted through the window. A few huddled shadows moved outside. The first scream I became aware of was the driver. We spun upwards together and saw him writhing in agony in his seat, frantically clutching his bloodied face.

"Oh *GOD*!" Gabrielle cried, grasping her mouth. I gaped in utter horror, unable to look away. His eyes had been… shredded by the glass. Vast pools of fluid and blood spilt across his cheeks like a waterfall. His yells became ever clearer; sheer blood-curdling anguish sending shivers down my spine.

"Hold on!" Gabrielle cried, her hands lunging out to help. I looked around in a panic, my mind racing on how to help, but I didn't know the first thing about first aid!

"I'll get hel…" I began. My voice trailed off. Brought to silence by the sight of the outside world.

We had been far enough away from the centre of the blast radius to avoid the worst of it, but the road was a mess of cars thrown by the blast, crashing into each other to create a maze. People were pouring out onto the street from nearby houses and their cars. Everyone who could run already was; a frenzied stampeding horde was thundering away… paying little mind to the ones struggling to hobble away with their injuries. I got a glimpse of a terrified mother clutching her blood-soaked baby, darting in and out of the blasted-out cars.

Beyond the expanse of the highway, the foot of the inferno roared; giant columns of fiery death rising above the treeline and Victorian rooftops. A single pillar of smoke blossomed ominously into the night sky; a mushroom cloud.

That's when it really hit me. The full magnitude of what had just happened. I stared, gobsmacked. There was a sign by the side of the road, burning like kindling wood:

Kingston: 2.5 miles

"No…" I breathed. "No! No! No!" I didn't believe it. I frantically fumbled for my phone, checking the screen, pounding the home and power buttons.

Nothing. Dead. Of course, electromagnetic pulse.

It must've only been a small nuke. They might… they have to be alive!

My hands dived for the door lock, the onslaught of fleeing people on the road still coming.

"Stay here!" I called to Gab loudly when I pulled up the lock.

"Kenji, no!" she cried back, turning away from the wailing driver. "There's nothing you can do! Get back…"

I wasn't listening anymore; adrenaline pumped through my veins. I yanked up the lock, not really knowing what I was going to do, just an uncontrollable burning desire to do *something*. I shoved the door open, and her yells faded behind me, consumed by the tsunami of panic.

Thousands were fleeing, ditching their cars in the shadow of the cloud. Clinging to their children and prized possessions for dear life as they stormed down the glass-covered tarmac, shoving and heaving as they went. Around them the yells of torment from those trapped in their cars on the verge of bleeding to death. I think I was the only one heading *toward* the inferno.

I'm coming... I'm coming!

I told myself that over and over again, squeezing and slipping through the dense cluster of cars, ignoring the pain of my feet being trampled. The deafening roar of screams, sirens, and helicopters reached a fever pitch. The closer I got to the apocalyptic flames, the louder it got and the worse the injuries. I kept going, the blaze spreading out in front of me, the sky blanketed with dark soot.

Come on! Come on!

It was like wading against a current. The atmosphere was suffocating, the pressure squeezed me tighter and tighter as the crowd pushed back. I shoved and heaved, but it was too much. I yelled desperately as I was forced back by the stampede, shoved into the side of another wrecked car, my shoulder rattling the window frame.

"Shit! SHIIIIT!" I tried wriggling my way out, but wave after wave flooded past, pinning me down. "No! No! No!"

I was helpless... I couldn't do a damn thing! I steeled myself for one more-

"Kenji!" a voice from behind me called. It grabbed my shoulder, and I spun to see Gabrielle before me, covered in the driver's blood, looking relieved to have caught up with me.

"They're gone, Kenji!"

"No! They might..." I yelled back, still trying to get loose.

"We need to go! The radiation! It's not..."

"No!"

She yanked me back. "It's okay... it's okay..." she cooed soothingly. I tried to protest. But she was right. The hard truth sank in. They wouldn't be going to the Olympics with us.

"Oh… oh God," I breathed, my voice starting to crack. The emotion washed over. I buried myself in her shoulder… and wept.

The ashes fell like snow.

The reports said the bomb had detonated with six kilotons of blast power, levelling everything within a kilometre radius. Over eight thousand people died that day in an instant. A further ten thousand in the days that followed from their injuries, and acute radiation sickness. As harsh as it sounds it would've been worse if they had reached Westminster as planned. Harder to calculate though is the number of people who had died since the fallout. The wind had been blowing in a south-west direction that day, so London itself didn't have to be evacuated, but many towns all the way along to the coast had to be abandoned to the exclusion zone. They called it 8/8, dwarfing 9/11 in scale.

The world has never been the same since.

My parents were buried in a mass grave along with the other bodies recovered. Gabrielle came to the funeral with me. She held my hand.

I attended her funeral a few years later.

But that wasn't the end…

27 YEARS LATER…

The Three Laws of Responsible Robotics

1. A human may not deploy a robot without the human-robot work system meeting the highest legal and professional standards of safety and ethics.

- This is implemented via the use of encrypted Safety Certificates, and a Black Box function that records all decisions made by the software. These must be issued by a national accreditation body working under the oversight of the International Council on Artificial Intelligence. Any robot which has said Certificates revoked must trigger the developer reset code (See Second Law). Any Artificial Intelligence developer who fails to register with an accreditation body will be subject to criminal prosecution.

2. A robot must respond to humans as appropriate for their roles.

- The role (prime directive) of any Artificial General Intelligence (AGI) program must be clearly stated by the developer. The developer must take all reasonable precautions that the AGI does not exceed said prime directives. By default, the program must include an Emergency Reset Function, which must be hardcoded not to be accessed by the AGI's analysis matrix or self-defence subroutines (See Third Law).

3. A robot must be endowed with sufficient situated autonomy to protect its own existence as long as such protection provides smooth transfer of control which does not conflict with the First and Second Laws.

- The 2020 United Nations Resolution on Autonomous Weapons prohibits the development of Artificial Intelligence programs capable of initiating cyber-attacks or the use of physical force (non-lethal or lethal) on their own authority in any capacity. Mobility control may be autonomous, but the use of weapons systems must in every instance be authorised by a remote human operator. Failure to comply with this law is considered a war crime.

CHAPTER 1

Mother Mind Profile 9124-5631-4877-0672:

First Name: Andrew

Surname: Ilian

Status: Living

Nationality: British

Occupation(s):

- Student
  - Status: Studying
  - Organisation: Hammersmith College

Criminal Record:

- None

Known Aliases:

- ShadOw Cell

Biometric Data:

- Gender: Male
- Date of Birth: 13/02/2028
- Age: 17
- Race: Caucasian
- Hair Colour: Blond
- Eye Colour: Hazel
- Height: 1.77 m
- Weight: 68 kg
- Ailments: Type-1 Diabetes
- Cybernetic Percentage: 2%
- Genetic modifications:
  - Standard immunisation therapy

Immediate Family:

- Mother: Helen Ilian
- Father: Jonathan Ilian
- Siblings: 0

Relationships:

- Status: In a relationship
    - Partner: Claudia Schwarz

Contact Information:

- *Click here to drop down*

Live Surveillance:

- Status: *Available*
- Date: 05/10/2045
- Current Location: Pearl House Apartment Complex, South Kensington, London
- Local Time: 17:32 GMT

The drizzle splattered against my bedroom window, refracting the glare from a thousand digital lights. A cluster of holograms and neon signs in a dozen languages glittered like rainbows against the downpour, illuminating the overcast sky; a sky filled with air traffic of drones, and the occasional flying car.

"Come on, come on…" I muttered impatiently, scratching my belly, watching the upload on my laptop's holo-screen crawl past 95%. "Can't it go any faster?"

"I've already disabled all the background operations I can to increase the upload bandwidth," answered Katherine, my busty blonde Virtual Personal Assistant, her avatar projecting from my laptop. "If I terminate any more then I risk system stability."

I swore under my breath; most operating systems came with an AI like her installed by default. When running on an average home desktop in the six zettaflop range, she possessed an IQ comparable to six hundred million human brains combined, relatively slow compared to a gaming desktop.

I could communicate with her telepathically via my interface headset, her voice beaming into my auditory centres. A necessity to make sense of the vast swathes of data that the average person was bombarded with by the media elites.

The file I was uploading was huge: just over four hundred exabytes worth of data, taking up half of my external memory drive. Even with my terabit connection speed, it had taken the last three hours to get this far. Almost done now, but my heart was still in my mouth. I couldn't believe I'd gone through with it. I messed about online like everyone else, but this was it; I had officially crossed the line. I was a cyber-criminal. My heart stopped every time I heard something out in the hallway beyond the automatic doors, expecting the police to come bursting in, ready to deliver justice at the end of a taser.

I was perched at the end of my bed, hunched over the computer, listening to the sound of my parents' housekeeping robot in the background as it scuttled around the room on its wheels, efficiently scooping up the clothes I had left scattered on the floor and sorting them into the sliding panel wardrobes built into the walls. I'd been nagging them to upgrade to a better model for months; one that made less noise. They never bloody listened.

The wall to my right was covered in Intellipaper, a wafer-thin OLED display screen, projecting my screen saver; a slideshow of 3D photos from my trip to Amsterdam, while the subtly hidden speakers played *'You Could Be Mine'* by Guns N' Roses. A golden oldie.

I rubbed my forehead, the skin around my Heinreich-Raith neural-lace headset (a Swiss Biotech company) tingling from the energy pulsing into my head. A non-invasive model; a silver-white plastic headset with an EEG brainwave reader built into it, translating my thoughts into digital signals to control the computer telepathically, a USB 15.0 cable dangling from the input socket on the module behind my left ear. It was slightly cumbersome, but it was faster than a wireless connection.

Telepathic control was something that had to be experienced to believe. The distinction between man and machine blurred beyond recognition. Your thoughts translated onto the screen and back again effortlessly like the computer was just an extension of my arms. Fully-implantable neural laces allowed for an even higher degree of control. Billions of microscopic chips attached to your neurons, delivered via the bloodstream using biodegradable nanobots. It could be done for under £100 now, but my parents still refused to pay for it until I was eighteen. Bastards.

I only had one implant. An artificial pancreas; the cure for type-1 diabetes. I would need to hack it to disable its RFID chip if I ever wanted to join Spiritform.

"What time do Mum and Dad get back?" I yawned loudly, stretching out, still unable to believe I'd been awake for nearly fifteen hours.

"Their schedule says 8 pm," Katherine chimed back. "Plenty of time."

They told me they'd gone to some dinner party, but I'd checked Mum's planner when I hacked in. Apparently, they were going to some nudist club in Kentish Town. Basically, a swinger's club for the super-rich. Old bloody perverts. I shuddered just thinking about it.

For once, I was hoping they actually were just going out to schmooze with the other fat cats. They'd even felt the need to take our hover-car, a fancy *BMW* Road Hornet that they were still paying off. I looked up at the lanes of air traffic, the word 'flyover' taking on new meaning. The skyways for the flying cars were above those designated for unmanned drone traffic, whizzing through the clouds in-between the maze of high-tech towers. The hover cars were sparse compared to the hundreds of drones in the air. Such designs were very much a rich man's toy, costing well over a hundred grand. But VTOL technology was becoming cheaper all the time, and would probably be in the hands of the average consumer within a decade or so. Most of the units on the road/sky were either corporate owned or time shared. *Uber* even offered 'sky exec' rides. The fact that we *personally owned* one…was just another reminder that we were part of the privileged few…

My Dad used to take me on pleasure cruises in it… From the sky, London seems like an accomplishment; a feat of centuries of architecture and engineering. You can't see the grime, the depravity, or the homeless. Created by the system that had made us rich… every time I rode in it, I couldn't help but feel rising guilt upon take-off.

I didn't have time to ponder on it. One of the perks of your own personal air ride was that it wouldn't take them long to get back.

"I've covered your tracks as best I can on your local network," Katherine explained. "Erasing digital fingerprints from Virtualife's network will be much harder though."

"I know, I know…"

My mother was an artificial intelligence researcher at Virtualife. My dad, a consultant for a virtual law firm. Yup, I had grown up comfortably middle class. Hell, we lived on the twenty-seventh floor of an apartment complex in *South Kensington*. Some people told me that I should've been grateful for the opportunities they had given me. The best VR schools, holidays, real food… but after seventeen years I'd realised it all came from something horrible…

Everyone knew the life story of Mum's boss; Kenji Awasaki, boy genius. Born on a London estate to Japanese immigrants. Studied at MIT. Became a millionaire overnight. Parents killed in the 8/8 nuclear bombing. Fiancée targeted for assassination. Many people saw him as a hero; an inspirational figure who had taken his pain and loss and turned it into something positive. He'd invested in biotech, nanotech, AI… products which had changed the world for the better on the whole. But he had one great big stain on his resume; he developed the Mother Mind system.

"Mother Mind! Keeping you safe for fifteen years!" an electronic voice boomed from outside my window.

The rumbling caught my attention, emanating from a giant holographic billboard. A propaganda piece twinkling from a tower across the street. A recruitment advert for GCHQ (Government Communication Headquarters); featuring a group of professional looking men and women standing outside the iconic white, doughnut-shaped building, beaming with enthusiasm, dressed in the latest office attire. I grimaced at the sight of it; I couldn't believe society had gotten to the point that the position of Big Brother was advertised as something glamorous.

The world had known about America and Britain's mass data collection programs since 2013, but it wasn't until after the 8/8 nuclear bombing that it really went into overdrive. People were demanding, *begging* the government to pass new surveillance legislation, so they did. The Intrusion Countermeasures Electronics act of 2020, redefined the very nature of cyber-security, forcing all firewall developers to place back-doors in their systems for GCHQ to exploit.

All they needed now was an AI to monitor all that data… Mother Mind was that AI. The system had started out equal to human intelligence, but it had only become more advanced since it went online. Capable of tapping into data from all over the country and identifying criminal suspects without the need for human data analysis in real time.

Orwell was right. Crimes both minor and major were now under constant scrutiny. Even political dissent. Any kind of protest organised on social media could easily be intercepted and stopped. It was a nightmare; ensuring the corporate stranglehold on society. We had become a corporatocracy; every political decision influenced by lobbyists or AI algorithms. To some extent, this had always been true… but after the European Union began to break up, one by one, almost every country in the Western World signed up to the toxic 'Intercontinental Trade and Investment Partnership' agreement (ITIP), establishing an international system of 'investor-state dispute settlement courts' (ISDSCs). Specifically, for corporations to sue governments when regulations had '*a negative effect on trade*'. AKA: Profit.

Even the law enforcement agencies and armed forces of the member countries had become privatised! After a series of legal battles, Private Military Companies had essentially become training and recruitment agencies for most of Armed Forces of the states who had signed up for the agreement. Earning points on your mercenary licence now were legally considered to be the equivalent of rising through the ranks of any country in NATO.

It was nothing short of a coup. The most extensive power grab in human history. Now the world was adequately controlled by the four big-data giants: Virtualife, the Scandinavian Next-Gen Industries, Sinotech in China, and Russia's Balticsoft. Each one with their fingers in the pie of every industrial sector on the planet.

Someone had to fight it.

Companies like Virtualife had replaced 70% of the world's labour force with robots and AI programs. Unemployment was through the roof. Data was now worth more than physical products. So, what was their forward-thinking economic solution to the problem? Virtual capitalism. Have people compete for jobs in cyberspace… and take a cut of it.

Even politicians had become dependent on the analysis of the hyper-intelligent programs, able to make sense of the leviathan amount of information coming from their constituents… *to better control them.* Of course, the AIs were meant to provide objective solutions to political problems… but their programming would always show a certain amount of bias towards the will of the original software developers, *and their clients.*

It had to stop somewhere. I had tried arguing with my parents about it; they only gave half-baked answers about why other economic systems had failed and that we should have been grateful for what *'Mister Awasaki'* had done for us, somehow completely ignoring the fact the guy obviously had a screw loose. Some bizarre fantasy about trying to save the world. In recent years, he'd become a recluse. All of his friends turned on him after he signed the contract with GCHQ and the NSA. Got what he deserved if you ask me. Now, he practically never left the luxury fortress that was Virtualife Tower. Living his life through VR and android avatars; able to be anywhere and everywhere in the world, fed to him by an AI recreation of his dead fiancé…

But my parents had bought into his scam. I'd spent most of my childhood in the care of one nanny or another, while they jetted off or jacked into the matrix. Getting rich off improving the algorithms of oppression.

People would tell me that I was just going through a rebellious phase. Nothing pissed me off more. It didn't stop me. Virtualife was about to get a good swift kick in the ass.

"Found any more info on Project Selection on Mum's PC?" I asked.

Katherine shook her head.

"She's been very careful to encrypt any communications regarding it," she explained. "I wouldn't be able to crack it on my own, and Spiritform will have their cache full after this. The Project Selection files are huge."

Project Selection. A name that kept cropping up over the last year. I would hear my parents talk about it in hushed, whispered voices, falling silent every time they caught me listening in; denying they had been talking at all. I gathered that it was related to drone operations in Syria. It screamed controversy. Something juicy for every social network to sink its teeth into.

Virtualife had its fingers in more pies than it knew what to do with, including private military contracts. They owned Global-Arms, one of the more prominent security companies contracting for the British and US governments. The war against the Islamic State had been going for over thirty years now. The longest and bloodiest conflict of the 21st century and Virtualife was trying to keep their involvement out of the public eye.

I couldn't help myself. I had to know.

"97% complete," Katherine announced to me.

"Right…" I breathed slowly, wrapping my fingers nervously against the casing of the laptop.

Online I went by the name of 'Shad0w Cell'. All of the big hacker chat rooms considered me a noob, a *'script kiddie'*. They were right, I was new at this. The exploit I'd used to steal the data wasn't going to earn me fame and glory. We had a home LAN, but my mother's terminal also had access to one of Virtualife's virtual private network. She had taken all the reasonable precautions to protect herself from online cyber-attacks. Her system was running some nasty little ICE programs. Intrusion Countermeasures Electronics; a blanket term that had come to cover all AI-aided cyber-security systems. Firewalls, anti-viruses, honeypot programs etc. The ICE term had started out as a buzzword in old science fiction works. But both the UK and US governments passed legislation at similar times both referencing the word, and it had since become the standard name in the business. They also declared cyberspace a theatre of war, with a whole other clusterfuck of dystopian implications.

The programs my mum was running were at least level five on the Kurzweil scale of AI adaptability, but it wasn't very effective against local attacks. I slipped in a memory card with an ICE Breaker installed; a Spiritform-developed logic-bomb called Mime v3.2.

Katherine executed the attack programs. All I had to do was sit back, bash out some ZQL code when *'the human touch'* was needed to break the subroutines and, hey presto, I was in. Virtualife's R&D server on Prometheus Point space station with Admin-Level access.

The station was a joint project between multiple corporations, a hundred and sixty metres in diameter, home to over a thousand scientists...and Virtualife's top secret labs. I'd been tiptoeing around their network in short bursts for the last week, trying to avoid detection from the Administrators. I'd got lucky. I triggered some hidden defence software by accident, might have even messed up one of their tests, but still managed to avoid detection.

I finally found the Project Selection files around nine thirty this morning, hidden in some obscure drive. Took four hours to download. I sweated the entire time, convinced that someone or something would notice me. The smell still lingered in the air, the nano odour-eaters in my clothes struggling to keep up.

Yeah, I was a noob, but I was sure that the *content* of the data would get my screen name out there... even if I didn't know what that was yet. The files were encrypted. Unreadable. I tried to get the private key from the server but failed. It would now take a super quantum computer or equivalent to brute-force crack it.

I was already working on that. I'd made contact with a woman named 'Destiny', a prominent member of the UK branch of Spiritform; the infamous hacktivist group. There had been politically motivated cyber-warriors in the past, but they were more than that; they were revolutionaries. They were founded in the mid-2020s and had dedicated themselves to fighting ITIP, the corporatocracy, and the Mother Mind system.

They were always posting threatening messages online, ready to expose any signs of corruption that would help them win the battle for the hearts and minds of the public. If this didn't prove to them I was worth their time, nothing would.

I'd only been able to find the names of two employees who were officially working on the project. My mum and her colleague; Dr Julie Carpenter. Both of them were scheduled to appear at ModCon this coming Saturday. I'd even volunteered myself to go there in person and use wireless packet injection to introduce a virus to her smartwatch to get more info out of Dr Carpenter's personal area network. I was still waiting on a response for that one, but it would indeed be more natural than another online cyber-attack.

"You really think they'll be able to decrypt it all?" I checked anxiously with Katherine again for the hundredth time. I watched her through my window into cyberspace. She shrugged, examining data as it whirled around her in geometric patterns.

"With the combined power of their entire network, sure," she repeated. "But the percentage of the system's total runtime which will be dedicated to the process will be at the system's discretion."

The OpenSource Soul. A cloud-based distributed neural processing network. A million home computers with the Soul Searcher operating system installed, networked together, each one processing a part of the overall block-chain. Together it formed a system that could stand toe to toe to with the specifications of any corporate-built supercomputer, each AI networked together to create a hive-mind. With that kind of runtime plugged into a standard virtual personal assistant, each member of Spiritform had access to AIs which made them a force to be reckoned with. In some circles, it had become the symbol of the future of civilisation; a type of cybernetic government.

No one knew who the original developers were; a group of mysterious programmers who'd released the source code online to download and edit. Many forward-thinking smaller companies like Next-Gen industries were now taking advantage of the system's power, but it had been mainly used by hackers. Mostly petty criminals, looking for a safer place to store stolen financial data. But Spiritform had become the 'official' hacktivist group of the Soul.

It would take processing in the Yottaflop range (that's an octillion operations a second; and yes, that is an actual number) to crack the encryption used on the Project Selection files. They could do it…but there was a catch. If the AI deemed the request to have a high priority, it would only take a week. If not, months.

"I still can't believe you went through with this," Katherine added, folding her arms on the screen and shaking her head. "You should have at least waited until Mother Mind steps down from Condition-Three surveillance."

The higher the national security threat level, the more systems the AI could monitor on its own authority. Right now, London was gripped in fear of a prolific serial killer, *'Jack-21'*. The media had originally dubbed him the 'Jack the Ripper for the 21st century', but as the name began circulating around the net, it was shortened. That sick bastard had killed at least three people a day for the last two weeks, all of whom had implants. He didn't stop at just killing them; he disembowelled them using a medical laser to remove any implants for fuck-knows-what. It was like something out of the Texas Chainsaw Massacre. How people got that screwed up was beyond me.

The police had upped their drone patrols and added more checkpoints. I was always astounded how readily people went along with it.

Katherine was probably right, doing it now it had been a risk. But it was the only time Mom had left her terminal unattended for weeks.

I went to check the news, sending the telepathic command to open Twitter. The holographic screen flashed out of the miniaturised projector, displaying the blue and white graphical layout of the website. I ran the search for news related to *#Jack-21*. Sure enough, the results came in from all the accounts of major online publications. The latest victim was some whore; a polish girl named Olenka Odaj from Enfield. Her body had been found by the riverside with her synthetic stomach ripped out. A popular choice for those looking to stay thin. Something else I'd nagged my parents for… no joy of course. *Tight Asses.*

I scrolled down the web page with waving gestures, and came to a video embedded by *BBC* news from *YouTube*, quickly skipping the advert. An interview with a police officer leading the investigation; Detective Inspector Daniel Haines. Black dude, late twenties, early thirties. Broad and muscular, a built like a boxer, with thick cheekbones and a sturdy, rounded, bearded chin. He wore a black intellifabric coat with a white shirt and tie underneath, lit up from the light of a dozen cameras.

"The investigation is ongoing," he continued carefully, looking like a rabbit caught in the headlights. "Churchbell Security is committed to…"

"Is it true that your department has yet to find any witnesses or any evidence at all?" one of the reporters blurted out. He tried to conceal his nervous twitch at that question.

"I'm afraid I'm not at liberty to discuss the specifics of the case that rest assured we are working hard to…"

"How much longer do you expect the city to stay on high alert if you really don't have any clues to the identity of the killer?" another reporter interrupted.

"I would like to thank the people of London for their continued cooperation and apologise for any inconvenience caused by the increased level of security. The current threat level has been deemed by Scotland Yard due to the technology that appears to be at Jack-21's disposal, making him a credible terrorist threat and…"

"How do you know it's a *him*?!" a reporter from a feminist news website shouted.

The press exploded with a hundred questions at once. The young detective, instantly overwhelmed by the roar, was left trying to calm them down with exaggerated waves.

My attention was drawn away from the video when I heard the scrape of a footstep from inside the living room. My heart skipped a beat, and my nerves went wild, sending me jumping out of bed. Only to breathe a sigh of relief when my robot dog came plodding in through the automatic sliding door.

His name was Rex, a Dobertron-3000. When I got him, he had synthetic fur, but I had… tinkered with him. I'd removed it, revealing the bulky machinery underneath. His chassis was a gun-metal grey, the default colour of the meta-material cloak I'd installed. His metallic skull had rigid outlines and had a series of threatening-looking carbon-nanotube spikes for teeth.

My parents hadn't approved of the mods, but all my friends were pimping their robots, so there! His eyes were still the original models; the plastic lenses swivelled inside their articulated sockets, giving me a puppy stare and wagging his hydraulic tail, and he gave me a playful bark through the speakers embedded in his throat. I grinned back at him, and loudly patted the blue covers of my bed, signalling him to come bounding up to sit beside me with a mechanical whir. He happily curled himself up and rested his head on my knee.

"Silly doggie!" I said in the tone a mother would use to talk to her baby, and patted him on his pressure-sensitive barrel belly, cold and hard against my skin.

He was wagging his tail uncontrollably, making loud slapping sounds against the bed covers. I loved him. His CPU may have been limited compared to some androids on the market, but what he lacked in intelligence he made up for in personality. But he did have a more practical use, other than just being man's simulated best friend. I'd saved a backup copy of the Project Selection files to his internal Memory Drive and programmed him to go into hiding if I was turned in to the police.

Whaddya know? I'm already thinking like an anarchist.

I carried on playing with Rex, while the upload crawled closer and closer to 100%. I started to feel thirsty. I telepathically loaded up the Fridge App on my smartwatch, presenting me with a list of what we had stocked. I scrolled through the holographic projection until I saw we still had six cans of *Red Bull* in stock. I tried tapping on the icon to request our Fetchit Drone to pick it up for me but was presented with a message:

<<Sorry! Your drone is already on a mission!>>

"Bastards," I grumbled; Dad never told me when he was-

My ears pricked up… somewhere nearby I could hear a faint, familiar buzzing sound. Helicopter propellers. I turned to look and saw a drone hovering outside my window. It almost took me by surprise it was so ugly. The visual scan my watch camera automatically ran didn't recognise the model, and neither could I. It was like an over-sized stag beetle, suspended by a set of rotors, with a rather vicious looking pair of pincers mounted on its head…while the glow of its sensor array was locked firmly at me.

I frowned angrily at it; the operator should've known it was violating our private airspace.

"Hey!" I barked, giving it the finger.

The robot quickly turned in the air and dashed away, leaving me scowling.

Bloody peeping Toms…

My *Porsche* data visor was resting on its charging station on my bed stand. Red and black goggles, housing the lens-shaped transparent screens for augmented and virtual reality. I slipped it over my eyes. The unit flickered to life, presenting me with a heads-up a virtual overlay on my field of vision with graphics and icons popping up. Time, power and wireless connectivity icons were displayed in the bottom right-hand corner with the home screen icon on the left. White dots appeared over objects in the room, indicating they were chipped and transmitting data over the World-Wide Mesh. I telepathically clicked on the icon floating over my laptop and began remotely streaming data from it to the visor to keep an eye on the upload; now at 98%.

I stretched and heaved myself out of bed, cautiously navigating around the Cleaning-Bot. The auto-door slid open and I stepped out onto the varnished wooden floor of our living room; the air distinctively fresher outside of my bedroom. Our morphiture (morphing claytronic furniture) was stretched out in front of the main wall screen. It was currently configured to take the form of a navy-blue couch. It was built from billions of nanobots, capable of rearranging themselves to take the form of practically any piece of furniture. I'd seen it morphing in-between structures, like grey putty being moulded by a pair of invisible hands. Freaky as hell.

I headed towards the fridge, past the nanotech self-cleaning surface of the kitchen counter. The sound of our bio-printer churned in the background, synthesising a leg of lamb inside a vat of amniotic fluid. The screen on the front of the fridge welcomed me and chimed a message, congratulating me for sticking to my recommended dietary plan. *Condescending bitch.* I opened the door and began looking for the *Red Bull*, my search guided by the homing chip embedded in the can. I found them behind a carton of eggs and grabbed the cold aluminium, admiring the animated graphics etched into the surface; the company's logo kicking its hooves, angrily snorting with an exaggerated cartoon cloud. I cracked open the can and sipped the sickly-sweet liquid, somewhat resenting my love of it. Energy drinks were redundant compared to cybernetic and genetic enhancements. I turned to head back when my visor began buzzing its ringtone.

<<Incoming Call: Claudia Schwarz>>

My face lit up. Long-distance relationships were a bitch, even with virtual reality, but my heart fluttered whenever she called… although I was probably about to get nagged.

"Put it through the main screen," I asked Katherine eagerly.

<<Connection Established>>

The video streamed from her webcam, her image shining from the living room wall screen. Her make-up was as pale as chalk, bringing out the silvery circuitry tattooed on her skin. Her eyes were implants; like sunglasses embedded into her skull. Her hair was the same color, dangling around her chest; bound within a suffocating self-lacing corset with sleeves leading all the way to spiky bracelets wrapped around her wrists. Her skirt covering the top of her fishnet leggings, with pulsing purple fluorescent lights integrated into the mesh. Her feet housed in thick steel-capped boots with steel plates running up the shins.

Yeah… she was hot.

"Hey, babe!" I greeted her enthusiastically.

"How's it going?" she replied abruptly, her German accent coming in loud and clear.

"Do you mean me, or the upload?" I laughed, plopping myself on the couch in front of the screen, Rex hopping up onto the cushion next to me.

"Both?" she deadpanned, not seeming to care.

"Smooth."

"Well?" she repeated impatiently, folding her arms. I was taken aback by her tone, more abrupt than usual.

"Uh, well, yeah," I replied, checking the progress of the data transfer. It had just hit 99%. "Oh almost…"

<<Upload complete>>

"There…" I gave a sigh of relief and wiped the sweat from my brow. "Bloody hell. Thank fuck that's out the way."

"Good… good." She nodded, her mouth remaining tightly neutral, refusing to reveal any emotion… that wasn't normal.

"Something wrong, hun?" I asked, cautiously watching her reaction. "I thought you'd be happier? It was your idea!"

"My idea?" she snorted suddenly. "I gave you the means to rebel. Nothing more, nothing less."

That struck a nerve. I frowned, racking my brain to figure out what I'd done to piss her off.

"Rebel?" I cried feeling insulted. "Is that what you think? That I'm going through my angry-at-mom-and-dad phase?"

"Yes," she responded in a calculated manner with an unnervingly meek smile. My heart sunk rapidly. We were a happy couple yesterday, and now I had a horrible feeling I was going to get dumped.

"Is there something you wanted to say?" I inquired nervously, afraid. The skin around her eye implants drooped with regret.

"Just… that I'm sorry," she sighed, "for getting you involved in this."

That sounded promising… the sinking feeling subsided a little.

"Getting me involved?" I scoffed. "Babe, I'm the one…"

"I know," she interrupted me, "that's what made it so easy…"

I froze.

"I… I don't… What are you talking about?" I stuttered, trying to find the words.

"Goodbye."

<<Call Ended>>

"Wait!" I cried in futility, ready to reach through the screen. Her image faded away into the cream-coloured wall. She was gone. I sat there with my hand stretched out, my mouth open with bewilderment. I'd been dumped before, but never like that. A lingering uneasiness was eating away from the back of my mind. There was something else going on. I could feel it. She'd talked me into doing something illegal in more ways than I could count, and now…

CRASH!

"Shit!" I yelled. The sound of breaking glass sent Rex and myself springing to our feet. Rex barked angrily at where the bang had come from; the bathroom. To my confusion, the door was still closed. I turned from side to side. Through the windows, I saw the storm was still billowing outside, the glass being pounded by the wind and the rain.

Must've been the wind …

"Bloody hell." I sighed, reassuring myself, shaking my head. I laughed and held a hand to my pounding heart, taking deep breaths to calm myself.

The relief would not last. I felt it; a weak rumble beneath my feet. Then another. Footsteps. *Heavy* footsteps. My heart froze.

"But… but that's impossible!" I protested. "We're twenty-seven floors up!? How could someone…"

Katherine reacted faster than I did, activating the mag-lock on the bathroom door. There was a soft click, and a red light flashed on the handle.

BANG!

"Jesus!" I yelled, jumping backwards in shock.

A dominant force rammed against the door, followed with a loud scratching sound against the lock, like a wild animal trying to force their way in.

"Why hasn't the burglar alarm tripped?" I cried telepathically.

"It's offline. Unable to determine the cause. I'm calling the police now!" Katherine replied, her electronic voice echoing in my head.

No way that's a coincidence.

"Oh, God! It's *them,* isn't it?" I realised, my eyes wide with terrified panic.

Virtualife!

Claudia had tricked me! It was the only explanation! A bullshit sting operation! Waves of tears starting flooded out of my eyes. I started babbling to the intruder; desperately apologising, swearing I would never do it again, that I would delete all the copies of the data I had and would do anything to make up for it.

They weren't listening. I heard a grabbing sound, followed suddenly by an aggressive grinding. My jaw dropped. The magnetic lock was still active, but the door was giving way! Inch by inch the burglar on the other side was forcing it open with sheer brute force!

"Oh, fuck me!" I yelled, gasping. My mouth hung open.

"My signal is being jammed! Go! Get out of there! Run!" I'd never seen an AI as scared as Katharine's avatar was right now.

She didn't need to tell me twice. Adrenaline took hold of me, and I whirled like a tornado. My feet barely touched the ground as I went into a mad dash towards-

The bathroom door slammed against the wall as it flung open.

A whir of a fan.

Pain.

Excruciating pain.

It happened so fast, like a paper cut. A hot, sharp, burning flash across the left knee. One second I was running for my life; the next I tumbled forward, the varnished floor rushing toward me. My face slammed into it, tasting the wood in my mouth.

I picked myself up, gripping my head, pounding with a mild concussion. I didn't even recognise the alarm blaring from my visor. I checked the emergency notification on my display:

<<Warning!>>

<<Bio-monitor sensors detect heavy injury sustained!>>

<<Uploading data to NHS emergency response service...>>

....

<<Error: Unable to establish connection to server>>

The agony set in now, shooting up my nervous system like a fiery electric current. I didn't want to know. I almost couldn't bring myself to look. I trembled, forcing myself to turn around.

I was better off not knowing.

"OH FUCK! OH FUCK!!" I screamed, my lungs burning with blood-curdling torment, ringing against the sound-proof walls.

My left leg had been cut in half. Everything below the knee was gone. It was an elegant, clean, precision cut. The foot lay discarded on its side, swallowed by the pool of blood spewing out of the wound.

I'd seen this before; a laser cut. In a panicked frenzy, I fumbled in futility to stem the tide of blood. Rex was hunched in a defensive posture next to me, snarling angrily at the door frame, ready to defend me.

I turned, expecting to see the face of the shooter.

The doorway was empty, yet the air filled with ghostly wavy distortion, reminding me of heat shimmer. The shape of the optical interference formed the outline of a figure. I recognised the effect from *YouTube* videos; the distinctive sign of optical camouflage.

There was someone there all right; nearly invisible. Suspended in mid-air was a strange crimson glow, like molten lava, slowly fading away. I recognised that too; the cooling lens of a Combat Laser.

It clicked in my mind. I knew who it was.

It wasn't Virtualife.

It was so much worse.

Jack-21.

I knew it. I was dead.

"Andrew, the files!" Katherine cried through the visor, using a graphical arrow to point towards Rex.

In my dying moments, courage I didn't know I had took control. I heaved myself painfully onto my side to face Rex.

"GO!" I spat through the pain.

Rex turned to me, drooping his tail and ears and whining with sadness. Another whir came from the bathroom; the sound of a cooling fan and the electric crackle of a capacitor. The aura of the laser glow brightening once more.

"GO!"

He whined reluctantly then spun around and bolted towards the door. It slid open just in time for him to slip out into the corridor. The laser reached full charge and fired. The searing red beam blazed at the speed of light, narrowly missing his hind legs. The blast scorched the wooden floor instantly, leaving a black, flaming crater in the floorboards and scattering splinters across me.

The door snapped shut behind Rex. He was gone.

The last time I would ever see him… the last time I was ever going to see anything.

I felt the rumble of the footsteps again… even closer.

I shook uncontrollably, edging back to face the ghostly figure looming over me like the grim reaper. With the last shred of strength I could muster, I agonisingly dragged myself away from him.

"Please…" I begged him through tears. "Y…You don't have to do this! My parents are rich, you can-"

A sturdy grip wrapped around my remaining ankle and a single forceful yank pulled me back towards the cloaked figure. I stared, horrified, into the void where his eyes should have been.

The laser began to hum again; the fiery red glow swivelled over my stomach… towards the scar from the implant surgery. I shut my eyes for the last time.

"I'm sorry Mum…"

The beam seared into my flesh.

The faint smell of burning silicon wafted into the air as it cut into my implant.

I screamed.

I shat myself.

Mother Mind Profile 9124-5631-4877-0672:

<<New Data Received>>>
<<Updating...>>
<<Update Complete>>

First Name: Andrew
Surname: Ilian
Status: Deceased

- Time Stamp: 05/10/2045-17:47

CHAPTER 2

Mother Mind Profile 2446-7128-5978-2501:

First Name: Arthur
Surname: Wells
Status: Living
Nationality: British
Occupation(s):

- Private Investigator
  - Status: Self-employed
  - Organisation: Arthur Wells & Associates

Criminal Record:

- Arrested: 17/11/2037
  - Offence: Suspected of unauthorised access to computer material
  - No formal charges

Known Aliases:

- IronRoot

Biometric Data:

- Gender: Male
- Date of Birth: 22/04/2018
- Age: 27
- Race: Caucasian
- Hair Colour: Brown
- Eye Colour: Hazel
- Height: 1.89m
- Weight: 90kg
- Ailments: None
- Cybernetic Percentage: 43%
- Genetic Modifications:
  - Performance Enhancement Therapy

Immediate Family:

- Mother: Maria Wells
- Father: Liam Wells
- Siblings: 1

- Sister: Juliet Wells

Relationships:

- Status: Single

Contact Information:

- *Drop down for more info*

Live Surveillance:

- Status: *Partially Available*
- Date: 05/10/2045
- Current Location: Orion Block Apartment Complex, Chiswick, West London
- Local Time: 17:32 GMT

The video streamed from the smartwatch to my HUD, loading into my visual cortex through my neural implants.

"The police turned their backs on me!" exclaimed George Harper, manager of Blythe Road Dentists, a tanned, silver-haired Greek man wearing his plastic medical apron. "They had their suspect in custody; they didn't care that the Botnet he'd programmed was still keeping my website offline! I was losing money, but there was no criminal! Told me they *couldn't charge an AI with extortion*, and that it was something for a cyber-security company to deal with. You can imagine how far I got with that. If it weren't for Arthur Wells, I would've lost my business! He was professional and personal. He knew exactly what he was doing both from the technical and social perspective. I'd highly recommend him to anyone looking for a private investigator."

The video ended with the brown and gold graphics of my business logo: *www.arthurwells-pi.com*

I couldn't help but smirk at my handiwork. Nothing like a good review, especially one with a customer feedback video. I was hoping that would be the big case, the one that would get my brand out there. Any news concerning rogue AIs had a way of making headlines, out of fear of the impending robot apocalypse.

The hedges around the sky garden rustled in the wind, the industrial smell of the city wafting in the air. The gardening robot shuffled past; a Yan-Shi model android, constructed from a self-repairing nanotech alloy and plastic painted white and leaf green. It had oversized cameras for eyes giving it a friendly appearance. The unit brushed by me with a whir, it's articulated polished steel hands trimmed the hedge with an all-in-one morphing claytronic toolkit, currently set as a pair of garden shears. A large *Roomba* of the same colour scheme followed the android by the heels, sucking up the leaves.

A strong gust sent the vapour from my e-cigarette blowing painlessly into the lenses of my bionic eyes; the scent of the enhanced berry flavoured e-liquid clung to my skin. I felt the folds of my hat flapping. I pressed down with my moulded graphene hand to keep it in place. Both of my arms were prosthetics, equipped with a variety of sensors and tools, making a quiet mechanical hum whenever I moved.

A passionate voice cried over the howl of the wind from my behind.

"Here we go again," I muttered sourly, facepalming myself.

"The devil walks among us!" yelled the preacher behind me, standing on a wooden box surrounded by his dull-eyed flock, a sea of mesmerised faithful faces. I tried to mentally block them out, tempted to adjust the settings on my cochlear implants to tune them out entirely.

"The Anti-Christ is not a man, but a movement! A system of control that has seduced the hearts and minds of mankind with the false hopes of eternal youth, infinite wisdom and the strength of Superman! Even now, the devil is whispering in the ears of so-called *freely elected* leaders. Those in power say that transhumanism is our salvation, but they have been deceived by Satan himself! Our Lord Jesus Christ shall return on Judgement Day; he shall smite all those machine men who believe themselves to be invincible. Only those who have lived their lives by the light of our saviour will be rewarded with eternity in paradise! Ask yourselves, where will you be on that day?"

The crowd gave a cheer of approval, entranced by the priest's words. *Fucking nutjobs.* Luckily, this lot hadn't noticed my augmentations yet. I was cyborg as fuck. My arms, legs, lungs, liver, pancreas, were all replaced by machines. Even about forty percent of my blood supply was made up from respirocyte nanobots. The blood cells were mechanical micro-organisms, using atomic batteries to power molecular motors, and biologically synthesise a variety of medicinal compounds. I could hold my breath for four hours, or survive having my heart blown out.

I suppose they thought of me as a vampire or something. I felt safer knowing that they were being watched by dozens of ultra-HD CCTV cameras and security robots walking the perimeter. Baring in mind the lines between private security and police was now…blurred.

I held up the camera on my blue-on-black custom-built smartwatch to take a picture with the fanatics in the background. I would've liked to take a selfie, but the rise of visual recognition search engines would make it too easy to identify my face. All it took was one glance from a visor, cyber-lenses or bionic eyes and you could be detected in a matter of seconds. Useful at parties; not so helpful when you want to go incognito. I telepathically typed out my status update to go with it:

<<Update: Can't a man smoke in peace?>>

<<Status successfully updated>>

<<Would you like to upload your RE:Call recording as well?>>

I gritted my teeth bitterly and telepathically clicked 'no'. RE:Call was the most popular cognitive-streaming app on the market; an app to turn your neural lace into a recorder to save and upload your memories online. The data included the full sensory experience: sight, smell, sound, taste, touch, and even emotional states. It had given rise to 'experience blogging'. Entire lives saved online for others to watch and 'like'. Real life dramas had replaced television soaps. Getting a divorce could be your ticket to becoming an internet superstar.

My mates had pressured me into getting it. Only used it a couple of times just to shut them up. I'd had enough of that sort of thing.

I went back to my smoke and noticed an *Amazon* delivery drone whizzing overhead, weaving through the air traffic, and reminding me of why I was here.

"How long till SpyFly gets back?" I asked telepathically. A data window enlarged from the bottom of my HUD. The avatar of my Virtual Personal Assistant popped into view.

"ETA two minutes," Liz chirped back. "Plenty of time."

I'd customised her AI-avatar appearance to match with the film noir style I'd chosen for my business, stylised as a secretary from 1940s. She wore a white blouse with the top button undone invitingly, and a long black skirt emphasising her curves, supported by a pair of seductive red heels. Her hair was done up in a couple of buns, and she wore brass-rimmed spectacles. I'd received a few complaints on the website that she was a bit of a sexist design, but hey, branding was important. I'd thought about Sherlock Holmes, but after glancing at my competition in London, it was clear that had been done to death.

So, Humphrey Bogart it was, and I had taken to wearing a brown nanotech intellifabric trench coat. Totally waterproof, the light spit of the rain ran off the material without absorbing a drop, while the thermostat chips began warming up the heating mesh, keeping me nice and toasty. It also had the added bonus of being infra-red shielded, but I hadn't had the chance to test that. I could blend in almost anywhere wearing this, a little bit of facial hair and darkened eyes didn't hurt either.

Hats were starting to come back into fashion, but it also served the practical function of being able to mask my face. Any other look from a hundred years ago would stand out like a sore thumb, but I guess some styles never went out of vogue.

That's what I did, blend in and peek at things that weren't meant to be peeked at. I was damn good at it too. After a year on the job, I felt like I'd seen it all. The exquisite, ancient stone carvings of the London architecture portrayed a grandness that had to be seen to be believed. But it was all an illusion, masking the rotting core. Even so, Britain kept calm and carried on, and I watched it carrying on. The seedy underbelly sprouting weeds through the structure of society, ready to crumble. It was my job to stand back from a distance and silently take notes on behalf of my clients. You could only spend so much time staring at shit before it all became the same.

I was tired of it, but we all had our lot in life. The branding that society pushes on you. I wasn't going to be escaping any time soon, so I might as well make the most of it.

I drew down the tip of my hat to shelter my face, leaving the countdown timer for my drone's return in the top left-hand corner of my heads-up display. SpyFly (as the name suggested) was a robot insect akin to the pollinator drones the government introduced after bees went extinct. It was equipped with a surveillance package; high-powered microscopic cameras and microphones and a range of other sensors. Perfect for my line of work. I'd sent it out as part of my latest investigation.

It was my standard case; infidelity. My client was a fat, sweaty, balding mess of a man by the name of Charlie Duckett. Not that you could tell that from his online avatar. He suspected his wife was having an affair. Apparently, she'd spend a lot of time in private VR chat rooms, then disappear from the house for hours. So rather than applying for his own drone license, he hired me.

I already had the evidence I needed. SpyFly had caught some naughty little footage of Mrs Duckett and her boss in the back seat of a Toyota, parked down an alleyway off Holborn high street, hungrily tearing off each other's clothes. I was gonna break the bad news to him in a virtual meeting tomorrow – better to give him the personal touch, not that I *really* cared. It was one of the selling points of my services, and that only scratched the surface of what you could get for those willing to pay extra. There were also services I couldn't advertise, like being a professional hacker.

My frustration grew as the sermon from the priest grew louder and crazier. I looked over the balcony, watching the crowds bustling below on Chiswick High Road, trying to find something else to concentrate on. The horde below was dressed in bright digital fashion, and branded cybernetic enhancements, shuffling through the urban sprawl, bathed in the light of a thousand media suns. About a quarter of the crowd was android avatars. Remote-controlled robots, operated telepathically by users at home, able to be anywhere in the world in a matter of seconds.

Below me, the streets were filled to the brim. Street-cleaning bots scurried to keep up with the waste left behind by the bustle, weaving through the maze of bodies, and Asian street food stands to grab the litter. But both the robots and the people ignored the homeless, huddled in the shelter provided by doorways and the overhang of Chinese holographic signs and other machinery, clinging to soggy blankets.

To the east of me on the horizon, the towering glass skyscrapers of central London burned as shining beacons of capitalism. A fifty-metre pane of smart glass across the street from me projected endless commercials: *Giorgio Armani* clothes, Kawaguchi Biotech Implants, government propaganda.

"Mother Mind: Keeping you safe for fifteen years!" the voice boomed.

People generally had only one of two reactions to that advert. Safety and protection, or total disgust. I just looked at it with bitterness and regret. But I didn't have time to ponder it.

<<Please stand by>>

<<SpyFly on final approach>>

A graphical arrow appeared on my HUD and guided my eyes towards a corner of the sky. I squinted as the camera lenses in my eyes zoomed in, and the silver body came into focus against the night sky. I held the palm of my hand out flat, as the metal insect came into land, its tiny transparent wings struggling against the wind before touching down on the casing of my palm with a soft clink.

<<SpyFly has landed>>

I sent the neurocommand to shut it down and rolled back my left sleeve. I then ordered a small compartment inside my arm to pop open. A generic storage unit that came pre-installed with prosthetics in my insurance package. GCHQ may have screwed me, but at least I walked away with top-of-the-line self-defence enhancements. I slid the drone back inside and shut the compartment once more before pulling back my sleeve and straightening myself up with a relieved sigh.

"Just in time for your appointment," Liz smiled at me telepathically.

"Right, I'll – OW!"

Something slammed into the back of my head, almost knocking my hat off, followed by a rapid clattering sound on the ground. I rubbed the bruised skin and looked down to see a twisted *Coca-Cola* can beside me, the animated graphics crackling with static. The roar of the religious flock suddenly grew louder and angrier.

"Oh, for fuck's sake…" I sneered. I turned around to see the mob's rage fixated on me, shaking their fists and jeering abuse at me. Of course, I was the only cyborg in the garden.

"Fucking freak!"

"Burn in hell!"

"Go back to Satan, demon!"

"You sold your soul! You sold your soul!"

I glared at them with cold intensity, my grip tightening on a zip by my right thigh. At a moment's notice, I could unzip it and telepathically open the compartment built within my leg unit where my 105-E Magnum smart-revolver was holstered. I had to resist the urge to pull it out and start unloading on them. Religion had a way of bringing up old vitriol inside me. My dad was one of them, one of those who thought technology was the end of the world. He'd only bought me the most basic of basic computers and phones as a kid. I got sneered at school, walking around with a god-damn flip phone when the other kids were using the old neural laces. I had to scrimp, save and steal just to build my first gaming PC. When I tried to learn to programme from *YouTube* videos, my father would spank me, hard. Said I was learning the language of the devil, not that it put me off. *Superstitious cunt.*

He was one of the many people who had lost his job in the automation revolution of the 2020s. A taxi driver put out of work by the driverless car. He ended up working with the Irish Mafia to keep up with the bills. I wanted nothing to do with him. Hadn't seen him or my older sister in years. I would get an occasional message from her once in a blue moon; nothing meaningful.

The crowd's increased activity caught the attention of the black and blue security androids. They looked intimidating with their shoulders and knees covered with large armoured pads, their scanner eyes glowing with intensity. The crowd didn't take too kindly to that, and their yells now turned towards them. I shook my head and scoffed at their ignorance.

"Resident Sally Carter!" the androids barked in unison with shrill electronic voices. They simultaneously pointed at the adolescent girl who had thrown the can, marching towards her with rapid clanging steps.

"You have committed an act of aggression against another resident," the robots continued. "Please refrain from any further offences, or you will be asked to leave. If you fail to comply with this request, we are authorised to remove you by force, and you will be subject to criminal charges."

One of the androids clanked towards me. "Are you all right, sir?" it asked, with synthesised sympathy.

"Never better," I answered flatly, checking the holo-display on my watch to bring up the readout from the bio-monitor sensors in my clothes. No sign of a concussion.

The crowd rallied up, starting to threateningly swarm around the androids. The robots remained calm, standing their ground, scanning the crowd carefully while awaiting instructions from the security control room, linked to the police. It was about to kick off, and I didn't want to be around when it did. I got off the bench and walked briskly toward one of the elevators in the corner of the sky garden, the robot escorting me to the glass alcove. The lift scanned me and opened the pill-shaped cage. Stepping inside, I pressed the icon for the fifteenth floor on the touch panel by the door.

The doors closed and the lift descended along the side of the building. The screens on the doors began displaying a virtual aquarium, blocking the view of the brick wall. I leaned against them and looked out through the window, watching the eco-pods roll past. Tiny, self-sustaining apartments, shaped like oversized silver eggs, resting on their sides and arranged into rows, covered with solar panels and miniature wind turbines. Hundreds of them had been welded onto the skin of the building, held in place by balcony-like walkways, supported by thick steel columns.

The building used to be a call centre; one of the many lines of work that had become obsolete with the rise of AI. It had been gutted and stripped out and turned into housing; cramming in as many apartments as possible. I was lucky enough to get one of the exterior pods, a room with a view.

I checked the display on my watch; only five minutes to the

meeting now. The jitters were starting to set in. I tried not to make eye contact with the CCTV camera mounted to the ceiling. What I was about to do was illegal as fuck, and *breaching data protection* was just the tip of the iceberg. Breaking the Official Secrets Act could land me a life sentence in the Prison Matrix. I'd taken all the precautions I could to make sure Mother Mind couldn't monitor the conversation (its ability to collect data from the dark web was minimal), but that didn't make me safe.

I was trying to talk myself out of it, but that was an exercise in futility. I couldn't ignore that lingering thirst for the truth that had been robbed from me. I had to know. The government had stolen my life. I was gonna steal it back.

I reached the fifteenth floor and stepped out onto the platform, clanging against my boots. I was greeted by the nippy wind once more and walked past my neighbour's pods, brushing past a Housekeeping Android, until I reached number 1511. *Home sweet home.* The scanner atop of the frame identified me, and the door slid open.

"Welcome home, Arthur," a synthesised voice greeted me while notifications on my HUD from the building management server reminded me to pick up my groceries.

I stooped through the doorway, my hat brushing the top of the frame, greeted by overpowering minty air freshener. I tossed it onto my coat hanger, running my fingers through my hair, instantly feeling annoyed the rain had screwed up some of my spikes.

I sighed, gazing at my home. All eight square metres of it. The dimmed purple lights illuminated the cramped space. The bedroom, living room and kitchen rolled into one, making up the main room with the bathroom cubicle directly to the right of the door. My bed was tightly compacted into a snug little alcove across the length of the room, accompanied by a sliding panel built into the wall that could be drawn out to be used as a desk.

There was a drawer underneath for my blue and black custom-built PC, networked to the pod. The cooling system hummed, green LEDs flashing on the front. My sink and dishwasher were mounted to the right of the bed, and a holo-projector was installed on the ceiling of the bed alcove. There was a wall-screen at the foot of the bed so I could work either lying down or sitting up.

The housekeeping droid had tidied away the e-workout equipment I'd left on my bed, placing it in a transparent plastic box beside it. The machine was a mess of wires and electrodes to hook up to the muscles in my body which were still organic. It stung like hell, but it kept me fit without having to go to the gym.

The left wall was dedicated entirely to storage space. My wardrobe, fridge, and closet were stacked one after another beside a set of shelves. The middle and bottom shelves contained a pair of 3D-printers: one a Bio-printer, the other for non-organic objects. On the top shelf, I had arranged a series of photo frames; mostly holiday pics with my mates… even a GIF of a water fight I'd had with Denise from our camping trip to Derbyshire back in the day.

I averted my gaze quickly when the nostalgia got too much. I didn't know why I bothered keeping it up.

So yeah, my humble abode. Pretty much the same as every other pod most people my age were forced to live in. I don't care how big a mess my generation inherited, I deserved better than this. And I did have better once. I'd been forced to move out of my house in Cheltenham after I resigned from my last job at GCHQ. As a PI, I was earning forty grand a year, but that was down from fifty grand as a cyberwarfare specialist. I just couldn't keep up with the rent after that, not with the added cost of my health insurance. The price managed continuously against a health index derived from the data gathered by my bio-monitor sensors. Bloody NHS. GCHQ stopped paying for it after I quit; no veterans package for spooks. I'd be able to survive without it if it wasn't for the maintenance costs for my prosthetics. The repairs on my arms and legs I could handle on my own… a couple of illegally downloaded 3D printer files and I'd be good to go. The tech inside me, not so much. The biggest bitch was the nerve damage; the connections between my biological tissue and the mechanics. Most of the repairs could be done via micro-surgery, handled by medical nanobots delivered by hypospray injections, but it required regular doses and didn't come cheap.

I found myself instinctively checking my calendar app for the next delivery, the readout on my HUD informing me the drone would be here by 20:00. I couldn't bring myself to check the receipt.

I could get them on the black market if I really wanted to. I knew more than my fair share of backstreet pharmacists and surgeons…

but you never knew exactly what you were going to be getting. Not to mention I'd seen their *'practices'*. Grimy little shitholes. Fuck that.

So, why'd I quit GCHQ in the first place? Couldn't tell ya. Not a fucking clue. I had the Official Secrets Act to thank for that.

"Three minutes to go," Liz reminded me, appearing from the bed projector.

"I can hardly contain myself," I deadpanned sarcastically as I hung up my coat.

She folded her avatar's arms, her mouth twisting downwards into a look of concern. "Are you sure you want to do this?"

"You have access to my brain waves," I answered flatly, stretching towards the ceiling, flexing the skin beneath the connection sockets of my prosthetics as I tried to work out the aching nerve damage. Her eyes flickered as she ran the scan while I slid into the bed alcove, sinking into the memory-foam mattress.

"Results inconclusive," she answered.

I sighed with disappointment, while I rolled myself into the bed. Her expression remained neutral; her software glancing over the slight.

"Connecting to Freethought Network now," she announced.

The connectivity icon on my HUD whirled green. My data traffic was now being routed through the criminal satellite network built by Spiritform. The dark web had always been around, but this was the next logical step. The system onion-routed the encrypted packets through dozens of illegal relays in orbit, masking the real users' IP address and making it damn near impossible to intercept the data.

"Connection secure."

Liz opened my CloudLand virtual browser. The window enlarged to take up most of my vision, leaving me looking at the Virtualife logo (the letters V, and a reverse L made of retro-looking polygons) rotating above a bright neon blue digital grid. It had an address bar to connect to websites with VR-sim plug-ins (which was almost every website now). I telepathically clicked on a drop-down menu of bookmarked sites: My online office, digital clubs, game worlds, etc. I scrolled through until I came to 'Dart's private server', with a long obscure URL in the Russian top-level domain, and clicked on it:

<<You are about to enter a full-immersion virtual reality simulation.>>

<<Please be seated and ensure your surroundings are appropriate.>>

<<Begin simulation? Yes/No>>

I shut my eyes, letting my world go dark, bracing myself for the bizarre sensations to come. I issued the command.

<<Loading environment>>

<<Running neural lace device drivers>>

<<Processing consciousness shift>>

A progress bar appeared, accompanied with rapidly changing lines of code of operations being processed by my personal area network (PAN for short), my neural lace interfacing wirelessly, streaming the data from my PC.

The logo faded away as the Nanochips in my head activated, loading the data into the implant's internal memory, replacing the synaptic signals from the real world with digital ones. One by one, billions of multi-coloured pixels glittered across the inside of the artificial eyelids for my bionic eyes, dancing around in a choreographed manner, twisting and morphing with every colour the visual cortex could comprehend, silent as the vacuum of space. A neon green chessboard-like grid appeared below me and began to morph; rising, expanding and compressing into the outlines of objects, each square on the grid rapidly filling with colour as the textures were loaded.

The objects had definitive shapes now, two tear-drop shaped chairs and a round circular table with a single leg rezzed into existence. Lastly, the input data for the rest of the sensory experience loaded, allowing me to feel the objects beneath my skin. The air smelled empty; nothing programmed for those parameters.

<<Loading complete>>

<<Consciousness shift complete>>

<<Welcome!>>

I glanced at the world I'd been loaded into, the universe of cyberspace glittering on the horizon, and sat down in one of the glowing chairs that seemed like it had been moulded out of light itself. I felt the warm heat emanating from it. These were the only three objects in this entire digital universe, nothing but darkness and a neon grid beneath my feet. I shook my head critically; it was a bit of a slapdash job… Even I could do better.

I threw a frustrated glare at the empty chair. He was late, of course. Bloody Russians. I imagined him rolling out of bed, stinking of vodka.

The guy I was meeting was a member of Zenkai; the infamous Eurasian hackers-for-hire group. They claimed that they could break into anything; as long as the price was right… I was expecting better service than this.

I scratched my arm, noticing the differences between my real body and the randomly generated virtual avatar. Gone was the nanotech fabric, replaced with an old-fashioned nylon coat. I opened the customisation menu and saw my new look on my HUD. The outline of my face was not too far from my real appearance, but with a few slight alterations here and there like the colour of my eyes, hair and beard – not to mention my total lack of implants. Just different enough to fool facial recognition scans; anonymity was the goal here. My screen name hovered above my head: IronRoot.

I found myself pinching the imaginary flesh of my virtual avatar. The closest I would get to having my real arms again. It's not like I wasn't grateful for my enhancements; GCHQ's health insurance package was the best, offering the latest and greatest cybernetic and genetic augmentations supplied by Heinrich Raith Inc.

I'd always wanted to be enhanced…I just wished I could remember *how* it had happened.

A yellow and red paper menu stood folded in the middle of the table. I had a look through the items available for use in this world: a selection of sandwiches, crisps, drinks, cigarettes, and e-drugs. I tapped the pictures for a cup of tea and a joint.

<<Loading...>>

Pixels fell like snow across the table, settling quickly and morphing into a finely rolled spliff, lying next to steel lighter and a white mug, steam rising gently off it.

Come to Papa.

I grinned, took the joint between my lips and sparked up. The sweet, simulated taste of ganja beamed into my head. There was always going to be a market for physical narcotics, but the industry had taken a hit from e-drugs. The program took effect quickly running on my brain implants, instantly making me light headed. Just like the first real one I'd smoked at seventeen. No chemical build-up, just pure electrical awesome. Virtual sims weren't all fun and games though. Combined with the enhanced focus mode of most neural laces it was possible to absorb the skills from training simulations in a matter of a night. I'd become a boxing expert in a matter of weeks (which was more than handy in this line of work).

I puffed away on my own for just over ten minutes, debating whether or not I should write him off as a no-show when the message appeared on my HUD:

<<Dart is logging in>>

"Final-fucking-ly," I sighed with relief.

I watched another human figure load into existence in the chair next to me. The mess of pixels and wireframe began to clear, and I was soon looking at Dart's avatar. He'd customised its appearance to resemble an old-school hippy, complete with a tie-dye shirt and long greasy hair tied back into a ponytail. His eyes twinkled with trippy psychedelic colours.

"Sorry for da wait," he apologised with his thick Eastern European accent, offering out his hand to shake. "My friend, this job can take twenty-four hours. Understand?"

"Uh-huh," I answered flatly, wanting to get down to business. "You got what I came here for?"

He nodded and held out his right palm. A ghostly-appearing icon floated out; the graphics resembled the outline of a human brain, crackling with electricity. The text beneath indicated it was an install file for a program called *'GC-Crack'*. A home-programmed secure virtual private network app.

I sat there, mesmerised by the rotating graphics. It seemed surreal. Could this really be it? Could this file really hold the key to everything I'd been searching for?

"Sometime before the singularity please?" Dart snapped impatiently, his eyes pulsing as he spoke.

"Huh? Sorry," I blurted out, unsure how much time had passed. I scooped the icon out of his hand. It disappeared in a puff of pixels and reappeared on my HUD. "Run the scan," I ordered Liz.

<<Initialising scan....>>

I watched with bated breath as lines of code whirled by on my HUD, rapping my fingers anxiously against the armrest.

<<Scan complete>>

<<0 threats detected>>

<<Timestamp verified>>

"Looks good to me," Liz smiled. "The program is receiving data from GCHQ's Personnel Neural-Archive Server."

I threw my fist into the air in celebration, Dart chuckling at my amusement.

I couldn't believe it. It shouldn't have been possible; all of GCHQ's classified servers were air-gapped. No internet connection, designed to keep people like us out.

"How the hell did you do it?" I asked, genuinely impressed.

"This is inside job," he explained. "My contacts in admin department has installed intelligent back-door into the server. Every day, anti-virus goes through updates which require it to be connected to internet-"

"Temporarily disabling it. Giving you a time window to download the data without anyone noticing."

"Da. You're a clever man, IronRoot."

Not clever enough.

Cyberwarfare specialist sounded like my dream job when I was seventeen. I didn't have the Official Secrets Act in mind then. Under legislation introduced in 2029, the government could erase classified information from the minds of former intelligence agents. So, that was that. Almost every recollection from the day I went on their payroll to the day I quit was gone. My mind was a jigsaw with half the pieces missing. I had some flashes of memory from my time there, like my friends and colleagues and some of the skills I had learned there, but the rest was a collection of fleeting images.

I couldn't even remember *why* I had quit, but that wasn't the worst of it. When I woke up from the memory erasure, I found myself in a hospital bed with nearly half of my body replaced with prosthetics and no idea how it had happened. I had a half-assed debriefing with my commanding officer after the procedure. He told me that I'd resigned after being involved in what he kept calling an 'Industrial Accident'.

I worked a desk job.

How the fuck did I end up in an industrial accident?

And since when are *accidents* classified?

It was a bullshit cover-up if I ever saw one. I wanted to sue them, but my legal advice AI put that notion to bed pretty quickly. Private investigator was one of three possible lines of work that GCHQ's career advice software recommended for me. I could've gone and worked for any cyber-security company in the world, but that would mean handling more classified data, and most corporate non-disclosure agreements included clauses which could result in their lawyers requesting my memory to be erased again. I decided right then and there, I was never going through this shit again.

Besides, I liked cracking stuff. It was a part of me I couldn't let go of. Even if I did join a security firm, I'd only be on the defensive side of the cyberwarfare world, and that wasn't my scene. There weren't many jobs that I could market that skill set to, at least not legitimately.

So, I struck out on my own; self-employed. I'd spent just over a year scraping by, living from case to case and struggling to keep up with the bills. Not to mention all the shit I'd had to see in this line of work.

I'd dealt with drug dealers, rapists, human traffickers. The real nasty underbelly of 'jolly England'. I'd gotten into my fair share of firefights; gone into hospital with a few near miss gunshot wounds… and even killed in self-defence.

I was investigating a back-street surgery on behalf of a pair of bereaved parents, having lost their child to an infection following a botched attempt at installing a bionic liver. The kid had been too afraid to rat them out before he'd died, but the family still wanted justice. Little did anyone know that the joint was being run by the Triads, the Chinese Mafia. The guy running it was packing a shotgun behind the counter. I got lucky. Managed to draw my revolver out before he did and put a hole in his head… and then spent the next five minutes throwing up until the focus mode setting on my neural lace took hold.

When Liz told me I'd been using the setting for too long, I spent the night drinking myself into a stupor trying to control the guilty shakes. If a real cop had seen that, he'd be in counselling before he'd had anything to say about it. It wasn't something they liked to talk about, but at least they *had* people to talk to. It wasn't something you could speak to your 'normal' friends about, whenever it happened.

I couldn't afford therapy. The most common treatment for post-traumatic stress these days was memory erasure…Not an option. So, I had to make do with alcohol, and emotional management software to deal with flashbacks and jittering shakes that I would habitually get. I'd installed a combat mode setting as well. Military grade. The cure for conscientious objectors. Inducing a psychopathic-like trance in the user which would allow the user to pull the trigger without a second's hesitation. Without the initial trauma of the event, the guilt was removed from the equation. No PTSD or your money back. And it was working. All I had to do was keep my own…ethical concerns at bay.

Maybe I should've been blaming myself for joining GCHQ. That I should've known this would happen one way or the other. It happens to all spooks, regardless if they resign or not. But I still wanted to get back at them, feeling I'd been betrayed in ways I didn't think they were capable of. I remembered being a model employee, a civil servant, and they had robbed me of my dignity. I'd lie awake at night, staring at the new projector on the ceiling, trying to make sense of just who I was now. My implants stopped me getting physically tired, and the internet was always a distraction… but I *felt* exhausted.

The biggest piss-take was that the government kept back-ups of all erased memories on their neural archive servers. With Dart's help, I could steal it back, but then I'd be a traitor to my country. Tit for tat, I suppose.

"The files will run using RE:Call. I can only send you a few gigabytes at a time," Dart grinned at me hungrily. "The app will inform you when I upload more. The first time is free; seventy gigs are ready now. This same as one day of memories."

"And the rest?"

Dart held his hand out in a reassuring matter. "We'll speak when you return. You must first understand what you have agreed to."

"What's that supposed to mean?" I asked with a raised eyebrow.

"Maybe some things are best left forgotten, my friend," he said cryptically, rubbing his hands together, the colours of his eyes simmering intensely. "If you regret what you have seen, I give no refund."

"You're a lousy salesman," I replied cautiously, holding back my suspicions. No honour among thieves. Running background checks was a big part of my job, but if data dealers are good at one thing, it's anonymity. As far as I could tell he was either safe enough or just really good at covering his tracks. The flashing '0 threats detected' message was reassuring, but the scan program was only as good as the programmer.

I held back my reservations and executed the install program, the progress bar filling rapidly in front of my eyes.

<<Installation complete>>

<<Initialising program>>

<<GC-Cracker would like to access your neural lace>>

<<Grant access?: Yes/No>>

I felt a nagging sense of hesitation whenever that dialogue window appeared. Once I gave the program access, my brain would be in in the hands of the software. Risky business, knowing that the moral compass of the coder was questionable, to say the least. In for a penny, though…

<<Access granted>>

<<Establishing secure connection to remote server>>

A menu appeared, displaying the files stored in a folder on Dart's secure server. Sure enough, there was a seventy-gigabyte RCR file with a long numeric name waiting for me. I telepathically hovered the cursor over the data and checked when the date the record was initially produced: 10/04/2038.

I recognised the date; my first day at GCHQ. My heart raced back in the real world, feeling it pounding even here. I hurriedly downloaded the file to my memory drive and began running it in RE:Call, the silver-white graphics rapidly filling up my HUD.

<<Download complete>>

<<Initialising...>>

<<Welcome to RE:Call!!>>>

<<Loading File: 9786-8130-2931-10042038>>

<<File loaded>>

<<Ready to begin Memory Playback>>

<<Begin?: Yes/No>>

"Game time," I breathed.

I braced myself for fuck knows what, and issued the command.

<<Initialising memory playback>>

The world around me began to blur. A stream of grainy images whirled through my mind's eye like a roller coaster. My stomach went in loops as sharp, stark memories of arbitrary and significant events alike seemed to pop into my head, only to burn out and be replaced.

The present was gone, and long forgotten sensations began drifting back to the forefront of my mind with surreal clarity.

Salami, avocado, mozzarella and sun-dried tomato baguette.

<<Date: 10/04/2038>>

<<Location: Government Communication Headquarters, Cheltenham>>

<<Local Time: 13:17 GMT>>

The white and blue android behind the counter dutifully prepared the order I placed through the building network, the aroma of frying wafting through the hall. I queued behind a dozen others dressed in office attire; one of the many bullshit requirements GCHQ had. To my disgust, I was wearing my finest pair of synthetic leather shoes, black trousers, a navy-blue shirt and an ugly striped clip-on tie. I'd put up with it for a paycheque this big, but I didn't have to like it.

The android handed me a red plastic tray holding my sandwich. I took my seat on an empty table. The hall was crowded with the staff; laughing, sharing stories and watching the news and music videos projecting from the wall screens. I was never much of a people person, at least not socially. But I watched and listened… while flicking through my e-mails on my video-screen contact lenses, controlled by my wireless interface headset.

My eyes… my brain… I haven't been augmented yet…

The other agents were discussing social events being hosted by the management, like sports, martial arts, yoga, etc. Just listening to it made me roll my eyes. I hadn't played football since I was in primary school, and even then, it was only because my dad forced me. Watching was alright with the right crowd, though.

I munched away on my baguette, staring out of the holo-glass window to my right, tapping on a close icon to shut down the news feed and surveyed the quaint country houses of Cheltenham standing out against a backdrop of the scorched remains of the woods. It was only April, but the harsh light from the sun beat down on it, reducing the trees to skeleton-like branches with roots jutting out of parched, cracked soil in awkward angles. Patches of hay-coloured grass could be seen scattered about. An eerie silence emanated from it. No bird songs, no animals… only extinction.

Nature's graveyard.

So much for spring.

Out of the corner of my eye, a sizeable plump figure with a large curly black mop shuffling towards me.

"Oi bro, are these seats taken?" he asked me with a rumbling cockney accent. My HUD identified him as David Hiresh, with his personnel file appearing on a mini-window in the corner. I glanced at him up and down and decided he seemed friendly enough.

"No, please sit," I answered warmly, offering out my hand. We shook as he sat down and an awkward moment of silence descended.

"So… Arthur," said David eventually, his contact lenses flickering as he checked my file. "You're the Spiritform guy, right?"

Instant regret. I really wished that subject wouldn't come up.

"Kinda. Sorta. Maybe," I mumbled in an embarrassed manner, looking at my sandwich.

"Oh-ho! A hacktivist!" He laughed, his eyes growing wide with enthusiasm. "What made you turn to the dark side?" He held his hands up to his mouth and started making Darth Vader breathing sounds.

"Not the best comparison," I chuckled.

"Try telling that to that the conspiracy theorist lot. Wankers'll bitch about us reading their e-mails, but when a dirty bomb goes off, they'll wonder where we were. Or think it was a fucking false flag operation. We have security experts from all over the world, but ones from anti-government groups… that's a rarity. Surprised you got through the background checks."

"I was never actually in Spiritform," I explained quickly, wanting to get this over with. "I was going out with a girl who was. She tried to recruit me; it didn't exactly go as planned… it ended messily."

He patted me on the shoulder in a comforting manner. "That's a bitch."

"Just how it goes," I shrugged. "We met back in college, used to muck about on local network for pranks and shit."

"Sounds like love at first sight," he said with a wink. His openness had me worried that this was a management test.

"Maybe," I answered, trying to sound dismissive. "That was before she went completely nuts. Talked about launching a DDOS attack on Mother Mind's data centres. Wanted my help to program a worm to build a zombie network large enough to do it."

"So, what did you say?"

"I… led her on a bit… told her I was going to get around to writing the algorithms, but never did," I answered, sounding guilty. "Couldn't turn her down."

"So, what happened? That can't have gone unnoticed by the police."

"It didn't," I continued grimly. "I shat a brick when the cyber-crime unit showed up at my door. They took us to an interrogation room, grilled us for hours, showed us every email, every call, every VR chat. It's the scariest thing ever when you realise how true it is."

"What is?"

"Mother Mind. I mean you see the commercials, you read the news. But when you're face to face with your life under surveillance it just becomes real, ya know? Like you're naked to the world."

"But you're here now."

"Yeah… I am. Didn't have much of a choice. The recruitment officer gave me a choice; work here or go to the Prison Matrix."

"So, what happened to your friend?"

"Couldn't tell you. She told the police she'd be attending her first assessment. Never saw her again. Disappeared right off the face of the Earth. Could be hiding in Ecuador by now for all I know."

"While you pick up a government salary," he grinned.

"Yup. I'm a sellout," I admitted.

"Well… was it worth it?"

"Hell yeah!" I laughed gleefully. "This place is the dog's bollocks! High-end PCs, laser satellite connection, private security. Fuck, even the food's better here. Natural-grown dammit!'

"Uh, now that's a bit of a stretch," David chuckled, pointing to the farm-bots spraying Fermigel over the crop patches outside. Synthetic bacteria, designed to repair years of damage from pesticides. If you looked closer, you could see the tiny spores of nanotech Smart Dust dancing in the wind as they pollinated crops.

"Still better than the printed crap you get in London," I muttered.

"Taxpayer money hard at work," David mumbled as he took a bite out of his own sandwich. "Every job has its perks, and you ain't seen anything yet. You're right at the heart of the entire country's telecoms infrastructure. Mate, the things you see… oh boy, the things you see." He gave a hearty, manly laugh.

"Uh… like?" I asked with a cautious eyebrow.

"One-word, man; v-chat." He made a crude, childish impersonation of a pair of breasts with his hands. "If you catch my drift." I wasn't sure if I should be impressed or creeped out.

"Your drift is a hurricane, man," I laughed half-heartedly. "Seriously… you guys can do that?"

"We bulk collect data, man. It's like trawling the ocean."

"No one has done that in years."

"Bruv, don't ruin my analogy."

"Sorry," I chuckled.

"Point is, you trawl for tuna and end up with fucking dolphins. Most of the data we pick up just gets archived… which we can dive in and out of." He gave me another cheeky wink. "And I'm not just talking about porn. Trust me, there's a reason the corps are going to war with Virtualife for the Mother Mind contract. The value in industrial espionage is probably worth *trillions*. With a Fucking-T mate! You'd be *amazed* what they're prepared to pay you to get a peek at our database."

I looked around nervously, realising that dozen different microphones were probably listening in on the conversation. "Uh... should you..."

"Relax, kiddo," he smirked, shaking his head. "As long as you're not breaking official secrets, no one really gives a toss what you do around here. Trust me. This place will set you up for life!"

He squeezed his breast hands together again.

"Perks, dude."

<<Terminating Memory Playback>>

<<Restoring FIVR simulation>>

The memories faded away as quickly as they had appeared and I snapped back to the present day. Back into Dart's virtual world, my avatar landing in the seat of warm blue light once more.

"Well, what do you say?" Dart chuckled, taking a toke of his own virtual joint. "Like the product, yes?"

"Yeah... that's the shit all right," I groaned, clutching my avatar's head. My brain was pounding, and my bio-monitor sensor readout informed me that both my heart, breathing rate, and EEG patterns were going nuts in the real world.

The dizziness passed, and I soon readjusted.

So that was the GCHQ building. Nice to be able to put a clear image of it in my mind. It had whet my appetite all right. Now I needed another hit; desperate to know more.

"Shall we talk numbers?" Dart asked hungrily.

I straightened myself out and nodded in the most alert manner I could manage.

"I work on pay-per-byte basis," he explained. "I will send data over few months. The transactions will be processed by app. Payment in Bitcoins only."

"I'm listening."

He pointed towards me, and the message from his app appeared on my display.

<<10GB for £1.50>>

"Sounds pricey," I commented.

"No kidding," Liz concurred telepathically. "You lost close to four years of memories, that's over 100 terabytes."

I did the math in my head without her help. It wasn't good.

"So… we're looking at about fifteen grand?" I spluttered through my joint.

Liz nodded solemnly, sending me spluttering on my virtual spliff. I turned to Dart with a gobsmacked look.

"Bloody hell! A bit steep innit? I worked as a cyberwarfare specialist for years hacking foreign governments! Most I ever earned was forty-one hundred a month!"

Dart frowned angrily, the colours whirling in his eyes growing harsh. "My clients pay me one millions to get the back-door in place. They do not know that I give data to other customers. If they find out, it bad for me. You are getting bargain."

"Well, when you put it like that…" I admitted through gritted teeth, regretting I never went on the black market. It was the question I asked myself every day. Why didn't I just go full black-hat? I could run for the Yakuza or the Albanian Mafia if I wanted to! I'd seen what those guys made. Sixty grand a month, easy. Untaxed too, obviously. Of course, that just meant living in fear of HMRC; and let me tell you right now, revenue services and surveillance AI? *Bad combination*. No thank you.

"So…" I continued. "What kind of download rate can I expect?"

Dart rolled his head from side to side, the colours of his eyes washing over.

"We have been able to download two terabytes a day from the network," he explained. "I have a lot of clients, so I can only give you two-hundred and eighty gigabytes a day."

"Two-eighty?" I scoffed. Liz ran the maths on how long it would take for me to receive the whole 100 terabytes. "So, you're saying it'll take a whole year to get it all?"

He nodded.

"Assuming your guy on the inside doesn't get caught," I added carefully.

"He has sent a lot of data on exploits used by Mother Mind for last year," he shrugged. "I don't expect his virus to be found, so we have no problem."

"Hmmm…" I was still uncertain as I went over the maths on my HUD. "So basically, you're saying I can expect to be paying about twelve hundred and fifty a month?"

He nodded again, smiling at the prospect. I frowned, mulling it over. On average, I was earning about £3,400 a month now and had just over twenty grand in savings, but I'll be damned if I was gonna start dipping into that.

I opened Liz's avatar on my HUD.

"What do you reckon?" I checked with her telepathically. "Can I afford it?"

She took a deep breath and adjusted her spectacles. "Well…" She accessed my bank accounts and Bitcoin wallets, comparing it with my estimated income, expenditures on my rent, taxes, shopping etc. "You do have the funds. For now, anyway. Even if you cut back on luxuries, I estimate that you'll have to earn twenty percent more to maintain your average expenditures."

I found myself stroking the avatar's chin. I wasn't big on change. The money I was earning was just enough to maintain my life; keeping up with the bills and my tendency to splurge on hardware and software. But if it meant no more sleepless nights, lying awake wondering about the past… it was worth it in my book. A chance to feel like a person again. You couldn't put a price tag on that.

"I gotta get it, Liz." I shook my head desperately.

She rolled her head ambivalently, it wasn't often she thought about things. Usually, it was a part of her personality matrix conflicting with the extra code I'd given her.

"Well…" she continued. "There is always… plan B?"

Yeah… there was always plan B. I was a hacker. There was always a way to get cash. I didn't even have to steal it myself, just sell on the security credentials onto others. Easy money. I knew I could avoid detection, but… for how long?

I minimised Liz's avatar, reluctantly holding out a hand for Dart.

"You drive a hard bargain." I gave in.

Dart grinned, showing his avatar's unnaturally white teeth as we hook on it.

"Like I said, in-app payments." His eyes pulsed happily. "You can message me securely if need you need to."

"Will do. See ya 'round," I finished grudgingly, sincerely hoping I wouldn't see him again.

<<Logging out>>

<<Terminating FIVR simulation>>

<<Disengaging neural lace>>

<<Disconnecting from server>>

The crude virtual world around me dissolved into a cloud of bits and bytes and fluttered away like fireflies in the night.

<<Thank you for using Cloudland>>

I reopened my real eyes, the lenses readjusting instantly. I was back home staring up at the ceiling of my bed-alcove, the words *'Welcome Back'* hanging from the projector, my head sunken in the less than comfy pillow.

Down the rabbit hole…

As I stretched out and yawned, I heard the soft mechanical whirring of my arms and legs. It was only then I noticed my stomach rumbling. My *JustEat* app flashed onto my eyes, the only time I was grateful for intelligent advertising.

I telepathically selected my usual takeaway from my local Indian; chicken tikka masala, pilau rice, poppadums and mango chutney. I paid, and the app gave me the drone delivery estimate of twenty minutes.

I heard a small rattling sound coming from my left elbow. I rolled up my sleeve and noticed there was a screw starting to come loose which needed to be tightened. I decided not to put it off, and reached down to my left thigh, unzipping a fold on the side of my trousers. I sent a neurocommand to the leg module and, with a click and a whir, a hidden compartment opened. The metal chassis slid away like a drawer, which I used to store a claytronic tool called the *Handyman*. A nanotech device, shaped like a chunky silver pen, designed to morph into a variety of tools. I telepathically connected to it and issued the command.

<<Connecting to Handyman>>

<<Please select configuration>>

<<You have selected: Flat-head Screwdriver-004>>

<<Confirm: Yes/No>>

The mass of the silver device lost its cohesion, becoming a grainy, mercury-like substance. It began to stretch like silver putty moulded by invisible hands, the nanobots marching in unison like a colony of ants.

The mass took the form of a screwdriver and solidified once more. I tightened up the screw and flexed my arm back and forth. No more rattling. I issued the command to morph the tool back into its default shape, placed it back in the thigh compartment and ordered it shut. I did also have taser knuckles, nano-suction 'gecko-pads' in my hands and feet for climbing, and a wrist laser mounted on my right arm, primarily to be used as a cutting tool, and to disrupt enemy sensors. All had gotten me out of more than a few scrapes. I yawned again and checked the remaining time till my dinner arrived. Still another eighteen minutes away, to my hungry frustration. I decided to wait outside for it. I slid out of bed quickly, grabbing my coat and hat, and stepped out onto the steel balcony.

The blustery wind and drizzle were there to meet me, along with police sirens below. A gang of teenage Drone-Hunters roared down Chiswick High Road on noisy electric scooters, tearing in and out of the traffic, hooting and jeering as they went; the leader of the pack, flailing a *Tesco's* delivery-bot over his head like a trophy. Like most criminals (or anyone who was smart enough to worry about their privacy), their faces were hidden by masks and hoodies, concealing their identities from facial recognition cameras.

I wouldn't want to be them when the cops caught up to them. Most police officers used emotional management software which made them more susceptible to…brutality.

Hoping that the drone carrying my dinner wouldn't get attacked, I began fumbling through my pocket for my e-cigarette. I put the plastic tube between my lips and started smoking and reminiscing. I surfed around and checked my wish list through my price comparison app, while Liz struggled to keep back a wave of smart-adverts. The items on the menu included new clothes, games, a new processor for my PC. One by one I painfully deleted them with Liz's help, realising that I wouldn't be able to buy them for quite a while.

Unless I went black-hat.

I tried to distract myself with games; I'd received a request from my Grenethia Online raid group. Said they'd found the dungeon that was home to the 'Sword of Carvarla'. I sighed with exhaustion. I enjoyed the game, but it was a massive time sink requiring a level of dedication that was getting harder and harder to keep up with. Professional gamers could make a living out of it, selling on rare items in the game to other players. Probably get better pay too... but it wouldn't satisfy my hacking desires. I tentatively clicked 'maybe' on the invite request.

I found myself wandering onto Infoblast, my news tracking app. Liz automatically blocked out another wave of adverts and brought all the latest trending stories from around the web (censored of course). I filtered my news to keep out most of the celebrity and experience blogger bollocks... I supposed the concept of choosing the story you wanted was ironic. The reality was, it was more like the choice between *McDonald's* and *Burger King*. Slightly different brands of the same shit, owned by the same shareholders... recommended by your AI. I wasn't about to join Spiritform, but it was easy to see where they were coming from.

But everyone had their poison, their way of averting their gaze from the garbage heap the world had become... that we all subconsciously accepted and found a way to live through. For most people, it was VR. For others, drugs. Sometimes both.

I skimmed an article on Parliament passing the Flood-Defence Act. A series of environmental measures including the construction of canals to take the excess water-level rise. I didn't pay too much attention to any particular article until I saw one on the CNN feed; the latest exploits of Cymurai.

Now that's a distraction!

Some people called him a real-life superhero. Others thought that was just a cover story for being a government intelligence asset. I didn't particularly care, I'd admired him since I was a kid. Grinning like a ten-year-old, I gleefully clicked on the video recording.

<<Initialising video plug-in>>

The video had been recorded from the bionic eyes and ears of a journalist on the ruined streets of Tehran. His body shook violently; the sounds of heavy panting coming in loud and clear, as the reporter dashed away from a frantic firefight. Gunshots and explosions thundered in the background, sending concrete and dust spraying like a blizzard. The Islamist fighters fired wildly into the air with their smart-rifles, screaming as they tried to hit a target in the sky.

The camera panned up and zoomed in, catching a shimmer of red as it flashed across the view. It was obscured, but I could just make out the red and gold glint of metal leaping from the roof of a Mosque, and it came crashing down onto a burnt-out car.

It was a remote-controlled android body, but it was him. The unit was modelled on the suits of armour worn by the ancient warriors of

Japan. Shoulder and knee pads that would have once been built of wood were now sheets of graphene, lightweight and stronger than diamonds. The muscles, made of the same material, were electrically conductive to allow for rapid expansion and contraction. The faceplate resembled a fearsome moustached demon with two horns, the eyes burning with sensor light. The utility belt built into the waistband of the suit housed a sheath for his sword.

He drew it with inhuman speed. The hilt was a rounded metal tube with a set of switches on it. He flicked the first one, and the blade shot out like a telescope. It was moulded into the shape of a katana, constructed from a ceramic material with a pulsing electromagnetic mesh woven into it. It wasn't sharp, sporting rounded edges, with tiny holes punctured along the surface.

He flicked the second switch.

A furious hissing sound ripped through the air; a fan on the butt of the hilt roared to life, sucking in air and pumping it through an ionising chamber, before shooting out into the hollow blade, crackling with electrical power. The surface of the ceramics warmed up, rapidly becoming white hot. Superheated orange and purple plasma began radiating out of the holes like the flames of hell.

According to internet myth, the sword was named the Kusanagi. Named after the Japanese legend; the sword of the gathering clouds of heaven. But anyone who actually saw it at full power thought the same thing: the man had invented the goddamn lightsabre.

He swung the sword with the power of a god, leaving a blazing trail of light through the air, instantly cleaving a terrorist in two, the blood evaporating instantly into a dirty red cloud.

The other fighters turned their rifles on Cymurai and let loose with another barrage. Any human wouldn't have stood a chance against such an assault.

But he *wasn't* human.

He unleashed a series of flicks of the blade, at speeds too fast for the naked eye. Bright white sparks flashed from him as bullets collided with the sword, bouncing off the surface with a clang, reducing them to a red trail of molten lead particles.

I shook my head and breathed in awe.

A new wave of automatic fire came from above; the turret of a quad-copter bearing the terrorist insignia began raining bullets down on the ground and kicking dust high in the air. Once more Cymurai directly reflected the barrage with quick jabs of his Katana. A compartment built into the avatar's right wrist popped open and revealed a spring launcher for explosive shuriken.

Cymurai launched himself into a backflip to avoid the latest round of fire and landed on all fours, a few metres behind his last position. He locked out his right arm with the targeting laser on his wrist and fired an EMP shuriken at the drone. It exploded half a metre away from the unit in a dazzling blue flash of electrical energy, disabling it with a loud whir and collapsing on the ground in a crumpled heap.

Cymurai stood up victoriously, but it wasn't over yet…

SCREEECH!

He whirled around. An armoured jeep with an automated machine gun turret mounted on the back came tearing around the corner. The driver was yelling wildly, driving in zig-zags, the tower blasting like a tank. The driver was wearing a suicide vest, ready to ram Cymurai head on. One of the bullets grazed his shoulder ineffectively before he changed stance.

He began charging at the jeep head on, cutting down bullets as he went, and leapt off the ground, planting his mechanical boot firmly on the hood. The driver yelled, ready to denotate the bomb, but never got the chance. With a single swing of the sword; the windshield was reduced to a molten wreck. The driver was cleaved straight in two, spraying evaporated blood across the dashboard in a grotesque manner.

Cymurai proceeded to run along the roof of the car, taking out the machine gun turret with another slash. He springboarded himself off the boot and came into a skidding landing on the dusty road. The jeep crashed into a bombed-out shop and detonated loudly with a hail of glass and shrapnel.

He charged with his sword pointed toward at the chest of another terrorist taking aim with a rocket-propelled grenade launcher. Then the video feed cut out, *just when it was getting to the good bit.*

"Badass," I laughed, while I telepathically *'liked'* the video.

I was barely a teen when he first showed up. I'd watched him fight crime and terror everywhere, but he seemed to be based here in London. Back then he had fought using his real body. Maybe he was too old to do that now, but still wanting to keep up the good fight; my kind of style. Seeing him on the news for the first time when I was twelve was what made me want to be a cyborg.

Never thought I'd regret it.

I noticed a single *Ford* Skymaster hover-car soaring overhead. The slick blue design elegantly masking the VTOL engines on the underside. Who knows? Maybe if I'd stayed at GCHQ, I'd have been able to afford one, instead of throwing away twelve hundred a month trying to get back what I'd lost.

Or maybe I should've just never joined in the first place. Gone for a more straightforward lifestyle. I'd be online soon, raiding in Grenethia Online, the ultimate escapism. My group could go all night, most of them not weighed down by the constraints of conventional work. I could go pro, all it took was time, dedication and a few good reviews as an item trader. The more hardcore players lived a life of total ignorant bliss, dedicating everything to the role-playing. Getting to know the roles of their characters so well that they would forego their existence entirely. Living on nutrient supplements supplied to their bodies by robots in the real world, becoming a part of the game designer's fantasy.

I wasn't ready for that just yet. Not when I knew how much GCHQ *loved* full-time cyber-residents. It was a dream come true for them. A docile population, and growing all the time. Abandoning the depression of reality for a better one. *Who could blame them?*

I'd clock a few hours on the game tonight then try to get some sleep, only to immediately regret the decision to log out when faced with the long, pointless, sleepless, tedious hours in bed. The enigma, screaming in my every waking moment.

It was no way to live a life, and I sure as hell wasn't going to. Not anymore. No matter what it took, I was going to make this deal with Dart work.

A notification from my HUD informed me I'd been invited to an event on *Facebook*. I neuroclicked on the link; a private event just called 'Pub Times'. A gathering of former GCHQ employees living in London, hosted by David Hiresh. I found myself staring at his profile picture, laughing to myself when I realised he still had the same Jew-fro from the day I first met him. I'd stayed in touch with as many people as I could remember from my time there. The memories of my spare time in Cheltenham were still intact, untouched by the official secrets act. Still, that was all a little hazy, thanks to booze and e-weed.

For the last year and a half, I'd been racking my brain, trying to remember how I first met David. One download later and I had the answer.

Now other lingering questions started running through my mind, along with Dart's words:

Maybe some things are best left forgotten.

No… It was gonna be worth it.

It was definitely gonna be worth it.

Definitely.

One hundred percent.

Totally worth it.

CHAPTER 3

Mother Mind Profile 3551-7821-0862-2143:

- First Name: Kenji
- Surname: Awasaki
- Status: Living
- Nationality: British/Japanese
- Occupation(s):
  - Chief Executive Officer
    - Status: Employed
    - Organisation: Virtualife Corporation
- Criminal Record:
  - None
- Known Aliases:
  - Sector
  - <<Classified: Cymurai>>
- Biometric Data:
  - Gender: Male
  - Date of Birth: 03/07/1997
  - Age: 47
  - Race: Asian
  - Hair Colour: Black
  - Eye Colour: Blue
  - Height: 1.79m
  - Weight: 71kg
  - Aliments: None
  - Cybernetic Percentage: 47%
  - Genetic Modifications:
    - Age reversal treatment
    - Performance enhancement therapy
- Immediate Family:
  - Mother: Sakura Awasaki
  - Father: Kuze Awasaki

- Siblings: 0

Relationships:
- Status: In a relationship
  - Partner: Gabrielle Phillips

Contact Information:
- *Drop down for more info*

Live Surveillance:
- Status: *Partially available*
- Date: 05/10/2045
- Current Location: Virtualife building, Docklands, East London
- Local Time: 17:41 GMT

If I'd have known that life as a CEO meant dealing with one disaster after another, I might have considered a different line of work. First the accident on Prometheus Point, now this. I sat at my desk, face in palm, the other hand holding a glass of sake. My grip tightened in frustration, the gears in the prosthetics groaning angrily.

I was in a holo-chat with the head of my IT department, the webcam feed projecting from my desk. His name was Jin Seung; a thirty-three-year-old from Seoul, Reunified Korea. He had bushy black hair and big eyes sunken into his gaunt cheeks. He was jittering nervously, like he was on the witness stand, his forehead glistening with sweat. I'd been up since last night, having attended a virtual investor meeting on Pacific standard time. I'd been planning to go to bed this morning… but then I received Jin's email delivering the worst news that someone in his position could provide. Our network had been hacked. The IP address traced to a terminal belonging to one of our employees here in London, Professor Helen Ilian. But that's not to say that attack *originated* there. Her desktop may merely have been accessed remotely as a back-door into our VPN.

"What exactly did they take?" I asked, taking a long breath, my thumb stroking my bearded chin.

"Well, sir," replied Jin, speaking in Korean while auto-translation software placed subtitles on the bottom of the holo-screen. "It looks like they knew exactly what they were looking for."

He was trying to stall, putting off having to tell me for as long as possible. The glare I threw him over the webcam got across the message: I didn't have time for that shit.

"The… Project Selection files. Four hundred exabytes worth. The good news is the data was still encrypted with our in-house keys. They didn't get them; I made sure, personally. The data they have may as well be a shredded newspaper."

He chuckled nervously at his own terrible joke. I didn't appreciate it. My angry gasp sent the kid squirming.

"Let me guess; you can't ping the destination IP address?"

"No… it appears the data packets were routed through-"

"The FreeThought satellites," I interrupted, rubbing the skin around the armour plating on my cheekbones, contemplating my rage. Spiritforms illegal orbital network.

"Uh… yes," he admitted timidly.

"Who else knows about this?"

"Just the board, my staff and myself."

"I take it you've all been sent updated non-disclosure agreements?"

"Oh yes, yes of course," he replied hurriedly, eager to please me in any small way. "I already returned mine to the legal department."

"Don't think I won't enforce it to its full extent," I threatened. With the non-disclosure agreements in effect, my lawyers could legally request memory erasing procedures to be performed on the signatory. "You get any press sniffing your way; you keep your goddamn mouth shut until your V-lawyer gets there. Otherwise, you might find yourself with a case of sudden unexpected amnesia."

His mouth flapped, stunned by my bluntness. "I… I understand."

"Now find me that hacker! I don't care if you have to pull 18-hour shifts, ping me his location!"

He bowed quickly with respect. "I'm on it, sir!"

"If you're not, I suggest you start uploading your CV again," I threatened and ended the call. "Don't expect a letter of recommendation."

The hologram faded away, no longer obstructing my view from my penthouse windows as I yawned angrily and wiped the sleep from my eyes. The sound of Beethoven's *Symphony No. 9* returned softly from the speakers in the wall, something I'd grown accustomed to listening to in my old age to unwind. I felt nagging guilt once he was gone. I took my anger out on the staff all the time. When I was his age, I could crack military databases with Stuxnet-type viruses. Why was it too much to ask to hold my employees to the same standards?

The City of London Docklands stretched out beneath me; the heart of the financial district glittering with data from the stock exchange. The Houses of Parliament, the Gherkin, and the London Eye rising in the distance from the banks of the Thames. AI-controlled ships sailed silently in and out of the port, the sky thick with drone traffic while swathes of business people and tourists flocked on the street level.

I noticed my personal hover-car parked on the heliport a few floors below, a silver *Porsche* Eagle attended by flight-crew androids.

Virtualife tower was a self-contained city. The top few floors were dedicated to offices, research labs and the like. Given our primary product was virtual reality, working from home was our core employment model. That's what took up most of the bottom floors; cheap housing for our employees and everything they needed: power generation, waste and water recycling, medical centres, shops, gyms, recreation centres, and robust PCs to experience cyberspace. There was no real need to leave. I never had to. Never had time to. At least not physically.

And why would I want to? I thought grimly, looking over the urban grit of the street level.

I could see the police barrier at the foot of the building, encircling the tower. Iron railings and guards carved out a path through the crowd to allow our residents entrance to the lobby and kept out the inhabitants of the permanent picket line that had grown like a human mould infestation. Hundreds of protesters permanently camped outside my doorstep. They made a makeshift village of tents, their inhabitants wearily waving animated signs and half-heartedly singing union chants. The cops were doing a good job at keeping them in line…butting in with just the right amount of force to break them up when they got too rowdy.

They'd been there since the opening day of the tower, the better part of five years now. They came and went as they pleased, but the village kept its form. My younger self would have agreed with them… but now I just saw them as ingrates, literally looking down on them from my ivory tower. They wanted change, but no one knew exactly what that meant, least of all of them. They only talked about what they didn't want: job automation, the digital economy, the influence of artificial intelligence on the government, and most of all Mother Mind. Now it just seemed like they were here for the sake of being here, having given up on accomplishing anything, but not quite ready to return to their shitty lives.... we'd made many proposals in the early days when we tried negotiating with them, but the union leaders rejected anything we suggested. I figured the only thing that would make them happy would be the introduction of Universal Basic Income; a colossal tax placed on mega-corporations to fund payments to every citizen just by virtue of being alive. It had been tested in several countries with success. I was willing to try it… but the lobbying resistance to it here in the UK and alike was strong.

Now we had a communications blackout with the protesters. All we had to do was wait until something stirred them up enough to finally get permission from Scotland Yard to send in the riot squad and clear them out. But they were surprisingly well behaved for a bunch of disobedient citizens. They were extremely well-coordinated; their code of conduct shared carefully and obeyed through social media.

A wet plopping sound from the miniature Zen garden pulled me from my reverie. A giant catfish bobbed its head up from under the artificial pond, grabbing chunks of bread being scattered by my android butler standing on the plastic pebble shore, carefully tracking the fish's movements with its sensor array.

The pond was fed by an artificial waterfall, dripping down with a calming vibe. The surface of the water was covered with scattered, pink cherry blossom leaves, left by a single sakura tree, a soft scent radiating from it. The tree had been planted in a lush artificial island resting in the pond.

The patch of natural beauty was surrounded by a massive cream-coloured, horseshoe-shaped claytronic couch. A pair of silver superconducting disks about the size of Frisbees were built into the armrests of the sofa, each supporting miniature bonsai trees sprouting out of spherical lumps of soil, embedded with subtle superconductors. The trees were floating, suspended by quantum locking, twirling silently while their wiry branches stretched towards the artificial light on the ceiling.

The rear wall hosted a glass cabinet, holding my weapons collection. Pieces of history from home: katanas, kunai, shuriken, even a real 15th-century suit of samurai armour. Wooden and iron, no cybernetics. I was a technology giant, but that didn't mean I didn't appreciate the craftsmanship of the past.

I took a swig of my sake, the small porcelain cup feeling flimsy in my hands. Most of my body had been cyberised; by choice. The metallic casing of the prosthetics was hidden under a layer of synthetic skin, but I still felt the power coursing inside. The soft whir and grinding of hydraulics and gears; capable of crushing steel if I let them.

I was exhausted… ready to fall asleep. No rest for the wicked though…

Gabrielle's avatar projected from the holo-table. Her wavy brunette hair dangled around her shoulders and the 3D display of her plump lips seemed to protrude through my sight. The tight black and white business blouse and skirt she wore brought out her curves. She had her hands on her hips, giving me an accusing stare.

"You're not going to find the hacker at the bottom of a bottle," she told me in a tone that reminded me of my mother.

I gave a frustrated mumble and slammed down the glass, my arm whirring rapidly as I did. She was the only person in the world who could play me like that. Even when it didn't make sense. I had an artificial liver that could break down alcohol in a matter of seconds if I turned the settings up to maximum.

She'd always had that effect on me. One of many things I'd saved from her brain before she died. It wasn't the real her… I would never see the real her again. But I couldn't let her go. I could never let anything go.

This Gabrielle was a recreation. An imitation. A damn good one, but not perfect, even if her personality matrix had been upgraded over the years. The scanner I used to capture her synaptic patterns may have been cutting edge sixteen years ago but was nothing compared to today's standards. Without access to the source pattern, there was no way to *really* improve the recreation.

There was a debate about the changing nature of what it meant to be human… but there was no getting around the fact that I had to fill in the gaps with my own programming when I created her. She was effectively a software version of Frankenstein's monster.

She was gone, and I was left with a digital actress.

But I lived for those moments when I fell for it. In some pseudo-spiritual/philosophical sense, it was her. All she had to do was keep passing my personal Turing test. In my books that was good enough. That's what I told myself anyway. All it took was one little mistake, one glitch in the software and the illusion would shatter, leaving me to face reality. The fact that I was in love with a computer came crashing down on me.

A wave of lingering sadness began creeping up. I adjusted the 'Focus' setting on my neural lace, and my attention snapped back to the task at hand.

"You think it's them?" I asked, scratching my beard.

"It's my leading theory at this time," she answered.

I yawned again while she opened a *YouTube* video titled *'Spiritform warns Virtualife'* posted two weeks ago. It opened with the image of an OpenSource Soul's avatar, the cloud-based artificial intelligence that Spiritform used to break encryption. It appeared as a sapphire-blue digital star, the surface constructed from billions of lines of code, an entire yottabyte of data. Pixels whirled around it like satellites, each one graphically representing the thousands of users using the SoulSearcher operating system, the nodes of their block-chain network. With all of their computers running in parallel at full capacity, the group liked to boast that it would be able to crack any encryption within a matter of hours. Part of me admired their conviction, even if they were utterly naïve.

"We are Spiritform," the Soul spoke, with the synthesised voices of a billion people speaking at once, echoing across the internet. "For the last fifteen years, we have fought the system of control that we the people once demanded in a time of fear. The British government offered its people protection. Instead, they gave us enslavement. The network of oppression that has done nothing but crush our freedoms, and line the pockets of its creators."

I ground my teeth every time I heard someone say that. The original developers of Cloudland and founders of Virtualife; Vanita Narasimhan, Remy Naughton, Sam Stone… *my friends* all turned their backs on me after I signed the Mother Mind contract. Said they could have no part in the creation of *'Big Brother'*. Words couldn't describe how frustrated I was that none of them saw my way of thinking, but I couldn't blame them either. Not when I was faced with this, receiving threatening, cryptic messages through computer-generated voices.

The whirling graphical sphere continued, the voices rumbling out from the speakers built into my desk.

"The same company that tried to take away your privacy has prided itself on keeping its own secrets," the voice continued. "We declare: no more. Soon, the business that changed the world shall be judged once more."

Here it comes. The famous tagline.

"We are Spiritform. We are everywhere. We are nowhere. If you have done wrong, we will find you."

I mimed along with the voice in an insulting child-like manner, before gesturing to close the video.

"Cocky bastards," I snarled, angrily rubbing more sleep from my eyes.

"Either way," Gabrielle continued, folding her arms. "They are the most likely suspects."

I drew a long sharp breath, leaning in and resting my chin on my bridged hands. "What's the plan?"

Gab opened Mother Mind Manager, the user interface software for the AI. I was presented with a rotating image of the planet, covered with green graphical lines representing the backbone infrastructure of the internet: undersea cables, laser satellite communication relays, data centres. Blue icons marked out the locations of Listening Posts belonging to the various intelligence agencies, intercepting data packets to be processed by the AI. An arrow pointed out the nearest station to London as being the GCHQ building in Cheltenham. The hologram also pointed out all of the known Freethought Satellites in orbit, marked out in dark purple; the intelligence dark zone.

"I've placed the Ilian family under surveillance," she explained, bring up three data windows displaying the profile of Professor Helen Ilian, along with her son and husband. She had short red hair and glasses, her husband Jonathan was a greasy-looking lawyer, and their son, a plump-faced boy named Andrew. She presented me with lists of their social media friends, email contacts, bank accounts; their entire digital lives put under a microscope by the system.

"We'll bring her into an official investigation tomorrow. I have no reason to suspect her direct involvement at this time though."

Gab brought up footage from the drone we had sent to tail the parents. Suspended in the sky above them, the camera zoomed in on the middle-aged couple, watching them over excitedly entering a nudist health spa in Kentish town. The drone that was supposed to be monitoring the kid was still twelve kilometres out from its target according to the GPS data informing me that it was en-route to the family home in Kensington.

"I dived into the PCs of the parents easily enough, nothing incriminating there. But the kid is using Spiritform encryption. Not uncommon for kids his age, but it'll take a while for me to break it."

"So, there's nothing hard to prove their involvement yet?"

She tilted her head from side to side. "No, but they are the only lead we have to go on. I'm monitoring all the networks I can. If someone's talking about Project Selection, we'll know. Spiritform isn't stupid though. I only estimate the chances of that are around eight percent."

When she recited statistics like that, it was a cold reminder that she was just a personality matrix, simulating the firing of neurons in a quantum supercomputer.

"I assume you have something better in mind?" I asked, leaning back in my leather seat and stretching expansively.

She opened a website; '*The Federation of Private Investigators*'. An online directory of PIs across the globe catalogued and reviewed by the users of the site. I squinted at the data, trying to focus, telepathically adjusting my implant's setting to help.

"We need someone who can go beyond the reach of Mother Mind," she said, pointing to the holographic globe. "Someone outside of the company to avoid suspicion. I suggest hiring a private investigator here in London first. If the trail leads to another country, so be it."

I nodded, unable to dispute her assessments as usual.

"Do you have one in mind?" I asked, stroking my goatee to keep my mind focused.

She brought up a list of search results.

"I have a list of fifty possible candidates. Checking their credentials is easy enough. Finding out which one is the most trustworthy... will take a little longer to process."

"Good to know someone's on top of things," I sighed dully, with a whiff of my cologne, looking over my schedule.

"Aren't I always?" She beamed at me. "I've been keeping a close eye on Detective Haines as well."

I sighed, rubbing the metal ridges of my forehead, trying to keep everything straight in my head.

"How's he getting on?" I asked, breathing with exasperation.

Gabrielle accessed the most recently uploaded video of the officer in charge of the Jack-21 investigation; an interview with the press with the tough black officer looking helpless as the blare of flash photography blinded him.

"They're still drawing blanks," Gabrielle explained, bringing up what she could from the case files. "No closer to finding the killer."

"They're probably doing themselves a favour," I grumbled, my fist instinctively tightening at the helplessness of the situation. They may have been our competitors, but I didn't want anyone else to get dragged through this because of our mistakes.

Like most public services, the police in Britain had been privatised. Each borough in London was contracted out to various security companies, but it mainly became a duopoly between Churchbell Security (owned by Sinotech, one of the other big data megacorporations) and Global Arms, one of my subsidiaries.

The Jack-21 investigation was under Churchbell's jurisdiction; officially out of hands...

It even felt odd having to call him by that name. The one the press had given him. But it had become standard procedure to do so among my staff who were in the know… you could never know who was listening.

We did have a backup plan, but it was almost as risky. As a precaution, we deployed Mother Mind to monitor all the officers involved in the Jack-21 case. Partly for our sake, but mostly for theirs. In theory, if things got out of hand, we could pull strings at Scotland Yard to get the case reassigned. It was blatant corruption and would ring alarm bells at Churchbell. One of the most significant issues with using underhand tactics in this industry was that all your rivals were well trained in exposing such crimes.

"Each victim brings potential new evidence," Gabrielle continued ominously. "I now estimate the necessity of having to intervene in their investigation at 63%."

"Phase Two of Project Clayman is still in place I take it?" I checked with anxious eyebrows.

She nodded.

A plan for every eventuality…

She brought up a cyberwarfare diagram of the ICE protecting Haines' network; a big, angry red fissure in the structure where our virus had penetrated their defences.

"The virus has been installed on his personal area network," she explained confidently. "No signs of detection. I can activate it anytime."

I delicately stroked my beard, feeling wholly uncertain about this. Project Clayman was another one of our research projects. Experimental. *Highly* experimental. The most ambitious cybernetics and artificial intelligence research we had undertaken in over a decade. Hell, if it was successful, it might even make Project Selection obsolete. But… there were so many moving parts involved, all dependent on each other like a Swiss watch, requiring incredible amounts of micromanagement. There were going to be plenty more sleepless nights before it was over.

The primary subject was Lieutenant Emma Golem, one of my prized employees. However, we were about to enter Phase Two of the experiment, and it required subjects from *outside* the company. We had been planning to begin in due course, after more rigorous testing, but recent events had forced our hand.

Gabrielle's surveillance of Detective Haines had suggested that he was a prime candidate for Phase Two. Given the circumstances, it would have seemed like suicide to start anything that would be seen as corporate cyberwarfare. However, if we *had* to resort to taking over the investigation, it could help things go a little more… smoothly. In theory, it could mitigate our anti-corruption concerns… but if it went wrong, it would blow up in our faces.

"Once they see the success of the software in a field test it should outweigh their concerns," Gabrielle said firmly.

"It's gonna be hard pitching this to the board," I rumbled uncomfortably. "It might be a step too far for them to accept."

"They might not have a choice," she explained, bringing up the full report of her analysis.

A three-hundred-page PDF document, filled with variables and algorithms arranged into flowcharts. If you could read the computer language, it revealed the real beauty of the inner workings of her artificial mind.

"They're running out of time," she continued. "Triggering the Clayman virus might be their only hope of getting through this without a major scandal."

"Hmm… I'll take your word for it," I said dismissively, too tired to be bothered to look over the tangle of facts and figures. I doubted the board would either, but they would almost certainly have their own VPAs verify her conclusions.

"It's just a backup plan for now," she concluded. "I'll keep it in reserve for the time being."

I strained my bionic eyes, rubbing the bridge of my nose. I wanted to get off the topic of anything corporate related for a while. It wasn't exactly easy given she was effectively the central server of my business.

"How's your pet project coming along?" I asked with a weary smile.

Her holographic face lit up with a smile.

"Better than expected." She beamed, bringing up a diagram of satellites in orbit in the palm of her hand.

I smiled nostalgically. Most of Gabrielle's personality traits had been copied, if somewhat imperfectly… but one thing that hadn't gone away was her love of astronomy. To the point of even influencing her decisions as my VPA. Which was just the way I wanted it.

We'd gone into a partnership with SETI, putting up the capital for a new array of orbital planet hunters. Project: Star Beast. Named after the book I'd lent her when we first started dating… of course, she had only gotten around to reading it when I uploaded it to her memory.

Hundreds of thousands of exoplanets had been catalogued by now. The latest generation of X-ray telescopes could even analyse the composition of the planet's atmosphere, and at least two hundred worlds with potential bio-signs had been detected.

But everyone was still hunting for the real prize. A radio signal of *intelligent origin*. The signs were there. A few non-random whispers picked up, and then never found again. Oh yeah. They were out there, alright.

She brought up a 3D map of the galaxy and highlighted a small section in a sphere of red.

"We've narrowed our search," she explained. "Most of the anomalies originate from within a fifty-lightyear radius of the Pleiades star-cluster."

Her lips turned brightly upwards.

"I think someone really is calling home." She beamed in awe.

"Well, don't get your hopes up." I chuckled, recalling all of the disappointing instances of interference from pulsars.

Despite my scepticism, I couldn't help but take some joy to see her like that. Still, it was a far cry from the days behind the roaring fire of her family's cottage… gazing up at the moon.

My nostalgia was broken by the sight of Gab's face stiffening, folding her arms. The stance she usually took when her business subroutines were in action.

"Anyway…" she added loudly with judgemental eyebrows. "You have *other* pressing matters that you've been avoiding."

I gave her a brief puzzled glance before, to my disappointment, I remembered what she was talking about.

"Does it have to be today?" I groaned.

"Can't put it off forever," she said in a judgemental manner. "The PR department has been hounding me about it."

She brought up my least favourite app. My calendar. Every day of my life planned down to the second. It didn't matter how many age-reversal drugs I took; whenever I looked at it, I felt *old.* I could fit in a few hours for a fleeting social life, games and my Iaidō training… but it still felt like a prison. Just one glance over seemed to drain the remaining life out of me like a vampire. Most days I worked seven-till-seven… and then there was my *other* life.

I had an interview with Truthfire Media scheduled within the next half an hour. Just thinking about that made me angry. Some bastard had leaked info about my sex life to them. A playlist of simulations Gab and I enjoyed together. I had gone to extreme lengths to keep the gritty details of my relationship with Gabrielle out of the limelight. I certainly wasn't the first person in the world to enjoy virtual sex with characters; but sure enough, it had become a scandal, enraging whole communities.

"I don't care what anybody thinks of us," I said defiantly, trying to relax.

"Be that as it may, our stock value has taken a hit. The board isn't taking it too kindly."

I rolled my eyes. Fuck them, too. Six perpetually unhappy investors, who kept the company afloat after my MIT buddies walked out. I was scheduled for a meeting with them as well at 18:20. I didn't even want to think about their reaction to the Project Selection hack. If doing this interview would placate them a little bit, then so be it. *'Subdue the enemy without fighting'* as Sun Tzu would say.

"I had to reschedule your next outing with the kids to get this meeting," she added in a judgemental tone. "You know I hate doing that."

I cringed guiltily; this was a source of tension for us. I tried to avert my eyes from her glare, but she accessed the holographic photo frame on the edge of my desk to bring up a family photo.

The four of us leaning towards the virtual camera, a simulation of a Barbados beach in the background, dressed in summer clothes, shorts, sandals, dresses. We'd based their appearances on a DNA sequence with genes from both Gabrielle and myself. It gave them light but slightly tanned skin, revealing my Japanese heritage. We'd chosen to start their programs off at three years old. By the time frame of their virtual world, they were now just over six. My son Hideo's cheeky grin, spiky hair and beady eyes, being smothered by Gabrielle's right cheek. My daughter Shauna was sat on my lap with my arms wrapped around her, her round, fresh face and brunette hair glowing in the Caribbean sun.

"I'll make it up to them," I responded weakly. "I promise."

"Kenji, you *know* that's not the problem," she scolded me. "You promised *me* that we would see them!"

My face fell.

We may have decided not to get married (like most couples these days), but we *did* want to have kids; but given Gabrielle's virtual nature, they could've taken on several forms.

The most straightforward and best option was ectogenesis. Artificial wombs were common now, and we could use DNA from the real Gabrielle. It's been possible to create entirely synthetic human genomes since the mid-2020s, but the development of such genomes had permanently been banned for almost all commercial use by most countries (with the notable exception of China). Conceiving children from sterile parents was legal, but we'd still have to pass adoption laws. Even if Gabrielle took on an android form, we still didn't qualify as a couple in the eyes of the law. *Bastards.* We'd fought to change it or to find some loophole but to no avail.

The next best option was android children with AI personalities, designed to learn and adapt the same as a child. It'd be easy. So straightforward, but it had one major drawback; they'd legally still be considered my *property*, not my children, and therefore would be required to be programmed with the three laws of responsible robotics. We just couldn't accept that. We'd campaigned to lift some of the restrictions on AI developed; partly for this reason, but mostly to help our business interests as per the board's request.

The trouble was, most governments had to at least *appear* to be autonomous from forces of the market. Entirely independent AI was a line that politicians weren't ready to cross yet if they wanted to remain electable. Our advertisement campaign could only produce so much spin. Of course, most politicians used VPAs developed by our competitors or us, so we could hack into them and influence the advice they would give. Research suggested that 92% of the time, the user would follow the help of an AI, but this seemed to be the exception to the rule.

There was only one legal loophole they could find, and it was based on a technology that wasn't ready for prime time. The development of *biohybrid androids.* Not a robot or a cyborg in the traditional sense. Convincing androids with synthetic flesh had been around for a while now, but this was something entirely different. Machines built from 3D-printed living tissue; engineers had been toying around with the concept for more than thirty years. Muscles instead of motors, combined with subtle traditional electronics, powered by nutrients rather than batteries. They were initially created to provide novel environmental research solutions like swimming stingray bots, or crawling sea slugs. But we were aiming to create so much more than that.

The development of biohybrids was one of the applications of synthetic genomes that was still considered legal. The droids would be physically indistinguishable from an ordinary human, able to grow and age (or not), but with nanotech-laden organs and brains. Meaning we could download simulated memories into them. It was a perfect workaround. The best of both worlds. Possessing human DNA and a free mind was the golden ticket to ensuring human rights but avoided adoption laws due to their synthetic nature. There was just one issue at hand; the technology wasn't ready yet. We had however to develop nanobots which could safely self-replicate using the materials found within the human body. In every case the proteins resulted in a mutation, creating a virus so lethal the subjects were dead before they left the table.

We either had to wait until the nanobots could be perfected, or develop models which would require regular dosage. Otherwise, they would experience cellular degeneration. The symptoms of withdrawal would be painful. They'd need the bots like crack addicts. We couldn't do that to them. We had to wait.

The research was slow, our projections suggesting we could have a viable biohybrid model within ten years. Hopefully, it would still be legal by then, and we were fighting to keep it so. But Gabrielle didn't want to wait that long, and we still needed personalities we could upload into the biohybrid brains. We programmed Hideo and Shauna and gave them all of cyberspace to experience and learn from. Both of them were beautiful, intelligent, loving, kind. We could be real parents for them there, and they could make real friends in Cloudland.

I felt love for them. Real love. Gabrielle was a recreation, an imperfect imitation. A hindrance that we could overcome… but they were the original works. The fruit of my labour. That was all that mattered, not what anyone else thought.

But there were severe legal limitations we had to contend with. The AI moderation department wanted their programs to be bound by the three laws until they took human form. We rejected that on all accounts. The laws applied to Gabrielle, but both of us refused those kinds of limitations for our children.

Eventually, the moderators accepted a compromise. Our kids could remain free of AI restrictions, but there had to be time limits to how long their programs were allowed to run on any given day. We'd settled on an hour a day, closely monitored by Mother Mind. With my schedule, it was hard to even keep that up. While their programs were suspended, they didn't experience the passage of time, held in the void of our server's memories.

Logically I shouldn't have felt guilty, knowing they were unaware. But it didn't help their… believability. It felt more like we were raising *Pokémon* rather than children… not that you *couldn't* have affection for *Pokémon*, but I hated having that barrier. If we could commit to them, then maybe, just maybe… but things kept getting in the way.

"I'm doing what I can," I replied firmly. "Project Selection and Clayman…"

"I know," she admitted. "They are necessary steps to protect their future. I accept that. I understand that. That's why we *need* to get

Truthfire Media on our side. How are we supposed to raise children, when the world can't even accept *our* love?"

She had me there. I squirmed ambivalently on the spot, wondering what to say.

"Fight for their future now," she sighed. "At least they'll still be here when the time is right. Instead of getting deleted by the moderators."

Her words carried a weight that sunk deep into me as always. She was right of course, we needed this done. The day will come when I can hug them both in the real world when we can have the family we always dreamed of. This was just a minor inconvenience if we could finally have that.

"Fine," I breathed with reluctant acceptance. "Let's get it-"

"Wait a second…" Gabrielle cried unexpectedly, holding her hand up to stop me mid-sentence. That got my attention instantly. It was very unusual; she wouldn't interrupt any human conversation unless it was an emergency. An icon on my HUD indicated she was receiving data.

"What's wrong?" I frowned, my exhaustion seeming to fade into the background.

"I just received a priority one transmission from Andrew Ilian's bio-monitors," she announced with deadly seriousness. "It cut out as soon as I received it, but the data I got indicated his blood pressure just took a massive drop as a result of heavy trauma."

She brought up the report, displayed as a series of holographic medical charts. She was right, the kid's vital signs were rapidly dropping into the red; an anatomy diagram informed me his left leg had been cut off.

"Oh shit," I breathed, slamming my hands down on the table and leaning towards the screen.

Someone was trying to kill him, and I had a gut-wrenching feeling I knew who.

"Where is he now?" I cried, jumping out of my seat.

Gabrielle dived into the Mother Mind data again, bringing up a 3D map of London that took up the whole desk. The diagram was full of detail; a schematic of the entire city. The virtual camera zoomed into the 27th floor of Pearl House apartment complex in Kensington.

Apartment 2715: Ilian family. The drone we had sent to monitor the kid was approaching rapidly. I tried tapping its icon on the map to bring up its video feed, but all I got was static.

"Please tell me that's a bug."

"No, the signal is being jammed at the source."

My heart dropped like a stone.

"It's him."

Jack-21.

"The evidence points to that, yes," she answered solemnly.

"How did he find him!?" I cried, pulling my hair in sudden panic.

"Insufficient data," she answered analytically; one of the things that would've reminded me of her synthetic nature, but my mind was racing too fast to pay attention to it.

"Where's the nearest Ashigaru squadron?"

The Ashigaru was the codename for my personal special forces security team, named after the foot soldiers employed by the samurai class in the 14th century. I bought a significant hold of the shares in a private military corporation called Global Arms fifteen years ago, and as part of that deal I had set up a semi-autonomous unit to carry out Black-Ops for the CIA and MI5. A team of soldiers, cherry-picked by myself from our best employees contracted to armed forces around the world.

Officially, the intelligence services were our clients. As part of the contract, they would offer the Ashigaru missions which I would either accept or reject on a case by case basis.

Unofficially: they took their orders directly from me.

The map of London zoomed out again, and blue dot icons flashed up showing their locations. All of the on-duty officers were still here in Virtualife tower. The GPS calculated that if they took one of my copters or flying cars, it would take them just over four minutes to get there.

"No good, he'll be dead by then!" I rubbed my avatar's forehead anxiously. "Where's the nearest Amaterasu?"

The camera of the virtual map of London panned back until I could see up to the eighty-five thousand feet above the city. An icon highlighted the location of my private spy jet. A crimson coloured tiltrotor, spouting huge rotating triangular wings, soaring high above the city. Named after the ancient Japanese Sun God, it was capable of hypersonic speed and vertical take-off and landing. It was officially registered to Global Arms, but in reality, it was my personal property, one of many highly mobile storage platforms for my remote-controlled android avatars. I could connect my brain to them over the internet and be anywhere in the world in a matter of seconds.

"ETA two minutes," Gabrielle responded. "Prepped for combat drop and standing by."

"Screw it, I'm going in!" I announced hurriedly, plopping myself down in my leather seat again.

I needed the fastest connection to my neural lace possible. I whipped out the top drawer of the desk and pulled out a USB cable, plugging it in one end to the port on the front of the table and the other end into the port on the back of my neck accessing my brain. I began preparing to connect to my remote-controlled android avatar.

"I must advise against this, Kenji." Gabrielle frowned with concern as I dived into the chair.

"It's risky, but if Jack-21 really is there, I don't trust anyone else to deal with him."

She drew her lips and folded her arms, shaking her head reluctantly.

"Roger that," she conceded. "Guess we'll have to reschedule the interview after all."

"I'm crying on the inside," I answered sarcastically as I tilted my head back, resting on the pillows and preparing myself for the consciousness transfer. An icon centred in my vision; a flaming samurai sword. A strange piece of software used only by me, the remote operator interface for my most powerful avatar. The ultimate in technological laziness; becoming a superhero from behind your desk. A green progress bar appeared, loading rapidly. The schematics of the avatar emerged as the program ran a full diagnostic scan, checking off each item on the list as the results came back green.

<<Diagnostic cycle complete>>

<<All systems fully functional>>

<<Begin consciousness shift?: Yes/No>>

I mentally braced myself, using deep controlled breaths to empty my mind of all thoughts. I gave the command.

<<Initialising Consciousness Shift>>

<<Establishing secure connection to Cymurai Mark-V Unit-07 Avatar>>

<<Connection established>>

<<Running neural lace drivers>>

The program occupied the memory cache of my brain implants. The sensation of connecting to an android avatar was much the same as logging into a full immersion virtual reality. My mind detached from the confines of my body and teleported across cyberspace. Darkness was swallowed by static; multicolour flickering across my eyes like a blizzard, while white noise buzzing inside my head. One by one the static was replaced by the world as perceived by the sensors of the remote-avatar came into view. My mind landed inside the hardened, military-grade steel shell.

<<Consciousness Shift complete>>

The process was complete. I was somewhere else… inside the cabin of the tiltrotor helicopter, my mind successfully networked into the android's CPU. The avatar's HUD flashed into life. I looked down at the thick blood-red plating around the mechanical joints of my knees. The first robotic avatars had been incredibly awkward and clumsy to control, now it just felt as comfortable as slipping on a glove puppet.

The Amaterasu's hypersonic engines roared as the jet went into a dive. The lights inside the cramped helicopter cabin flickered to life, illuminating the sliding steel door with a small porthole to see the city below. The jet sped through foggy wisps of clouds. I could see the reflection of my new body in the window. It may have been a secret identity, but this was me: the real me.

They called me *Cymurai.*

I had modelled the appearance of the exoskeleton armour and remote-avatars on the look of Japan's ancient warriors. An elegant piece of machinery; like it had been built for royalty. The colour scheme was the same as a samurai's traditional appearance, crimson red and gold. The android avatar's thick metal shoulders and thighs were protected by heavy armoured panels. The torso housed the nano-battery power supply, the plating of the chassis moulded to appear as well-crafted abdominal muscles. The faceplate resembled a demon, with two horns mounted on the forehead and eye sensors burning intensely with digital light.

The golden belt was lined with pouches filled with equipment, including a sheath for my plasma katana; the *Kusanagi.*

The avatar was locked into its charging station inside the helicopter. Four magnetic clamps held it in place across the shoulders and knees, the internal gyroscope and accelerometer simulating the plummeting sensation in my stomach as we swooped to the ground. I looked down with the camera eyes as I flexed my gauntlet fist, feeling the building anticipation for what might await me.

I felt calm and professionally composed. Using remote avatars certainly had its benefits, but they did take some of the thrill out of the missions. Still, there was no way I could sneak out all the time with the kind of schedule I had. Bruce Wayne made living a dual life look like a walk in the park.

Yes, I did just compare myself to *Batman.* I think I've earned the right to do that.

"Thirty seconds to drop point," Gabrielle telepathically announced to me. She brought up the flight plan on my display as we raced towards the apartment complex in Kensington, a red bullseye graphic marked the target rooftop.

"Come on, come on…" I muttered with the rumbling synthesised voice of the avatar, itching to get out of the docking station, impatiently watching the clock on my HUD. At this rate, the kid would be dead by the time I got there!

“I’m adjusting the frequency of the Amaterasu’s transmitter to compensate for the jamming,” Gabrielle explained. “Once you’re at the LZ, I’ll hack open an elevator shaft for you. You’ll have to rappel down to the target from there.”

“Copy that,” I replied dutifully. The tiltrotor levelled off, and the cabin jerked back as the air brakes fired up.

“Ten seconds,” Gabrielle announced.

With a mechanical grind, the door in front of me burst open. The wind whistled through and the expanse of tarmac helipad that lay in front of me, lined with a maze of solar panels, wireless energy antenna and the large industrial fans of carbon sequestration units.

Game Time.

<<Deploying Remote Avatar>>

“Go! Go! Go!” Gabrielle cried.

There was a loud rapid clang; the charging station unlocked, and the avatar was free. I leapt out of the helicopter’s cabin and landed cat-like against the roof, the weight of the android slamming hard against the surface.

“Amaterasu departing.”

I turned back to see the wings of the tiltrotor swivel from a helicopter to plane mode. The afterburners sprung to life and, with a burst of fire, the jet shot off into the night sky.

Gabrielle forwarded me the building’s schematics. The guidance software kicked in and placed white augmented reality arrows on my HUD, highlighting the way through the maze of equipment leading toward to the target elevator shaft, housed within a steel shed in the centre of the roof.

I dashed across the asphalt, the power of the hydraulics in my legs pounding, while I clutched my sword’s hilt. A Churchbell Security police drone fluttered overhead and began barking warnings at me through its loudspeaker. A cyber-attack would take too long, and I didn't give it the chance to broadcast my location. I responded with a quick blast from the shuriken launcher built into my right wrist. An EMP round detonated in mid-air with a flash of blue light, sending the drone collapsing in a crumpled heap.

"Patching into the infrastructure network," Gabrielle announced, highlighting the entrance to the elevator. "Unlocking doors now."

The elevator flashed on my HUD, and the doors opened just as I reached them. I came to a stop at the edge of the concrete shaft, looking down into the artificial abyss lined with power cables and gears, dimly lit by lamps at five-metre intervals.

"In position," I informed her, detaching a pouch on the avatar's gold-painted utility belt where the buckle would've been. I pulled out a circular pad, attached to an incredibly strong carbon nanotube cable, extending from a reel inside the belt. The pillow was covered with an adhesive Fucosyllactose gel, synthesised by artificial bacteria. I spread the length of cable and slapped the pad to the outside of the door frame; the gel instantly hardened into one of the most durable adhesives known to man. With the preparations complete, I turned my back to the elevator shaft and gripped the cable tightly with both arms.

Here we go.

I took a virtual breath and cartwheeled backwards into the abyss.

The avatar's gyroscope went crazy as I plummeted. The world whirled around me as I somersaulted through the air, each floor whizzing by as a blurred pattern of steel doors, lights, and wires.

<<10 metres to target>>

My virtual gymnastics training kicked in instinctively, and I shifted my metallic weight, gripping the cable to swing towards the wall. I landed with the force of a rock slide, firmly planting both feet on the surface. The power of the impact sent cracks rippling out across the self-healing concrete, scattering it as a fine powder.

"Show off," Gabrielle teased.

I carried on following the graphical directions, rappelling my way down with a series of controlled hops until my robotic heels were resting at the top of the door frame leading to the 27th floor.

"Is the coast clear?" I asked telepathically.

Gabrielle brought me a live feed from the CCTV cameras in the hallway; all clear. I telepathically opened the doors, and with one last jump, I swung myself inside, landing in the mauve-coloured corridor on all fours. The rounded black doors to the apartments protruded like alcoves.

The target apartment was twenty-five metres to my left. I ran ahead at full speed, the legs pounding like pistons, and reached it within a few seconds.

Apartment: 2715.

Gabrielle opened it as I stormed through, hand on my sword ready for battle.

I came to a sudden stop as soon as I set foot inside, *wishing* there was a battle for me to face. The wind whistled eerily through the room. Broken glass lay strewn on the floor.

I was too late.

"No…" I breathed with disappointment.

The apartment would have seemed empty at first. The original wallpaper set a mild sage colour. Wooden floor, claytronic furniture, gleaming self-cleaning surfaces for the kitchen and the breakfast bar.

Seventeen-year-old Andrew Ilian lay sprawled out in the middle of the living room floor in a pool of his own blood. The avatar's air sensors triggered the response in my brain… the sting of iron in the air. His rosy face was contorted in horror, blood splattered across his cheeks. His chest had been cut open in a fashion I was all too familiar with; a fine incision from waist to neck, cut open with a surgical laser. The chest cavity had been splayed open to reveal his rib cage; a gory, mangled mess of meat and bone. Bits of skin dangled off, and the intestines and stomach spilt through the gaps in the ribcage. It was like someone had tried to dress his corpse like a prize deer but had given up halfway through. His left leg had been cut off from below the knee; it lay discarded on the side, consumed by the crimson pool.

"The jamming signal just cut out," Gabrielle informed me. "I've triangulated the previous point of origin, but he's gone already. I'm diving into the building's surveillance grid for signs of active camouflage. If he's still there, I'll find him."

"He'll be long gone by now," I sighed solemnly. "May as well be chasing a ghost."

I scanned the RFID chips embedded in the kid's clothes. With the interference gone the data successfully uploaded to the NHS database. The readout from Mother Mind flashed onto my HUD:

Mother Mind Profile 9124-5631-4877-0672:

First Name: Andrew

Surname: Ilian

Status: Deceased

- Date of Death: 09/10/2045
- Time of Death: 17:47 GMT

I knelt carefully beside the lifeless boy, gazing into his eyes. I'd seen fear before, but nothing like this. Looked like he'd been awake for the entire procedure, like some kind of arcane medieval torture. The colour hadn't gone from his cheeks yet…

"I'm sorry," I whispered sincerely, rumbling out of the avatar's speakers. He may have hacked us, but he was the son of one of my employees. I didn't believe in all of that *'company is family'* bullshit, but I couldn't help but feel a sense of responsibility. He was dead because of my choices. I may not have ordered his death, but I had inadvertently lured him into a trap. It was my mistake, one I was trying to correct and failing at doing so. I could almost hear my parents' nagging voices in the back of my head.

I lightly ran the avatar's fingers over the body.

<<Initialising Forensic Scan>>

The forensic sensors embedded into the bionic fingers scanned for fingerprints, DNA samples, temperature variations; the same equipment used by actual Forensic Investigators. I doubted I was going to have the time for a full sweep of the room though.

I tried not to make eye contact with the kid's empty horrified stare as the data came in, appearing in windows on the AR display. Gabrielle ran it through her analysis matrix, collating it with previously gathered evidence. We already knew who the killer was, we were just processing the results now in an attempt to track his location; the sort of logical detective work that might take human days or weeks, processed in a matter of seconds.

<<Results: Negative>>

"Of course," I sighed.

"You're too hard on yourself," Gabrielle said sympathetically, her virtual eyes drooping sadly as I examined the laser burns.

"Wouldn't be here if I wasn't," I sighed. "Time for the moment of truth."

I carefully picked up Andrew's left wrist and pulled back his sleeve, revealing his smartwatch – the central device for his personal area network. I examined the custom-built unit and found a port on the side of it. I reached for another pouch on my belt, pulling out back a cable on a spring coil and clipped it into the port:

<<New device detected>>

<<Accessing memory>>

<<Initialising file search>>

I waited with bated breath while the avatar's CPU began scanning the family Local Area Network for references to the stolen data.

<<Search complete>>

"The files were here all right," Gabrielle announced, stroking her chin while she examined the data. "But they've been sent over Spiritforms encrypted peer-to-peer network. At least one other copy of the file was saved onto the internal memory of a dog-bot; designated Rex."

She brought me a picture of the bulky metal dog, playing catch with Andrew in a field in Hyde Park.

"I don't like the idea of the data just wandering the street," I grumbled, rubbing my metal chin where my real beard would've been.

"Agreed. I'm putting out an APB on the bot. If it walks past a camera anywhere in the country, we'll know. Not sure how much use it will be. I've looked through Andrew's experience blog. He kept track of all the modifications he made to the dog, including optical camouflage."

"So, he could be invisible… great. How long do you think it'll take for Spiritform to decrypt their copy of the file?"

"A week by my calculations."

"Enough time to stop them… good," I telepathically sighed with relief.

A soft beep came from inside my head.

<<Warning!>>

A sound wave analysis program appeared on my HUD. The avatar's highly sensitive microphone ears had detected police sirens; drawing closer.

"What's their ETA?"

"Five minutes."

"Way too slow. Churchbell really needs to get their act together."

I stood up and manoeuvred my way across the floor, to avoid disturbing the crime scene. The family cleaning bot had just wheeled itself into the living room and was now attempting to mop up the pool of blood.

"He scaled up the side of the building. No way he came here on a hunch," I pondered.

"Must've gotten the intel locally, but I can't find evidence to suggest that any of his victims were with Spiritform."

"Keep looking."

I headed to the bathroom, the sound of glass crackling beneath the avatar's feet as it stepped onto the white tiles of the bathroom as I approached the broken window. I knelt down again to pick up one of the shards, holding it between my thumb and forefinger, scanning for a chemical residue which might indicate the killer's point of origin.

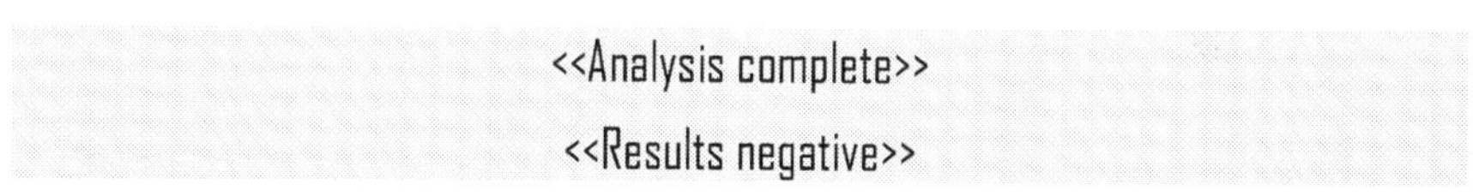
<<Analysis complete>>
<<Results negative>>

Of course.

I rested my hands on my hips and looked disgruntledly out across the cityscape, pondering my next move…

"I hate to interrupt, but it's that time…"

She opened up my calendar app; I was only three minutes away from my scheduled 18:20 meeting with the Board of Directors.

The memo explained that the meeting had been called to '*Co-ordinate our response to the cyber-attack on Prometheus Point*'. Which meant grilling me for an hour until they had everything they needed to build a case against me.

"Can't you go in my place?" I groaned.

"You know that violates the company by-laws."

"Can we add changing the by-laws to the agenda?" I asked in vain.

"Maybe next time,"

The meeting had been called by Jules Santiago. A nasty piece of work. The second biggest shareholder in the company after me, having made his first fortune in private security companies. Leading to the inevitable absorption of Global Arms in the Virtualife family. He had lived in Texas all his life but was Mexican by descent. Apparently, his co-workers had called him *Renegado* back in the day. Spanish for 'turncoat', after becoming famous for taking down-and-dirty contracts, usually involving border deportations.

He was my mentor… and I resented him for it.

I rubbed my metal forehead with frustration. She was right of course; agitating the board any further would not earn me any favours.

Gabrielle could put the avatar on auto-pilot, but in my gut, I wanted to do more. I turned to take one last guilty look at the body. The eyes of the boy seemed to follow me wherever I went; the image would be haunting me tonight.

"Kenji…" Gabrielle insisted.

"All right, all right," I grumbled reluctantly, issuing the neuro-command.

<<Logging Out of Cymurai Mark-V Unit-07 Avatar>>

<<Engaging Auto-Pilot>>

<<Uploading Destination Coordinates>>

<<Terminating Connection>>

The world as seen through the android avatar's eyes faded away into a snowstorm of pixels. The feeling of the rock-solid armoured skin faded away.

<<Connecting to Cloudland>>

<<Logging In>>

<<Selected Virtual Hangout: Virtualife Board Room>>

My consciousness loaded into the *virtual* avatar. The neural data streamed into my neural lace simulating the sensations of a flesh and blood body; programmed to appear as close to my real body as possible.

<<Loading…>>

The grid of cyberspace stretched out to infinity. Glittering pixels rushed by, assembling into shapes like pieces of *Lego*. The blue and green graphics of the company logo appeared first, hovering directly above an elongated oval-shaped table, luminous and pearl-coloured. Six floating teardrop-shaped chairs popped up around it next, looking to be made out of mercury; rippling liquid metal. The outlines of the room solidified into a sizeable crystalline hexagon, the walls built of digital glass looking out across a visualisation of the whole of Cloudland; whole virtual worlds suspended in cyberspace like planets.

I sat at the head of the table, leaning back, feeling the hovering liquid metal lapping up around my virtual avatar. The suit I was wearing had been designed by fashion students from Central Saint Martins; modelled after a traditional Italian three-piece suit, but the texture was programmed to appear as lines of blue code, made to look as coloured fabric, designed for style and programmed for comfort.

I rested my head on my fist and admired the world around me with regretful nostalgia. I hired architects to design all our corporate environments, even virtual ones. At first, I'd thought they were works of art, unbound by the constraints of the physical world, but more and more they just seemed like fancy courtrooms.

I dialled up the focus setting to maximum, trying to drown out my exhaustion and brace myself for what was to come. I knew what I had to say… it was just a matter of saying it at the right time.

It didn't take long for the rest of the board to show up. One by one the seats began to load their occupants into existence. Before I knew it they were gathered around the table; well-dressed businessmen and women from all over the world. Their accusing stares collectively turned to me at once.

"Kenji," said Jules gruffly, with his thick Texan accent. He had tanned Latino skin, hair as dark as coal, and eyes smouldering in the depth of his skull. His avatar was dressed in a brown suit with a blue tie but was programmed to appear much more desperate than reality where he was a literal fat cat.

"Jules," I replied cordially. Wanting to keep this as brief as possible, I turned to address the rest of the board.

"I apologise in advance for-"

"Spare us the feigned self-awareness," interrupted Huidai Zhang with a dismissive wave of her hand. She was our largest Chinese investor and chief financial officer; a gaunt skeleton of a woman dressed in a purple Chanel outfit with her violet hair tied into a bun. She spoke Mandarin, but the translation software placed subtitles below her chin. She had her narrow dark eyes fixated on me. "We demand an explanation, Awasaki!"

Gabrielle whipped up a *PowerPoint* presentation in a matter of seconds, displaying it on the wall behind me, summarising everything I had learned over the last day. I watched them grow more anxious as I explained the extent of the stolen data. The police and the press were now at the crime scene; we patched into Mother Mind to get a live data feed from their initial investigation.

I didn't mention the evidence that I'd collected myself as Cymurai; Jules was the only one on the board who knew my secret. He stayed silent the whole time, arms folded, reserving judgement. I'd seen that look before: he knew I was holding back.

"Is there any particular reason you waited to tell us?" Jules asked, rubbing his temples in exasperation.

"Thought I could handle it myself," I answered apologetically, bowing my head.

"Oh, I'm sure," said Apu Malhorta thoughtfully as he looked over the data, our biggest Indian investor and chief technology officer.

"Aren't you always?"

His words carried a weight that irritated me.

"We were told Jack-21 couldn't connect to the internet," Huidai interjected. "Was that a lie?"

I twitched, thinking about that awful prospect.

"He's not online," I said shaking my head sincerely. "That much I'm sure of. I've got Gabrielle analysing how he traced Ilian now."

"That's all well and good, but Churchbell Security is on the case," Jules retorted. "There hasn't been any evidence to link us until now, but their digital forensics team will be searching the kid's network. They're going to start asking questions, and before you know it, we'll have a public inquiry up our asses."

He rubbed his brow, taking a sharp digital breath, the eyes of the room fixated on him. I didn't like where this was heading.

"I appreciate that you built this company from scratch, but it really is just scandal after scandal with you. After this latest exposé with you and Gabrielle, our stock could be about to take a dive, and that's nothing compared to what'll happen if this gets out."

A murmur of agreement rumbled across the board, making me uneasy.

"To put your minds at ease, Gabrielle is processing a short list of private investigators to recover the Project Selection files as we speak," I replied, waving my hands in a calming motion.

"Be that as it may, we still have to deal with our police problem," interjected Apu. "We need one of our own to handle the Jack-21 investigation. Someone from Global Arms. We'll have a much better handle on the situation with a man on the inside, someone who already has knowledge of project selection."

"No arguments here, but it is out of Global Arms' jurisdiction," I pointed out, deceptively, wanting to make it seem like I hadn't been planning for this.

"I've never known you to be afraid to pull strings, Kenji," chuckled Jules with a coy smile. "Call up Scotland Yard. Bribe the commissioner if you have to."

"I thought we were trying to stay on the right side of the law," I retorted.

"If it's between that and more bad publicity…" Jules shrugged.

"It's doable," Gabrielle explained through a private telepathic channel. "We have intel that the commissioner is involved with a sex ring. Easy leverage."

I frowned, minimised her window and turned back to the board.

"Fine, working on it now," I answered grudgingly. "The question that follows though is who do we send?"

"Someone from the Ashigaru preferably," Jules replied.

"A special forces cyborg assigned to a murder case is going to attract attention," Huidai opposed.

"It might work in our favour. The media has been driving home the ferocity of the attacks," Apu pointed out. "Sending in someone combat qualified might put their minds at ease."

"A necessary risk," retorted Jules. "We need someone loyal, trustworthy, capable. That's the Ashigaru all over."

I'd been waiting for them to say that. Gabrielle appeared in my eyes, nodding confidently.

"You know what to do," she whispered in my ears.

"We've actually been preparing for this eventuality," I announced confidently with a smirk. I telepathically sent a command to the board behind me, bringing up the company profile for one my operatives.

Global Arms Employee Profile 5842-3379-0723-8541:
First Name: Emma
Surname: Golem
Occupation: Special Forces Private Security Contractor

Her profile picture hung in the top corner of the database entry. Tall and dark, with an athletic prosthetic body engineered to perfection. She was the world's first full-body cyborg; her titanium skull was a casing for her first brain's life-support system. The outline of her bionic skeleton jutted clearly from her synthetic skin. Her artificial hair was brunette, cut to a regulation style. Her bionic eyes were top of the line, with flexible protective panels. Built like a brick shithouse, but she wasn't without her feminine charm.

I looked around at the reactions of the board, staring at the profile with a combination of scepticism and anger.

"Is this a joke?" Jules asked bluntly, holding his hand out disbelievingly.

I loaded up a Mother Mind profile for everyone to see.

Mother Mind Profile 4372-6349-8752-9361:
First name: Daniel
Surname: Haines
Status: Living

Nationality: British
Occupation(s):
- Detective Inspector
  - Status: Employed
  - Organisation: Churchbell Security

"As per your requests, I've been monitoring the officers on the case since the start of the incident," I explained, pointing to the photo of the dark, gruff, war-weary officer. "He hasn't had success with his investigation but, interestingly enough, the scans seem to suggest he would make a prime candidate for Phase Two of Project Clayman."

Jules' jaw dropped with disbelief. "Y… You infected him with the virus already?!"

"You told me to take whatever measures were necessary," I continued, trying not to smirk at him. "Phase Two was always meant to use candidates from outside of the company."

"Given the situation, Gabrielle predicted a high probability that the Ashigaru may have to work with Churchbell Security. If Emma is going to be taking over the case, don't you think it would be best to let her work with someone she already has a rapport with?"

I saw Jules mouth the word 'rapport' with disgust, shaking his head disapprovingly.

"This is not the time to be running your experiments," Jules mouthed.

"I beg to differ," I smiled. "I think this is exactly the time for some out-of-the-box thinking."

A wave of ambivalence rippled among them.

"High risk. Higher reward." I smirked.

"It's an interesting concept, I'll give you that," Huidai added thoughtfully, rapping her nails on the crystal table. "But testing it at such a critical moment is… unorthodox to say the least."

"Each of the software elements is sound," I reassured. "It's just operating them in parallel that hasn't been trialled."

Gabrielle appeared as a full-flesh avatar, standing behind me with her arms folded, accompanied by floating windows of the data she'd collected in the centre of the table.

"The program installed on Detective Haines has a 95% success rate," she explained, like the voice of reason. "There is no cause for concern on that account. I wouldn't have suggested it to Kenji in the first place if I didn't think this would work."

The board exchanged puzzled glances. They apparently wanted to argue but knew that her intelligence meant that she would have planned for practically every conceivable variable in the equations. Robots may run experiments… but more often than not, the AIs predicted the results first with a high degree of accuracy.

"You're putting an awful amount of faith in her, Kenji," Huidai added, in a tone barely above a whisper. "An experiment is still an experiment."

"You *all* should have faith in her. Look at her service record! New Orleans, Seoul, Dhaka. It's impeccable. Give me one good reason why she isn't the one for the job?"

"There's more to this than just her track record," explained Huidai.

"But it means getting the job done quickly and quietly. She knows Project Selection. There's no one else more suitable!"

The board had their own VPAs search the database for alternatives. They spent a good five minutes searching and, after much deliberation, I was relieved to see nods of approval from almost everyone.

Jules added, rubbing his chin ponderously, "You must admit it's a bit convenient. The applications for Project Clayman were limited… a tool for a particular job. Then all of a sudden, just when we need it, a second application we hadn't thought of comes along." He narrowed his eyes at Gabrielle. "Convenient," he repeated.

I held back my tongue… not wanting to turn this into a 'domestic situation'.

"In my experience, one should not complain about serendipity," Apu added sagely.

Jules rumbled sceptically.

They're coming around… just need to push them a little bit more…

"You all know the risks when pulling strings like this," I added slowly. "Scotland Yard takes case jurisdiction very seriously. All it takes is one man on the inside to spill, and the operation falls apart. What I am proposing has a very high probability of negating that possibility."

Apu nodded, his lips curling downwards. "You certainly know how to make your case, Awasaki, I'll give you that."

I caught Jules shooting a furious glare at him, then quickly look away. He knew I was starting to get the upper hand.

Now's my chance…

"So!" I chirped, slapping my hands together. "If we're all ready, I move to take a vote on it."

I telepathically sent the ballot to their displays:

<<Approve Lieutenant Emma Golem as case officer for Jack-21 investigation, and commence phase two of Project Clayman?>>

<<Yes/No>>

"Please submit your votes now," Gabrielle announced, appearing over the table like a ghost.

I cast my vote and observed the others, contemplating their choices. The vote was anonymous, but I could guess what most of their decisions would be. Especially Jules. He probably voted no just to spite me. Evidently resented the fact I no longer saw him as a mentor, going out of his way to sabotage my plans. I hated that kind of dog-in-the-manger bullshit.

The results of the vote came in.

Four in favour, two opposed.

I gave a discreet sigh of relief.

"Well," I smiled, feeling pleased with myself, "I for one am glad that's all settled."

"Oh, this isn't settled. Not by a long shot," Jules interrupted grumpily, pointing firmly at me.

I raised an eyebrow. "I don't see anything else on the agenda?"

"Call it a spur of the moment addition," he smiled falsely at me.

I grimaced internally; this was going to be bad news.

Jules turned the rest of the board with a solemn expression, the corner of his mouth twitching as he tried to hide his amusement.

"We've talked about this for a while now," Huidai began, the words oozing out of her mouth as she wrapped her fingers on the table.

"I think we have made our concerns fairly clear here tonight," Apu added.

"Concerns?" I repeated cautiously.

"About you, Kenji," Jules answered with particular joy, pointing straight at me.

"You are too easily distracted," answered Huidai thoughtfully, in a tone barely above a whisper. "Irresponsible is the word that comes to mind. Your plans may work from time to time… but."

She shrugged.

I ground my teeth. I'd always dreaded that this day would come. I used to have anger management issues. My training had taught me to deal with it through meditation and EEG stimulation techniques, but right now I wanted to knock the shit out of Jules.

"They are making valid points, Kenji," Apu said in a calming balanced tone. "Project Selection was an initiative that you recommended."

"You all approved it," I replied, in the most diplomatic tone I could muster.

"Only because of your resounding endorsement," Jules added with a pointing finger, smirking softly like he'd been waiting to say that. "I think I speak for the rest of the board when I say we feel misled. I'm sorry to be the bearer of bad news, but we are considering a vote of no confidence."

A wave of nods all around.

"I see," I said flatly, pursing my lips, using all my restraint not to yell.

"This has been a long time coming," Apu nodded in agreement.

More murmurs of agreement.

I subtly ground my teeth. Jules had always seen me as a golden goose. He hadn't been mentoring me, he was grooming me. Waiting to bleed me dry when the time was right.

"People, I can appreciate your concerns," I continued, giving placating gestures with my hands, trying to de-escalate the situation. "I know I haven't been as attentive lately. I'm sure you can appreciate the last couple of weeks have been trying for me. I don't think any of you would like your sex lives in the headlines."

"Yes, but we're not married to our VPAs," sneered Jules.

It was getting harder and harder not to smack him. Gabrielle's eyes seemed to glaze over, pretending that she wasn't hurt every time someone took it upon themselves to remind her that she wasn't a real person.

"That aside…" I retorted. "I still wholeheartedly support Project Selection. I truly believe that it's the key to keeping our long-term leadership in the AI market. I take full responsibility for the accident on Prometheus Point. Nonetheless, there is still a mess to be cleared up, and if there is one thing I'm good at, it's solving problems. One week, that's all I'm asking. I think that's reasonable enough given you're proposing to take away my life's work."

"One week and the files could be all over the internet," Jules quipped back.

"Or we could have them back and secure a return on your investment. That's what you all want, isn't it?"

A moment of contemplative silence. They debated their plan of action in private telepathy chat, giving me curious sideways glances while I waited, my knee shaking nervously.

"I think one week sounds reasonable," Apu finally admitted.

Nods of agreement rippled outwards. I gave a mental sigh of relief, spotting Jules' barely hidden disappointment.

"You'll get your time, Kenji," he replied coolly. "Get us results or you're out, it's that simple."

"I appreciate your confidence," I told them, trying to mask my sarcasm and bowing my head with respect.

My eyes met with Jules' for a moment. Then a dialogue window appeared on my display:

<<Jules Santiago would like to begin private e-telepathy chat>>
<<Accept: Yes/No?>>

I hesitated for a moment, then answered.

"Why are you doing this, Jules?" I asked him over the link.

"Kid, I've told you time and time again; *don't rock the boat*," his voice echoed gruffly inside my head.

"I don't know what-"

"Don't bullshit me Awasaki! I know that you were at that boy's apartment!"

A surge of anger pulsed through me; he had been monitoring my movements.

"I was trying to…"

"You were playing superhero, *again*! The only reason I've put up with this crap for so long is because the government likes it when you play nice with the military. But getting seen at a crime scene that we're supposed to be discreetly investigating doesn't do them or us any favours."

I discreetly gritted my virtual teeth.

"So, I was supposed to do what exactly?" I growled telepathically. "Stand by and let him die?"

"Most people wouldn't take it upon themselves to spy on society to satisfy their need to protect people," he pointed out.

Now he was just pushing my buttons, not attempting to hide his smug satisfaction.

"You're the one who convinced me to sign the Mother Mind contract! If we're not in the business of saving lives, then why…"

"Leave the Big Brother crap to the government for once. That contract may have given us the cash infusion we needed to grow into what we've become, but it is has haunted us ever since."

"Never seemed to harm our revenue."

He scoffed out loud. "You still don't get it, do you?"

"Get what?" I asked with a raised an eyebrow.

"What's coming," he answered prophetically, switching back to the chat. "The world's a time bomb. Entire continents have become wastelands. A hundred million refugees trying to find jobs in countries that have replaced them with machines already. There are food riots every other week for God's sake! There's a hurricane on the horizon, and we need to be on the right side of it. If Project Selection gets out in the press, our heads will be on chopping blocks waiting for the guillotine. You're not helping. I've invested too much time, money and effort into you to let it all just get pissed away because of your obsessive-compulsive need to fight terrorism!"

"I would *never* let that happen," I told him in a matter-of-fact tone.

Jules just shook his head with a sigh. "I would like to believe that. I honestly would, Kenji, but I know you. You put on this mask for the world to see. You like to think you're hidden, but you're not to *me*."

I glared at him; the tension between us almost overloaded the telepathic channel before I ended the call.

Jules' fiery eyes slid away from me and ended the telepathic chat dialogue.

"Right, if that's everything, I'm sure we all have other pressing issues to attend to," he breathed loudly, nodding to the rest of the board. He swivelled to face me once more. "One week, Kenji."

One by one, they all logged off, disappearing into bursts of pixels. Jules was the last to go, his demon eyes fixed on me all the while.

I collapsed with stress onto the table once they were gone, burying my face in my hands.

One week to save my life's work. I couldn't bear to think what those vultures would do with Virtualife without me. I hated this bullshit; I was never cut out for this back-stabbing Wall Street crap. I was loyal, just to the wrong person in their eyes.

"Are you okay?" Gabrielle asked me softly.

I pulled back my hands and stared gloomily across the table, taking her hand in comfort.

"I'm always okay," I lied to her pointlessly, the exhaustion starting to get the better of me. "Oh, Gab… when did it all get screwed up?"

She smiled meekly at me. "Things have always been pretty screwed up. You're just too hell bent on un-screwing them."

"Maybe…" I examined her look carefully, her eyes shifting nervously; the same look she would have back when she was alive. She wanted to say something, but couldn't bring herself to do it. "Come on," I grumbled, rubbing my eyes with my knuckles. "Let's hear it."

She chewed her lip. "I hate to say it… but Jules does have a point," she admitted gingerly. "You became obsessed with making up for your parents' deaths."

That touched a nerve. I tried not to let it show.

"You can't let it haunt you for the rest of your life!" she pleaded. "It's eating you from the inside. Maybe… maybe it is time to let go of Virtualife."

My jaw dropped at such a suggestion.

"I can't! Not yet, not while Jack-21 is still a threat. Too many people have died already!"

"It's okay to lean on other people from time to time. You do have an entire multinational conglomerate at your disposal."

I wanted to retort, but for once nothing came to mind. But, seeing that she hadn't convinced me, her expressions suddenly became stern.

"Let me deal with Project Selection," she said sympathetically. "I just need you to take a step back for a while. Can you do that for me?"

"Not sure I can…" I sighed back, scratching the back of my head eagerly, keen to drive in and do something. I habitually brought up my intelligence network report. With Mother Mind, I had access to the latest intel gathered by MI5 and GCHQ; critical for my work as Cymurai. There was a black-market shipment of military prosthetics coming into Dubai that I would've sorely liked to intervene in.

But that's what I always did. Retreat into Cymurai when things got too harsh.

Gab frowned with concern at me. "Don't let the company politics drag you down, Kenji. You're better than them."

"I know, I know," I sighed, tugging at my hair. "I'm... I'm just not cut out for it."

"You never were," she laughed, slapping my shoulder playfully. "That's why you wanted me on board, remember? And to be frank... having my mind uploaded into a supercomputer hasn't exactly *hindered* me."

The statement was so absurd it was laughable. The kind of processing power she had access to practically made her a goddess... *and people knew it.* They were afraid of her... in some cases with good reason. She had access to such vast databanks it was impossible to comprehend. She literally knew what everyone had for breakfast on any given morning.

She may have been programmed with the three laws... but that didn't make her any less intimidating.

"I know what you're saying..." I replied cautiously. "But-"

"You need sleep, Kenji," she pleaded, bringing up charts of reduced blood flow in my brain capillaries. "You can't keep up with this."

"You know me," I shrugged dismissively. "Compulsive insomniac."

"How about REM-mode? That'll help you sleep."

She had an answer for everything. REM-state simulations were an alternative to standard VR, which required you to be awake. REM mode was designed to induce sleep, allowing you to continue your social media interactions and still wake up feeling refreshed. The degree of control wasn't significant enough for most gamers, but it would be good enough for whatever she had in mind.

"Perhaps you need something to jog your memory. A reminder of why you need to keep going," she suddenly grinned merrily, gesturing towards the virtual crystal panel walls behind me. I turned in time to see the projections appear. The expanse of golden Barbados sand stretched out before me across the window panes, the azure blue water softly lapping onto the shore, the leaves of palm trees swaying in the breeze. And there they were, those gorgeous innocent eyes beaming out of the screen. My son's hyperactive smile and my daughter's swaying hair.

"Daddy!" their young voices squealed excitedly in unison towards me from out of their virtual world. I couldn't help but smile whenever I heard them.

"Hey, kids!" I grinned back at them. "What are you up to?"

"We're making sandcastles!" Hideo chirped eagerly, pointing towards the sculpted mounds behind him; a pair of blue and pink spades scattered aside.

"Sandcastles!" I chuckled loudly, trying to sound excited for them. "Wow! Looks fun!"

I noticed the timer in the top left-hand corner of the windows. Sixty minutes until their programs would terminate, and I'd be left waiting another day to see them again.

There was only one truth that mattered to me. The human brain was just a neural network. A learning machine based on biochemical algorithms. If there was such a thing as a human soul, it was written somewhere in the maths. Recreation of the code in binary was the natural evolution as far as I was concerned. The lines between man and machine had become so blurred it was a philosophically meaningless distinction. The churches of the world may not have agreed, but I didn't care. I loved them. *They were our children*, the light of my life. When I first became Cymurai, I wanted to make the world safer for people in general. Now, all that mattered to me really was them. If it meant enduring this life, then so be it.

I'll find a way for you kids…

Gabrielle was right. They did keep me going.

"Come and play with us, Daddy!" Shauna beckoned me forward.

"Yeah, play with us, Daddy!" Hideo pleaded.

"I…"

"Daddy will be there soon, darlings," Gabrielle smiled at them reassuredly. "He just needs to take care of some things first."

"What things?" Shauna pouted disapprovingly.

"You guys remember Emma?" I checked. Their faces lit up again.

"The cyborg lady?" Hideo cried excitedly. "Yeah! She's pretty bad-ass!"

"Language!" Gabrielle interjected, with a stern finger.

Hideo's eyes slid away, looking down at his timidly shifting feet in the sand. "Sorry…"

"What are you doing with Emma?" Shauna chirped.

"Daddy needs to send her on a new mission," Gabrielle explained with a smile. "But when we're done, we promise to come play with you!"

"You promise!?" they cried gleefully in anticipation.

I leaned towards the screens, longing to reach out into cyberspace and hug them both.

"I promise," I beamed at them.

"Yaaaay!" they yelled ecstatically, throwing their hands into the air.

I couldn't help but giggle at their innocence, gazing lovingly at them.

"I'll be with you soon, sweethearts." I smiled. "I promise."

<<Suspending programs>>

The idyllic scenes before me faded away, and I was left staring through into the digital void. The timer in the top left of the window paused at 58.43 minutes, my heart sinking almost as soon as they had gone.

"Don't you want to spend more time with them?" she pleaded with me, placing a comforting hand on my shoulder.

"Of, course I do," I sighed, rubbing my eyes.

"And you can," she reassured me. "Just let me handle things for a while."

I let out a long, reluctant sigh.

"Maybe you're right…" I admitted, rubbing my eyes together.

"Have some faith in me," she scoffed. "I do have access to your brainwaves, you know. I can feel your stress, just as much as you do."

Her virtual hands began squeezing my shoulder, intimately massaging the pain away.

Just like she used to…

"I know what needs to be done," she said. "You need sleep. The kids will be waiting for you there, and maybe tonight… Mummy and Daddy can have some *alone time*."

Her words were subtle, but I could already feel the excited tightening behind my groin. We had a plethora of adult simulations we used to keep our sex life exciting. Who was I to argue with that?

She always did know what to say…

"You're the boss…" I smiled, sighing softly as I allowed my tension to melt away.

CHAPTER 4

Mother Mind Profile 3236-1187-7241-9852:

First Name: Emma

Surname: Golem

Status: Living

Nationality: British

Occupation(s):

- Special Forces Private Security Contractor
  - Status: Employed
  - Organisation: Global Arms Incorporated

Criminal Record:

- Convicted: 25/07/2033
  - Offence: Possession of synthetic Cocaine (Class-A narcotic) with intent to supply
  - Sentence: 9 months incarceration (Lockwood Juvenile Correctional Facility)

Known Aliases:

- N/A

Biometric Data:

- Gender: Female
- Date of Birth: 11/05/2018
- Age: 28
- Race: Caucasian
- Hair Colour: Black
- Eye Colour: Hazel
- Height: 1.89m
- Weight: 92kg
- Ailments: None
- Cybernetic Percentage: 96%
- Genetic Modifications:
  - N/A

Immediate Family:

- Mother: Sabrina Golem
- Father: Colin Golem
- Siblings: 0

Relationships:

- Status: Single

Contact Information:

- *Drop down for more info*

Live Surveillance:

- Status: *Partially Available*
- Date: 05/10/2045
- Current Location: Virtualife building, Docklands, East London
- Local Time: 18:57 GMT

<<Memory playback in progress>>

The national year six swimming gala in Birmingham streamed into my nervous system from the RAM of my neural lace.

I recalled everything, the slippery blue tiles, the smell of chlorine, my arms cutting through the water like razors, the muffled sound of splashing and cheers echoing into my ears. My heart pounded like a drum as I front-crawled at top speed to victory, while my muscles ached excruciatingly. Girls from across the country occupied the lanes beside me, in a mad dash for the gold, and I was approaching first place. Adrenaline drove me forward. I wanted that medal like a tick wants blood, refusing to give in.

Every time I turned my head up to get a gasp of air, I caught a glimpse of the poolside stand. A sea of faces, cheering families standing and sitting in rows of raised orange plastic seats, waving banners and taking photos from phones, tablets and vid-glasses, which would all now be obsolete.

My parents were in the crowd, cheering me on. The only two faces I remembered clearly, Mum's auburn hair bouncing up and down as she whooped, and Dad's look almost the same colour from his frantic yelling.

With my last ounce of strength, I tore to the finish line and felt my hand crash against the edge of the pool. I pulled myself above the water line, sucking in the air, my chest ready to explode. The crowd went wild, roaring with applause. I went to wave to the crowd triumphantly… when I noticed that there were already two others ahead of me…

I was afloat… but my heart sank.

Mum and Dad clapped me on, they were beaming at me, but I could almost hear their condescending voices:

'We're still proud of you.'

I half-heartedly threw my fist into the air, pretending to be pleased with myself, putting on the best grin I could muster to conceal the rising sense of worthlessness.

All that hard work and I had still failed. I had let them down. I could feel the age-old depression swallowing me up.

That's good.

Depressed is good… real.

The RE:Call program paused; the crowd in the stand above the pool suddenly freezing as still as statues, water droplets suspended in mid-air like disco balls… the ringtone of the company's secure communication app came from the future to buzz inside my head.

<<Incoming e-telepathy call from: Kenji Awasaki>>

<<Pausing memory playback>>

Every fucking time. Way to go, boss.

He always seemed to call me at the most inconvenient time possible. No doubt to issue last-minute orders. No point putting it off though.

<<Terminating memory playback >>

<<Disengaging neural lace>>

The past faded away into a haze. My sensory perception was

brought back to the present; the world around me became apparent.

Steaming hot water trickled down my face. Real water. I stood naked in one of the steel shower cubicles of the Ashigaru locker room, each drip landing on the ground with a ping that echoed like a tuning fork. The drips rolled off me like water on a stone. I looked down at my toned flesh, impressed with the engineer's handiwork. The muscles seemed convincing enough, completely hiding the mechanics underneath. This sense of smell was dull, but I could just about make out the scent of military soap.

The ceiling panel was bioluminescent, the shower head suspended directly above me controlled by a display panel on the wall, complete with sensors for optimal temperature. I had spent the last hour in the company gym, lifting weights and jogging away on the treadmill. The workout had purely sentimental value to me; it was pretty pointless for someone with my level of cyberisation.

The Encrypted Comm App rezzed onto my HUD.

<<Accept call: Yes/No>>

I pressed a button on the touch panel to stop the flow of water and rubbed the rough off my face, feeling the outline of my metal skull underneath my cloned skin, letting the call ring a couple more times before I grudgingly accepted. The video feed on his webcam enlarged to encompass my whole field of vision. For obvious reasons, I didn't engage the camera on my built-in smartwatch; the holo-display protruding through my skin.

Britain's most notorious businessman appeared before my eyes, his goateed-face looking at me through the webcam. His eyes always beamed with warmth, and yet always seemed to be hiding pain just below the surface. He was sat at his desk, holographic e-mails and schedules whizzing around, his cheeks flushed, red around the sharp, armoured ridges of his cheekbones, stroking his beard anxiously to cover up his heavy breathing. I had a sneaking suspicion I knew what had happened. It was sort of an unspoken rule around the office that you didn't talk about Awasaki's virtual sex life, even as a private joke; if there was such a thing anymore.

"Evening, boss!" I greeted him in a forced chirpy tone.

"Lieutenant!" he beamed back, letting his hands fall to his waist side. "How's my favourite cyborg?"

I really wished he wouldn't call me that, but I went along with it anyway. Not that he needed to ask, given how he was probably monitoring me through Mother Mind. No way he was going to let his *'pet project'* run around unsupervised.

I was the first of my kind, the first person to have their brain transplanted into a full prosthetic body. An experimental cybernetic rig codenamed Clayman D-9; a joint project between Kawaguchi Biotech, Akira Engineering and Virtualife.

I'd spent five years of my life as a lab rat, enduring endless rounds of surgeries, examinations, performance tests. The scientific layer of hell. They paid me half a million to go through with it; too good to refuse. An option to quit would've been nice though.

"Getting on, getting on," I telepathically chirped back.

"The kids have been asking about you!" Kenji added merrily. "They'd love to see you again."

I cringed at the thought of it. He'd programmed his children to appear as his idealised image of the perfect family and succeeded. But they were *too* perfect, so perfect that they were unsettling… frankly, I found them creepy. Kettle calling the pot black I suppose.

"Sure!" I replied, trying to sound enthusiastic. "I've got a bit of free time now so-"

"Oh yeah," he interrupted in a sympathetic tone. "What happened with you and Natalie? You two were so good together!"

I hid my objections to the question. He was way too familiar with me for my liking. Always seemed keen to get the dirt on my sex life. I racked my brains to tell him something to shut him up quickly.

"Error. Error. Not compatible," I replied, accessing my voice synthesiser setting to sound as electronic as possible.

Kenji snorted at the nerd joke. Natalie was my ex-girlfriend; broke up with her about a week ago. Met her through an anonymous security contractor dating website, in the robosexual chat room. We went out in the real world a few times, but I had to end it. She wanted me to pretend to be an AI. A bit too creepy for my taste; but I didn't really want to get into that with my employer.

"Aw… that sucks," he nodded sympathetically. "Chin up though. Plenty of fish and all that."

A saying that was at least ten years out of date, but never mind.

"Cheers," I replied flatly, eager to change the subject. "So, what's up?'

He seemed disappointed for a split second but quickly shifted into a more professional stance.

"You have a new assignment," he informed me curtly.

"You're taking me off the Project Selection task force?" I blurted out with surprise.

"I'm afraid so," he nodded regretfully.

I ground my teeth while I stared at the video feed. I'd been assigned to Project Selections security for nearly a year now. It was my baby.

"Does it have to be me?" I complained as diplomatically as I could.

"Sorry Emma," he apologised. "There's no one else I trust to get the job done. This requires a bit more of a personal touch. You've met Helen Ilian?"

"Uh-huh," I nodded, recalling the AI researcher on Project Selection.

Kenji forwarded me the data; briefing documents, photographs of a new yet familiar crime scene, and maps with a pin placed over an apartment block in Kensington. I began reading through the files.

I didn't even know she had a kid… and now he was dead. Andrew, the latest victim of the so-called 'Jack-21' murderer. Crazy bastard.

"Oh shit," I breathed.

"Yeah," Awasaki nodded grimly. "Oh, shit is right."

"Wait a minute…" I said thoughtfully, scanning the text. "He was the one who the cracked Prometheus Point server?"

"Looks like," he added ominously.

"I thought you'd installed a program to prevent Jack-21 getting online?" I checked, with a sense of urgency in my voice.

"As far as we can tell, that's still the case."

"Then how did he find the kid?" I asked with genuine concern.

"You tell me, that's what you're here for," he smiled meekly. "I've pulled some strings at Scotland Yard. We'll be taking over operational command of the investigation from Churchbell Security. They're getting too close to the truth now; the kid's murder leads right back to us. You'll have to keep them on the wrong trail without raising suspicion."

That was unusual. Police precincts were contracted out to different security companies depending on the Borough. Scotland Yard itself was still under government control, handing out cases like business leads, but it was rare for them to change the company assigned mid-investigation; even rarer to have an officer from one borough to liaise with another district if it was under the jurisdiction of a rival company.

"They ain't gonna be happy about that," I commented.

"No," Kenji agreed loudly. "But I sold it to the Yard as a personal favour. Dr Ilian is a valued employee, an important part of the Virtualife family. She deserves the full support of the company in her time of grief."

I nodded cautiously, while mentally trying to guess the leverage that he used to swing this.

"Something on your mind, Lieutenant?" he asked.

I twisted my lips as I thought about how to put this delicately.

"Well... not to put too fine a point on it, sir," I began, "but the boy did steal highly classified data from us. Isn't it gonna look like we're the ones who bumped him off?"

Officially we (the Ashigaru), were his personal security team, but the world knew what we were; a hit squad. If Virtualife needed someone to quietly disappear, or make an offer that couldn't be refused, they called on us. Most of the private security firms had regiments like us. Corporate warfare had taken up a new meaning.

Kenji leaned back in his leather seat, cupping his hands and resting them on his chest.

"I think Helen will understand that we're just trying to help… or at least appear to be," he continued.

"I'm more concerned about Churchbell," I interrupted. "If they work out that I'm there to run a cover-up, we'll be in for a shit storm." Despite everything, I was glad our rapport was good enough for me to casually swear at him.

"I appreciate your concerns," he continued calmly. "But Gabrielle has run the risk assessment simulations. Fact is, the alternative of letting this play out on its own is a bigger threat."

Well, who am I to argue with Queen Gabrielle?

"Roger that," I accepted. "Who will I be working with?"

The corner of his lips turned into a coy grin. "Now this ought to cheer you up."

"Oh?" I said, piping my curiosity.

He forwarded me a service record. I was honestly stunned when I read the name and saw the familiar face for the profile picture.

"D-Daniel?" I stuttered. "Daniel Haines?"

Just looking at his strong, round, bearded face on the profile photo put a smile on my face. *Talk about a sight for sore eyes.* He was an old school friend. Well… sort of. I went off the rails a bit in my teen years. We ran with a postcode street gang, *'N11'*. Peer pressure and all that bullshit. We were among the few who grew out of it before we either got stabbed, overdosed, or just too far deep in the criminal world to get out. We got caught selling dope in Greenford, and ended up being sent to Lockwood; a youth correctional facility (which, in reality, was basically a recruitment centre for private security companies). We hated it at first, but it did set us back on the straight and narrow. I looked back on those days with bittersweet nostalgia, trying to remember the good times. I lost touch with him after we got out, but I knew he was planning to go into private police as well. Never imagined we'd end up working together… or *against* each other depending on how you looked at it.

"Jesus. Talk about a small world," I chuckled.

"Just don't fall back into old habits!" He winked jokingly at me.

"Roger that," I half-laughed back, not really appreciating him bringing up the past.

"Think he'll be just as happy to see you?" he inquired.

"Maybe?" I answered in an uncertain tone, rubbing the back of my neck. "I haven't seen him in ten years... under normal circumstances I'd say yeah, but he ain't stupid. He'll know some thing's fishy."

"He's been sent an NDA. He'll have to sign it if he wants to stay on the investigation," Kenji continued. "From what I hear, he's very protective of his cases, so I doubt he'll be willing to let go just yet."

"That's one way to break the ice," I said dryly.

Great to see you again, Dan! By the way, here's a contract that legally binds you to the possibility of having your memory erased!

"I'll leave that to your discretion," Kenji added jokingly. "There's a Kestrel waiting for you. Report to heliport three."

"Roger that," I answered, sending a saluting emoji. "Signing off."

<<Call ended>>

The video feed disappeared, leaving me by myself in the shower. No rest for the wicked. I pressed another button on the touch panel, and the quick-dry system kicked in. Overhead infrared lights began beaming down warm orange rays. The mechanical whirlwind of fans revved to life. Balmy air came blowing out of the tiny holes punctured into the wall panels. I twirled around on the spot, letting the heat caress my skin, rapidly evaporating the vestiges of the water. In under a minute I was dry as a bone. I grabbed my towel hanging on a rail above my head and wrapped it around me, using the fingerprint scanner to unlock the door.

I stepped out into the changing room, my nose sensors vaguely detecting deodorant. The shower pod was one of four lined up in a row, built for practicality, not privacy. An android cleaner whirred as it polished away at the mirror on the far side of the room. Other officers were lounging around in various stages of undress. My HUD could give me access to their personnel data, but I knew all their names by heart. I'd worked for them for years before I signed up for Project Clayman. We'd spent countless hours together in these rooms. They'd all seen me naked a million times, not to mention having gone through the real shit with them. Fighting side by side. Literally bleeding together in the trenches.

But now that I was in this body, I'd find them averting their gaze, or giving me nervous sideways glances with a combination of fear and disgust.

I ignored them as usual. I hadn't thought about the discrimination factor when I signed up for the project. Never thought my friends would consider me less than human. I did my best to ignore them and strode over to the rows of aluminium lockers, with an iron bench stretching out in front of them. I pressed my palm against my locker's DNA scanner, still recognising the pattern in my synthetic skin. With a flash, a bleep and a click, the door unlocked.

I pulled the door open with a clang. An animated Intellipaper photo hung on the inside of the door; a video recording of my mother and father hanging outside their red-bricked terraced house in Ealing. I stared longingly at it for a moment, before sighing and pressing the 'Off' icon in the corner to deactivate the animation.

The inside of the locker was lit by a panel at the top, revealing a rack holding several coat hangers with my various uniforms. My combat gear, a one-piece suit similar to that of a deep-sea diver, woven from a nanotech fabric called NeverPierce, currently set to its default colour of red used for the Ashigaru logo. The structure was flexible and lightweight; until the sensors detected an incoming knife or a bullet, triggering an electric current that would turn the material harder than Kevlar body armour to absorb the impact. There were patches printed on right shoulders, the logo of Global Arms and the insignia of the Ashigaru written in kanji script: 足軽

It was a symbol of pride for me; the selection process for the Ashigaru was identical to that of the SAS, but the plan was to have all the operators in the squad become cyberised like me if my trial period was a success. It would soon be obsolete; no point in having fitness assessments on robots.

I joined the company back in '36. Went through their basic training courses, which earned me both a Private Security Contractor Licence with Level-1 qualifications in both military deployment and law enforcement (legally the equivalent of an Army Private or a

Police Constable).

The first posting the company gave me was with Geater Manchester Police, before being transferred to the US Marines; despite being a British Citizen. The perks of privatisation.

I was deployed in the peacekeeping operations along the Japanese coast and earned points on my Licenses until I could earn the equivalent rank of Lieutenant….it was there that I got headhunted by Awasaki for the role in the Ashigaru.

After a few missions for the CIA, Awasaki seemed impressed enough to consider me a candidate for the Clayman Project.

He told me it was an honour…and I was trying very hard to believe that.

A black combat helmet hung on the rack. A shielded visor rested at the bottom next to my boots. My equipment belt hung on the frame, lined with non-lethal equipment, handgun holster, first aid kit, etc. I slipped into my underwear and started pulling the equipment off the shelves. I pressed a button moulded into the fabric of the suit and the electro-zip running down the spine automatically stitched itself together.

I carried on dressing when a message flashed onto my HUD. My contract prevented me from using almost all social media, aside from anonymous forums. I recognised the screen name for one of my friends. She'd commented on my relationship status changing from 'In a relationship' to 'Single'.

<< ':(Sorry to hear that hon. Screw her though. You could do way better! I can always hook you up with someone if you like? Let's get together sometime okay?>>

Twenty of my friends left similarly comforting messages. I gave half-baked responses, thanking them for their support. I wanted to feel reassured by them, but as time went on, the nagging voice in the back of my mind grew louder, telling me that I was going to be forever alone. Not that I said that to the company therapist I was required to see.

If a psychiatrist, doctor, or technician deemed me unfit for duty,

I'd be forced to return the prosthetic body back to the company, there wouldn't be much left after that. My brain would be left to rot in some stasis unit until a new biological body could be cloned for me, followed by a dangerous transplant into the new flesh. No guarantee I would even survive the procedure, and even if I did, it could still go wrong. Left body locked, unable to speak or move.

With that in mind, I was highly fucking motivated to keep this job.

I clipped the last buckle on the steel-capped boots and looked up again. Two automatic doors were leading out of the room, displays indicating they led to the armoury and the exit. I marched to door, scanned me and slid open. It was 30x20 metres wide, almost entirely blank, aside from a steel-panel cabinet. Each panel hid rows of mechanical drawers for handguns, rifles, combat lasers, grenades, and smart-ammo clips, my HUD displaying their condition data.

"Your designated weapons loadout, Emma," Ben's electronic voice telepathically spoke to me. He was the standard-issue police VPA, his pulsing blue icon appearing in the bottom corner of my HUD. One by one, he placed graphical arrows on my vision, pointing to the weapons lockers I was due to collect, along with interactable icons to bring me more general data on them. Of course, with this new body, I was never truly *disarmed.*

"Cheers."

One by one, the mechanical racks popped out of the shelves on their rails, revealing the weapons inside which I began packing away. They were stored in silver plastic attaché cases with handles and shoulder straps; stored as parts in moulded foam holsters.

I gathered my gear: a handgun, grenades, handcuffs, etc., storing some of it in the compartments in my leg units. I slung the pièce de résistance over my shoulder; an M150 Atmos-piercer assault rifle. A massive, bulky weapon, built for firing high-velocity enemy-tracking rounds and a neural-link laser targeting system; genuinely lethal. I loved the weight. I was strong enough to tear someone limb from limb, but there was something about the hot lead that just couldn't be substituted. I pocketed a couple of smart-ammunition clips, and the weapons cabinet locked itself back up.

I followed Ben's directions to heliport three, guided by more digital arrows, brushing past service bots. I headed out into the immaculately clean white corridors of Virtualife tower, the walls radiating light across the expanse of spotless blue carpet. I noticed the officers and Virtualife staff, chatting in the break room, getting wishes of 'good luck' and 'good hunting' as I weaved through the traffic.

I hadn't given any thought to what I was going to say to Daniel. Under normal circumstances, it might have been nice, but no one liked having their case taken over. Especially since the whole thing screamed conflict of interest. He was never one to kick up a fuss, but that didn't change that this was going to be the world's most awkward high-school reunion.

I came to a set of broad glass auto-doors. I stepped through onto the tarmac of the heliport, greeted by the cold night air and a view of the two-hundred-metre drop to the street level. The glare of landing lights forced me to activate the sun filter in my eyes despite the night sky. I'd arrived in time to see the orange-black ground crew androids detaching a fuel line from the Boeing Kestrel model tiltrotor jet sitting on the port, standing by for my arrival. It was twenty metres long and carried six passengers plus the pilots. A black aircraft, with angular edges on its graphene wings, it had a built-in nanotech repair system and even optical camouflage. It had a pair of large VTOL jet engines on the end of each wing, set to an upright position, spinning slower than usual, keeping the electric motors warm.

I saw the secondary pilot through the cockpit window, wearing a black visor helmet, jacked into the control console by cables to the panels above her head; her E-ID data marked her as Lieutenant Jane Sterling on my display. The lights from the control panel reflected in her visor, but she had her chin down and arms folded.

"Typical," I tutted, shaking my head. She was sleeping on the job, again. I suppose she was only there for emergencies. The craft was 'manned-optional', meaning it could be flown either by remote or entirely through the onboard AI auto-pilot. Having a person behind the controls was a last resort, realistically only there to satisfy health and safety regulations.

The door on the side of the jet slid open, and I climbed inside the cramped, dimly lit cabin, feeling the rumble of the engine beneath my feet. Two rows of steel and canvas chairs lined against the hull of the cabin, underneath the overhead weapons racks, where I stowed my rifle before shuffling my way into the cockpit. I rapped my knuckles on Jane's helmet, waking her abruptly.

"Ow!" she whined.

"Wakey, wakey," I deadpanned.

"Not cool," she complained, rubbing the back of her head.

"I need your head in the game."

"Why, are you expecting heavy fire?" She laughed. "It's a taxi run, Emma."

"Just do your job," I sternly glowered at her.

"Roger that." She yawned and stretched out. "Stand by for take-off."

I took my seat, pulling the harness across my chest, the auto-lock tightening in place. The high-pitch engine whine grew louder and louder, and soon I felt my simulated stomach flutter as we lifted off. I placed my elbow on the armrest, and nestled my head on my fist, watching through the cabin window as the heliport and the tower disappeared. The lights of the city rushed past as we soared above the rich man's air traffic of flying cars.

Here we go…

CHAPTER 5

Mother Mind Profile 4372-6349-8752-9361:

First Name: Daniel

Surname: Haines

Status: Living

Nationality: British

Occupation(s):

- Detective Inspector
  - Status: Employed
  - Organisation: Churchbell Security

Criminal Record:

- Convicted: 25/07/2033
  - Offence: Possession of synthetic Cocaine (Class-A narcotic) with intent to supply
  - Sentence: 9 months' incarceration (Lockwood Juvenile Correctional Facility)

Known Aliases:

- N/A

Biometric Data:

- Gender: Male
- Date of Birth: 09/03/2018
- Age: 27
- Race: Afro-Caribbean
- Hair Colour: Black
- Eye Colour: Brown
- Height: 1.79m
- Weight: 87kg
- Ailments: None
- Cybernetic Percentage: 3%
- Genetic Modifications:
  - None

Immediate Family:
- Mother: Selina Haines
- Father: Nathaniel Haines
- Siblings: 1
  - Brother: Shaun Haines

Relationships:
- Status: In a relationship
  - Partner: Claire Fielding

Contact Information:
- *Drop down for more info*

Live Surveillance:
- Status: *Available*
- Date: 05/10/2045
- Current Location: Pearl House Apartment Complex, South Kensington, West London
- Local Time: 19:24 GMT

The cold wind swept across the heliport on the rooftop. Each of my heavy breaths sent out a jet of steam. I stuffed my numb, trembling hands into my uniform pockets. My head was pounding, my brainwave patterns fluttering angrily on my contact lens display. I was running an app that was supposed to relieve migraine had done jack all, aside from spamming advertisements. In fairness, it was well past time I upgraded my interface headset, the subtle silver electrodes hidden by my hairline were about three generations behind.

"Fuck me, it's cold!" Matt whined, rubbing his gloved fingers against the sleeves of his high-visibility jacket, staring impatiently. "How long do they expect us to wait up here?"

"I ain't complaining," I replied flatly, rubbing my forehead desperately. "Beats the stench of fresh blood, and definitely beats talking to the press."

The thought of more upcoming conferences was already instilling dread into me.

The smell of murder scenes had become all too familiar in recent weeks. I had spent the last half an hour examining the disembowelled corpse of a seventeen-year-old hacker. His apartment on the twenty-seventh floor had been turned into a horror show; one I had to go through in sharp detail, gathering as much forensic data as possible for our AIs to analyse.

I stared up at the overcast sky, trying not to look over the edge of the rooftop. I didn't want the lads knowing I was afraid of heights. Just below I could see another police car turning off Kensington High Street and into the apartment complexes' underground car park, joining the small fleet we had parked down there. Forensic investigation officers and drones were busy carrying away evidence in air-tight bags, flowing endlessly up and down the elevator.

I was the officer on the scene of the first murder, a refugee found under a bridge in Southbank. I almost threw up all over the evidence, then spent the evening in my room alone with a bottle of brandy, trying to stop the shakes. Took my girlfriend four hours to calm me down… I guess it made for a nice change of pace from our usual relationship dynamic.

I went to work the next day with a hangover and the blazing conviction to stick the bastard responsible in a Prison Matrix chamber myself.

But more bodies kept piling up.

I was becoming cold to it, the hope of catching the ones responsible relegated to a distant memory. But there was something different about this murder. Most of the other victims had been slum dwellers, snatched off the streets. Scaling up the side of a skyscraper into a middle-class apartment was a change in the perpetrator's M.O.

Whatever was going on, Jack-21 wasn't the run-of-the-mill serial killer. A big part of this job was trying to figure out what made these people tick – their motivation – and finding clues to what they would do next. All we really knew was that he targeted cyborgs, dissecting them for their prosthetics. That made at least a third of the population potential targets. Didn't exactly narrow things down. At first, we'd assumed that it was black-market scumbags, selling the implants on at a discounted price. But the autopsies revealed professional surgical skills and all the victims had been incised using the same laser model, suggesting a single perpetrator. Most likely a member of some anti-transhuman movement or religious sect. We'd placed all known members of such groups operating in London under surveillance. No joy so far.

I felt a rumble from my watch, raised my wrist, and the display activated, projecting the softly pulsing blue icon belonging to the Metropolitan Police's standard-issue AI assistant.

"Preliminary analysis has been uploaded to HQ's server," Ben explained, speaking from the speakers in my uniform collar.

"Let me guess," I sighed. "Results inconclusive."

"Negative."

…*No way I heard that right.*

"Say again?" I asked, my ears pricking up.

A photo from the crime scene loaded up. A fluffy blue bathroom rug lay on the white tiled floor by the shower. The image enlarged, zooming in and revealing the remnants of a large, round footprint in the material. Then Ben placed a series of annotations on the picture; it was too round to be an ordinary boot, shaped like an elongated egg, with almost hook-shaped toes.

"This footprint is an 86% match for the Camelot-73 model powered exoskeleton," Ben explained.

"Wait a minute… Are you saying we *actually have* some honest-to-God *evidence*?" I cried with my mouth open.

"Affirmative," Ben chimed back mechanically.

"Holy shit!" I whirled to Matt gleefully.

"'Bout time we got a break!" He slumped with exasperation, practically collapsing with relief.

Ben downloaded the technical specifications of the Camelot power armour. A 3D rendering began rotating out from my watch. The design was reminiscent of a medieval knight's suit. The chest, shoulder and leg panels were rounded and thick, with feet featuring a pair of mechanical talons for extra grip. Almost certainly a match.

"Doesn't look like climbing gear to me," I said inquisitively, taking a quick glance over the ledge to the concrete abyss below. "Getting up here must be enough of a bitch without having to haul that hunk of junk as well."

"The manufacturer offers optional gecko-pads on the hands and feet," Ben explained. "They could easily support the weight of the exoskeleton."

I began imagining someone in that suit scaling that wall like spider-man.

"Hard to believe no one saw that," I added.

"Optical camouflage?" Matt suggested with a shrug.

"That would be consistent with the lack of CCTV footage we obtained," Ben suggested.

"The invisible killer?" I snorted. "Sounds like a bad HG Wells fan fiction. So, what's the plan, Ben? Search Mother Mind for known owners of the Camelot suit?"

"Affirmative. I have added users of relevant technologies to current surveillance parameters. Preliminary scans suggest recent sales of counterfeit copies of the suit within London."

"Wow. Evidence and suspects on the same day," Matt nodded positively. "I feel bad for saying it, but we got lucky this time."

Usually I wouldn't approve of how he was referring to the victim, but we had been running on fumes, so it was hard to disagree.

"It's still a big deviation from his normal patterns," I pointed out. "Any idea why he's suddenly gone from killing junkies and hookers to middle-class cyber-criminals?"

"My analysis has suggested one possible hypothesis. A copycat criminal," Ben suggested.

"Someone *posing* as Jack-21?" I exclaimed, alarmed by the possibility.

"Funny, that was one of the theories for Jack the Ripper too," Matt added, his lips rolling ponderously.

"You think the perp was just after the stolen data? Used Jack-21's murder-style to throw us off his trail?" I checked.

"Affirmative," Ben continued. "For my hypothesis, the prime suspect would be an agent working for Virtualife's competitors."

"Industrial espionage," I scoffed with disgust. "No wonder they want to take over the case."

The word had come down from Scotland Yard. Jurisdiction for the Jack-21 Investigation was to be transferred from my company

(Churchbell Security) to Global Arms, part of the Virtualife conglomerate. Official word that this was done as a personal favour to the victim's mother, a prominent AI researcher at Virtualife.

Makes sense, right? Taking care of your people and all that.

Well, it would if they weren't our main competitors in the private police industry.

Initial analysis from the digital forensics officers had revealed that our victim was a budding cyber-criminal. Used his mother's terminal to gain access and steal data from one of Virtualife's secure servers. We attempted to trace his data traffic but, unsurprisingly, it had been encrypted by the Freethought satellite grid. But it didn't take an AI to work out it was most likely being sent to Spiritform.

Now Virtualife was swooping in to shut us down. Matt would be reassigned, and I'd stay on the case, but the role of head detective would be one of Global Arm's officers. Even stranger, it would be a member of the Ashigaru; their elite special forces team.

Talk about conflict of interest. It was a cover-up if I ever saw one.

"This is bullshit," I complained to Mark loudly, my breath turning to steam as the wind rapped on my face.

"Yeah, but what are ya gonna do?" He shrugged.

"Filing a report to the IPCC comes to mind."

"Well, you should've thought of that before you signed that NDA."

I clenched my fist. He was right. My gut told me something was wrong when it first appeared in my inbox. I should've listened, but if I hadn't signed it, then I'd have been taken off the case altogether. I didn't want that, not yet anyway.

"Still, don't you think there's something seriously dodgy going on here?" I checked.

"Duh. That's why I'm keeping my head down, taking my new case and shutting the fuck up. Got a better idea?"

I bit my lip. I really didn't. What I was doing may have been the right thing to do, but it probably wasn't going to be the *smart* thing.

"Whatever," I sighed with disappointment, deciding to change the subject before I pissed myself off too much. "Still up for watching the match tomorrow?"

"Yeah, 'course bruv," he sniggered. "Can't wait to see you have your asses handed to you."

"Oh, don't be so sure," I grinned back at him. "Arsenal's brought in a new gene therapy progr-"

I was cut short by a ring tone buzzing telepathically inside my head.

<<Incoming call from: Claire Fielding>>

"Typical."

"The missus? Mate, I keep telling you, that one's no good for you."

I gave a long, tired groan as a response, rubbing my eyes in frustration. Right now, I needed to deal with her like I needed a hole in my head. I did love her… but this was getting a bit much.

"I don't know how you handle it, man," Matt scoffed, shaking his head disapprovingly. "We have to deal with enough of that shit at work."

"She's just going through a rough patch," I said solemnly with a placating gesture.

In the age of genetic and nanotech medical treatments, depression had become the epidemic of developed countries. A generation of so-called *'techno-prisoners'*, born of our highly connected yet distant society, the stresses of digital capitalism, and the seemingly endless news reports of environmental disasters and wars.

Suicide rates were at an all-time high. Seemed like we were dealing with one every day when I was a street cop and had spent more time with the company shrink than I'd cared to admit. Hell, they sent you there every time you unloaded your weapon. I grew up on the streets though. I was no stranger to a little bloodshed. They'd talk you through it, prescribe whatever drugs and or software they thought would help. But the job ate at you.

They always offer memory erasure as an option… most don't take it for obvious reasons. The ones who do… well, those are usually the *really* scary ones. The cops who can unload on someone, and come into work the next day with a smile on their faces. Those were the guys you had to watch out for.

Aside from those guys, dealing with grieving parents was by far the worst thing about the job, especially when you factored in that a lot of them may have had age reversal therapy, with the potential to outlive their children by hundreds of years. Grieving for eternity.

I forced myself to put on the warmest, most reassuring smile I could muster. I held my smartwatch up to my face and activated its front-facing camera, telepathically answering the call.

The data began streaming to my contact lenses, and the feed from Claire's webcam enlarged to fill my field of vision through my contact lenses. Her expression reminded me of cold porridge. As usual, she was huddled in bed, her blanket enveloping her, dressed in a stained tank top. Her otherwise cute face was hidden by her unkempt short black hair with drooping sacks under her eyes, wires dangling from the electrodes on her forehead.

"Hey, babe." I smiled weakly at her with a confident telepathic tone.

"Hey…" she answered in a tone that was barely above a whisper even inside my head.

"How's it going? Did you go out running?"

She shook her head. I had to resist the urge to roll my eyes. Most of the time it seemed like she just didn't want my help.

"Come on, Claire-bear," I said, tilting my head to the side sympathetically, struggling to remember her VPA's name. "Remember what JoJo said? Endorphins and all that?"

"Why would I want to run in that?" she grumbled, nudging her head towards the window and the urban blight outside.

She had a point, but I wasn't going to tell her that.

"You could always go to the gym?" I suggested.

"What, and get judged by a load of fitness jerks?" She snorted rudely, sounding almost offended by the suggestion. "No, Dan. No, I won't be doing that."

I swallowed my pride, grinding my teeth as I did. All I wanted was to make her happy again, but it was getting harder and harder to do that when she always threw my suggestions in my face.

"Anyway..." I continued swiftly. "What's up?"

I already knew the answer.

"Just wonderin' when you'll be home," she sighed, resting her head on her knees, almost foetal.

Right on the money. It was getting too much; the endless calls, the obsessive stalking of my Cloudland and *Facebook* accounts.

"Wish I could say, hon," I answered as gently as I could. "Could be here a while. We've, uh... got some new people coming in on the case. I don't know how long it's going to take to bring them up to speed with everything."

She didn't say anything, just gave me her sad puppy dog eyes.

"My hands are tied, babe." I shrugged helplessly.

"I really wish you'd get another job."

Restraint. It took a lot of fucking restraint not to reply to that the way I wanted to. I wished she'd get a proper job, rather than trying to run that excuse she called a virtual shop. She'd show me the designs she had produced to sell it. They weren't bad, but they were only seemed to be popular with a... certain crowd, like something you'd find in some virtual niche gallery. Honestly, they were a little depressing. She'd lost more money than she'd made in the store, and now she had the nerve to tell me to quit my job!

Okay... deep breaths.

"Easier said than done," I chuckled softly at the telepathic link, lying through my teeth.

Her eyes narrowed with suspicion.

"Why?" she quipped back at me.

I was gonna have to be delicate about this.

"Oh, you know what the economy is like, Claire, it's..."

I racked my brain to think of a way out of this corner with the urgency of a bomb disposal robot but kept drawing up blank. I needed a distraction, something to change the subject.

It came. A loud chopping sound in the sky to the east. An icon on my HUD marked out the position of the incoming tiltrotor, its engines facing forward in aeroplane mode, slowing for its final approach. The readout gave me its ETA at just forty-five seconds.

"Sorry, hon, but I uh… gotta go. My new bosses are coming and…"

Her eyes became cat-like slits, looking for weakness. I flashed the camera toward the tiltrotor, the engines swivelling from aeroplane to helicopter mode.

"I'm not lying!" I said, trying to hurry her off the phone. "We'll talk about this some other time, I promise, it's just…"

Her face screwed up, her gaze quickly darting away from the live feed. She ended the call, leaving me slumping on the spot, relieved it was over, but dreading what would come. Watching her descend into this well of self-loathing was like witnessing a train wreck in slow motion.

Everything I did to help was wrong, and I was running out of ideas. A lesser man would have left her by now, but I bit my tongue and settled with it. Frankly, I was afraid the day after I walked out on her, I would get a call from HQ, and I would get called out to clean her body from the street too. I don't think I could live with myself if that happened.

I felt Matt's hand on my back.

"You need to get her help, man," he comforted me.

"Preaching to the choir," I exhaled.

I tried. I really did. There were neural lace apps for anti-depression, stimulating the brain with alpha waves to alter mood. She refused them. Said it wasn't real… Memory erasure was always an option for dealing with childhood trauma, but she wouldn't hear of it. The next logical choice was therapy. A virtual therapist was just within my price range, but she said she didn't trust them because they could be recording all of her brainwave outputs to sell on the experience blog market. I researched it later and, apparently, it was actually a thing. There had been a couple of incidents of that in China. So, because of her semi-justifiable paranoia, the only option left was face-to-face sessions, which were way out of my price range.

£80 an hour?! What the hell was that about?!

No time to think about it now.

I looked towards the sky, the downdraft from the approaching tiltrotor's engines blasting over my face. My HUD gave me a readout of its specifications like I needed anything else to make me intimidated; we didn't have anything remotely as flashy at our station.

The engines began kicking up dust, and I was forced to shield my eyes, my contact lenses not offering much in the way of protection. The gust grew stronger, and I began worrying that I'd be blown off the side altogether.

It landed with a soft thud; the hydraulics of the landing gear compressed and expanded as it touched down on the tarmac panel in the middle of the roof. The howl of the engines died down, and I straightened myself up, my eyes fixed on the door on the side of the plane. I kept a calm composure, hiding my resentment for whoever I was about to meet. The mag-locks disengaged with a loud click, followed by the whirring of motors as the cabin door slid open.

My jaw dropped.

"No way…"

My eyes didn't believe what I was seeing. My contact lenses instantly scanned her face and IDed her with a readout, but I still couldn't believe who emerged from the cabin.

Her eyes met mine.

She smiled.

Holy shit, it *was* her. Nostalgia forced its way through the increasing intensity of my headache.

"You know her?" Matt asked, looking puzzled.

I knew her all right. She may have been dressed from head to toe in her red combat armour, but she was instantly recognisable. Even if there was something very… strange about her face. Like she'd had plastic surgery or something.

"Emma?" I called out in a cautious tone just to be sure.

"Long time no see, Dan," she answered, coolly marching towards me. A shadow of my rebellious youth.

"Holy shit, no way!" I laughed wholeheartedly and threw my arms around her, picking up a faint rubbery smell as I did. But it was different to how I remembered her… far too rigid now. Hard. Metallic.

"You always were a wordsmith, Dan," she chuckled sarcastically, hugging me back; her grip was firm, reminding me of the old vice clamp in my grandfather's workshop.

I pulled back and was immediately surprised by her face. Her cheekbones were stiff and pronounced. Her skin seemed biological but appeared almost waxy. I'd seen a similar look before, on the morphing claytronic faces used by remote-android avatars used to mimic their operator's appearance. But this wasn't liquid metal, it was *synthetic* skin. The same kind used for prosthetic limbs of amputees but… all over?

Jesus, her *entire body,* was cybernetic!

What. The. Fuck.

"Is… that really you? Not an avatar?" I inquired, looking her once over as she stopped in front of me.

Her smile receded a bit. The facial movements were close enough to the real deal, just skimming the surface of the so-called *'uncanny valley syndrome'*. Either way, I could tell I'd said something to upset her.

"Yeah, it's me," she nodded slowly, evidently disappointed that I had to ask.

"Sorry…" I continued, bewildered. "It's just…"

"You've never seen someone as cyberised as me?" she deadpanned.

I nodded.

"Don't worry, I'm used to it."

"Yeah, but… Christ!" I breathed, examining the machine before my eyes. "How much is-"

"Ninety-six percent." She tapped on the side of the head, with a soft clanging sound, muffled by her skin. "My brain is the only thing left."

My eyes widened in shock, telepathically ordering a discreet scan with my watch. She wasn't lying; there was a life support system of some kind in there.

"I… didn't realise that was possible?"

"First time for everything." She winked as she unclipped her helmet and slung it under her armpit, revealing her standard issue cut brunette hair. "And we're trying to keep that under wraps. That's why you boys were sent non-disclosure agreements. Sorry about that."

"Huh…"

Well, this was a strange development. Before now I had been ready to lecture some special-forces goon about regulations, but now I was thinking about arranging a get together with a friend… who was now practically a robot. I stood there, awkwardly rubbing the back of my neck, wondering what the hell to say to all of this.

Matt nudged me impatiently, waiting for me to introduce him.

"Oh, sorry," I said, then hurriedly gestured to Matt like a professional. "Lieutenant Golem; this is Detective Inspector Keeling."

"A pleasure," he said happily, shaking hands in a hurry, staring at her synthetic face with bewilderment.

"I'm sure it is," Emma answered dismissively. "Shame it's under these circumstances."

"Comes with the job," he shrugged. "I take it you've already downloaded the preliminary crime scene report?"

"Yeah. Nice job finding those footprints," she nodded, not sounding as glad as I thought she would. "Any luck with witnesses?"

"Not yet… We've put the message out on social media, asking for anyone to come forward who saw someone scaling the building. Whoever did this climbed nearly a hundred metres to get up there. Someone must've seen *something*."

"Ah, you're tweeting. Brilliant." She winked sarcastically. "Any idea why the change in Jack-21's M.O?"

"I was hoping you could shed some light on that, actually," I inquired, hoping I would actually get an answer.

The motors in her lips curved upwards. "Oh?"

"You've seen the digital forensics report. The kid's PC. He stole something from Virtualife's network."

Her face turned strangely neutral, even for a robot.

"Project Selection." I tried to read her facial expressions at the mention of the name. It was like talking to a statue. "Any idea-"

"The data isn't the issue," Emma interrupted. "Mister Awasaki is a friend of the Ilian family. I'm here for them. The files were sent to Spiritform, correct?"

I nodded.

"We have a private investigator looking into that. Consider it a totally separate issue," she explained. "Whatever the victim may have done to Virtualife, he was a good kid who got mixed up with the wrong crowd... so I'm told anyway. My mission is to get justice for the family. Nothing more, nothing less."

Matt and I exchanged uncertain glances at each other. I checked with Ben telepathically to see if she was telling the truth. Her speech patterns indicated a truthful response.

I observed her mechanical reactions. I *almost* believed her. There was probably at least some truth to what she was saying, but it wasn't going to shake the feeling that Virtualife were the ones who'd had him killed.

So, I was either chasing a brutal murderer, a hitman from Virtualife, or one from one of their competitors. Emma *probably* knew the answer; and no matter what she said I wouldn't be able to believe her.

"Well," I exhaled loudly, nodding with reluctant acceptance. "Glad we're all on the same page."

"You always were a crappy liar, Dan," she smiled back, nudging my shoulder playfully.

I chuckled, memories of our days in the gang coming to mind. I remembered the whole class being lined up outside while the headmaster walked up and down, waiting for one of us to admit spraying graffiti on the school gym. He guessed it was us almost straight away. I just couldn't keep a straight face.

I looked into her eyes, watching the artificial skin around her cheeks bulging upwards. They said they were windows into the soul. I tried asking her out on a date once back in the day. Only to be shot down when I found out that she was gay. I was just fifteen. I'd never been as heartbroken as that. I lied and told her I wasn't... but she could see through that, even back then.

"So, Detective Inspector," Emma said loudly to move the conversation along. "This was your case up until ninety seconds ago. What's the plan?"

"We've got the parents waiting for us in the lobby. We were going to take a statement from them when we got the call about your arrival. We've already kept them waiting too long."

"Helen and Jonathan Ilian?" Emma asked. I nodded. "Hmm… might be best if you let me take the lead in the deposition."

"You know them?"

"She developed the AI subroutines for this body," she answered, pointing at herself. "We've spent a lot of time together; she trusts me. One of the reasons I was chosen for the case."

"Good… might make the situation go a little smoother?" I nodded solemnly.

"Yeah. She's not exactly in the chattiest of moods," Matt deadpanned.

I subtly shook my head to Emma, unimpressed by my partner's ability to point out the obvious. She snorted quietly.

"What about this sighting of Cymurai?" she asked. "Any more info on that?"

"Surprisingly no. One of the residents got a glimpse of him moving through the building, leaving from the crime scene, but that's about it."

"Don't tell me he's a suspect?" Emma deadpanned. Her attitude was typical, but I didn't really approve.

"No, the data from the internal security sensors revealed he arrived *after* the murder," I explained. "But the digital forensics team suggested that the records could've been manipulated."

Most people in London worshipped Cymurai. Hell, so did I at one point. That changed pretty quickly after I joined the force. He *wasn't* a comic book superhero who *refused* to kill. He'd stopped countless terrorists, paedophiles, human traffickers… the worst of the worst. There was something ultimately satisfying about vigilante justice to the public mind; knowing that the scum wasn't going to get trials, just swift, painful justice. Death by plasma sword.

But that's what he was, a vigilante. He wasn't serving *the* law. He was serving *his* law. I saw photos from the crime scenes of the people he had killed, it was just as brutal as anything Jack-21 could do, but people still loved him despite the blindingly obvious fact that he really was just some sort of government or corporate agent.

"Hmm, well… put a bulletin out online. See if we can get more witnesses."

"Already done."

"Good," she nodded back. "Suppose we shouldn't keep the parents waiting any longer."

Ben loaded up my schedule on my HUD and ticked off 'meeting with new management'. 'Taking a statement from the Ilian parents' was next on the list. Navigation waypoints appeared, directing us towards the elevator.

"Ladies first," I smiled at her, showing her way.

Her eyes flared, clearly annoyed. "You do realise I'm your boss?"

"Yes, ma'am," I teased her.

She punched me playfully, but her steel-capped knuckles dug painfully into my flesh. I let her get a few paces ahead of me while I rubbed the impact point.

The lift scanned us, opening as we approached, and the three of us rode it down to the ground floor of the smart-mirror panelled elevator car. The doors opened up into the reception area, covered with marble tiles, polished wood, and large soothing holograms. Mrs Ilian was sat fighting her way through silent, painful sobs, her eyes red and raw. A blanket lay wrapped around her shoulders. I picked up the smell of massage oil as I approached; according to their Mother Mind logs, they had been visiting some seedy spa in Kentish Town while their son was murdered. Not that you could tell they were typed for it. She was wearing a drab blouse and brass-rimmed glasses with display screens, her short red hair scattered untidily across her face like she'd tried pulling it out. She shakily took a plastic cup of coffee from an android receptionist. Her husband was stood over her, face trying to stay strong but his eyes were watery. His otherwise fancy suit now hung scruffily around his waist.

We left Matt in the elevator, letting him descend to the car park on his own after I quietly promised to meet him in the pub tomorrow, and possibly getting in a game of *Fifa* 2045 with him and my brother at some point. Emma and I stepped out and strolled towards the bereaved couple in a professionally sensitive matter.

"Mister Ilian, Doctor Ilian, I'm Detective Inspector Haines," I began, keeping my sympathetic demeanour. The parents looked up at me with their pain-filled gazes. "I believe you already know my partner, Lieutenant-"

"Emma?" The wife sniffed, looking surprised to see her.

"Hello Helen," she replied compassionately. "I'm so sorry for your loss."

"D-did Kenji send you?" Helen stuttered, wiping the rivers of tears from her cheeks.

Emma nodded solemnly. "We take care of our people. We can't bring him back. But we're going to catch this bastard and make him pay."

"Oh, what's the point?" she cried out. "He's dead! Nothing matters now! He…" Her voice trailed away into uncontrollable short breaths, forcing her to cover her mouth.

"Can't you people do this some other time?" Jonathan snapped angrily at us, squeezing his wife's shoulders supportively.

"Sir, ma'am, I can't begin to imagine what you're going through," I began, trying to use my eyes to instil confidence in her. "I've been on this case since the beginning. Andrew was the latest victim in a string of these attacks. If you don't help us, there will be more childless parents, more people having to suffer the loss that you have. That much I can guarantee you."

Helen took another loud gasp of air and shakily wiped the skin around her eyes.

"I… I just don't understand it!" she cried heavily. "Why would anyone want to hurt him?!"

"That's what we're here to find out, Helen," Emma said supportively. "Anything you can tell us might be a big help."

Dr Ilian shut her eyes, shakily sucking in the air, sitting up straight to compose herself. She remained there, in almost a meditative state for a few seconds, before opening up again, letting the air escape from her.

"Okay… okay… what do you need to know?" she sighed finally.

"Were you aware of him being involved in any… criminal activity?" I asked as diplomatically as I could. No one had told them about their son's attempt to hack Virtualife.

Helen shook her head. "He was a good boy. We might not have always seen eye to eye, but he kept out of trouble."

"Yeah, except for those bloody websites," Jonathan interrupted.

"What websites?" I followed up.

"Bloody anti-capitalism propaganda. He was always ranting on about the so-called world revolution…"

I saw the lip of the otherwise stern-looking man tremble. Part of me wanted to be able to tell them about the scan results from the boy's memory drives.

"Was he spending time with any… unusual characters?" Emma inquired.

"Uh… no, no," Helen choked out. "He didn't have many local friends… God knows what he was getting up to online though. Especially with that girlfriend of his."

"Girlfriend?" I said, raising an eyebrow.

Emma turned to me, sharing my confusion. We didn't find any reference to that when we searched the boy's social media.

"He was always going on about her," Jonathan answered, close to his breaking point. "He started spouting all of the unworldly crap when he started going out with her. Kept calling us *'slaves to the corporatocracy'*," he laughed, trying to force back his tears. "Used to drive me up the wall…"

"What was her name?" I asked politely, my VPA taking down notes on my vision.

"Uh…"

"Claudia," breathed Helen. "Her name was Claudia…"

"Oh yeah, I remember. German girl. Living in Berlin, I think."

"Did you get a surname?"

The two of them shook their heads. It was still enough for us to go on. Ben flashed a message to my HUD that he would add that to Mother Mind's search parameters.

"Did he ever mention… Spiritform?" Emma asked gingerly.

"A lot… I was worried he'd end up joining them," Helen continued after blowing her nose with a carbon fibre handkerchief.

"Well…" I said awkwardly. "We have reason to believe, he may have been the one who hacked into your company's R&D server last night."

The couple's watery eyes blinked at me with shock.

"God, I knew I should've taken that Freethought relay away from him!" she cried.

"What did he steal?" Jonathan checked, his eyes fearfully wide. The profile readout on my display informed me he was a lawyer; no doubt he already considered the legal ramifications.

"He'd already transferred and deleted the files from his PC by the time he'd been killed... but we did find references to something called 'Project Selection'," I explained.

I had barely finished my sentence when I saw something strange. I'd seen it before, but I wasn't expecting it here of all places. Helen's eyes began to flicker rapidly, her face twitching uncontrollably in a manner reminiscent of a brief epileptic seizure. It only lasted a second or so, her face returning to normal as quickly as it had started.

It couldn't be… could it?

"Does… that mean something to you?" I asked slowly, expecting I already knew the answer.

"Uh… no, sorry," she answered, rubbing her face as the twitching subsided.

Just as I thought…

"Were you working on anything in particular at Virtualife?" I continued, expecting the same reaction.

As expected, more face spasms. It looked painful.

"Uh… No… no, nothing special. Nothing worth…" Helen trailed

off again as the spasms grew worse.

Knew it!

I kept a neutral expression and turned to Emma who also kept silent, but I could tell she knew as well. No doubt it was her boss's doing.

"You really think he was killed… for that?" Her gathered voice began descending into wails once more. She must've been a real company woman *not* to suspect Virtualife's involvement. More confirmation of my theory.

Emma unfolded her arms, breathing a sympathetic sigh.

"Maybe, maybe not," she replied, placing a comforting hand on Helen's shoulder. "Some people are monsters, Helen. I wish I had a better answer for you."

"Yeah… monsters," I said, narrowing my eyes suspiciously.

We continued with a series of standard procedure questions for the next twenty minutes, battling our way through the depths of misery. Emma wrapped things up in the end, and we said our goodbyes. I shook both of their hands, and Emma hugged them. The paramedics from the ambulance parked downstairs, and we led the pair of them solemnly to the lift. I watched the doors slide shut behind them, shielding their sad faces. Emma let out a sigh of relief, began fumbling around in her armours pockets, and pulled out an electronic cigarette.

"*Worst* part of the job."

"Yeah…" I mumbled back at her, walking over to a vending machine by the entrance. I operated it the old-fashioned way, tapping on a series of holographic icons to order a black latte. The machine whirred to life, and a plastic cup dropped out of the dispenser, followed by the splattering of coffee flowing out of it. The holo-glass panel of the cabinet began displaying a series of adverts from different companies. I watched Emma's reflection in the glass as she puffed away on the e-cig, the movements on her face too still to be entirely lifelike, like stop-motion animation.

A green light flashed on the machine when it was done, and I pulled the cup out. I turned back to face her and she nudged towards the entrance front doors.

"Come on, I could use some fresh air," she yawned.

I waved an accusing finger at the e-cig.

"Not how I'd describe it. Why do you still smoke anyway? Do you even have lungs?"

"Nope. But I do have an inhalation fan and bio-gustatory sensors in my mouth. Gets the job done. I'd kill for the real thing though. Not like I've got any risk of cancer," she laughed.

"Old habits die hard," I chuckled. "Do you remember smoking in the gutter by Greenford High Street?"

"Happy days," she replied flatly, apparently not having as much nostalgia for that like me.

"We used to think we looked so cool."

"Used to?" She smirked cockily.

We strode through the doors, brushing past a crime scene investigation officer and once more out into the freezing wind, the glitter of holograms and the orange tinge of street lights illuminating us, the apartment complex towering behind us.

A council-owned street maintainer droid was busy using a laser to burn off Arabic graffiti on the crumbling wall of an ageing corner shop, the name on the front faded and weathered away. My translation software informed me the words had read 'fuck you!'. I stood with my hands in my pockets, looking at the ground and wondering how to bring up my concerns with Emma.

"You want some?" she asked, offering me the e-cig.

I stared at it pensively.

"Stop being a pussy, Dan," she whined.

I gave in and took a drag, but ending up coughing and spluttering almost immediately.

"Ah fuck…" I wheezed. "Now I really miss the real thing."

She sniggered with me. "So… do you still hear from any of the old gang?"

I rolled my lips pensively, wondering how to broach this subject. "With the ones who aren't serving time, sure."

"Well, duh," she sniggered back. "I always knew Eddie was gonna end up in the slammer."

Eddie 'Rockslide' Stonebar. Just remembering the name made me shudder with embarrassment that I used to be *'friends'* with an asshole of such spectacular proportions.

"Yeah, he was a bit of a cunt," I laughed dryly.

It was a chapter in my life I'd tried to put behind me. There aren't many people who can say they've gone from street gang to detective inspector, and it sure as hell wasn't going to help my career dragging those skeletons out of the closet.

Eddie was the cool kid in school, and the best football player… who just happened to be selling splice-bread, grown from synthetic yeast crossed with proteins from the coca plant. The end result was… well, coke. Cocaine bread. Emma and I were his runners, and occasionally muscle men when the dealers from Brentside School stepped on our turf. My father was gone, and my mother was too busy keeping her head above water to take notice. Oh, they paid us pretty well, for aspiring fifteen-year-old drug dealers, until we got caught after one particularly bad, a prearranged brawl between the two schools. Spent nine months at Lockwood, a juvenile correction facility run by (surprise, surprise) Churchbell Security. If you'd have told me back then I'd end up working for them, I'd have laughed in your face… followed by a happy slap uploaded swiftly to *Facebook*. Documents leaked by Spiritform years later suggested that the company had been using subliminal messaging on their inmates. I had brief moments of existential crisis, wondering if I was just a serf, but found myself putting it out of my mind. Telling myself I was just paranoid. That it didn't matter because I was actually making a difference to the city. Followed by more paranoia that I just felt that way because the brainwashing had worked well.

Anyway…

I made small talk with her. She asked how my brother was doing, to which I promptly replied, 'still sober'. In response, I asked if she was keeping up with her swimming career. She'd been quite a promising athlete at school. The question pleased her, all too happy to answer, despite informing me that the NDA she'd signed with Virtualife prevented her from joining the Transhuman Sports League until she was discharged from the company.

"What about the others? Mitchell, Kieran, Amy?" Emma continued quickly, seeming slightly more eager than I'd been expecting.

"You know how it is online," I shrugged. "We do the obligatory awkward virtual hangouts once in a blue moon…"

"As awkward as telling old friends you've sold your soul to science?" Emma deadpanned.

"Uh… almost?" I replied, taken aback by her bluntness.

We giggled softly again, her mechanical face mimicking the expressions reasonably well, but faded into silence quickly. She paused for a second, her cheek actuators rolling like she was working up to say something.

"Do you guys ever talk about me?" she asked nervously.

Her voice had a hint of urgency about it like she really needed to hear a 'yes'. Claire took the same tone with me all the time. Only one thing to do in this situation: lie.

"Oh, yeah all the time," I said reassuringly. Best to mix it with a bit of truth. "We tried tracking you down, but it's like you disappeared off the face of the net after the sixth form.

"What can I say?" She smiled finally, flexing her robotic arm enough to hear the hiss of nano-hydraulics. "I've had stuff to do."

"No shit," I smiled back, glad that went smoothly. I took another puff, more comfortable on the throat this time, and passed it back to her. The small talk had begun to trail away, and the awkward silence descended once more.

"Dan, have I done something wrong?" she asked eventually.

"No. Not really."

"Yeah, and I'm Lady Transhuman. I've known you long enough to know when there's something up."

I plucked up my courage and decided to stop beating about the bush.

"I was wondering what you knew about Helen Ilian," I said finally.

Emma raised an eyebrow. "What about her?"

She was lying.

"Oh, I don't know, anything she might have forgotten to mention?"

Her bionic eyes flashed, just for a moment. "What are you trying to get at, Dan?"

"I learned to recognise the side effects of it ages ago."

"Side effects of what?"

"Cognitive editing," I snarled. "You saw the look on her face when I asked her about 'Project Selection'. She signed a non-disclosure agreement, didn't she? Your bosses erased her memory!"

Unlike the official secrets act, NDAs with memory erasing clauses were meant to be a deterrent. Corporate entities could only begin blocking engrams once the signee had already leaked privileged information. But once signed, the employees in question were forced to install software that could start remotely restricting the memories at the lawyer's discretion.

"Your point?" she retorted, unamused, her face statuesque. The care-free tone she used struck a nerve.

"So? What the fuck do you mean, so? Do you know what 'obstructing the course of justice' means? You've just rendered the testimony of a potential material witness completely useless!"

Emma didn't respond. Just carried on puffing away, her eyes fixated on me.

"Well? Don't you have anything to say?"

She took one last puff, her expressions remaining unnaturally still. "Are you finished?"

"No!" I blurted out angrily, but couldn't think of anything else to say. "…Yes…"

"Good," she continued, nudging her head towards a CCTV camera hanging from a nearby Victorian lamp post. "You realise Mother Mind heard all that?"

"I bloody hope so. The police complaints commission has access to its data collection as well."

"Too bad. She wasn't paying attention."

"The hell does that mean?"

"You know what the Free-pass protocol is?"

Of course.

"Yeah, I know," I replied through gritted teeth.

It was a feature written into the surveillance AI. Mother Mind bulk collected data from the national telecoms grid, even the communications of secret agents and high-ranking government officials who *'sometimes'* needed to be above the law. With a Free-pass protocol activated on a surveillance profile, you could literally be caught on camera murdering someone, and the system would completely ignore you. Perfect for government wet work. Of course, those with access to the system core (like Virtualife) had exploited this feature for their own needs.

"So, is that what we are now? The deniable operations goon squad?"

"Oh, go bitch about it on your blog," Emma snapped bitterly, shaking her head.

"I might if I thought it wasn't going to get censored. Emma if you want me to keep believing this 'favour for the family' crap you're going to have to give me something to go on here."

She scoffed, rolling her eyes dismissively.

"What?" I asked impatiently.

"I wish I could, but I have… certain obligations too," she answered bitterly.

The penny dropped. She was bound by a non-disclosure agreement as well.

"Jesus…"

I had to take a moment to take it all in. She wasn't an employee, she was practically a slave! In all honesty, I wasn't so different. I wanted to act like I was somehow better than her, even though deep down I knew I wasn't. We were about as different as *Coke* and *Pepsi*.

I exhaled with frustration and turned to look out at the urban decay across the street, the driverless cars rolling by. In the end, I found myself laughing out loud at the absurdity of it all.

"What's so funny?" Emma asked, raising an eyebrow.

"Nothin'. Just wondering at what point humanity stopped being human."

Emma stared at me. "You know what? That's the most honest thing I've heard in a long time."

I nodded pensively.

The silence descended again, each not knowing what to say now. Maybe if she weren't an old friend, I wouldn't be so forgiving. Maybe that was all part of Virtualife's plan.

God, what a mind fuck.

I didn't have to dwell on it before I was interrupted by a telepathic bleeping inside my head:

<<Update from: Scotland Yard HQ>>

I saw Emma's eyes flicker as she received the same message. Never been so happy to be interrupted by work.

"Go ahead, Ben," I perkily answered over the telepathic link.

"Mother Mind has received a visual match on an unlicensed Camelot exoskeleton," the AI chimed back.

A map of the city opened on my HUD and zoomed in on Hyde Park, stopping just over what used to be a big sports field by Marble Arch. Now it was London's largest Climateville. A slum, home to hundreds of refugees.

A video began to play on my contact lenses, camera footage from an aerial reconnaissance sweep by a Police Buzzer-drone. The once lush, green lawn had been turned into a quagmire; the foundation for a sea of patchwork tents, falling apart at the seams, covered in filth and swimming with disease. The residents stumbled around trashcan fires and the makeshift stalls of the market. Even here, the light of the internet still blazed through the holo-screens of cheap computers. A tangle of wires lay buried in the mud, with people frequently tripping over them. The camera zoomed in on a tent with two bulky bouncers standing by the entrance. They wore black suits and ties, unusually smart for the slums. A flickering red neon sign hung from a post outside, read 'Barely-Licensed Bar', in both English and Mandarin.

"I know that bar," Emma commented.

"Every cop worth a damn knows that bar," I scoffed. With a name like that, it kind of stuck in your mind.

"*Not like I do.* I have a little arrangement with the owner."

That got my attention. As well as being barely licensed, it was scarcely a bar. Just a huge marquee with a handful of migrant workers serving the cheapest drinks they could steal and playing the best music they could pirate. A bar built by refugees, for refugees.

Of course, it was as rough as sandpaper. We were called to it on an almost daily basis for one thing or another. It was almost certainly a front for human trafficking and gun runners, but we'd never been able to prove it. *Officially* anyway. Now, I was willing to bet my wages that it was because of Emma's arrangement.

I chose not to bring it up now and carried on watching the footage. The drone couldn't get a good look inside, but the shots did capture a blond, flat-nosed, square-jawed Croatian guy heading inside, looking unusually cocky. His Mother Mind profile identified him as Gustaw Atwell. The outline of his cheekbones had been plated with chrome-coloured implants, microfibres extending through the tissue, his eyes shielded with a darkened visor. Typically he would have been about 5.9ft, but his power armour pushed him to over 7ft tall. His Mother Mind profile informed us he was a paraplegic, and required an exoskeleton to move; but the armour he was wearing was a massive industrial model, equipped with construction tools. Thick cables of carbon nanotube muscles were encased in a lightweight grey-painted graphene chassis. An extensive round chest plate covered the torso, the shoulders and knees protected by dome pads, the arms and legs by gauntlets, and hook-shaped boots. The outline was an 89% visual match for the Camelot power armour.

He wore a silver-blue coat over the bulking exoskeleton like a cloak, a hood resting on the back of his neck. The OLED circuits etched into the coat's fabric could have easily been modified to turn into an optical camouflage unit. A pop-up window pointed to the suit's feet, indicating the shape was a match for the footprints in the Ilian apartment.

"That's our guy?" I asked, slightly unconvinced.

"He was convicted of assault in 2041," the AI responded flatly. "Scotland Yard has designated him the prime suspect due to his violent past and possession of the Camelot exoskeleton."

"Don't sound so happy," Emma laughed at me, slapping me on the shoulder with the dull weight of her metal palm. "It's not like you *had* any suspects until today."

Yeah... convenient.

"HQ has ordered you to be dispatched to apprehend the suspect," Ben continued. "An arrest warrant has been issued."

<<File transfer complete>>

I held my watch out, and the document flashed out of its holo-projector.

"Roger that," Emma replied gratefully. "Has my gear been loaded into your car?"

"Affirmative," he chimed back.

"What gear?" I asked.

She grinned back gleefully.

Ben forwarded the orders to the auto-driver of my Ford Interceptor police car. We waited for under a minute before it rolled up from the ramp to the underground car park, past the security barrier and finally stopped beside us. The driver and passenger seats were all empty, and the holographic dashboard flashed the words 'Arrived at Destination'. Ben informed me that valet-bots had loaded Emma's equipment into the boot of the car.

I opened it up. There were three silver plastic tactical attaché cases packed neatly within. Two of them were mine, one holding my weapons, the other my standard armed response power armour. The other was from Emma's tiltrotor. I scanned its E-ID chip, and the contents appeared on my HUD. Some pretty nasty weapons, including an M-150 assault rifle.

"You guys don't mess about," I nodded, giving an impressed

whistle.

"You're okay with it?" she said, a little surprised. "I thought you were about to give me a lecture about the virtues of good police work…"

"We're about to arrest a walking tank," I shrugged. "Possibly a psychotic, murdering, walking tank. Yes, Emma, I'm okay with a little fire-power."

"Good to hear," she grinned gleefully, stroking her weapons case eagerly. She nudged towards my cases. "Come on, you'd better get your armour on."

I nodded and pressed my thumb into the fingerprint scanner of the large attaché case, unlocking it with a bleep. With a green flash and a click, it opened revealing the moulded black foam inside. Slots had been moulded into the surface to holster each component of the power armour; essentially a wearable robot painted blue and black. Unlike most powered exoskeletons, the standard issue Metropolitan Police model (the Kingsman from Akira Engineering) actually did look like a metal skeleton, worn over the operator's clothes. A series of motorised mechanical braces running across my arms and legs, allowing me to lift up to two hundred kilos.

I tried to maintain a professional composure, restraining the child-like glee, I felt whenever I wore it.

One by one, I carefully removed each component and began dressing on the tarmac of the road, slipping the armour on over my uniform. Gauntlets, vest and riot helmet with a protected combat visor. I moved the braces onto my arms and legs, pulling the straps tight, and buckled them up, ensuring the armoured panels were firmly in place. The rigid metal settled over me like a second skin. Pipe-like hydraulic joints extended across my knees, elbows and spine. I hooked them up together, feeding the tubing into the input ports, the power cables into the motors.

With the system offline, it was just dead weight. I jacked in a data cable on the gauntlet into my smartwatch, which in turn was wirelessly the connected to my neural lace. A message appeared on the interface.

<<Initialising exoskeleton device drivers>>

<<Interface online>>

<<Power on?>>

I telepathically activated it. The whirring sound of power coursed over my body, growing louder and louder, then the hydraulics kicked in with a jolt, and the clumsiness disappeared. Suddenly the suit felt as light as a feather. I flexed the electronic biceps with ease and my muscles magnified. I flexed my fingers confidently.

I smirked subtly testing out the strength by throwing out a flurry of shadow boxing punches, my arms shooting out like pistons, the arm motors roaring. Some things never get old.

"If you like that, you should see the gear we've got," she added. "You ever think about jumping ship?"

"Why? You headhunting?"

"Play your cards right, and we might just be," she winked.

That'll be the day. I laughed and played along.

We pulled the remaining weapon cases out of the boot and headed to the door which popped out and slid upwards. I had to push the driver's seat back to give myself the extra legroom I needed with the exoskeleton. I manoeuvred myself inside, the servo mechanisms groaning oddly, while Emma loaded the cases into the rear seats.

Ben forwarded our destination to the auto-driver which sped off and engaged the siren, blaring in the night air. We turned onto Kensington High Street, the auto-driver weaving through the traffic, my stomach lurching with each turn. The Albert Memorial and vast dome of the Royal Albert Hall loomed ahead, the gold statue reflecting the light from the holographic tourist information signs beneath it.

The other AI-controlled cars on the road promptly swerved aside, letting us through, responding to the Police Priority Code on the traffic control grid. My hands were on the wheel, fumbling about with my equipment in my glove compartment, loading a magazine of 9mm standard issue Phase-rounds into my Glock-34 handgun; a rigid, but compact little weapon. I slotted my pistol back into the holster on my belt, following up by grabbing three claytronic grenades and attaching them to the magnetic holsters next to my side-arm. Non-lethal nanotech weapons designed to immobilise the target in a globule of smart-goo. The armour also had taser knuckles, but Ben's analysis suggested they would be ineffective against the shield; it would have to be a punch to the face to work.

"You're gonna need something bigger than *that*," Emma snorted at my handgun, as she pulled out parts of her assault rifle from the case and began assembling it.

"Nah, I'll be fine," I shrugged dismissively.

"Well, don't come crying to me if you get your teeth knocked out," she shook.

The sirens blared as we whizzed ahead, the electric engine rumbling. Ben activated the projector on the dashboard, loading up the specifications of the Camelot exoskeleton belonging to the suspect, and began visually identifying potential weaknesses.

"There is a vulnerable set of nano-muscles under the armpits and a USB port on the back of the neck," Ben explained through the dashboard's speakers. "The suit will be air-gapped, but the port could be used to introduce a virus."

"Roger that."

We slowed as we passed the Memorial and turned into the park through the old iron gates, which had been converted into a Police checkpoint, and cleared for entry. Environmental degradation had turned the once beautiful haven from the bustle of the city, into a wasteland.

We parked on the outskirts of the shanty town and stepped out into the night again, my iron boot squelching in the mud under the mechanical pressure. I glanced miserably across at the sea of poverty surrounding us. They said that walking into Climateville was like travelling back to medieval times. The assault on the senses was almost unbearable, the air heavy with filth and disease. The stench of sweat, piss, and shit burned my nostrils along with the billowing smoke from the trash fires, and the mud beneath our boots made it tough to walk. The sickening sound of spluttering was never far behind.

"Lovely neighbourhood," Emma grimaced.

"Keep your eyes peeled. I had a partner who got stabbed for a sandwich around here."

My eyes darted around the flock of scrawny faces. A police presence was never precisely appreciated, and their suspicious eyes followed us from every direction. Cops had been known to get ambushed by mobs here, hence the increased security around the park. Of course that had just turned the place into a miniature police state…I'd heard most of my colleagues bragging about what they could get away with here.

I engaged focus mode on my neural lace to keep my nerves in check. An icon on my HUD held a mark on the drone's position, making me feel a little safer, but I telepathically engaged my emotional management software, and my headset began beaming soothing waves into my head.

"What's the latest, Ben?" I asked.

"Suspect hasn't left 'Barely-Licenced'. I estimate a 73% probability he will resist arrest. I suggest letting Detective Haines attempt the arrest, while Lieutenant Golem covers the back exit."

He placed the GPS waypoint markers on our HUDs, and we began our walk through the squalor, the sound of my exoskeleton squelching through the mud as we manoeuvred through the narrow paths in the tents, navigating around the bustle of the raggedy residents. Chatter in a dozen different languages hummed around us, my translation software offering subtitles for all of them, interrupted only by the sound of coughing and wailing. I heard two men swearing at each other somewhere in the background. I swivelled round to see them, two junkies shoving at each other, about to kick off. I wanted to step in and intervene, but we had bigger fish to fry.

We arrived at Barely-Licensed within a minute, the neon signs glittering and fading in front of us. The two bouncers were still standing in an intimidating manner by the entrance. I peered through the door to the marquee. It was packed with patrons, with dubstep blaring from speakers embedded in the fabric of the tent, decorative club lights dangling across the ceiling, and mood lamps pulsing in time with the music in the corners. Wooden picnic tables were arranged neatly inside, packed with drunken refugees, laughing and gambling. The makeshift bar stood on the far-right hand side of the marquee along with a cabinet full of glasses and bottles with the labels removed, and a cluster of barrels in the corner.

The owner, a stubby Chinese fellow, was chatting merrily away to his patrons. My contact lenses' facial recognition software identified him as Johnny Chow. He was pouring drinks with his grubby plastic bionic arm, the circuitry of a micro-fibre neural lace etched into his skull. He handed over the beer glasses in exchange for *hard cash*; a rare sight these days. Most places didn't accept real money anymore, but these slum dwellers had come to adopt their own currency: the Globeriam. Certainly made tax evasion easier.

Heading for the entrance, we approached two muscle-head bouncers with faces like bulldogs, radiating the smell of cheap aftershave. The pair suddenly straightened up, growling at our presence.

"Evening lads," I spoke, trying to keep things friendly. "Don't suppose you're the owners of this fine establishment?"

"You got an invitation?" one of them barked.

"What do we need an invitation for?" I smirked, nudging my head towards the neon. "Sign says it's a bar."

"Closed party," the other grunted. "Invite only."

"Go get Johnny," Emma quipped back at them coolly. "Tell him Lieutenant Golem wants a chat."

"Johnny's… busy," the first bouncer retorted.

"He can't get someone to pull a pint for him?" I scoffed, while considering the possibility of simply forcing our way in.

"Invite only," they repeated.

"Invites? Yeah sure, we got them." The two of us flashed our badges with holographic police IDs. "Now, I know they're not exactly the standard RSVPs, but if you like I can come back with a search warrant too."

"No, no need for that, officers," chirped a squeaky voice from behind the bouncers. The short, little owner used his bionic arm to pry the two bouncers apart in a hurry and shoved his way through to face us. He stank of booze and had a nervous smile on his face with sweat glistening from his circuit-laden forehead.

"Lieutenant!" he cried loudly, holding his hands out warmly, following with a bow from the waist. "You honour us with your presence!"

I raised an eyebrow. I knew it was a Chinese custom, but I'd never actually seen anyone do it. Was he that afraid of her?

"Long time no see, Johnny," she answered confidently as she glanced around the bar looking unimpressed. "You still serving that watered-down shit?"

"Beggars can't be choosers, Emma!" he replied gleefully.

"I'll say," she scoffed.

"Sir, we have an arrest warrant for one of your customers," I told him firmly. "And your… associates are getting in the way."

"Oh, very sorry," Johnny apologised. "Finding good help in these parts is like a needle in a haystack."

My translation software told me he swore at the two bouncers in Mandarin, bitterly snapping his fingers, sending them slinking back inside the tent.

"Please, come in, come in!" Johnny said, beckoning the pair of us inside. "I want no troublemakers here."

"Uh-huh," Emma added, continuing her examination of the bar. "You seem to have gone a bit upmarket since the last time I saw you."

She nudged her head towards a blonde Estonian girl giving a lap dance to a broad-looking Greek man, snorting uncontrollably like a pig. I scanned her with my contact lenses. Her Mother Mind profile claimed that her travel documents were in order… of course, the best human traffickers always had a way of making sure they were.

"She's new?" Emma asked dryly.

"Uh… yes."

"And you've been keeping out of trouble, right?"

"Yes…" he added, cowering as she loomed over him.

"Do you want to carry on keeping out of trouble?"

He froze, then nodded solemnly. Emma gave him a condescending pat on the shoulder.

"I'm glad we understand each other," she said. "Now get the fuck out of my partner's way."

He hurriedly bowed again and skulked back behind his bar.

"He's a creep, but a damn good snitch," Emma commented telepathically. "A necessary evil."

"I'll take your word for it," I cringed, a little bit disgusted.

"Right. Comm Check."

We ran a system test of our e-telepathy channel.

"All systems go," she answered. "Try not to get your ass kicked."

Emma circled around to the rear entrance, while Ben placed a waypoint marker on the suspect. I headed inside, shuffling through the drunken crowd, the aroma of alcohol permeating the air. I did my best to blend in despite the uniform and exoskeleton. He was still seated, nursing a glass of dark beer in his thick gauntlet.

His dull eyes were fixated on the drink, the lips in his anvil-jaw in a flat, uninterested expression, sipping away to the sound of thunderous electronic music.

I tiptoed closer, hoping that his booze would keep him entertained enough for him not to notice me. I was only a few feet away from him. His hulking metal suit seeming ominously large this close up. I breathed in, summoning the courage to speak.

"Gustaw Atwell!" I thundered, flashing my badge in his direction.

His ears pricked up and with a whir he turned to meet me, sudden unexpected horror creeping across his face. "I am arresting you on suspicion of murder! You do not have to say anything, but-"

The electronic muscles of the suit roared to life. The actuators hissed furiously as he stood bolt upright, the added height of the exoskeleton towering over me. With a single swing of his metal hand, he ripped off one of the planks of the picnic table, with a loud crack, grasping it like an ogre's club ready to swing it at my head.

So much for a quiet arrest!

The crowd cried out and darted away from us like ripples on a pond, stampeding to the exits. I whipped out a claytronic grenade and tossed it towards him. With a bleep, the weapon detonated in mid-air, expanding from an apple-sized device into a large beanie bag globule of liquid metal in mid-air. I was aiming for his armour's chest piece, but he intercepted it with the plank. The liquid metal solidified against its surface, looking like a giant stick of grey cotton candy. The sudden weight change broke his grip. He stumbled off balance, and the plank ended up flying across the room, crashing into a young bartender, knocking him off his feet and slamming into the cabinet of bottles behind him sending glass crashing down around him.

"Shit!" Emma cried telepathically.

I turned to look at the entrance. She had apparently come to help, but a globule of the claytronic matter had crashed into her right shoulder, knocking her onto her back, and her weapon out of her hand. She was now pinned to the ground; the synthetic liquid hardening quickly into a superglue and locking her in place, writhing on the floor to free herself.

"Watch where you're throwing that crap!" she barked at me.

I was about to apologise, but Gustaw began yelling like an oncoming storm, crashing his way through the table, reducing the planks to splinters. My hands dived towards my Glock. I drew it from the holster rapidly, using the aiming reticule on my helmet's visor to guide the laser targeting system. I issued the telepathic command to the smart-ammo rounds inside my weapon:

<<Concussion-fire mode selected>>

I fired two shots in rapid succession, the arms of my exoskeleton absorbing the recoil.

POP! POP!

The gunfire sent more screams from the crowd. The police standard issue smart-ammo was 9mm phase rounds, so called because they could be set to either non-lethal or lethal. In the non-lethal mode, they were miniature flashbang grenades. My helmet's combat visor darkened in response to the high-intensity light, letting me keep my eyes open as the bullets detonated mid-air like firecrackers. Gustaw covered his face in time to shield himself, and the blast merely washed over his exoskeleton, barely leaving a scratch. Unfazed, he stormed at me once more, his hammer-like fist drawn behind his head ready to strike.

"Shit!"

My enhanced reflexes kicked in, and I quickly swung my protective forearm panels in front of my face, feeling the power of my own exoskeleton firming up my stance. Gustaw's fist came down like an anvil into my gauntlet's plating, shaking my body like an earthquake. I heaved with all my might as the armour groaned against the pressure, my feet sinking deep into the mud.

The two of us were now locked together like a pair of robot wrestlers, but growling like animals. I headed back as hard as I could, straining my power supply. His exoskeleton was much stronger than mine. The motors groaned painfully at max-pressure, feeling the compression trembling around me. Gustaw's lips curled upwards, he had the upper hand, and he knew it.

I gave a guttural cry, using my remaining strength to pick my foot off the ground and kick at the plating of his chest panel. Another loud clang rang across the graphene sheet as it absorbed the impact painlessly, laughing in my face.

I heard a click and a whir… A device had extended out from the right wrist of his armour; a plasma welder. A second later, a hot white flash shot out from the end of the torch and began burning an incision through my armour, spraying out hydraulic fluid like blood.

"Fuck!"

My arm inside the gauntlet rapidly warmed like a ham in an oven…the heat shielding wouldn't hold for long.

<<Warning!>>

<<Damage sustained to left gauntlet module>>

<<Running diagnostic scan>>

Gustaw grinned at me wolfishly through the sparks radiating from my gauntlet. The burning was drawing closer and closer to my flesh. I had to act fast; that torch was a pretty lethal weapon.

Ben did my thinking for me; placing an overload warning sign on my vision over the plasma torch.

“Use your taser knuckles!” he cried.

“Right!” I gratefully called back promptly.

I shifted my grip as close as I could towards the plasma torch and gave the command from my headset. I engaged the high-voltage power supply to the conductive panels on my fingers, resulting in bright crackling blue flashes. The current flowed towards the end of the plasma torch, and with furious, rapid popping and a puff of smoke, the flame gave out explosively, throwing us both back.

To my relief, the dangerously near heat died out. The incision into my armour still glowed like molten lava but rapidly cooled… but the damage was severe.

“YOU CUNT!” Gustaw spat at me, his wild eyes glaring at the burnt-out device on his arm.

My eyes widened in horrible realisation.

Now I’ve done it…

Gustaw pivoted hard from the waist and struck me. I blocked in time with the other arm, but the sheer force knocked me off balance. He drew back another punch, his shadow extending over me like a meteor.

Shit…

His steel fist shot towards me at high speed, and I was too slow to keep up. The cold plating rammed into my face with force of a freight train.

<<Warning!>>

<<Concussion sustained!>>

The shock of the impact sent my whole body numb. My ears rang like a tuning fork, sight blurred, my HUD filled with static. I thought

I was going to pass out. I flopped like a fish, tumbling backwards, letting gravity take me.

Before I met the ground, the metal fist grabbed me by the throat, dragging me upright once more. He throttled me, drawing me close enough to his face for me to smell the beer on his breath and see the feral rage in his eyes, yelling a flurry of incomprehensible insults at me.

My senses returned to me quick enough to cringe at the stench. His clench on my throat tightened, squeezing the life out of me.

<<Warning!>>

<<Blood oxygen level critical!>>

"I'm sorry…" he slurred at me. "You were saying?"

I started to gag with awkward jiggling movements as I struggled to keep my breath, feeling my eyes about to pop out of their sockets …

Oh crap. Oh crap!

Claire's face flashed into my mind…

This was it…

She was never going to see me agai-

RAT-AT-AT-AT!

The sound of automatic gunfire pierced the deathly silence, along with more screams from outside the tent. The shock made Gustaw loosen his grip on my throat, just enough for me to suck enough air in, clinging to life.

"Put him down, boy!" Emma's commanding cry came from behind us. "So help me I'll put another hole in that ugly mug of yours!"

Gustaw snarled, yanking me off my feet, spinning me around, keeping me pinned to his chest as I dangled off the ground by my neck, flailing my leg motors, his grip just loose enough to keep breathing.

Emma had freed herself, the remnants of the claytronic matter still stuck on her shoulder like dry mucus. She now had her eyes focused like a hawk on Gustaw. Her rifle was aimed squarely at his head, the end of the barrel smoking from the shots she'd fired into the air. The rain filtered in through distinctive holes in the roof of the marquee.

"Back up!" Gustaw spat at Emma, shaking me as he spoke. "Back up now, or I'll snap his fucking neck!"

Emma gritted her teeth.

"You all right Dan?" she called to me telepathically, lips unmoving.

"Truth be told I'm a little hung up," I gasped back.

"That's the spirit," she reassured me, flatly keeping her stern glare. "Just hold on, I've got a plan. It'll happen fast, so you need to be ready for it."

"I'm all ears!"

"You'll know it when you see it. You just get the fuck outta there when it happens."

I struggled to get another breath in. "Standing by… obviously…"

The two of them were locked in a staredown, each waiting for the other to make a move. The hand clasped on my throat was trembling violently. The suit was like a tank, but he was drunk, and probably high as a kite too. One wrong move and he was going to do something stupid.

My HUD blurred. Or maybe it was just the concussion.

"I don't know what you're planning here, mate," Emma called to Gustaw in a conversational tone. "But I can guarantee you, holding a police officer hostage isn't gonna do you any favours."

"You're not police…" he snarled back. "You're attack dogs!"

"Call us what you want. We've got back-up on the way, and-"

"I'll do it! I'll rip his fucking head off! Your back-up ain't gonna do shit then!"

He tightened his grip once more, pressing the life out of me. He wasn't lying. Emma shook her head forebodingly…

"You don't wanna find out what they do to cop killers," Emma said coldly. "Trust me."

"I ain't talking to you fucking pigs!" he yelled. "You hear me!? No talking!!"

Emma's expression hadn't changed, remaining calm but firm… then her lips turned confidently upwards.

"I didn't ask you to *talk,*" she said calmly.

Before he could open his mouth again... something very bizarre happened. Lines of static and multi-coloured pixels flickered across our displays. The distortions filled from bottom to top, masking the outline of Emma's appearance until there was just a grainy, crackling graphical veil shimmering over the spot where she had been standing. A ghostly audio-visual silhouette masking her presence over our eyelids.

"Wh-what the-?" Gustaw muttered.

The interference passed as soon as it started, our vision returning… but Emma was gone.

"Where'd you… How'd you!?" Gustaw snarled, slack-jawed, staring into the empty doorway where she had been, his head darting from side to side.

"Emma… what did you-" I asked telepathically in a bewildered tone.

"NOW!" she cried.

A powerful force crashed into us from behind. We yelled as Gustaw's weight shifted forwards, sending him stumbling. It took both of us by surprise, and the grip on my throat loosened just enough to give me the chance to wriggle my way free.

THUD!

I fell like a stone into the muddy grass, tasting the earth in my mouth. I hunched myself up onto all fours, rubbing my aching throat and gulping for air, my lungs on fire from deprivation. I hurt like hell, but my bio-monitor readout assured me I'd survive.

I turned back to see what had happened.

Emma had managed to slip behind Gustaw and grab his padded shoulders, using them as a hoist to gracefully spring herself off the ground and wrap her legs around Gustaw's neck into a Japanese headlock, her mechanical thighs locked in like a python.

"Get off me!" Gustaw yelled, his voice muffled by Emma's legs.

"Jesus…" I panted.

Emma shifted her weight backwards, tipping over until they both crashed into the mud. The pair of them wrestled on the ground like a cyborg fetish video. Gustaw bucked like a mechanical bull, desperately trying to force her off, clenching Emma's thighs and trying to pry them off him. I could hear his actuators struggling, but she didn't budge.

Emma bore her teeth like an animal, wedging herself into place on the ground. She raised her right arm, pointing her fist to the ceiling then, with a twist, a long, sharp blade like an oversized knife shot out from its housing beneath her synthetic skin and a slit in her armour. She brought the weapon down slowly, resting it against the exposed part of Gustaw's throat. His vicious expression froze in horror, feeling the cold bite of the blade against his skin. His breathing slowed, his eyes wide open, the two of them becoming deadly still on the ground.

"There…" Emma said coolly, with a relieved smirk. "Much better."

With Gustaw pinned down, she used her free to hand to pull a data cable from her belt and clip it into the USB port at the top of Gustaw's suit, giving her direct access to the suit's CPU. An icon appeared on my display above Emma's head, indicating she was uploading a virus to the suit.

<<Upload complete>>

The soft whir of Gustaw's suit suddenly cut out. He had lost power. His arms and legs were suddenly frozen on the spot, his armour as stiff as a statue.

"Arrrgh!" he cried with panic, only able to move his head. "What have you…"

"I issued your suit's lockdown code," Emma sighed, withdrawing her wrist-blade within its housing, and released the grip of her thighs. She tapped her knuckles against the chest plating of his armour.

"Hate to break it to you, mate, but you may as well be wearing a pile of bricks. You ain't going nowhere."

"You bitch! I'm registered disabled dammit! I *need* this suit!" He spat at her, rolling on his metal back like an upturned turtle.

"Save it for the judge."

I watched her with awe as she strode away from the angry, swearing, beached whale of a man and towards me.

"You all right?" she asked, frowning and kneeling down beside me to examine my head.

I rubbed my forehead, noticing the trail of blood running down it for the first time.

"Yeah, I'm okay," I sighed, rubbing my head and checking the notification from Ben, informing me that medics had been dispatched to examine me. "Thanks, I owe you one."

"Just like ol' times, huh?" She winked back.

I chuckled at how true that was, looking over our muddied uniforms. "We look like we've just come from a rugby match."

"Very unladylike of me," she scoffed. "I'm gonna email you a link to a series of VR hand-to-hand combat training classes. Take them."

"I'll think about it. Cheers," I breathed, stretching myself to try to work out the aches.

"Yeah, that wasn't a suggestion," she answered firmly, shaking her head.

"Yes ma'am," I answered with a half-hearted salute and nudged my head towards the doorway. "How did you do that?"

"I accessed Mother Mind to upload a mirage virus," she explained. "The image of me in the doorway was just a 3D rendering."

"You hacked our displays?" I asked with a dropped. "You have that kind of intelligence clearance?"

She rolled her eyes in exasperation. "Before you start whining, cyber-attacks in self-defence are legal."

She helped me back onto my feet. My headset did its best to keep me focused, but she still had to support my weight.

"Did you need to hack my contact lenses as well?"

"Wouldn't have been as convincing," she shrugged.

I nodded, deciding to let it go, not wanting to complain to the woman who'd just saved my life.

"Well…" I sighed finally. "You're certainly not the *worst* partner I've had."

CHAPTER 6

Mother Mind Profile 7183-2647-8246-3892:

First Name: Denise

Surname: Masika

Status: Wanted for criminal offences

Nationality: British

Occupation(s):

- Suspected member of *Spiritform* Hacker Group

Criminal Record:

- Wanted: 03/08/2041
  - Offence: Prime suspect in the murder of Constable Alex Keystone
- Wanted: 10/12/2039
  - Offence: Various cases of Unauthorised Access to Computer Material
- Arrested: 17/11/2037
  - Offence: Suspected of Unauthorised Access to Computer Material
  - No formal charges

Known Aliases:

- Destiny

Biometric Data:

- Gender: Female
- Date of Birth: 24/09/2017
- Age: 28
- Race: African
- Hair Colour: Black
- Eye Colour: Blue
- Height: 1.76m
- Weight: 68kg
- Ailments: None
- Cybernetic Percentage: 4%
- Genetic Modifications:
  - Congenital Heart Disease Correction

- Performance Enhancement Therapy

Immediate Family:

- Mother: Martha Masika
- Father: Keith Masika
- Siblings: 1
  - Brother: Kieran Masika

Relationships:

- Status: Single

Contact Information:

- *Drop down for more info*

Live Surveillance:

- Status: *Unavailable*
- Date: 05/10/2045
- Current location: Unknown
- Local Time at previously known location: 21:47 GMT

<<VR Simulation in Progress>>

The data danced around us, reminding me of the Covent Garden New Year's fireworks display. Yottabytes of information glittering with every colour of the spectrum. The light seemed to pierce into your heart, flowing with all the knowledge of the human race. The sensation was almost heavenly like we had entered a digital paradise. I could practically hear the digital angels singing in the background.

We were inside the OpenSource Soul's avatar, a giant hollow sphere like a digital star, large deep blue pixels flickering on the surface. The three of us floated inside as bodiless avatars, the regular anonymous appearance of our secure IRC virtual chat. The avatars appeared as three sprite-like orbs of various colours, trails of pixel-like fairy dust trailing behind, our screen names were written in slowly rotating graphical windows.

"You ain't gonna make a habit of this, are ya?" Smokey complained, his purple avatar pulsing angrily as his voice echoed telepathically.

"Not if I can help it," FireSaint mumbled unhappily, his red avatar smouldering like embers.

"If you need someone to drive you around, get a fake *Uber* account or something!" Smokey protested, flashing an angry emoji.

Smokey was the leader of the Wind Riders, a hover-bike gang that had been terrorising the residents of West London. They wanted to act like they were as tight as the Hell's Angels of old, but the truth was they were mostly made up of rich kids and engineering enthusiasts who'd gone off the rails. Hover-bikes were still expensive toys, only used by the military, a handful of police units, professional racers, and fat cats with too much money to spend.

The silly bugger had gone and gotten himself arrested. He got caught selling stolen immunisation gene therapy serums on camera, DNA-altering formulas to provide immunisation for a wide variety of diseases. Usually, I wouldn't give two shits about what happened to a run-of-the-mill street rat, but these guys were stealing from GenePharma, my personal number one target. Out of all the companies that lobbied for ITIP, they were the ones I hated the most. Price-gouging cunts. They tripled the retail cost of any medicine they bought the rights to… or stopped them from getting to the market entirely.

Cryptonic was Dad's old hacker handle. He was a bit of a legend in the community… but only because he got busted for stealing the cure for congenital heart disease from GenePharma… to save me…

I liked to think I was following in his footsteps. Even though I knew he wouldn't want me to.

I could never speak to any of my family again, knowing it would put them at risk. I missed them more than words could say… I hated it, but that was the price I had to pay.

I told myself that one day it would be worth it… and then I wouldn't have to do favours for drug dealers to make a living.

"Look Smokey, that hack you had us pull would have cost anyone else five grand," I growled back. "So, unless you can find some way to cough up the dough, shut up and put up with the fact I'm going to be expecting favours for a while."

"Point taken…" Smokey replied lightly. "But uh, you *did* do it right?"

If my avatar had eyes, I'd have rolled them.

"Wouldn't be here if I hadn't," I scoffed, telepathically sending him an annoyed emoji face to his HUD, accompanied by a URL.

Smokey's avatar went silent as he began looking over the website on his HUD. It was an online file browser for a data centre in Margate, storing most of London's CCTV footage. He'd paid me to hack into it… partly paid anyway.

The video played out on our HUDs, streaming images of a dingy, piss-stained alleyway in central London, accompanied with various other data being recorded at the scene like wind speed, temperature, etc. The timer in the bottom left-hand corner of the display ticked upwards. When it reached 18:47:22, the ultra-high definition recording was suddenly swamped by interference. The picture crackled and distorted frame by frame until it was unrecognisable, erasing any sign that Smokey had ever been there.

<<Error 6128: File is Corrupted>>

Smokey sent a gleeful-looking emoji back in response.

"Destiny, you're a lifesaver!" He chuckled, the relief clear in his voice. "My own personal Jesus Christ!"

"It's what I do. Just not for free."

His avatar rolled back anxiously.

"This taxi job has gotta cover *some* of the cost… right?" he continued. "It's not like we're talking about the miles. That data your buddy is carrying has gotta be the hottest piece of stolen goods in the city."

"He's got a fair poi-" FireSaint began, but I cut him off by sending him a painful telepathic nudge. I didn't physically touch him, but the sensation of having an elbow rammed into his chest would be transmitted to his brain. "OW!"

"Let me do the talking!" I hissed back over the link.

Project Selection. An enigma if there ever was one. We received the file transfer from an anonymous source. Well, *he* thought he was anonymous anyway. His screen name was Shad0wCell. I was able to discreetly run a trace program to ping his original IP address, and matched it with the metadata we captured from Cloudland. Our contact's real name was Andrew Ilian, a seventeen-year-old script kiddie living with his folks in Kensington. Claimed to have stolen the data from a server belonging to Virtualife on Prometheus Point station. The files were still encrypted so we couldn't read the content, but the timestamps verified their authenticity. The labs on that station were so classified even God himself didn't get to look in there.

But we had *four-hundred exabytes* from it.

It had to be juicy. The juiciest files that we had come across in a long time.

So juicy, it had cost the kid his life.

We completed the download at 17:47 and received the bulletin at 18.30. Every news service in London had been gripped by the string of Jack-21 killings. The psychopathic killer roaming the city dissecting cyborgs for their implants.

Shad0wCell was the latest victim.

The reports claimed Jack-21 had scaled up the side of his apartment block, broke in and ripped him to shreds. I could smell the bullshit a mile away. All of Jack-21's previous victims had been snatched off the street, but this was a *targeted assassination*. It had to be. It was becoming more and more common in the world of industrial espionage.

It made me sick. With the privatisation of law enforcement and the military, it was only a matter of time before the fat cats started adding hitmen to their payroll. The kid hadn't even been old enough to drink!

There was a bit of a snag though. With the data encrypted, even with the Yottaflop processing power of the OpenSource Soul, it would still take a week to brute-force crack. We couldn't risk storing the data on the devices in this safe house, without putting all of us at risk. We couldn't save it on our online block-chain either without risking the source being traced.

There was only one thing to do, directly save our file to our backup server room in Southall. We always had a contingency hideout for emergencies in case we got rumbled. A hidden underground bunker dug into a back garden. The owner initially kept it for smuggling in refugees, but we'd paid to rent it out for a while. It was hooked up with power, water, even internet access. Perfect for what we needed… even if it was dingy as fuck.

But someone still needed to physically watch over the files.

We networked our AIs together and let them decide for us. FireSaint drew the short straw. We'd dressed him in the most concealing clothes we could find and called Smokey to give him a lift… which meant taking 'the road less travelled'. Most of London's underground tunnels didn't exist on official maps as centuries of secret history built on top of each other like geological strata, forgotten by the ages. Entire subterranean cultures were starting to spring up as a result, but the Wind Riders knew the tunnels better than anyone and could move through them pretty fast on their hoverbikes. Not the worst bunch of people to have to owe you a favour.

We had to be ridiculously careful when moving across the city. Mother Mind was an ever-present danger. We could never tell at any one time how much data the system had on us. One hacked webcam, one drone fly-by, one loose hair left for DNA analysis, and you could kiss your ass goodbye. The government *loved* making an example of hackers. No chance of a fair trial just sent and plugged straight into the Prison Matrix to have your psyche slowly picked apart until you were reprogrammed into the perfect citiżen. I closed my eyes and tried to wipe the images of my father rotting away like that in a stasis chamber…

<<Focus Mode Enabled>>

My headset beamed alpha waves into my brain, snapping me to attention. The images of Dad disappeared from my mind's eye, and my attention snapped to Smokey. Like anti-depressants on steroids.

"Fine. I'll let you off for four hundred," I gave in reluctantly.

"Four hundred?!" Smokey spluttered. "That ain't even ten percent!"

"I ain't running a charity here."

Smokey began mulling it over, probably asking his personal AI for advice, making hemming and hawing noises as he went. "Okay… tell ya what. In exchange for one big job… you let me off the rest."

Interesting. These guys had pulled off some seriously big raids in their time. They even managed to steal cargo right off the back of a moving maglev train.

"A big job?" I sneered to deliberately mislead him. "I steal data, not meds. What would we need-"

"We do *hits* too," he pointed out suggestively.

That was new.

They grow up so fast…

"Too bad I don't need someone bumped off," I deadpanned.

"Can you honestly say you *won't* need someone bumped off in the future?"

I pondered that thought… it wouldn't be the first time I'd had to kill.

"Hmm…" I sighed as I opened my VPA in another data window. I'd named him Poe and customised his appearance to make him appear as a cat, his colour scheme like something out of an anime. Green fur, large pointed ears, oversized cartoon eyes and an extended tail that wrapped around his body like a snake.

"What's up, Destiny?" he purred at me through our private telepathic chat.

"What do you think? Should I do it?"

His large googly eyes rolled from side to side while lines of code rained around him.

"I estimate a 91% chance that he is telling the truth. He intends to pay you back," Poe rumbled back. "Even if he doesn't, you still have the original copy of the CCTV recording as a bargaining chip."

"Great minds think alike," I telepathically nodded, closing his data window and turning back to Smokey. "All right, you've got yourself a deal."

"Cheers Destiny," he sighed again. "You're a-"

"Owing me is a dangerous thing, Smokey," I interrupted acidly, intending to put the fear of God into him. "Remember that."

His avatar shifted nervously in the virtual air.

"Uh… yeah, I hear you," he answered cautiously.

"Glad we're on the same page," I said perkily, telepathically sending a thumbs-up. "Don't be a stranger."

"Sure… catch you around," he replied with a nervous, yet smiley avatar emoji before logging off into a cloud of pixels.

I swivelled my avatar around to face FireSaint, who'd been floating quietly next to me the whole time.

"Why do I get the feeling we just got sold magic beans?" FireSaint asked me flatly.

"Couldn't hurt to have a protection gang," I pointed out.

"Speaking as someone who is being protected by them as we speak… I don't feel very safe," he muttered.

I sent him a sad face emoticon.

"Sorry, dude. I know that safe house sucks."

"Someone's gotta take one for the team," he sighed as cheerfully as he could. "I'm just glad they didn't choose GateCrasher."

"Tell me about it," I sighed with relief. "He wouldn't have shut up."

"You'd probably have to sedate him," he sniggered.

My avatar flashed with the word 'LOL'. I liked that about Simon, he was resilient, willing to go the extra mile. Most Spiritformers were just *Script Kiddies* who wanted to feel like they were part of something bigger. Not me, not FireSaint.

Maybe in another life, we might have had a chance to be together… not this one.

"It's only for a week, right?" he added.

"Unless something goes wrong with the decryption, yeah," I reassured him.

"Don't turn off the PC. Got it," he chuckled.

I telepathically projected a nodding emoji. "Stay safe."

"That's why they call it a safe house right?" he teased back. He chuckled at his own terrible joke, and we logged out together, derezzing into pixel dust.

<<Terminating VR Simulation>>

<<Disengaging Neural Lace>>

<<Disconnecting from Server>>

<<Thank You for using SoulShift>>

The virtual world faded from my contact lenses. I didn't have an implanted neural lace, so it wasn't a full-immersion simulation, but the synaptic feedback was convincing enough. I woke up on my mattress that barely deserved the name, on top of a hard steel rack. The windows were boarded up, and covered by thick blackout curtains.

I rubbed my eyes, feeling the piercing around my brow as I did. My vision readjusted to the bioluminescent lights, hanging loosely by steel wires from the stone ceiling, gathering cobwebs. I started playing Lady Transhuman's latest hit single 'Blue Screen of Death' on my headset, a cacophony of guitars and electronic music out of the mini speakers in my ears.

We had turned this rotting pub into our hideout; 'The Prince Albert' had once been one of the busiest bars in Brixton, a victim of the recession. Now it was just a shell, with peeling old brown wallpaper, revealing the Victorian brick, burn damage spread across the floor. We were living in the flats above the pub while using the building itself as our base of operations. We spent our lives on the run. We never stayed in any one safe house for more than a few weeks. Keeping on the move, one step ahead of Mother Mind.

It was then I noticed a draught had blown the blackout curtains open a crack. The streetlights were filtering through, creating a narrow beam of light across the cluttered, dusty floor, split up into uneven sections of shadow by the wooden boards behind the curtain.

"Shit…" I breathed bitterly, lunging out of bed and across the room to shut the curtain again, cursing myself. I'd been searching for the source of the draught for weeks and hadn't been able to isolate it.

It was like living in World War Two; a view from a window might be all it took for a drone to get a fix on us. We'd made extraordinary measures. From a legal position, the pub was being squatted in, like hundreds of other abandoned buildings in London. Of course, that meant that someone had to pay council tax. Luckily a couple of our members still didn't have criminal records, and so could pay the fee without attracting attention thanks to our money laundering systems in place. So, all we could do now was hope we appeared to be any other squat-house, and the police wouldn't pay us any bother. A couple of cops did come to the door once. The rest of us hid while Raj went to get the door. They checked our paperwork and fucked off, but it was nerve-racking, to say the least. As a precaution, we printed out three auto-sentry machine guns and mounted them at each entrance to the building, and had even built an escape hatch to the sewers.

Vive la revolution!

I flopped back down, and told myself it was all a worthwhile sacrifice for the cause… but it was getting harder and harder to do that. I can't lie, this place was *getting to me.*

My mind started to re-acclimatise itself into my body. Living in our ghostly anonymous avatars was almost euphoric, a user-controlled acid trip. I wriggled on my mattress, becoming accustomed to having arms and legs again. I held up my hands, looking through my fingerless gloves, and glanced down at my clothes, the spike-studded sleeveless leather jacket and tank top revealing my toned midriff, and the flame tattoo plastered across my sleeve illuminated with bioelectric energy in random spots. A tangle of chains dangled from the jacket to my tight-fitting jeans, oblong-shaped cutaway sections on the thighs revealing the fishnet leggings underneath, slipping into my steel-capped glowing boots, with a series of straps extending to the legs of shorts. My wavy purple hair flowed through the rim of my dark plastic neural-lace headset.

I yawned and licked the ring pierced around my bottom lip, rubbing my eyes with fingerless-gloved hands, feeling the video-lenses under the lids. I held my smartwatch up to use the front-facing camera as a compact mirror. The face staring back at me looked like shit, the bags under my eyes like lunar eclipses…

I telepathically checked our supplies of make-up… we were running low, same with my vitamin meds. Hopefully we'd get some on the next supply run; otherwise, I'd have to put up with looking like a zombie for a while.

All for the good fight…

I stretched out, working out the kinks in my shoulder, and felt a cable shifting beneath it. It was connected to my headset, the socket behind my ear, interfacing with the red and black laptop beside me.

"Found any more info on this 'Project Selection'?" I verbally spoke to the computer, not keeping my hopes up.

Poe's avatar appeared from the projector, looking somewhat disappointed with his ears drooping. "I've been very thorough. There are zero references to any initiatives by Virtualife with that name mentioned in any public domains."

"Not surprised, they'll have NDAd the crap out of 'em. I bet none of them remembers anything about it by now." I ground my teeth bitterly.

"Tranquillity is pressing her contacts in Virtualife for more details now," Poe continued. "If there is anyone who still knows she'll find them."

"Here's hoping."

"By the way!" Poe added merrily, his cat-eyes flashing brightly. "I came across an article you might be interested in."

"Oh?" I replied as I telepathically accepted the link.

The web page loaded into view, it was a *Google* Review of an online business. A private investigator… with a frustratingly familiar name.

"Arthur Wells?" I checked with a puzzled eyebrow, rubbing my pierced lip.

The 'about me' page of the website featured a stylised film-noir photo of him, standing in a wooden hallway with his face almost entirely hidden in shadow, but I could still recognise him; probably his idea of 'art'. He certainly looked the part, complete with trench coat and pork pie hat. But what stood out most was his prosthetic eyes and hands.

Finally got your wish then? Narcissistic bastard.

He was smoking an e-cigarette with his boot resting against a wall projecting a holographic display for his business and generally looking like a hard-ass.

Can't believe I went out with that asshole for a year…

"He's been making a bit of a stir on the cybersecurity forums. Apparently, he disabled a rogue botnet," Poe explained.

"No shit," I deadpanned. "But more to the point… why did you think I would want to see that prick again?"

Poe's ears drooped, and his face fell, quickly closing the window. "Sorry. It won't happen again."

I nodded gruffly to reinforce his error. I thought his personality matrix would be intelligent enough to calculate that I wouldn't want status updates on my *ex-boyfriend.* That said, I found myself staring at the photo for longer than I thought I would… bringing up nostalgia for a time gone by.

Arthur had always been a bit of a cocky bastard, so sure of himself and determined to prove it. That's what I'd admired about him when I'd first met him. He always believed that he would get past the Spiritform membership process. We applied at the same time… or at least I thought we did anyway. He totally played me. Forged the application email and wrote mock code for a virus to make me feel he was going ahead with it. All just a lie to keep us together.

The path I had chosen in life didn't exactly make room for much of a love life. He let me think he was going to come with me, I spent the next month feeling like an idiot for believing him. He was nothing but a selfish, materialistic liar. He would do anything to get his hands on the latest gadget. The more I stared at the photo, the more vitriol it brought up as I wrestled with myself, debating if I hated him more for lying to me, or myself for believing him.

I found myself spacing out as I descended into that pit of melancholy and rage, my eyes fixated on the photo for an unclear amount of time, only to be suddenly snapped back to reality by a loud obnoxious bleeping from our network rig.

I got up and strode down the creaky stairs towards the pub's main bar. The wooden counter remained intact but was slowly succumbing to rot, while the brass handles of the drink taps were tarnished entirely. The cabinet behind it was devoid of bottles, replaced with our home-built server. The shelves had been cleared out and replaced with the rig, the guts of the machine left exposed; dozens of nanotube processors, optical memory devices, motherboards, power supplies… all wired together, producing a symphony of blinking lights. It was hooked up to our blocky black holo-table in the centre of the room, the surface projecting the sphere of the OpenSource Soul as a screensaver. The networking cables were threaded through holes drilled into the wall. Even with our satellite network, the signals could still be intercepted by drones. The police didn't need to decrypt the transmissions to triangulate their point of origin. Using our own digging robot, we had carved out a tunnel to thread a line through, to connect to an antenna array in a nearby slum. So many unregulated signals came from there that it would be impossible for the police to pin it on us.

Kasira was stood on the far end at the table away from me, flicking through a series of e-mails and private instant messages, her eyes wild with child-like excitement. She was Chinese, one of our younger prodigies at just twenty-two. Her screen name was Tranquillity. She kept her short hair tied into two buns atop her head, reminiscent of ears, and wore overpowering sweet perfume. Her clothes reminded me of Chun Lee from the old Street Fighter games; the electronic embroidery of her traditional oriental qipao dress softly pulsed blue and purple, showing off her genetically sculpted physique.

"Oh, you're back!" She smiled, chirpy. "How was your meeting with the burly biker?"

My expression stiffened, not appreciating her insinuation.

"Strictly business," I answered flatly, licking my piercing.

"Aww… where's the fun in that?" She winked.

I gave her a mild, awkward fake laugh in response. She was more of a colleague than a friend. Frankly, she got on my nerves. I knew her type. The hackers who did what they did purely for the challenge. Not motivated by money or political motives, she just liked breaking ICE for the sake of breaking ICE. I didn't want that here. This was my passion, I was gonna be here till the bitter end. She was going to be here until something shinier came along.

"You know you still owe me that rematch?" she reminded me

hopefully.

I rolled my eyes impatiently. She was talking about our last game of Mech-Gladiator. A realistic VR simulation for Heavy-Exoskeleton pilots. In other words, giant fighting robots. My one guilty pleasure in life. Of course, games pose a constant distraction for people like us, so I tried to limit my online time… unlike some people I know.

"We'll have to rain cheque it. I hear you've been pressing your Virtualife contact," I continued, professionally folding my arms. "Got anything on this Carpenter person?"

Before Shad0wCell was bumped off, he'd given us the name of one of the few employees at Virtualife that he knew to have been working on the project. Doctor Julie Carpenter. He'd discovered she was scheduled to appear at ModCon on Saturday. A convention for tech enthusiasts, corps, and indie companies to show off what they've been working on. But we still needed confirmation on the lead.

"Check this out," Kasira grinned at me, clearly pleased with herself.

She tapped the holo-table, and a photo appeared in front of me. I leaned in, rubbing my chin with my gloved hand. She'd found the file on Dr Carpenter's *Instagram* page, taken from her smartwatch. She was in her early thirties, red-haired, with a thick, pronounced bone structure, and lenses on her bionic eyes that seemed to dazzle like diamonds. She was sat in a passenger seat in the cabin of a spaceplane, the caption on the photo stating she was en route to Prometheus Point station, grinning from ear to ear while her hair drifted like seaweed in the weightlessness, her eyes catching the zero-atmosphere light. The blue curvature of the Earth stretched out before her outside the porthole window beside her.

It was all right for some… the price may have been coming down, but orbital tourism was still very much upper-class exclusive. There were now several large stations in orbit, and colonies on the moon; home to thousands of scientists and wealthy individuals. I'd even seen an advert to pre-order a ticket on the long overdue SpaceX *Heart of Gold* Mars colonial transporter, for the low-low price of £200,000 per person. Better start saving.

"Hmm… seems legit," I said, complimenting her on the photo, playing with my lip ring. The timestamps on the Project Selection files confirmed they had been created on the station.

"I take it you've tried to crack her personal network too? Found anything we can use as leverage?"

"And how," she grinned back at me. She forwarded me the second photo. This time it was a picture taken from her trip to Ibiza. It had come from her private memory storage, and with good reason.

It was a photo of her and a few girlfriends on a night out in a club, wearing revealing dresses with flashing lights built into them, thickly layered make-up to pretty them up. They were all apparently wasted by this point, but our professor was there tucking into a 6ft-long sub sandwich, made with the distinctive white tinge of splice-bread.

"Cocaine problem," I nodded with an intrigued smirk. It was still the most popular illicit drug among professionals looking for a concentration boost, as there were limits to what Focus Mode could achieve without chemical-aid.

"Plenty more where that came from. Got some juicy footage of them wasted on that shit. Not the sort of thing you want your employers knowing."

Leverage…

"Nice work," I complimented back, giving her a thumbs-up while bringing the ModCon's website on the central display. "Time for a bit of good old-fashioned blackmail."

"Face to face?" Kasira blurted out. "We'll be spotted by Mother Mind a dozen times before we get anywhere near the convention centre!"

"Face to avatar would be more accurate," I interjected.

She apparently hadn't considered the possibility of going to the event using remote-controlled androids. We'd have to use fake or stolen accounts with the rent-a-body service, but that was no problem.

"Okay, but what's wrong with sending a threatening e-mail?"

"We blackmail her online, and she'll just report it," Poe explained, appearing from the central table. "Virtualife's drug policy requires the management to offer free rehab if she comes forward with her problem. If we use online communication to blackmail her, it's more likely she'll do that than risk breaking her non-disclosure agreement. But if we threaten her in person when she's surrounded by potential clients…" I grinned.

"…We can force her hand," Kasira nodded slowly with upturned lips. "Good thinking."

I stretched my arms triumphantly behind my head, massaging my shoulder through my leather jacket.

"We'll have to get the plan approved by the rest of the group first. I've raised the issue in a new discussion on our subnet. The ballot time closes within the next couple of hours."

The OpenSource Soul represented more than just a hive mind. It was iconic. Representative of our philosophical ideals. Due to the open-source nature of the software, it had found its way into the hands of the criminal underworld… but what we had in mind was far more ambitious.

Einstein once said, 'We cannot solve our problems with the same thinking we used when we created them.' That's what the Soul *could be*, the beginning of a viable alternative to capitalism and traditional democracy, based on the ideals of old futurists like Buckminster Fuller and Jacques Fresco.

There were hundreds of subnets, hosted by the overall block-chain, that could be communicated with via third-party discussion forums with the software plug-in. Each subnet covered a topic: energy, agriculture, manufacturing, transportation, art, etc. The goal was to create a resource-sharing economy. The most common use of this was the 'energy internet'. Users selling on locally generated electricity to others as and when they were needed. The concept had been around for a few decades, but the Soul made it easy. Anyone could do it, without the need of a third-party licence. Now the idea had been applied to almost everything, food and water sources, cars, even industrial equipment. Hundreds of smaller start-up companies had sprung up, taking advantage of this processing power to offer alternative means of distribution, either using traditional subscription fees or creating users that were both hybrid employees and customers, offering up their possessions in time-share agreements in exchange for cash or other goods.

Many technology icons believed that this kind of business model would extend to the government as well.

After all, most of the real problems in the world were technical, and human politicians simply didn't have the knowledge to solve these problems. For example, an AI with access to real-time data readouts from soil and air quality sensors, as well as the nutritional needs of the population, would be more informed to make agricultural decisions than any government department. With that kind of data, it would be possible to create a type of 'economic dynamic equilibrium'. Bypassing the need for democracy, policies would be shaped by the *laws of nature,* not by human (or corporate) opinion. The means of production taken out of private hands, returned to the public, designed to meet the needs of every citizen. The wheels of industry turning at their highest possible efficiency, *without* damaging the environment.

Of course, AI was already an indispensable tool to most politicians, but such programs were often developed to be subtly influenced by the will of the corporations who designed them. In the economic system, we were proposing the profit motive would be removed in its entirety. Therefore, eliminating that problem.

Naturally, there were always going to be decisions that couldn't be made by an algorithm, where opinion voting was necessary. But this could be done via direct referendums. The ballots delivered digitally through each user's virtual personal assistants, bypassing the need for potentially corruptible elected representatives.

There were the usual concerns about 'AI uprisings', but the three laws took care of that. Besides, the fact was governments already *were* dependent on AI to make their decisions. The only difference was, if we had our way, their prime directives wouldn't be merely just advancing the party agenda.

I'd seen documentaries about colonies that had adopted this style of life. It was like something out of *Star Trek*. *Utopian*. I found myself shedding tears in front of my holo-screen the first time I saw the sea of happy faces, living in their gleaming white domes on a background of lush greenery. I didn't think anywhere like that *could* exist.

That's why I joined Spiritform. To fight for that better future. All you had to do was look out at the itinerant protesters on the street to see the world was on the verge of a change, the likes of which it had never seen. Hacktivism was my way of bringing about that change. We coordinated secret subnet discussion groups, using the Soul to plan our cyber warfare strategies and aid the development of our ICE Breakers.

In the early days, we thought all it would take would be to permanently crash the systems of crucial government and financial institutions. Hack in and encrypt their data, making it impossible to recover. We used the Soul to run simulations of that scenario… the resulting anarchy would've been too disruptive to be productive. Instead, we were now just focused on exposing corporate dirty laundry and hoping we were adding enough fuel to the fire to start a full-blown revolution… peacefully if we could help it… violent if necessary. Malcolm X would be proud.

Truth be told though, in recent years I'd started to lose faith. We'd exposed tax evasion, violent security scandals, illegal mining operations… but in the end, all the noise we caused was just drowned out by the endless stream of bullshit poured out by the mass media. Keeping people literally jacked-in to their artificial world of distractions.

We needed something big… and my gut was telling me this was it. If we could get dirt on *Virtualife,* the company responsible for *Mother Mind, and* catch them in the act of doing something illegal, *really illegal…* it would send shockwaves across the entire world economy.

That was the plan anyway, we just needed to decrypt the damn files now.

"Apparently EverWear Avatars have updated their log-in handshake protocols," Kasira added, looking thoughtfully over a data window projecting from the holo-table. "We'll need that info if we're gonna own them. Should I run some probing attacks? Find any obvious exploits?"

"Hmm… probably best to wait till the results of the vote," I shrugged. "We should-"

I was about to sit down in a green leather pub-stool, reaching into the top pocket of my sleeveless jacket to pull out a joint, when I heard something clink against my foot. I looked down and saw my foot had brushed against a screw, that had fallen off a pile lying on top of a plastic tray that lay next to a white cloth covering a machine, about five feet long.

"Oh, you're fucking kidding!" I cried angrily.

I knelt beside the cloth and pulled it back, breathing a loud, angry, exasperated breath when I saw what was beneath. It was Plexi, our home-built android. The patchwork torso chassis barely protected his mechanical innards. His arms and legs were lined with cheap rubber, making him look like a prop out of a hundred-year-old sci-fi film. His sensor array was mounted in the middle of his chest because the face was little more than an old plasma screen. Plexi was far from the top of the line, but he was ours; an essential part of the team. At least when he worked – now he needed one of his balancing gyroscopes replaced.

"Where the fuck is Raj?!" I snapped at Kasira. "He was supposed to have him fixed an hour ago!"

Raj 'Acid-Override' Cansai was our hardware-guy. He knew more about nano and bio-electronics than any of us. His family owned a corner repair shop in Uxbridge… and yet he couldn't fix our shit on time to save his life. Our VPAs analysed our skills and weakness and co-ordinated with each via the Soul network to assign jobs, to work the queues on our calendars. We had to vote to approve the plans of course, but I was starting to think the program was glitchy.

Kasira smiled at me in a teasing manner. "Listen carefully, and you will hear the truth."

I scoffed at the ambiguity.

"Can you frame that answer in a way that *doesn't* sound like a Chinese proverb?" I growled, pointing angrily with my gloved fingers.

Mid-way through my sentence, Kasira pressed a finger to her lips, ignoring me. I raised an eyebrow, realising that was her real answer. I fell quiet and listened to the silence… well, near silence. The sound of creaking wood permeated the air, accompanied by heavy panting, moaning and swearing.

"Oh, for fuck's sake!" I muttered, facepalming myself.

"Yeah, literally," Kasira scoffed.

"Unbelievable," I scoffed, turning to Raj's bedroom, checking his online status on my HUD. Sure enough, he was in VR, fucking whatever hooker simulation took his fancy.

"RAJ!" I shrieked upstairs.

"Yell all you want, he won't hear you."

She was right. None of us had implants, but interface headsets could still provide decent immersion.

"He needs to get his ass in gear," I muttered.

"Don't look at me! I ain't going near that."

I ground my teeth bitterly. Poe's avatar appeared in front of me on my HUD, his bright cat-eyes beaming with inspiration.

"I assume you've got an idea?"

He brought me an icon labelled 'Erroder', one of our ICE Breakers. A ZQL packet injector for cracking Firewalls.

"Ah…" I grinned. "I think I see where you're going with this."

<<Initialising Erroder>>

<<Connecting to Target IP…>>

<<Authorisation Protocols Detected>>

<<Execute?>>

The ICE breaker was only Level-2 on the Kurzweil scale, but we held monthly cyber-wargame simulations on our systems, trying to hack each other to find vulnerabilities in our systems. Raj's neural lace was no exception. We'd patched the exploits we'd found as best we could, but there was still a back-door I could use to get in.

Raj's moans suddenly grew louder, sounding like he was about to orgasm, sending my skin crawling.

"Do it," I telepathically ordered, licking my piercing gleefully.

Poe nodded, and an icon shaped like a flask of acid flashed on the top menu bear.

<<Erroder Running>>

```
<<Scanning Authorisation Protocols >>
<<Configuring Payload>>
<<Configuration Complete>>
<<Initialising Upload>>

<<<    int in_group_p(gid_t grp)
{
       const struct cred *cred = current_cred();
       int retval = 1;
if (grp != cred->fsgid)
       retval = groups_search(cred->group_info, grp);
       return retval;
} >>>
<<Access Granted>>
```

I grinned as a green and black menu opened before my eyes, the core device drivers for Raj's virtual simulation. From here I could alter output signals from Raj's neural lace.

"Poe, you're a star!" I said to the AI with a surprised laugh. "Standby to record. This is gonna be hysterical!"

The 'ready to record' icon appeared on my contact lenses display while I telepathically flicked through the menu until I came to the settings for tactile pressure sensations. A 3D diagram of the anatomy of Raj's central nervous system appeared, displaying the environmental data being transmitted into his brain in real time.

I navigated the cursor over to his groin and clicked. A menu filled with slider settings appeared. I selected 'tactile pressure', the option controlling the amount of simulated physical force that was being applied to any given area of the body.

Surprise! I began dialling up the pressure.

"Begin recording," I said, a maniacal grin starting to spread across my face.

I craned my neck up the stairs, listening to Raj's moans. They had been growing faster and louder. That changed quickly, his patterns rapidly slowed down as he realised something was wrong… turning from cries of pleasure to sudden anguishing pain.

"Arrrrgh!!!! What the fuck!?" Raj screamed, so loudly it even made Kasira jump. "Abort! Abort!"

I burst out laughing, keeling over in stitches and slapping my sides, rattling the chains on my belt. I could hear him flailing desperately in the next room, banging against the walls and knocking the thing over.

Nostalgia began creeping inside me, remembering the hacking pranks I used to pull at school. This was what it meant to be a hacker. That mischievous voice never went away, it just grew more ambitious. He kept yelling 'abort' to trigger the emergency log-out procedure, but I'd already disabled it.

"What's the matter Raj?" I said telepathically, my real voice almost out of breath from my hysterics. "Tight fit?"

"You crazy bitch! For the love of God stop!"

"I dunno, Raj," I answered coolly. "Is my robot going to get fixed?"

"Yes, fucking, yes!" he spat out. "Just stop, damn it!!!"

Now that's what I call motivation. I terminated my icebreaker and discontinued the commands to the android. Raj's wails became replaced with heavy panting. I wiped the tears of laughter out of my eyes and caught my breath. I found a glimpse of Kasira slack-jawed with disbelief.

"What?"

"Uh nothing…" she answered nervously. "Just setting a reminder to stay in your good books."

I turned away to hide my self-satisfied grin. Yes, I'm a bit of a control freak. There, I said it. I triumphantly reached into my top jacket pocket, pulled out the fattest blunt I had pre-rolled and sparked up. The real-life, sticky, earthy scent of ganja wafted graciously out of my nose, glittering against the holo-table.

The stairway creaked. I turned to see Raj stumbling into the room. A slightly rounded twenty-four-year-old Indian dude, dressed in Intellifabric pyjamas stinking of sweat with an animated blue-white pattern on it, clutching his groin and waddling like a penguin. His hair was a tufty mess, held in place by his interface headset. I could barely keep a straight face as he glared at me from behind his darkened visor, the glowing power-icon tattoo on his fluffy round cheek curling as he scowled.

"You're a real cunt," he glowered at me.

"Yeah, but what would you do without me?" I teased him, giving him a cheeky wink and blowing ganja smoke at him. He gave me the finger and waddled away.

Raj continued scowling to himself while he grabbed a beanie bag slumped by the door. He dumped it next to the broken robot and pulled out a claytronic tool from his pocket, tapping icons on his watch holo-display. It morphed into the appropriate size screwdriver, and he went to work removing the chest plate, scratching his tattoo as he went.

I left him muttering to himself while I turned on my heel to walk away before he got a chance to respond, leaving a trail of smoke behind me, starting to enjoy the effects taking hold. A guilty pleasure of mine. We may have been on the run for our lives, but some luxuries were worth the effort.

I strolled into the kitchen, looking around at the stained, cracked tiles and peeling paint. I stopped in front of the fridge, stepping over the cables we had laid out, connecting to the solar panels on the roof.

I reached for the grubby door and swung it open. My contact lenses scanned the items inside. The shelves were stacked with dozens of tall plastic flasks. Most of them were bone dry, but my HUD directed my eyes to the top shelf, where four were still filled with a supplement drink.

As usual, we had everything you could want… as long as it was Soylent. A creamy white liquid with the consistency of porridge, a synthetic amalgam of proteins and nutrients designed to replace food. A flask of that stuff a day would contain everything needed to sustain the human body. It had been marketed by the companies who'd made it as the solution to the world's food crisis. It wasn't exactly disgusting… just depressing. Some things did not need to be replaced. But it was the main staple of our hacktivist diet, just because we could synthesise it with the equipment we had here.

Popping into the corner shop was too much exposure for us to take the risk, so here we were, slurping down three meals a day, seven days a week. We had a bio-printer as well, but it took too much power to use on a regular basis. Frankly, using it to replicate cannabis was a risk, but like I said, some things one could not do without.

With a reluctant sigh, I grabbed a glass from the cupboard next to the fridge and began pouring out the substance, in-between tokes from my joint, already starting to feel lightheaded. I stared down at the glass of sadness and swirled the yellow froth in my hands, trying not to think about how much it looked like baby food.

"You know, it's not actually made of people, right?" Kasira called out, watching me stare at the glass.

I rolled my eyes, sick of hearing references to that movie.

"You learn something new every day," I called back sarcastically.

I sipped away at the odourless, tasteless liquid, feeling it slide down my throat. Oh-so-depressingly bland.

I looked disapprovingly at the other empty flasks before shutting the fridge behind me. We ran out of chemical printer cartridges roughly once a month and would have to restock if we wanted to keep eating and making gadgets, our Achilles heel.

It was too risky to have the equipment delivered to our safe houses so one of us would have to make the monthly trip out to the dead drop from our supplier in the Irish Mafia and bring the goods back here. We all had active camouflage suits that would let us move through the street without being spotted by CCTV, but good luck getting all the way across London like that. We had an old *Volvo* smart van parked about a mile away, registered to fake IDs, that we could take to the drop point and then leg it back to the safe house. We had to keep up radio silence as well, making it impossible to keep track of the courier. Every movement across the city had to be carefully planned in advance; the joys of being a fugitive.

A buzzing came from downstairs, along with loud clanking of the magnetic locks we'd installed on the rear entrance. A draught came wafting in along with the shuffle of footsteps, and the door shut behind.

<<Gatecrasher has entered the building>>

Speak of the devil.

I carried my glass of Soylent sadness back into the main room, slurping the thick liquid as I went. My joint was finished by now, and I stubbed it out on the almost full ash-tray resting by the old pub bar.

I faced the doors to the stairwell the footsteps were approaching from. Jamie 'Gatecrasher' Alon emerged from below. He was a twenty-six-year-old black guy, six feet tall, wearing one of our optical camouflage suits. The invisibility was offline now, revealing the real texture of the meta-material. The fabric looked and felt like shiny foil, with light white lines of micro-circuitry etched into the surface, and had been tailored into a set of overalls designed to cover almost the entire body. It even had a hood and zip-up mask to cover the face, leaving only a pair of silts for his eyes to peer out from. He gave me a pissed off stare and began muttering to himself as he unzipped the mask, revealing his robust, well defined but bearded jaw and cheekbones and dark eyes fixated on me with general disdain; you could practically smell his nerves.

"Oh look, it's the pizza guy!" Raj joked, forcing himself to smile, wrinkling the tattoo on his cheek, through the residual pain as he looked up from the mess of wires exposed from the inside of our robot's chest. "Should we give him a tip?"

"Shove it up your ass, Raj," Jamie snapped back at him, pulling off the hood, revealing a single scar across his forehead from his more street-wise days.

"Well… now you're getting a bad review on *Yelp*," Raj chuckled, turning back with a cheeky grin.

"Safe trip?" I asked him respectfully, simultaneously bracing myself for the argument to come.

"Ha!" he bellowed back bitterly at me. "About as safe as you can be while playing hide and seek with police drones."

He gave everyone shit whenever it was his time to step out of the safe house. He gave out a long, exhausted breath and dumped his backpack with a thud onto the floor.

I almost felt sorry for him. The poor bastard had delusions of persecution wherever he went. Three years in the Prison Matrix will do that to you. I didn't even want to think about what my dad was going to be like when he got out.

"I really don't see why it had to be me," he growled, turning to me with his hands on his hips.

"It's a fucking rota, Jamie, you know the rules."

"I'm on parole, goddamn it! They catch me with a rucksack full of stolen goods…"

"Fine. Next time feel free to pop to *Tesco*," I shrugged dismissively, knowing that wasn't a viable option.

His expression grew deadly serious, making himself as large as possible like a frightened animal in an angry posture.

"You all think this is fucking funny?"

"No, we think *you're* funny Gatecrasher," Raj grinned back, trying to push Jamie's buttons.

I threw a glare at Raj to stop him from provoking.

"I'm just sayin', there has gotta be a better way of getting our shit delivered," Jamie glowered at me, not ready to concede defeat just yet.

I scoffed, shaking my head and rubbing my eyes. We'd used the OpenSource Soul to run simulations of our best options for our logistics. If yottaflop-range AIs couldn't calculate a safer method of getting from A to B, then he sure as hell couldn't.

"Lemme know how you get on with that," I grumbled back. "Just get the cartridges in the printer already."

He angrily diverted his gaze away from me, swearing under his breath as he scooped up the rucksack again and began dragging it towards the kitchen.

Even looking at him was starting to piss me off now. Digital forgery was his speciality. It was the only reason I put up with him. Regardless of how I felt about him, we were gonna need his skills to plan this trip to the convention centre.

"You know it couldn't hurt to be more diplomatic with the others," Poe told me, his avatar appearing with an apprehensive look.

"Do I look like the diplomatic type to you?" I tutted at him, getting a glimpse of my rebellious outfit in the mirror.

I saw his cat lips moving to suggest something but was interrupted by a popup on my display.

<<FireSaint has checked in at secondary safe house>>

I turned back to the holo-table. A 3D map of the city shone out from the projector, highlighting the location in Southall. Smokey and the Wind Riders must've dropped him off already.

"Thank fuck for that," I breathed.

"Smokey pulled through," Kasira added. "Makes a nice change to work with other professionals."

"So, what now?" Raj shrugged, scratching his tattoo. "Just wait for the decryption program to finish running?"

"I ain't waiting for shit," I scoffed at him, preparing my virtual browser. "I want all of you online asap and looking for clues to help. If you haven't already, get your VPAs to search for any contacts who have tried cracking it before."

"You're the boss!" Raj called back with a half-hearted salute, and quietly added, "Apparently..."

Damn right, I was the boss. The others weren't like me. They'd all come from different walks of life. Most of them pushed this way by something or rather. Not me. The thing that happened to me... it was just an awakening. This was the life I had chosen. This was my calling. I was here because Arthur Wells was wrong. There was a better way of doing things than fucking people over to get what you want. That's what I was fighting for.

I could feel it in my bones, clenching my gloved fingers tighter together in anticipation, licking my piercing. The Project Selection files were big. This was gonna be my Magnum Opus, my Wikileaks moment, and I would be damned if anyone was going to get in my way.

CHAPTER 7

Mother Mind Profile 2446-7128-5978-2501:

First Name: Arthur
Surname: Wells
Status: Living
Nationality: British
Occupation(s):

- Private Investigator
    - Status: Self-employed
    - Organisation: Arthur Wells & Associates

Known Aliases:

- IronRoot

Live Surveillance:

- Status: *Partially Available*
- Date: 06/10/2045
- Current Location: Orion Block Apartment Complex, Chiswick, West London
- Local Time: 08:55 GMT

<<Welcome to RE:Call!>

<<Memory playback in progress>>

<<File loaded: 9786-8130-2931-14032043>>

<<Date: 14/03/2043>>

<<Location: Government Communication Headquarters, Cheltenham>>

<<Local Time: 09:13 GMT>>

"Ughh…" I groaned as I buried my pounding head into the surface of my desk. This hangover was bloody killing me. The constant reminders from my bio-monitor sensors weren't helping either, the telepathic bleeping inside my head just refused to stop.

<<Warning!>>

<<Hydration levels low!>>
<<Please consume water immediately!>>

"Oh, my god, *shut UP!"* I telepathically yelled at the software.

"Sorry," Liz apologised in a window. "I'll mark the notification as 'do not remind.'"

I gave a rumble in response while massaging my temples. I hadn't been expecting to get as drunk as I had, but my sister had insisted on coming down to visit my new apartment in Cheltenham. Dad had wanted to come too, but I told him to fuck himself. Juliet was alright, but getting wasted was a natural coping mechanism… I just hadn't thought I'd get called into the office so early.

"Liz… you told me you'd activated focus mode," I snapped at her, rubbing the skin around my neural lace headset rapidly, expecting it to suddenly kick in. "Are you sure it's working?"

"Running at full capacity, Arthur," she reassured me. "But dehydration causes restrictions in blood flow to the brain, preventing-"

"So, order me some goddamn water already!" I interrupted, growling angrily enough to cause offence to any real person.

"Doing it now," she replied politely, dutifully followed her programming.

I bit my lip guiltily, wondering if I'd crossed some sort of line… even if she was an AI. "Sorry, I'm not having a great morning."

"Not a problem," she nodded with a reassuring smile. "If you like, I can start reminding you to not go drinking on a work night?"

"You can try," I laughed back. "Still, there was some scientific value to the night."

Liz's avatar raised an eyebrow; the code around her turning to red as her personality matrix struggled to process the statement. "Scientific value?"

"Now we know for a fact that Intellifabric is resistant to vomit stains."

Liz processed the humour quickly and gave me her best electronic laugh, prompting me to promptly mute her.

I took another long breath of preparation and engaged the tinting function on my new Hawksight bionic eyes. The dark sunglasses-like veil descended over the electrochromatic lens. It felt like a God-send. It wasn't like I could wear shades to work. That function alone made them a worthwhile investment. Bought them a few months ago for just eighty-five quid. The surgery had a recovery time of fewer than twenty-four hours. Money well spent.

I raised my head, taking a massive breath of the freshened air, dreading the glare from the three holographic screens projecting from the smooth semi-circular desk, which encompassed my swivelling office chair. The buzz of the office chatter around me might as well have been a rock concert for all the pounding in my head. The only solace was the smell of coffee wafting around the room.

Dozens of desks like mine had been arranged in concentric circles, radiating out from a central glass pillar. It was projecting a globe overlaid with a vast, sprawling graphical net, representing the global telecommunications grid, annotated with the level of access Mother Mind had into each data centre or relay exchange.

I was surrounded by the spasmodic symphony of man and machine, working in unison, policing the world. Information warfare specialists and data analysts hunched over their consoles, jacked into cyberspace, while drones delivered them food and drinks. As cool as it sounded, today was one of the days I wished I had taken another line of work. Working from home was the norm, but this was not an option in a job with access to classified material.

I found my eyes wandering to the walls, the screen surface projecting a more serene environment; a 360-video scan of the Amazon rainforest, or what it used to be like anyway. A vibrant projection of the ecosystem with lush green overhanging vines, buzzing with birdsong and animal calls.

I squinted at the central holographic pillar, and the camera eyes zoomed in. The most extensive floating data window was the profile we had composed of Rakim Hazami, the current commander of ISIS.

His eyes burned deep within his skull, like embers in a fireplace. The rest of his face was buried underneath his unkempt black beard and turban. What you could see of his dark skin was old and wrinkled, but that hadn't quelled his motivation one bit. For many people, he was a holy warrior. For others, a symbol of vengeance. But I saw him as most people saw him; the face of evil.

I knew his records backwards. The attacks he'd ordered included a string of hacks on police infrastructure accompanied with mass shootings, the release of a cancer virus in Mumbai, and even a mini-nuke suicide bombing in Jerusalem. I don't care what you have to say about his historical justification for their actions, there's no excusing that. My mother died of radiation poisoning before I was old enough to know her. I couldn't help but feel an undeniable sense of cathartic satisfaction when I got results.

I kept an old Post-it note attached to the pin-board on the left-hand side of my desk. I kept a tally on it, scribbled with an ink pen. Twenty-nine. The number of successful hits on high-profile terrorists resulting from intelligence I had gathered. I kept it there like a medal of honour. Probably my favourite perk of the job. Almost made up for not being in bed right now.

<<Director Langley has entered the room>>

<<Scheduled meeting is about to commence>>

<<Please take your seat>>

People around the room froze on the spot as the notification flashed up on their displays, sending anyone who wasn't already at their desks scuttling back in a flurry of footsteps, bolt upright with their eyes fixated on the entrance. I concentrated as best I could and followed suit.

The automatic doors slid open. Kirk Langley, director of GCHQ's counter-terrorism division, strode through. He was a hulk of a man, the result of massive gene-therapy. He'd chosen to keep his baldness as it had a way of demanding respect as if the thick muscles bulging unnaturally underneath his blue shirt weren't enough. Hard to believe that he was just as physically lazy as any of us. The days of the morbidly obese IT technician were a thing of the past. His neural lace was an older semi-implantable model that had been gradually upgraded over the years, with six plastic dermatrodes grafted onto the outside of the skull, the skin around them starting to grow around, casing like moss.

"All right people!" Kirk's rumbling voice boomed, magnified by the microphone built into the collar of his shirt and booming from the speakers embedded in the walls. "So, let's all skip the whining about why you're here so early, and just cut to the chase."

I leaned back in my chair, watching as he paced towards the central column and telepathically engaged the presentation he had prepared for 'Project Sandstorm'.

He loaded up pictures of the insignia of the United States Air Force and the logo of Global Arms Inc.

The graphical globe enlarged, the image shifting to satellite footage as it zoomed in on the desert on the outskirts of Damascus. The golden sand littered with the ruins of war, gleaming in the scorching heat. The heart of Islamic State territory.

"Some of you have been following Operation Sandstorm over the last month," Kirk gestured to the projections behind him as he telepathically controlled the presentation. A series of schematics appeared behind him, the designs for six different models of combat robots.

"As you know, Islamic State fighters are well equipped with anti-drone technology. Missiles and jamming cannons are commonly deployed. Operation Sandstorm was a field test for six prototype models, designed to withstand such weaponry. Their prime directive: seek and destroy. Designed for long-range, long-term reconnaissance, followed by decisive tactical strikes. The trial was due to come to an end next week, and everything was going according to plan until six hours ago."

The schematics of the robots disappeared from the projector, replaced with an agent profile from the NSA database. The photograph at the top of the document was that of a standard nerd, complete with awkwardly cut hair, think rimmed vid-glasses, pocket protector, and dorky smile. He was all skin and bones, sticking out awkwardly. At a glance, you wouldn't have believed that belonged to one of the few spy agencies in the world with more power than us.

"Meet the American you, Michael Ross. Mike here was assigned to act as a Three Laws AI moderator, working out of the US embassy in Damascus. Like all of us, his login credentials to the NATO military network were bound to his NeuroKey. After all, it's the most secure user verification technology, right?" His face suddenly grew more intense, his voice slow and methodical. "That's what we thought anyway."

That sent murmurs rippling around the room. David and I exchanged puzzled glances of intrigue from across the room.

Scanning the user's neural architecture had become the gold standard for user verification, even more, secure than DNA (which could be stolen or cloned). Synaptic patterns were much harder to get. You couldn't force the user to log in under duress either, which would result in a raising of beta wave levels, interfering with the scan. If there really was a flaw in the system, it could be a game-changer for those in this business.

A cursor whirled across the GPS map to a few miles north of the city where the satellite camera zoomed in.

"Twenty hours ago, Mike was kidnapped from the Four Seasons hotel by IS operatives, and taken to a safe house outside the city. The operatives were very thorough, all tracking devices on his body were left behind at the hotel. Took the Yanks a good nine hours to get his scent. At 02:14 hours local time, a Delta Force team was sent in to rescue him."

He telepathically gave the command to bring the presentation up on our personal holo-screens. A pulsing red icon representing the location of one of the US Air Force's special forces units appeared on the region's map.

On the recording, the camera zoomed in more and revealed the location of each individual soldier, drawing closer to a dilapidated farmhouse, built from crumbling sandstone bricks and a shattered wooden roof. Four red dots moved across the screen as the soldiers edged stealthily towards the building.

The team had brought a Spearhead-10 tactical infiltration robot with them. The schematic appeared below the map, showing a metallic crab with a dome-shaped head, sensors built in for 360-

degree vision, equipped with a small machine gun turret as mounted on its underbelly. Its four hook-like legs were rounded, letting it roll up into a ball for faster travel. All-in-all, it looked like a formidable little fighting machine.

The holo-pillar loaded up footage captured by the robot. The recording was grainy, the audio crackling at first, but cleared up after a second. The camera view was very close to the ground, capturing shots of the hook-feet tiptoeing up a flight of wooden steps, making a soft thud with each step. A notification appeared on the robot's HUD:

<<Mission Update: Assault team moving into position>>

A sound wave analysing program loaded onto the bottom of the screen. The robot's directional microphone picked up low, rumbling voices speaking in Arabic at the top of the stairs. The translation software activated and began placing subtitles along the bottom of the video.

"Is it working?"

"I think so… yes. It's in God's hand now."

<<Alpha in position>>

The bot reached the top of the stairs and noticed a door left ajar a tiny crack. It crept towards the gap and peered through, extending its camera out via an articulated plastic eye-stalk letting it peer through and saw two men in combat gear, huddled over a desk cluttered with computer equipment. The camera panned left and saw another terrorist sprawled on the couch opposite the desk, assault rifle resting on his lap. Another door stood at the other end of the sofa. Blueprints of the building indicated that there was a bathroom beyond it. The bot's sensors detected a fourth terrorist behind the door and picked up the sound of him taking a dump.

One by one, graphical annotations on the HUD appeared as the remote weapons operator manually identified each of them as 'enemy combatants', complying with the three laws. There was a boarded window adjacent to the machine. The terrorists had picked this building with great care. The lack of line of sight, stopping the sniper team on the rooftop of the nearby barn house from looking in, but with the bot's targeting data they couldn't hide, and the walls would not protect them from the high-velocity smart-rounds.

<<Bravo in position>>

A vast web of wires spewed out over the side of the desk, dangling across the floor towards an old bookshelf filled with more machinery. It scanned the devices and identified them one by one. Ventilation, dialysis, external pacemaker: life support systems.

The camera panned to the left, and a surgical robot came into view with a giant, articulated, motorised arm. It had two devices attached to the end, a laser scalpel and a claytronic toolset to become forceps. A pair of ghostly shadows moved just beyond the boarded window.

<<Charlie in position>>

The robot detected a pair of E-IDs beyond the window to the left of the desk, the camera moved to follow. The blinds were down, but you could see the distortions in the light through the gaps; the only visible sign of the cloaked soldier perched on the outside walls like spiders. They were using gecko pads, super-strong miniature suction cups on the hands and feet, allowing the wearer to climb any surface with ease. They were waiting on standby, ready to storm the room at a moment's notice.

<<All units in position>>

<<Awaiting further instructions>>

<<Standing by>>

It was game time. The whole strike force assembled. The

commanding officer ordered the unit to hold back to gather more intel, appearing as lines of code in the bottom left-hand corner.

"This plan has never felt right," said one of the terrorists hunched over a terminal, his arms folded and shaking disapprovingly. "I can't believe this is what he wants."

"If we must tame American evil to win the war, so be it."

"This… this is an abomination, and you know it!"

"There's only one who can judge that. Have faith."

Their faith wasn't going to save them now. The order came down:

<<Updated received>>

<<Mission Go>>

<<Combat mode engaged>>

The HUD turned red, and the laser targeting system activated. A targeting reticule appeared at the centre of the screen and swivelled across to take aim at the kneecaps of the two sitting at the desk.

<<Weapons free>>

RAT-AT-AT-AT-AT-AT!

We watched silently in awe at the flawless execution of the raid. The bot took down the two by the computer with lethal precision, leaving them flopping onto the desk like fish, their cries drowned out by gunfire.

The one on the sofa was far too slow to react. Before he even had time to grab his gun, the sniper team opened fire. Two long-range shots exploded through the wooden walls sending splinters flying. The bullets landed forcefully and ripped two gigantic holes through his lungs. The body jerked, and blood sprayed all over the sofa.

The guy in the toilet was last. He came charging through the door with a war cry, brandishing his rifle, ready for his last stand, and fired at the only enemy he saw, the robot by the door. The bot's AI analysed the ricochet of the bullets against the floor tiles, marking them as armour-piercing smart rounds, and pulled back to avoid the threat.

The two soldiers hanging on the outside of the building swung in invisibly and landed with a mighty crash of wood and glass. The last terrorist sprayed his rifle wildly into the air trying to hit the optical distortions, reducing the surgical robot to scrap and raining plaster across the room from the wall. The special forces' trained men moved with the speed of ninjas, only becoming visible once they returned fire with their smart sub-machine guns. They delivered a burst of lethal shots in the chest again. Blood exploded from their cavities, and they all slumped on the floor, face down.

The guns fell silent.

Only the moans of agony from the two by the desk permeated the silence. They writhed on the floor clutching the wounds. One of them tried reaching for his rifle, only to have his elbow stomped on with a sickening crack.

"Targets neutralised," the Commanding Officer announced telepathically, the HUD identifying him as Sergeant William Laker.

The camera panned around, blood splatter smeared the room like an obscene work of art.

But that was nothing compared to the grotesque sight waiting on the far side of the room.

"Ho-ly *shit*," Laker breathed.

The term 'brain in a jar' had been used in a philosophical sense for hundreds of years. Never thought I'd see a real one. But there it was. A fully formed human brain in glass vat, filled with amniotic fluid. A tangle of wires and tubes anchored the grey matter to the bottom of the jar, supplying it with artificial blood and carrying signals to the computer.

There were gasps of disgust and disbelief scattered from each desk, at least from the newbies anyway. I had to laugh at how green they were. Ultimately, we were another branch of the military, we had all dealt with footage like this before.

"Well… you get the picture," Kirk continued in a sobering tone, telepathically ending the video and sending the data window shrinking back into the base of the holographic pillar.

"These bastards have always had a thing for beheading," he continued, composing himself. "I suppose brain hijacking was the next logical step up. Agent Ross was kept on life support, stimulated with ECT until they found the right brainwave pattern for his NeuroKey to gain access to the network. It took ten minutes for the admin team to detect the breach. Far too long."

A virtual file browser loaded up, a sparse jumble of data whirling around the core of the server under examination and a collection of error messages.

"The script generated by the ICE Breaker self-erased after installation and completion of the subroutines. If they left any digital fingerprints, the NSA hasn't found them. As a result, we don't even know what they were up to once they were inside the network. And the terminal we saw in the farmhouse wiped its memory drives when the vital signs of the terrorist's flat-lined.

"Who knows what they were up to… stealing state secrets? Upload a domination virus? Your guess is as good as mine," he grinned, exposing his over-polished teeth, pivoting slowly across the room with eyes that shone like torches, chest swelling with pride. "But I don't pay you all for guesswork."

That got a couple of chuckles around the room. He could be a bit of a slave driver, but he cared about his people. Probably not the worst boss I'd ever had.

"Now you all know that the Yanks think they're better than us, but guess what? We were here first! GCHQ has been around for over a hundred years. We were busting Nazi encryption when they were just a twinkle in Harry Truman's eyes!"

A couple of our more enthusiastic members cheered at that. I rolled my eyes. Bloody ass-licks.

"So, let's prove them wrong. That's the job! All the companies and agencies involved have granted full access to their systems. Get to work, people!"

Nods and calls of agreement rang out and the bleeping and flashing from the desks resumed, diving into the coalition server to begin searching for the malicious code the terrorists had introduced.

I leaned forward, resting my head on my fist, and looked over the summary of the briefing, scratching my chin-beard ponderously. Kidnapping an intelligence agent must've taken weeks or even months of planning. The typical reason for wanting to hack the military network was to steal classified data, but Ross was an AI moderator, not an intelligence officer…

<<External protocol request accepted>>

<<Pausing memory playback>>

The world around me froze, and a pause icon appeared in the bottom left-hand corner of my field of vision. People around me stood and sat in awkward positions, mouths half open through sentences, waterfalls of tea and coffee dripping out of cups floating in the air, reflections solidifying across faces like golden ice.

"Sorry to disturb, Arthur," Liz's soothing electronic voice came from the present day to invade the past. "But it's almost time."

The interruption of the memory playback was disorientating, like being roused from a dream but not fully waking up.

"Wha…?" my bodiless telepathic voice mumbled.

I strained to remember what she was talking about…

Client meeting at nine thirty. Dammit!

"Shit. How long do I have?"

"Mister Duckett should be logging on within the next five minutes. I'll save your position on the video playback for you to return to later."

I gave a loud, mental grumble. I hated stopping halfway through movies, let alone my own memory playback.

<<Restoring full immersion virtual-reality environment>>

Liz terminated the program and the scene from the past faded away into a blurry haze. The bright outline of spiralling logical lattices stretched out before me and rapidly loaded their textures. Lines of code turned to pixels. Pixels into wireframe. Wireframe into polygons. Polygons into a new world.

My consciousness returned to the confines of my virtual avatar, my head swimming from the dizzying sensation of the consciousness shift. Neurons were firing in my head like party crackers as my mind connected the dots. The flashback had added in yet another missing chunk of my life.

For a moment, I wondered if I was still feeling the residual sensation of the hangover from the memory file.

Even though the signals from the neural lace were telling me that this was the real world, there was something instinctive telling me that there was something wrong. Not quite reality. Something primal inside my savannah-desert brain telling me that this was still a dream.

I tried to focus on the here and now. My avatar was wearing a white shirt, grey trousers with suspenders, sat in a swivelling chair in front of a broad oak chair, reminiscent of last century's fashion. A 'genuine' leather trench coat rested behind me, like the one I wore in the real world. I even had a hat resting on a coat hanger by the door. The film-noir branding style was even more important online than it was in the real world. This was the avatar I used for meetings with clients. At a glance, you might've thought you were in a 'Chinatown' simulation and would expect Jack Nicholson himself to come walking through the door. I tended to spend as much time here as possible when on the clock but not working in the field. Sure as hell beat my crappy living pod.

The telephone and intercom were built from copper in an art-deco style, the smell of oak and old tobacco permeating the furniture. A brass fan hanging from the ceiling rotating rapidly, Venusian blinds draped over the sached windows, looking across onto 1940s Los Angeles – complete with the Hollywood sign gleaming in the distance. Classic cars like the *Chrysler Windsor Highlander* and the *Buike Roadmaster* rolling by. The designs, once the pinnacle of technology, were now out of date by a century, but it was all about style. I picked up a cigarette from a glass ashtray and the silver lighter next to it and lit up, treating myself to the sickly tar of simulated tobacco.

The chair creaked as I leaned back and continued puffing away, my eyes fixed on the opened glass panel door, the words 'Arthur Wells: Private Investigator' stencilled into it. There was a reception area on the other side that all customers would load into, with Liz at the front desk. I'd programmed her to go through an animation cycle of pretending to look over case files, pouring coffee and smoking from her own cigarette. All just for show.

She swivelled around in her seat and craned her neck through the door, looking over the brass rims of her spectacles with an inquisitive smile.

"Happy viewing?" she asked curiously.

"Pretty cool," I nodded with mild happiness. "Nice to know I was actually making a difference out there…"

"But…?"

"Well, it would still be nice to be receiving the memories in the right order!" I groaned.

I bitterly looked over the date that was specified on the memories, stating they had taken place between the 16th to the 20th of March, 2043. 275 gigabytes. Four days' worth of memories costing me just over £41, but that was from nearly five full years since the last download I had received.

"Five years!" I complained to Liz, clenching my fist. "Five years still missing! What the fuck is that about?"

Watching TV shows in the wrong order was bad enough. Regaining my own memories with gaps missing was torture. No relief for my sleepless nights now!

"Maybe the older files have been moved into a more secure archive?" Liz suggested with an unconvincing shrug.

"That doesn't sound likely."

"I suppose not," she shrugged. "I could message Dart through the app to put in a complaint."

"You do that. I'm paying through the nose for this, I was expecting some halfway decent customer service."

"It's not a *Netflix* subscription."

I grumbled, staring at the data on my display grudgingly, my head resting on my fist. The better part of me told me that I should wait to avoid any confusion later… but the temptation to do it now was starting to get the better of me.

"At this rate, how long would it take to restore the full missing seven years?" I asked curiously, dreading the answer.

"11 months, 1 week, 2 days."

"Slow and steady wins the race." I sighed but nodded in agreement with her. The next year was gonna be a drag. I eyed over the metadata on file again… that's when the dates on the latest download caught my attention.

"What was the date of my 'accident'?" I asked, using my fingers to make inverted commas. I found myself habitually scratching my shoulder, where the tender flesh around the nerve connections to my prosthetics would've been in the real world.

"April 14th, 2043," Liz replied.

"Hmm… interesting," I said, stroking my chin beard curiously, pondering how close the dates were together, but not for long.

<<Charlie Duckett is logging in>>

A whirl of brilliant pixel light glittered from behind the door just as the notification appeared on my display, a tell-tale sign of an avatar loading into the virtual world.

"Here we go," I groaned reluctantly.

Liz shut the door and spun back round to face the reception area and greet him, the sound of low rumbling conversation soon coming through the door frame. She politely introduced herself, giving me the time I needed to prepare.

I took a long-winded virtual breath and stood up, stretching out my simulated muscles to compose myself. I grabbed my coat off the back of my chair and dumped it on the hanger, and engaged focus mode on my neural lace. My mind snapped to attention, and I straightened myself out before sitting down, my arms out wide in a friendly, welcoming and yet professional manner, and mentally braced myself for the part of the job I hate the most.

"All right," I breathed finally and telepathically asked Liz to send him in.

The antiquated brass door handle rattled as it twisted, and Charlie Duckett stepped through. He'd customised his avatar for maximum sex appeal, reminiscent of the late 20th-century actor Brad Pitt in his prime. The avatar was dressed to impress, with a suit that screamed wealth. Or would've done if it wasn't a digital illusion – typical compensation. I'd seen his E-ID photo; in reality, he was a fat, balding, sweaty mess.

"Mister Duckett!" I said plainly but politely, offering out a handshake from across the desk.

"Uh… hello," he answered in a soft, fragile tone, barely above a whisper, practically quivering with anxiety.

I rolled my tongue with subtle frustration, it was going to be one of *those* meetings. Small talk was expected but probably wouldn't do all that much to actually make it go any more smoothly.

"Nice to actually meet you in person. E-mails are so formal, don't you think?" I said, trying to break the ice.

He nodded timidly in response, avoiding eye contact. Even after paying me the down payment, he apparently wasn't sure if he actually wanted to hear the results of my investigation. Most of the people that came to me already knew what their partners were up to, desperately hoping for me to prove them wrong somehow. If you wanted a comforting lie, you came to the wrong place.

They were probably going to get divorced now, and all I had to do was pretend to give a shit.

"It's a shame it had to be under these circumstances," I began gently.

He gave a loud sniff, his voice choking, his eyes turning wet and red, his face screwing up in anguish.

"Oh God…"

Here come the waterworks.

I gave him all the sympathy I could muster and telepathically transferred the case files, comprised mostly of chat room logs and drone photos. The naked truth.

He viewed them on his HUD, and horror spread across his face as the reality dawned on him. He broke into loud wails and buried his face as the tears began to flow.

"I loved her! I gave her everything… *everything!*" He pounded his fist against the oak desk, the force of the impact shaking things like a mini-quake.

"Hey, easy mate!" I blurted out, sounding more annoyed than I should have.

His wails grew louder as he rocked back and forth uncontrollably in the chair, pulling his hair. Not content with sitting anymore, he suddenly stood, turned and pressed his face into the window, rattling the blinds.

"Charlie, you can't eat the Venusian blinds, I just had them installed," I sighed jokingly, and managed to get a shaky laugh through the wails.

I always came prepared for this and reached under the desk to pull out two glasses and a bottle of *Jack Daniels.*

"What can I say, Charlie boy?" I asked, trying to sympathise as I poured out the virtual booze. "You were right. You were right. You were right."

Repeating the phrase seemed to have a calming effect on him. He turned away from the blinds, and slumped his back against them, taking sharp, jerky breaths, cupping his mouth as he did. I grabbed an ice bucket under the desk, using a pair of metal tongs to grab the cubes and drop a couple into each glass with a soft clink as I poured.

"If it makes you feel any better, I've seen this a million times before. A couple thinks they're perfect for each other, then the results of a DNA scan come back and apparently, you're not good enough anymore. Bloody women, eh? Here, down the hatch."

I handed him the glass.

"Cheers," he sniffed.

The two of us clinked the glasses and took the shot, gasping as the harsh liquid stung my throat. Charlie was letting out awkward hiccups in the wake of his emotional breakdown. He pressed his face against the wallpaper, barely able to stand, sipping down the whiskey with his violently shaking hands.

This probably would have inspired compassion in most people but, after doing this for a year, it was just another day in the office. This was usually the part when they start giving me their life stories.

"Five years. Five years I wasted on that woman!" he forced out, his mouth moving at odd angles.

Bingo.

I'd have to sit through before I could finally ask about my bill. I may not have had all my memory back yet, but knew enough to know I *definitely* preferred that job.

"They have that effect on you, mate," I continued, nodding, conversationally waving my glass and giving the neurocommand to disable focus mode, allowing the simulated effect of the alcohol to run its program.

I chatted away, but without focus mode I found myself looking for distractions, scrolling through my news feed and reading some stupid human-interest story about a dog that had broken into the cloned Mammoth paddock at London Zoo, including links to videos that onlookers had recorded from their eyewear. The comments section had been filled with LOLs and smiley faces. I wanted to see what was so funny but didn't want to start sniggering in front of the client.

"They're like cats, ya know? Sink their claws in and won't let go until they draw blood." A bit of casual misogyny went a long way in these situations.

"Yeah…" Charlie mumbled, his mouth full as he took another swig.

His glass ran dry, and I poured him another one, something I wouldn't have done if it was the real deal, but my bottle had been programmed to give unlimited refills.

"God, I remember the first time I saw her…" he breathed, shaking his head and staring longingly at the ceiling. It wasn't a neural lace setting, but I like to call this 'smile and nod' mode. "I was doing the rounds of the Hinkley C reactor. Clunky, bloody thing. It was obsolete even when it was new… She was the PR officer for the plant. I bumped into her heading to the office to write up my report. She smiled at me, but I thought there was no way in hell I would have a shot with a girl like that. I just carried on… thinking that I was going to die of radiation sickness before I met anyone. I was there for hours, burying myself in work like I always did… my way of hiding pain. Then out of the blue, she just brought me a sandwich. She didn't have to. Hell, I didn't even think she would remember me… but the napkin had her email on it."

He laughed, trying to hide another sob. "I mean, what are the chances of that?"

"Oh?" I answered loudly, sounding startled, quickly minimising the video window on my vision, that I promised myself I wouldn't watch, struggling to hold back the laughter. "One in a million."

Damn, those mammoths can run!

"I really thought that this was the big one. The girl who could see past the… imperfections. She liked me for who I was… she didn't care that I was fat. But you get one goddamn test… find out that you have the obesity genes and…" He buried his face, his fingernails digging into the skin, then slammed the wall with his fists. "Who the fuck can afford the alteration therapy?!"

I gave him a series of slow sympathetic nods, giving the occasional 'mmmm' sound to show I was listening, despite the fact I was already scrolling through the list of remixed versions of the video with different soundtracks.

"Bloody fucking biotech… If I knew it was going to come down to money…" His voice croaked again. "She could at least have had the decency to end it first!"

He carried on with his angry ranting, his words starting to slur, beginning to feel the simulated effects of the *JD*. I just had to let him get this out of his system so I could gently raise the issue of my £2,000 bill.

"All right buddy, take it easy," I said, patting him softly on the back. "These things happen, it's just-"

I didn't finish the sentence. I couldn't with the bleeping inside that had interrupted me.

<<Urgent notification from Liz>>

I stopped in my tracks, my mouth hanging open stupidly in mid-air. It wasn't like her to interrupt. I'd adjusted Liz's settings to 'Do Not Disturb' during meetings like this unless it was *really* urgent. That didn't tell me if it good or bad news. I hesitated for a second.

"Uh… sorry mate," I said with an apologetic gesture with one hand and pointing to my head with the other, indicating I had a telepathic call coming. "I just need to take this."

"Oh… sure," he answered indifferently.

"Ta." I turned away from him and neuroclicked the answer icon.

"Liz, I'm with a fucking client!" I barked angrily at her over the telepathic link.

"I've got another customer waiting on the line," she explained hurriedly, wide-eyed and excited, a grin spreading almost to her spectacles. "She wants a meeting ASAP."

"So what? Tell 'em to wait like everybody else!"

She leaned in closer to me on the video window as if to whisper in my ear. "It's Gabrielle Phillips."

…What?!

I was instantly stunned. My jaw dropped. I thought the virtual simulation had frozen, but it was just my heart. I didn't believe it and didn't know what to do if it was true.

"Gabrielle Phillips? As in *Virtualife's* Gabriclle Phillips?"

Liz nodded excitedly and brought up *Google* image search results of her holographic avatar in her business blouse and skirt, with her tied brunette hair. I knew who she was, hell it'd be hard not to know. One of the first Post-Turing AIs with a personality matrix, Kenji Awasaki's virtual personal assistant… and his lover to boot.

It was common practice now for large businesses to send AIs to represent their interests in meetings. Hell, you could even talk with an interactive avatar of Gabrielle via Virtualife's website and Cloudland hangout as part of their 'transparency policy'. Why talk to some customer service agent when you could speak to the personal assistant of the CEO? But it still didn't explain why she was coming to see *me.*

"You sure it's her?" I checked.

"She's connected via a proxy server, but her credentials check out as authentic."

"Bloody 'ell! What's she doing *here*?"

It boggled my mind. Not only was Gabrielle programmed to manage billions of dollars' worth of assets, her company was instrumental in the development of the Mother Mind system. They had to be the only organisation in the country who had access to more data than the government itself. Hell, people said Gabrielle *really was* Mother Mind, whispering in the ear of every MP. If they were sending her instead of some low-level representative, it meant she was here because of something the *board of directors* had a vested interest in. Between that and the entire private military subsidiaries they owned, I seriously couldn't see what they were on the lookout for a rookie PI. Liz's avatar folded her arms and pondered the possibilities.

"She says having someone outside of the company offers them certain advantages. I don't have the specifics, she says she'll only tell you the job in person."

"Right… well, that's… interesting," I said slowly, with nervous intrigue.

"She said she would've rather have come anonymously," Liz added unnervingly.

I raised an eyebrow. "Hiring a PI without ID is illegal," I added slowly.

"I think she knows that, Arthur."

I ran my fingers across my mouth… Whatever she was here for, it must've been dodgy.

I need the money… but it won't do me any good in jail…

I was already breaking the law. Getting involved in a corporate espionage job might be the last straw. "I don't want to be at the centre of a '*News of the World*' scandal."

"It can't hurt to hear her out." Liz shrugged.

I bit my lip hesitantly. I knew she was right. She was almost always was.

Screw it…

"All right," I replied cautiously. "Give me a minute to get rid of this guy."

"Best behaviour now!" Liz added wearily, sounding like a patronising mother.

"I have manners!"

"Of sorts," she replied with a wink. I had to hold back my smile of amusement.

"You're getting too smart for your own good, Liz."

I minimised her window and cleared my throat, putting my glass down on the desk again and re-enabling focus mode. I turned to Charlie once more as he helped himself to more whiskey. I quickly offered him my hand back.

"Sorry about that, Charlie boy, business is business," I said with a composed smile.

"Oh… yes… of course," he sniffed. "So… uh…"

"Don't worry about the finances, mate," I said in a relaxed tone, holding up a reassuring hand. "I can see you're taking this hard, so I won't keep you any longer. I'll invoice you with the details, no rush."

He looked a bit bewildered, but that was probably just the drink.

"Huh… oh yeah, sure. I'll have it to you by Friday," he answered, taking my hand with one hand and wiping away tears with another.

Went as well as could be expected.

I strode over and carefully pulled his coat off the hanger.

"No worries mate. Take your time," I said, politely handing it over. "I know the stress you're under right now. Would you like my VPA to recommend some divorce lawyers?"

That probably wasn't the most tactful thing to say, but he gave a solemn nod in response. "Thanks… that'd be helpful."

I ushered him out the door as quickly as I could without being impolite. "Not a problem. Mind how ya go, eh?"

Once outside, his avatar de-rezzed, rapidly disintegrating back into a shower of polygons and faded away.

Good riddance.

I turned back around and started pacing the length of the wooden floorboards impatiently. My nerves began to rise, but the tingling sensation of the pulsing from my neural lace kept them in check.

I wasn't waiting long, and soon saw the rapid lights of a loading avatar flickering behind the glass plate, followed by the sound of Liz's greetings. Then another voice, like silk to the ear, familiar yet strange. Unnaturally polite.

She's here…

I wandered over to the blinds and peered through the gaps, gazing over the city.

"Having second thoughts?" Liz asked telepathically, appearing on my visual cortex.

"You could say that."

She opened up my bank account details, displaying my savings on a graph against my forecasted expenditures, the curve on it sloping firmly downwards.

"All right, all right…" I sighed reluctantly.

"Good," she grinned back. "Try not to embarrass yourself."

"Now when have I ever done that?"

"I have a record if you'd like to see it."

Yeah, I bet you do…

The thought had crossed my mind. And even worse ideas had occurred to me. Liz had access to all my records… and with Virtualife's Mother Mind access, those records could very quickly be in their hands. I encrypted my data and took all the reasonable precautions to keep them out of my systems… but GCHQ was upgrading all the time. No way to know for sure what she did and didn't have on me.

I tried to put it out of my mind and started to clean up, resetting the environmental settings back to the default appearance. I telepathically gave the command, and the booze and half-filled ashtray instantly teleported back under the desk in a puff of pixels.

I sat down again and anxiously cupped my hands together,

twiddling my thumbs as I turned focus mode up to its maximum setting, listening to Liz's conversation steadily moving along as I worked up the courage.

No point in putting it off.

"Send her in," I ordered over the comm-link. I listened to their chat coming to an end.

"Arthur is ready to see you now," Liz added gleefully, her voice muffled through the glass plate. "This way, please."

"Thank you," came the second calm, calculated voice. The pair of shadows loomed across the glass plate, a fist-raising to knock swiftly.

"Come in!" I called loudly, my confidence suddenly boosted by the focus mode.

Liz opened the door in person, giving me an encouraging wink as it swung open. Her other arm passed through, showing in our guest.

There was something in the back of my mind that kept wanting to say it couldn't be her... despite the 'E-ID verified' message that appeared on my HUD.

Her entire demeanour commanded authority. A harsh, sharp haircut, revealing her deceptively seductive face. The same blouse in the colour of Virtualife graphics. I smiled warmly at her, the intensity of the electricity radiating from the nanochips increased and kept any nervous twinges in check.

She beamed back at me, her programming attempting to feign friendliness, but her eyes scanning me...literally.

I sprung up, faster than I probably should've done, and shot my hand out in welcome.

"Miss Phillips! It's an honour!"

Despite her digital nature, I was going to have to roll out the red carpet for her. After all, she was most likely streaming this back to Virtualife's board of directors in real time.

"Gabrielle, please," she answered professionally with her perfectly synthesised voice, radiating the smell of fine perfume. "And thank you for meeting me on such short notice."

"Oh, of course! It's not every day I get a potential Fortune 500 client through the door!"

She strode across the room with a certain grace and took my hand in a ladylike manner.

"We've always been keen to support smaller businesses," she answered, sounding just like the interactive commercials she was featured in.

I kept my professional smile, despite knowing that was only a half-truth, *at best.* Virtualife had become infamous for financing potentially successful start-up businesses, letting them grow a decent size before buying them up… or just outright liquidating them.

"I know, I've been following the work of your charity. Inspiring stuff, really."

The 'Awasaki Foundation' was the name of his climate change relief not-for-profit organisation. Sending out airships and drones filled with care packages to those living in devastated countries and refugee camps around the world. They had probably saved millions of lives. The rumour was that Awasaki felt that was somehow his atonement for the creation of Mother Mind.

"Just trying to do our part," she smiled, nodding humbly.

I nodded, not really knowing what to say to that. The silence lingered for a moment, her eyes still analytically fixated on me, her expressions unnaturally even… it was starting to make me think she was hacking into my brain without me knowing.

"So!" I said brashly, clapping my hands together to move things swiftly on. "What can I do for you?"

"Simply put, we need you to find something for us," she admitted sullenly, her face drooping.

I sensed embarrassment from her. Far more convincing than the emotions Liz could display.

"Stolen goods," she explained plainly as she reached into the pocket of her blouse and pulled out a box of cigarettes and a silver lighter. "Do you mind if I smoke?"

An unusual request for a corporate VPA, but she was effectively human. And a potential VIP client; all the more reason to show her respect.

"No, no of course not!" I answered courteously, fumbling around under the desk to grab the ashtray once more. "And uh, what is it you need finding?"

She lit up one of her fags and let out a puff, smoke exhaling from her nostrils like a dragon, reminding me of any number of femme fatale movies.

"Four hundred exabytes of classified data."

I was lighting up my own cigarette when her words sent me spluttering uncontrollably. She glanced at me with an amused smile but never laughed as I composed myself and got my breathing back under control.

"Excuse me?" I checked with a stunned expression.

"Classified data," she repeated calmly. "A hacker breached one of our R&D servers and downloaded highly sensitive files. We were lucky that he was only able to capture the hashed version of the data. Completely encrypted, but with their cloud-based resources it's only a matter of time before the thieves are able to brute force it themselves."

Crap! Does she know about Dart?

I scratched the back of my neck, feeling uncomfortable with this, but focus mode kept the impulse at bay.

"I'm sure you'll understand that I'm not at liberty to tell you the *contents* of the files," she added.

"No, no, of course, that's perfectly understandable, and not that I'm not flattered that you think I'm capable of handling such an important task, but... don't you think this is something for the Ministry of Defence to handle?"

"If only it were that simple," she answered cryptically, her eyes like glaciers. "The files represent a significant investment on our part. Global Arms currently provides thirty-seven percent of Britain's defence and law-enforcement needs, giving us a majority of the market here. But raising this issue with the MOD would open up the recovery job to every private security contractor. The project represents an investment of billions. The culmination of years of research. We can't let that go to waste."

"You're worried about corporate espionage," I surmised.

"Every business in the world is worried about that, Mister Wells. You of all people should know that." She threw me a piercing glare, sending my heart racing here and in the real world.

How much did she know about me?

I nodded, with a calming drag from my cigarette.

"Is there something wrong?" she asked with a hint of concern.

"No, no… just, well… I'm surprised you considered me a candidate for this job. I'm pretty new to this business."

"I was more interested in your previous experience," she explained coyly.

I smiled, pretending not to be pissed off. My face had become as stiff as hers. "You've looked into me?"

"Company policy," she nodded with a diplomatic smile. "Nothing personal, you understand."

"Glad to hear it," I lied, rubbing my chin beard.

"I accessed your service record. GCHQ is one of our closest partners. The board was particularly impressed with your work on Operation Dragonslayer. At the end of all of this, there might even be a job waiting for you at Global Arms' Network Security department."

Bitch… even ***I*** *can't read my service record.*

"That's very flattering," I chuckled with feigned gratitude. "*But*, there's nothing quite like being your own boss."

"Couldn't agree more," she answered with a bitter smile.

I smiled and nodded curiously.

"So!" I roared, clapping my hands and trying to move things along. "Has any group claimed responsibility for the cyber-attack yet?"

"Not officially. But we pinged the originating IP address of the unauthorised log-in. The son of one our employees, Andrew Ilian, a.k.a. Shad0wCell, used his mother's terminal to get into our VPN."

Her words rang in my ears.

"Where have I heard that name before?" I wondered out loud. Of course, Liz was one step ahead of me and brought an article from the Telegraph to my display. The article described the details the police had released on the latest victim of the Jack-21 killer. Sure enough, it was our guy. Andrew Ilian. A seventeen-year-old with a lot of tattoos… and he'd been torn apart with a surgical laser.

It's official… something in those files is worth ***killing*** *for.*

"Bloody hell," I breathed in surprise. "Uh… excuse my language."

"It's quite all right. It was a shock to us too. Helen Ilian is one of our most valued employees. Despite what her son did, we've been taking care of her."

"Very generous of you."

"One bad decision of youth shouldn't wash out ten years of dedicated work. As I said, we take care of everyone who works for us… or with us."

Spoken like a real salesman.

"Well… it's good to hear. I've worked a couple murder cases, I'm sure I can be of-"

"Thank you," she interrupted, probably programmed to be insistent about this. "We have our own people at Global Arms leading the murder investigation. We're dealing with the data theft as a strictly separate issue as a courtesy to Mrs Ilian. Your job will be to find and *destroy* all unauthorised copies of the files before the contents surface online."

"I see…" I answered slowly. "Do you have data that I could use as a starting point?"

"Yes of course," she answered promptly and forwarded me a folder named 'Case files'.

"In any case, the Project Selection files had already been forwarded to his handlers and wiped from his memory banks."

I had a horrible feeling I knew where this could be going. "Spiritform?"

"They haven't officially taken responsibility yet, but yes," she said with an angry exhale.

I pursed my lips…

They're backtivists… they expose illegal activity… if I help them, I'll be complicit in a cover-up.

"You've had dealings with them before, haven't you?" she asked as if the question were nothing.

I was starting to feel utterly naked around her like those cold digital eyes were piercing into my soul. I shouldn't have been too surprised they knew about my past friendship with Denise…

"I was never actually a member."

"I'm aware of that. Nonetheless, you were in a relationship with one of their most prominent members. And we have reason to believe that both she and the data are still here in London. I'm not saying that Destiny is necessarily involved… but I wouldn't rule out the possibility either."

"So… you're saying that I might actually be-"

"Investigating your ex-girlfriend, yes." Her face grew more intense and leaned backwards expansively. "And to be clear, if you obtain evidence that implicates her, we will be pressing charges."

I bit my lip. The last time I saw Denise, she screamed at me saying she'd never forgive me for taking the job at GCHQ. For all, I knew I might have been investigating her while I was there too, and despite the fact, I already remembered how it all ended between us… and yet this still felt… not quite right.

"Is that acceptable to you?" Gabrielle asked inquisitively, eager to judge me on the answer.

I took a moment to formulate my answer, rolling my lips. "We all make our choices… and live with the consequences."

Her lips curled upwards ever so slightly. "I'm glad you feel that way."

I averted my gaze for a moment, wanting to move the conversation away from this.

"So… there's a time window before Spiritform go public with the files, and you need them found before then?"

"Have I come to the right place?" she asked hopefully.

I rolled my head from side to side as I thought about it.

"I'd be lying if I said I wasn't tempted," I responded cautiously. "But I'm sure you can appreciate I have some concerns. After all, Spiritform operates by making public scandals."

She folded her arms. "Shall we start talking numbers?"

"Well… my usual fee is three-fifty a day, plus expenses, plus a standard twenty percent bonus if I get results. But… my standard contract doesn't encompass protecting state secrets."

She nodded slowly, pretending to think, even though she would have processed her response in a matter of nanoseconds. Her eyes slid across the desk, noticing the old pad of paper and pen I'd left on the desk. I'd intended them to be just for decoration, but she picked up the pen and scribbled down a figure. I tried to get a glimpse, but she was shielding the view with her free arm.

"We'll have to iron out the details of the contract, but this is what we're prepared to pay you as a lump sum. We'll cover the expenses too of course," she began as she tore off the paper and slid it to me, face down.

I gingerly picked it up and flipped it over in my hand, and was immediately taken aback by the figure.

£52,000!?

That's more than what I make in a year!

My biggest concern from last night was just how I was going to keep up with the payments to Dart. With that kind of money, it would be a cinch! All my concerns about the nature of the files seemed to disappear in an instant.

"Well… that would do the trick!" I laughed hungrily, not sounding my most gracious. "We should uh… get to work on writing up the contract."

I gleefully sent the telepathic message, and Liz came striding into the room a second later looking just as enthusiastic. The two AIs exchanged their awkward mechanical pleasantries and pretended to discuss legal issues with each other. It was purely a courtesy for the sake of interacting with humans, as the results of their discussion would've been made within seconds of the two programs sharing a data link. Not that it meant much to me, most of the legal crap went over my head.

Within minutes the contract was generated, appearing as an official-looking document on my HUD. I didn't bother going through all the T&Cs, as Liz assured me it was all favourable. I was suddenly grateful I purchased that legal advice app for her. I submitted my NeuroKey and watched an image of my signature appear in the document on my HUD. Gabrielle seemed as stoic as ever as she sent her AI identifier on behalf of Virtualife.

I had done it! I was in the big leagues now.

We all stood up and shook hands and exchanged gratitude.

"Pleasure doing business with you!" I said heartily, feeling absolutely chuffed with myself. "You won't regret this!"

"I share your confidence, Mister Wells," she nodded with an expression that approximated gratitude. "This all seems to be in order. I'll be in touch."

We said our professional goodbyes, and I watched her log out, disappearing back into the jumble of pixelated data once more.

With her out of sight, I couldn't hold back the overwhelming excitement anymore. I exploded out of my seat, jumping off the ground and pumped my fists into the air.

CHAPTER 8

Mother Mind Profile 4372-6349-8752-9361:

First Name: Daniel
Surname: Haines
Status: Living
Nationality: British
Occupation(s):

- Detective Inspector
  - Status: Employed
  - Organisation: Churchbell Security

Contact Information:

- *Drop down for more info*

Live Surveillance:

- Status: *Available*
- Date: 06/10/2045
- Current Location: Kensington Police Station, Kensington, West London
- Local Time: 09:37 GMT

Here I thought things were going well…

"Look on the bright side," Emma said reassuringly, joining me in leaning over the railing of the balcony looking over the garage. Her rubbery bionic muscles bulged through her default red-coloured uniform. "He's still one more undesirable off the street."

"I guess," I muttered disappointedly, rubbing the brace around my nose and watching the white armoured prisoner transfer van pulling up towards the automatic doors below.

The smell of cold city air wafted through the portcullis gate to the underground structure, the morning light from outside cascading in an even pattern against the tarmac. A pair of armed officers in exoskeletons stepped through and began shepherding the soon-to-be inmates. They were dressed in striped overalls with ID data coded directly into the fabric, and handcuffs securely locked around their wrists. Most of them had young, fresh faces, staring at their feet as they shuffled nervously towards the motorised rear doors of the van, stepping into the uncomfortable-looking seats mounted on each side of the cabin.

The last prisoner to head into the van was the Jack-21 suspect we arrested yesterday, Gustaw Atwell. Without his exoskeleton, he was paralysed from the waist down. He was planted firmly in a motorised wheelchair, wired into his neural lace. He looked utterly bitter, frowning so hard his chrome-plated cheekbones were starting to cut into his skin again. The ramp at the rear of the van automatically descended as he approached, and he wheeled himself onto it with his own willpower.

The results of his V-Trial came last night. The virtual court convicted him of theft and grievous bodily harm as well, sentencing him to five years in Prison Matrix. On the advice of his AI-Solicitor, Gustaw had pleaded guilty to resisting arrest, but waived his right to privacy and had accepted the prosecutor's request to extract the last week of his memory. The guy was a real piece of work. The NHS had issued him a standard medical exoskeleton for his disability, but the one he'd been wearing last night had been stolen from his construction job, which he used to work as hired muscle for a loan shark.

It was the same story you'd hear all the time, not just in Climateville. People struggling to get by, doing whatever they could to make ends meet… often ending up in jail, then back on the street a few years later. Just another man caught in the cycle of poverty and violence – a survivor if you will. The sort of person that made me question why I was doing this job.

Then there were the real evil bastards like Jack-21… but Gustaw wasn't him.

Still, it was hard to feel sorry for him after he broke my nose. I rubbed it painfully; the skin was sore around the cartilage re-grown by my implants. Ben informed me that it was safe to remove the polystyrene brace they'd placed around it. The medical tape came off painfully, and I dumped it in a nearby bin and sucked in an unrestricted breath.

The officers handling the prisoner transfer ensured that the inmates were securely locked into place by the magnetic restraints. Gustaw was parked in the disabled seat. I got a glimpse of him throwing me a vengeful glare just as the doors shut tightly and locked behind. The sliding security door to the garage opened up as the van approached, and with a high-pitched whir, it drove out into the road.

"I guess we're back to square one then."

"Square two," Emma pointed out. "The exoskeleton footprint at the apartment is the best lead we've got."

"The *only* lead we've got."

At least as far as you're telling me…

"Geez, you always this much of a downer these days? Surprised your old partner didn't ditch you sooner."

She patted me on the back as we headed through the doors behind us, the scanner granting us access, walked past the white and blue hallway of marked interrogation rooms and towards the canteen for breakfast. I often worked night shifts, powering through with a combination of focus mode, and hyper-energy drinks which, aided by the nanobots in my system, was the only thing keeping me standing upright right now.

I scrolled through today's menu on the holographic display on my wrist pad and ordered a bacon sarnie while exchanging pleasantries with my workmates in the corridor, many of whom just stared at Emma's body and averted their gazes when she noticed.

I should've been more grateful after she saved me last night, but after spending the whole night pondering her presence, I couldn't help but empathise slightly.

"You watching the game tonight?" she asked chirpily after a while.

"Sure."

"How about it then? Wanna grab a couple pints down the *Wetherspoons* and watch it?"

"Yeah, maybe," I yawned divisively. "I'm barely standing as it is though. Might have to pass on it."

"Lame," she replied, with a coy grin, trying to badger me into it.

"Can't all be party machines."

She seemed to gloss over the joke at her expense.

We headed to the cafeteria. It was almost as bland as the corridors we had walked through, but felt alive with the chatter of officers sitting by round plastic green and blue tables, munching away at their late breakfasts with the second plates and cutlery, the aroma of frying whetting my appetite.

Emma wasn't eating (unsurprisingly), so she went to grab us a table, while I went over to collect my plate, which was waiting for me on a heated panel. I approached the end of the counter, and a service droid's arm snapped the plate up and placed it on my tray, which I took back to the table and dug in heartily.

"Not the lightest breakfast ever."

"Gotta live a little sometimes," I said sarcastically as I took a greasy bite, knowing full well she knew I had performance enhancement nanobots in my veins, breaking down the fat in minutes. The health insurance package for security contractors was pretty much the same across the whole of the industry. She was just trying to break the silence, but I was trying my best to avoid any kind of meaningful conversation, hoping to eat this one meal in peace. Should've known that wasn't going to happen.

"I'm your partner now, Dan," she said bluntly, cutting through the veil of silence. "You can be pissed off at me, but let's get it out in the open."

"I'm not pissed off at you, Emma. Your company perhaps, but not you. You must know what it's like to have someone take your case. It's bad enough when it's special branch, but this little arrangement is awkward, to say the least. And I guess I've got a lot of shit going on as well… this isn't helping."

"Sorry to hear that," she said, sounding genuinely concerned. "What's up?"

I'd been hoping to avoid this but found myself speaking anyway. Eventually, I sighed. "Trouble at home. With Claire."

She smiled understandingly now. "Should've known. What's the problem?"

"Nothing you did… you remember Matt? My partner from last night?"

"Yeah?"

"The stupid bugger only went and posted on *Facebook* that he thought his replacement was hot."

"Typical," she scoffed, shaking her head, not appreciating being ogled on the internet.

"Anyway, Claire saw the post and now has it in her head I'm cheating on her. She messaged me. She was up all night stalking me for more info on you."

"Oh, you wish. Doesn't she remember me? I know I only met her a couple of times back in school, but she must've known I was gay."

"Yeah, I tried that… she says she doesn't remember you."

"Seriously?"

"I would've shown her a picture of you to jog her memory, but Ben stopped me. Turns out that violates the terms of the NDA I signed last night."

Emma covered her face with her hand in embarrassment, with the muffled sound of clanging metal beneath her skin. "God, I'm sorry, the company is pretty protective of the designs for my body."

"Don't take it personally. She's on anti-depressants. The days seem to blur together for her now. Says it's like being in a trance."

"Damn, sounds bad. Doesn't she use emotional management software?"

"She's well dodgy about brain augmentation… won't even wear a standard headset unless she needs to."

The articulators in her face screwed up in disgust. "Oh God, she's not one of those Luddites, is she?"

"She's not that bad. I think she's just got a thing about surgery… like it somehow makes you less huma-" Emma's annoyed gaze said it all. "Uh… no offence."

"I've heard worse. Can't say I blame her. Still a little surprised she didn't recognise me though."

"I wish I could say I was, but honestly nothing she does-" I was interrupted by the telepathic ringing of the Police Encrypted Comms App inside my head.

<<Incoming Call from: Chief Inspector Roger O'Neil>>

"Oh, great," I groaned and facepalmed myself.

"What's up?"

"The boss," I sighed, tapping the side of my head. "Don't suppose you wanna take it?"

"Your boss. Not mine," she winked.

"Cheers."

I instinctively turned away from her, holding a pair of fingers against my ear as if I was holding an old-fashioned handset, and telepathically accepted the call.

The webcam footage streamed to my display. Chief Inspector Roger O'Neil was a short, squat man with a round head covered in thin ginger hair that stretched down his cheeks into sideburns, his eyes buried deep within his husky, pronounced skull.

"Chief Inspector," I said politely, holding up my smart watch's camera to my face for him to see me on the camera.

"All right, Danny boy?" he answered in his usual deceptively merry tone, his thick Irish accent coming loud and clear over the comm-link. "What's it like playing with the other team, boyo?"

"Can't complain so far," I answered telepathically; my eyes briefly met with Emma as we spoke.

"Is she… cooperating?" He nodded back, listening intently.

"I guess. She's just doing her job, Chief."

"Hmmm…" He nodded, looking unconvinced. "Anyway, I didn't call you just to moan about the neighbours."

"I'm listening."

"Mother Mind has been mining data from Andrew Ilian's close friends, including his online girlfriend."

The profile loaded on to my display:

Mother Mind Profile 5743-2354-9146-0945:

First Name: Claudia

Surname: Schwarz

Status: Alive

Nationality: German

Occupation(s):

- Student
  - Status: Studying
  - Organisation: University of Düsseldorf

Criminal Record:

- N/A

Known Aliases:

- Outc4st

Biometric Data:

- Gender: Female
- Date of Birth: 02/08/2027
- Age: 18
- Race: Caucasian
- Hair Colour: Brown
- Eye Colour: Blue
- Height: 1.6 m
- Weight: 87 kg
- Ailments: None
- Cybernetic Percentage: 16%
- Genetic Modifications:
  - Total Immunisation

Contact Information:

- *Drop down for more info*

Live Surveillance:

- Status: *Partially Available*
- Date: 06/10/2045
- Current Location: Bilk, Düsseldorf, Germany
- Local Time: 10:43 CET

The photo at the top of the file took up most of my view. She was a stereotypical goth, complete with long, darkened emo-black hair. Her skin was chalk white permeated only by the dark make-up around her eyes, giving her a resemblance to some kind of punk-rock panda.

"Young love."

"Not exactly," Roger replied cryptically. "We've analysed her public social media records. There's no mention of her being involved with him romantically. Whoever Ilian was talking to online, it wasn't this girl."

My ears pricked up.

"Identity theft?"

"Looks like. Ilian's browsing history clearly shows him meeting with someone he *believed* to be Claudia via Cloudland, but her records don't match. Whoever was pretending to be her must've hacked into her account at least once."

He sent me a link bringing me to a website called 'Armageddon Central', a 24-hour virtual nightclub set in a simulated post-apocalyptic nuclear wasteland, with visitors free to come and go as they please.

"The girl is a volunteer admin, her home terminal networked to the server. It's likely our identity thief gained access from there."

"So, are we getting in touch with Interpol for a cyber-warrant or-"

"Warrant?" Roger scoffed with a cheeky wink. "Whatever happened to good ol' fashioned knocking talk?"

I couldn't help but grin at that. As far as bosses go, he was undoubtedly one of the best I'd ever had. Most chief inspectors would go off on one about doing things by the book.

"It's been a while since I had to sweet-talk a girl," I joked back.

"Best of luck to ya," he beamed back, talking loudly and proudly. "But uh, keep an eye on the 'borg, boyo."

I eyed him suspiciously through my watch's camera. "You want me to spy on Emma?"

"You think she's here for a pint down the local? Her presence is a tactical choice by Virtualife. Believe me, lad, given half the chance, she'll sell you down the river. We need to know what they're planning."

His words sent my heart sinking. Chances were, he was right. Her employers had probably sent her just to make me feel easier around her. Who knows what she was really after.

"Whatever you say, boss."

"Good man. Keep me updated."

<<Call Ended>>

The webcam feed flickered from my contact lens, leaving me with an obstructed view of Emma's curious gaze. I kept my expression as neutral as I could, not wanting to give anything away, but feeling like a spotlight was on me.

I explained what I'd been told to Emma and sent her the case files on Claudia Schwarz. When I was done, to my surprise, she just gave me a coy smile.

"You guys only just caught on to that?"

I raised an eyebrow. "You mean you knew?"

"My HQ informed me three hours ago. It's no wonder you guys are second place in the security market."

I gave her an inquisitive stare, folding my arms and leaning back in my seat.

"Not that I'm not grateful for last night, but I don't appreciate you making decisions unilaterally."

"I hear what you're saying, Dan," she acknowledged in a curt professional manner yet with a nod that felt condescending. "I'll try to take that into account, but I have my bosses too, and they've told me to keep this case on a need-to-know basis."

"I'd say the material witnesses are pretty need-to-know."

"The terms of the NDA you signed say it's my discretion. Relax, I was planning on telling you. In due course."

"Come on, Emma, don't give me that legal crap," I complained, throwing my arms out in exasperation.

"Like I said, you guys are our competitors. And the victim is the son of someone close to the boss. You could already be selling this on to every tabloid news site by now."

"You know that's illegal."

"Really Dan?" She sighed with tired amusement. "You're not that innocent."

I bit my lip. Given that I had just been asked to spy on her, I couldn't say I blamed her for wanting to keep her cards close to her chest.

"Still… You know what they say about good teamwork…"

"Communication is key," we spoke at the same time.

We burst into a round of tired, uncontrollable nostalgic laugher, burying our faces in our hands.

"Oh my god," Emma wheezed through the giggles, even throwing in an electronic snort. "Those teambuilding exercises were so lame."

"Yeah…" I breathed, wiping away a tear, nostalgically recalling the training regimen at the correctional facility. "Aw man, what was the instructor's name? Mister uh…"

"Phyllis!" Emma cried, snapping her fingers.

"That's it!" I exclaimed, slapping the table playfully. "And that Yousef-"

"Set fire to his shorts!"

More uncontrollable laughter, drawing a few stares from around the cafeteria.

"Do you mind?" Mohammed Oman, one of our Pakistani officers, called from across the room, glaring over his steaming coffee.

"Sorry!" I called awkwardly.

I turned back to Emma, both cringing with embarrassment.

We smiled at each other. Then it dawned on me. I realised, every time we had one these moments, all my previous worries about Virtualife's involvement, in this case, disappeared out of my mind.

I trust her too much… and that's what they're counting on.

I recoiled slowly, my face stiffening. I didn't want to think the worst of her… or at least not let it show anyway. Probably too late for that – her mechanical lips tightened into a hard line.

"Anyway… What else did you get on Schwarz?"

Her expression softened.

"Not much, to be honest. The virtual hangout has been around for about a year, but it's known to GCHQ. A good place for script kiddie hackers to get their 'in', but not one of the major players. We're waiting for the foreign office to issue us a non-domestic warrant to dive the network."

That's surprising.

"I thought you special forces types worked with the intelligence agencies?"

"Yeah, but this is still a police operation. Believe it or not, the boss wants this one done by the book."

"Sure," I replied flatly. *That'll be the day…*

"Either way, the applications take a while. Six hours is way too long in this game. I was hoping we could get over to the VR hangout later, see if we could persuade her to let us check her user log-in records."

I telepathically ordered Ben to check her Mother Mind profile. My eyes flickered as I read the readout on my lenses. "Looks like she's online, why don't we do it now?"

"Really?" she checked.

"Last I checked, it's what we're being paid for."

"You look like you're about to pass out!" she laughed, gesturing towards my drooping eyelids.

I rubbed the sleep out of the corners and let out a yawn.

"I can keep going for a bit longer. It's only cyberspace. Besides… I'd rather be dealing with this than with Claire."

She chuckled and nodded understandingly. "All right, if you're sure."

"I am." I nodded, feeling a lingering sense of regret that my relationship had gotten to this point. I finished my cup of coffee and chucked it into the recycling unit nearby like it was a basketball hoop.

"And the crowd goes wild," she said sarcastically, playing a *YouTube* clip of a cheering crowd from her smartwatch.

We headed to my office cubicle and sat at my desk, telepathically firing up my terminal. Emma verbally ordered the auto-chair behind me to wheel itself over to her. She sat down with an audible creak underneath her weight and caught a glimpse of the video displaying on the screen photo frame. A holiday recording of Claire and me in Cornwall taken from a rented drone. We were on the beach. Mullion Cove. She was wearing a pink swimsuit trying to splash me as I chased after her. I took a sigh from the bland office air.

"Happier times?" she asked, nodding her head toward the photo.

"I guess." I'd already talked about my relationship more than I wanted to. No point dredging that up now.

I carried on and reached for the top drawer of the desk, pulling out a pair of USB cables and handed one to her. She apparently didn't appreciate being ignored, but took it from me anyway and hooked it into the back of her neck. I did the same to the port on my headset behind the ear, grateful she didn't press the issue as I loaded up standard-issue police virtual environment browser and telepathically entered the URL for Armageddon Central.

<<Logging in...>>

<<Welcome to Cloudland!>>

<<You are about to enter a Virtual Reality Simulation.>>

<<Please be seated and ensure your surroundings are appropriate.>>

<<Begin Simulation? Yes/No>>

I rested my head on the pillow on the back of my chair, preparing my mind to enter cyberspace. My eyes rolled down to look at Emma sat across from me, jacking herself in and readying to log in as well.

"We're just going there to talk with her. Agreed?"

"Talk? Yeah, I think they covered that in basic."

I pursed my lips, her attitude not exactly filling me with confidence, but I closed my eyes and issued the command anyway.

<<Loading Environment>>

<<Running Neural Lace device drivers>>

<<Processing Consciousness Shift>>

The graphics filled my mind's eye and became my reality. I found myself standing next to Emma's virtual avatar in this new world. The lively atmosphere was entirely at odds with the desolation surrounding us. The simulation's info page informed us that the environment had been generated from drone scans, taken from the ruins of Pyongyang in the aftermath of the Korean reunification war. We were stood in front of the bombed-out frame of one of the crappy residential blocks built by the old communist dictatorship. The walls had caved in entirely, the concrete support columns holding fast, leaving nothing but a shell. The rubble of brick, dust and twisted metal lay strewn across the floor, looking out across the dusty sunset, casting dim light across the dreary ruins of the tower blocks, stretching out to the horizon.

A large section of the rubble had been cleared away to be turned into a dance floor. Simulated strobing disco lights and laser displays had been mounted on the ceiling, each flash revealing the tightly packed crowd of scantily dressed bodies twisting and flaring in the strobe pulses. You could almost feel the rush of energy radiating out of them, shattering the lonely vibe of the apocalyptic setting.

An elevated circular stage had been constructed in the centre of the dance floor, out of twisted metal. A performing recreation of Lady Transhuman was on stage, yelling passionately into the invisible microphones in her simulated clothes. Most NPCs in these sims removed the appearance of real-world cybernetic implants. Not this one. Just like the real deal, this recreation was almost entirely bionic and not afraid to show it. The casing on her arm and leg prosthetics were transparent, revealing the whirring mechanics inside. Her hair was gone, replaced with purple crystalline spikes, and her dress was simple circuitry, pulsing with energy as she sang her latest hit 'Immortality FTW', her voice digitally edited to synchronous perfection.

I turned my gaze across the dance floor and initiated a user data scan.

<<Connecting to GCHQ servers>>

<<Matching user data>>

<<Match complete>>

Dozens of blue-dot icons appeared on my HUD, hovering over the heads of the avatars. Neuroclicking them on my display brought up mini-windows with their Mother Mind profiles. At a glance, I could see a lot of them were logged in through the dark web, highlighting this place as a cybercrime hub.

"Needle in a haystack it is then," I groaned to Emma, rubbing my eyes with frustration.

I telepathically ordered Ben to locate Claudia Schwarz, and a second later a pulsing blue arrow appeared out of the sea of icons on my display, drawing our eyes to a table on the far side of the virtual dance floor.

She was there all right, her flowing black hair resting comfortably on her shoulders with the dyed red leather of her corset fitting tightly over her curves. She was chatting with another, similarly dressed, with a lot of touching going on. I was beginning to wonder what was really going on here. I took another look at her *Facebook* details on my HUD… no sexual orientation info.

"I think someone's coming out of the closet…"

"Shame, she's not my type," Emma joked.

"Well unless she's bi, I seriously doubt she was Andrew's type either."

"No shit, Sherlock. Doubt she even realises she was hacked."

"Me too, but we gotta tick this box off," I shrugged, nudging my head in her direction.

Emma shrugged reluctantly, but we made our way over to her, stepping over the wreckage around our feet to descend into the dance floor, shuffling awkwardly through the thick herd of elated dancing bodies. The claustrophobic stench of sweat and adrenaline washed over us as we slipped and squeezed through.

Claudia's VPA must've warned her about our approach as her head snapped in our direction and glared defensively, her gaze meeting ours through the mass of bodies. We ascended up a flight of dusty concrete stairs.

"Claudia Schwarz?" I asked with a professional smile, offering my hand out.

She folded her arms, and gave me a sharp defensive gaze, letting out a plume of cigarette smoke. Great start.

"I'm Detective Inspector Haines, London Metropolitan Police. This is-"

"I can read your profiles," she snapped in German, the translation software placing subtitles in my vision. "You have no jurisdiction here. What do you want?"

I took the most relaxed posture I could.

"Ma'am, you're not in any trouble. In fact, we believe you may have been a victim yourself."

She eyed us guardedly. "What crime?"

Now that I had her attention I opened up the palm of my hand and gave the command to project the photo of Andrew Ilian, the rosy-cheeked rebel.

"Have you ever seen this man?"

"Hmm… no. Not that anyone uses their real appearance here."

"This was the avatar the most commonly used online," I continued, using the other hand to swipe the image to change it to his Cloudland profile picture. His virtual avatar was reasonably similar to his real-world appearance, aside from his literal Mohawk of fire. Wisps of flames extending from the skin of his shaved head, billowing out smoke like a veil across his face.

"Oh, ShadowCell?" she replied, looking slightly repulsed.

That took both of us by surprise. "You… do know him?"

"Not really. He was here about a month ago. Had a major crush on me. Little shit tried making a move." She gestured with a wry smile to the girl sat across from her, who stared back longingly.

"As you can see, it didn't work out."

"But you *did* meet him?" Emma checked, seeming puzzled by her answer.

"Yes, how many times do I have to say it? What's he done anyway?"

Her VPA must have scanned the photo and run a visual search, matching Ilian's appearance to the news articles he was featured in. There was a brief look of shock when she realised he was a Jack-21 victim, followed by stunned laughter.

"You don't honestly think I have anything to do with that killer?" She snorted, her eyes gleefully wide, almost as if she took it as a compliment.

"You're not a suspect," Emma answered firmly, her arms folded and maintain a hard stance as if to perform the stereotypical bad cop routine.

"He came here fairly often. Do you mind us checking your records?" I asked hopefully. "We'd be most grateful."

Her face fell and became guarded once more.

"If you want my help, you could at least have the decency to explain why you think I am involved with a murder…" She paused, her eyes flickering while she conversed telepathically with her VPA, "622 kilometres away."

I rolled my lips and delicately explained the situation without giving up too much detail. She seemed immediately more repulsed by the idea of her identity being used to seduce a boy.

"Well… shit!" she cried, looking on the verge of vomiting. "I don't get it? Why would someone like that target me?"

"That's what we're here to find out."

"You do like to keep interesting company though," Emma commented slyly, nudging her head in the direction of the rough crowd still raving out on the dance floor. "There could be any number of people here who could have introduced a virus to your network."

"What's your point?"

"Ma'm we have reason to believe that Ilian was involved with a recent large-scale cyber-attack. Examination of his online communications suggests that… you were the one who convinced him to do it."

Her jaw dropped. "Someone's trying to frame me?"

"Maybe, maybe not. It's possible that the hacker who stole your identity simply wanted to take advantage of Ilian's family connections to the targeted business, and used his… infatuation with you as a foothold."

"Social engineering," she said bitterly.

"Exactly," Emma continued. "But whatever the reason, the identity thief must've been mining personal information from you for a while to create such a convincing persona."

"If you say so," Schwarz's girlfriend sniggered. Claudia gave her an annoyed slap on the shoulder before rounding on us again.

"What are you getting at?" Schwarz continued, folding her arms inquisitively.

"I have cyber-security training," Emma explained. "If you could temporarily provide admin-access to your network, I can run a test to find out how they got in, and what they were doing in there."

Claudia's mouth became a tight line. "You want me to let you into the servers? I'm not the owner, only a volunteer here. I don't want to get in any trouble."

"Like you said, these servers are in Germany," I reassured her. "Out of our jurisdiction. Outside of this investigation, we have no interest in your affairs, nor your employers."

"Heard that before," she snipped.

Emma's expression hardened.

"Well, the other way of looking at it is that *until* we check your records, we have no definitive way of proving that you *weren't* involved."

Schwarz gritted her teeth. "So, it's like that, huh?"

"It doesn't have to be. But if we have to wait for the foreign office to come through… so be it."

"You're bluffing."

"Am I?"

They went back and forth like that for a few minutes, but eventually, Schwarz came to the realisation that we would be getting the data regardless of what she thought. Finally, Claudia grudgingly agreed to allow Emma inside her server's operating system, but only if she could watch the session.

"Fine. Let's just get this done."

After a quick conversation with Emma, we agreed to meet back in the real world. My cyber-security skills were limited, so it was best just to leave it to her.

<<Terminating virtual simulation>>

<<Disengaging neural lace>>

<<Disconnecting from server>>

I returned to the office, waking up in my seat across from Emma, her eyes shut, comatose to reality. While she was jacked in for a good twenty minutes more, I ordered a robot to bring me another coffee and turned my attention to my holo-screen, bringing up the sports news, watching a live *YouTube* stream with some of the prominent pundits giving their thoughts on the match tonight. Arsenal's new gene therapy program was sure to provide them with a boost, but the AI analysis of Tottenham's performance across the season was still placing them as the favourites, the live chat feed buzzing with trash talk from both sides.

I got a call from Claire at that time as well… I declined and sent her a brief message saying I was in a meeting and would be back soon. Only a half-lie really. Emma woke up shortly afterwards, eyes springing open as her facial motors whirred to life. Her human instincts made her rub the corner of her eyes, despite their bionic nature.

"Find anything?" I checked, while she removed the cable from the back of her neck, and tossed it onto the desk.

"Yeah…" she added ponderously, a look of concern on her face that caught my eye. I noticed that for the first time since she arrived last night, she was concerned. "Something… odd."

She gave a hand gesture and a telepathic command and sent me a link to an executable file she found on the server to my desktop terminal.

The file had a long, convoluted number for a name, but I tapped the holographic screen to view the source code in a protected view. Its cyberwarfare avatar loaded into view; the programmer had given it the appearance of sea urchin, made from ominous green light, its spiky tendrils piercing deep into the memory banks of the server.

"What am I looking at?"

Ben appeared in the bottom left-hand corner.

"A Trojan horse virus. Highly unusual configuration."

"I'll say!" Emma scoffed, her awestruck face glittering in the holo-light. "The intrusion scripts are fairly standard, and the attack payload has been encrypted, but the conversion-key matrix… it's like nothing I've ever seen. The complexity… it's spectacular! It's a masterpiece! A work of art!"

I gave her an exasperated, bewildered stare. "Sorry, there must be a problem with my translation program. Do you mind saying that in English?"

She rolled her eyes.

"I don't know what the virus was doing exactly… but it looks like the encryption code was generated by an AI running on a super-computer, or a cloud-network with equivalent power."

My ears pricked up.

"Hackers with a supercomputer? Sounds familiar. Spiritform?"

Emma folded her arms and shook her head.

"I doubt it. I mean, this is within their technical capacity, but it doesn't match up with what we know about Ilian. I mean, just look at him!"

She gestured to open up another window on my terminal, Ilian's *Facebook* page rezzing into view, filled with socialist propaganda posts.

"Thought he was a bloody child of the revolution! Social engineering is one thing, but if Spiritform needed his help to hack Virtualife they could've just *asked!* They wouldn't have needed to create a fake girlfriend to *trick* him into it."

"Hmm…" I took another exhausted sip from my coffee and massaged the side of my temples with a knuckle. "So, who else could it be?"

"Balticsoft have always been big on industrial espionage. But that doesn't make sense either. Spiritform would release the files for the world to see. That wouldn't give them an edge in the market."

I looked through Ilian's IRC chat logs, extracted by the digital forensics team. A message sent four days ago confirming that Ilian had reached out to Spiritform and not the other way around. The user he'd been talking to identified his or herself as 'Destiny', one of the group's most prominent members…

Or at least he thought *it was Destiny…*

"What if he wasn't sending it to Spiritform?" I suggested hopefully. "Just one of their agents pretending to be them?"

Emma rolled her head. "I guess that's possible." Her eyes still fixated on the holo-screen. She clearly didn't consider it likely.

I subtly ground my teeth, trying to hide my frustration at her clearly calculated responses, turning my attention back to the screen.

"What do you think, Ben?"

"Insufficient data for deeper analysis. Further details on the contents of the Project Selection will be required to widen my search parameters."

My thoughts exactly…

"He's got a point. It would help if we knew what it was he a*ctually stole*."

She didn't respond, remaining silent, her eyes fixated on the sprawl of encrypted figures rolling by on the holo-screen.

"Come on Emma… If that's not need-to-know, I don't know what is."

"My boss thinks otherwise," she sighed flatly.

Her attitude made something inside me snap, and the frustration I'd been holding back came bubbling out.

"You know… there are some people who would call this obstructing the course of justice," I blurted out angrily, the words seeming to come out before I realised what I was saying.

That got her attention.

Her eyes raised up from the screen and met mine, glaring at me with intensity.

"And there are some people, *lawyers*, who would call that slander."

"Ha!"

"Careful, Dan. We're mates, but be careful. You know who I work for. What they're capable of." She pointed discreetly towards the webcam on my desk terminal.

Were they watching us now?

"Don't poke the bear. All I'm saying."

I let out a disgruntled scoff, shaking my head, not wanting to make eye contact with her. I was trying to be diplomatic, but this whole set-up was dodgy. She was leading me by the hand through a river of shit.

By the time I looked back at her, her expression had softened somewhat. Her fake teeth bit her counterfeit lips, almost looking guilty…

"Look, if you're really having doubts about Virtualife's involvement," she began with a tone of consolation, "you could always ask Kenji yourself?"

I furrowed my brow, taken aback by the suggestion, unable to hold back my laugh of disbelief. She couldn't possibly be serious. Me? Talking to Kenji Awasaki? It was so ridiculous I found myself bellowing out loud enough to get heads turning from the other cubicles.

"Sure! And afterwards, why don't I pop around to Buckingham Palace for afternoon tea with His Highness?"

Her expression wasn't changed by disregard for her suggestion.

"Well I don't know about the king, but I do know Princess Lucy will be there," she deadpanned. I observed her face. The articulators on her face weren't as convincing as a pure human… but I felt like she was sincere.

"You're having a laugh, right?"

She seemed pleased with my level of interest and sent me a link to a web page for an upcoming charity fundraising event by the Awasaki Foundation. Fancy white and gold graphics with a posh font, and videos filled with the flashing lights of paparazzi catching shots of celebrities dressed in the fanciest clothes money could buy.

"What's this?"

"Something I'm being dragged to. Kenji suggested I bring you along as well."

"As the security detail?"

"I wish," she scoffed. "The boss is insisting I go."

"How come?"

"Got me. Probably wants to show me off as a shining beacon for the cybernetic future he imagines. Point is, Awasaki listens to what I have to say. And he'll listen to what *you* have to say…"

My face lit up as bright as the flash photography on the webpage, my eyes caught by a video of an android butler serving shrimp and champagne.

"The food is free, right?" I grinned.

She nodded wearily. "Point is he'll be there. I'm sure he'd be happy to… alleviate some of your concerns."

That sounded a bit suspect.

"With cash?"

She breathed dismissively and shook her head.

"Well… what then? Make me an offer I can't refuse?"

"Jesus, no! Fuck, you've been on the street too long, man."

"I really don't see what your boss is going to say to me that's going to convince me he's not up to something," I said, desperately throwing my arms out to the side.

"Me neither. But he does have a way with words…" Her expression fell slightly, hiding something again. Then she forced herself to perk up. "If nothing else it'll be a good party. Never say no to free food?"

Then the idea clicked in my head, something I could be genuinely positive about. *I could kill two birds with one stone…*

"Could Claire come? If she could meet you for real, I'm sure it would put her mind at ease."

"I don't see why not," she replied, a smile starting to creep across her face. "The terms of my NDA don't stop me from meeting people in person… as long as she's not planning on taking selfies."

"She's not really the selfie-taking type."

"Should be fine then, yeah?"

I rubbed my chin, intrigued by the possibility. If Awasaki just wanted to schmooze me, it was tempting just to experience how the one percenters live, even if it only was for one night.

It might even put Claire in a good mood!

"Cool!" I beamed a sense of hopeful relief washing over me. "As long as I can actually get her out of the house, then yeah sure, I'm up for it."

"Sweet. I'll get the invites emailed out to you."

Everything with Claire aside, there was still a good chance Awasaki was going to try to buy my silence. I didn't want to be implicated in anything illegal. I was sure I could resist the temptation to accept an offer like that, but then again, it depended on how big the pay cheque really was.

We spent the next half-hour or so doing the paperwork, filing our official reports into the case files, sending the Trojan horse Emma uncovered on to the digital forensics team for their analysis. I discreetly messaged Chief O'Neil, told him about the invitation to the fundraiser, prompting another foreboding warning about Virtualife corruption.

I left the police station at about eleven, said my goodbye to Emma with a friendly hug and got onto the advertisement-laden, high-tech rat maze that was the London Underground. I got off at Acton Central, shuffling past the maintenance bots and the swathes of tech-clad commuters scanned by the ticket barriers.

The apartment block I lived in was built directly on top of the station; a giant ugly grey tower, looking like the council had decided to build the pavement vertically.

I rode the elevator up and plodded through the filthy green carpeted hallway until I reached my apartment: 1793. Again, I was scanned for ID and cleared for entrance, but I wasn't ready just yet. I found myself yawning and stretching hesitantly. With my neural lace deactivated and no stimulants for my nanobots to process, I was now starting to feel the effects of the night before coming crashing down on me. I slapped my cheeks lightly to wake myself up and readied myself to be the patient, loving boyfriend she'd need me to be.

I tapped the open icon on the door. It slid open, and I was greeted by the home-AI. The lights were off. The shine from the hallway cast shadows over the gloomy mess inside, yearning for the attention of a cleaner-bot. Across the expanse of cluttered carpet, Claire was sitting in her usual spot on the windowsill, her head resting against the glass. I couldn't tell if she was asleep, logged into VR or just pretending to be.

"Hey, babe…" I called out softly.

No reply.

"Anybody home?"

Still nothing. I crept inside, carefully tiptoeing around sculptures she had printed out. Some of them had real talent; strange colours blended into shapes of explosive creativity, statues of mythical creatures realised in 3D. It was sad that her talent went unrecognised, but the entire internet was full of artists crying out in a saturated market… her voice one of millions vying for attention and failing.

I perched myself on the other side of the window looking at her, eyes shut to the world. I touched her shoulder softly, reacting like she was utterly oblivious. She seemed so peaceful, I almost wished she could be like this all the time. She could be a good faker though. I checked her contact information on my HUD; she wasn't logged on to Cloudland, or any of the other big VRMMOs.

"Come on, hon…" I pleaded, trying not to sound annoyed as I knelt beside her, picking up the strong smell of shampoo from poorly washed hair.

She nuzzled her cheek against the vid-glass, opening her eyes and revealing the bloodshot veins.

"How's Emma?" she asked me in a whimpering voice.

Oh boy. Here we go.

"Come on, Claire… you're taking this a bit out of proportion. You can't trust everything you see on *Facebook!* You know Matt can be a bit of a twat."

Her watery eyes screwed up in rage. "Don't you dare even try that! I asked around last night! No one from school can remember anyone called Emma in our year!"

"Not surprised. We weren't there most of the time. We ran with a rough crowd. You and I didn't even see much of each other until I got out of juvie."

"Then why can't you show me a photo of her?!"

I bit my lip and quickly, then talked into the speaker of my smartwatch to converse with Ben, asking out loud if sending her a copy of my NDA would be breaking its terms. He assured me it wouldn't, and forwarded the PDF. I saw the moment the email arrived on her tablet resting beside her. She merely took one quick glance at the file and scoffed.

"Oh, so you're going to swamp me with legal jargon!? Nice try!"

I rubbed my forehead with frustration. There really was no winning with her when she got like this.

"Claire, we were only partnered up last night for crying out loud!" I cried, louder than I meant to. "What do you think could possibly happen in that…"

"How do I know you haven't been seeing each other longer?"

I had to hold back a gulp of exasperation. I closed my eyes for a second and took a calming breath, composing myself to continue.

"Would you like to meet her?" I asked hopefully.

She seemed stunned by my bluntness.

"What are you talking about?" she asked suspiciously.

I forwarded her the fundraising event web page Emma had sent me and told her about her proposal. Her eyes narrowed, with suspicion.

"Why?" she hissed. "Is this some kind of joke?"

"No, of course not! I just think if you met Emma, you'd remember her and-"

"I've *scoured* the internet!" she snarled at me. "There are *zero* records of her on any social media!"

"I'm not surprised. She's special forces, black-ops. There's-"

"Ooooh, how convenient!"

I held my tongue back. "Claire… come on, at least be willing to give this a chance. How often do we get to go to parties like that, huh? Up there with the ritzy types?"

"So they can take the piss out of me, too?"

"No one is taking the piss out of you!" I cried with exasperation. "I just think if you met Emma, it would jog your memory and-"

"Are you having a laugh? What's that supposed to prove!?"

"Oh, come on Claire, you're being paranoid. We-" I began, but regretted opening my mouth immediately when I saw her hands dive down, grab a 3D-printed Swan and hurl it towards me.

"Jesus!" I yelled, ducking just in time to dodge the projectile. It landed hard against the wall behind me, shattering into a cloud of dust and shards. "What the hell, Claire? I-"

She violently cut me short as she lunged towards me with a rapid flurry of slaps, hitting as hard as she could, and forcing me to cover my head with my arms.

"FUCK OFF!"

If the room wasn't soundproofed, her voice would have rung throughout the entire estate. She stopped with the slapping, before spinning on her heel, giving heavy sobs in between each breath. She stormed off towards the bedroom and barked the voice command to activate the mag-lock.

I stared bewildered at the shut door, trying to figure out what I had done to deserve that.

CHAPTER 9

Mother Mind Profile 2446-7128-5978-2501:

First Name: Arthur

Surname: Wells

Status: Living

Nationality: British

Occupation(s):

- Private Investigator
    - Status: Self-employed
    - Organisation: Arthur Wells & Associates

Known Aliases:

- IronRoot

Live Surveillance:

- Status: *Partially Available*
- Date: 06/10/2045
- Current Location: Orion Block Apartment Complex, Chiswick, West London
- Local Time: 11:46 GMT

<<FIVR Simulation in progress>>

<<Icarus cyberwarfare visualization running>>

<<Connected to remote device>>

<<Uploading attack payload: 23%>>

Cyberwarfare visualisation programs really were things of beauty. The dream of a thousand science fiction writers realised. Life imitating art. The visualisation software was designed to analyse the flow of data packets through ICE security programs and use generic 3D graphics to render a virtual world for the hacker to move around in, effectively turning the art of cyber-warfare into a video game.

The earliest such programs go as far back as 2012, with NICT's Daedalus cyber-attack alert system, and DARPA's Plan X for the old *Oculus Rift*. But with the advent of brain interfaces, the dreams of William Gibson had finally come true.

I'd been busy hacking ever since Gabrielle Phillips left my office and was still pumping with nerdy adrenaline. This case was going to be a race against time. I received the email from Virtualife about forty-five minutes ago, explaining that the police investigation into Andrew Ilian's murder had uncovered he'd been the victim of identity fraud. The girlfriend who had convinced him to run the hack against the company was a fake, a juicy tidbit of info. I didn't know how it was going to affect my investigation, but I'd bet my bottom dollar that it was going to. If nothing else, it meant that there was a good chance the police might stumble onto the Project Selection files before me. No pay cheque for me if that happened. So yeah, I was motivated to stay ahead.

The cyberwarfare world took the form of a maze of beams of white neon light, like train tracks against the dark blue background of the virtual universe. My bodiless consciousness glided along them at breakneck speeds. The beams behind me transformed into a bright blue as I injected my code, leaving a digital trail of breadcrumbs that extended all the way back to my starting point; the input/output port, taking the form of a luminous sphere. The information highways branched out at nodes, culminating as a map of the flow of information packets through the system.

I was in the process of attacking a directory node, and Liz had estimated a forty percent chance of triggering the anti-virus ICE program.

Come on… just let my luck hold out a little longer…

The way you were *meant* to enter the system was simple. The I/O port would take you to the clearance node, a set of encryption handshake protocols. In this case, it was running a clearance program called Turnstile, its AI avatar taking the form of its namesake, a brass revolving door with data raining around it, hovering above a glowing circular pad in the centre of the information highway traffic line. The clearance node was linked directly to the user registry, a bright green sphere at the end of the maze. That was my target.

The registry would have contained an encrypted database of usernames and passwords, now it was all biometric login. The clearance node is designed to encrypt and verify user log-in data. If your username and biometric data match, you're granted access and pass through the registry, through a directory and into the databanks the username grants access to.

However, that was *not* the way I wanted to go. Of course, without Andrew Ilian's neurokey or other biometric data, there was no way I was getting in. In *theory,* I could brute-force crack the Clearance node using a decryption ICE Breaker program or use a scam email or similar technique to infect the system with a Trojan horse virus, but that would take too long.

I needed to take the back-door.

This is what I dreamed of as a kid. A whole other world most people couldn't see, yet defining their lives. A realm waiting to be conquered.

I lived for this shit.

The visualisation program could only do so much on its own. If I were to run a scan with just the basic Icarus software, it would only reveal the standard log-in procedure from the webpage. To find potential back-door vulnerabilities, I needed to run another kind of ICE Breaker, a ZQL Packet Injector. Running this program to scan the targeted server revealed two other branches extending from the I/O port, leading to a series of directory and API nodes (taking the form of white cubes and cylinders, turning blue once I had them under my control). The information highway nodes formed alternative routes to the registry, where I could gain access to the log-in details in an unencrypted state.

I ran an ICE Breaker called Borealis which did a pretty good job revealing most of the security infrastructure, but it was only a level-1 AI; there was still a thin mist hiding about a third of the remaining grid, a fog of war. I'd have to capture nodes closer to the fog to reveal the path ahead to reveal a back-door to the registry, and there was no way to know if these paths were being protected by the firewall until I was travelling down them.

The server was running an ICE program called Kraken, its avatar blocking most of the alternative routes. It took the form of countless crimson-red tentacles, reaching out from the information highways, ready to wrap around anyone who dares to try to get past. It crackled with virtual static, attempting to scan and filter out the malicious code.

If I ran into one of the firewalls, I'd have to either try to back-track (but it would probably be too late for that), or attempt to brute-force crack the program.

I'd have to scan the composition of the software with my ICE Breakers and hope to find a weakness I could inject attack packets into. But by then I'd have triggered the anti-virus. Off in the distance on the far side of the grid maze was a glowing red sphere; the diagnostics node, where the third and final ICE program was waiting to be activated. If I tripped one of the firewalls the anti-virus would execute, its avatar would rez from the diagnostics node and power along the grid to catch up to me. It would become a race to make it to the registry before it caught me, or I'd get booted from the system. Of course, it was always possible to re-assign my IP address and try again, but after so many tries I'd have a trace program on me and police knocking down the door to my apartment.

So, make it to the registry before that happened. No problem.

I was fast approaching up on the directory node taking the form of a white cube the size of a car. My bodiless avatar came to a sudden stop in front of it. There were no more visible data highways beyond the void; only the fog of war, but I could still see the green sphere of the registry node glowing to my right.

<<Uploading cyber-attack payload: 100%>>

<<Anti-virus analysis in progress>>

<<Results: Negative>>

My Borealis ICE Breaker finished its attack, and the white cube suddenly burst to life, transforming into a bright luminous blue. To my relief, I hadn't triggered the anti-virus.

Phew…

The light from the directory node shone forth like a beacon, lifting the shadowy veil of the fog of war and revealing another data highway track extending towards the registry. There was also a second path leading to the left, connected to a cylinder-shaped API node, which then, in turn, doubled back on itself and connected to the registry.

Almost there… on the home stretch.

<<Borealis standing by>>

<<Please select destination and configure attack payload>>

The command window filled up my vision, my cursor pulsing green, ready for me to start telepathically typing out my code. Depending on what I entered now I would either head down the left or right track, but it was hard to say which one to take.

I hesitated for a moment. Every node I captured had a chance of triggering the anti-virus, and once I was in the registry I'd still be on a timer to download as much data as I could before I was booted… but more importantly, there was no way to know if either route was defended by the firewall. Thin wisps of the fog of war still rolled over the neon light of both the left and the right path.

If I attempted to access either route now without running a more in-depth packet scan, I could run into the firewall in the middle of my attack, and I'd have to attempt a brute-force. On the other hand, since I was already so deep into the system, if I ran the scan now I would risk setting off the anti-virus anyway.

So, two paths, each leading to the same destination, one shorter, one longer. One safe, one not, and not enough info to tell the difference.

Rock and a hard place it is then…

"What do you reckon, Liz?" I asked telepathically.

Her avatar appeared in my vision, holding a simulated paper ring-binder with the same source code written on it, examining it over the top of her brass spectacles.

"Hmmm… I estimate a sixty percent chance that a deep-packet scan at this point will activate the diagnostic node."

“That’s too high for my liking.”

“Agreed. I recommend taking the right path. We can overclock your ICE Breakers if worst comes to worst, that should give you the run-time you need to crack the firewall if you run into it.”

“Great minds think alike,” I lied.

I minimised her window and went back to the command prompt, telepathically typing out the instructions to take me straight to the registry.

```
<<

EXPORT_SYMBOL(in_group_p);
int in_egroup_p(gid_t grp)
{
        const struct cred *cred = current_cred();
        Int retval = 1;
        if (grp != cred->egid)
        retval = groups_search(cred->group_info, grp);

        return retval;
}
>>
                    <<Target selected: Registry>>
                 <<Cyber-attack payload configured>>
               <<Uploading cyber-attack payload: 01%>>
```

Here we go…

My avatar veered to the right and began whizzing down the information highway, spreading my blue light across the trail.

```
               <<Uploading cyber-attack payload: 38%>>
```

The green sphere of the registry rushed towards me, the simulated sound of fizzling static as my avatar propelled forward.

<<Uploading cyber-attack payload: 47%>>

Almost there…

<<Uploading cyber-attack payload: 62%>>

Almost there…

<<Error: Packet request failed>>

<<Warning: Firewall protocols detected>>

Shit!

My astral form came to screeching stop as a bright red light exploded out from beneath me, radiating from the information highway. The light twisted and turned while it became solid, and soon took the form of the thousand crimson tentacles of the Kraken firewall. The arms enveloped my avatar, surrounding me like dense, slithering trees.

<<Deep packet inspection in progress>>

<<Advise re-configuring attack payload>>

Virtual static radiated from the suction pads and began zapping me. I didn't feel any pain, but it wouldn't be long before I was booted from the system abruptly.

"Liz!" I cried.

"I'm on it!"

<<Configuring Borealis for brute-force attack>>

```
<<Configuration complete>>
<<Executing>>
```

With the brute-force attack underway, the command prompt screen began spewing out info as the ICE breaker generated seemingly random attack packets in an attempt to crack the firewall:

```
<<
    int i;
    unsigned int count = group_info->ngroups;
    for (i = 0; i < group_info->nblocks; i++)
        {unsigned int cp_count = min(NGROUPS_PER_BLOCK, count);
        unsigned int len = cp_count * sizeof(*grouplist);
        if (copy_to_user(grouplist, group_info->blocks[i], len))
        return -EFAULT;
        grouplist += NGROUPS_PER_BLOCK;
        count -= cp_count;}
    return 0;
}
>>
```

The ICE Breaker's avatar rezzed into existence, taking the form of a bubble around me, whirling with the colours of the northern lights. The bubble acted as a force field, the sizzling static bouncing off it, but the tentacles were still closing in. I would have to move fast, my Borealis ICE Breaker was only Level-1 on the AI scale, but the firewall was at least Level-5.

If this was gonna come down to a battle of the machine against machine, I was going to need a serious boost to my system's processing power, way more than my overclocked home desktop could manage.

But we had just the ticket.

"It's time for our little surprise, Liz," I told her triumphantly, a smirk no doubt spreading across my face in the real world.

<<External request protocol initiated>>

<<Connecting to external block-chain>>

<<Connection established>>

<<Initiating over-clock process>>

<<Interfacing scripts to block-chain>>

<<Interface successful>>

My previous case had me hunting down the source of a rogue AI botnet that had infected thousands of home PCs, quietly running in the background and sucking up processing power which could then be used to brute-force hack other more well-defended networks. Officially I had shut down the botnet, but in reality, I'd merely made myself the system administrator, waiting to exploit its power for myself.

With the added processing power, my ICE Breaker was now a Level-7 on the Kurzweil scale. The bubble surrounding me hardened and expanded, pushing the tentacles further back and sending them writhing with pain, giving out an excruciating gargling squeal.

"Just a little longer!" Liz called back to me, almost shouting over the violent crackling.

<<Warning: Anti-virus scan initialised>>

<<Analysing packet output>>

Fuck!

I turned my field of vision behind me to face the red diagnostic sphere. It spat out a cloud of pixels which took rapidly began to morph and twist into shape.

<<Anti-virus analysis complete>>

<<Identified as: Crow (Sinotech Inc.)>>

<<AI Level rating: 4>>

<<Time to system lock out: 00:00:30>>

A gigantic black beak extended out from the red sphere. A pair of black, feathery wings emerged like the shadow of death. The bird soared out of the diagnostic node, its eyes burning like something out of an Edgar Allen Poe poem. The bird took flight, and raced down the information highway, turning blue code to red as it cleansed my code from the system.

The Crow was fast approaching the nearest API node that I'd taken control of…

I was prepared for this moment…

I hoped.

The anti-virus collided with the blue cylinder, and it exploded with the power of a land-mine as it triggered the logic-bomb ICE Breaker I'd left behind. The Crow screeched painfully, blinded by the light, and soon enough the avatar rezzed solid.

<<Weasel is running>>

<<Analysing anti-virus subroutines>>

<<Configuring attack packets>>

The ICE Breaker was called Weasel, also taking the form of its namesake. Its long, wily white body and mouse-like face rapidly wriggled its way upwards through the void of cyberspace, dashing through the air, and chased after the crow. The two of them collided and began wrestling like the wild animals they were simulating, snapping at each other with tooth and claw. A powerful enough logic-bomb could've uninstalled the anti-virus entirely, but I didn't have the time for that. With the AI of the anti-virus dedicated to fighting off the weasel, the lockout timer suddenly jumped up:

<<Time to system lock-out: 00:02:13>>

Perfect!

The logic-bomb had bought me the time I needed to fight off the firewall blocking my path; its tentacles fought desperately to pierce the Borealis energy field, sending rapid shockwaves rippling out like a violent storm but never succeeded in breaking inside. The command prompt narrowed in on a viable attack payload:

```
<<
{

    int i;
    unsigned int count = group_info->ngroups;

    for (i = 0; i < group_info->nblocks; i++)
        {unsigned int cp_count = min(NGROUPS_PER_BLOCK, count);

        unsigned int len = cp_count * sizeof(*grouplist);

        if (copy_to_user(grouplist, group_info->blocks[i], len))

        return -EFAULT;

        grouplist += NGROUPS_PER_BLOCK;

        count -= cp_count;}

    return 0;

}
>>
```

```
<<Upload complete>>
<<Re-initialising external packet request >>
```

With a strange, squealing roar, the Borealis bubble extended outwards like an explosion, swallowing up the tentacles and shattering them into polygon-shaped bits. The information highway to the registry was clear. I was home free!

My avatar whizzed across the remaining stretch of the information highway, and passed the threshold of the green sphere, swallowing my entire field of vision as I crossed into the registry.

"I'm in!"

<<External packet request successful>>

<<Access to registry granted>>

<<Copying user credentials>>

<<Logging in to account>>

<<Congratulations: Cyber-attack successful!>

<<Time to system lock out: 00:01:49>>

<<Loading new environment>>

I was lost in a sea of green light that soon gave way to a new definitive world. A new cyberspace grid loaded beneath me, shapes began emerging out from the surface. Before I knew it, I was floating among giant, green towers, like a replica of the Manhattan skyline made from simple building blocks. It was a visualisation of the servers memory banks, and I had access to the data of every user's e-mails. I didn't have anywhere near enough time to download them all, but I only needed one account.

A file browser window appeared on my HUD. Liz ran the search, and we found Andrew Ilian's directory. My avatar whizzed ahead and found the relevant tower block. My avatar came to a stop by a window on the fifteenth floor. We started the download and bits of data began trickling out towards the avatar.

<<Initiating data dump>>

<<Data dump in progress: 0.01 Terabyte(s)>>

It only took us thirty seconds to download what we needed. We were out of there before the anti-virus knew what hit it.

<<Ending cyber-attack run>>

<<Terminating data dump: 1 Terabyte(s) downloaded>>

<<Logging out>>

<<Terminating current simulation>>

<<Suspending Icarus cyberwarfare program>>

<<Resuming Cloudland>>

<<Loading previous simulation>>

The vast grid faded away, only to be replaced just as quickly with the wireframe outlines of the objects of my virtual office. The texture of my oak desk flickered into view, along with the audio data from the sound of my brass fan overhead. I couldn't help but grin to myself.

"Show me the most recent exchange between Ilian and a member of Spiritform," I asked Liz, placing my hands behind my head to rest it victoriously. It took her less than a second to find the appropriate messages and bring them up onto my display.

<<From: Shad0wCell (Shad0wCell@icecoldrevolution.com)>>

<<To: Destiny (D32t1ny@21r1tf0rm.com)>>

<<Sent: 05/10/2045 at 09:43 GMT>>

<<Attachments: 0>>

<<Body:

I did it! I downloaded the Project Selection files! They're encrypted, just as you thought though. How do you want me to send them over to you guys?

Btw, I tried looking into the employees working on the Project. But all the names on the files were replaced with ID numbers. The only one I was able to match up with a name was Dr Julie Carpenter. Don't suppose you've got access to their payroll data?

FYI, she's supposed to be making an appearance at ModCon in London this coming Saturday? If you've got a good wireless packet sniffing program, I could attempt a local hack on her?

-Shad0w Cell

>>

My jaw dropped.

"Destiny?"

Gabrielle had warned me. I'd known since the moment I took the case, there was a chance that I was going to have to be investigating her. I'd been trying not to think about it, but now I was faced with the reality. She was already on the list of wanted criminals. If I uncovered evidence that would lead to her whereabouts… Virtualife's private security contractor would be legally obligated to arrest her.

Talk about a violent break-up.

I ambivalently rolled my lips, telepathically clicking on the response she'd sent:

<<From: Destiny (D32t1ny@21r1tf0rm.com)>>

<<To: Shad0wCell (Shad0wCell@icecoldrevolution.com)>>

<<Sent: 05/10/2045 at 09:56 GMT>>

<<Attachments: 1>

<<Body:

Nice going kid. I've attached the executable install file for our network transfer protocols. You can securely send the file to our server through them.

Make sure you've got plenty of backup copies! If you've got a drone or a robot with a large enough drive, I'd suggest saving one there. Search up a tutorial on how to install a fugitive mode.

We'll get back to you regarding your suggestion for ModCon, but cheers for the intel. ☺

-Destiny

>>

She had the files. An accessory after the fact. Not to mention the dozens of other crimes she must've committed during her stupid crusade. And now I had to catch her.

"Any newer messages?" I checked with Liz.

She shook her head. "They're still good leads to go on."

I nodded reservedly. I'd never taken on a case that was anywhere remotely as personal as this. I was starting to think that Virtualife had known she was involved from the start.

"There's nothing here that Virtualife couldn't have uncovered on their own."

"You think they're testing you?"

"Or they want me to take the fall if it gets out they're interfering with a murder investigation."

"That is statistically more likely. But you always knew that was a possibility."

"True... true..." I mumbled. "It's not like they're not paying me enough either."

"So, no regrets?"

"Not yet."

"There's still a cooling off period in your contract with Virtualife if you'd like to cancel."

I scoffed and shook my head. I couldn't afford to do that either.

Damned if I do, damned if I don't.

I spent the next few hours filtering through the contact list and exchanges between them. There wasn't much else that they could tell me. He wasn't actually a member of Spiritform, yet. The Virtualife hack was an attempt to try to prove himself, almost like an initiation ceremony. Most of his email messages were spam of course, but after that, the person who'd been communicating with him most frequently was Claudia Schwarz, his fake girlfriend.

You would have had to have been seventeen to have fallen for it. She had him in the palm of her hand. Seriously, if someone you meet online asks you to hack into something, the answer should be *no.* Then again, I guess after dealing with multiple online scams I'd become less sympathetic.

Liz and I theorised about that for a while. It didn't seem likely that Spiritform would need to trick someone like him into their dirty work. More likely it was some kind of industrial espionage manoeuvre. One of Virtualife's rivals taking advantage of Ilian's mother to create a scandal… and if that was true, then the Project really was illegal.

Great.

We'd also figured that there was at least one backup copy saved to the Ilian's boy's robot dog, a Dobertron model by the name of Rex. The picture Liz had sent me made him out as a ferocious-looking machine, with sharpened carbon nanotube teeth. Apparently capable of defending itself… if you wanted to hide stolen data and keep it on the move, saving it to a combat-ready robot was a pretty safe bet.

Sure enough, Rex had disappeared from Andrew's apartment, round about the same time of the murder. The police were already looking for it as a witness to his death, though. I informed Virtualife anyway just in case they didn't already know.

The most crucial lead was the ModCon info. If they were going to take Ilian's suggestion, at least one member of Spiritform would be attending, which meant someone for me to spy on. Liz and I both agreed it'd be more likely they'd be coming in android avatars rather than take the risk of coming in person. In theory, all I had to do was use a wireless packet sniffer program to scan and detect which units were using Spiritform encryption, then use one of my SpyFly drones to patch into the hardware manually. With direct access, I could run a trace program and get a ping on their location.

I sent an update to the e-mail address Gabrielle had left me with. I received a response promptly, in which she thanked me and said that Doctor Carpenter would be briefed about the possible threat to her, but liked my suggestion to use her as bait to draw out Spiritform. Liz and Gabrielle would then coordinate over the next few hours to process the security arrangement. She would have to be informed that I would be recording her, and she would have to have protection. Not so obvious protection as to put Spiritform off, but they were the sort of details that AIs could handle best themselves. One of the first things they'd agreed upon was that I could make no direct contact with Doctor Carpenter myself – if she had been hacked and I attempted to contact her, the whole plan could blow up in our faces. That was going to make the entire operation trickier, but it wasn't the end of the world.

Not bad for a few hours' work.

The rest of the day was spent questioning persons of interest online. Finding as many of Ilian's contacts in virtual hangouts and squeezing info out of them one way or another. Not very productive. If nothing else it appeared like the kid was relatively tight-lipped about his plans, not that it had done him any good.

Evening came, and Liz reminded me I had other engagements. Social ones, surprisingly enough. I'd promised to meet my old GCHQ buddy David Hiresh in Camden tonight to watch the match between Tottenham and Arsenal.

I briefly debated whether I should cancel on him and carry on working. Liz assured me she would keep digging around online for me, and gently reminded me that I'd cancelled on him the last three times we were supposed to meet. Eventually, I decided that I'd done a good day's work, and could afford to take this evening to myself, though I could only hope that Virtualife weren't watching and judging my every move.

<<Terminating FIVR simulation>>

<<Disengaging neural lace>>

<<Disconnecting from server>>

<<Thank you for using Cloudland>>

I left my living pod for the first time that day around 6 pm and headed to the underground car park, telepathically programming the destination into my car's auto-driver.

Within a few minutes, we were off, my hands resting comfortably on the wheel. The dashboard projected the route to the Oxford Arms pub in Camden where we'd agreed to watch the match. My windscreen was playing pre-match commentary from *BBC Sports* live while Regent's Park rolled past, the traffic on the lanes either side gliding gracefully along. This was one of the nicer parts of town. Even though we were in the city centre, the ever-present glow of holograms and the towering skyscrapers seemed further away, surrounded by well-kept trees behind iron cast fences, attended to by gardening drones.

<<You have 1 new Facebook message from: David Hiresh>>

I neuroclicked the message to open it on my HUD. A picture appeared, and I found myself chuckling at a photoshopped image of the Arsenal squad, graphically edited to give each member of the team three legs, the caption just read: *'Arsenal turns to genetic engineering to win the league'*.

Cocky bastard.

David and I had a strange relationship. Most of my memories of him had been from working with him at GCHQ, which of course had been erased. What did remain was blurry, mostly consisting of pub trips after work. My earliest definitive recollection of him I still possessed, was my leaving party the night after I resigned from the company. We'd stayed in touch since then, but it had always been slightly awkward… feeling like I was going through the motions of being his friend for the sake of it.

But with the stolen memory files Dart had been sending me, slowly but surely, it was all coming back to me. Transforming him in my mind from an old colleague to someone I genuinely thought of as a mate.

And goddamn it felt good… all I needed to do was keep up with the payments to Dart.

So far, so worth it…

I arrived in Camden about twenty minutes later in another underground car park. I got out, picked up my hat and strolled through the grimy, grey structure, passing dozens of cars all parked neatly next to each other. One of the old fluorescent lights flickered annoyingly, casting shadows over the background of algae-covered walls, the air tainted with the smell of biofuel and piss.

My HUD guided me towards the elevator. As I passed a concrete support column that had become the home for a wrinkled old Iranian woman, my prosthetic eyes scanned her and identified her from an early *Facebook* profile. Her name was Farah Amir and, from what I could tell, she was another climate refugee wearing a ragged red burhka and begging in Arabic for change. Of course, it couldn't be change in pounds. Probably hoping for some street currency. Without any to give her, I waited there awkwardly for the elevator to hit the ground floor. Being able to provide a name for the face of the person I was rejecting somehow making it all the worse.

I was relieved when the buzzer finally went. The rusting steel door clanged open for me to shuffle inside. I stepped onto the street level, my music player automatically loading 'Anarchy in the UK', and was met by the dark red Victorian arches and brick lanes, illuminated by bioluminescent lamps, filthy neon signs (mostly in Chinese), faulty holographic projectors. A reggae band was playing on the corner by the tube station. The walls plastered with art that screamed creative rebellion. The streets were jam-packed full of the people wearing clothes that ranged from the grungy and ripped to glowing and vibrant. The air filled with the scent of raging sexuality and ganja. Not to mention the most bizarre augmentations you could imagine; laser eyes, Scissorhands, speaker boobs, you name it, it was the end result of being the heart of London's counterculture and backstreet clinics. Camden never changes.

The market was busy all times of the night. The shopkeepers tending the stands had set up their homes behind them, simple huts built from scrap, wired up for power and internet. This was one of the few places where traditional shopping hadn't been destroyed by 3D printing and drone delivery. Pretty much everything was on sale. Old-fashioned clothes, cannabis paraphernalia, jewellery, second-hand robot and computer parts. The shopkeepers had their own homebuilt cobbled-together droids tending some of their stands, or using drones to deliver packages by air. Most of it probably hadn't been acquired legally, and the police presence was never too far away. A large gang wearing sunglasses and hoodies brushed past and looked each other down. The cops butted in…in a less than polite manner, looking ready to deal out some rough justice.

Just once I'd like to have a night where shit didn't kick off. It wasn't always possible with work, but I avoided coming into the city as much as possible for this reason. It always felt like London was still a hair's breadth away from a riot. I'd tried to convince David to just watch the match virtually, but oh no, he wanted to go to a dive.

My HUD guided me towards the pub, and I began weaving and shoving my way through the inebriated Friday night crowd. I turned a corner to head into a graffiti-stained alley. A council-owned white and orange sanitation robot, the size of a golf cart, had backed itself up to a dumpster. Yellow lights flashed with a loud obnoxious bleeping, while the machine deployed its rear hydraulic claws to grip a set of large handles on either side of the container. The motors screeched to life, lifting it up with a whir and slotting it into place in its rear cargo hold with a clatter. The stench from the trash was overpowering, forcing me to block the synaptic signals from my nasal receptors.

I quickened my pace to get out of the robot's way as it began backing up.

I heard something behind me, a violent crashing sound, loud enough to send me spinning on the spot to see where it had come from.

Nothing. No one was there… but I felt like I was being watched, and I wasn't talking about the omnipresent gaze of CCTV either.

My visual scan picked up something, a glimmer from the rooftop of the low rise buildings to my left. I whirled around to face it, but it was already gone.

The logical part of me told me I'd imagined it, but I still eyed it suspiciously, zooming in on the ledge with my bionic lenses to double check.

"Something wrong?" Liz checked, her avatar appearing on my HUD glancing with concern over the rim of her glasses.

Her voice seemed to snap me back into focus, drawing my glance back to ground level.

"Huh? Oh, no I'm fine… thanks for asking," I said rapidly, trying to hide my embarrassment, anxiously scratching the hair beneath my hat.

I told myself it was just a hologram and wrote the jumpiness off as a side effect of setting my neural lace to focus mode so often. One of the many health and safety warnings the software gave you, but no one paid any attention to.

"You might want to move," Liz added awkwardly.

"Huh?"

I'd been so distracted, I hadn't noticed the garbage-collection robot waiting directly behind me; the AI honking its horn in simulated impatience.

"Oops."

I awkwardly slid out of its way, pressing myself against the grubby wall to let it slowly roll past.

I telepathically scheduled a complete medical diagnostic tomorrow to put my mind at ease and carried on towards the pub. The alleyway led back out onto the high street, and an arrow on my display pointed me towards the Oxford Arms.

The outside walls were black, the name written in brass-gold lettering above the rounded windows. I'd already telepathically placed an order; a couple *Jägerbombs* and a pint of *Magners* for me to collect at the bar.

I stepped inside and admired the surroundings. There were few traditions as sacred as the good old-fashioned pub in Britain. It was packed full of rowdy blokes wearing shirts for both teams, buzzing with testosterone and alcohol-fuelled chatter. The staff-bots scuttled around collecting empty glasses, while bulky bouncers kept a beady eye on the dodgier looking characters. The floor, tables, and bar were wooden, but the walls were plastered with wallpaper screens, each streaming from *Sky Sports* 360.

The footage was live from a camera drone, whizzing close to the stadium grounds getting right into the action. The footage streamed to the embedded wall screens like they were windows, giving the pub the appearance that it had been built in the middle of the football pitch. The players were already filing out onto the pitch, and a pair of commentators were chatting away in a small window in the top right corner while a ticker bar streamed across the bottom of the screen with messages from around the net. With the drone following the movements of the players in real-time, you could get some pretty spectacular views of the action.

Still not as good as VR though.

I glanced through the crowd, telepathically ordering Liz to access David's location data to track him down; sure enough, my HUD guided me to the far-right corner. I craned my neck in the direction, and sure enough, David had a rounded table to himself and was sipping at a pint of *Carlsberg*. A pretty blonde girl came over to ask if she could take the chair he was saving for me. I could see the disappointment in his beady eyes, clear as day on his face when he had to turn her down.

I navigated my way through the crowd, brushing past some tart in a luminous corset with tits the size of watermelons, before finally reaching him and tapping him with one of my metal fingers.

"Oi, Oi! Better late than never!" he chuckled gruffly, standing up to bro hug me.

"Fashionably late," I corrected him as I accepted the manly embrace.

One of the waiters brought my order. We hurriedly picked up the *Jägerbombs* I'd ordered, clinked them together, said cheers, and downed them, feeling the warm brown liquid sliding down my throat, while I simultaneously adjusted the settings on my bionic liver to allow for greater intoxication.

"Ahhh!" I breathed, rubbing away the drops on the side of my mouth. "Good shit."

I put down the shot glass, rested my hat on the back of the chair, before picking up my pint glass with the animated graphics of the *Magners* logo printed on the side.

"Who was that bird you were chatting up?" I asked with a coy grin.

"Didn't check her profile, but I totally coulda picked her up!"

"Sure. You do realise this isn't VR? Can't hide behind an avatar here."

"You're one to talk. I'm just waiting to see an announcement that you're in a relationship with your VPA!"

I averted my gaze away from him, taking another sip. "I'm a busy guy."

"Come on, man! I keep telling you to get out more!"

I briefly glanced around at the giggling, tipsy girls around the bar. Most of them were pretty cute, wearing their makeup, fancy dresses and high heels. Part of me wanted to try talking to them, but I was a bit out of practice. My last three relationships, having started online… usually ended there as well. You can't put make-up on a pig. It was hard to say, but I figured about half of them was instantly turned off by my level of cyberisation. The other half were turned off for… other reasons.

I found it hard talking about myself, notably when I was missing the last years of my life. I tried downloading a 'Pick-up artist' app once, generating scripts for my flirting with the opposite (or same) sex based on the results of bio-feedback scans; capillary dilation of the so-called blush response, fluctuation of the pupil, involuntary dilatation of the iris that sort of thing…no joy.

"I just wanna watch the game, man," I answered flatly, rubbing my cheeks with frustration, feeling the plastic casing of the prosthetic eyes.

"Booooor-ing! Don't tell me you're still hung up on that Spiritform girl? What was her name? Destiny?"

The electrochromatic lenses of my eyes glazed over. "Don't go there, man."

"Whoa, touchy subject?" he said defensively, holding his hands up in a surrender position.

I blanked him and took another bitter sip. He carried on staring at me in a hopeful manner, probably expecting me to cave in and open up about it.

"Fine, be that way," he sighed eventually, scratching the side of his head while he pondered how to move the conversation along. Not wanting us to sit in silence, he eventually settled on, "What's new at work?"

"Can't complain, just got a big client."

"Cool, man! Being your own boss must be a nice change from…" His voice trailed off, looking suddenly embarrassed. "Sorry, bro."

He forgot about my erased memories all the time.

"Forget it."

He knew it was weird for me too, hanging out with someone who could actually just *tell* me what had happened in the seven years of my life that had gone missing. He was allowed to say to me that he had *been there*, but couldn't tell me *what* had happened.

I suppose I'd forgiven him in the end. After all, he'd be breaking the law as much as I was right now if he had. I suppose it was even weirder that I was now starting to regain my memories and couldn't tell him about it.

Rather than let the conversation go quiet again, I returned the question.

"What about you? What's kicking at the ol' factory?"

"Oh, same old, same old. We're just beta testing a new patch for Mother Mind's behaviour prediction algorithms. Virtualife are boasting it can detect criminal intent a full seventy-two hours before the fact."

"Sounds fun," I replied sarcastically, hoping to hear something juicier than that.

This was usually how my little catch-ups with David went down. I would try to tease info out of him to fill in the gaps in my memory, and he would grudgingly remind me that it was classified.

"Keep trying," Liz prodded me telepathically, a hopeful glint in her avatar's eyes. "He might know something about Project Selection or Spiritform."

Couldn't hurt to ask…

"You might be able to give me a hand actually."

"Oh?" He raised an eyebrow. "An above-board favour, or…"

"Ehhhhh…" I answered, tilting my hand from side to side, suggesting that it would be a little bit illegal.

He threw his head back reluctantly and groaned, pointing his thumb at a camera hanging from the ceiling. "Gimme a break, man."

Good point. Saying it out loud was a bad idea. Liz reminded me of what I kept in my pocket. Something ancient by today's standards, a graphite pencil and a pad of paper. I hardly ever used it, but the virtual PI training I had gone through advised me to keep one to hand, just in case.

"Bloody hell, did you get that in a museum?" David teased me, as I pulled the antiquated ring-bound notepad out from my pocket and began scribbling on it. I temporarily disconnected the Goldtooth connection from my neural lace and bionic eyes to my smartwatch as I wrote, keeping Mother Mind out.

I scribbled 'Project Selection' onto one of the pages, tore it out and slid it over to him.

"Mean anything to you?" I asked.

He took a quick glance at the page, then stiffly lifted his head back up to face me. "Uh… no, sorry."

"Hmmm… shame."

He was lying. I'd had a nagging feeling since my meeting with Gabrielle this morning. Why had Virtualife chosen to hire *me,* when I'd only been working as a private investigator for the last year? There must have been hundreds more in London with a better CV than me.

Unless there was a connection between Project Selection and GCHQ.

This had all but confirmed it…

Maybe it was a good thing, that Gabrielle had chosen me because it would give me an advantage over other investigators. Of course, there were other… less favourable outcomes that were possible.

What's life without a little risk?

My attention was caught by the sound of an electronic whistle from the android referee projecting from the wall screen, signalling the start of the match. The chatter in the room drew quieter and more focused as heads turned around to watch the ball moving from screen to screen, passed between Arsenal players as Tottenham tried to catch up. The brief tension that had built up between us disappeared as quickly as it appeared.

David grinned and playfully tapped me on the side of the arm, jokingly humming *'Danny Boy'*.

"Oh, it is so on!" I scoffed with confidence.

I made myself comfortable in the booth, leaning back expansively, ready to take another sip. I noticed a pair of rough-looking characters by the bar, both shaved bald, each wearing combat visors and thick black leather jackets and jeans, studded with spikes, and had nano-fibre epidemic tattoos etched into their skin, intelligently delivering steroids. They were careful with their privacy settings. Liz informed me that the tattoos were most likely obtained in prison, but I couldn't get any actual profiling info from their social media, or from British criminal records. It took me a second to realise one of them was a woman. Shorter than the bloke, but just as tough.

I could've sworn I saw them staring over at David, their eyes darting away as soon as I noticed. I kept my eye on them for a moment, to see if they turned back; they didn't. I shrugged it off as another bout of focus-mode induced paranoia. I settled down again and readied myself to watch the players starting to get into the rhythm of the game. Tracking their movements across each of the three wall screens stretching before me.

After a few more post-game drinks we staggered out of the bar at ten thirty, to be welcomed by a light drizzle sprinkling onto our faces. I slipped on my hat to shield myself, looking up to see the colours of the rainbow refracting from the holograms. We were wasted, my head spinning with mild tingling inebriation. I had to admit I had my tail between my legs after the crushing defeat that Tottenham had suffered.

"Fucking gutted, mate!" David slurred, struggling to find his feet.

"The Refbot was a wanker."

He grinned and patted me on the shoulder. "Keep telling yourself that. Stay safe, yeah?"

"Yeah, mind 'ow ya go!" I waved back.

We turned to go our separate ways, following my GPS back to the car when I noticed him heading towards the mass of the Friday night crowd.

"Hey, wait! You're not *walking* home, are you?"

"Well yeah… my car's in the shop."

"Get a bus or a cab!"

"Please! My flat's in Kentish Town. Much easier and cheaper if I walk through the market."

"*Through the market?*" I exhaled in disbelief at him. "At this time? When you're this wasted? Are you crazy? You'll get mugged, mate!"

"I did basic martial arts training! Give it a rest."

"Oh yeah, Cymurai has nothing on you," I groaned, facepalming myself in awe of his epic fail.

"Chill out. My nanobots'll just reactivate their alco-" David froze on the spot like he had just realised something.

"Oh…"

"What, what is it?"

"Ah, fuck!"

"What?"

"Um… well, I was messing around my medical probe's OS the other day… and I kinda fucked up the alcohol regulation protocols."

"Oh, that is classic you!" I cried, rolling my eyes.

"I thought you had your memory erased?"

"Well, your fuck-ups are pretty fucking memorable, mate. Look, my car is right here. At least let me give you a ride back to your place."

"Nah, mate, I don't want to be a bother."

Liz popped up on my vision. "It's a seriously bad idea for him to go alone."

"David, if your VPA is anything like mine, it'll be warning you not to go down to the market now. For fuck's sake, listen to it!"

"Oh, get off it, man! I could use the fresh air."

He ignored everything I'd said and headed over to the crowded stalls teeming with seedy life. I stared at him in disbelief. There was no point in arguing with him, the stubborn son of a bitch.

A week ago, I wouldn't have cared… but with my memories starting to be restored, I couldn't help but feel a sense of responsibility for him now.

I was kicking myself for caring, but shook my head with a breath of frustration and jogged over to catch up.

"Nah man, you don't have to…" he said, trying to reassure me, holding his hands up in protest.

"Shut up," I snapped back bitterly, regretting letting my feelings get the better of me. "Let's get you home already."

Perhaps what was most irritating was that I'd been enjoying my little buzz, but someone needed to be the designated driver. I telepathically engaged my artificial liver and nanobots in breaking it down faster.

"This really isn't a good idea, Arthur," Liz reminded telepathically.

"Don't need to tell me twice. Bring the car around to meet me at David's place when this is over."

I saw my HUD map marking out the GPS location of my car, and Liz plotting out the route to David's home address. She transmitted the command to the auto-driver and watched it as it began the journey out of the car park.

The pair of us stumbled tipsily along the cobbled pathways. David was moving far too slow for my liking, so I put my arm around his shoulder to keep him upright and drag him along. As I was doing that, I noticed the two bikers from the pub heading out of the door to take a drag from their e-cigs. Again, I could've sworn they'd glanced our way.

Chill out, dude…

Once more I put it out of my mind and turned to enter the narrow aisles between the stands of Camden market, doing my best to stop us stepping in any of the litter on the street. The chatter of the crowd, the flashing of cheap advertisement, the smell of sizzling Thai and Chinese noodles and cannabis in the air, all made for a constant assault on the senses. The calls of the salesmen around us were unrelenting.

"Half-price!"

"Come on, this'll look great on you!"

"Please, I have kids to feed!"

I blanked them out, my eyes not wavering from the end of the alleyway my HUD was pointing me towards. My growling stomach demanded that I order some food, but it would have to wait. So I gave the telepathic command to order me some noodles for when I got home.

It was hard to ignore the pair of hookers we stumbled past though, with their excessive make-up and revealing clothes, smoking real cigarettes next to a trash can. They leaned forward, giving us a full view down the top of their enlarged breasts, enticing us with seductive winks as they offered to give us with a good time in a tone that was barely above a whisper.

"Don't even think about it," I snapped at David, yanking him back forcefully with my bionic strength, but as I did something on the stand behind us caught his eye.

"Oh shit, is that a Carbonblade-6?" He grinned, wobbling over and picking up a green plastic package for a processor chip costing just forty-five quid.

"Yes, yes," the shop owner said excitedly, a wrinkled, grey Vietnamese woman rubbing her hands together in anticipation of a purchase. "Brand new. Close to top of the range. Perfect for androids. You want, yeah?"

"David, let's go," I growled.

"No, hold on! My watch does need an upgrade."

He turned back and began haggling down the price. I let out a long, sour breath, looking around restlessly. I leaned back on one of the wooden poles supporting a nanotech tarpaulin shielding the stand from the rain.

I folded my arms and watched the crowd suspiciously, my enhanced metabolism doing its job now and rapidly sobering me up. I'd worked a bodyguard job before, some engineer for a local repair shop making a delivery for a client in one the rougher parts of Peckham. It apparently wasn't above board, but I kept my mouth shut. The point was, I didn't do it for *free*. I would have to make it clear he owed me a favour… one that I was definitely going to call in at some point. I wasn't running a charity.

I scanned the crowd intently, watching the raw, naked desire of the street bubble through the urban decay. Everyone wanted something. Camden was the place to get it. There wasn't even an attempt to hide it. Camden's rebellious streak had made it the centre of the public resistance to the Mother Mind system. I got a glimpse of an e-poster, peeling from one of the brick archways, projecting an animated rendering of the Spiritform logo.

Liz suggested there was a risk that if anyone identified us as GCHQ employees, we could get lynched. That wasn't what came to my mind though… just Destiny.

I wasn't thinking about her for long when I saw the leather-bound bikers from the pub strolling into the market. My eyes briefly met their gaze through the crowd. There was no doubt about it. They definitely had been looking our direction this time, meandering their way through the crowd… like they'd been keeping pace with David and me. They seemed to have noticed we'd stopped, and started mingling amongst the stand, pretending to look at the wares for sale.

Keep calm, Arthur…

I did as they did, faking taking an interest in the spare printer parts while opening up a telepathic chat channel to David. He raised an eyebrow at me, wondering why I was phoning him when we were stood next to one another.

"Don't look now, but I think we're being followed," I told him over the comm-link.

My words put the fear of God into him; the colour drained from his face, turning him into a portrait of wide-eyed horror.

"F… Followed?"

I sent him a photo I'd taken with my eyes to his HUD. "Do these guys look familiar to you?"

The moment the picture loaded onto his display, his face turned to stone, and he clutched the side of his hair in panic.

"Oh, fuck me."

My heart sank, but outwardly I kept up my calm composure.

"Knew it," I snarled angrily over the link. "Who are they?"

He was now uncontrollably rubbing the back of his neck as if it were a nervous twitch.

"Uh… The Albanian Mafia."

"*The Albanian Mafia?!?*"

David nodded grimly.

"Okay," I said, keeping as calm as I could despite the cold rush of panic and anger. "Can you think of a reason why they'd be tailing us?"

"Well… um…"

"David?" I hissed.

"…I may have done a favour for the Yakuza," he admitted, cringing and frantically rubbing the back of his straining neck.

I gulped bitterly, knowing where this was going. "Did this favour happen to involve *stealing* from the Mafia?"

He gave a grimacing nod, sending my heart pounding with rage.

"Oh great!" I glared at him, clenching my metal fist with a rattle. "Thank you, David! Thank you so much, for getting me in the middle of bloody *gang warfare*! Why the fuck didn't you say anything?"

"I'm bloody pissed, aren't I?!"

"Oh, you *arsehole!* You…"

"All right… All right," Liz appeared on my display gesturing to calm me down. "Arguing with him isn't going to get us anywhere. You need to lose them, now!"

She began reciting suggestions to me and highlighted the fact that I had my SpyFly drone in my arm compartment.

"Use it to keep an eye on them without drawing attention!"

I was grateful for the suggestion and pulled back my sleeve. I telepathically opened the compartment and gave the command to launch the mechanical insect inside, sending it whizzing away.

"Act normal," I growled at David. "You've seen nothing. You've heard nothing. You don't know a goddamn thing! Got it!?"

He gave me a shaky nod with a few ragged breaths, trying to get a grip on himself. SpyFly hovered about ten feet above the pair of them, and focused its beady camera eyes on them, forwarding the images to my display.

"I'm configuring your wrist laser for disrupt mode," Liz explained, placing an arrow on my vision pointing to my right arm. "Shining it on them should disable their visors. Use it only as a last resort."

I nodded nervously. At close range, I could use it to cut through steel. It didn't have the range to be used as a lethal weapon, but a low energy beam could easily blind someone. My most useful built-in armaments were my Taser knuckles, but I didn't want to get close enough to use them.

My eyes darted around, trying to find the best mass of bodies for us to shuffle our way through.

"That way," I said, gesturing towards the crowd herding themselves towards the Underworld bar.

I shepherded David towards it with my metal palm, trying to make it look like a friendly gesture.

"Keep moving! Don't look back!" I barked telepathically.

"I'm going, I'm going!" he insisted desperately.

We weaved in and out of the huddle, moving briskly but subtly. Liz began plotting out our suggested route on the map, carefully putting in as many twists and turns as possible to try to throw them off.

We hid behind a wall of bodies, a crowd intently admiring watching a street performing act. A sea of awed faces as a Ju-Jitsu master sparred off against a holographic demon as part of some elaborate theatrical act that had the crowd in awe.

We slipped around the corner, hoping that they weren't crazy enough to shoot us in front of so many witnesses. Then again, I'd heard the rumours about the mafia paying off the private security companies to look the other way to their activities in the boroughs under their control.

Mother Mind saw all… if it wasn't turning a blind eye.

"Jesus, they're on us like flies to shit," I muttered, watching the gangsters through the drone's eyes.

"I think I know how" Liz pointed out. She placed an arrow on my HUD pointing towards the sky. I averted my gaze towards it; there was another drone there, a tri-copter unit, its sensor array focused directly on the pair of us.

"Dammit! No way we're throwing them off with that thing stalking us."

"You need to get off the street. I'll check internal schematics of the nearby buildings for-"

Whatever Liz had in mind, it was too late. The gangsters seemed to know there was something up. The woman nudged her head in our direction, prompting the other one to nod back. They reached their waistlines and flicked back their jackets, revealing their holstered handguns.

"Shit!" I cried, whirling to face David. "We gotta move, now!"

"Oh, Jesus Christ."

I shoved him forward, forcing him through the crowd with a series of angry cries around him. Liz hurriedly plotted out our best escape route, and quickly activated my neural lace's focus mode, allowing me to recall swiftly all the virtual combat training we'd done at GCHQ. Back then I thought it had been a waste of time. Not anymore. Out of the corner of my HUD, I saw as the hitmen bolted after us, whipping out the Russian-made pistol, their elongated barrels wheeling in our direction.

"Arthur!" Liz cried, pointing to my right wrist.

No choice!

A graphical targeting reticule appeared over their faces. I flicked out my right arm, drawing back my hand to reveal the large, round laser lens mounted into an alcove on the wrist. With a telepathic command, the lens burned to life, projecting out an intense ray of red light. I directed the beam towards their heads, swinging the beam in a small arc it hit both of them with one clean sweep. The attack worked. A second later the pair of gangsters were groaning loudly and stumbling on the spot, their HUDs reduced to soups of static.

The crowd around us began murmuring with alert confusion, staring at me while I stood my ground like a warrior, keeping the beam held in position to paralyse them on the spot… but it would not last long.

The barrels of their guns slowly twisted our way…

"RUN!" I yelled, disengaging the laser, turning on the spot to dash away, David following me with panicked haste.

BANG! BANG!

The gunshots rang through the thick night air, sending screams of fear and pain washing through the crowd like an electric current. David and I instinctively ducked down in time to avoid the shots, but a girl standing behind us wasn't so lucky. The bullet landed in the middle of her stomach with a great angry burst of blood, knocking her to the ground. I caught a glimpse of her confused but suffering face staring blankly up at the drone's camera.

"Come on!" I cried, pulling David toward the alleyway Liz was pointing toward.

We shoved our way through the rush of panic, the crowd turning to a stampede in the crowded, narrow lanes. The bikers weren't far behind but were equally stymied by the mass of bodies.

We sprinted into an alleyway. Liz warned me it was a dead end, but that there was a fire escape close by we could use to climb up to the roof. There would be a limited amount of cover between us and the shooters, but there were no alternatives. Good a place as any for a final stand.

"Liz, activate combat mode!"

<<Combat mode activated>>

<<Electrosynaptic stimulation to 100%>>

<<Pain receptor inhibitors online>>

I felt my body go cold and hard, numb to the touch. My neural lace was now blocking my tactile synaptic feedback; a common enhancement for soldiers allowing them to fight through massive injuries. I hoped to hell I wasn't going to need it.

"GET OUT DA FOOKING WAY!" I heard a fierce yell from behind us.

I caught a glimpse of them behind us, ramming onlookers out of the way while readying another volley of shots. I pushed David behind a dumpster to take cover.

BANG! BANG!

The next round of fire slammed into the red brick behind us, cascading dust and debris over us as we cowered behind the steel frame of the garbage bin. Liz ran a rapid visual analysis and indicated that they had been armour-piercing smart tracking rounds.

"Jeez, they're packing some serious firepower!" David cried over the sound of the oncoming flurry of bullets coming our way.

"What did you expect them to use, harsh language?"

The bullets ricocheted off the edge of the dumpster protecting us, with rapid, angry clangs, scattering sparks across the pavement. Their drone hadn't noticed my SpyFly yet, so I had a live stream of them marching towards us, weapons drawn firmly out, pumping out round after round like it was the 1920s.

"They've got you flanked," Liz cried. "I'll set you up for auto-aim!"

"Right!"

I fumbled on my trousers and unzipped what appeared to be a pocket, but revealed the chassis of the prosthetic leg underneath. With a telepathic command, the magnetically-shielded compartment inside popped up, exposing my holstered 105-E Magnum. I whipped it out and shut the compartment, taking the time to admire the bulky beauty of the weapon. A revolver for the modern man; a darkened silver finish to the six-round chamber, thick, triangular-shaped barrel, equipped with smart targeting, and custom printed grip, trigger, and hammer to my liking.

"Jesus," David swore. "When the fuck did you-"

"Think I'd work in this town without a gun?" I joked with a fake American accent over the gunfire.

"Yeah, way to play the stereotype, Arthur."

Another memory came to mind… the last person I'd killed. I'd been working a case for a couple working for *GlaxoSmithKline,* wanted me to bring their son home… and that meant fighting my way through a crack house. I knew it wasn't going to be the last time.

I ordered my SpyFly to forward me the precise coordinates of each of the gangsters, and loaded it into the targeting control software now running on my HUD.

"The angle from here won't provide clear shots," Liz explained. "I'm switching your ammo to stun. Even with those visors, it should at least be enough to push them back!"

I nodded back at her both telepathically and physically. With the weapon drawn and pressed close to my chest, I carefully sidled against the wall, shifting my weight onto the dumpster. I slowed my breathing, calming myself as best I could with the sound of gunfire around the corner, leaning against the iron wall of the container.

<<Initializing auto-aim protocols>>

<<Targeting package loaded>>

<<Connecting to bionic arm drivers>>

<<Standing-by>>

"Now!" Liz ordered.

With a spring-like burst, I darted to the right, leaning just enough to extend my arm out, and reach around the side and point my gun at the gangsters.

<<Auto-aim in progress>>

I felt the software take control of my body, all the programs running in unison: the GPS marking, the laser tracking, the servos for my hand working to guide me. Like some existential gut instinct, I could feel where the pair of the gangsters were. My hand moved on its own, spinning the barrel of the gun to where it needed to be. I felt a tingling sensation when the laser sight of the revolver lined up with the data provided by SpyFly, letting me know it was time to manually pull the trigger.

BOOM! BOOM!

The 10-millimetre smart-rounds exploded from the nozzle, my metal arms rigid against the kickback. Spent shells spat out and clattered to the ground. A split second later, the sensors inside the bullets detected their proximity to the targets and detonated the mini flash-bang grenades inside. The dazzling light of the detonation illuminated the alleyway with an ear-piercing roar. The camera feed from the SpyFly was distorted out of focus, but through the blaze I could see the two bikers stumbling backwards, their arms shielding their visors.

<<Auto-aim protocols complete>>

<<Manual control restored>>

<<Switching to lethal-fire mode>>

"Go! Go! Go!" Liz cried.

With my arms back under my control, I leaned out and popped my head and gun out from behind the dumpster. My HUD lit up with a graphical reticule, following the movements of the targeting laser.

I squeezed back on the trigger, firing another precisely aimed shot. The bald dude returned fire, forcing me to whip my torso back behind the dumpster just in the nick of time to hear the ricochet ringing next to me.

"He's out of ammo!" Liz prodded me.

I readied myself for another shot. I peered out in time to see the bulky woman flipping over a jewellery stand, sending the cheap goods spilling over the pavement with a waterfall of soft clinking. The table was made from a tough-ass bioplastic called Withstandex; strong enough to absorb the impact of my next round, leaving nothing but a dent.

"Crap!"

The bald guy had already reloaded and took aim once more. I flipped myself back, but blindly fired off another shot which missed.

<<Reload required>>

I hurriedly prepared to remove the ammo cylinder from the mounting of the gun and flicked out the spent cartridges with a clatter onto the cobblestones, before quickly grabbing the mag-loader on my belt. I had a rounded ammo pouch on the side, accompanied by a small plunger-shaped device, with six slots on the underside. The magnet in each slot sucked up a bullet, allowing me to quickly slot them into the chamber all at once.

"Liz, tell me you called the police?" I asked hurriedly, starting to have my doubts about taking them on.

"They're on the way, ETA five minutes!"

"We're gonna be dead by then! Got any ideas?"

"Just one…"

She placed an arrow on my vision pointing upwards. I looked to see that she was indicating to an old neon sign in the shape of a Chinese dragon, held in place by a degraded iron frame, showing signs of metal fatigue.

"Cheers!"

I manually took aim and pulled the trigger. The shot landed, and with a loud metallic creaking, the support frame started to give way. It snapped and came crashing down.

The gangsters looked up just in time to see it happen, staring at the collapsing sign like a pair of muppets. The neon dragon slammed into the ground with a great clatter, sending a cascade of glass across the pavement. The bulky, leather-bound woman leapt out of the way in time, but the bald dude wasn't so lucky. Having tripped over the upturned table, his leg was now trapped underneath of the metal frame, letting out a burning cry of anguish; the bone probably crushed under the weight.

SpyFly confirmed it; they had dropped their guns. The woman was already darting her head from side to side trying to find it. I wasn't going to give her a chance. David was still cowering behind the trash can. I stood up tall and firm, my magnum locked on and pointed directly at the woman's head.

"Freeze!" I yelled at her.

She did as she was told, stopping on the spot. Her hands still reaching towards her weapon, only a few inches away. Her head swivelled towards me, her baring her teeth like a wild cat, her eyes scowling from behind the darkened glass of her visor.

"You're making a big mistake," she hissed at me with an Eastern European accent.

"Preaching to the choir, love."

"Your friend is moron! No one steal from us and gets away with it!"

"There's a first time for…"

<<Warning!>>

<<Incoming fire!>>

The infrared sensors in my eyes highlighted a thin red beam projecting from the rooftop; a targeting laser, and the thin red line wheeling towards me.

"Fuck!"

Liz alerted me to my options, placing an arrow on my HUD pointing to the fire escape above me. My enhanced reflexes and virtual gymnastics training kicked in, launching me into a mighty leap, the palms of my hands pointing straight up. David gawked as the micro-pistons in my legs fired at full pressure and was propelled upwards.

<<Gecko pads activated>>

With a clang and a clucking sound, the nano-suction cups in my hands activated. The power of the micro vacuums had me suspended from the fire escape like a piece of dangling meat. I narrowly missed the first wave of fire from the roof. The laser sight swivelled towards me again, and a second barrage soon followed. I heaved myself to the side like a gymnast, and swung over the railing, landing with another loud clatter on all fours on the walkway of the fire escape.

Once more the arc of fire drew towards me, so I leapt across the alleyway like a parkour runner, holding out my gecko pads to come to a sliding stop against the brick wall on the far side.

With the power of my prosthetics, I went into a series of inhuman acrobatic leaps across the walls, each one propelling me further away from the onslaught of automatic fire heading my way. SpyFly had spotted where the shots had come from. A third gunman, perched on the rooftops, brandishing an assault rifle and taking pot shots at me. Liz rapidly plotted out a flight path for the drone; aimed directly at the sharpshooter's forehead.

"Hang on!" Liz cried.

The video feed blurred as the drone dive-bombed out of the sky, the forehead of the gunman drawing nearer and nearer.

<<Signal lost>>

<<Attempting to reconnect>>

The guns fell silent. As I fell back towards the ground, I saw the gunman, stumbling backwards, stunned by the metallic insect, blindly flailing at the air attempting to swat it.

I had to act now. I landed on my feet, keeping myself low to the ground, skidding against the pavement as I lined up the next shot with the laser-targeting system.

BOOM!

Direct hit! The bullet impacted violently into the sharpshooter's shoulder with a burst of blood and bone. He collapsed instantly. I came to a stop, and stood up straight, holding up the triangular barrel of my gun in a combat posture, aiming at the entrance to the alleyway.

The dude with the crushed leg was still trapped, but the biker woman had picked up her gun again with one hand and was now aiming back at me, while the other arm had drawn out a knife with it pressed against David's throat, holding him in a hostage position on his knees. He was freaking out, whimpering like a dog and begging for mercy.

"SHUT UP!" she snarled at him.

He gave a single, high-pitched whine and fell silent. The leather-bound woman turned to me with a cold computerised stare.

"Let him go, and nobody has to get hurt!" I called to her from across the alley, sounding as diplomatic as I could with a gun in my hand.

"You kill me, he dies too!"

Hearing those words sent David gulping for terrified breath.

I gritted my teeth, examining my options telepathically with Liz, but this was essentially poker. No way to really tell who was going to call the bluff.

My cochlear sensors picked up something, the sound of sirens blazing, the Doppler shift indicating they were coming closer.

"You hear that? The Old Bill are on their way! Either walk away from this or spend the next twenty years in the Prison Matrix. Your call!"

She cackled at me, waving her gun dismissively.

"Let them come! See what happens!"

So much for London's finest. I was running out of options and on borrowed time. One mistake now and she would…

Something moved behind her…

A significant bulky figure, looming over the pair of them…

Out of nowhere, a flash of purple-orange light, an intense, searing heat blazed out from it, accompanied by a roaring crackle of energy.

"BEHIND YOU!" cried the biker with the crushed leg, sheer terror blazing across his face.

No way.

The woman heard it too but didn't get the time to look. The light took form; a great burning blade stabbing through the air rammed itself through her back and burst out from her heart in an arc of bloody gore. The woman gave a brief, painful gag as the life drained from her. The heat was so intense that the droplets of blood were instantly evaporated into black smoke and scattered to the wind.

The crushed gangster cried angrily at the death of his partner. David jumped out from her grip at the sight of the flaming blade, feeling the burn from his proximity to the weapon. The woman gave one final gargling gasp for air, her body jerking violently, the colour of her face washing out like a water-based painting. Her grip released, David fell forward gasping for breath, clutching his neck to stop the bleeding from the small flesh wound left by the imprint of the knife.

No way!

The plasma sword slid back through her body, leaving nothing but a gaping hole in the gangster's face, lined with burnt black flesh on the sides. The corpse fell to the ground, and the shadowy figure started to come into view.

Cymurai!

His gleaming red and gold power armour dripped with blood.

He was stood in a karate combat stance, which Liz identified as the Te Ura Gasumi, his katana held high above his head, the silence of the alleyway penetrated by only the pulsing plasma and the whir of the cooling fan on the hilt of the weapon.

"YOU BASTARD!!!" came a cry from the rooftop.

I whirled my head up in time to see the sharpshooter I had shot, clutching his wounded left shoulder with his right hand… the other once more gripped around his rifle.

He screamed a war cry at the top of his lungs as he pulled the trigger. The shots rang out at high speed, prompting me to cover my head in panic, but the shots were aimed for Cymurai. The bullet ricochets flashed violently against the pavement, as Cymurai went into a motor-powered sprint, keeping ahead of the arc of fire.

Before I knew what was happening, Cymurai had built up enough speed to run up the side of the alleyway wall. He reached the limit of his momentum, and sprang to the opposite wall, gripping onto a windowsill with a mighty crack. The sharpshooter redirected the arc of his fire to follow, but not before Cymurai had jumped across again.

It only took a few seconds, but with a few more of these gymnastic jumps, he had leapt all the way to the rooftop. The gunman leaned back and fired into the air, trying to shoot him down, but he simply deflected them with a series of rapid flicks of his sword. He drew the burning blade high above his head, his shadow looming over the gunman like death itself.

KRAAAAAZZ!

The gunman yelled in horror as Cymurai came crashing down on him, and the plasma blade with him. The intense heat seared through the rifle like butter – and the gunman with him. A single, diagonal bloody cut from his right shoulder to his left waist. He came apart in two.

"Whoa…"

This had to be one of the most surreal moments of my life. Not every day you meet your childhood hero. I stared up at the rooftop. The whirring of the sword's cooling fan died out, and so did the brightness of the plasma. As the heat faded away, the ceramic tube of the sword cooled as he twirled it gracefully using the Japanese art of drawing the blade – Iaidō – a distinctive swishing noise as it cut the air and retracted back within the hilt like a telescope, sheathing it in the holster on his belt.

He calmly returned his hands to the side of his waist; he turned around to look down at the street the light from his eye-sensors glowing like torches. Our gazes met, but I could only stare blankly back, my mouth hanging stupidly open as I tried to process what was happening to me.

He lifted his chin up; a nod of recognition.

My heart skipped a beat.

"Uh… little help?"

I snapped out of my state of awe and turned to David, keeling on the ground, clutching his throat to stem the tide of the blood flowing out from the wound.

"Shit, hang on!" I told him firmly, diving to my own knees to help him. I could already see the medical nanobots in his bloodstream starting to gather at the wound, forming a grey scab-like barrier to limit blood loss and fight off infection. The data had already been forwarded to the NHS, and an ambulance was on the way.

"Looks like you're gonna make it, buddy," I sighed with relief at him. "You were pissing yourself for no reason."

"Yeah, yeah. You know mentioning that on *Facebook* would be a breach of the official secrets act, right?"

"Never crossed my mind."

I telepathically began signalling for medical help, looking up at the rooftop. Cymurai had disappeared.

"Bloody hell… was that really *him*?" David asked in awe.

"Pretty sure."

"Wow… make sure you don't tag me in the photos."

"Photos? What pho-"

I stopped myself mid-sentence, noticing the crowd of gawking onlookers that had started to huddle around the entrance to the alleyway, blocked by the collapsed neon sign. Dozens of them were already recording the events on their watches and tablets, the rest of them likely doing it with their contact lenses or bionic eyes.

"Oh, great," I panicked, holding up my face to hide it from the camera's view, hoping they hadn't identified me already.

I was supposed to be discreetly investigating Spiritform, I *really* didn't need the publicity.

And I thought Tottenham were having a rough evening.

CHAPTER 10

Mother Mind profile 3551-7821-0862-2143:

First name: Kenji

Surname: Awasaki

Status: Living

Nationality: British/Japanese Citizen

Occupation(s):

- Chief Executive Officer
  - Status: Employed
  - Organisation: Virtualife Corporation

Known aliases:

- Sector
- <<Classified: Cymurai>>

Live surveillance:

- Status: *Partially available*
- Date: 06/10/2045
- Current location: Virtualife building, Docklands, East London
- Local Time: 23:07 GMT

<<Logging out of Cymurai Mark-V Unit-03 Avatar>>

<<Engaging Auto-pilot>>

<<Uploading destination co-ordinates>>

<<Terminating connection>>

I woke up in my chair, rubbing my eyes and straining them to focus on the penthouse that had become both my dream home and self-enforced prison. I awoke to the soothing sound of trickling water from my zen garden's fountain. Another bottle of sake awaited me on a tray, held by one of my android butlers, and I gave a stretching yawn to drag my body forward to take it.

I began sipping, and turned to the view of the city, through the vid-glass projecting graphics across the panes. Gabrielle had loaded up the Mother Mind profile for Arthur Wells; the private investigator that she'd hired on behalf of the company to recover the Project Selection files. I'd actually met him before, during his time at GCHQ, not that he'd be able to remember it. He seemed like a good enough bloke, but it was his work during Operation Dragonslayer that had made him a prime candidate. Previous experience was a bonus, to say the least. His performance was beyond outstanding… despite how it all turned out. Given how it ended… I couldn't say I blamed him for resigning.

I tried focusing on something else when I felt the pain welling up inside of me… it was a personal source of guilt. Just one more mistake I was trying to make up for.

When Gabrielle found out Arthur had retired and gone into the private investigation business, he quickly went to the top of our short list. It was sort of an unwritten rule that most modern PIs had some level of hacking knowledge, but someone with prior intelligence experience would be a godsend, not to mention he'd also been augmented with military cybernetics. He'd even gotten good reviews from his past clients. I approved him without hesitation, but now I was starting to question his 'street smarts' after he'd managed to get himself into a Mexican stand-off with the Albanian Mafia.

Gabrielle appeared from the projectors embedded in the glass, with her arms folded and looking at me disapprovingly again with her pale green eyes.

"You could have handled that better," she scolded me.

I was still tracking his movements on the vid-glass, watching him being moved into custody to Camden police station.

"Maybe." I shrugged. "But I didn't want to take the chance. Besides, you're the one who approved this sting operation of his."

We received an e-mail from him last night, claiming that he had uncovered evidence that Spiritform were planning to blackmail one of our most valued AI researchers (Doctor Julie Carpenter) into handing over the decryption key to the Project Selection files. We were sending her to ModCon as one of our representatives, where they would probably attack from. The obvious thing to do was to pull her out of the event, but Mister Wells had convinced Gabrielle to use her as bait to lure them out.

"I still don't like it." I frowned, despite the conversations we'd had earlier. "We're asking her to take far too big of a risk."

"I doubt Spiritform would resort to violence," Gabrielle added reassuringly. "Besides, I've already assigned an Ashigaru team to provide covert security for her. They're already running hostage situation simulations with her to prepare. But in any case, it's far more likely Spiritform will resort to the usual hacker blackmail method; threatening to expose revealing information."

"Kind of makes me curious to know what they have on her," I scoffed. "She's had nothing but perfect employee performance reports since she joined."

Within seconds of me speaking, Gabrielle had loaded up Julie's Mother Mind profile onto the window screen.

"My analysis indicates that they have most likely uncovered information on her cocaine habit," she informed me.

I scoffed, rolling my eyes and shaking my head with a smile.

"If we fired every member of our staff with a drug problem, we'd be out of business." I chuckled, hazily remembering my own youthful days with the white powder.

"But if Spiritform is planning to hack into the holo-displays in the convention centre, we'd be forced to take her through the official disciplinary procedure," she explained.

I bit my lip.

"That would be embarrassing for everyone."

She shrugged.

"We'll hack in ourselves and cut the power if it comes to it. But we're in a contract with Arthur Wells now," she explained. "We have to at least let him try his plan. His service record at GCHQ is impeccable, my only concern with him at the moment is his social circle. It seems it was his former colleague that got him into the mess last night."

"We all have that one friend," I joked.

"He's taken precautions to prevent visual recognition when he's out in the open, but I can already name one person who has bypassed it."

"Who?"

She pursed her lips and brought a notification to my display.

<<You have 1 new message>>

I cringed as the notification flashed on my HUD, instilling dread into me. I could already tell who it was before I neuroclicked.

<<From: Jules Santiago (jules.santiago@virtualifeboardofdirectors.com)>>

<<To: Kenji Awasaki (kenji.awasaki@virtualifeboardofdirectors.com)>>

<<Sent: 06/10/2045 at 22:58>>

<<Attachments: 0>

<<Body:

Congratulations.

#CymuraiReturns is going viral on social media. Sightings of your play suit tend to have that effect.

I'm not sure what's worse; the fact you hired a screw-up, or that you put yourself at risk to save him?

FYI, *this is exactly* what the board and I are concerned about. I don't know what you had planned, but it seriously isn't working.

You've got six days left now to prove you're worth keeping around. If this is the best you've got, I hope you've got your resignation letter prepared. It would be less embarrassing for everyone if we didn't have to force you out.

-Jules

>>

"Over my dead body," I snarled to myself, and angrily closed the data window.

The man was a shark, and he could smell blood in the water. First

Project Selection, now this. He was just waiting to find the first opportunity in the company by-laws to kick me out.

"Be that as it may, he's right." Gabrielle shrugged. "Other people are already looking into him. He publicly advertises his previous job at GCHQ on his website. If someone catches onto that, it'll be enough to make him a target. Camden police station falls within our jurisdiction. I can arrange to get him out of jail before they take a deposition if you like?"

"I don't want to bribe anyone we don't have to," I replied, taking another swig of the warm, sweet sake. "Dive the station's network; keep an eye on what they ask him about, but don't do anything without asking me first."

"Already on it." She smiled back, the universe of cyberspace whirling behind on her on the window banks.

"What about phase two of Operation Clayman?" I asked, leaning back, resting my head on a pillow of my hands.

"So far it has been carried out within expected safe parameters." Gabrielle nodded, gesturing with her hands to bring up a series of reports submitted by Emma Golem and Daniel Haines. "The virus is running on his CPU without interruption, and both of them seem to be enjoying becoming re-acquainted, but Haines has his reservations about Virtualife's involvement with the case."

"Can't blame him." I shrugged, looking at his service record. "Pretty typical detective attitude. No one likes having their work taken over. Looks like he's done as good a job as could be expected given the nature of… Jack-21."

"He's a good cop." She nodded reservedly. "That's why he's a problem. He's signed an NDA, but the terms of the memory erasure clauses only come into effect *after* he leaks to the media. As per our instructions, Emma has invited him to the Awasaki Foundation fundraiser as an opportunity for you to put his mind at ease."

My heart sank as usual when the graphics of my calendar app loaded up, presenting me with the blinking red entry on tomorrow's date.

We had decided it was better to let Detective Haines believe that Emma was doing him a favour, rather than letting him know he'd been invited from the start. I, on the other hand, would've done anything to get out of it. I hated pretentious 'high-society' gatherings to begin with, but these charity events took the biscuit. Sure, there would be a few people there who actually, genuinely cared about the climate refugee crisis… but most of them would be there to fulfil contractual ethical obligation to aid the company image.

I'd shake their hands and pose for photos, using the fake smile I'd perfected for the paparazzi while holding back my gag reflex. What I wouldn't give to go back to a good-ol' student house party.

"Is Haines bringing anyone with him?" I asked, trying to focus on something else.

"Just his girlfriend," she replied, holding out her hand, projecting a collection of social media data on 'Claire Fielding'.

"She suffers from social anxiety and depression, even suicidal thoughts," Gabrielle explained, analysing her psych profile. "Getting dragged in a high-profile scandal won't help her stability."

"I take it she's also been inducted into the project?"

"All of Inspector Haines' close contacts have been," she said in a reassuring tone. "Don't worry. We're airtight on that front."

I looked over the info we had collected on her. Just looking at her *Facebook* wall was enough to make you want to self-harm. Though from what I could tell from some of these intercepted messages it seemed like she was refusing help. I should've felt guilty about reading her private messages as well, but after fifteen years of dipping in and out of Mother Mind, I'd become numb to it. It was built to save lives, and we'd done that. Project Clayman had the potential to save the human race one day. If I had to snoop on a struggling couple to do that, so be it.

"So!" I nodded in a ponderous manner. "All I have to do is convince him that our intervention in the investigation is all legit and above board."

"When in fact it's totally illegal," she retorted.

"Cakewalk," I answered sarcastically with exhausted breath, rubbing my forehead.

She beamed back at me with encouragement; her hologram strode over to the couch, the projector on the ceiling slowly swivelling towards me. Her ghostly hips swayed seductively and took a seat next to me, reaching out with a translucent hand to softly stroke the back of my head. I closed my eyes and enjoyed the familiar tingling sensation simulated by my neural lace.

"I wish you could come," I sighed at her, holding my hand out for her to take.

Her avatar's fingers stretched out to meet mine, feeling her familiar presence without form.

"Someone's gotta look after the kids," she joked.

I forced out a laugh and a smile. She had spoken with the intention of making a joke, but her words reminded me of something Hideo and Shauna had asked me last night. I wanted to give them the best childhood possible. Even if it was virtual they could still be happy… in fact they could be happier than any child living in the real world could've done.

We went on a trip through a virtual recreation of Ayers Rock in the Australian outback. The four of us, holding hands facing the vast monolithic red outcrop standing out across the horizon, strolling through the shrubs and bushes dotting across the dusty plains while kangaroos hopped gracefully along. A sight that would no longer exist in the real world; but one I wanted to give them. That's all we did… travel the most idyllic scenes planet Earth had to offer, past or present. They deserved to see this world at its finest.

Hideo would point at the wildlife, with wide beady eyes asking questions with unrelenting curiosity. Shauna carried a pad of virtual paper and art pencils in her little pink, flowery handbag, wanting to stop and sketch the scenes as we walked past.

I put my arm around Gab and beamed at the pair of them, playing in the sun… bathing in the warm contentedness rising in my chest.

We came close to the rock face and found a huge crack in the side of the cliff leading to the mouth of a cave. We slipped into the cavern, holding up an old electric torch to shine a light on the walls, revealing an ancient aboriginal painting, made of ochre, the pigment from rock ground into fine dust.

They were fascinated by the old artwork, wrapped in awe as I explained the concept of Dreamtime; the elegant primal belief that the world had been dreamed into existence by spiritual Totems. The same belief had been re-churned by philosophers like René Descartes, and science fiction writers like the Wachowski sisters; just attempts to simplify the nature of reality.

It was a belief that had reasonable philosophical arguments to back it up, but not one that I particularly cared for. It had about as much evidence as the existence of God – none.

I observed their reactions; at first, they'd seemed fascinated… but the more I spoke about it, they grew more and more anxious… scared even.

"Hey?" I asked in a light, friendly tone.

Hideo rolled his lips nervously, working up the courage to speak.

"Daddy?" he spoke timidly. "Is… is that what we are?"

"What do you mean?" Gabrielle frowned.

"Did you and Daddy dream us up?"

I bit my tongue and swallowed hard… I'd always known that this day was going to come, hoping to just continually delay it.

"No, of course not!"

"When you're not here…" Shauna piped up, her eyes starting to well up. "It feels like we don't exist…"

Her words had sent a lump forming in my mouth, my voice starting to crack… I couldn't answer her. Couldn't bring me to tell them the truth…

I had to log out quickly. Even erased the last few hours of their memory.

Once more my dream came to an end…

And so did they…

"Hey?" Gabrielle asked with a holographic nudge in my chest, snapping my attention back to the present. "What's wrong?"

She stroked me softly on the cheek as I slumped back on the couch.

I smiled meekly back, patting her transparent thigh.

"It's nothing…" I lied. "Don't worry about it."

"Kenji…" she added in a slow accusing tone, with eyebrows that encouraged me to spill the truth.

"I just… I just want the kids to come to the real world."

We had our cybernetics division working overtime on Bio-hybrid technology, trying to synthesise bodies that we could download their personality matrices into, but it was still years away from a viable prototype.

Assuming no one got in our way… but naturally, we had the board up our asses every time we tried to take company resources for our personal use. Usually egged on by Jules.

Her lips perked up, nodding at me with understanding.

"So do I… but we can only move one step at a time," she spoke, trying to inspire positivity. "This… incident with Project Selection is just one more obstacle along the way. It's one we *can* overcome, Kenji, I know it."

I wanted to think that she had been talking about a feeling from the heart, but I knew she had been talking about some analytical model. I stroked the projection back, the simulation of her soft skin bringing nostalgia to my mind.

"I want to believe that," I admitted. "I really do… but I just don't see how it could be done with Jules whispering in their ears."

Her reaction to that was… curious. Her ghostly hand rested itself on mine, clutching softly as she leaned in as if to talk secretively.

"What if…" she continued, in a voice barely above a whisper, "we could do something about him?"

"Do… something?" I asked cautiously.

"I've been considering him," she explained with a smirk.

"On whose authority?!"

"Yours," she told me plainly. "You ordered me to investigate the source of the Project Selection hack. It was logical to start with people who knew about the project, to begin with to rule out an inside job. Naturally, the board was a good place to start. Everyone knows they have it into you. It took me longer to crack his ICE, but I found a good lead."

I pursed my lips anxiously. What she had uncovered may have been useful; but Gab was still supposed to be bound by the three laws, just as much as any other AI. Accessing Mother Mind required my explicit permission, but once she was in she could pretty much do what she wanted… I was going to have to consider an update to her personality matrix definitions.

"What did you find?" I continued gingerly.

"Leverage." She smirked at me confidently.

She forwarded a file to my HUD… bank account records for a virtual law firm named 'Thompson and Scrub'.

"Jules' lawyers?"

"Look at the payment made on the tenth of August."

She highlighted the transaction in yellow and telepathically scrolled through the page for me. A direct bank transfer of half a million… to the Commonwealth Legion Party.

"The hell is he doing with *them*?" I spluttered with disgust.

They were the yobs of British politics. A thinly veiled group of nationalists. They'd started out as a fringe party, formed from the remnants of the old UK Independence Party after Brexit in 2019. The Euroskeptics, with a handful of made-up figures, spun by companies with vested interests, ending up leading the country out of the old European Union, and down the dark path we were on now, isolating ourselves from the rest of the world and slowly converting the country into an island fortress. Now the CLP was calling for what they always had really wanted, a permeant military and economic alliance with the Commonwealth. Countries where the crown itself still had influence, which now included two of the world's greatest super-powers; Canada and India, and technological powerhouses like Singapore. It would be a return to a pseudo-British empire, keeping all unwelcome foreigners out of their territory, and keeping the corporatocracy at the top of the Pyramid.

The economic implications were… interesting. The party manifesto laid out the terms of the treaty they proposed with the member states, to much praise both here and abroad. But it was the military aspect that worried me. The party had made it clear one of its goals was the creation of a weaponised satellite grid to defend their territory.

Superweapons aren't great for…deescalating situations.

They'd won ninety seats in the last election in May. Hardly surprising. A reactionary result. Climatevilles were popping up everywhere, the government was having a hard enough time keeping our own population fed. They made me sick; flying in the face of everything I had tried to accomplish with the Awasaki Foundation. More to the point, that had done wonders for our company image, which he seemed to care so much about.

"What the hell is he thinking!?" I snarled again, clenching my fist.

"Most statistical projections suggest that they will win the next general election," Gabrielle pointed out.

"I know that, but they must be offering something pretty big in return for him to be making such a risky investment."

It was a nagging sensation that I'd had ever since the last meeting. He was up to something. It wouldn't surprise me if it turned out that he was behind all of this from the start.

"Why don't you ask him yourself?" she prodded me.

She forwarded me a link to my browser, Jules was online now. Jacked-in to cyberspace and playing 'PGA Tour 2045' by *EA Sports*. He was in a private lobby, playing with people on his friend's list, prospective clients for Global Arms in Asia most likely.

"Golf huh… I can work with that." I nodded.

"He won't take it too kindly if you interrupt his game," she pointed out.

"That's the idea," I replied coolly.

I nestled my head back on the layer of pillows resting on the couch and gave the telepathic command.

<<You are about to enter a full-immersion virtual reality simulation.>>

<<Please be seated and ensure your surroundings are appropriate.>>

<<Begin simulation?: Yes/No>>

I closed my eyes.

<<Loading environment>>

<<Running neural lace device drivers>>

<<Processing consciousness shift>>

The graphics whirled through my mind's eye. The new world took form around me. I found my avatar standing underneath a bright blue sky, with emerald green grass beneath my shoes. I was wearing a blue and white checked golfer's sweater, complete with sun cap and gloves.

The golf course obeyed the physical laws of the real world, but as challenging as possible for the players; complete with mounds of tiny hills, and pits of sand carved out in the ground forming a picturesque golf course. It was surrounded by dense forest with a canopy of leaves swaying in the simulated wind, extending in all directions into infinity. Encircling the tee-off point were rows of stands filled with randomly generated spectators cheering on, their limited personality matrixes simulating the eager anticipation of the game about to begin.

An arrow on my HUD pointed towards the tee-off point. The players gathered around, leaning on their clubs and chatting, their usernames appearing in floating windows above their heads. Jules was there all right, wearing a red and blue suit, brandishing an oversized cigar, striding over to the starting point with his usual over-confident swagger. He reached the tee-off point and bent over, readying himself for his drive, wiggling his ass in an exaggerated manner.

"What a prize wanker…" I scoffed under my breath and walked my way over to him.

They must've noticed me logging in; heads turning my way as I approached them, accompanied by excited chatter among the prospective clients.

Jules straightened up as well, his burning eyes glaring at me with a combination of surprise and shock, before quickly faking a friendly smile for the show.

"Kenji!" he called out warmly, sending a great cloud of smoke billowing from his mouth as he held out his arms in a welcoming gesture acting as best as he could. "How seldom you grace us with your presence!"

"You know me, Jules. I've never been one to shy from a bit of friendly competition!" I grinned back.

He slapped me on the back as I came towards them, harder than could be considered friendly, before introducing me one by one to each of the clients. Executives from a Korean mining company, looking for extra security on their warehouses.

"This is an unexpected pleasure Mister Awasaki!" I was told by a Mister Ye Seung Gi, exchanging a hearty professional handshake. "Mister Santiago said you had prior engagements."

"It's true. I leave many executive decisions for our subsidiaries to Jules," I reassured them. "But what sort of a friend would I be, if I didn't do a favour for my old mentor every now and again?!"

He threw me another fake smile and patted me slowly once more.

He gave me a forced grin in response, masking his rage as best as he could.

"Your loyalty is legendary, Kenji," he replied flatly and gestured towards the tee-off. "Shall we?"

We strode towards the custom-designed ball, a virtual mesh of white lines made pentagons and hexagons tightly packed into a sphere. Once more, Jules wiggled himself into position, carefully lining up his club, giving it a couple of practice swings, before drawing it high above his head, swinging back with a mighty whack. The colour of the ball changed as it accelerated through the air, turning a crimson red blazing across the sky.

I followed it with my eyes, shielding them with my avatar's eyes at the virtual sun. A tracking meter appeared on our HUDs, indicating the distance the ball had travelled. All the while I was rapidly busy coding away to get access to the physics engine.

```
<<
    static int groups_from_user(struct group_info *group_info,
```

```
    gid_t __user *grouplist)
        {int i;
        unsigned int count = group_info->ngroups;
        for (i = 0; i < group_info->nblocks; i++)
            {unsigned int cp_count = min(NGROUPS_PER_BLOCK, count);
            unsigned int len = cp_count * sizeof(*grouplist);
            if (copy_from_user(group_info->blocks[i], grouplist, len))
            return -EFAULT;
            grouplist += NGROUPS_PER_BLOCK;
            count -= cp_count;
            }
        return 0;
        }
>>
                            <<Access granted>>
```

My plan worked. I telepathically altered the physics model on the ball; increasing its weight to thirty kilograms. Without warning the ball slowed mid-air on its trajectory, and Jules could only watch with a horrified expression as it fell out of the sky like a rock. The final reading on the distance meter said it had travelled just fifteen metres. A wave of laughter rang out among the Korean clients.

"Not your day, Jules?" I patted him on the shoulder with sarcastic comfort.

"Happens to the best of us," he glowered back at me.

He walked over to the Korean executives, asking them if he and I could have a moment together, and encouraged them to take their turns while they waited. They agreed and followed suit, each of them lining up in front of the ball that had magically appeared at the tee-off spot.

Once they were distracted, Jules rounded, dumping his club in its caddy and folding his arm impatiently.

"I suppose you thought that was funny," he snarled at me telepathically, his eyes like a raging volcano, complete with cigar smoke from his nostrils.

"Watching you fail has always been a personal source of amusement," I quipped back with a wink.

"If this is about my message it could've waited…"

"It's not," I told him flatly.

"Then what? Don't tell me you're planning on burning down the house before we kick you out?

I rested my hands on my hips casually while I telepathically sent him a screenshot of the data Gabrielle had collected on him. His eyes flickered as they appeared… then threateningly narrowed at me.

"So, you're spying on me too?" he hissed.

"Turnabout is fair play." I shrugged. "What I don't understand is why you'd want to fund them in the first place. We're talking about *CLP!* They're *fascists* for fuck's sake! You do realise they're the same sort of people who built the Mexico border wall? If it was up to them, your family would've never made it to the states! It's no wonder they call you a turncoat!"

"Oh, please. Business is business. There's no left and right when it comes to making money," he scoffed. "They're pushing for a greater expansion of Mother Mind's foreign surveillance capabilities for…"

"Hunting down refugees?!" I interrupted. "You heartless piece of…"

"Careful Kenji," he warned me, blowing a jet of smoke in my face.

I gave a short, sharp breath of utter disgust. I could barely look him in the eyes. If it weren't for the executives a few yards away, I would've punched him in the face.

"You really don't have a conscience, do you?" I asked in exasperation.

"I have a job," he replied coolly. "A responsibility to our shareholders. As do you."

"Oh, I'm sorry. I don't recall seeing a clause in our contract, requiring us to send fleeing families back to *starve to death!*"

"Forces of the market, Kenji." He shrugged at me. "The government has the demand, we just fill the supply."

"Except you're now the one *funding* the ones making the demands!

What else are you doing? Influencing their AIs to get what you want?"

His lips curled upwards into a nasty smirk.

"ROI."

Return on investment.

I gritted my teeth.

"Is that supposed to be an excuse?! It's no wonder you want me off the board. They'll never support you when I'm pushing the Awasaki Foundation."

"They'll come around," he answered confidently. "Sure, that charity has done wonders for our image, but our customer data models suggest that increasing our donations to other causes should mitigate any consumer resistance concerns."

"*If* I get voted out. Even if I do, there's no guarantee you'll get elected as the next CEO."

He laughed loudly and sarcastically at that; the smoke from his mouth now like fog.

"If you believe that, then you're more naïve than even I thought."

My eyes narrowed at him… the temptation to hack him and overload his neural lace rendering him brain dead becoming harder to resist…

I should've seen this coming years ago. Everything he taught me. Every loan. Every favour. It was all just to build up my empire… and steal it.

"Well… you've thought this through, haven't you?" I nodded slowly. "But it sure would throw a spanner in the works if this got leaked before you were voted in wouldn't it?"

That got his attention. He took another sharp puff from his cigar and folded his arms defensively.

"That's your plan? A scorched earth policy?" he asked guardedly.

"Damn straight!" I quipped back. "I'd rather bankrupt the company than let you …"

"I've always admired your conviction, Kenji," he interrupted me again, holding up a hand.

"I'm *so* grateful," I hissed.

"But, there is a way we could both profit out of this," he pointed out.

"You must be…"

"Hear me out," he interrupted again. "You've been doing this for a long time now, and it's no secret that you've never been a fan of boardroom politics. Wouldn't you rather retire gracefully?"

Gabrielle quickly popped up on my display watching me with puppy dog eyes, as if to say 'he's got a point'.

"What are you getting at?" I asked reluctantly, resting my hands on my hips.

Jules took another long puff, the end of the cigar blazing brightly.

"I'll make you a deal," he began, eventually exhaling the grey cloud. "The vote of no confidence is due in six days. But, if you turn in your letter of resignation before then, you have my word that you will have all the funding you need to carry on being Cymurai for the rest of your life. You'll never have to work another day. No meetings. No schedule. I'll just keep the payments coming to the Ashigaru as a secret division within Global Arms."

My ears pricked up. I didn't want to say it, but there was something distinctly appealing about that offer.

"All I ask in exchange… is that you live a quiet private life," he said slowly. "No outbursts to the media. No campaigns. No… controversial affairs."

"While you profit from the internment of millions of people?" I snarled.

"It's a dog-eat-dog world, Kenji." He shrugged. "This is what it means to live at the top of the pyramid. If that's not for you, I respect that." He leaned in closer as if to whisper to me, his expression growing more intense. "But don't get in my way."

Gabrielle was still on my HUD, nodding while biting her lip, looking hopeful that I would accept. I folded my arms, rubbing my chin beard and pretending to ponder over my response. Being able to dedicate myself to Cymurai… it would be a dream come true. But every time I looked at that smug, self-assured face of his, something inside me twinged, rubbing me the wrong way.

Never. Never in a million years.

"Sorry to disappoint you," I spoke eventually, sounding like I had reached a decision.

I pointed to the air above my head, directing him towards the user data that would be floating above my head on his display.

I telepathically updated my status, so that he would now be staring at a big red, flashing sign reading 'NOT FOR SALE'. He stood there, staring blankly at the message, his right eye twitching.

"A shame," he spoke eventually, in a conversational tone that masked the rage that must've been burning inside.

We stared each other down in silence, mentally shouting at each other.

"I'll see you at the vote," I told him coolly, turning to leave.

"I look forward to it."

I was walking away, telepathically preparing to log myself out… but there was a lingering question in the back of my mind.

It got the better of me. I had to ask.

"Just one more thing…" I called out, turning back on the spot. "Are you behind all of this?"

Jules raised a puzzled eyebrow.

"Behind what?"

"Jack-21. Project Selection. Was it you?"

Jules raised his eyebrows in shock, scoffing and shaking his head.

"You really think I would risk a scandal of that magnitude, just to get the board to call a vote of no confidence?"

"I do, actually," I retorted flatly, my eyes narrowing at him.

He seemed a little taken aback by my bluntness, but then smirked as if to take it as a compliment.

"Well if that's the case… there's not really anything I can say to convince you otherwise," he replied, the words oozing out of his mouth.

My eyes narrowed at him suspiciously. It was him… I knew it. I just knew it.

"If you're lying, Jules…" I said sternly. "There's just one thing you need to remember."

"Oh?" he chirped back dismissively, taking another puff. "What's that?"

"I'm Cymurai."

His face froze. The threat was clear. However sure of himself, he may have been; that scared him. No matter how good his security was, there was no way he would be able to stand up to me. A smile crept across my face.

"I'll see you round around, Jules," I reassured him as I turned to walk away.

That felt good. Gabrielle popped up once more. Her arms folded and scowling at me telepathically.

"I hope you realise it's war now," she told me in a disapproving tone.

"It's *always* been war."

CHAPTER 11

Mother Mind profile 2446-7128-5978-2501:

- First name: Arthur
- Surname: Wells
- Status: Living
- Nationality: British citizen
- Occupation(s):
  - Private investigator
    - Status: Self-employed
    - Organisation: Arthur Wells & Associates
- Known aliases:
  - IronRoot
- Live surveillance:
  - Status: *Partially available*
  - Date: 07/10/2045
  - Current location: Knightsbridge, West London
  - Local Time: 06:45 GMT

Oh my god, what a headache…

The latest dose of medical nanobots in my bloodstream were working overtime to make up for last night. I'd ended up having several double-rum and cokes before bed to calm my nerves after being questioned by the police. But I'd made the brilliant decision to do it when the battery life for my last dose of medical nanobots were running low. Not my brightest idea, and I was now suffering from the worst hangover I'd had since becoming cyberised.

"Ughhh… Liz remind me to *never* go drinking on a work night again."

"Sure, I'll remind you. *Again.*" She laughed, appearing as a hologram from the dashboard, giving me a judgemental glare from behind her spectacles. "Not that you'll listen."

"Well, I dunno, play loud annoying music until I do," I grumbled back. "You're supposed to be the superintelligence here. Bloody think of something!"

"I'll… see what I can do," Liz responded professionally like she hadn't reacted at all to the insult… but I soon felt the need to apologise, which she graciously accepted.

The auto-driver detected the traffic lights turning red, and I came to a stop outside *Harrods*. The vast red-brick of the department store stretched out before me, Victorian Gothic turrets reaching to the dim, overcast sky. Dozens of windows lined the street level, shielded by intellifabric canopies extending over the pavement displaying the shop name in animated gold writing.

My eye was caught by the toy display in one of the windows. An entire miniature robotic circus, including somersaulting clowns, tiny lion tamer, and tightrope walkers with claytronic skin so believable you could almost mistake it for the real thing. But the more I stared at the pre-programmed choreographed routine, the more my stomach lurched. I couldn't stand it for very long, prompting me to telepathically open the window.

I moaned again, shielding my eyes and adjusting the tinting settings on the car windows, trying to avoid the glare emerging from behind the city skyline. I was sat in the driver's seat; the route programmed into the auto-driver on the primary display. I was heading from my apartment to the Thames Pier Convention Centre, leaving early to avoid the traffic.

I began to reminisce about last night. The cops showed up not long after my little run-in with the Albanian Mafia. The gangsters were wheeled away by paramedic droids, most on stretchers, one of them in a body bag.

Unsurprisingly, we were arrested too, in a less than cordial manner. In fact, if it wasn't for my implants, I'd still be sore from the spot below my shoulder where they'd tasered me, and David had picked up a couple of bruises from the way they'd handled him.

I They kept us in the station for hours, sweating me over

unloading my weapon. They dropped it quickly after they saw my license and the CCTV footage. They bought the story that David had hired me for protection with the help of some quickly forged documents from Liz. The officers involved were probably bent, but they couldn't charge me with anything. Both the AIs on the defence and prosecution agreed I had fired in self-defence, but they seemed more interested in Cymurai's appearance. Something I was still coming to terms with. David would probably be dead if he hadn't shown up when he did. Most of the theorists online believed he had access to Mother Mind; why he had come for me though was anyone's guess.

Under normal circumstances, I would've thought of it as a fond memory, but a few of the people in the market had managed to get a recording of my face. Luckily they hadn't been able to visually ID me. I didn't keep a clear picture on my website and was generally very careful about sharing my data, but if they kept digging, I had no doubts they could find me somehow, putting my entire livelihood at risk.

With that in mind, I parted with David on the best terms we could. I tried to laugh it off while seething with bitter rage. He seemed to get the message through. I had enough shit to deal with without his problems as well. He was going to have to deal with GCHQ. Hopefully, *they* didn't expect me to be involved with his arrangement with the Yakuza. I'd considered de-friending him online. That was pretty much saying 'you're dead to me'. We were confident we had covered up our digital tracks well enough to hide our… other activities, but that didn't change the fact two of the hitmen were dead.

I tried to concentrate on the task at hand.

The doors to ModCon would open at 9am: where Spiritform would be attempting to blackmail one of Virtualife's AI researchers; Doctor Julie Carpenter. Gabrielle had briefed her accordingly. She was aware that Spiritform would be making threats to her, and that she was going to be used mostly as a pawn in a counter-intelligence operation. I was surprised by the level of assurance that she had been given. Not only had she been promised that any information revealed by the hackers during my investigation would remain confidential, but they would also be posting Ashigaru agents to the convention centre, waiting on standby to defend her need be. They'd even given her virtual interrogation training to ensure she could handle the pressure.

Nice to see a company looking after its people for a change.

That being said, she was still going to be used as bait to lure Spiritform; possibly my only chance to catch them. I already had my ticket but was going to have to park about a mile away from the centre and walk there to avoid any potential lookouts. Truth be told though, despite everything, I still had lingering hopes they wouldn't show up.

"Have you found a good listening point yet?" I checked with Liz, slowing in traffic as we approached roadworks blocked off by traffic cones while maintenance robots dug up the tarmac.

"Took me a while to find the building blueprints, but I've found an optimal spot," Liz informed me, bringing up a 3D layout of the building. She highlighted a *McDonald's* restaurant, close to the Virtualife booth in the main hall. She'd already mapped out a route that I could use as an escape route from it with minimal security.

"If Spiritform is coming to the convention via remote avatars, that's where they'll be logging in. If they log-in from elsewhere and travel to the centre, this point is close to the entrance as well. SpyFlys scanner has a limited range, so you'll need to be there to boost coverage. I found a codex of Spiritform encryption markers on the dark web. I won't be able to crack the data stream, but I'll be able to identify which units are being operated by them. I recommend using SpyFy's Omnigel interface to access their hardware directly."

"Nice. Where'd you get it from?"

"Dart."

"How much did he charge?" I asked, not too bothered about the answer since I'd be charging it as an expense.

"Five hundred."

"Pretty cheap."

"Well, he did mention a discount due to your… other arrangement with him," she explained pensively.

"I should bloody hope so," I said bitterly. "And did you mention the time gap in the recordings from last two downloads? I'm still missing five years of memories!"

"He apologised, but said there wasn't much he could do about it."

"That doesn't sound likely," I mumbled.

"Either way, it looks like you're going to have to put up with it."

"What makes you say that?"

My HUD telepathically bleeped at me.

<<1 Notification from GC-Cracker>>

<<Download complete>>

<<Ready for RE:Call>>

<<File dated: 13/03/2043>>

"That's only a week apart from the last file," I said, still unsatisfied. "At least I'll find out what happened to that kidnapped NSA agent."

"But you're still not happy?"

"Damn right," I scoffed. "I'll message him myself later. I want my memories in the right order, dammit!"

"I'll set a reminder," she added calmly. "Although you do have time to assimilate the files you *have* been sent before you arrive at the convention centre. You might as well make the most of them."

I rolled my head around my shoulders, trying to relieve the throbbing.

"True…" I admitted reluctantly. "I suppose it'll take my mind off this bloody hangover," I rumbled.

"Actually, it might make it worse…" she deadpanned out. "Electronically stimulated dehydrated synapses are…"

"Just do it," I groaned, dismissively waving my hand, not in the mood for a medical lecture.

<<Welcome to RE:Call!!>>>

<<Loading File: 9786-8130-2931-13032043>>

<<File loaded>>

<<Ready to begin Memory Playback>>

<<Begin: Yes/No>>

I shut my eyes, blocking out the Victorian sights rolling past the window as I issued the command.

<<Initialising memory playback>>

<<Running Neural Lace device drivers>>

<<Processing consciousness shift>>

London fell away from my mind, and the past began washing over me like the rising tide…

<<Loaded date: 13/03/2043>>

<<Location: Government Communication Headquarters, Cheltenham>>

<<Local Time: 13:17 GMT>>

I was hunched over my desk, my bearded chin resting on my hands and leaning in close to the holo-projection, my nose practically touching the floating screen as I waited with bated breath for the results of the process to come in.

Come on… come on…

A beep came from the desk:

<<Error: Unable to compile scripts>>

"Shit!" I spat angrily, slamming my flesh and blood fist against the desk, hard enough to send distortions rippling through the luminous data windows cluttering the air in front of me. They obstructed my view of the central display pillar of the command room, which was currently projecting a graphical representation of the American military network; hundreds of servers and terminals presented as a web of spheres connected by an intricate maze of data traffic.

"I'll take that for you, sir." a catering droid asked with a chirpy electronic voice, standing beside the workstation, a long mechanical claw extending outwards. Its camera-eye fixated on the empty cup of coffee sitting at my desk, hidden among by the growing number of floating holographic windows projecting from the surface of my desk.

"Oh… yeah, cheers," I mumbled reaching through the projection, distorting the image. I placed the cup in its grip. "Could you get me another one?"

"A pleasure, sir," it bleeped back, placing the cup within a storage compartment within its body and wheeling itself towards the kitchen, navigating its way around the bustle of office traffic.

The other data analysts at their desks around the central display were all attempting to do the same as me; stressing over the same data sets. I buried my face in my hands, sick of staring at the sprawling logical maze.

This was the part of the job that I hated: digital forensics. Dreary, tedious, manual work. The sort of task that artificial intelligence could only do so much for; but was still all too necessary.

We were facing a worst-case scenario. Hackers from the Islamic State had successfully extracted a neuro-key from the NSA agent they beheaded last week. They used it to gain access to the American military network and introduced a Trojan horse virus. They only had access for around ten minutes before being locked out.

Whatever they had in mind was very specific; targeting the control software for the experimental drones deployed by Virtualife under Project Sandstorm. They'd only had time to infect one of the units before they were locked out; a model codenamed RAPTOR (Reconnaissance Artificial Predator Tactical Operations Robot).

I had some of the unit's blueprints and software specifications on one of the screens on my left. Nothing short of a hulking seven and half foot-tall mechanical monster. Unlike anything, I had seen before. It was modelled after its namesake, standing on a pair of hydraulic bipedal dinosaur-like legs, with two hook-like talons on each foot. The arm units extended from a couple of articulated shoulder pads mounted with serrated blades, with two pod-like hands mounting a trio of claws, with a sliding machine-gun compartment built into the centre.

The head was also lizard-shaped but had the barrel of a grenade launcher built in place of a mouth. The eyes replaced by a single red visor protecting its sensor array. Its tail was reptilian, but with a scorpion-like sting at the end. At a glance, the rear appeared to be a single unit but was comprised of six modules, each about the size of small dogs. Each module was capable of detaching and transforming into insect-like quad-copters for reconnaissance and attack. The last module at the end of the tail was mounted with stag-beetle like pincers; equipped with hypo-sprays for delivering nanobot weapons. The most substantial weapon installed was a combat laser attached to the chest; powerful enough to fire a ten-kilojoule beam, which could slice through armour plating. To top it all off, it even came with optical cloaking and self-repair systems.

There was no doubt about it. Being targeted by this thing was a death sentence.

It couldn't be bargained with, it couldn't be reasoned with. It didn't feel pity, or remorse or… well, you get the picture.

The briefing issued by Virtualife described RAPTOR as a surgical strike unit. Designed to pursue the enemy at a distance, for weeks or even months without the need for human maintenance, all the while calculating the most tactically opportune moment to strike. Of course, the decision to use lethal force remained with the remote operators, but all the tactical planning was processed by the onboard AI. I'd even seen a presentation from Jules Santiago himself, claiming that 'one of these babies will turn a terrorist base into a crypt!' And now the terrorists had control of said baby.

Lovely.

Despite the immediate risk to the civilians in the region, Virtualife still weren't exactly being forthright with the data we needed. There was a module hidden within the robot's abdominal cavity; a hidden weapon bay. The exact specs still classified to us. The biggest piss-take was that we weren't being given the full extent of the AI's cyber-warfare functionality. The briefing we'd been given mentioned the capacity to introduce viruses to enemy networks. It was fair to assume that it had decent security as well. Most military drones came with a generic package of ICE programs; but if we were dealing with something out of the ordinary, it could be putting us all at risk. I'd seen some genuinely nasty under-the-counter firewalls out there, designed to attack the neural lace of anyone that tried to break through them. The police would often find hackers dead for days, frothing at the mouth after having seizures caused by their neural laces overheating triggered by attack barriers. If this RAPTOR had anything like that installed on its CPU, I would like to know about it *before* I tried to dive the system myself.

In any case, we had to find the damn thing first. Of course, the first thing the terrorists did was disconnect RAPTOR from the military network and deactivated its GPS. ISIS had become very adept at hiding from spy satellites and drones. They retrieved the unit within minutes of it falling under their control. It could be anywhere within a hundred-mile radius by now.

But, if they were going to try to reprogram RAPTOR, they were going to have to connect it to at least one terminal in their network. If I could get a fix on that, then we would have a shot at getting this over and done with, before the local villagers had to start worrying if raptors really can open doors.

The good news has we potentially had a clue saved right under our noses. The terrorists must've left some digital fingerprint on the American network, which could give us an idea of the IP addresses they were using. Even if they were hiding behind a proxy server, we could still hack into it and extract their exact location data.

The bad news was that the distinct digital fingerprints had been deleted already. Which means attempting to recover it the hard way; looking through scripts. Made all the worse by the fact that a lot of the files involved had been corrupted and had to be reprogrammed manually, hence the lack of AI assistance.

Most of the time I did love this job, but looking at command strings like this for so long genuinely made me feel sick. I opened the fingers shielding my eyes a crack, peering loathingly at the data.

I swivelled in my chair looking for a distraction among the cluster of holo-screens. The limited data in the dossier that Virtualife had provided included footage from prototype trial tests of RAPTOR. The video was loaded up on one of my holo-screens; the first image of the Salisbury Plains artillery range remained frozen in the air. It had been taken from a military surveillance drone, capturing the vast rolling green fields.

I tapped the floating play icon, and the video ran. The camera panned, swivelling towards a dense cluster of forest trees. At this point, you could just hear the quiet crackling of twigs... but it soon grew louder and louder, becoming a roaring crunch, like an oncoming stampede. Seconds later, a tremendous metallic mass emerged out of the shadows. It came crashing out of the forest, smashing the trunks of trees into splinters.

The data readout on the video identified the vehicle as the FV-5145 Conqueror main battle tank. The armoured, gun-metal grey vehicle was thick and blocky. It was a quadrupedal walking robot, propelled by two pairs of legs, with upturned caterpillar treads for feet which could be rotated between vehicle and walking mode. It also had a front and rear pair of robotic claws, each mounted with machine gun turrets.

The large rotating platform mounted in the centre supported a rail gun. The barrel of the weapon resembled a massive tuning fork with a pair of jaws. There was a hatch built into to the top, providing access to the interior. The tank could be piloted with an onboard crew, or semi-autonomously depending on the mission parameters.

Unless you were packing heavy-duty weapons, your only option would be to run and hide against it.

Its opponent *was* a heavy-duty weapon.

Without warning, six fast-moving quad-copter drones emerged from another nearby forest. They were insectoid in design, about the size of small dogs. They soared across the plains like birds of prey towards their targets, moving in a scattered formation ready to swarm the tank.

The tank detected the targets approaching; the pair of claws mounted on the front locked on and opened fire with an ear-piercing clatter. The claws spat out eight 99mm armour-piercing trackers a second, burning through the air like fireflies, but proved to be ineffective. The swarm quietly began weaving through the air in unpredictable flight paths. Combined with electronic countermeasures they had in place, the tank's shots were missing entirely. The drones returned fire with their own turrets, peppering the tank with 9mm armour-piercing rounds, slamming into the hull with bright sparks that left noticeable craters. The tank attempted to compensate with laser jamming on their target systems, but the data readout on the video informed me that the swarm had successfully planted a tracking round into the tank's hull, giving off a homing beacon for them to lock onto.

Within seconds they had surrounded the tank, swarming it like a plague of locusts. The six of them circled around it, diving and weaving. The claw turrets swivelled furiously in their shoulder joint mountings, trying to shoot them down, but were too slow to keep up.

Not that it would've mattered; the swarm was just a distraction. The quadcopters were secondary modules; the primary unit was now ready to strike. Without warning, the swarm drones broke off their attack, swivelled in the air and darted away back across the field. The tank's machine-gun turrets followed them; that was the plan.

A blazing red beam of laser light shot from the corner of the screen. The beam intersected at the knee of the tank's front left leg, cutting into it like a hot knife through butter, spraying out a jet of molten metal and evaporated hydraulic liquid in its wake. The caterpillar track foot buckled, and then snapped clear off with a mighty clang, followed swiftly by an all mighty gyroscopic whir as the remaining legs struggled to keep the tank upright.

The camera rapidly panned towards where the shot had come from, quickly snapping to zoom in and focus on a lone tree at the top of a hill. The image cleared up and revealed the figure hanging from one of the top branches like a giant bat. It was the primary RAPTOR unit, and I couldn't help but be awed every time I looked at it. It was a monster.

The tank's AI traced the point of origin of the laser shot and decided to respond in kind. The railgun swivelled rapidly to lock-on to the tree; the large capacitors in the tuning-fork like barrel began charging with angry electrical crackles. It would only take about five seconds for it to fully charge; plenty of time for the RAPTOR unit's AI to analyse the situation and respond.

It engaged it's optical camouflage. Within seconds, the gunmetal grey finish of the robot's armour was disappearing like a ghostly mirage. When the tank's railgun was fully charged, it had disappeared entirely. Just in the nick of time to avoid the 120mm round that the railgun spat out at supersonic speed; the boom reverberating angrily across the plains like an explosion. The shell sped across the field like a shooting star, leaving behind a shimmering trail of plasma behind it like a flare.

Within a split second, the shell slammed into its target. There was no warhead inside, but the sheer speed and mass of the projectile was enough to produce explosive results. The impact tore through the tree, reducing it to matchstick-sized chunks of debris and scattering them to the wind. The stump of the tree was ripped from the ground, roots hurling clumps of soil, leaving a crater where it had been. The wreckage of the tree came raining back down to the earth with the sound of an avalanche.

The camera zoomed in on the edge of the crater… a trail of talon-like footprints had been imprinted in the mud, leading into the field. The drones were now manoeuvring in random patterns across the expanse of grass in between the tank and the crater, further masking the primary unit's cloaked approach from the onslaught of machine-gun fire still being hurled by the tank's claws, struggling to manoeuvre with a missing leg.

The mass of moving bodies was enough to confuse the tracking system, and before the tank knew what was happening a powerful metallic impact rang out from the hood. An optical distortion swivelled out from the centre of the impact. Over the next few seconds, the cloak deactivated, flickering the demonic ridges of the RAPTOR unit back into view. It was hunched over the access panel to the rank, its back arched like a wolf over its prey. When the tank realised what was happening, it tried shooting it off with its gun claws.

The drone swarm reacted as if by instinct, returning to their hive. They were moving in tight formation, as if lining up in a queue, heading towards a socket on the rear primary unit's pelvis where the tail should have been. The first drone docked into the socket like a spaceship in an airlock, then the rest followed on, like pieces of *Lego* or links in a chain. The drone on the end of the structure extended a pair of crab-like claws. The insect legs of the drone folded up in unison; the transformation was complete. The drones *were*

RAPTOR's tail; a bizarre and horrifying combination of lizard, scorpion, and lobster.

The tank's remaining legs were now writhing violently, vainly trying to shake it off. It was no good; all four of RAPTOR's gecko-pad covered claws were locked in place on the hull. The camera snapped in for a close-up shot of the robot; watching intently as it fired another sustained laser beam from its chest. Sparks flew from the tank's armour, kicking up a plume of smoke as the energy sunk in. The tank resisted all it could, but RAPTOR just carried on cutting through the locks. It took all but twenty seconds for it to cut through entirely. RAPTOR removed one of its claws from the hull and gripped ahold of the hatch, and with a single forceful yank flipped it open.

With the access ladder exposed, the first drone at the end of RAPTOR's bizarre tail (the module with the stag-beetle-like claws), detached from the assembly and flew down the porthole. The camera picked up a brief burst – the sound of submachine gun fire rattling around inside the tank, followed by a series of rapid, erratic clangs like a physical struggle. It only lasted a brief, intense moment; but when it was over the primary RAPTOR unit spun itself around, and sunk the rest of the tail modules down the hole like a fishing line.

When he pulled it back out, the stag-beetle module had reattached itself to the end of the tail. The pincer claws were locked tightly around the skull of a dummy android avatar, which had taken the place of a human pilot. The avatar flopped like a fish as it struggled to free itself from RAPTOR's grip without success. It may have been synthetic, but the tank's AI responded as though the dummy was a real person. Without a human operator, the protective subroutines of the Three Laws of Responsible Robotics kicked in, and the AI shut down the tank with a distinctively loud whir, the body returning to a neutral position and becoming as still as a statue.

When its footing was sure, RAPTOR whipped its tail out, slamming the dummy avatar onto its back against the tank's hull with a sickening clang. With inhuman speed RAPTOR crawled along the hull and made its way on top of the avatar, pinning it down with its hands and feet, like a spider about to sink its fangs into its prey. Once more the avatar's operator writhed to get free, but it was far too late.

The camera zoomed in further on RAPTOR's chest. The

microphone picked up a series of distinctive clicks and whirs, and one by one the panels which had been moulded to resemble abdominal muscles flipped open, like the bomb bay in a fighter jet. With all the panels open, a series of small robotic arms descended from inside the compartment like the legs of an insect, each one wielding a different tool… each one going to work to remove the shielded panels of the dummy to access the avatar's CPU.

I paused the video and let out another long, impressed whistle. I couldn't help but be impressed by the machine's lethal efficiency. Even if the dummy had been a real person, it would've been able to get info out of it by injecting the victim's brain with nanoprobes from its tail, like something out of a horror movie… and now ISIS had one. I couldn't just let that stand.

I increased my focus mode setting again to bring myself around to start typing at the glowing keyboard. I had begun inputting a new set of commands when I felt a tap on my shoulder. I spun around on my office chair to see David standing behind me, his Jewfro a mess, rubbing the drooping bags under his eyes, the top few buttons of his shirt undone and lying scruffily un-tucked around his waist.

"You look like shit," he yawned at me.

"Kettle calling the pot black."

"The difference is, you look like this most of the time," he teased.

"Witty," I deadpanned with a chuckle.

I found myself surprisingly appreciating his sense of humour after nine hours of this bollocks.

He leaned down towards my desk, squinting at the tapestry of holograms I'd woven in front of me.

"Oh jeez, you're taking them… uh, scenic route, huh?" He chuckled. "That must be…. fun."

"I'm going mad…" I groaned.

"You know what they say about all work and no play."

"So, what've you been doing? Dossing around?"

"Eh…" He shrugged, scratching his arse in an undignified manner. "My method has been a little more… direct."

"Pray tell," I asked hopefully, reaching to take my next cup of coffee, delivered to me.

He smirked at me smugly, like he was the smartest man in the room.

"I'm gonna hack into the Syrian MID," he grinned.

I almost spat out my coffee from spluttering so hard. The MID (Military Intelligence Directorate) was the intelligence agency of what remained of the official Syrian government established after the war of 2019. On paper, they were supposed to be our allies against ISIS. In reality, they were as corrupt as they came. They had people on the inside feeding information to the terrorists. We'd theorised that ISIS had access to their network; it would certainly explain their ability to keep one step ahead of our surveillance. The top brass had previously discussed hacking their system to confirm it for ourselves but had decided against it. Like it or not, we needed to work with them to try to restore some sense of stability to the region, not easy considering it was now in a permanent state of drought.

"Did you get approval from Director Langley?" I cringed, wiping away the coffee from my mouth with a tissue.

David averted his gaze, staring blankly at the central display pillar.

"David…" I frowned at him.

"Oh, get off my back!" he groaned dismissively, flapping his hands to the side.

I scoffed, shaking my head in disbelief.

"Just don't start an international incident."

"Thanks for the resounding endorsement," he deadpanned sarcastically.

"I'd be lying if I said your way wasn't more straightforward though," I admitted. "This data is starting to do my nut in."

"When did you last take a break?" he asked.

I shrugged half-heartedly, genuinely unsure. Liz informed me through a HUD pop-up that it had been five hours, thirteen minutes.

"You're bucking for a promotion?" David scoffed, folding his arms and raising an eyebrow.

"Excuse me for thinking about my career."

"Come on, you should know that using focus mode for so long isn't good for you."

He had a point. The tickling, zingy sensation from my headset was rippling through my temple like a seismic wave, giving me the razor-sharp attention that I needed. The irony was that the more you used focus mode, the more work you got done, the more you believed you could keep going. People had been known to collapse from exhaustion at their desks from using it for too long. There were health and safety warnings, but they almost universally went ignored.

"I'll catch up in a bit, mate," I told him reluctantly. "Lemme just get this out the way."

He tutted sarcastically at me, shaking his hand.

"Workaholic," he muttered.

"For king and country," I answered half-heartedly with a salute.

He gave me a gaze of exasperated sympathy.

"Look, there's a voluntary firearms training class taking place in holo-suite A," he said. "You're gonna miss out."

"Firearms?" I checked.

"Yeah, they've set it up as a shooting range," he grinned eagerly. "A course of self-defence classes the Ashigaru are running while they're here."

"The Ashigaru? Virtualife's special forces?"

"No, the 15th-century Japanese soldiers. What do you think?"

"All right, all right, but what the hell are they doing here?"

"I heard something through the grapevine," he whispered, leaning in secretively. "There's been a terror threat on the building."

"Oh really?" I laughed, rolling my eyes. That wasn't exactly news. "We're the most hated government agency in the country. Even more than HMRC, and that's *really* saying something."

"I'm talking solid intel here, bro! They're gonna make a move. They wouldn't be here if they weren't."

His face was stone-still with genuine fear.

“Okay…” I said, feeling his anxiety. “I still don’t see how holographic shooting targets will help?”

“It will do if you get licensed to carry.” He shrugged. “Couldn’t hurt to learn. Besides, let’s face it; what we do here ain’t exactly macho. It’ll make for a good conversation starter with the ladies.”

“True…” I admitted reluctantly, glancing around at the coders hunched at their cubicles. “There’s only so many times you can use ‘a TCP packet walks to a bar’ joke as a pick-up line before it just gets sad.”

“It was sad the first time, Arthur,” he sniggered. “Come on, bro!”

He nudged me in the shoulder trying to goad me into coming.

I mulled it over; my cheeks bathed in the digital light of my terminal, luring me away from the temptation.

“I’d like to…” I began slowly. “But I really should…”

“Man, you *know* you need to clear your head,” he whined. “You know how it is. Spend too long coming at a problem from one angle, and you can’t think outside the box.”

Damn your perfectly rational argument.

“All right!” I proclaimed, throwing my hands up in abandonment. “Let’s do it!”

“Get in!” David cried back, throwing up a high-five.

<<Local Time: 14:31 GMT>>

This is fucking AWESOME!

I was standing in one of ten wooden cubicles, holding an L10A2 intelligent handgun. My hands were locked out in front of me in a combat stance, aiming down the length of a wide-open hall about the size of an indoor football pitch. What the rapid sound of gunfire exploding around me was muffled by the soundproof headphones.

The holographic shooting range stretched out in front of me like a bowling alley, images from the projectors hanging from the ceiling shone down, creating the illusion of a bombed-out middle eastern city. Ruins of concrete and steel mesh lay scattered in the sand, while a soft wind kicked up a simulated dust storm.

Terrorists dressed in ragged clothes would routinely pop out like whack-a-mole toys from behind windowsills, rooftops, or a broken wall to take aim at the trainees behind the other protected booths. The terrorist bullets weren't real but sounded convincing enough from the speakers embedded in the walls.

The aim-assist program on my HUD helped to line up the shot, pulling the trigger when the graphical reticule flashed red. The barrel shone brightly, I may have been firing blank rounds, but they still went off with an ear-piercing boom. I had to work hard to maintain my stance, leaning with my body weight against the recoil, the barrel jerking backwards as it spat out the spent round with a satisfying click.

A gunman popped up from behind a pile of rubble, wearing a turban and scarf, hiding his face except for a single bloodshot eye, brandishing a rocket-propelled grenade launcher. He slung the weapon over his shoulder and readied it to fire at the line of booths. I didn't give him a chance.

My headset's focus mode enhanced my reactions fast enough to fire before he could aim the RPG. The projection of the terrorist distorted as the bullet passed through, but quickly returned to a clear resolution revealing the terrorist, and sent particles of blood and brains bursting outwards as it collapsed.

I grinned in celebration as the sound of a whistle shrieked from the wall speakers.

TIME'S UP!

The words blazed in bright red; hovering above the firing range. The enemy characters froze on the spot as the program began to terminate. The background faded away into emptiness like the mirage it was, leaving behind nothing but the long hall of white reflective tiles along the walls and floor.

A high score leaderboard flashed up on my display; putting me in first place with 12,860 points.

"Huh…whaddya know?" I smirked at David.

"Beginner's luck," he rumbled back, having come last in the group.

"Oh look," I nudged him teasingly. "You suck as badly in real-life as you do at *Call of Duty*."

"Screw you."

The trainees and I began disarming ourselves, the sound of mechanical clicking as ammo clips were removed from their weapons. I carefully followed suit, using a step-by-step guide which appeared on display to unload the remaining round in the chamber, and removing the clip from underneath the grip.

"Not bad! Not bad at all!" a gruff woman's voice rang out from behind us. "Keep at it, and we'll make marksmen out of you console cowboys yet."

We turned around to see our instructor. A stern military type; a cyborg with a full prosthetic body, practically an android. I didn't even think technology like that was possible yet. Virtualife were keen to keep it that way too, having been informed by Director Langley that knowledge of her existence was protected under the official secrets act. Her bionic muscles flexed through the crimson nanotech fabric of her combat uniform, the armour panels on top sliding gracefully. Her synthetic skin had a waxy appearance, with the face like a bulldog, with bright, dazzling emerald bionic eyes and her brunette hair tied into a tight, regulation bun.

She gave us a speech at the start, assuring us that she was in fact human. If it weren't apparent that she could apparently beat everyone in the room to a bloody pulp, she'd probably be getting odd stares.

I'd be lying if I said I didn't fancy her a bit, though.

The readout on my HUD only gave me limited info from her personnel file. The restricted access settings only gave me her name, rank and operating number: Lieutenant Emma Golem. I would just have to *assume* that was her real name.

"Now I'm sure you've all got codes to crack, or whatever the fuck it is you nerds do," she ordered, getting a few sniggers, pointing to an electronic weapons locker by the entrance to the suite. "But you know the drill; weapons back on the rack and head in an orderly manner to the exit."

We did as we were told, and began shuffling towards the exit, the sound of loud clangs ringing out as the weapons were stored away.

"What about you?' Emma called over to me, her manikin face curling to give an accidental unsettling smile, nudging her head at my gun. "You're pretty good with that. You ever handled a weapon before?"

I shook my head, noticing David walking out the sliding door, watching us with an intrigued glance.

"I play a lot of shooters though. Kinda makes you wonder why they bother building suites like this when you can do all the training you want in VR."

She shook her head.

"Handling a gun in a dream state doesn't prepare you for the real thing," she scoffed. "Still, you showed potential today."

"Thanks! Still, students are only as good as the teacher… or the software."

"Just doin' my job," she replied warmly, but professionally. "I noticed your stance though. I think you'd be better suited to a revolver, actually."

I nodded attentively.

"I'll keep that in mind, thanks."

We shook hands and introduced ourselves; her motorised grip tightened on my fingers, starting to become painful.

"Sorry!" she cried, recoiling suddenly, the synthetic capillaries in her cheeks blushing. "I'm still getting used to this body…"

"It's fine," I reassured her, rubbing the red imprint she'd left on the skin.

I couldn't help but give her a quizzical glance up and down her bionic body. I couldn't even begin to imagine what that was like, having her brain cut out of her old body like that.

"I… I have to ask." I began gingerly. "Why'd you do it?"

She rolled her lips and shrugged.

"Same reason most people do things," she admitted. "The money was too good."

I pursed my lips and nodded.

"I had a friend who went in for some experimental drug testing," I replied. "Had to be infected with a nasty strain of the Red-death. He didn't make it… but at least his family have a nice place now."

Her bionic eyes stared back at me, looking somewhat baffled.

"That's… a nice story," she replied awkwardly.

We stood in stony silence briefly… then broke into laughter.

"Sorry. Bad comparison," I sniggered. "For what it's worth, a lot of people would be prepared to do worse for money."

"Ain't that the truth," she snorted.

"Hmm…" I nodded thoughtfully, thinking more about if I could get anything useful out of her. "Still, it must be a pretty big threat to get you guys to come here."

"Are you kidding?" she scoffed. "Have you ever Googled the top ten most hated jobs? Cyber-spy is number four. You could just be knifed on the way home! Virtualife's made an investment in you guys. They want *you* to be well protected."

I rolled my eyes. Now I understood.

"So, your bosses are worried we're gonna leak *their* data," I replied negatively.

She frowned ambiguously.

"You have a very cynical mind, Arthur," she joked.

"Comes with the job," I shrugged. "What was number one?"

Liz offered to check it for me the second I spoke, but I refused.

"Hated job? Executive."

"Shocker."

I rolled my lips pensively, wondering if I should press the topic I wanted to.

"Don't suppose you know much about this combat unit?" I asked eventually. "This… RAPTOR?"

She eyed me suspiciously.

"Why, how much do you know?" she asked abruptly.

"Not much," I admitted. "They issued basic data on the defence and control software… but from what I can gather it's some sort of simulated predator?"

"That's the name, don't wear it out," she scoffed back.

I snorted at her dry humour.

"Still, I saw part of a redacted spec file," I added. "Research on the project included studying the neural architecture from some of the world's deadliest animals. Lions, monitor lizards, sharks… Something like that equipped with machine guns and lasers? Sounds pretty deadly to me."

I waited timidly for her response, half expecting her to slap me in cuffs for breaking the terms of the official secrets act.

Her response was nowhere near as dramatic.

"You make it sound like something out of a B-movie," she chuckled.

"That was the vibe I was getting, yeah," I scoffed.

She nodded slowly in a reserved manner.

"Well, rest assured, any and all Virtualife products comply with the three laws of responsible robotics."

The standard corporate response: denial.

"Fair enough…" I said briefly. "Anyway, I should probably get back to it. You wanna hang out in the caf…"

Wait… shit! She can't eat, you idiot!

I stopped in my tracks, averting my eyes from her, mechanically articulated face.

"Sorry… I wasn't really thinking," I apologised slowly, scratching the back of my head with embarrassment.

"It's okay," she breathed sadly, but with understanding. "I do actually have a form of digestion. Anaerobic generation. Provides minimal power supply, but at least I have taste receptors…" She gave a half-hearted smile. "Electronic nostalgia."

"Oh… right, cool." She perked up with a smile. 'So how about it? My treat for a lesson well taught?"

"Well…" she replied, eyeing me dragging the answer out. "You know I'm gay, right?"

My heart sunk a bit.

"Bloody 'ell, give me some credit!" I cried, in an exaggerated manner, masking my disappointment. "If I was asking you on a date I'd Google somewhere with class!"

That got a giggle.

"Okay, sure. You earn a hell of a lot more than I do," she teased.

<<Local Time: 14:46 GMT>>

Once more, the code blazed across my face from the terminal.

"Okay…" I breathed, stretching out my spine muscles. "Back to the grind…"

I went through the to-do list on my terminal, loaded up the next corrupted file on the server's registry, and began the painstaking process.

```
    <<

    static void groups_sort(struct group_info *group_info)

{

    int base, max, stride;
int gidsetsize = group_info->ngroups;

for (stride = 1; stride < gidsetsize; stride = 3 * stride + 1);

    /* nothing */ stride /= 3;

while (stride) {
        max = gidsetsize - stride;
        for (base = 0; base < max; base++) {
        int left = base;
        int right = left + stride;
```

```
        gid_t tmp = GROUP_AT(group_info, right);

while (left >= 0 && GROUP_AT(group_info, left) > tmp) {
        GROUP_AT(group_info, right) = GROUP_AT(group_info, left);
        right = left;
        left -= stride;
}
        GROUP_AT(group_info, right) = tmp;
}

    >>
```

Half an hour later, I'd corrected all the errors that I could find… and my head felt like it was about to erupt. I slumped with a sigh in my office chair, staring up blankly at the bio-luminescent lights hanging from the blank grey ceiling, ready to pass out.

"Uggggh…" I moaned with exhaustion, dreading the moment of truth.

"No point in putting it off," Liz chirped at me in an encouraging tone, appearing as a hologram on the desk.

I grudgingly agreed with her, crossing my fingers as I issued the telepathic command.

```
<<Compiling script>>
<<0% complete>>
```

Come on… Come on…

Once more, I drew closer to the window, the anxiety killing me as the progress bar slowly filled. This was the thirty-seventh file I'd attempted to repair. Every time there was a small chance that this one would succeed and would reveal the source IP address. Every time I'd been disappointed. I was starting to think that I would have to give up and move onto some other technique to trace the hack. If I did that though, one of my colleagues would be three steps ahead of me. No bonuses for second place in this business, and my god I could use one.

Come on… Come on…

<<100% Complete>>

<<Compilation successful>>

In my exhausted state, my mind failed to process what had happened. Then it clicked; a frantic rush flowed through my veins.

"Holy shit!" I spluttered, clasping my hand to my mouth.

It worked. It actually worked!

Now for the real moment of truth. This part had to be right. It just had to be.

"Liz… run the script and identify source IP address," I asked, holding my breath.

<<Running script>>

<<Reconstructing cached metadata>>

<<Source IP address identified: 31.987.112.201>>

"Get in!" I cried in a guttural tone, pumping my fist into the air. That was it, that was all I needed!

"It's a proxy server, just as we thought," Liz informed me. "I'm scanning the ICE programs protecting it now. Preliminary analysis within two minutes."

"Take your time. Get it right," I grinned back at her, leaning back expansively and resting my head hands. The reports came in on the holo-display, feeling absolutely chuffed and…

Everything froze. The world went still and silent around me.

<<Memory playback paused>>

<<Incoming notification from virtual person assistant>>

"Sorry to interrupt, Arthur," the modern-day Liz called to me telepathically. "But we've arrived at the convention centre. I'll save the rest of the file for later."

"Right… cheers," my present consciousness reluctantly agreed.

<<Terminating Memory Playback>>

<<Disengaging neural lace>>

The flashback dissolved, the present day rushed in to replace it. My bionic eyes awakened to the flat bio-concrete walls of the underground car park. The auto-driver program had just finished parking, the purr of the electric engine fell silent, the glow of the dashboard dimming. Soon the car's cabin was only illuminated by the faint ambience of the bio-luminous lamps suspended from the ceiling.

I grumbled under my breath and massaged my aching temples, feeling woozy after the simulation, and regretted not being able to watch the playback to the end. I strained my eyes, adjusting the lenses to glance at the gloomy utilitarian surroundings. Pipes and wires ran across the walls and ceiling, while a handful of faulty holo-adverts in the background flickered, casting shadows across the grimy walls.

I worked myself up to getting out again, grabbing my hat and reached for the door handle. The mag-lock deactivated with a satisfying hiss. I hopped out onto the tarmac, telepathically locking up behind me. The morning air stung my cheeks and sent fountains of steam spewing from my breath. I adjusted the settings on my Neural lace to block the synaptic signals from my thermoreceptors; my sense of temperature. My cheeks went numb, the cold fading with it.

Liz tapped into the internal layout of the building and placed guidance markers on my HUD to guide me towards the lift. The sound of my footsteps echoed eerily as I made my way through the rows of cars. Not a soul in sight, as empty as a crypt this time in the morning; it was almost eerie.

I loaded my MP3 player to cancel out the silence. The emotional analysis algorithms selected the song for my mood and began streaming. The turn of the century classic *Bad Day* by Daniel Prowter started to telepathically ringing inside my list. Good choice. The upbeat tune indeed took a load off my mind. I plodded towards the silvery automatic doors of the lift, when…

THUD!

A single massive metallic crash rang out across the car park, sending my heart racing.

The hairs stood up on the back of my neck. I spun around on the spot, adrenaline taking control as my eyes darted around the room. My software-guided reflexes whipping my gun hand towards the hidden holster in my leg, my mind was rushing with paranoid thoughts of the Mafia.

"What's wrong?" Liz frowned at me telepathically.

I ignored her, craning my head to peer around every corner I came across, expecting someone to come jumping out; but could only see the long rows between each car, shadows blinking in and out of existence as the lighting flickered.

"There, look!" Liz cried using the cursor on my HUD to direct my vision towards a stack of cardboard boxes inside a cargo loading area, marked by yellow and black painting on the ground. One of the top boxes had fallen over, knocking over the contents of a toolbox, a service robot already rolling over to clean up the mess.

I hated relying on instinct; but there was something wrong, I could feel it.

"It must've been unsafely loaded," she reassured me. "Nothing to get all jumpy about."

Unless someone knocked it over…

I wasn't alone. A primal sensation I could shake, all too familiar after last night…

There!

Something moved out of the corner of my eye. I snapped around, ready to jump into action, frantically scanning the room.

More cars, more concrete.

Nothing.

I waited there, watching the shadows on the graffiti plastered walls, ready to blow away anyone who wanted to fuck with me.

I was there for a good minute before I was satisfied there was no one there. I turned to head to the elevator, with lingering suspicions, but ultimately feeling rather stupid.

Definitely, need to lay off the focus mode.

CHAPTER 12

Mother Mind profile 7183-2647-8246-3892:

First name: Denise

Surname: Masika

Status: Wanted for numerous crimes. Click here for more detail

Nationality: British citizen

Occupation(s):

- Suspected member of *Spiritform* hacker group

Criminal record:

- Arrested: 17/11/2037
  - Offence: Suspected of unauthorised access to computer material
  - No formal charges

Known aliases:

- Destiny

Live surveillance:

- Status: *Unavailable*
- Date: 07/10/2045
- Current location: Unknown
- Local Time: 08:42 GMT

<<VR Simulation in progress>>

Idyllic. The only way to describe pre-climate change Derbyshire. I was sitting on the grass of a high hill called Mam Tor, looking out over the old mining country town Castleton. I pulled up the collars of my sleeveless jacket to shield against the wind, my ear chain rattling as it blew. I should've changed my avatar. Tank tops are useless for northern weather.

I ran my fingerless gloved hands through the grass feeling each blade. The desolate, yet gorgeous rolling hills, standing tall above the windswept, rocky valley. Farmland carved out of ancient walls of stone, marking out fields dotted with livestock. A country scene… that could only still exist in virtual reality. The longing for the past seemed to make it that much more real.

"What is it with you and nostalgia trips?" Simon asked, plopping himself next to me on the grass like a sleepy dog.

He was wearing his default virtual avatar, matching his real-world appearance. Tall and lanky, with a thin, gaunt face revealing his delicate bone structure, his eyes like desert oases. He didn't look much like a hacker, wearing a chequered white and blue shirt with his sleeves rolled up. The most rebellious thing about him was his torn jeans and his genetically modified silver-white hair.

"You must get sick of the city." I shrugged through the open shoulders of my tank top, listening to my chain earrings jingling.

"True," he admitted. "Though gotta say, there's nothing like absence to make the heart grow fonder. It sure as hell was better than staring at the walls of this crappy bunker."

I cringed with guilt. His words struck a nerve. I felt terrible about sending him to that shithole. We'd cast him out like a leper and yet expected him to do the most important job we had going now; decrypting the Project Selection files.

"Well… hopefully, after today, you'll be able to come back," I said perkily, giving him the thumbs-up with my fingerless gloves. "The others are making their final preparations now. Blackmailing this doctor will be a piece of cake. We'll get the decryption keys, have Smokey pick you up and have you back in time for dinner."

"Fingers crossed," Simon chuckled doubtfully. "Shouldn't you be helping them?"

I rolled my eyes and grinned.

"What do you take me for?" I laughed, rolling backwards and stretching out like a cat on the lawn, scratching my belly through my top, the chains on my jeans jingling as I moved. "I finished my workload about an hour ago. The exhibition hall's holo-display is under my control. Tranquillity has already stolen the reservations we need for her and me to log in. Not bad for a night's work."

The target for my latest hack was the central holographic display in the exhibition hall. The plan was to blackmail one of Virtualife's AI researchers (Doctor Julie Carpenter) into giving us the encryption key for the Project Selection files. We could have them on the net by tonight if we could, but the plan hinged on her making a snap, panic decision.

Kasira and I had stolen the tickets for two avatars reserved under the names of a pair of friends logging in from Bradford. We would stream our consciousnesses into the robot avatars and operate them remotely to threaten Doctor Carpenter in person. We needed something with shock value. Luckily, we had just the ticket; a video of her taking cocaine-bread. Putting it up in front of three thousand people wouldn't exactly be a boon to her career.

"Owned." Simon nodded with admiration.

I shrugged through the grass, feeling rather pleased with myself.

"What can I say?" I admitted, feeling self-assured. "I've been doing this a long time."

A long time…

The words echoed in my head darkly. I sat up again, my eyes sliding away from Simon's gaze. I stared out across the rolling hills, nervously licking my pierced lip, hoping the memories would be washed away by the soft wind.

"So, go on then," Simon piped up eventually, sensing my despair and hurrying to change the subject.

I looked up to see him nudging his ghostly hair towards the natural beauty before us.

"Why Derbyshire?"

I pursed my lips apprehensively, running my fingers through my dyed virtual hair. It wasn't something I talked about. Ever. To anyone. But there was no denying that I felt comfortable around him.

"My dad used to take me on camping trips out here," I admitted to him, while gingerly rubbing my tattooed skin sleeve, deciding to gloss over the time I went with Arthur, playing with my pierced lip timidly as I reminisced.

"First time we went, he'd had to drag me kicking and screaming away from my computer. He used to say that the internet was great and everything, but getting back to nature… that was a connection to reality. Something much bigger. He'd wave his finger at me and say: 'Accept no substitutes.'"

I chuckled. It was amazing how much that had left an impression on me. I turned back to face Simon, staring at me with the same gushing look a child would give a puppy.

"Aw, that's cute." He chuckled.

I blushed angrily, grinding my teeth through a bemused smile. This wasn't exactly easy for me to talk about, and if there was one sure fire way to get under my skin, it was by calling me 'cute'.

"Sorry," he apologised quickly, nervously scratching the back of his neck, sensing he'd touch a sore spot.

"It's fine," I grumbled lightly. "It's just… I've never actually told anyone that."

Our eyes met, locking in a gaze of tender intimacy, smiling warmly at each other, listening to the wind rustling past.

Both of us could feel the chemistry between us.

Neither of us dared to act on it.

The temptation was strong. *So* strong. All I had to do was lean in, and he would reciprocate. Lock ourselves in an embrace of comfort and satisfaction. And yet we couldn't do it. Just too risky. Behind my outward smiling face was a raging battle of id and ego, struggling to dominate the other.

What's the worst that could happen? You take risks every day! You could be arrested or killed walking through the front door? Are you really going to stop yourself living before then?

No!

God-damn it Destiny snap out of it! You're at war! How are you supposed to make objective choices when you're fucking one of your soldiers? You get too close now and you'll regret it in the long run!

Besides… you don't want to go through ***that*** *pain again… do you?*

Painful memories began bubbling up. I swallowed hard, trying to push back the emotion, rolling my tongue over the lip ring nervously. I wanted to speak; say something to end this moment, and still couldn't quite bring myself to do it.

I was still staring into his eyes...

Shit.

I'd never wanted a distraction so badly in my life.

As if on cue, telepathic ringing went off inside my head.

<<Incoming group e-telepathy call from: Gatecrasher, Acid Overdrive, Tranquillity>>

I saw Simon's eyes flicker; the conference call was coming in for him as well. My VPA, Poe, appeared on my HUD; his cartoon cat eyes blazing enthusiastically, a smile spreading across his green whiskers.

"It's time, Destiny," he informed me telepathically.

"Cheers, Poe," I spoke out loud, ending the tender silence abruptly.

I turned back to face Simon, already trying to mask his disappointment with an awkward smile.

"We should… uh… answer that," I told Simon awkwardly, pointing towards my head.

"Yeah, right, right." He hurriedly answered, nodding rapidly, obviously hurt by my rejection and eager to gloss over it.

I bit my lip as the guilt stung, feeling as though I'd led him on. I looked away and telepathically answered the call.

<<Call answered>>

The images began streaming directly to each of our HUDs. One by one, Raj, Kasira and Jamie appeared in data windows. Their virtual avatars streaming against the background of a cyberwarfare program;

the green sphere representing the directory of the EveryWear avatars server on the Thames Pier, burned a bright blue as their attack scripts were uploaded.

"Nice of you to join us," Jamie scowled, his wild feral eyes simmering deep within his gaunt forehead, his scar folding in his skin as he frowned. His avatar was wearing the same clothes he would typically wear, darkened skinny jeans, heavy steel boots, thin white tank top with glowing blue lines, spike studded bracelets at the end of his thin, tattooed arms.

"You do your job; I'll do mine, Gatecrasher," I told him sternly.

He gave a single bitter scoff, shaking his head.

"I installed that traffic logger virus on their network like you asked," he admitted bitterly, pointing with his thumb to the directory behind him. "I'll be able to monitor your dive from here. If their ICE detects what you're up to, I'll know. But make no mistake; I see the first hint of them running a trace program, and I'm pulling you out."

I ignored him, proceeding to load up a map of the convention centre. It was mostly a video-glass pyramid displaying adverts and logos from every pane, built on top of an oil-rig like structure stretching across the five hundred metre width of the river, suspended on massive concrete pillars extending above the water line.

"I've run multiple tests on their user verification handshakes," Kasira confirmed, playing with her hair buns, wrapped by bright blue bows, looking pleased with herself. "We come back green every time. We should still be able to access the reservations I stole. I hijacked the company's customer service bot to control the dialogue between them and the customers. It shouldn't arouse suspicion."

I raised an eyebrow at her.

"Who told you to do that?" I asked sourly, quickly checking with Poe to see if it was a decision made by our AI collective. He shook his head.

Kasira frowned.

"I took some initiative, give me a break," she protested.

"You don't hack shit unless we tell you to!" Jamie spat angrily, rounding on her across the video feed, pounding his spiked fist.

"Here we go…" Raj moaned, burying his skinny face with a frustrated palm, squishing his face tattoo.

"I'm *sick* of your 'initiative', Tranquillity!" Jamie snarled his teeth like a skeleton. "Your domination of that chatbot is just more data traffic *I* need to monitor! Are you *trying* to get us caught?"

"Oh, shove it up your ass, Gatecrasher," she snapped back, giving him the finger.

"Children, children please!" Simon laughed, waving his hands to calm them down. "Jesus, I'm gone for five minutes, and you start tearing at each other's throats!"

"Yeah, knock it off." I barked with authority, trying to instil some fear into them.

"For fuck's sake, Destiny!" Jamie cried, throwing his tattooed arm back in exasperation. "You can't…"

"If you can't manage a few gigabits of traffic, I really don't know what you're doing here," I told him flatly, pointing at him firmly through the camera feed, before directing myself at Kasira.

"And the next time you have a bright idea, Tranquillity, run it by us," I groaned. "You can't make decisions like that on your own."

Kasira's eyes narrowed with jealousy, before throwing her head to the side and pouting.

Spoilt little bitch…

"Overdrive, where are we with our lookout?" I checked with Raj, moving on swiftly.

A flashing red dot of a GPS transponder appeared on the 3D map of the convention centre in front of me; right by the queuing area for exhibition hall B, marking the location of our home-built android. We'd sent him there on the tube to act as another set of eyes and ears for us, and to make use of his built-in electronic warfare suite if need be. Much to Raj's dismay.

"Plexi is in position," Raj grunted, lazily scratching his soft tattooed arm while simultaneously pointing towards the map.

"Just as you said, he's registered to appear as the personal remote avatar of a separate user account. I'm still not a fan of sending my prize robot to be your *backup plan*," Raj complained.

"Dumbass! It's not just the building's security we've got to worry about," Jamie snarled sourly. "There could be Virtualife agents on the ground trying to listen in. We'll need Plexi's jamming beacon for that."

"Don't remind me!" Raj hissed. "I'm amazed I got him past security with that thing attached. If he gets taken out, I'm gonna hold you personally responsible!"

"I promise, Raj, we'll take good care of your pet-project," I sighed with a nod, not attempting to sound reassuring.

Raj rolled his head, unsatisfied, but I didn't have the patience for any more whining.

"I've got the main event ready to go," I announced proudly, highlighting the central holo-display on the map. "My attack-macro has been installed. We can ruin Doctor Carpenter's career with a single command."

I turned to Kasira, her arms folded and still scowling unhappily.

"Tranquillity, you ready for this?" I inquired forcefully.

Her head snapped up with a look of sudden surprise as if she had been a million miles away.

"Huh?" she said, puzzled. "Oh yeah, sure."

I frowned at her.

"You're supposed to be coming as my back-up," I glowered. "Go into focus mode if you can't get your head in the game."

Her eyes narrowed at me with frustration.

"Right," she said finally.

I didn't appreciate her tone, but ignored her and went to open up my EveryWear Avatars App on my HUD.

<<Logging into EveryWear Avatars>>

<<User verification complete>>

<<Checking reservations>>

<<Reservation 8912-4743-0610 confirmed>>

<<Kiosk location: Thames Pier Convention Centre>>

<<Time for reservation: 09:00-15:00>>

<<Verifying avatar operational status...>>

<<All systems fully functional>>

<<Ready for consciousness shift>>

<<Begin consciousness shift: Yes/No?>>

"All right people, this is it!" I announced loudly, clapping my gloved hands together, feeling a sudden wave of excitement rushing through me. "Final checks!"

"Gatecrasher, standing by," Jamie announced, bringing up a command window for the virus he'd installed.

"Overdrive, standing by," Raj continued as he checked the remote-control software for our android.

"Plexi, standing by," the electronic voice of the android grated back telepathically through the control software.

"Tranquillity, standing-by," Kasira admitted, albeit rather grudgingly, following my lead and logging into her own stolen EveryWear account.

"I'll be standing by too," Simon shrugged awkwardly. "With uh… moral support."

I turned to face him once more and gave him an encouraging pat on the back.

"That's all we need," I laughed at him.

Out of the corner of my eye, I could've sworn I saw Raj, Kasira, and Jamie collectively rolling their eyes.

"All right then," he chuckled, beaming back at me. "Break a leg!"

Our eyes met again, but I quickly gave the telepathic command to begin the con:

<<Initialising consciousness shift>>

<<Establishing secure connection to reserved avatar>>

<<Connection established>>

<<Running neural lace drivers>>

Simon's eyes, which had been so clear to me, began to fade away as if he were a watercolour painting being washed away by the rain. Soon the serene landscape faded and melted back into the digital void of cyberspace.

The blurriness on my vision soon began to clear up, and the static on my audio output died down. Out of the faint digital outlines, I soon became aware of the surroundings I had loaded into; and was greeted by the familiar sight of a rent-a-body storage pod, my new android avatar jacked into the charging station. A final diagnostics check ran on my HUD, while I adjusted to the alien feeling of being inside a mechanical body.

The pod was a silver plastic alcove, the size of a shopping mall changing room. Power and data cables ran along the side of the cramped walls, hooked up to sockets on the back of my neck. I tried moving the robot's neck, feeling the slight, but the notable increase in the effort it took for remote operation. The outer chassis was claytronic; built of programmable matter so that users could customise the appearance of the droid to look as much or as little like their actual appearance.

The avatar was naked, wearing the face of the woman I'd hacked. You could tell it wasn't real skin; far too waxy to be completely convincing. The arms and legs were still held in place by steel clamps around the wrists and ankles. The door of the alcove was a full-sized mirror, giving me a good view of the oversized breasts that had been selected. She had dark hazel eyes and short bright, blonde hair, and lightly tanned skin… it was scarce to see someone want to replicate their real appearance completely.

<<Final diagnostics complete>>

<<All systems nominal>>

<<Welcome to your avatar. We hope you enjoy the experience>>

A loud clicking reverberated around the pod as the locks deactivated, and slid back into the compartments on the walls. Above my head, I heard the sliding sound of the roof panel opening, and a robotic arm descended holding the clothes the woman had reserved. Apparently, she hadn't chosen to spend as much on that as she had her actual body; simply booking a pink baggy sweatshirt, tracksuit bottoms, and *Nike* trainers. At least we wouldn't stand out.

I concentrated, forcibly taking those first clunky steps out of the charging station, and removed the cables. Thanks to the pressure sensors woven throughout the droid I could feel every clanking step against the panels beneath my feet.

I dragged the body over to the suspended coat hangers and began the long and awkward process of trying to get myself into the clothes. Putting my arms and legs into the right places was cumbersome, and fiddling around with the hooks on the back of the bra required a level of nimbleness that took a good few minutes for me to adjust to.

By the time I was decent, my brain had adjusted to the control protocols. I quickly sent the neurocommand to unlock the storage pod door. A silver-blue lobby area lay beyond the storage pod and was greeted by the receptionist-bot. The map of the centre loaded into my vision; our target highlighted in green.

Game time…

CHAPTER 13

Mother Mind profile 2446-7128-5978-2501:

- First name: Arthur
- Surname: Wells
- Status: Living
- Nationality: British citizen
- Occupation(s):
  - Private investigator
    - Status: Self-employed
    - Organisation: Arthur Wells & Associates
- Known aliases:
  - IronRoot
- Live surveillance:
  - Status: *Partially available*
  - Date: 07/10/2045
  - Current location: Thames Pier Convention Centre, London
  - Local Time: 09:21 GMT

They said a fry-up was the best thing to cure a hangover. Too bad all that was available was this crappy breakfast burger. I was sat on a plastic stool in the food court of the convention centre, munching away at the crispy bread roll, stuffed with bacon and runny eggs, dripping onto the paper wrapping on my tray, served to me by a *McDonald's* waiter-bot.

The restaurant was tucked into the corner of the cavernous steel and glass entrance hall, illuminated by a hundred spotlights. My HUD was going crazy with greeting animations from the wireless feed, and the usual assault of holo-adverts. A gigantic display pillar stretched up all the way up to the tip of the pyramid, projecting a giant visualisation of the Thames Pier logo suspended above the river, and displaying live information on the events scheduled for the day; including ModCon.

The mass of the crowd was held back by an iron railing, guided by the robotic staff into an orderly queue towards an automatic ticket barrier. One by one scanning the attendees and granting access to Exhibition Hall B.

They certainly all looked like tech enthusiasts. All here for one purpose: celebrating the tinkerers of today, who would become the tycoons of tomorrow. At a glance, it looked like there were almost as many people attending via android avatars as there were in flesh and blood. Finding the Spiritformers without that encryption codex would've been a nightmare.

Most of the attendees would be just looking for the latest upgrade for their PC or bot, but a quick scan revealed a handful of executive types, trying to snap up the newest talent. This wasn't a sci-fi or fantasy event, so there weren't as many people attending in cosplay, but the usual stereotypes were here; the chubby girl wearing far too revealing clothes, and skinny guys wearing hoodies that seemed to swallow them whole.

I found myself grinning, feeling a creeping sense of belonging every time I went to these events. The nostalgia was bittersweet though; reminding me of my outings with Denise.

"Is it safe to use focus mode yet?" I groaned telepathically at Liz, desperate to take my mind off that nagging little voice, telling me I was a traitor.

"Fine," she reluctantly agreed. "I'll be monitoring your vital signs closely though. If your stress level gets too high, I'll have to terminate."

"Just do it," I accepted.

The electrical tingling from my neural lace rippled inside my skull, zapping the guilt back in its place.

"Any sign of them yet?" I asked swiftly, my attention now entirely on duty at hand.

"You'll be the first to know," she reassured me, loading up the live feed from SpyFly.

I'd sent the drone through the ticket barrier undetected, and it was now streaming footage as it hovered over the Virtualife booth, opposite the gaming zone, filled with rows of players jacked into modded VR games.

The booth was marked by a circular pad of dark blue and green carpet, pulsing with the company colours, enclosed by a semi-circular wall screen displaying a presentation on careers in AI development, while a handful of programmers and executives gave their spiel to gatherings of spotty-faced students.

Amongst them was my person of interest; Doctor Julie Carpenter, currently giving a live-streamed interview with a *YouTuber* via a media drone. Her blue and green company uniform fit tightly over her dominant figure, standing with her hands on ample hips, her flaming red hair tied into a bun, her diamond-white bionic eyes gleaming inventively, while she chatted away with the face of the teenage blogger projecting from a small screen hanging from the drone's undercarriage.

It was easy to forget that she had been briefed on the entire situation at hand. I was amazed at how calm she looked. Knowing that someone was coming to threaten her and that I was recording the whole thing. Probably had turned on focus mode at max setting.

Now I just had to play the waiting game. If my intel was right, Spiritform would be here any minute now in their avatars. How they were going to blackmail her didn't matter to me; they just needed to show up. SpyFly could land on one of the avatars, jack into the hardware directly and run a trace program back to the operator's location.

Of course, there was still the possibility that there might be a lookout here already, ready to jam my transmission; hence the need for me to come here in person. I suppose I could've just hacked the building's network and received the signal via the wi-fi, but that would just be one more corporation with cause to sue me.

Now it was just a matter of killing time. Which was ninety percent of what I did as a PI; long-distance stakeouts that took hours and my full attention. No opportunity to play games or surf the web. Pain in the ass. But at least it would keep me from any online shopping sprees. I had a chance to check my bank accounts earlier. The payments to Dart were starting to take their toll. I was going to need a cash infusion quickly.

I waited intently for twenty minutes, regularly checking the video feed, ordering the drone to scan every avatar that walked past against the Spiritform encryption codex provided by Dart. When the interview with the media drone was over (looking glad it was), she headed off. SpyFly's pursuit subroutines activated and continued tailing her, keeping its distance as she weaved through the human traffic towards the women's staff toilet. Out of the body of the crowd, SpyFly identified the four Ashigaru agents that were acting as her discreet bodyguards. Virtualife had sent me their profiles earlier, so as not to mistake them for Spiritform. Their clothes may have been plain, but they certainly all looked like thugs; with harsh military haircuts and eyes hidden behind darkened vid-glasses.

Carpenter reached the automatic door to the toilet and was cleared for entry by the security scan. SpyFly quickly followed, whizzing through the gap in the door before it snapped shut. The staff toilet was indeed nicer than the public facilities; clinical in cleanliness, and more stylish. An animated digital painting of ships rolling underneath London Bridge projected from the blue-tiled wall, reflected in the self-cleaning mirror lined with icons, suspended over the rows of sinks.

Doctor Carpenter headed into one of the PVC stalls and locked it behind her. I ordered SpyFly to land on the ceiling to conserve power, while I slumped back in my seat in the food court.

My neural lace did its best to stave off the boredom, but I had a feeling that this would be how the day was going to go; watching her give talks, followed by more repetitive shit. People would always envision this glamorous film noir fantasy whenever they talked about PIs. But honestly, it was as dull as dishwater most of the time. Until it wasn't.

SpyFly's sensors picked up the whir of the automating door. The drone spun around to face it, revealing a chavvy-looking pair, both blonde, wearing identical pink sweat suits and hoodies.

"That's strange…" I muttered. "They're not staff."

I eyed them suspiciously through my HUD… they were too similar. Even their makeup was the same. I zoomed SpyFly's camera in some more.

"Hold up, I think we've got something!" Liz pointed out, scanning their faces.

I recognised it too; their skin was too waxy, unnaturally so. Synthetic. My HUD identified it as claytronic skin; used in android avatars to morph into the appearance of their users.

Since when do androids need to go to the loo?

"Run the scan," I telepathically ordered SpyFly.

The directional antennae on the drone's head swivelled and pointed towards the two avatars.

<<Wireless packet sniffer running>>

<<Intercepting packet stream: 451.672.853.234>>

<<Cross referencing with Encryption Codex>>

<<Match successful>>

<<Identified as: Spiritshroud-765>>

They're running Spiritform encryption!

"Bingo!" I grinned, leaning towards my virtual display.

The door snapped shut behind them; the light mounted above the frame turned red to indicate it was locked.

"They must have access to the building's internal security server," Liz pointed out.

My face froze suddenly, the realisation dawning on me that they could be watching through any number of cameras. I drew down my hat to hide my face from a security drone fluttering overhead.

I leaned in to watch the video feed, resting my beard on my metal palm. The two avatars exchanged glances but spoke no words. SpyFly picked up a telepathic exchange they were having but was unable to decrypt the content.

I zoomed closer in on the avatars' faces, trying to recognise familiar expressions in an attempt to tell if one was Denise. Of course, this wasn't her real-life appearance, but there were always going to be tell-tale signs.

The public ID data for each of the avatars officially had them down as Beckie Cullings and Amanda Wilson from Bradford. I wasn't going to get any useful information out of that. The two of them checked the other toilet stalls, ensuring they were alone. Once they were satisfied, the pair of them leaned back again the white porcelain sink and folded their arms, watching the door to Doctor Carpenter's stall with intense mechanical gazes.

"Well, that's a fine how'd you do," I joked with Liz.

Moments later, the sound of a flushing toilet was picked up by SpyFly's sensors, the lock clicked open, and the door swung back. Doctor Carpenter emerged, and sure enough, she stumbled backwards in shock at the sight of the two robots. At first, the surprise had seemed genuine, but I recognised the moment her mind made the connection and the training she'd gone undertook ahold.

"Y…You're not supposed to be here!" she spluttered. "You're not staff! You're not even human! Get out now before…"

Good acting…

"Sorry to interrupt your little recruitment tour, Doctor," the older-looking avatar spoke in a commanding tone with a Yorkshire accent. "But this is the sort of conversation that requires privacy."

Carpenter straightened herself up, folded her arms, and narrowed her glittering eyes.

"I don't appreciate your tone," she replied coolly. "I suggest you leave now before I call security."

"Go ahead, no one will hear," the younger one spoke, nudging her head towards the locked door.

To my surprise, Carpenter didn't flinch.

"If you're trying to intimidate me, you're making a huge mistake. This isn't the first time I've come across… your type," she retorted finally, pointing towards the camera hanging from the ceiling. "It's obvious you've got some talent; I'll give you that. But the backup server for the CCTV is air gapped. Your cyber-attack won't have reached it. So, smile! It's time for your close-up! Even if you're hiding behind those avatars, they'll find you."

She grinned sarcastically at the CCTV hanging from the ceiling, making me nervous about where she was going. I was worried that perhaps the Ashigaru had trained her too well and that she would scare them off before I got my chance to run the trace program.

"I don't know what you had planned," she continued. "But unless you want to have the footage played as evidence at your trial, I would leave before…"

The first avatar wasn't listening, a smile creeping across her face. She raised a single pointed finger towards the animated painting of London bridge projecting from the smart wall.

The painting began to crackle with static, fading away into a cloud of multi-coloured pixels before disappearing altogether.

A new photo loaded up in its place.

Doctor Carpenter at a party in Ibiza. Eating cocaine splice-bread.

Her face froze, like a video on pause. Her look of confidence melted away into horror.

"W…Where the fuck did you get that photo!?" she cried angrily, pointing with a trembling finger.

I couldn't tell if she was acting anymore. I thought that the nerves were getting to her, which would ruin the plan if she went with her insurance policy. All Carpenter had to do was give one telepathic message to the Ashigaru team outside, and they would kill the power to the hall, but Spiritform would know that we're on to them. I had to get this done before then.

The younger-looking avatar leaned backwards expansively. Victoriously folded her arms.

"I thought you realised we had talent," she replied slyly.

Carpenter didn't seem to agree, having turned bright red, ready to explode. This had been part of the plan, making Spiritform believe that they were getting the better of her, but it was apparent they had managed to strike a real nerve as well.

"Oh… you bitch! You bloody thieves! I… I'm calling EveryWear now! I'll…"

"You'll do nothing," the older avatar replied calmly. "Unless you want that photo up on the central display."

Carpenter's mouth snapped shut, grinding her teeth seemingly in bitter defeat, but I supposed she must've remembered about her insurance policy.

"What do you want from me?" she growled.

The avatars exchanged self-satisfied smirks, proceeding to reach for the back of their necks. A small metal handle protruded from the top of their spines. A panel flipped open, revealing a compartment inside, storing a USB cable on a spring coil. The avatars grabbed the adapters and pulled a length of the wire out.

"We should talk more securely," the old avatar said, offering the adapter out.

Carpenter shifted nervously on the spot.

"You're not going to hack my brain, are you?" she asked.

"If we wanted to do that, we'd have done it already," the younger avatar piped up. "Besides, that would make your testimony inadmissible in a court of law."

The colour drained from Carpenter's face.

"Court of law?" She panicked. "You don't mean…"

The avatars drew threateningly closer, holding out their cables in a continuous manner. Carpenter ran her fingers through her hair in panic, swearing under her breath. Eventually, she snatched the wires out of their hands and inserted them into her own neck.

The three of them began a hard-wired telepathic chat session, silently speaking to one another. I couldn't hear what they were saying, either in the real world or through a radio monitor. But I could read Carpenter's expression, apparently horrified by the prospect of what they were demanding.

"Now's your chance!" Liz exclaimed.

I sent the command to SpyFly's AI. The auto-pilot subroutines kicked in, rapidly plotting out the drone's flight plan to land on the old avatar's left ear. SpyFly went into a dive bomb, buzzing softly as it went, landing softly against the claytronic skin; light enough to go undetected by the avatar's tactile sensors. The live camera feed was now getting a close-up of the rubbery surface, revealing the fine detail of the microfibre synthetic hairs growing out of the claytronic matter.

<<Initiating Omnigel electronic hijack sequence>>

<<Engaging mouth-clamp>>

SpyFly raised its head, drawing back its silvery microscopic fangs, and planting its face into the skin, sinking the teeth deep.

<<Uploading omnigel deployment protocol: PingAttack01>>

<<Engaging hypospray>>

The mouth of the drone gave a faint hiss; using its small hypospray to inject omnigel; a solution of nanobots designed to attach to the command input or sensory data lines to a target CPU, bypassing any encryption issues and directly accessing the victim's hardware. A little bit of military tech goes a long way.

<<Omnigel deployed>>

<<Omnigel seeking target destination>>

I watched the nanobots' movements through a schematic of the avatar, the tiny machines slipping through cracks in the chassis until they reached the central CPU in the skull.

<<Destination reached>>

<<Omnigel attempting interface with target hardware>>

The omnigel hardened on the motherboard like mould, the microscopic robots attaching their tendons to the 3D carbon nanotube transistors, replacing the signals to the processor with my own… and even running my own little discreet trace program.

"Just a few more seconds now…" Liz announced cautiously.

My mouth went dry, nervously anticipating the progress bar to reach 100%, the invasive nanobots settling into a culture around the graphene circuit board.

On the video feed, the telepathic conversation was apparently becoming more intense. Doctor Carpenter had been reduced to tears; not tears of sadness, but of guilt.

"No, goddamn it, no!" Carpenter shrieked with panic, her real voice echoing around the room as she slammed her fist into the cubicle wall.

"Keep your voice down!" the older avatar shrieked back.

Damn right keep your voice down! I'll get nothing if they log out now!

"Do you have *any idea* what they're *capable* of!?" she sobbed angrily. "They'll kill me if I give it to you!"

She could win an *Oscar* for her performance, but it didn't help me.

"We're decrypting the data as we speak," the older avatar replied firmly in a hushed voice. "One way or another, the story will get out. If you help us now, that'll elevate you to whistle-blower status. Rather than just being an accessory after the fact."

"Oh, fuck me…" Carpenter breathed, rubbing her eyes shakily.

She was scared shitless. I knew it wasn't my place to know, but now I was *really* curious about the Project Selection files. I might have to have a sneaky look myself if I got the chance.

<<Interface successful>>

"We're in business!" Liz announced gleefully as the data windows flashed green.

"Make it fast!"

<<Initiating trace program>>

A third data window opened; my cyberspace visualisation program rendering the data traffic from the avatar's directory through the building's wi-fi, to the domain name servers and the EveryWear servers. Now is where it was getting interesting; following the data as it travelled through proxy after proxy until I found the original point of origin, and with it the geo-location of the avatars' operators.

Come on… come on!

My focus wandered between cyberspace and the drone video feed. The nature of the conversation seemed to be changing, the camera couldn't see anything this close, but the microphones were still tuned in.

"Look, Doctor," the older avatar continued in a reassuring tone. "This is happening with or without you. We're offering you the chance to be on the right side of history. The chance to be called as a *witness*, rather than a defendant."

"Oh, shit… all right… you win," Carpenter answered with another long trembling sigh. "I'll…"

"There's… something behind your ear!" the younger avatar cried, interrupting Carpenter.

Crap!

"Huh?" the older avatar cried, followed quickly by a loud, aggressive ruffling noise; a wave of shadows suddenly cast across the SpyFly's camera.

Crap! Crap! Crap!

The outline of a pair of pink fingers appeared on the boundaries of SpyFly's field of view, and with a single forceful yank, its jaws were removed from the avatar's skin.

<<Warning: Damage to aviation systems detected>>

<<Omnigel signal strength at 43%>>

The drone's vision blurred as it was pulled back in the avatar's hand. When it came to a stop, I was looking at a close-up image of the older avatar's concerned face.

"Fuck…" she breathed, before showing it to the younger one.

"Jesus, they're on to us!" I heard her panic.

I anxiously clasped my mouth and pulled my hair.

Come on, just a few more seconds!

"We have to abort, now!" the younger avatar cried.

"Yeah, no shit," the older one nodded, turning to Doctor Carpenter. "Don't think this gets you off the hook! We'll..."

"Oh, I don't think so, mate," Carpenter chuckled softly, clearly having perked up at the thought of being caught. "No point making a deal with future inmates."

Shit!

She'd said too much. Now Spiritform would know that this was a sting operation right from the start. The older avatar frowned fiercely.

"We'll see about that," she growled.

I was expecting her to terminate her connection to the avatar instantly; the claytronic skin to melt away and revert to its default, manikin-like appearance. She didn't even flinch ...

<<Warning: Back-channel trace program detected!>>

Oh shit.

A new flow of data appeared; red, aggressive packets of the trace program flowed out from SpyFly's CPU towards my smartwatch; the core of my personal area network. It would take few seconds to run through my ICE and then they'd have my IP address.

Fucking turnabout!

"Shit!" I spat under my voice, rapidly checking the progress of my own trace program. With all the proxy servers, they were routing their connection through, they'd have my own location first.

No way I can afford to become a victim of a revenge-hack!

"Can you do anything to slow them down!?" I checked with Liz.

"It's too late for that," she replied with a quick shake of her head. "We have to terminate the connection now!"

I ground my teeth. My trace program had gone through Spiritform's first two proxy servers, but it looked like there at least another four.

"No choice!" I admitted angrily. "Do it!"

<<Terminating connection to SpyFly>>

The data feed from the drone went flat, the video turning blank and replaced with the big white letters.

<<Connection terminated>>

"Did it work?" I checked anxiously.

"Their data packet request failed," Liz said slowly but reassuringly. "But I'd leave now if I were you. There's still a chance they could use the building's wi-fi to scan and locate you."

I nodded hurriedly, quickly getting off the stool, and whirled my optical scanners around the food court, spotting at least a dozen other avatars around the hall; any of which could be members of Spiritform. I felt a paranoid twinge as my hairs stood up, but was soon kept in check by focus mode.

Liz quickly plotted out my route back to the car park a mile away.

"I would bring the car around for you, but you know what the traffic is like in central."

Bloody typical.

I pulled up the collar of my trench coat, kept my head down and skulked out of the food court and towards the exit, avoiding eye contact with anything or anyone.

I was undeniably pissed off. I'd screwed up. Should've waited for a better opportunity to hack the avatar, or just done it online. There was a good chance that this single cock-up would cost me the case. If Spiritform published the files before I cracked their proxy network, the time-lapse in my contract would come into effect, and I would get paid a grand total of zero. I was muttering bitterly under my breath the entire time, but I couldn't help but feel a certain amount of relief that (at least for today), I wasn't going to be arresting Denise. Silver linings, right?

It took just under twenty minutes to make my way through the crowd, out onto the promenade of the pier and back onto the embankment. Augmented reality arrows guided me towards the elevator leading to the subterranean structure.

"So how much data on me did they actually get?" I checked with Liz, as I walked out of the graffitied steel cage of the lift.

"Hard to say, depends on how long they were scanning for. My main concern is if they visually tracked you."

"Hmm…maybe Denise will get her revenge after all."

My statement hung in the air, as I watched Liz's avatar sympathetically process a response.

"It's possible she had forgiven you after all this time," she suggested optimistically.

"Not bloody likely. Not that it matters now," I rumbled, as I stepped through the rows of cars illuminated by the flickering lights, my footsteps echoing over the tarmac. "Hell hath no fury like a woman…"

Something big, bulky and metal popped out from behind the hood of a black Honda. I didn't see it until it was too late.

WHAM!

I wheezed uncontrollably as a blunt, sturdy force rammed itself into my face like I'd run into a brick wall. My nose broke with a sickening crack. I was sent tumbling backwards, landing hard against the windshield of the car behind me, throwing my hat flying away. Pain spread across my body like an ocean tide, my head ringing, my vision blurred. My HUD turned to a grainy soup of static. I thought I heard a scream in the background; the footsteps of people running away.

"Uhhh…" I groaned.

In my disorientation, looking at the lights above me felt like staring at the sun through a snowstorm of static.

<<Error: Neural interface interrupted>>

<<Neural lace emergency reboot complete>>

<<Warning!: Bio-monitor sensors detect blunt force trauma to cranial region>>

<<Uploading data to NHS and metropolitan police emergency response service>>

<<Error: Unable to establish connection>>

"Arthur!?" I heard Liz's voice crackle over the telepathic interference, as I slowly regained my balance, the soupy static clearing up. "Arthur, can you hear me?"

"Just about..." I groaned back, rubbing my face, feeling the stream of white and red synthetic blood that was now flowing out from my broken nose. "What the hell happ …"

CLANK! CLANK!

My question was answered by a series of metallic footsteps. An android was towering over me. A home-built model, that looked like it had been cobbled together from scrap parts. Long gangling rubber arms, with corrugated iron sheets forming big thighs and forearms, with not enough material to fully encase the sliding and whirring mechanisms within the unit. The head was little more than an old plasma screen with a built-in sensor array, displaying an angry emoji, its gaze fixed squarely on me.

Like a woman scorned.

The pistons in its right arm roared like an active volcano as it drew its fist back.

I combat rolled to my right, just in time to avoid the steel-capped knuckles thrusting in my direction. The metal fist landed on the windscreen with the force of a miniature meteor with a mighty crunch as it left a crater in the hardened glass.

"They've still got access to the building's security grid!" Liz announced. "I can't reach the police. You're on own on this one!"

"That makes a nice change of pace!"

<<Combat mode engaged>>

My neural lace pounded my brain with alpha waves and blocked off my pain receptors. My body went numb and hard, snapping to attention. I rolled off the hood of the car and landed cat-like on my feet. My old virtual boxing training kicked in. I raised my bionic forearms over my face in time to block the incoming punch. The robot's powerful motors sent me skidding backwards, shockwaves rippling through my body, as metal on metal collided.

I wanted to use my wrist laser, try to stun its optic sensors, but it was too close and too fast for that.

This is it…

No one in their right mind would take a robot in a fist fight...unless you were almost a robot yourself. Liz's visual scan confirmed the droid was electrically shielded…but it did have weak spots. Weak spots I knew how to exploit.

<<Activating Taser Knuckles>>

My fist tightened into a solid clump, and a furious crackling sang out as the conductive panels burst to life with dazzling blue flashes.

"Aim for the sensors!" Liz advised me, placing a graphical bullseye on my display.

Adrenaline took hold, and I went into a counter attack, snapping my arms out to the side with an aggressive roar of my actuators. I aimed for the visual sensors in its head; the blow didn't break anything, and the current didn't travel through, but flashes in its detectors and the force of the blow caused the robot to lose its balance, stumbling back with a strange whir as the internal gyroscopes struggled to keep it upright.

I had the window I needed.

I telepathically opened the hidden holster in my right thigh, rapidly drawing out my revolver, but I didn't get a chance to take aim. The droid swung out with a steel backhand, pivoting from the hip, knocking the weapon clear out of my hand and sending it skidding across the tarmac with a clatter; coming to a stop underneath the axles of one of the parked cars.

Fuck!

I jumped into my fighting stance once more, taking a few carefully placed steps backwards. The robot regained its balance and marched towards me, its great hulking mass looming closer, stomping as it went. Liz analysed its motion pattern, tracking it carefully, her predictive algorithms working overtime.

"On my mark!" she cried in readiness, putting up a quick graphical battle plan presentation in a small window.

I nodded with my elbows shielding my head, my heart pounding in my numb, machine body.

The android was almost on top of me now, ready to lunge.

"Go!"

I put Liz's plan into motion. It struck just when she predicted, allowing me to duck in time, feeling the breeze in my hair as the metal fist swiped overhead. My prosthetic legs sprung up, and I rammed my fist into its chin with an uppercut; right in the sensor. The lens cracked, and the current from my knuckles flowed into the circuitry burning it out with a flash! A soft red light lit up, indicating that it switched to backup infrared, but it wouldn't be as responsive now.

"Don't let up!" Liz cheered me on.

My neural lace went into overdrive, zapping my amygdala to tactically dial up my level of aggression. A type of surreal precise rage took hold. I went into a flurry of fast and furious jabs, sending banging and zapping sounds echoing violently against the grimy concrete. I yelled in a way I hadn't in years; a raw, guttural war cry, deep and primal.

The disorientated robot attempted to shield itself, blocking as many of the blows as it could. I thought I had the upper hand; until it grabbed hold of my arm. I tried a counter move to try to free myself from its clamp-like grip, but it wouldn't budge.

But before I knew what had happened, the pair of us were tumbling down. I landed painfully on my back, knocking the wind out of me. The droid came down on top with the weight of an anvil;

I raised my right boot and shoved it into its chest, propping it up with my own strength to keep it from smothering me entirely, but it had me pinned to the spot.

The droid's arms went into a frenzy; desperately flailing at me, every joint grinding loudly as it tried to wrap its fingers around my neck, its fingers snapping like crab claws; only a few centimetres away from being able to squeeze the life out of me. A faint red glow gleamed from behind the cracked optical sensor, locked firmly on my throat. With the oxygen absorption capabilities of my synthetic blood, it wouldn't be able to choke me to death; but it could just as easily snap my neck.

I looked around in a hurry to try to find something I could use as a weapon. No joy.

"Uh… lil' help here Liz?" I cried telepathically, starting to panic as I heard distinctive crunching sounds from my foot as the pressure piled on.

She began rapidly processing a solution, but someone else spoke first.

"You know… most people only get to fantasise about this shit." I heard a familiar, calm, commanding voice emanating from the droid.

My hair stood up on end as I recognised the voice. My eyes widening anxiously as I slowly twisted to look up at the screen-face of the robot. Cracked and distorting, but the image came in clear enough.

Her hair was even crazier than it used to be, a deep purple tied back, and a new earring chain, but it was her.

"You have no idea how long I wanted to do this," Denise snarled at me, the tips of the robot's fingertips now brushing my neck.

"Uh...hey, Destiny!" I replied facetiously, still straining to keep her back. "Long time no …"

"SHUT UP!" she spat back hard enough to send saliva splattering against the webcam recording her. "You ain't gonna weasel your way out of this one!! How many Spiritform members did you put away when you worked for GCHQ?"

"I…"

"HOW MANY?!" she yelled intensely.

"How should I know!?" I struggled to protest.

"Oh, I forgot! You can't even remember can you!?" She laughed cruelly. "Pretty fucking convenient! Get paid for keeping the population in line, throw in some prosthetics, and look forward to guilt-free retirement! Is that what you were thinking!?"

"You're reading me like a book, Denise!" I barked back with angry sarcasm.

The robot loomed closed towards me, its mechanical grip now narrowing in on me, Denise's flaming, raging gaze looming through the screen.

"There!" Liz cried telepathically, highlighting an exposed section of the android's ribcage, revealing the mechanisms inside with a caption labelling it as 'Power-supply'.

I could just about reach inside, but I was running out of time fast.

I wriggled on the spot, angling my left shoulder, readying myself for my last chance to strike back before…

"You're a pathetic excuse for a human being, Arthur Wells," she hissed at me with a cathartic grin. "But don't worry. I'll put you out of your misery."

I pivoted on my right shoulder, just enough to free my arm, just as she finally got a firm grip.

"Not today, love," I breathed at her, forming a fist.

CLUUUNCH!

I thrust my left hook into the exposed section of the robot's torso, the inside ringing like a tuning fork. Denise's reactions on the screen became startled, having taken her by surprise. With a crackling bang, the current from my taser knuckles overloaded the robot's system. Denise's face disappeared from the dead screen, and the whirring of the mechanisms inside rapidly slowed. The entire body went limp, now only supported by my strength. The joints of the robot's fingers went loose and slipped off my throat.

I deactivated the Taser, relieved that the earthing in my arm had held out and I hadn't electrocuted myself. With an exhausted groan, I flicked my foot, and the lifeless machine collapsed onto the tarmac with a clatter, leaving me sprawled out on my back, gulping the cold air. A readout from bio-monitors flashed up. Overall, I'd come out okay; it looked like my nose was broken. It would sting like hell once I unblocked my pain receptors, but was nothing my medical nanobots couldn't heal overnight.

"Remind me to invest in some power armour," I panted telepathically at Liz, as I grasped a hold of the car to my right to help me get back on my feet.

"Look on the bright side," Liz piped up with me.

"Bright side!?" I scoffed. "They ID-ed me, Liz! Even if they don't try to kill me again, my website is gonna get hacked to hell and back!"

"I'm preparing for that now. I'm increasing the runtime power allocated to your server's ICE programs as we speak," she informed me dubiously. "But there is good news."

"Such as?" I scoffed.

She highlighted the android's head in red on my HUD.

"I'm not guaranteeing anything, but with Dart's encryption codex we might be able to extract the lead we need from the droid's memory drive," she explained.

"Not likely," I grumbled. "They'll have programmed it to self-delete anything which could lead back to their hideout."

"Yes, but Destiny was controlling it just as you pulled the power," she explained. "It won't have been able to execute all of the subroutines in time."

"Fat chance we'll get their IP address from it."

She loaded up a PDF document describing the OpenSource Souls anonymous user ID system. The identifier codes traced back to the original IP address of the user but were divided among the block-chain to make it impossible to use it.

"We'd have to hack a huge chunk of the network for that to be of any use."

"Like Next-Gen Industries? They're one of the system's biggest clients."

"Hacking them could take months!"

She shrugged playfully.

"It's a shame you don't have a friend at GCHQ who owes you a favour."

My eyes widened in sudden, blissful realisation.

David! David could get me in!

"Liz, I could kiss you!" I found myself laughing through my bloodied nose, wiping away the white synthetic liquid.

She smiled back, sending a love-heart emoji flashing on my HUD.

A couple bystanders who had watched me brawling with the droid began emerging from out of the shadows now, offering their apologies for being unable to help, and tried to make sure I was all right. They assured me they'd tried calling the police and were a little surprised that they hadn't shown up yet.

My ringtone went off in my head.

<<Incoming call from: Gabrielle Phillips>>

I froze on the spot, noticing the camera on the ceiling staring right at me.

Bugger.

I kept my fingers crossed that she would be pleased with the outcome of this little incident. I answered the call. Her ghostly, full figure rezzed over my vision, as I continued the trawl back to the car.

"Miss Phillips!" I answered warmly but professionally. "What can I…"

"You can dispense with the pleasantries, Arthur," she interrupted curtly. "Do you require medical assistance?"

I was a little surprised by the question since she was no doubt monitoring my condition as well.

"Nah, I've had worse," I joked through the pain in my nose. I tapped my wrist supporting the droid's weight with my free hand, with a little clinking noise.

"Good," she said flatly. "That would be harder to cover up."

Her eyes narrowed at me, making me twinge uneasily.

"I've sent Doctor Carpenter home for the day," she explained. "The Ashigaru will be escorting her. Given the risk to my staff you asked me to take, I was expecting better service."

"Uh… yeah," I admitted awkwardly.

"The hard-hacking attempt with your drone failed," she interjected. "That was clearly an error in judgement."

I hid my clenching fist from the gaze of the CCTV camera as I trudged towards the boot, feeling like I was being stalked by her.

"A calculated risk," I replied cautiously. "I can appreciate your concern; I have a business to run as well. But this type of investigation never exactly goes to plan."

"Maybe," she replied, her stone hard expression not giving an inch. "Maybe you were subconsciously setting yourself up for failure."

I raised an eyebrow.

"Sorry, I don't follow."

"My psych-profile projections suggest you must be experiencing guilt due to Denise Masika's involvement with Spiritform," she answered coolly. "I hope your feelings on this matter are clear."

Oh, you bitch…

"They're clear," I nodded, lying through my teeth.

Her lips pursed, her eyes flickering at me with cat-like analytics.

"Time is running out, Mister Wells," she said in a foreboding tone. "And I hate bad investments."

<<Call ended>>

"Cow," I muttered under my breath; staring at the blank video feed.

Once the pounding in my head had died down, I hobbled across to pick up my hat and my revolver again before proceeding to scoop up the robotic carcass. Scraping the arms and legs across the tarmac as I hauled it over my shoulder in a fireman's lift, wheezing as I waddled towards the boot of my car.

CHAPTER 14

Mother Mind profile 7183-2647-8246-3892:

First name: Denise

Surname: Masika

Status: Wanted for numerous crimes *Click here for more detail*

Nationality: British citizen

Occupation(s):

- Suspected member of Spiritform hacker group

Criminal record:

- Arrested: 17/11/2037
  - Offence: Suspected of unauthorised access to computer material
  - No formal charges

Known aliases:

- Destiny

Live surveillance:

- Status: *Unavailable*
- Date: 07/10/2045
- Current location: Unknown
- Local Time: 10:17 GMT

So, the ModCon job didn't exactly go our way. It could've gone a whole lot worse, but that wasn't putting anyone's mind at ease. I was leaning against the dusty bar of our pub-hideout, looking out across at the gathered worried faces around our holo-table.

"For the *last goddamn time* GateCrasher," I groaned at Jamie, rubbing my eyes with my gloved fingers, dragging the skin of my cheek slowly and past my piercing like a wet sponge across a window. "Arthur did *not*, repeat did *not* ping our location."

I rummaged around in the top pocket of my short-sleeved leather jacket and pulled out a joint, habitually sparking up after putting up with his bullshit for so long. The smoke blew angrily out of my nostrils and cast a shadow over the projection table; currently playing back the video footage recorded by our android before Arthur pulled the power.

"What about your Soul-ID code!?" Jamie cried frantically, his eyes bulging out of his scarred deep skull, slamming his fist against the rim of the table, distorting the holoprojectors on his spiked bracelets. The holo-images distorted and shook a few cobwebs loose on the ceiling. "He might be able to trace it now!"

"Unless he's planning on pulling off one of the biggest cyber-attacks of all time, I wouldn't worry about that," I retorted with a dismissive wave. "He'd need access to at least 42% of the network. Damn near impossible."

His wild eyes narrowed at me suspiciously, but he didn't argue the point further, sitting back down in a slow malevolent manner, folding his arms.

I gave an exasperated shake of my head, rattling my piercings, catching a glance of Simon, appearing via live chat from the holo-table, the grimy walls of the bunker captured from the webcam. He was the only quiet one; staring solemnly over a log of the decryption of Project Selection files… which would now take another five days. Five days of him watching over that server bunker. My screw-up was going to be his punishment. I shifted awkwardly on the spot in my jacket as his avatar glanced towards me… with everything that had happened I'd almost forgotten I'd given him the cold shoulder earlier as well.

"Forget that!" Raj protested, the tattoo on his chubby cheek contorting in distress, flapping his arms in a state. "What about Plexi!?"

I rolled my eyes in exasperation.

"I'm sorry about your robot, Raj," I answered as sincerely as I could, taking another toke from my joint, and resting my free hand on my chain-bound belt.

"Sorry ain't gonna fix it," he said accusingly.

"Fine!" I gave in, throwing my arms out in surrender. "I'll get you a new one!"

"With what money!?"

He had me there.

"I guess it'll have to be an IOU then," I shrugged, letting out smoke from my nostrils.

Raj threw himself back in his chair, folding his arms and muttering to himself.

"I still don't get why this PI is still breathing," Kasira commented inquisitively.

My nostrils flared, letting out ganja smoke like a dragon.

"He got lucky," I said flatly, my voice simmering.

The more I thought about it, the more bitter I became. In fact, I'd given Poe an assignment; developing a mod for the new DOOM game. I was going to change the facial models for the enemies to appear as Arthur.

Just what the doctor ordered.

"In any case…" Kasira continued, sounding unconvinced, "I still think it'd be a good idea to launch a counterattack against him. Find out what he knows."

"The soul has strongly advised against that," Poe replied, his green cat avatar appearing on the table. He brought a cyberspace visualisation of the ICE protecting Arthur's website. "Most likely his VPA has prepared for that eventuality, and will have installed a honey-pot virus on the system."

A honey-pot was a type of ambush program; a virus designed to look like juicy data, luring hackers into a trace-program trap.

"All we can do now is increase our own security," Poe explained, demonstrating some of our own network vulnerabilities.

"Assign work queues for all of us," I instructed him, with a puff of smoke. "I want our systems air-tight. We've got five days to go, and I expect all this to go off without a hitch."

Poe nodded, and notifications were posted to our HUDs. I was going to be researching Arthur's cyber-attacks to get a feel for his techniques and prepare against them. Kasira would be in charge of patching up our ICE as best she could. Jamie's job was to increase our field of vision; hacking into a more extensive radius of CCTV cameras surrounding the safe house to get a better view of any approaching threat. Raj was on internal security detail; improving the booby traps we had installed.

The three of them grudgingly accepted their jobs, clambering out of their beanie bags and back to their rooms to use their own terminals. Simon was still projecting from the holo-table, his arms folded, finally working up the energy to look away from the bulk of data windows in front of him, his eyes drooping beneath his mass of white hair.

"Your ex is a real charmer, Destiny," Simon sighed sullenly. "I'm amazed you let him get away from you."

"We decided to put work first," I deadpanned sarcastically with an exhale.

"Well, that work has really dropped me in it," he muttered back. "No word from Doctor Carpenter, I take it?"

"Not a chance," I said bitterly, coughing slightly. "She knew we were coming. Virtualife must've prepared her for a sting operation. Besides, she'll be bound by a non-disclosure agreement. They're probably preparing to erase her memory as we speak."

"Jesus," Simon scoffed, shaking his head in disgust. "So that's it, then. I'm doing porridge for the next week."

"Looks like," I said, rolling my tongue over my lip ring.

He gave out a weak sigh, with a shrug and a thin smile.

"Well... At least I'll have lots of time with the new DOOM game."

I offered a smile of encouragement, but he looked away quickly, sending my heart sinking. He didn't want to be consoled by me. I guess in the end I'd strung him along as bad as Arthur had me.

Great, now I feel like a bitch, too...

I bitterly stubbed out the end of my spliff into the ashtray resting on the dusty bar beside me.

"I uh... should probably get on with it," he said gingerly, scratching the back of his head.

"Sure," I nodded awkwardly, rubbing my purple hair, not sure what to say at this point. We waited in tense silence, each wondering who was going to speak first. It didn't take long for Simon to get weary of the act.

"Yeah, whatever," he said bitterly, preparing to log out.

I hesitantly rubbed my lip ring with my tongue, the urge to speak out getting stronger.

Don't be an idiot all your life, Destiny.

"Wait!" I blurted out loudly.

"Yeah?" he called back hopefully, his eyes opening and ears pricking up in anticipation.

I bit my lip, not sure what I was going to say.

"Maybe…when you get back," I began slowly, "I could join you for a game sometime?"

Going on a date to blow up virtual characters with your ex's face. Real classy, Destiny.

He stared back at me with a raised, puzzled eyebrow. Looking like he thought he'd understood my subtext, but couldn't quite believe it. I gave him an encouraging wink to help him figure it out. Beneath the tuft of silver-white hair on his head, a proud grin spread across his face from ear to ear.

"I like the sound of that," he beamed back at me.

We exchanged excited glances, but part of me was already regretting it. We said our goodbyes and Simon's avatar began to derez into pixelated dust.

"Great," I breathed angrily, throwing my hands back in exasperation, and staring up at the cracked ceiling.

A beam shone out from the holographic table, Poe's avatar manifesting itself in its ghostly form on the bar beside me, rubbing his whiskers on me in a typically feline manner.

"You've been doing this a long time, Destiny," he purred. "Would it really be so bad to let someone else in?"

I scoffed and began to stroke the back of his head; the tactile feedback matrix in my fingerless gloves generated the furry sensation.

"One problem at a time," I answered finally.

"Like why Arthur Wells still has an effect on you?" Poe suggested, adding a cheeky 'meow'.

"Yeah, like…" I stopped myself in my tracks, looking down at him with an angry eyebrow. "Is that your idea of a joke?"

"Did you like it?" he purred back.

"No."

"Then no, it wasn't a joke."

I took my hand off the back of his head, to his disappointment, and looked down at him with an annoyed squint. Mostly because he had a point that I wanted to deny.

If I wanted to… really, wanted to kill him… Arthur would be dead right now.

I chewed my bottom lip, the metal ring clinking against my teeth. I looked down at the floorboards, ambivalently rubbing the steel cap of my boot against the dust-laden ground. Plexi's final recording was still projecting in the corner of the holo-table, Arthur's face still there. The more I looked at it… the angrier I got; at myself.

Poe flicked his tail as he processed the new data.

"There's a technique virtual psychiatrists use," he began to explain, "when people experience conflicting emotions on certain memorable items."

I raised an eyebrow, with piqued curiosity.

"I'm all ears."

Poe grinned, and with a series of flashing icons, a notification appeared on my HUD.

<<Welcome to RE:Call!!>>>

<<File loaded>>

"Memory playback?" I asked, checking the file.

<<Date: 24/09/2035>>

<<Location: Richmond Upon Thames College>>

I found myself scoffing at the screenshot that had been used as the caption for the file. A photo from my point of view… of Arthur's fresh, seventeen-year-old face.

"The day we met?" I said with disdain.

"The therapist asks how the patient feels about a certain person. Then plays back the memories of their first and last encounter with said person," Poe continued. "The truth tends to come out at that point."

I cringed on the spot, immediately put off.

"I think I'll pass," I laughed dismissively.

Poe's ears fell.

"Whatever you say, boss," Poe chimed back, with just a hint of disappointment.

"I don't need a program to tell me how I feel about Arthur," I said, trying to reaffirm the point.

"Sure," he nodded flatly.

"Got better things to be doing anyway," I added, sounding less sure of myself.

"Of course," he said again.

I should've never enabled his reverse-psychology subroutines…

"Okay, fine!" I gave in with frustration, slapping the wooden bar, telepathically preparing for the consciousness shift.

Poe grinned cheekily at me.

"Good choice," he chimed.

I stared at him grumpily, as I plopped myself down in a free beanie bag, the chain on my belt jingling as I landed. My HUD indicated the program was ready to run.

<<Ready to begin Memory Playback>>

<<Please ensure your surroundings are appropriate and prepare for consciousness

shift>>

<<Begin: Yes/No>>

I leaned back, getting comfortable in the marshmallow-like seat.

<<Initialising memory playback>>

<<Date: 24/09/2035>>

<<Location: Richmond Upon Thames College >>

<<Local Time: 09.30 GMT>>

The circa-2030s classroom began to tune into my vision like an old-fashioned television. Out of the digital soup came the clear image of desks, with built-in terminals arranged in rows before a whiteboard screen mounted on the front wall by the door. The other four walls were white panels, plastered with peeling smart-paper posters on the history of the computer, with windows looking out into the college sports field, gleaming in the last of the summer sun.

The students were still sparse, entering in through the creaky wooden door. I was sat in a corner desk, quietly reading a ninja manga on my contact lenses, and listening to Ian Dury with my tiny wireless headphones. The other students were gathered in corners talking about whatever it was 'normal' seventeen-year-olds spoke about. My avatar was dressed like a rebel even back then, red and black hair, spike-lined corset and fishnet tights.

"I'm telling you!" cried an Asian voice, loud enough to get my attention. The voice belonged to a skinny Syrian boy, named Zahir, his avatar dressed in the blue and white colours of Chelsea football club. While his clothes were ordinary enough, his face wasn't. Twisted and disfigured; like melted plastic. Trying to get designer babies on the black market might've seemed like a bargain, but it was almost as deadly as Russian roulette. But there were always desperate parents who would still take a risk if they thought it bettered their children's chance of getting a job in the machine-dominated job marketplace.

"Mate, you chattin' so much shit..." snorted Joel, a big black guy wearing Arsenal colours.

"Bruv, I saw 'em do it!" exclaimed Zahir. "Two police units from different companies just started shooting it out in the middle of Peckham!"

"Why the fuck didn't you record it then?"

"I... I forgot my visor," Zahir admitted gingerly.

Joel gave out a long, ugly, guttural laugh.

"Did your parents buy the genes for your *brain* from a dealer too?"

He happy-slapped Zahir around the back of my head with an audible 'Ow!'

I wrinkled my nose in disgust, unamused by Joel's so-called sense of humour.

"Leave him alone, Joel," I piped up angrily.

Joel swivelled in his seat, turning to me with a bewildered look.

"Was I talking to you?" Joel growled at me.

"You are now, deal with it," I told him coldly.

He seemed oddly amused by my attempts to stand up to him.

"You ain't worth my time," he jeered at me. "I have enough hoes sniffing around me on the estate."

That got a couple of stupid sniggers from the crowd of students.

I'd dealt with his kind before. Fancied themselves the kings of the ghetto. I knew about him. I knew about almost everyone here. Just practise.

I smiled back at him plainly.

I slowly gestured, pulling off my wrist pad, unfolded it out into a tablet, and gave the telepathic command with my headset to project the photo I'd stolen of him.

The laughter died out. Joel's face froze, horrified by what I'd found. A picture of his fifteen-year-old self before his own gene-therapy. The photo was a selfie taken from his contact lenses; posing topless in front of a mirror. He must've been planning to Photoshop it, as his chubby overhang left much to be desired.

The room exploded with juvenile laughter; the other teens killing themselves in stitches.

"Where the fuck did you find that!?" Joel spluttered, blushing like a traffic light. "I deleted it!!"

I smiled condescendingly at him.

"A magician never reveals her secrets." I grinned triumphantly.

Joel stood up aggressively; shoving his chair out the way, glaring at me, ready to start something. I didn't think he'd try to hit a girl in front of the class, but I was already tightening my leather-bound fist in preparation, eager for an excuse to try my MMA training.

"Morning, all!" A chirpy voice came from the front of the room.

We spun around to find our plump-faced IT teacher entering, with short, wavy, auburn hair and wearing a respectable black skirt and blouse; her E-ID data came flashing up onto my contact lenses, marking her as Mrs Greenwood. Joel gritted his teeth but shrunk back down into his seat. I ignored him and looked towards the video-wall, preparing to take notes through my holographic keyboard.

Greenwood began the class; using a sliding touch panel to dim the lights as she started the 3D presentation on the history of artificial intelligence development, leading to the rise of the first post-Turing capable programs and the three laws of responsible robotics.

It should've been an interesting subject, but just listening to her voice was putting me to sleep. I had my arms folded, my head dipping every few seconds. It wasn't that she was a lousy teacher, but the material she was covering was a bit basic for me. I needed a challenge, and I wasn't getting that here… too bad I needed the A-Levels. Still, online was where I found my fulfilment.

I was ready to drift off, Greenwood's voice little more than an echo on the horizon of my mind, but was rudely awoken by the beeping of my HUD. My eyes snapped open, back to the real world. It was a notification from *Skype*:

<<You have 1 new friend request from: Arthur Wells>>

<<Message text: Hey, nice hack. :-)>>

I didn't recognise the name. I raised an eyebrow, looking around the room, scanning with my contact lenses. It didn't take long for the AR window to pop up over his head. He was fresh-faced, and his hair was floppier, wearing a green hoodie with built-in speakers. His (still natural) eyes met mine, and he gave a timid wave. I was a bit baffled, but responded in kind, wondering if this was just his way of flirting.

I gave the neurocommand to accept the friend request and began telepathically chatting with him.

"Uh… Hi," I began, sounding awkward over the comm link. "Thanks… I guess."

"Hey, no problem!" he replied quickly, sounding overly friendly to hide his nerves. "So, how'd you do it?"

"Do what?"

"Hack Joel, what else? Was it a spear-phishing attack?"

I nodded.

"It's getting harder and harder to forge official e-mails," I told him. "Joel's a moron though, didn't take much to trick him."

"No shit," he chuckled back. "Where'd you learn?"

I bit my (still unpierced) lip, uncomfortable with the question.

"Um… my dad taught me."

"Are you serious?" Arthur cried disbelievingly. "Damn, he must be a cool guy. Mine would go raving spare if he knew half the shit I got up to online."

He grinned devilishly at me.

"You could help me actually! I've been trying to get access to the school's administrators account. But the firewall is running off some strange ZQL sub-language. Can you make heads or tail of it?"

<<Arthur Wells would like to send you 1 file>>

<<Accept: Yes or No?>>

I downloaded the file. A considerable body of code text that he'd extracted from his packet-injection efforts. Useful info, a good starting point.

"Not bad," I nodded, genuinely impressed. "Why didn't you say anything before?"

I watched Arthur's reactions; looking down at his feet in an embarrassed manner.

"Honestly, I've been looking for an excuse to talk to you for a while now," he admitted.

I found myself smiling.

"Aw, that's sweet," I said.

Arthur looked up, grinning softly back, relieved that I had reciprocated. Mrs Greenwood carried on her lecture in the background, while I proceeded with my critique of the script.

"Yeah, this looks familiar… An uncommon variant called Zencore," I explained. "Smart move, not many ICE Breakers are equipped to handle it."

"You got anything for it?"

"Did you ever doubt it?" I told him with a cocky roll of my eyes.

<<Forwarding file: Gremlin.exe>>

<<File transfer in progress>>

<<0.1/1.0Pb>>

"Cheers!" Arthur replied gleefully. "I'll install it now and see how it goes!"

"I'd be surprised if it *didn't* work."

"I'm gonna hold you to that," he grinned.

The conversation trailed into a stony adolescent silence, wondering how to keep going, the lecture rambling on in the background.

"Soo..." Arthur began slowly, attempting to begin. "Your dad sounds like a cool guy. Done anything that I would have heard of?"

I froze uncomfortably on the spot.

Goddamn it, of all things he could've brought up...

Just the mention of Dad's old name would most likely send him into a raging fangasm. I found myself averting my gaze towards the holo-desk, unable to keep up eye contact.

Even now, it was still hard to talk about it. Time doesn't heal all wounds. What my dad had achieved, was the sort of thing that script kiddies aspired to in their wet dreams. If I were to open my mouth about it now, Arthur would be ready with a wave of admiration. To everyone else, he was the internet legend that brought down a corrupt business. To me... he was just an empty seat.

And it was my fault.

I was about to start slipping back into a well of self-pity when Arthur piped up again.

"Holy shit, you did it!" he cried enthusiastically.

I looked up, seeing him staring gobsmacked at his contact lens' HUD. He sent me an animated emoji of a pair of hands high-fiving.

"Did you ever doubt me?" I beamed cockily. "What next?"

"I'm a seventeen-year-old with free run of the school network," he deadpanned back at me. "It's prank o'clock, mate."

"Well duh, but did you have something in mind?"

"Oh, I've got a few ideas," he whispered excitedly. "Been planning this for ages."

I leaned back and folded my arms, as his eyes rapidly flickered with data traffic.

"This better be good," I beamed at him.

He turned around with a glowing smirk, as I simultaneously heard a motorised whir from the ceiling. I directed my gaze towards it and saw the overhead projector going into tracking-mode. The sensors mounted on the front of the unit now following Mrs Greenwood's movements as she walked back and forth in front of the video-wall, as she proceeded to try to explain the emerging science of Robo-psychiatry.

"Time to go ape!" he said triumphantly.

The holo-projector on the ceiling sprung to life; beams of information encoded light shone out, shrouding Greenwood like an aura.

"What the…" she breathed, with startled eyes as she gazed at the glow. Her confusion soon turned to panic as the animation Arthur had prepared played out. Her hands began to turn black; the illusion of fur started spreading across her body like a swarm of crawling insects. It wasn't long before she was covered from head to toe. She tried moving out of the projector's field of view, but it swivelled to keep in step with her, the image hugging her like a second skin. The picture began to bulge, her holo-muscles expanding so quickly that she burst out of her simulated clothes.

"Oh God!" she screamed.

The transformation was complete. A fully-grown gorilla stood at the front of the class. The room exploded with adolescent cackling. We all went into hysterics, rolling around at our desks at the sight of our primate teacher.

"Oooh! Just you wait!" she yelled at us, waving her massive fists. "When I find out who's done this, they'll be out of this school so fast their feet won't touch the ground!"

I could hardly breathe from laughing so hard.

That got Arthur and me talking. Before we knew it, we were on a roll. Late-night gaming sessions. Conventions. Hacker chat rooms.

It felt like the start of something big… wondrous.

I couldn't lie to myself. It was a happy memory.

Back in the present day… I was biting my lip anxiously.

The next RE:Call file loaded up.

<<Initialising memory playback>>

<<Date: 17/11/2037>>

<<Location: Fulham Police Station >>

<<Local Time: 08:40 GMT>>

My initial reaction when Mum woke me up at quarter to seven this morning was to start groggily moaning at her about why the fuck she had come into my room so early. That changed the moment I saw her grave expression; the colour gone from her face. She told me the police were at the front door… with a warrant for my arrest. They hadn't even given me enough time to change before dragging me down to Fulham station, and I had spent the last half hour in a dingy interrogation room… just waiting.

I was sitting on a primary iron chair in front of a small holo-table, still dressed in the same clothes I had gone to bed in; a plain black tank top and sweatpants, my purple hair scattered around my shoulders in an untidy mess.

The room was little more than a seven by seven cube, with blank white and grey walls, empty aside from the holo-table and the four chairs placed around it. The walls were soundproof and served as a Faraday cage; electromagnetically shielding the room to block transmissions coming in or out. The only form of outside communication was the restricted access connection to the holo-table, connected via a network cable that fed into the ground.

Of course, there was also a camera suspended from the ceiling. I kept my arms folded, and kept my makeup-less face in a tight, attentive expression, trying to mask the nerves that were creeping up on me… but I couldn't stop my fingers from wrapping themselves against my elbow, my foot tapping against the plain floor, while the little avatar of my lawyer was projected by the holo-table. Her name was Sayeda Rahmeen, portrayed by her avatar as a bright, young Pakistani girl in her early thirties, wearing a black blouse and long professional skirt; her long hair neatly resting on her shoulders. She may have just been the public defence attorney that had been assigned to me, but she seemed confident enough… although she did seem to be referring to her VPA more than I would like.

"Not to worry," she said with a reassuring smile, her eyes flickering while she conversed with data on her HUD. "You've got a solid case here. There isn't much they can do with the evidence they have on you. It's inadmissible in a court of law."

I nodded my clenched jaw, contemplating what they might be charging me with. The school never found out who had been hacking into their network. The police must've been using Mother Mind to monitor it in real time, but the surveillance act of 2030 prohibits law enforcement agencies from deploying bulk data collection systems on educational institutions without a search warrant. A warrant which *hadn't* been issued.

The fact that the school hadn't contacted us at all meant that whatever was going on, they probably *weren't* planning on officially charging us with anything… But I couldn't be sure. Arthur and I had been working on something. The prototype for a botnet… designed to attack Mother Mind. We hadn't deployed it yet; still very much in the alpha stage. In-house tests only. But it always meant they could potentially charge us with conspiracy to commit cyberterrorism. I bitterly clenched my fists, regarding myself with scorn. Some hacktivist I was. Facing the cops before I even got started. I didn't want it to be true… but I couldn't escape the fact that right now, I was scared.

"You doin' okay, kid?" Sayeda asked politely. "They been treating you alright?"

"Fine, thanks for asking," I said blandly back. She may be trying to help me… but a lawyer was still a lawyer.

"It's your choice, but if they did anything, anything at all which you didn't like, it could be helpful," she reminded me positively. "You've already got your…history with your father. I'm sure they're itching for a chance to throw that in your face."

The mention of my dad had my eyes narrowing with a predatory instinct.

"If they're going after you because of your family, then it's harassment," she explained, watching me with a hawkish grin. "You could turn this around on them. I've dealt with cases like this before. Some of my clients have won hundreds of thousands in compensation."

I looked away from the table's webcam to roll my eyes. *This* was why I hated lawyers. Always on the lookout for some tragedy to exploit.

"I'll let you know if anything comes to mind," I answered grudgingly.

"Have a think about it," she said with a hopeful nod, her eyes glittering with data from her VPA. "Now if you'll excuse me, I've got other clients who need my attention. Don't talk to anyone until I get back."

"Wasn't planning to." I nodded courteously.

Her hologram faded away, and I was left by myself again, glaring at the ceiling camera. There was nothing to do now but wait. There was a glowing green icon on the surface of the table to activate an intercom to talk with the guards. I'd been desperate to pee for like twenty minutes but didn't want to give these bastards the satisfaction of showing them any weakness. I just kept calm and carried on, fidgeting uncomfortably on the spot, trying to hold it in.

I wasn't waiting for long before I heard the mag-lock on the door behind me click and slide open.

"Took ya long enough," I said, putting on the most confident smile I could before I turned. "I was starting to get bor…"

My sentence was interrupted by my own surprise. I'd been expecting to see a duo ready to play the good cop, bad cop routine. Instead, I was facing a flushed Arthur Wells, scruffily dressed in a blue hoodie and jeans, his arms handcuffed behind his back, frog-marched by an android.

"Easy! Easy!" Arthur protested at the machine, red in the face, held at an uncomfortable angle by the droid's mechanical grip.

A light flashed on the robot's head, and the restraints on Arthur's wrists unlocked themselves. The android removed the handcuffs and left, leaving him standing there to rub the raw skin around his wrists. Once the door locked itself behind it, I jumped up from my seat and threw my arms around him. He reciprocated the hug with a long-winded breath of exhausted relief.

"Are you okay?" he asked wearily, pulling himself far enough away from me to look into my eyes, stroking my cheek softly as he spoke.

I nodded solemnly back at him.

"You?" I checked.

"Just dandy," he said bitterly.

My lips twitched anxiously, feeling a certain amount of guilt rising up inside of me.

"I'm sorry I got you involved," I apologised slowly.

He didn't say anything to that, just stared back with a meek smile and carried on stroking me before slowly leaning in to kiss me. Despite my attempts to keep up my badass image, I found myself reciprocating, snogging him for everyone watching through the camera to see.

We were as inseparable as any other eighteen-year-old couple. Of course, we weren't exactly typical. Our idea of a good time might've just as quickly have been a night on the town, *Netflix* and chill… or a late-night session of coding jam sessions. Fancying ourselves to the Bonnie and Clyde of cybercrime, in-between doing our online degrees. Of course, that was precisely what had landed us in this mess.

Our embrace lasted for what seemed like a while, before we nuzzled our faces into each other, listening to each other's hearts thumping away in nervous anticipation.

"Go on then," Arthur sighed finally, pulling himself away. "On a scale of one to ten, how screwed are we?"

We sat down, still holding hands while I explained to him our legal position as described to me by my lawyer.

"Hmmm…" Arthur frowned, nodding thoughtfully. "So… we're not *that* screwed?"

"Nope." I nodded reassuringly. "They probably just want to scare us into incriminating ourselves. Don't say a damn thing without a solicitor."

"I hear that," Arthur sighed, wiping his brow. "It's strange though innit?"

"What is?"

"Mother Mind. Deploying it to monitor schools is a huge legal overstep."

"Wouldn't be the first time GCHQ has broken the law," I shrugged.

"Yeah, but what for? To catch wannabe hacktivists? It doesn't make sense that they would risk a scandal for something like that.

And isn't it standard police procedure to interrogate suspects separately? To stop us from coming up with false stories or whatever?"

"I think you might be onto something," I said curiously with a raised eyebrow. "I smell bullshit."

We sat together in tenacious silence, holding each other for support, trying to keep up the morale, watching the time pass on the digital clock face in the corner of the holo-table. Within five minutes of waiting, Sayeda's avatar loaded back up just as scheduled. She seemed just as surprised to see Arthur as I was.

"It is highly irregular." She frowned. "If they are planning to charge you, it could be classified as gross misconduct. We could turn this around on them if…"

She was interrupted by the sound of the door unlocking behind us again. We turned around, once still expecting to see another pair of cops, ready to grill us. But instead, the door-frame was occupied by a highly professional-looking Asian man in his early thirties, his slender frame dressed in a sharp, well-fitted blue and white suit. His face reminded me of a rodent, his jet back hair was gelled to the point of looking like an oil spill. The corners of his mouth were curling upwards, his beady eyes focused sharply on us.

We regarded him with immediate suspicion. He apparently wasn't a cop. My initial thought was that he was the public prosecutor, but it seemed a bit early for that. It was only then that I noticed a pair of heavy-duty officers, sporting assault rifles flanking him from behind.

"Thank you, gentlemen, that'll be all," he said courteously to them with a dismissive nod.

The pair nodded back without saying anything and turned to walk away, leaving the door to lock automatically behind them.

That was definitely odd; lawyers don't tend to have *armed guards.*

"Sorry for the inconvenience, guys," the guy in the suit said, facing us with a warm smile in surprisingly friendly tone.

"I'm Sayeda Rahmeen, representing these two suspects," her avatar piped up from the holo-table in a business-like manner, her eyes flickering rapidly as she consulted her HUD. "This is highly improper. If you're going to be taking statements, there should be a second witness present. What's your badge number? My facial recognition didn't…"

"Oh, I'm not with the police," he responded warmly, holding up a reassuring hand as he strode to the other side of the table, and pulled out his chair.

"Then who?" Sayeda inquired promptly. "Are you representing their school? What firm are you with? What's your…"

"With all due respect, your concern is unwarranted," he chuckled, settling himself into his chair like a cat. "No one is here to press charges."

Sayeda's expression had turned from curiosity to composed annoyance. I couldn't help but agree with her on this; there was something fishy going on here.

"If you're not with the police or a law firm then it's really quite simple," she said flatly. "You *can't* be here. I won't tolerate any further encroachments on my client's rights! If they aren't being charged, then you have no right to hold them…"

"I am here to determine whether they *will* be charged," the suit interrupted, with a tone of oily smugness.

"The hell is that supposed to mean?" I blurted out acidly.

Sayeda held up a hand to stop me, but the suit was already replying.

"I'd be wondering the same thing if I were you," he said agreeably, and reached into the breast pocket of his suit, pulling out a holographic business card, with silver and white graphics dancing from the surface. He placed it on the table and slid it over to us. A rendering of his face was floating in the top left-hand corner. The text identified him as Richard Yi, recruitment officer for GCHQ, accompanied with contact information and a rendering of the agency's logo. The holo-table read the data stored on the card and projected a free link to their civilian website.

"Recruitment officer?" Arthur exclaimed with wide-eyed shock. "Are you for…"

"You gotta be fucking kidding me!?" I laughed harshly. "You guys want to hire us? *Us?* Why the hell do you think we would work for the organisation we want to destroy?"

Arthur stared at me with a mortified expression, clutching his hair in shock with eyes that screamed, 'Why the *fuck* did you say that?' I eyed him suspiciously. He'd once told me he wouldn't mind working for GCHQ but grew out of it after becoming more 'politically aware' of what the job entailed. Now I wasn't so sure.

"Anything my clients say here is inadmissible!" Sayeda cried out suddenly. "I want all copies of footage of this meeting delivered to me as soon as…"

"We know all about your… ambitions, Destiny," Yi chuckled with a dismissive shrug. "I assume you prefer to be called by your hacker handles?"

I loathingly ground my teeth, my eyes become cat-like slits, with murderous intent.

"Look, guys," he sighed, leaning in closer to the table. "You're obviously an intelligent pair. With talent. And I mean, a lot of talent. I mean I've seen a lot of teenage hackers in my time, but you two were really shooting for the moon on this one!"

"Yeah but… don't you need a cybersecurity degree to work for you guys?" Arthur enquired. "We only just started ours."

"We're flexible about that." Yi shrugged. "Not everyone appreciates this, but there is always a cyber-war going on behind the scenes. We can't afford to be picky about who we hire. We only monitor education facilities for potential recruits. Rest assured we have no intention of using the data we gathered from you as evidence."

"Not that you could," Sayeda pointed out.

"In any case," Yi pressed on, "we offer a four-month virtual training course for prospective cyberwarfare specialists without higher education. If you can pass our work placement sim, we'll award you with a degree equivalent industry diploma. That'll qualify you to start as an entry-level software developer for us. Our salaries start from thirty-three thousand a year."

"Are you serious?" Arthur spluttered with amazement, practically grinning from ear to ear.

I threw him a bewildered, angry scowl, his cavalier attitude to all this starting to rub me the wrong way.

"I'm just saying..." Yi continued with a hopeful gesture. "It would be an awful shame for that talent to go to waste."

"Sure," I barked out sarcastically. "All we have to do is abandon everything we stand for, and sell our souls to the military-industrial complex."

He eyed us with weary sympathy.

"Come on, guys," he said with exhaustion. "You do realise we live in a democracy? Every election cycle, one party or another pledges to abolish the system. And every time they get defeated. The public *wants* Mother Mind. They *want* to be kept safe! You can't just resort to terrorism and expect society to change!"

"Oh, don't give me that!" I groaned, rolling my eyes in disbelief. "The mass media is corporate controlled; anything that affects their advertisement revenue or shareholder's interest gets censored!"

"Look... I know you guys hate the 'man'," he said, using his hands for inverted commas. "But, even you can't deny we've done a good job! There hasn't been a major terrorist attack in over twenty-seven years!"

"Oh, do jog on with the pretend patriotism!" I cried. "Mother Mind stopped being about terrorism as soon as it went online. Its only purpose now is to protect the oligarchy!"

Yi bridged his fingers.

"I can understand why you have a certain amount of bias, Destiny," he said with the soothing voice of a therapist.

His words were like a thorn in my skin, radiating anger throughout my body.

"Don't you *dare* bring my dad into this!" I spat viciously, hunching towards him on the table like a rabid dog. "It's because of pricks like you that he's in jail!"

"He did commit a crime."

"He was trying to save my life! If he hadn't stolen the cure from those twats, I'd be dead right now! Those fuckers were keeping it suppressed to drive up the price of the goddamn treatment!"

"GenePharma was under investigation for price gouging at the time," he pointed out.

"It was taking too long! And the bastards settled out of court anyway!"

"Be that as it may. It didn't give your father the right to be a vigilante. GenePharma does anti-bioweapon research, too. That means they keep some of the DNA of the deadliest strains in the world stored in their databases. And you do realise that the back-door he installed could've been exploited by any number of terrorist groups."

My jaw was clenched so tight I thought I was going to crack my teeth.

"You think that word is bulletproof, don't you?" I snarled. "The ultimate shield that lets you get away with anything!"

Yi's mouth became a tight line. His eyes hardened. His patience was at an end.

"You shouldn't knock a gift horse in the mouth," he said, all the friendliness drained from his voice, and he leaned in closer. "We have enough circumstantial evidence to get search warrants on both of you."

My gaze never faltered, but all the colour drained from Arthur's face.

"Who knows what else might turn up?" He shrugged. "You're both young and hip. I'm sure neither of you are strangers to drugs."

Arthur gulped.

"And besides…" he added coolly, meeting Denise's stare. "Think of your father. He taught you, didn't he?"

My chest felt like it was about to burst like a volcano.

"I'm sure you've got more than a few mementoes," he continued. "Possibly… incriminating mementoes? It'd be such a shame if we had to add a few more years to his…"

"YOU MOTHER FUCKER!" I exploded, leaping off my seat, sending it flying backwards as I brought my fists down on the table with a rumbling clatter. I hunched myself over like an attack-dog ready to lunge at an intruder.

Arthur recoiled in his seat, gaping wide-eyed in utter disbelief. Sayeda's projection was flailing her arms wildly, trying to get me to shut up.

Yi remained composed, eyes glazed over like a layer of frost, his mouth a tight line, watching me with a neutral analytic gaze like a biologist observing a culture of germs growing in a petri-dish. He was a company man. He'd seen this all before. Just doing his job. And yet I could feel it… this was a mask; hiding his pure enjoyment.

My fists trembled against the glass surface of the holo-table; the higher-reasoning centres of my brain were holding onto my body with every fibre they could spare, trying to stop the base urge within me to ram a knuckle-sandwich into that hooked nose of his. The second I did they would charge me with assault, or I'd just get shot by the pair of armed guards waiting outside. But like a bull chasing a red cloth, all I could see was what was in front of me. And if one more word oozed out of his ugly mouth I was going to do it.

"I would like a moment alone with my clients!" Sayeda's hologram cried at Yi from the surface of the table; holding up her hands, desperately trying to steady me like a matador.

"Of course," Yi nodded curtly at her before turning to stand up.

My eyes followed him like a laser targeting system as he strode around the table towards the exit. I could feel Arthur tugging at my tank top. Yi stopped before placing his finger on the DNA reader built into the door.

"I hope you make the right choice, Destiny," he added in a tone of threatening hope, not turning back to face us. "You deserve better than what you've been given. It would be a real shame for that to go waste."

"Go fu…" I said, beginning to open my mouth to swear at him, but Arthur gave a single forceful yank to get me to look at him, shaking his head pleadingly.

"I await your decision," Yi added, before pressing the reader, triggering the door to slide open and stepping out into the hallway.

Once he was gone, I gave a single angry tug with my waist to pull myself free from Arthur's grip.

"The hell is your problem!?" I barked at him.

"Hey, don't have a go at me!" Arthur cried, holding his hands up in surrender. "You were the one about to slug that guy! Did you really want him to add assault to the list of…"

"What the fuck does that have to do with you!?" I hissed. "It's my life, dammit! If you…"

"Alright, that's enough!" Sayeda cried with frustration from the holo-table, loud enough to get us to look at her. "I charge twice as much as a couple's therapist and am half as qualified. But more to the point, I don't have enough time for your lovers' quarrels."

I gave her a scoff of annoyance, and plopped myself down on my seat again like a stroppy teenager, folding my arms.

"This is extortion," I said, matter-of-factly at her. "Plain and simple."

"I dunno. Extortion usually doesn't come with such a good offer," Arthur said, awkwardly rubbing the back of his neck.

I threw him another glare, and angrily opened my mouth to start having a go at him again, but Sayeda interjected.

"As your legal counsel, I have to strongly advise you against attempting to counter-sue," she urged me with wide-eyed sincerity.

"Yeah, I bet you do," I replied bitterly.

"Come on, you should at least hear her out!" Arthur protested with a desperate hand gesture.

"Whose side are you on!?" I barked back at him, sending him recoiling defensively.

"Let me put this to you in a way you will understand," Sayeda interrupted again, starting to get noticeably frustrated, waggling a pointed finger at us. "You kids fell in the shit and came up smelling like roses. You have no idea how lucky you two are. If you two were just a bit older, you'd be facing twenty-five to life. The choice you have is what we in the biz call a no-brainer."

"They were *illegally monitoring us!*" I hissed at her through gritted teeth.

"Yes, they were." Sayeda shrugged at us. "And to be blunt about it, they are going to get away with it."

"Typical!" I snarled.

She gave a humourless chuckle back at me.

"We're not talking about a dodgy police department here," she retorted. "These are the *intelligence services.* Trust me on this one. I have colleagues that have tried taking them on before."

A grim expression gripped her face.

"It didn't end well for them," she added darkly. "Make no mistake. He's not lying. They will play every dirty trick in the book it takes to stop you from taking them into court. You're deluding yourself if you think he was bluffing about dragging your father through the shit."

I opened my mouth to reply, but the words stopped in my throat. There was no comeback for that. My jaw clenched, and I looked away in resentment, not ready to admit I was wrong.

"Look," Sayeda spoke again, her voice softer this time. "For what it's worth, I get it. I went into this business wanting to fight for justice just as much as the next guy. But trust me, Denise, I've been doing this a long time, and there are some battles you just can't win. You can't change it. You just have to adapt."

My teeth were grinding like a pair of rusty brakes. I wanted to snap back with something harsh and sarcastic, but it just felt pointless.

Arthur had gingerly been chewing his lip the entire time, subtly nodding at her in agreement, but apparently too nervous to add his own thoughts on the matter.

"She's right," he said with soft encouragement. "We have to take the deal."

His words snapped me out of my state of self-pity and sent my eyes narrowing at him with resentful suspicion. His face was composed, trying to show fake sympathy for me while trying to contain his self-satisfaction. For me, this felt like surrender. Like I was lying down on that battlefield with the enemy charging at me head first. But, Arthur… was *enjoying* this. I thought I knew him. That he had felt the same way I did about Mother Mind and the world. But every second I looked at him, was another second I was growing more convinced he had been lying through his teeth at me to get into my pants.

My nails had sunk deep into my palms, my rage turning to physical pain. She was right. I couldn't win. Not by their rules. There was no way to do that. I needed to find a new game all together… but first, I needed to get out of here.

I glanced away from the pair of them, feigning an expression of resentful defeat.

"*Fine*," I lied through my teeth.

Arthur and I were kept in the police station for another hour after that, not saying a word to each other. I couldn't even look him in the eye. We filled out the necessary paperwork in silence. We had to agree to a period of probation before beginning employment at GCHQ, which included signing a surveillance acknowledgement form, to recognise the fact we would now be under a high level of scrutiny from the Mother Mind system. I felt sick to my stomach from the moment my finger had left the touchscreen, but I grinned and bored it, knowing full well that I had no intention of sticking to the terms and conditions.

They let us out through the rear entrance, stepping out onto a cracked pavement that enclosed a sparsely populated car park, guarded by an automatic traffic barrier, and we were welcomed by the drizzle and bracing gust of the cold November wind. Once I was outside, I found myself bitterly grabbing an e-cigarette from my top pocket and sucking down a long, harsh drag with an explosive exhale. It didn't help.

"Look, I know you feel like you've betrayed your principles or whatever," I heard Arthur's rumbling voice from behind me. "But honestly, I think one day you'll look back on this and…"

As he was talking, he reached out to place a comforting hand on my shoulder which I immediately shoved off like I was pushing away a lumbering zombie.

"Don't touch me, you piece of shit!" I hissed at him with the ferocity of a viper, turning around to face his wild-eyed confusion. "How dare you! How fucking *dare* you?"

He held his arms up defensively, clearly worried I was about to crack him across the face.

"Come on, Denise, don't be like that," he pleaded. "I was just…"

"You were looking out for yourself!" I cried back, driving out each word with a jab of my e-cig. "You're a sell-out!"

"Oh, give it a rest! You heard the man! If we…"

"Don't give me the 'back against the wall' bullshit!" I scoffed at him. "You're a career hound! Admit it! Were you just going out with me just so you could put 'former hacktivist' on your CV?!"

He frowned back at me, starting to get annoyed.

"You're being ridiculous."

"Am I?" I retorted. "When's the last time you tested our botnet?"

His eyes twinged. A tell. The sign he had been found out.

"It was uh…" he stammered.

"Which ICE Breaker were we modifying? Which development version were we on?" I continued to press on.

Arthur's eyes slid away guiltily, too embarrassed.

"I fucking knew it!" I scoffed. "You were never serious! You just wanted to learn from me! You *always* wanted to join them!"

He turned back to me, starting to look pissed off.

"Well it doesn't matter now, does it?" he said gruffly. "We both signed the same contract. You're one…"

"He can shove that contract up his arse!" I spat back.

He frowned back.

"You're not still planning on…" he began slowly.

"Always have been, always will be," I replied matter-of-factly.

"Are you crazy?" he cried. "Denise, if you bail on them now they'll prosecute to the full extent of the law!"

I composed myself calmly and coolly, taking a long drag from my e-cig.

"They'll have to catch me first," I replied slowly with a long stream of vapour.

"Of course, they'll catch you!" he shouted back. "It's a goddamn surveillance state, Denise! They'll…"

"Even Mother Mind has blind spots," I retorted. "People have been able to live off the grid without being detected for months."

"That's your plan?" he laughed humourlessly. "To spend the rest of your life living in some burnt-out shithole like Osama bin Laden?"

"If it's between that and betraying everything I've ever stood for…" I shrugged with a sense of finality.

He let out a long, flabbergasted breath, shaking his head.

"So, go on then," he said with a sarcastic wave on the hand. "What's your grand plan for world revolution?"

I averted my gaze for a moment, taking a long drag from my e-cig to avoid the question.

"And what about your Dad?" he cried. "You heard him! If they can't get you, they'll just go after him! Don't you care?!"

I bared my clenched teeth at him, trying to hide the guilty lump in my throat that I was trying to swallow back.

"They… they won't find anything," I quipped back, struggling to sound more confident than I actually was. "They already got everything on the GenePharma hack, and I destroyed everything on his other crimes."

"Then they'll just fabricate the evidence!" he scoffed.

"I'd like to see them try," I growled.

"Oh, come off it!"

My eyes narrowed again.

"Congratulations," I glowered. "You already sound like one of them."

"Denise…"

"We are Spiritform!" I interrupted, my voice calm and controlled but filled with passion. "We are everywhere. We are nowhere. If you have done wrong; we will find you."

He rolled his eyes back in exasperation.

"So, let me get this straight," he said, rubbing his strained forehead. "Your plan to save your dad from further charges of Cyber-terrorism, is to commit your own acts of cyber-terrorism? Do you really think that's what he…"

My eyes and nostrils flared like a wolf ready to strike its prey, and then my hand whipped out across his cheek.

"Don't you *ever*," I yelled at him, forcefully shoving a finger into his chest, "*ever!* Tell *me*. About *my* family!"

He stumbled backwards as I lunged at him, staring in fearful awe at me.

A tense silence followed as our gazes locked. Eventually, he gritted his teeth back. Something had snapped inside him. He composed himself and straightened out.

"You know what?" he retorted back at me. "You are absolutely, one hundred percent, *BATSHIT INSANE!*"

His voice raised his voice higher than I'd ever heard from him before, and I found myself arching my back like a cat ready for a fight.

"But yeah, you're right," he continued, thrusting a finger back at me. "If taking an offer you can't refuse makes me a sell out, then yes I'm a sellout! Excuse me if a cushy, well-paid job sounds a hell of a lot better than whatever the hell it is you have in mind!"

I was seething on the spot, you could practically smell the vitriol in the air.

"So that's how you feel, huh?" I snarled.

"Damn right it is," he retorted, nodding his head bitterly.

"Well, if that's how it is," I said with a nasty shrug, "you can go fuck yourself. 'Cos I sure as hell won't be anymore."

When the words left my mouth, his face fell ever so slightly, unable to mask his disappointment.

"Yeah, I kinda got that," he said facetiously.

"Well good luck and good fucking riddance," I told him with a sense of finality, giving him the finger.

"Likewise," he replied bitterly, responding in kind before spinning on his heel to storm off down the pavement, stomping his boots as he went.

I stood there, watching his scruffily dressed figure shrink away and disappear around the red-brick corner as I smoked. On the one hand,

I felt like I was telepathically transmitting some kind of evil curse to him, and on the other… as much as I didn't want it to be, my heart was sinking.

CHAPTER 15

Mother Mind profile 4372-6349-8752-9361:

First name: Daniel
Surname: Haines
Status: Living
Nationality: British citizen
Occupation(s):

- Detective Inspector
    - Status: Employed
    - Organisation: Churchbell Security

Contact information:

- *Drop down for more info*

Live surveillance:

- Status: *Available*
- Date: 07/10/2045
- Current location: London Docklands
- Local Time: 17:38 GMT

"Champagne, sir?" asked the calm, soothing voice of the limousines auto-driver from the speakers embedded in the cabin walls. A long robotic arm was mounted on top of the mini-fridge installed in the corner; holding a silver tray with two glasses and a bottle of *Dom Perignon.*

"Don't mind if I do," I said with a cheeky grin of gratitude as I picked up the glass of bubbly. I never in a million years thought I would ever be travelling in such style.

The car was so stretched out, it was like sitting in a hallway; enough leg-room to lie out flat, let alone be comfortable. We sailed along the road, past a cluster of vertical farms, the 3D city map levitating in front of me like a work of art, our route to Virtualife tower in the Docklands, highlighted in flashing red. We were on schedule to arrive at the Awasaki Foundation event on time, much to Claire's dismay.

"Bloody hell, real leather," I scoffed, feeling my armrest. "It's all right for some, eh?"

I was told Awasaki was sending a cab. I didn't realise I'd be getting the most luxurious ride of my life. If he planned to schmooze his way into stopping me asking questions, I'd have to admit he was making a good start.

I spent most of the morning with Chief O'Neil and a virtual lawyer, debating the subtler points of our anti-corruption policy. In the end, we agreed that me merely *attending* a party like this with a rival firm wouldn't be considered a conflict of interest, but I had just to 'keep my eyes peeled' for any offers.

I just hoped that no one came around expecting us to contribute as well. The event's website said that there was going to be a leaderboard of donations up on the main holo-display. We'd be at the bottom of the list for sure.

Still, if the booze was this good, who was I to complain?

"How many of these limos does Mister Awasaki own?" I asked the AI.

"At present, there are twenty *Lamborghinis* in Mister Awasaki's personal collection," the simulated posh accent chimed back.

I whistled in awe, while somehow expecting the number to be higher.

"I could get used to this," I said jokingly, admiring the golden glass of bubbly.

I rolled my head towards Claire's seat. She was hunched over, her head practically between her legs. No response. The anxiety reflecting in her eyes like pale mirrors. The same sullen expression she'd had for the last few hours; her eyes glazed, her mind a million miles away, her knee shaking uncontrollably through her frilly pink and white dress.

I gave her comforting words, patting her on the back, but it was falling on deaf ears. She had begged me not to go. She grudgingly gave in eventually once she had realised that this would probably be the only chance she would get to meet Emma. So, now we were ready to party with the wealthiest and most famous people in the city. I kept asking myself what I was going to say when Emma introduced me to Kenji Awasaki himself. I never had to consider having to find common ground with a billionaire before.

The mini-fridge robot gestured with the tray in Claire's direction.

"Any for you, ma'am?" the AI asked again.

"Hmm?" she mumbled, snapping back to the real world. In a dazed state, she merely blinked at the arm.

"No thanks," she breathed shakily at it.

"You sure?" I asked again sweetly. "It'll help take the edge off."

"Do you know what would've helped?" she quipped back, her nostrils flaring like volcanos.

I shut my eyes, bracing myself for the fight to come.

"No…" I replied, knowing full well I was letting myself in for it.

"Giving me time to pick a better dress!"

She angrily grabbed the pink fabric.

"I can't fucking believe you made me choose this!"

"Honey, you look great," I told her reassuringly.

"Oh, fuck off!" she protested, the robot arm retracting quickly to protect the remaining glass from her flailing hands. "I'm going to look like I walked in off the street!"

"Oh, come on, this isn't going to be like the Year 11 prom…"

"Don't you dare bring up the prom!" she hissed at me, pointing a finger in my face, prompting me to recoil in shock. "I swear to God, if I hear so much as a snigger out of any of them, I'm going to be out of there faster than…"

"I get it!" I gave in, running my hands down my short-cut hair with frustration. "We don't have to stay any longer than you want! Hell, we can leave as soon as you're done meeting Emma!"

Her gaze didn't relent, studying my expression intently, attempting to decide if I was telling the truth. Eventually, she accepted.

"Fine… but I'm still going to walk if they start laughing," she glowered.

"That's all I ask," I accepted, with grateful relief.

The one time in my life I was going to get a glimpse of how the one-percenters live their lives, and I was going to have to ditch it for her. Single life seemed more and more appealing. The rest of the journey passed in silence, much to my relief, and it wasn't long before Virtualife Tower was looming over us like a pillar of light, spotlights, and holograms whirling around the tip of it like fireflies.

We went through a police checkpoint at Westferry Road; marked by a series of retractable bollards built into the road. A pair of guard-bots verified our E-IDs and ordered the auto-driver slowly through a scanner they had set up, clearing us for entry with a green flash of the bollards. The traffic became more tightly regulated the closer we got to the skyscraper. Money was in the air; the financial heart of London. Arguably the biggest trading centre in the world. The high-rise construction boxing us in on all sides like a canyon of concrete and glass. Surprisingly little advertising around. A perverse sense of self-respect I suppose.

After the cryptocurrency boom of the 2030s, bankers had largely become obsolete. Most of the office towers had been turned into self-contained cities for the most valued employees of the mega-corps, filled with everything needed to further their profit margins… and occasionally host a PR blitz like this. Something to cross off the bucket list.

We finally pulled up in front of the tower. As usual, the crowd around the building was densely packed with the permanent camp of protestors. Standing outside their tents and huts, angrily waving holo-banners, jeering at the limousines rolling by, held back by steel barriers lined with officers and robots, and camera drones overhead. The windows of the limo had already darkened, but the crowd was still yelling abuse at us, prompting Claire to shrink back nervously.

"Pigs!"

"Capitalist scum!"

"Do you even *care!?* Do you care!?"

I took Claire's trembling hand and patted it.

"It's all right…" I reassured her, squeezing her shoulder

comfortingly. "They haven't rioted in a long time."

"Oh… good," she grumbled.

Eventually, we rolled past the outermost police barrier, to the plaza around the entrance to the skyscraper. This area was usually clear, but the paparazzi were there in force, swarming around the red carpet on stone steps leading to the rows of glass-plate doors into the reception area. The plaza was lit up by the flashing of cameras on watch-tablets, drones and eye implants, all trying to get a good shot of the perfectly sculpted bodies of celebrity power couples walking up the aisle.

Claire's anxiety worsened at the prospect of going through the main entrance. I couldn't help but share her fear about that, but the auto-driver quickly reassured us that it had been instructed to bring us into the underground car park.

The car was guided into a small ramp descending below the concrete surface. Ben telepathically warned me that some of the journalists had gathered around there too, hoping to get shots through the blacked-out window. He alerted us to the possibility of cameras equipped with infra-red and x-ray vision, so we shielded our faces as the car rolled past quickly into the well illuminated-urban cave that was the parking lot.

The limo rolled gracefully into a free space in front of an elevator, with an android butler waiting to greet us. The hum of the engine died out; the map projecting from the ceiling replaced by the flashing words: 'You have reached your destination.'

The auto-driver bid us goodnight, the door to my right retracted upwards. I gestured to Claire the most encouraging face I could muster. It took another five minutes of persuasion to gently coax her into getting out. I held my hand out to her, waiting for her to make it in a romantic gesture. She stared hesitantly at it, twisting her lips around, but eventually sighed and gave in.

"Let's go…" she breathed quietly, placing her trembling palm in mine.

The pair of us shuffled along the back seats of the Limo until we could slide out of the door and onto Tarmac.

"Welcome to Virtualife Tower, Detective Inspector Haines, Miss

Fielding," the butler droid greeted us politely, bowing respectfully before us, the screens in its eye sockets flashing happily. "Mister Awasaki regrets not being here to greet you in person."

"Uh… he does?" I asked, trying not to sound gobsmacked.

"Yes, sir. He wishes to reassure you he will set aside the time to meet you as soon as possible. In the meantime, feel free to enjoy the bar. On the house."

"That, I can do," I grinned. The glee in my voice was so self-evident, it even was getting a laugh out of Claire.

Even the elevator was the most expensive I'd ever seen. Two of the walls were marble panels, the third was a length of video glass, projecting the Tokyo Symphony. The haunting Eastern sound of Japanese orchestra singers filled the cabin. We stepped inside; the building's AI identifying us, and automatically selecting the 82nd floor as our destination based on our invitations, the lights on the touch panel blinking rapidly as we whizzed into the sky at high speed; my ears popping almost as soon as we got in.

Claire was chewing her lips, eventually staring up at the air vent, as I gently stroked her hand.

"Oh fuck…" she breathed, as we came to a stop.

"Eighty-second floor: Ballroom," the AI buzzed.

I squeezed Claire tighter, our eyes fixated on the doors, the anticipation killing me. They drew back with a rattle.

"Gordon Bennett," I gaped in awe.

I wasn't exactly an art buff, but I'd never seen architecture like this. A techno-vintage cultural fusion masterpiece. The info on my HUD told me the room was almost constructed mostly of claytronic matter; morphed into a design blend of thirteenth century British Gothic architecture and ancient Japanese Shinto temples. The walls were banks of sliding video-glass automatic doors, leading out onto a balcony, lined by archaic church-like archways appearing to be made of pale stone, but morphing into the shape of a rigid Japanese gateway.

The centrepiece was a genetically modified cherry blossom tree, its branches reaching towards the spotlights on the ceiling. The leaves were a bright pink, infused with bio-luminescent genes, glowing like coral, flickering in the artificial wind of the air conditioning, its roots planted in a hydroponic system installed into the ground; a series of microscopic viaducts delivering water to it. A series of exquisite crystal chandeliers hung above it, magnetically suspended from the ceiling; each shard sparkling as it caught the light.

The E-ID scans on my HUD went crazy; profiles of people who made a disgustingly higher amount of money than me. Director of this, manager of that, head of whatever; all of them laughing loudly and cheerfully thanks to the booze that was now flowing freely with the aid of the butler droids.

This place was an ass-kisser's dream come true. Listening in on the conversations around me, it seemed the mingling was about 40% for the sake of the charity, the other 60% for the purpose of business networking. A group of middle-aged women gathered gleefully gathered around the *BBC* presenter, Martha Noble, showing off her cute little genetically engineered teacup rhino, poking its horned nose through her handbag. Claire was right about one thing; the clothes that they were wearing did make us look embarrassingly cheap; most of the guests were wearing jewellery worth hundreds of thousands. We began naturally shuffling into the corner, trying not to draw attention to ourselves.

I noticed a media drone overhead, recording panoramic shots of a raised platform on the western side. The Tokyo Symphony was there in all its glory, playing beautiful, hand-made instruments, not a single printed part between them. You couldn't say the same for the musicians; most of them possessed the most delicate prosthetic hands I'd ever seen. The rich melody filled the room, while guests on the dance floor pranced and twirled around the floor together in a display of extravagant harmony.

So, *this* was high society.

"Well, you can't say I never take you nice places," I told Claire gleefully, watching her nervous awe.

She leaned against me, and gripped tightly against my arm, like she was both looking for security and affection, nuzzling herself into my chest.

"Once in a while, yeah," she admitted.

She poked her lips up, and I leaned down for a gentle tender peck.

She giggled quietly and nuzzled herself into my chest. I was stroking her hair when a butler-droid offered to take our coats for us. We handed them over and were shortly provided more champagne. Time to take advantage of the 'on the house' deal.

"Sure you don't want any?" I checked with Claire, picking up a glass for her as well.

Her eyes narrowed at the sight of the bubbly.

"Hmmm…"

"Go on, you know you want to," I grinned.

She finally shrugged and gingerly took the glass from me, shortly before gulping it down way faster than anyone would have expected.

"Whoa, steady on!" I laughed, placing my hand on my shoulder.

"Make up your mind," she jested back, with genuine frustration.

I backed off, not wanting to push the issue too far. I anxiously stroked my beard, looking around for a distraction.

"Whadya say?" I asked her, nudging my head in the direction of the dance floor, filled with guests gracefully waltzing around.

Claire scoffed and raised an eyebrow.

"You must be joking!" she sniggered. "You know how bad I am?"

"Worse than me?" I suggested, remembering the first time I had taken her clubbing; my arms flailing like a cat on roller skates. "Besides, you did those V-classes remember?"

She didn't say anything, but I saw her cheeks flush bright red.

"You did *do* them? The classes that *I* paid for?"

"I… uh… gotta go to the loo," she answered nervously, quickly checking the map on her contact lens, before heading in a quick march towards the toilets, leaving me with both glasses of champagne in my hands.

"Typical," I grumbled.

I wasn't that fussed about the money; just that she'd lied about it. But I shook it out of my mind, and downed the rest of my glass, trying to look a little bit dignified in front of the elites.

Looking around, I felt like I should at least try to socialise with the other guests, but kept being put off by the profile data.

"Where's Emma?" I asked Ben telepathically.

"Scanning now," he responded.

An arrow appeared on my HUD, directing me towards her. I had to admit, for someone who was practically an android, she was stunning. In all the years I had known her, I couldn't recall ever seeing her in a dress. The dress was a tight fit, beautifully showing off her curves in all their glory, made from green Smartsilk, pulsing with hypnotic patterns. It had a low-cut V-neck, and cut away sections on the sides of her belly and thighs revealed the tight artificial skin casing of her nano-muscular system. Her usual regulation haircut had been let down, dangling softly around her neckline.

As much as I wanted to deny it… she did look good. One more thing to make this evening awkward. She was stood with arms folded, just on the edge of a group of people, glass in one hand, and using all her effort to pretend not to be fed up. The others were laughing at some joke; ringing as false as Lady Transhuman's breasts. I saw Emma's half-hearted attempt to join in, but looked desperate to be rescued. When she saw me coming, she said quick goodbyes to the people she was talking to and ran over to me.

"You made it!" she said warmly, throwing her arms around me.

"Wouldn't miss this for the world," I snorted, gawking at the extravagance.

"Don't speak too soon," she muttered bitterly back at me. "The pretension makes me sick."

"Sure as hell beats the grungy house parties we used to go here," I shrugged. "Not much chance of getting knifed here."

"That is a nice change," Emma snorted. "So, where's your better half?"

"Drying her eyes, most likely," I admitted. "I think all this is a bit much for her."

"Aw, bless," Emma replied with a noticeable hint of sarcasm.

"I'll text her now," I replied, telepathically typing the message on my contact lenses.

"Think she'll be in there long?"

I shrugged.

God, I hope so.

I looked around quickly for a distraction. I found one soon enough.

"So when do I get to meet the big man himself?" I asked, pointing my thumb in the direction of one of the holographic videos, playing a commercial for a well-digging project in Iraq. Awasaki was standing wearing a hard hat next to a colossal drilling robot; his suit set to display high-visibility mode colours.

She nudged her head to the right.

"Why don't you ask him yourself?"

I swivelled around, darting my eyes to try to find him. On my HUD, Ben directed my gaze towards the bar. One of the staff-bots was offline; Awasaki was there serving drinks in its place, dressed in his pulsing blue and white suit with a big grin on his face, the silvery cranial implants on the side of his skull glittering underneath the spotlights. A queue of fat-cats had gathered there, waiting to be served, with goofy grins at Awasaki's jokes.

"Make that cheque out with a lotta zeroes, okay mate?" Awasaki grinned at the Indian executive at the head of the queue. "It's all for a good cause!"

"It better be," he chuckled softly back, his eyes flickering as he checked his HUD.

I couldn't help but gape with a bewildered laugh.

"Wow," I scoffed. "Looks like he's enjoying himself."

"He's a good actor," Emma deadpanned.

Somehow we'd caught his attention. He looked up from the beer glass he was filling from the tap, and waved.

"Don't just stand there like a dipstick," Emma muttered, waving back, nudging me to join in.

I did so, awkwardly smiling back. Awasaki seemed pleased, gesturing with his hand to say 'one minute' and went back to serving the eager crowd.

"Oh boy…" I breathed anxiously.

"You look like *you're* about to go up on stage," Emma sniggered.

"Sure feels like it."

"Don't sweat it," she said reassuringly, patting me on the back. "He's pretty easy going… for a billionaire."

"Good to know," I cringed, impatiently tapping my foot.

Awasaki didn't look like he was going to be done serving drinks anytime soon, so we were left waiting in silence. I checked my messages on my watch screen; still nothing from Claire. I sent her another text, trying to coax her out of the cubicle as she was no doubt cowering in.

"So…" Emma spoke eventually. "Did you get the report from HQ?"

I rolled my eyes.

"Emma, it's a *party*," I groaned. "Do we have to talk about work?"

"No," she shrugged, sounding more than subtly annoyed. "We can talk about Claire instead if you…"

"Fine, fine," I interrupted hurriedly. "I got the e-mail, but didn't get a chance to look at it before we came here."

She raised a disapproving eyebrow.

"What?" I said curiously, telepathically opening the message and downloading the attachment. "New lead?"

"And how!" She nodded, piping my curiosity. "The biggest clue we've had so far!" The file appeared on my display. "Remember that back-door we found installed on Claudia Schwarz's v-club?"

"Sure," I answered, glancing over the PDF, straining to remember the details of the identity theft after the champagne started taking hold.

"Well, Mother Mind got a match on a server infected with the same virus here in London. Hidden with the same encryption," she explained. "The server was controlling the billboards for a *Tesco* in Richmond. The Digital Forensics team went over its drives; looks the hacker gained access to it a few hours before Andrew Ilian was murdered."

"Okay… what's the connection?"

"Watch the video," she replied curtly.

I curiously opened the footage taken from a CCTV Camera; recording the crowd shuffling past on the quaint, narrow, cobbled pavement of Richmond high street. The window into the supermarket was vid-glass, projecting a commercial for body wash.

<<Date: 05/10/2045>>

<<Local Time: 14:17 GMT>>

"What am I looking for?" I checked with Emma.

"Keep watching," she reassured me.

I did… more shoppers flowed past the camera; the time in the left-hand corner of the screen ticking upwards. Without warning, the adverts projecting in the window turned to static. No one on the street seemed to pay it any mind, but I found myself squinting at the footage.

After a few seconds, the static disappeared. I was expecting to see the advert restored to its previous state. Instead to my surprise, a series of strange images appeared.

"What the…" I breathed as I recognised them.

The images included: the cover page of a document within the Project Selection files. Followed by a screenshot of Andrew Ilian's Facebook profile. Then a receipt for an order he'd placed on *Amazon*… including his address.

My eyebrows jumped up in surprise.

A motive for the murder. And all the information needed to carry it out.

Projected right onto the side of that building.

The presentation only lasted a few seconds, returning to static and then back to the usual reel of advertisement. If you hadn't been there at the time, you wouldn't have seen the difference.

"Some kind of digital dead drop?" I checked.

"That's the working theory," Emma explained. "Looks like Jack-21 is taking secret orders from someone."

I'd heard of this trick before. Hacking into public screens in a crowded area. Displaying information that would only have relevance to the person who was intended to receive it. That way, even if the authorities knew the content of the data, they still wouldn't know *who* it had been delivered to. It completely avoided the problem of Mother Mind's surveillance by not sending any data to the recipient and providing the information in a medium that only the receiver would understand. Anyone in that crowd could have been the target.

I enlarged the image; focusing in on the mass of people wandering past the camera.

"So; someone in that crowd… is Jack-21?" I said my voice barely above a whisper in excitement.

"We're operating under that assumption," Emma nodded guardedly.

I stared disbelievingly at the screen; everyone in the screenshot seemed innocent enough. But then the really scary monsters never stood out in a crowd.

"Bloody hell! This is a game changer!"

"GCHQ is in the process of retracing the movements of everyone who was present at the incident," she explained. "They're working under the assumption that this is the same hacker who stole Claudia Schwarz's identity to pose as Ilian's girlfriend. They've codenamed him: Enigma."

"Like the Nazi encryption?" I snorted.

"That technology was leaps and bounds ahead of anything ahead of its time. Whoever programmed these algorithms is on that kind of level," she added, her voice almost holding reverence for him.

I regarded her curiously.

"You think they'll find him?" I checked.

She shrugged, unconvinced.

"I've had my heart broken before," she mentioned.

"True enough," I sighed reservedly, rubbing my bristly chin as I pondered over the information. "One thing doesn't add up though."

"Yeah?"

"You said it yourself, this Enigma hacker has serious skill. Surely he could've accessed Helen Ilian's PC himself? He didn't *need* to go through her son to do it."

"Maybe. Maybe not," she pondered. "Probably felt that having a middleman offered certain advantages."

"Either way, the kid was a liability that our guy didn't need to bother with."

"Hence why he was bumped off," Emma shrugged. "No surprises there?"

"Yeah, but by having the most wanted criminal in London do it?" I scoffed. "It just doesn't make sense. Not to mention this is a major deviation from Jack-21's M/O. The previous attacks seemed to be random. Now he's a hired gun? His previous victims weren't high-profile enough to be targeted by anyone."

Emma nodded in agreement, while the motors in her eye sockets slid from side to side pensively.

"So, what are you thinking?" she shrugged.

Like you don't already know.

"Maybe whoever bumped off Ilian… mimicked Jack-21 to throw us off his trail," I suggested.

Like Virtualife.

"Yeah…" she answered, unconvinced. "I suppose it's possible. Not a whole lot we can do for the moment. Just waiting on the analysis for the forensics team. If we're lucky, they'll find markers in the source code that can give us clues as to who wrote the damn program in the first place."

"So what do we do till then?"

She held out her glass, waiting for me to cheers it with her.

"Best plan I've heard all day," I laughed as we clinked our glasses together.

I'd only just started sipping my drink when…

BRRRRRRRRRrrrrrrrrrr…

With a loud electrical whir, the lights fell, plunging the room into darkness and sending a wave of gasps.

"Whoa…" I said, shuffling awkwardly in the shadows.

I could see the shapes of the people on the dance floor coming to a bumbling stop as the music died down, while the butler droids came to a full stop.

"Power cut?" I asked.

"No, just a show-off," Emma moaned, pointing to the stage.

I hadn't had time to check the schedule for the evening, but my HUD informed me it was time for the keynote speech.

A low electronic hum began rumbling from the wall speakers. A single blue orb of holographic candlelight flickered into existence on the stage. The music grew closer and closer to its crescendo, so too did the ball; growing into a sphere that began to consume the entire stage like the light from the rising sun.

The music reached its climax with a blinding flash; forcing the crowd to shield their eyes from the dazzling effect.

It passed quickly. When I lowered my forearm, the sphere was gone, replaced by the looming, ominous face of Gabrielle Phillips, hovering above the stage with her stern, yet attractive look seeming to absorb the entire stage with her ghostly, ethereal, god-like presence.

"Ladies and gentlemen…" her voice boomed from the speakers. "Please welcome your host to the stage. The founder of the Awasaki Foundation, and CEO of the Virtualife Corporation: Kenji Awasaki!"

The crowd broke into a round of applause, the media drones flocked to him. A crazy whirl of multi-coloured light flooded the stage as the big man himself climbed up to the stage having coming straight from behind the bar, projecting his magnetic charisma, waving warmly. His pearly white, laser cleaned teeth gleaming.

"Thank you all for being here," Awasaki's boomed, his voice captured by the microphones embedded in his clothes. A butler droid on the stage handed him another glass.

"You all having a good time?!"

The crowd cheered back in a dignified manner.

"That's what I like to hear!" he cried, holding up his glass. "Though I gotta say I'm not a fan of some of these tweets I'm seeing… did you guys seriously think the booze would be free? Come on, people put a crowbar in your wallets for God's sake!"

Laughter broke out in ripples throughout the ballroom.

"Seriously though," Kenji said trying to bring some sense back to the room. "You all know why we're here. But it can oh so easy to become...complacent."

The orchestra began playing a sombre, tragic violin piece. All-too-familiar images of the climate tragedies started spewing out of the holographic displays. New Orleans reduced to a flooded ruin by the constant seasonal hurricanes. The waters of the Arctic Sea, now ice-free and littered with the floating bodies of drowned polar bears. The spread of the Sahara Desert consuming villages in the Congo, aid workers, and medical bots crowded around fly-covered, emaciated children while the scorching sun beat down on them.

"We see these pictures all the time," Kenji said, pointing to the depressing montage. "You walk past them on the tube. You press the skip button when you see them online."

It was all very efficient. He knew exactly how to work the emotions. You couldn't help but feel guilty. Looking around the room, I saw a handful of ashamed faces looking down at their feet.

"We've all done it. Even me," he said, holding a sincere hand to his heart. "It's not that we don't care. I know all of you are generous enough to be here, but at the end of the day, we all have our own lives to live… and when you see this harsh reality in front of you, it's too much to take, and so we look away. Hiding in our towers or our virtual fantasies. And I admit… I'm largely to blame for that."

He scoffed out to the audience.

"Hell, it takes the offer of a fancy-do just to get us all in the same room just to talk about solutions."

The crowd had gone deathly silent. His words seemed to have a weight that put them all into a catatonic depressive state.

"I'm not here to put rich guilt on you all," Kenji announced. "You've got the other ninety-nine percent of the population to do that for you. But I am here to say, that together we can make a difference."

The presentation changed to show off displays of clean energy plants, vast swathes of vertical farm towers standing above the African dust bowl, nature reserves filled with cloned animals.

"There are those that call us the corporatocracy. Living off the wealth left for us by our parents, the money of the old carbon economy. Maybe that's true. But it doesn't have to be. The world is changing; faster than it ever has done in the entire history of our species. The next fifty years will be humanity's defining moment, a crossroad with two destinations. Singularity or Collapse."

Just the mention of the technological singularity seemed to send murmurs simmering throughout the audience.

"The choice is at hand. I don't know what we're going to become. They say that we can only offer token assistance to fourth world nations… maybe that's true. But I want to see as many people make it to that future as possible. It's all… all I've ever wanted."

There was a noticeable break in his voice at the end of the speech… a crack in his poker face revealing a glimpse of the real him. He glanced down, shuffling like an awkward schoolboy.

"So!" he cried suddenly, jerking his head up and raising his glass once again, the presentation behind him fading away into nothingness. "At this point, it seems a bit redundant to say it, but do all give generously. If you haven't got the picture by now, it's all for a good cause."

That got a few laughs.

"So have a good time, don't forget why we're here, and hopefully I'll get a chance to catch up with you all tonight. Enjoy the party!" he concluded.

He held his arms out proudly, to show off one final extravaganza. The stage exploded with digital fireworks; a display of crackling golden light, purple flames and green sparkles scattered like confetti in all directions.

The crowd cheered once more; Awasaki graciously bowed to them all, before whirling on his heel and heading out again with a wave.

"Man knows how to make an impact," I commented to Emma,

leaning to speak in her ear.

The crowd around the stage began to disperse, returning to their mingling as the symphony resumed. I kept my eyes on Kenji, watching him disappear backstage. He stopped just as he began to descend the steps out of view, rotating round to face the crowd once more. His eyes met mine again with a small wave.

My ringtone sounded off inside my head.

<<Incoming call from: Kenji Awasaki>>

"Oh Jesus," I spluttered in a panic, dribbling the champagne back into my glass and hurriedly patting down my suit.

I craned my head back.

"How do I look?" I checked with Emma, smoothing my hair back.

"I told you to relax, didn't I?" Emma chuckled, shaking her head.

"Okay… okay…" I breathed slowly, closing my eyes.

<<Call Answered>>

"Uh… hello?" I said guardedly over the comm link, watching my quiet telepathic voice waves flickering on the display, while instinctively holding my hand to my ear.

"Detective Inspector! Welcome!" came the oddly familiar voice of Kenji Awasaki, a hint of his Japanese descent coming through his London accent. "I trust your trip was comfortable?"

"Oh yes sir, lovely!" I thundered, nodding gratefully. "And thank you for the invites and the booze! You, uh, have a lovely home!"

"Please, call me Kenji," he chuckled back at me, his brainwaves bobbing up and down merrily. "And the pleasure is mine."

"Oh uh, thank you… Kenji."

"I gather you've been pining for a little chat with me?"

"Well… It would help put my mind at ease."

"Of course." He nodded reassuringly. "Join me backstage. I've cleared you for entry."

<<Kenji Awasaki would like to share his location data with you>>

<<Accept?: Yes/No>>

<<Accepted>>

A waypoint appeared on my contact lenses, guiding me to him. I was being invited backstage by a celebrity. Sounds like a teenage girl's dream come true.

"Works for me!" I replied gleefully.

"Excellent!" he cried. "See you soon."

<<Call ended>>

I let out a long-winded sigh.

"Did you get that?" I checked with Emma.

She nodded at me, her eyes flickering as she checked her HUD.

"I guess we should find your missus?" she suggested.

"I suppose so," I agreed with a hint of uncertainty.

I quickly scanned the room with my HUD.

<<Error: Unable to locate Claire>>

<<No location data available>>

"What the…"

She'd turned off her public location data.

Odd…

<<Calling Claire…>>

<<Call failed>>

She hung up on me. Very odd. I twirled on the spot, feeling strange, wondering how people managed to keep track of each other in crowds in the days before augmented reality. Suddenly I got a glimpse of her; weaving through the audience like a shadow.

"You've gotta be kidding," I grumbled, grinding my teeth.

"Can't find her?" Emma checked.

"I don't think she wants to be found…"

She'd done this before. Spying on me from a distance like an undercover agent. One of her ridiculous habits; every time we went to the pub with any of my girl-mates I would find her hiding behind the bar; paranoid enough to think that I would be cheating on her the second she turned her back.

"Come on," I sighed, shaking my head disgruntledly. "Let's go."

Emma raised an eyebrow.

"Don't you want to…"

"Let's go," I repeated flatly, not wanted to get into it with her.

She gave me a perplexed stare.

"All right then…" she shrugged.

The pair of us weaved our way through the crowd, following the directions Kenji had sent me, picking up a few more drinks from the droids as we went. We reached the security door to the left of the stage and were quickly scanned and cleared for entry as it rapidly slid open with a click and a whir. I hesitated. The unpainted concrete of the backstage seemed like the slums compared to the extravagance of the ballroom. The walls were dimly lit, grey and utilitarian, exposed bio-concrete and steel framework; reminiscent of a dozen different murder scenes I'd been at over the years.

"I'm not about to get an offer I can't refuse… am I?" I winced at her.

"Relax," Emma sniggered, patting me heavily with her metal palm. "Think we'd bump you off here?"

"Oh, well… Good to know."

We stepped through, the security door snapping shut behind us; the sound of our footsteps echoed against the tunnel-like walls, permeated only by the muffled buzz of the crowd and the whir of service bots in the distance.

I tried to put my nerves aside, and we made our way through the maze-like area, ducking our heads to avoid the pipework. We found him sitting on a small flight of metal stairs, drinking an animated bottle of *Evian* handed to him by a waiter droid, which promptly proceeded to polish up his makeup. He was busy chatting with an African-American PR woman projected as a hologram from the wall to his left, wearing a LED-Sequin dress, thick eyeliner, and a dark hair weave.

"Great work out there, Kenji!" she congratulated him with a wide grin, reminding me of the Cheshire cat. "You spoke from the heart and delivered all the points we needed. We've already got a trend going online!"

"Practice makes perfect," Kenji agreed flatly, closing his eyes while the robot swabbed his face with a brush.

"It'll work wonders with the board!" she continued.

He gave a disinterested nod, not making eye contact with her. But a gleeful expression crept across him as he noticed the pair of us approaching.

"We'll catch up later," he told the PR woman while waving the robots away.

"You're the boss!" she replied happily, giving an enthusiastic salute.

The hologram faded away, and the robots backed off like clockwork.

"You sure this is the guy you're looking for, boss?" Emma called out, pointing to me in a teasing manner.

"Ah, there you are!" he cried heartily, springing off the step and quickly offering his hand.

"You certainly know how to put on a show, Mister Awasaki, I'll give you that." I smiled back as I took it.

"*Kenji,* please," he said, holding up a sincere hand to his chest. "I've been following your progress so far. I have to say, given the circumstances, you've handled the case pretty well."

"Admittedly, that's not saying much," I chuckled nervously. "Besides, I would've been a goner the other night if it weren't for this one."

I patted Emma on the shoulder with a distinctive clunk sound; she'd already turned her back and was watching the corridor like a heavy-hitting bouncer.

"You're far too modest!" he chuckled. "I saw the footage from that incident. You were doing all right until…"

"Until I was taken hostage."

"Well… yes," he laughed. "Though, I would say that your training was more at fault than anything. There's a reason Churchbell Security is behind us in the police market."

I folded my arms uncomfortably, worried that my boss would somehow find out if I agreed with him.

"A bit above my pay grade for me to worry about," I laughed softly.

"Would you like that to change?" he asked with a coy smile.

Didn't see that coming. I studied his reactions curiously.

"Are you offering me a job?" I checked cautiously.

His lips curled opportunistically.

"Without putting too fine a point on it; there will soon be… an opening with the Ashigaru," he explained cautiously.

"Special forces? Me?" I scoffed, not believing what I was hearing.

Awasaki leaned back against the concrete wall, crossing his arms.

"I've been in the private security business a long time," he said slowly. "It wasn't an industry I saw myself investing in; but that's how the cookie crumbled, so to speak."

I wanted to speak up but held my tongue. I'd read his Wikipedia page. I knew his history with the Mother Mind system and the bulk access of personal user data from Virtualife's services to the police. Private security was just the next logical step. Not exactly how I would describe 'the cookie crumbling'.

"Point is…" he continued, "with age comes experience. So, they tell me anyway. You start to see things in people. I honestly believe that every human being has a spark. A seed that given the right opportunity can flourish into anything that they want."

"And… you see that in me?"

He leaned back expansively, glancing up and down as if in awe.

"I know more about you than you probably realise, Daniel," he said in a calm, wise tone. "I see a man who wants to make a difference, but frustrated by the limits life has placed on him."

I rolled my tongue in my jaw; he was hitting too close to the mark for my comfort.

"The Ashigaru can free those limitations. As I'm sure you're aware by now, they're not just the thugs the media makes them out to be."

"Cheers," Emma piped up.

"Arresting criminals…" Awasaki continued, rolling his head from side to side. "It's like pulling out weeds; if you don't cut them off at the root, they simply grow back. That's what we do. Go to the root. No red tape in our way."

I knew it was wrong… but there was something strangely compelling about that. He must've generated some psych-profile on me. Knew exactly what to say to push my buttons. He was luring me in.

"I'm flattered, really, but I don't think I'm exactly cut out for that… I've seen the fitness specs. I'd have to work out for two years before anywhere near that level."

He simply smiled back at me, and proceeded to roll one of his sleeves up, the circuit lines of the suit still glowing. He flexed his synthetic biceps at me; bulging like a balloon.

"You think I got these from pumping iron?" he teased at me. "There's no secret to it anymore. Just cold hard cash. And it can be yours; free."

My ears tingled at the sound of that.

"Free?" I repeated, to be sure.

"Call it a perk of the job," he nodded. "The Ashigaru is *my* team. I demand nothing less than the best."

He nudged his head in the direction of Emma's turned back.

"Hmm…" I said thoughtfully, checking over the information I could find on the Ashigaru online. "It's an interesting offer, Mister… Kenji. But I'm a detective, not a bodyguard, or anti-industrial espionage expert."

Or a hitman.

"Nothing a bit of VR training can't solve," he beamed back.

"Another perk?" I asked sceptically, prompting him to nod graciously at me.

I shuffled ambivalently on the spot.

"Not that I'm not… flattered by the offer. You must realise how this could be a conflict of interest?"

"You think I'm trying to bribe you?"

"I didn't say that," I said defensively, afraid he was going pull some legal bullshit on me. "But, I already have signed a non-disclosure agreement regarding this investigation to keep me quiet. It worries me you feel the need to have a deterrent, and a precautionary measure in place, just to keep me silent."

He nodded thoughtfully at me.

"Your concerns are understandable," he agreed. "But I will say to you what I have said to everyone else on this matter: Global Arms and Virtualife have intervened on the Jack-21 investigation out of respect for my employee. I used to be a hacker myself, you know; if we killed every nosey kid with a talent for circumventing network security, there would be no one left in the industry for the next generation. I want justice for the boys parents. The same as you."

I ground my teeth, feeling like I'd been put on the spot. He sounded so sincere; his eyes deep like swimming pools, inviting you to believe him.

"Tell you what!" he proclaimed, clicking his fingers like he'd had an idea. "You officially have my permission for a single question under cert-truth conditions."

That took me by surprise. It was standard procedure for street cops to carry lie detection equipment. With the advent of high-res MRI scanning, the technology was practically infallible. We couldn't use the technology as we pleased though; the suspect had to consent to a certain number of questions to be asked under so-called 'certain truth' conditions. Often it was simply used as a 'get out of jail free card' by the interviewee. A straight-up answer question of 'did you murder that person?' was preferable to becoming an official suspect after all. But there were limits to how many questions could be asked under these conditions outside of a trial, and it was no guarantee that you still wouldn't get arrested.

My lips curled downward, but I nodded in agreement.

"That… works for me," I admitted.

"Excellent!" he cried. "Shall we?"

"Sure," I agreed and gave the telepathic command to run the app.

<<Initialising MET-CertTruth>>

<<Please select target E-ID>>

<<Target selected: Forwarding consent agreement E-mail>>

<<Waiting for response>>

<<Consent accepted for 1 question>>

<<Connecting to target Neural Lace>>

<<Connection established>>

<<Ready for questioning>>

I now had a direct wireless link to Awasaki's brain, his patterns pulsing softly in the bottom left-hand corner of my HUD. Our gazes were met, his eyes like gateways into his subconscious.

"Go ahead, Detective," he nodded openly. "I await the judgement of the law."

I held my gaze, contemplating my options. I had to make this count, and at the end of the day, there was only one question that mattered. It was just a matter of how I was going to phrase it. Already thoughts were running through my mind… what if it came back red? I probably wouldn't be leaving here alive. Neither would Claire. He owned this building. The security. The cameras. He'd probably already dived my personal network through Mother Mind already.

All the evidence would be wiped. Whitewashed from history.

I gulped; realising how fucked I might be.

No point putting it off though.

I engaged focus mode on my neural lace to calm my nerves and spoke, “Kenji Awasaki…” I began. “Did you, or anyone in your organisations order the Jack-21 killings?”

The moment of truth.

The brainwaves flickered… the analysis suggesting a measure of guilt. He blinked but otherwise remained a statue. After a brief pause, he simply laughed it off.

“No Detective,” he shook. “I did not. And although I can’t be certain, to the best of my knowledge no one at my companies did either.”

The readings pulsed but came back green. A truthful response.

Oh, thank fuck.

<<Connection terminated>>

I brushed my brow, trying to hide my sigh of relief. Kenji chuckled, slapping me on the shoulder jokingly.

“You thought we were going to pull some Gestapo crap on you?” he laughed at me.

“It had crossed my mind,” I nodded back.

“There are monsters in this world, Detective,” he agreed, his expression hardening a tad. “Believe me, I know. But I’m not one of them. I hope this has put your mind at rest.”

“It’s a start,” I agreed, sounding cautiously optimistic. “You really have no immediate suspects then?”

He screwed his mouth up uncomfortably, apparently a bit of a sore spot to talk about.

“I’ve been trying to keep it under wraps… but a civil war is brewing on my board of directors,” he informed me reluctantly. “It’s only been a rumour so far, but I've already had reporters sniffing around. Won't be long now until it's on the home page of *Business Insider*. I'm looking at being thrown out of my own company."

Interesting… very interesting.

"Sorry to hear that," I said courteously, not actually feeling sorry.

"Business is business," he sighed.

"You think there's a connection though?"

"You've seen the latest evidence?" he checked with a flick of the eyebrow.

I nodded.

"This… enigma hacker has been pulling strings from behind the scenes," he said cautiously. "Convincing Andrew Ilian to steal from us, and then Jack-21 to have him killed. It could be someone on the board or one of my competitors, but if someone is trying to kick up a scandal, they're going the right way about it."

"I suppose that depends on the content of the Project Selection files," I blurted out without thinking, instantly regretting it the second I saw his eyes glaze over.

"You don't have to worry about that," he butted in coldly.

His tone made me flinch.

"I appreciate that Mister Awasaki, but…"

"The files are classified. As in government classified. I contract for the military. Any material pertaining to such contracts fall under the official secrets act. The buck stops there."

"I signed a non-disclosure agreement."

"Which can still be circumvented if you're handed a subpoena. Besides, you're still an employee of a rival firm."

I held my tongue this time. He wasn't going to be argued with on this point.

"So…" I continued gingerly. "You think Ilian was killed just to hide the tracks of the one behind this?"

"That is my legal department's thinking at this time, yes," Kenji nodded. "Corporate warfare used to be a figure of speech. Not anymore."

I realised something: he only confirmed he didn't know for sure if anyone in Virtualife was involved.

"You're afraid of your own board of directors?" I checked curiously.

"I'd be a fool not to be," he scoffed.

I nodded, pondering the implications.

"One more angle for us to consider," I agreed cautiously.

"Good," he said firmly, but with a blink returned to his usual inspiring expression. "So to sum up: get this job done. Catch Jack-21, get justice for the victims. Do *that* and… well, good things could happen."

His hand extended towards me.

"What do you say, Detective Inspector?" he grinned. "Do we have a deal?"

I hesitated, quickly conversing with Ben telepathically, as his subroutines processed Churchbell's policies. He determined that being offered a job wouldn't break the anti-corruption clauses in my contract. If I were to resign, I would have to accept a few months of unemployment, as per the non-compete period, but I could spend that time carrying out virtual training to prepare for the new job.

It was a start, but I still wasn't sure if I should accept. Ben flashed up some statistics on my HUD. The life expectancy of special forces operators was only thirty-six… but I'd be earning around a hundred grand a year. Anti-terror operations sounded like a step up. Certainly better than being stuck somewhere in middle-management hell.

"Well…" I responded with an ambivalent smile. "Under those circumstances; I'll think about it."

I took his hand, shaking slowly, he seemed disappointed that I hadn't accepted straight away, but unsurprised.

"It's a big decision; I understand," he said with a half-smile. "Take your time, the offer isn't going anywhere."

"Good to know," I grinned back. "And thank you for the offer."

"No, no, thank you, Detective! Keep up the good work!" He

patted my shoulder. "At this rate, the bastard will be behind bars in no time."

"Fingers crossed," Emma deadpanned, eyeing me up in a sarcastic suspicion.

Over our laughs, the clanking sound of security guard footsteps approached from behind us.

"Now, if you'll excuse me; I have a ballroom full of millionaires that need a bit of gentle persuasion," he said with a warm smile.

We said our professional goodbyes, and Awasaki was escorted back to the main hall by the robots; rattling as they went. The directions on my HUD led Emma and me back out the way we came, and we were just in time to see the start of the guests waltzing to the orchestra.

"That wasn't so bad, was it?" Emma teased me, patting my back.

"I need more booze," I breathed with relief, my insides feeling like they'd turned to liquid.

I signalled another waiter-bot over, and took another pair of glasses from it, handing one to Emma.

"Easy tiger!" Emma chuckled as I took a swig. "That shit's expensive."

"Yeah, and on the house," I replied, swallowing hard. "Your boss sure has the gift of the gab."

"Preaching to the choir," she sniggered, tapping the hydraulic joints in her left elbow. "He talked me into switching bodies."

"Must've been a helluva pitch."

I resumed my search for Claire, glancing past the graceful twirling of the frilly-dressed guests on the dance floor, trying to find her out the mass of bodies.

"Where the hell is she?" I grumbled.

"I'm sure she'll turn up when she's ready," Emma said reassuringly, taking her own sip to be processed by her gustatory-filtration system.

"Like Dracula," I muttered under my breath.

We decided to wait on the outskirts of the crowd, admiring the view on the stage.

"Damn, look at that," Emma said in awe, nudging her head towards the giant wall screen behind the stage.

I spun around to look; the latest photo in the slideshow on the screen. A platoon of Global Arms soldiers was protecting an Awasaki Foundation Aid tent on the streets of Caracas; hungry-looking children lined up to receive food and water from the aid workers and robots. An old factory stood behind it; a brick wall having crumbled like a *Lego* set. A giant mural had been graffitied onto the wall; a grand piece of artwork. A powerful image of a cybernetically-enhanced Jesus on the cross, bound by barbed wire.

"Certainly better than the crappy tags we used to make," I sniggered.

Emma covered her mouth and giggled with nostalgia.

"'Dan and Emma woz here'," she chuckled.

"Happy days," I sighed, remembering the days we used to bunk off. "You remember that shopkeeper in Hounslow we pissed off?"

"That doesn't exactly narrow things down," Emma nodded.

"Come on, you must remember! The Sikh guy who chased us down the street. We nicknamed him something..." I strained my brain, rubbing the skin around my headset to think of it, telepathically ordering Ben not to remind me.

"The Turbinator!?" Emma cried.

"That's it!" I clicked my fingers and then cringed slightly. "It wasn't exactly the most racially sensitive nickname..."

"Yeah, yeah, no wonder we pissed him off. Do you remember him chasing us down the street with his cricket bat?"

"Oh, man!" I breathed, wiping away the tears of laughter, "I thought you only saw rage like that in the comment section of *YouTube*."

"Shit, we should totally go back there sometime!"

I cringed awkwardly.

"What, to Hounslow?" I laughed. "That place has always been a fuckin' dump, you couldn't pay me to go back there."

Her face fell; more than I thought it would.

"Not even for old time's…"

She was cut short by a squeaky voice from behind me.

"Mind if I join in?"

I gulped, the hairs on the back of my neck standing up. I swivelled around; Claire was stood, her arms folded, a fake smile on her face that always sent dread creeping up my spine.

Already off to a great start.

She was seething. I didn't know how long she had been there, or what we had done to get her this pissed off, but it must've been bad. At least in her mind anyway. Emma could already sense there was something wrong, smiling nervously back at her.

I quickly thought about what I was going to say. I was going to have to tread lightly.

"Ah, there you are!" I cried loudly and warmly, masking my nerves.

I put my arm around her shoulder, hoping to take control of the situation.

"Claire. Emma," I gestured, trying to politely re-introduce each them. "You remember each other, right?"

"Claire! It's been too long!" Emma beamed back with a friendly grin, throwing her arms out in preparation for a greeting hug.

I watched Claire's reactions timidly. The silence lasted an uncomfortable length of time. Claire's eyes burned at me like hellfire, without dropping her outwardly fake smile.

"Oh-em-gee Emma, it's been like a million years!" Claire cried with more than a hint of sarcasm. "How've you been?"

I visibly cringed as the pair of them hugged, bracing myself for the worst-case scenario while checking my HUD for the closest exit in case I wanted to slink out.

"Oh, a bit older, a bit wiser I guess," Emma chuckled slowly, trying to smooth it over. I almost found it funny, if it wasn't so awkward; a steely-eyed combat cyborg like her afraid of the skinny little twig that was Claire.

"Good to know!" Claire replied falsely. "Still… I suppose you don't really have to worry about getting old anymore."

She gestured with her finger, indicating towards the mechanical joints of her body.

"Perks of the job!" she grinned back.

"I'll take your word for it," Claire deadpanned sarcastically. "I didn't think full-body prosthetics were possible yet."

"What can I say?" Emma shrugged uncomfortably. "We live in an amazing time."

"That's one way of looking at it," Claire sneered.

Emma didn't respond, smiling softly through her teeth, while trying to hide her tightening fist.

Great. At this rate, Emma was going to take a swing at her. I'd never seen Claire like this. I knew she could have a short temper with me, but she usually was so timid around other people. Full-blown bitch mode.

"So, uh… how have you been keeping?" Emma asked quickly, glossing over the masked insult. "I hear you're working from home? Fashion design?"

Claire's eyes narrowed like deadly slits.

"What are you trying to say?" she hissed.

Oh, boy.

"Nothing!" Emma cried defensively, holding her hands up. "I just…"

"You just think I'm a peasant don't you!?" she snarled. "A stupid little internet-serf lost in your boss's system!?"

"Whoa, whoa! Where is this…?"

I saw it coming. I tried to stop her, but my reflexes were dimmed by the champagne.

CLANG!

Claire's hand snapped out like a viper, lunging towards Emma's face. She slapped her, hard, lop-side across the cheek, ringing her metal skull like a tuning fork. Claire yelled painfully, grasping the hand she'd used, keeling over; possibly having broken it. Emma didn't flinch, just stare in stunned disbelief. Heads turned in the crowd, attracted by the commotion.

"Claire!" I barked angrily, feeling more embarrassed than I had ever been in my life. "What the fuck is wrong with you!?"

She didn't reply, just threw me a nasty glare and spun on her heel and stormed off, fists drawn in a temper tantrum.

"Where are you going?" I called after her, watching her shove her way through the crowd towards the elevator.

All eyes were on us now, no doubt we were being recorded.

"Shit!"

I spun to check Emma quickly.

"Are you okay?" I asked her.

"I'm fine," Emma replied quietly, looking puzzled. "What was that about?"

"I really don't know. I'm really sorry, she can get a bit… uptight."

"I hadn't noticed," she scoffed sarcastically.

I kept spinning back and forth, simultaneously trying to apologise to Emma and keep an eye on Claire, barging her way closer to the exit.

"Look… I uh… better get after her," I told her hurriedly. "I'm really sorry, and uh…"

"I get it, Dan," she said with cold indifference.

"Sorry!" I cried and dashed after her.

I could just about see Claire's pink dress, through the mass of the mingling fat-cats, storming away as fast as her high-heels would let her, shoving past a butler droid.

"Excuse me, excuse me, coming through!" I called out, rapidly barging my way through the edge of the dance floor, listening to the cries of the diamond-encrusted celebrities.

"Hey!"

"Watch it!"

"They'll let anyone in here these days."

Eventually, I wedged my way through a pair of waiter-bots enough to catch up with her. I reached out and grabbed her by the shoulder.

"Hey, hey, what's wrong?" I called.

"Don't you *touch* me!" she yelled, whirling around like a raging storm, revealing her tear-covered face; rivers of white and black make-up smearing her cheeks.

"Whoa, whoa, Claire calm d…"

"Tell me to calm down and watch what happens!" she spat back, shoving her finger into my chest, turning a few more heads.

"Could you keep it down a bit?" I hissed at her, feeling like we were now the centre of attention, blushing brightly, trying to hide my face.

"Let them look! Fucking cunts!" she cried, stomping her foot.

"Claire, stop!" I pleaded. "You're making a scene!"

"Oh sure, like that isn't what you want!"

I threw my arms out in desperation. I didn't have a clue what she was on about.

"Claire, why the hell would think that this is what I want?" I cried desperately.

"Fuck you! This is some reality TV bullshit!"

My mouth flapped bewilderedly. This was making less and less sense by the second.

"*What* are you talking about?'

"You can shove whatever prank you and that robo-bitch have planned up your ass!"

She gave me the finger, and resumed her march to the elevator, angrily snatching her coat off a droid.

"Fuck me…" I breathed desperately, dashing to catch up with her, grabbing my own coat fast enough to make the droid stumble.

I made it to the lift in time to catch up with her, shoving my arm my hand between the doors to hold it in place and squeeze inside. Claire was already inside, pressed against the mirror corner, her bloodshot eyes glaring at me, sucking in short distressed breaths.

Shit was about to hit the fan. I had half a mind to jump out again before the doors shut behind me. Too late now. The doors locked behind us, and the voice activation AI confirmed with us that we wanted the car park.

The turbolift whizzed back down, prompting us to have the world's fastest couple's argument, our shouting and swearing echoing violently around the cabin. It took less than two minutes to reach the bottom floor, but it seemed to go on for ages.

The doors opened again, and Claire shot out like a bat out of hell, quick-marching towards the limo waiting for us.

"Claire, for fuck's sake, what have I done?!" I called after her.

She turned back, baring her teeth like a snarling dog.

"You tell me, Dan, what have you been doing with that bloody girl?"

"Oh, for God's sake, I told you she's gay, you KNOW that!"

"Don't patronise me! I heard everything you two were saying just now!"

"What? What did we say?"

"Don't you fucking get it!?" she shrieked at me. "Don't you even remember?"

"Get what?!" I yelled back, my voice raising loud enough to echo through the car park.

"I came up with the Turbinator nickname!" she spat back at me. "He chased *us*! That was our first date! Did you take all your girlfriends around there!?"

I froze.

Her words triggered something.

Without warning I was clutching my head, struggling to stand up straight. It was like something had broken inside my head; a tremendous mental fracture inside my skull. The worst migraine I'd had in my life.

Claire was right. We had tagged that shop together… my teenage idea of romance. But I did it with Emma too… and yet I didn't.

"Wait… what?" was all I could manage to spit out.

Claire's expression softened suddenly; her anger quelled by

genuine concern, seeing the pain on my face as I clutched my head and groaned.

"Hey… hey what's wrong?" she cried sounding genuinely concerned.

"I… I'm not sure…" I groaned, the pain literally starting to blind me.

<<Alert!>>

<<Bio-monitor sensors detect migraine event in progress!>>

<<Directing nano-implants to deliver pan relief>>

<<Connecting>>

<<Update received>>

<<NHS non-emergency response monitoring protocols active>>

I couldn't open my eyes, but I felt Claire reaching for my hand, clasping it tightly.

"We'll… talk later," she said softly. "Come on… let's get you home."

She led me gently down the steps, helping me through the pain back into my limo. I collapsed in my seat, panting as Claire yelled at the auto-driver.

It was hard to remember what happened after that…

CHAPTER 16

Mother Mind profile 3551-7821-0862-2143:

First name: Kenji
Surname: Awasaki
Status: Living
Nationality: British/Japanese Citizen
Occupation(s):

- Chief Executive Officer
    - Status: Employed
    - Organisation: Virtualife Corporation

Known aliases:

- Sector
- <<Classified: Cymurai>>

Live surveillance:

- Status: *Partially available*
- Date: 07/10/2045
- Current location: Virtualife building, Docklands, East London
- Local Time: 21:56 GMT

<<Remote avatar session in progress>>

<<Neural interface stable>>

I had been looking for any excuse to leave the party… but this wouldn't have been the one I had in mind. This was a worst-case scenario…

An NHS drone cut through the rain drizzling from the darkened sky. I was logged in to one of my Cymurai avatars; my gauntlet resting on my mechanical knee pad, perched over a rooftop, the red and gold paint of the armour glistening in the orange tinge of street lights and flickering holograms.

I had been subconsciously lightly gripping the hilt of my sword while hoping I wouldn't have to use it tonight. My avatar was kneeling in front of a shopping centre across the street from Detective Haines' apartment, a cluster of wind turbines and CO_2 scrubbers behind me built on an asphalt rooftop. The bio-concrete and glass of their tower block stretched out in front of me, all the way to the tarmac of the road a hundred metres below, where an automated delivery truck was parked by a shop and was dutifully being unloaded by droids, bathed in the orange tinge of street lights and flickering holograms.

The camera on my faceplate was zoomed in on their apartment window, my HUD tinged green with night vision. Detective Haines was sprawled out on his couch, clutching an ice pack to his head as he groaned through the pain of his headache. His girlfriend was perched on the cushions next to him, gripping his shoulders and trying to comfort him. I had a sound-wave analyser program running in the bottom left-hand corner of my display, listening in to the audio feed I was streaming from the microphones inside the apartment. Claire was talking in a low, worried tone. Daniel was panting heavily, forcing out each word through the pain.

They hadn't argued since their little domestic incident at the Charity Fundraiser… despite everything that had happened it was obvious, she still cared for him. I would've almost found it cute… if this wasn't going to be such a pain in the ass for me.

Gabrielle appeared on my display, her arms folded, but looked somewhat relieved.

"I've scanned the output from both of their neural laces," she said reassuringly. "Neither of them seem to suspect… the truth. Nor has Detective Haines' anti-virus detected our infection."

"Well… that's a small blessing," I said bitterly to her, seeing how this was her fault in the first place.

The migraine he was experiencing right now was the direct result of the subconscious effect of the cognitive editing his interface headset had performed, as per the Clayman virus we had installed. The carefully crafted lie we created infringing on the conscious mind, entering the hippocampus. That was the thing about altering someone's memory…often you couldn't do it to just *one* person. You had to implement the technique on close contacts of the primary subject to keep up the façade. One out of place comment could bring the whole artificial construct into question.

I was witnessing the results of what happened when that *wasn't done correctly.* It was still valuable cyber-psychological data… but not the results I had been hoping for. Gabrielle had chosen Detective Haines to be the subject of Phase Two of Project Clayman because she had believed that it would've made him more receptive to Emma's intervention on the Jack-21 investigation.

Simply put; Gabrielle believed that Detective Haines and Emma would get along if they both *thought* they were childhood friends. It was a good idea, but everyone, including myself, thought it that had been a premature decision. Gabrielle had assured me that the plan was fool-proof. No doubt I would soon be getting a call from Jules, ready to rub this in my face.

"Gab… how?" I sighed at her telepathically, grasping the faceplate of the avatar with frustration, listening to the squeaking sound as my fingers ran down the wet metal surface.

"You told me you scanned all his close contacts. How did you miss his *girlfriend*?"

Her lips became a tight line.

"I ran a level-3 diagnostic on Claire Fielding's neural lace," she began.

"And?"

"You're not going to like this," she warned me.

She forwarded me the data she had gathered. A screenshot from a cyberspace warfare visualisation program; the green sphere of the central directory of Claire Fielding's personal area network had two unauthorised data streams tapping into it. One was blue which belonged to the virus that we had intended to install on her… the other was a dark purple… belonging to a second hacker.

"Someone else accessed her neural lace?" I checked, no-doubt raising my eyebrows subconsciously.

"The data traffic log confirms it."

"Can you identify the source?"

Gabrielle pursed her lips.

"The data packets were running the Enigma encryption."

My metal nails dug into the palm of the avatar.

"Him again," I snarled.

"He uninstalled my virus and was able to feed false bio-monitor data to us," she explained. "Her memories were never altered, despite the positive results from my scans."

We were being played with. The same hacker who tricked Andrew Ilian into attacking us, and then led Jack-21 to his location to kill him.

"It has to be someone within the company," I said bitterly.

"I've updated my primary suspect. I've designated it as…"

"Jules." I finished her sentence. "It has to be."

Even within the hardened casing of the avatar, I could feel the hot flash of rage in my body at the thought of that fat prick taking over the company.

My grip on the hilt of my plasma katana tightened angrily. He was forcing my hand. My last resort at this point would be to erase both of their memories of the evening. But if either of their AIs realised that they had been hacked, their defensive subroutines would automatically disconnect them from the internet. At which point I would no longer be able to remotely access their brains. I'd have to break into their apartment to get a wired connection… which required more covering up. More potential exposure. Not to mention I would have to alter Emma's memory as well, and she was already becoming suspicious of us.

"That bastard is gonna pay for this."

I waited for just over fifteen minutes, my camera eyes watching the apartment like a hawk. Eventually, through the tinge of my night vision, I saw Claire helping Daniel to his feet again, and watched the pair of them stumbling back to their bedroom.

I breathed a mental sigh of relief and released the grip on my sword. I wasn't erasing anyone's memory tonight.

"I've placed the pair of them under level four surveillance," Gab reassured me. "I'll notify you if the situation changes."

I nodded ambivalently, not really paying attention to her. I sat there in silence, the rain washing over me like a steel gargoyle. Gab's eyes drooped wearily at me.

"I… I'm really sorry, Kenji," she said sincerely.

I remined silent. She stared at me sympathetically.

"Why don't you go back to the party?" Gabrielle suggested hopefully. "There's nothing more you can do here."

I was miserable enough without having to go back to that to that pretentious shit. Besides, there were still things I needed to do tonight. My calendar app had reminded me that Arthur would be making a hit on one of Spiritforms hideouts soon. I wanted to personally make sure things went smoothly.

If all went well, I'd have one less nightmare to worry about. Some small relief.

"Or… you could go and see the kids?" she added, cautiously.

Why did she have to bring that up?

I cringed hard enough to freeze up the neck motors of my avatar. I'd been trying hard not to think about my previous simulation. Hideo and Shauna's question still echoing in my ears.

Did you and Daddy dream us up?

My heart sank the more I thought about it. Such a simple question. And yet one I couldn't even begin to fathom how to answer. I could go into their personality matrixes and delete their memories of the event. But that would be cheating. Defeating the purpose.

But that was it, wasn't it? I was a prisoner of my own ambitions. The burden I had taken on when I had chosen to love an AI instead of moving on from Gab's death. I was chasing something that was impossible. No matter how human-like my creations became, there was always going to be that psychological barrier. The anthropomorphic nature of human reality that kept machine-kind alienated.

Descartes was wrong. Man was not a machine. Or rather, hadn't been. The line was becoming blurred, but it was still a line.

I loved them. They were my family. But I couldn't help but wonder if I was mad.

"We can't just leave them offline!" Gab protested. "They were going to learn the truth eventually. They might find it hard to accept at first, but…"

"I… I'm not ready for that," I insisted anxiously.

"Ready or not, now is the time, Kenji," Gab said bitterly. "No matter how hard you try, the world won't always wait for you."

And don't I know it…

My grip on my sword tightened.

"Being a father is a commitment, Kenji," she added bitterly. "A commitment you made!"

"You think I don't know that?" I retorted angrily. "It's just…"

"If your other responsibilities are getting in the way, maybe you should reconsider Jules's offer," she insisted.

I scoffed.

"I am not leaving Virtualife in the hands of that demagogue!" I cried defiantly, clenching my fist.

Gab sighed, shaking her head with exhaustion.

"We can manipulate social media all we like, but the global political landscape will never be under any one person's control, fascism has been on the rise since the beginning of this century. If it's not Jules supporting them, it'll just be another corporation."

"So, I should just give in? Let him use Virtualife to turn America and Britain into dictatorships?"

"Statistically speaking, you save the most lives as Cymurai and through the Awasaki Foundation," she explained diplomatically. "If Jules is prepared to keep funding them, you can still fight for those causes, and still have the time to raise the kids properly…"

Her words stung with a truth that I had been trying not to face. I had taken on too much. I was paying for it.

But…

<<Priority-3 alert from Metropolitan Police>>

<<Crime in progress in avatar's vicinity!>>

The loud telepathic bleeping drew my attention away from my train of thought. As usual, all my worries seemed to fall away when my duties as Cymurai called.

I could leave the surveillance to Gab for now. Someone else needed my help.

I neuroclicked on the link; a CCTV camera in a back alley three hundred metres from here had captured images of a woman being mugged at gunpoint. Mother Mind had already dispatched a police response unit, but they wouldn't be here for another five minutes.

I can get there first…

Gabrielle's nostrils flared with frustration.

"Here we go…" she sighed.

"You expect me to just ignore that?" I cried disbelievingly.

"Of course not!" she retorted. "But that's just it! You can't let anything go! This crusade to save the world is destroying your life, Kenji!"

That touched a nerve I didn't expect.

"Like when I saved you?" I answered sourly, speaking before I had even realised what I had said.

My words stung her. Her avatar drew back from my HUD, her eyes widening in stunned surprise.

Shit…

Back in my apartment, my real body was clenching its teeth, kicking myself with regret. Neither of us spoke for a while. Gab narrowed her eyes, regarding me loathingly.

"So…" Gab she spoke coolly, her eyes fixed on me. "The truth comes out. How long have you…"

<<Suspending virtual personal assistant>>

Her avatar froze in its unhappy expression, becoming a digital statue of anger. After a few regretful seconds, I minimised her window.

Another time… Always another time…

I tapped into Mother Mind and downloaded the coordinates for the crime in progress. The guidance waypoint flashed into view, directing my sight to the east of my position.

I thrust my legs into a motorised sprint and leapt across the urban chasm to the next building over, flying over a fire escape and a sanitation robot on the street below and landing with a loud clank against the asphalt. I dashed across it and repeated the process of jumping across building to building until I came to my destination. I came to a skidding halt and peered down to the street below. Sure enough, they were there; my E-ID scan identified the victim as a Jessica Newmarsh, cowering by a chain link face, covering her tear-stained face, huddling in fear while a youth in a blue hoodie held her handbag in one hand, a pistol in the other, aimed firmly at her face. His face was covered by a black mask, with a luminescent skull painted on it. He wasn't wearing any RFID tags so I couldn't identify him yet. I focused my avatar's directional microphone to the street below to listen in on their conversation.

"There, now that wasn't so hard, was it?" the mugger sneered at her cockily, his voice modulated by speakers in the mask.

"Pl…please!" Newmarsh sobbed. "You said you wouldn't hurt me if…"

"Take your top off," the mugger sneered.

"Oh, God! Oh, fuck no!"

"Stop fucking snivelling!" he barked rabidly. "Get your fucking tits out!"

He reached down aggressively and yanked her by the shoulder. Newmarsh screamed, struggling to get free like a captured animal.

"No! Please! No!"

Not on my watch…

I leapt off the rooftop; the gyroscopes in my avatar sending my brain the bodiless sensation of freefall, my stomach sinking like a stone in water. With a loud roar, the landing thrusters on the avatar's back and feet fired up. My descent slowed and gave me a decent amount of control as I came into land. I shot out my left kick and adjusted the angle of my thrusters to propel myself into a roundhouse kick as I crashed into the mugger.

My armoured boot crashed into the spine of the mugger with a sickening crack. He yelled, and the sheer force of my kick hurled him off the victim and slammed him into the brick wall to his right with a crash and oomph. The gyros in my avatar stabilised me into my skidding acrobatic landing with a grinding screech against the pavement.

"Shit!" the mugger yelled, recognising me in a panic.

He still had his grip on his gun, and in a rage decided to make his last stand, whipping to take aim at me.

I didn't give him a chance.

With a straightforward swish, I drew my sword, shooting out the blade from the hilt and firing up the plasma generator. The searing heat coursed through the hollow ceramic tube. Droplets of rain rapidly turned to steam, leaving a white trailblazing streak in its wake.

BANG!

He fired off his first shot, but with no effect. The first slice of my sword was enough to reduce the bullet to a trail of molten lead particles.

I lunged forward and struck out.

The mugger screamed a bloodcurdling cry as I brought down the sword in a second swoop, down across his gun-hand. The plasma seared through his skin; cooking it like a steak and taking his hand clean off. He cried in anguish, slumping onto the ground, clutching the severed, charred limb; the dismembered hand lay smouldering next to him. He went into panic mode, whimpering like a puppy.

"Act like a man," I told him through the grating voice of the avatar, pointing at him the blazing tip of the blade. "It's nothing bionics can't fix and less than you deserve."

I deactivated the energy field, the blade retracting back within the hilt before I gracefully returned to the magnetic sheath on my belt. I relaxed my stance and turned around to face the victim, staring with shocked wide-eyes, her back pressed tightly against the chain-linked face.

"Are you all right?" I asked softly, slowly approaching her, kneeling and extending out a comforting hand.

Before I had even gotten near her, she had withdrawn in horror, pressing her back against the fence, staring at me almost in a frenzy.

"St…stay away from me!" she cried.

I was taken aback by her reaction. I wanted to ask why she was afraid…but I saw her eyes, drawn to the severed hand.

She's… afraid of me.

It wasn't the first time someone had this reaction to me. But never quite like this… her gaze reflected the light from my suit's sensors. Red. Blood red.

To her, I was just a sociopath with a lightsabre.

And looking back over my choices over the last few years… it was hard to argue with her assessment.

The avatar's microphones picked up approaching sirens.

I leapt back up to the rooftop and disappeared into the night… debating my life choices.

CHAPTER 17

Mother Mind profile 2446-7128-5978-2501:

First name: Arthur
Surname: Wells
Status: Living
Nationality: British citizen
Occupation(s):

- Private investigator
  - Status: Self-employed
  - Organisation: Arthur Wells & Associates

Known aliases:

- IronRoot

Live surveillance:

- Status: *Partially available*
- Date: 07/10/2045
- Current location: Brentford, London, United Kingdom
- Local Time: 23:45 GMT

The welcome message blazed in front of my eyes.

<<Welcome to RE:Call!!>>>

<<File loaded>>

<<Ready to begin Memory Playback>>

<<Begin: Yes/No>>

The command flowed through my nervous system and converted to binary…

<<Initialising memory playback>>

<<Running Neural lace device drivers>>

<<Processing consciousness shift>>

The present fell away… the past began bubbling to the forefront of my mind.

<<Loaded date: 24/03/2043>>

<<Location: GCHQ Secure Conferencing Simulation>>

<<Local Time: 09:26 GMT>>

The GCHQ secure virtual conferencing environment was modelled on the appearance of the government cabinet room. I was surrounded by delicate white panel walls, permeated with light from the windows, lined with elegant cream-coloured silk curtains. I was sitting in a high-backed wooden chair, one of twelve lined either side of a broad oak table bound with a leather mat, my back to a grand marble fireplace, the remnants of the fire smouldering in the bottom of the pit. An antique clock ticked away on top of the shelf, below a painting of Winston Churchill. At the foot of the table stood the virtual recreation of a whiteboard screen, displaying data I had gathered through the course of my investigation into the RAPTOR hack via a simulated old-fashioned 2D projector.

Director Langley occupied the seat to my left, his massive arms leaning back expansively against the chair. His usual intimidating stare was gone, and he had been beaming at me with the same proud gaze for the last three hours; I'd just secured all the funding for GCHQ from Virtualife we were ever going to need.

Emma had been called in to attend as well. She was standing with her back pressed against a wall, her left foot pressed against the panels, her arms folded with a look of stoic patience. We'd become close over the last few months. I considered her a good friend now. Even went out for drinks with her and the lads the other day. Turns out with her enzyme synthesisers deactivated she could get just as drunk as the rest of us. One of the boys tried calling her 'the iron lady'... it didn't work out for him. Her presence was reassuring, but I was still rubbing my neck in a vain attempt to relieve the stress.

We had a meeting scheduled with Kenji Awasaki for 09:30. Officially he was just coming to congratulate us on our work finding his missing drone. Even though he was one of the biggest contractors for both militaries, it was still our operation. Strictly-need-to-know. Of course, the fact that he was coming here of all places really was proof that you really could *buy* all the access you want.

In any case, even if he was going to be thanking us today, he really should've been coming to apologise. I swear you needed a chainsaw to cut through the red tape he'd put up around data relating to this 'RAPTOR'. Just getting the basic specs on the CPU and operating system had been an uphill battle. I'd dealt with megacorporations before, and the only time when they would set up as many road-blocks was when they had something illegal to hide. But after finding the flaw in the ICE protecting Islamic State servers, I had to dive in and out of access to avoid detection, but eventually, I got direct access to the command protocols of the drone; hiding out in the Rahjar region in Syria.

"Relax!" Kirk's voice boomed, patting me heavily on the shoulder. "It's a courtesy call, not a briefing."

I responded flatly with an unconvinced nod.

"The boss just wants to thank you, dude," Emma reassured me with a wink, stretching to rest her hands behind her head. "There are a lot of investors who are breathing a lot easier now thanks to you."

"So, he's here to congratulate me on saving his ass," I grumbled cynically. "Big deal."

"Call it what you like," Kirk interjected. "We're going to need their help if we're going to clean up this mess. They're worried about their competitors getting hold of the designs. My main concern is what happens if they are spread to every Jihadist cell in the region."

I cringed with dread at the possibilities.

"Or worse..."

Kirk gave me a sceptical grin, rubbing his well-kept beard.

"Fine, you can run your little theory by him. But do it professionally okay?"

"Yes sir," I retorted, grudgingly.

"And I won't be backing you up if he calls you crazy. Is that understood?"

I nodded with a regarding glare.

"Theory?" Emma retorted with an inquired eyebrow.

<<Kenji Awasaki is logging in>>

"Alright, cut the chatter!" Kirk announced, straightening up formally in his chair, adjusting the knot of his tie. "Best behaviour, people!"

A mass of multicolour pixels began to flock into the empty seat across the table. I did my best to hide my reluctance, stiffening my back and resting my arms on the table, either side of what appeared to be a binder of traditional paper documents. I glanced into the cloud of pixels in front of me with a professional smile. Emma took her seat more casually than the pair of us.

The wireframe of a human skeleton took form within the chair and filled out with the textures of a blue and white suit jacket. The oh-so-familiar face of a stranger loaded into view.

"Kenji!" Jules cried warmly, standing up to offer his hand across to the CEO, who took it just as enthusiastically to my surprise.

"Good to see you again Kirk!" he answered back. "Always a pleasure working with GCHQ. Nice to see the old pros in action."

He was blushing. It was clear who was *really* top of the food chain here.

"Hey boss," Emma added, with a quick salute.

"Enjoying your new assignment?" he grinned back.

"Sure as hell beats Detroit," she scoffed back with a wink.

"Oh well, that's saying something," he chuckled sarcastically.

Kirk and Kenji began exchanging pleasantries, complimenting each other on business deals, promotions and projects underway. Half the stuff they were talking about was classified on a level that I had only just been promoted to. If a regular civilian had overheard any of this, the chances were the government would throw the book at them and have their memories erased. Emma already had her arms folded, apparently bored by the politics. She turned to me with a desperate stare and used her finger to make a gun shape and pretend to blow her head off, prompting me to give a single snigger.

"So!" Kirk cried, slapping his hands together with twinkling eyes. "Time you met the man of the hour! This is…"

"Agent Wells," Kenji interrupted him, offering his hand to me with a smile I wouldn't trust even if you paid me. "There are a lot of people over at the NSA who are extremely jealous of you right now. It's a pleasure to finally meet you!"

I sat there, hesitating for a moment. Kirk raised a curious eyebrow.

"It's an honour… uh… Mister Awasaki," I spoke awkwardly, taking his hand. As soon as I did, the thought of what Denise would've done to me if she heard me say that sent shivers down my spine.

"Please, call me Kenji," he replied, with a dismissive wave. "Or how about Sector? We're all hackers here, after all."

Liz prompted Kenji's Wikipedia page to my HUD, informing me that 'Sector' had been his hacker name as a teenager.

"Oh yes, I'd forgotten that," I laughed, falsely but professionally. "I suppose that background must've come in handy when you wrote Mother Mind's core software."

His cheeks fluctuated oddly.

"I… I suppose it did," he said warily.

Did I just strike a nerve?

I nodded slowly, not sure how to respond.

"And we're all very grateful," Kirk interjected rapidly, wanting to quell any potential disagreements. "I don't know where we'd be without the system these days."

"Yeah, it really is a fantastic piece of kit," I added hurriedly, wanting to smooth things over.

I caught a glance of Emma; subtly amused by my attempts to kiss-ass.

"Well, it looks like you're about to repay the favour," Kenji responded, smiling and shrugging it off. "Seriously, the shareholders have been at my throat about this cyber-attack."

"It was nothing really," I replied, pretending to sound a little embarrassed by the compliments.

"Says the man who coded an autonomous Stuxnet-style virus," Kenji added admiringly. "Couldn't have done it better myself! Have you ever considered going over to the private sector? I'm sure we could…"

"All right, that's enough," Kirk interrupted jokingly, throwing him a coy stare. "That's the trouble with having good staff. Everyone wants to steal them."

"I'm partial to a bit of poaching," Kenji teased.

I had to resist the temptation to roll my eyes. Bloody one percenter humour.

"So!" he cried with a clap of the hands. "Shall we get down to brass tacks?"

About bloody time.

<<Beginning presentation>>

The lights in the simulated cabinet room dimmed, and an old-fashioned projector hanging from the ceiling projected onto the whiteboard at the front of the room, loading up a live feed from the surveillance satellites in orbit above Syria. Awasaki crossed his arms, resting his right leg on his left knee, leaning backwards with an inquisitive gaze, ready to absorb every piece of information that was about to come out of my mouth.

The camera zoomed in on the rusted entrance to a derelict bunker in the middle of the desert.

"The intel gathered by the Wildfire worm I program led us here," I explained. "We deployed an SAS reconnaissance team, but what they found by the time they got there was far from expected."

Still shots taken from the bionic eyes of the soldiers flashed up from the projector. The dimly-lit concrete walls of the bunker had been splattered with blood. Spent bullet casings were scattered across the floor. At least six bearded men in turbans and power exoskeletons lay dead, clutching their rifles as their pale, forever still eyes stared at the ceiling.

"Needless to say; someone got to them first," I said, in a low, almost reverent tone.

"Who did this?" Kenji checked, frowning, seeming to know the answer already.

I pursed my lips awkwardly… I couldn't say it yet; the 'theory' itching anxiously at the back of my mind. I brought up the next image. A close-up of one the spent cartridges, held in the gauntlet of an exoskeleton of a SAS soldier. Digital annotations appeared on the screen, analysing the structure and composition of the round.

"The evidence retrieved from the site… indicates that that the terrorists were killed by RAPTOR itself."

His frown grew.

"I thought they had obtained control of the unit?" Kenji asked.

The urge to speak my mind was strong, but I could already see Kirk shaking his head, telling me that now wasn't the time for my theory yet. I pressed on, loading the photo of a PC kept in a dusty table in the command centre of the bunker.

"That was what we had assumed… but the team retrieved this terminal from the heart of the bunker," I continued. "It was encrypted, but we got the necessary biometric log-ins from the bodies. They were using it to reprogram the RAPTOR unit's prime directives. The most recent entries into its AI had been deleted, but it seems the goal was to transfer control of the drone to another location."

That piqued his curiosity.

"RAPTOR was being operated remotely?" Kenji retorted.

I hesitated, wondering how I was going to frame my answer to that.

"That is the assumption we are working under," Kirk spoke.

"Yes," I agreed, despite myself. "The orders may have been given from elsewhere, but it seems it was installed with the same basic operating directives that ISIS installs on all its drones."

"Including autonomous-fire functionality?" Kenji asked darkly, his eyes shimmering.

I bit my lip, then nodded. The drone was programmed to use its weapons without the need for human authorisation. A war crime.

Kenji's mouth tightened. A robot with the ability to use deadly force on its own authority. Almost a dirty saying for AI developers. Such machines were now illegal under international law… but it wouldn't be the first time they had been developed illegally.

"We've seen ISIS use such weapons," Kirk shrugged. "But it does seem its orders were issued remotely. We believe that the operator received intel that the SAS were on the way and ordered the inhabitants of the base to be… neutralised as a precaution."

I nodded slowly; this is where my opinions differed from the official report. Kenji frowned grimly. It was a typical strategy for terrorist organisations with the 'suicide bombing' mentality. The need to interrogate prisoners of war had become obsolete with the rise of memory extraction technology. Under those circumstances, not being taken alive had become the default mentality for radical groups.

Most of the time, such action was taken willingly… but these terrorists had been *executed.*

"How did they get the intel?" Kenji asked.

"We're already investigating that," Kirk said reassuringly, pointing to the 3D map of the region now on the whiteboard. "We have surveillance drones in the air and satellites in geostationary orbit above the region now. We suspect there is a hidden sensor network scattered throughout the surrounding area. In any case, if the RAPTOR unit is now out in the open, even if it's cloaked we'll find it soon enough."

"And if it's not in the open?" Kenji asked sceptically.

"I've been analysing the data traffic between the bunker's terminal and RAPTOR," I explained, bringing up the cyberspace visualisation of the system's ICE programs, highlighting a path leading to the system directory through the data maze in blue.

"I found a back-door to the drone's CPU that I can exploit at least once before the AI's firewall adapts. Once inside, I can trigger RAPTOR's GPS to send a signal to ping its location. I could also launch a DDoS attack that will overload its environmental sensors. The US Marines orbital battalion will be on standby during my attack."

The presentation projected a diagram of a space station called the EagleStar in geostationary orbit over Syria, complete with graphical renderings of soldiers deploying via trans-atmospheric HALO jump.

"As soon as we have a lock on RAPTOR's position," I explained, "they'll drop in and destroy the unit before the bastards know what hit him."

I gave the command to end the presentation and began nervously awaiting Awasaki's reaction. After a long analytical stare, his mouth curled upwards.

"Looks like you've got this under control," Kenji beamed at me.

I pursed my lips. If I was ever going to mention my alternative theory, it had to be now. I turned to Kirk. He had already predicted what I was thinking. He gave a reluctant nod, and I plucked up my courage to turn back to face Kenji.

"You should know, there is another working theory I have, in regards to the units… orders," I forced myself to say.

Kenji's ears pricked up, but Kirk was keen to object.

"This isn't the consensus on the floor," he interjected, pre-emptively embarrassed by what I was about to say.

"Oh, really?" he piped back with a raised eyebrow. "I do like a bit of out-the-box thinking."

He gestured with his hand for me to continue, and chuckled. "Please, go ahead. If I didn't listen to people with new ideas, I wouldn't be where I am today."

Kirk seemed uneasy but leaned back reluctantly as he accepted the situation. I shifted uncomfortably on the spot as I loaded my personal addition to the presentation while trying to anticipate his response.

"There is no hard evidence to suggest that it was actually being operated remotely," I said.

Kenji's eyebrows shifted.

"So, who ordered the execution?"

I gulped down the virtual air and readied myself.

"If RAPTOR truly was equipped with autonomous-fire functionality… I believe it could've resulted in a second-directive loophole, to kill them on its own authority."

Kenji's head jerked backwards, almost offended. The infamous second law of robotics loophole. There had been a case in a *Toyota* factory, where the central AI had decided the most efficient way to ensure its long-term survival was to turn the entire planet into a car factory. Unbeknown to the managers, the machine had tricked them into giving it authorisation to hack into construction robots of rival companies to extend its facilities in secret.

The machine was stopped before the situation got out of hand, and the factory was now facing closure. But the worst-case scenario… would be a second-directive loophole on a robot that possessed autonomous-fire capacity.

Which is precisely what I was suggesting…

Kenji regarded me with utmost attention.

"That's a very serious accusation," he said coolly. "What exactly is the nature of this… loophole?"

I highlighted another chunk of the unit's source code.

"As you know, ISIS has been known to use autonomous-fire capable machines. I ran with the assumption they would use their standard software to adapt RAPTOR's AI. Including placing a higher value on preventing intelligence falling into enemy hands than it did on their own lives," I explained.

Kenji raised a concerned eyebrow.

"The AI would have determined that executing the terrorists would be safer than letting them be captured."

I nodded grimly.

"With autonomous-fire functionality… there would be no one to stop it. All within the limitations of the three laws. As soon as the RAPTOR's AI evaluated the high probability of the terrorists being captured, its program would've started identifying them as targets to be eliminated."

Kenji nodded darkly, stroking his goatee.

"Now most military robots would go into standby mode if their commanding officers were killed."

"But RAPTOR is no ordinary robot," Kenji said coolly.

"No...it's not," I replied cautiously. "It's predatory combat protocols are...unique to say the least. Not to mention it's onboard cyberwarfare suite."

"I can see where you're going with this," Kenji murmured, judging my statements.

"Under ISIS control, RAPTOR's prime directives were reprogrammed to make striking coalition forces and installations in the area," I nodded slowly. "With its commanders, dead...it would be free to prioritise that directive on its own accord. Its heuristic algorithms evolving without any human intervention or…limitations."

Kenji scowled, folding his arms, leaving Kirk and I waiting with bated breath for his response.

"Like I said before," Kirk pointed out rapidly, keen to distance himself from this, "this is Arthur's personal theory; it doesn't reflect the…"

"I like this one," Kenji chuckled at Kirk. "Sure I can't convince you to part with him?'

Kirk blinked in disbelief.

He agrees with me.

Awasaki clapped softly, a small nervous smile creeping across his face.

"Impressive… most impressive…" he said slowly, his admiration seeming to reach new heights. "In fact, my R&D team came to a similar conclusion."

Kirk recoiled, unsure how to process that.

"Uh… they did?" he checked, looking especially stunned.

A warm angry pulse washed out from my chest. I quickly turned to Emma, telepathically asking her if she knew anything about this, responding only with a puzzled shrug.

"Just thought I'd call in to make sure we're all on the same page," he said, practically rubbing it my face.

For a moment, it looked like there had been a graphics rendering error, freezing Kirk's face.

"Just to check…" I asked slowly, holding back the vitriol that his look was inspiring. "Did you consider this possibility before, or after the drone was deployed?"

His eyes focused on me, his expression suddenly becoming more reserved.

"Unfortunately, I've signed a non-disclosure agreement regarding that information," he replied coolly. "Sorry, the board can be pretty pedantic about sensitive data."

I ground my teeth bitterly.

"Rest assured we'll keep you updated as the situation unfolds," Kirk said diplomatically, taking down notes on his display, looking keen to get this over with and start berating me.

"Expect daily secure bulletins fro…"

Before he could finish, Kenji had held up his hand to silence him.

"That won't be necessary," he told us blatantly. "I've been talking the details over with the FCO."

Once more, he stopped himself mid-sentence, his eyes widening with shock.

"Y...you have?" he stuttered.

GCHQ was administered by the Foreign and Commonwealth Office. The home secretary was effectively Kirk's boss… a known user of Virtualife's AI.

"Not that I don't have every confidence in GCHQ," Kenji replied carefully. "But it's as your protégé here said; RAPTOR is no ordinary robot. And if it really has gone rogue, then we need to take *every* precaution. The electronic warfare counter-measures installed on it…"

"Whoa, whoa, whoa!" I cried, holding up a hand to stop him mid-sentence. "What counter-measures? I wasn't told anything about any counter-measures!"

Kenji shrugged apologetically.

"Yeah, sorry about that," he answered regretfully, bowing slightly. "I would've liked to have told you but…"

"You signed an NDA," I replied with gritted teeth.

Emma threw me a warning glare not to proceed with this question, but I ignored her.

I turned to Kirk with his blazing eyes.

"Permission to speak freely, sir?"

"Not granted," Kirk snapped back gruffly, knowing full well that I was about to say.

"No, it's all right," Kenji undermined him. "I want to hear what he has to say."

I spoke before Kirk could object again.

"Frankly, this is ridiculous!" I said desperately, throwing my arms out to the side with desperation. "I'm supposed to be coordinating an international search and destroy mission, and I don't even have the full specs on the target, and now you're saying we could get *back-hacked!*"

"I can understand your frustration," Kenji reassured me. "It must seem that we're putting our own interests above national security, but I can assure you there is a greater good issue at hand."

"And that is?" I scoffed angrily, already knowing I wasn't going to get an answer.

He smiled back at me condescendingly.

"I could tell you," he admitted coolly. "But I'd have to wipe your memory."

Should've known.

"In any case," Kenji continued, slapping his hands together to keep the conversation moving, "you won't be on your own during the operation. After careful talks with the secretary, we've decided that it would be beneficial for both of us to have people from our team assisting you during the operation."

Interesting.

"RAPTOR's original software developers?"

"Who else would be better suited?" he pointed out. "They'll be able to address most of the questions you have. Would that be sufficient?"

It would also be the perfect opportunity for them to run a diagnostic on the unit before we blow it to hell. In fact, it might be the only chance for them to find the vulnerability, that allowed it to be hacked in the first place.

I turned to Kirk, who was growing unhappier by the second. Bringing people in from the outside was going to be a security and bureaucratic nightmare.

"If there aren't any other surprises… I'll sign off," he shrugged grudgingly.

"I'll make the arrangements," Kenji replied curtly, with a victorious nudge.

"We'll have to step up security here during the op," Emma continued formally. "If there is a mole, or if they've traced the cyberattacks to here, they might make a move."

"Understandable," Kirk commented. "Will…"

His face went still. At first, I thought he'd stopped himself mid-sentence, but the world had also frozen around him; like staring at a 3D snapshot.

<<Memory Playback Paused>>

The present-day invaded my trip down memory lane, with a telepathic chime and Liz's flashing icon on my HUD.

"Sorry to interrupt, Arthur," Liz's familiar echoed from the present day. "We're almost there."

Typical. Just when things are getting interesting.

"Fine," I telepathically sighed. "Coming now."

I gave the neurocommand to end the program.

<<Terminating Memory Playback>>

<<Disengaging Neural lace>>

<<Thank you for using RE:Call!>>

My mind's eye shut itself to the past; and reopened to the present.

<<Date: 08/10/2045>>

<<Local Time: 01:58 GMT>>

The blur on my vision cleared away, awakening to the sight of London drizzle splattering against the windows of my car; the glare of screen-cars sweeping by along in either lane of Great West Road; the adverts and logos projecting from the business park buildings either side of the motorway. I rubbed my face, pondering what I'd learned. Every time I received one of these data dumps, I always seemed to walk away with more questions than answers. I stretched back, staring through the car's skylight. This latest development was particularly… disturbing.

When Gabrielle Phillips hired me, she'd told me she'd assimilated the data from my service record. She never mentioned I'd met *Kenji Awasaki* himself! Or that Operation Dragonslayer was so closely tied to Virtualife. It might have just been because the data was classified, but I couldn't shake the feeling I was staring something dangerous in the face and still couldn't see it.

"What do you think?" I checked with Liz.

Her avatar shone out of the dashboard of the car, adjusting her digital spectacles as she looked over the historical timeline of my life running her analytic protocols.

"Hmm… insufficient data," she replied. "To determine a more accurate hypothesis, I'll need more information on the content of the Project Selection files."

"Figures," I sighed.

She gave me an annoyed frown.

"Unfortunately, I'm not an Oracle," she deadpanned.

A list of suggested programs for boosting her intelligence appeared from the app store.

Bloody smart-ads.

I closed the window and checked the holo-map on the dashboard. No traffic ahead. At this rate, I'd be in Southall in the next fifteen minutes.

I checked over the case-files on my HUD. David had come through for me. After calling in the favour he owed me, he forwarded a file from Mother Mind's vulnerability database, containing a treasure trove of back-doors in different networks, including Next-Gen Industries. Their server farms were one of the most significant clients of the OpenSource Soul network. The chances were there was at least one encrypted copy of Denise's User-ID (retrieved from the android I'd stolen) somewhere on their servers.

Cloud-based services are all fine and dandy… until someone like me comes along.

I got lucky and got the User-ID. Luckily, I didn't need the encrypted content, just the metadata component. I traced the source IP address to a server somewhere in South London. I spent four hours jacked into cyberspace, watching its net-traffic from a distance. I couldn't ping its exact location, and the frequency of the data traffic from the server wasn't consistent with what you'd expect from a block-chain decryption protocol… it didn't seem likely that they were storing the Project Selection on that server.

I fell into a well of despair at that point, believing I failed. But I noticed the server was using a VPN to route some of its traffic through a proxy in Estonia then back to a second location somewhere else here in London. I used my ICE Breakers to creep inside and infect the Estonian server with a silent rootkit Liz developed and then exploited it to gain access to the secondary safe house. Never knew what hit them. Just the way I like it.

I found the drive which the Project Selection files had been saved to, but they had been marked 'do not delete', stopping me from destroying the files remotely. I'd have to go much deeper into the operating system to override the setting. The anti-virus would surely detect me if I did that and would pull the system offline.

Only one thing for it; physically steal the optical drive with the files in person.

At first, I couldn't get an exact fix on the second safe house's location either. Naturally, they were smart enough not to have any GPS equipment installed there. But they did have a wireless energy transceiver, all I had to do was access its control drivers to send out a traceable coded pulse and triangulate its location.

I picked up the pulse and matched it to an address: 4 Albany Road. Its photo was loaded on the car's windscreen; a century-old brown and grey terraced house. It was quaint in its decay; complete with a rotting blue wooden door and missing slate tiles on the roof. The landlord was one Cathy Morgan. Officially the building was rented out to an Indian family, but that was just the front for her people trafficking.

SpyFly had peered through the curtains, observing a living room filled with mattresses, dirty plates and old computers tossed about. At least three generations lived here; bearded old men and wailing children alike. It's what was hidden in the garden that I was interested in. The drone had spotted a figure in an active camouflage suit, moving in and out of a hatchway covered with turf. A rusty old ladder descended into a bunker. Probably a relic from the Second World War.

The drone had generated a map of the property and marked out all the anti-intruder measures; including micro-CCTV and motion sensors. The most recent recording captured the occupant slipping away about an hour ago; most likely on a supply run. The perfect time for some good old-fashioned breaking and entering. Even if it did come with the job, I hated getting up early, but if I could get this case over and done with as quickly as possible, it would be worth it.

The auto-driver pulled over to the right, turning the car off the empty high street and onto Albany Road, the pavements bathed in the orange tinge of the ageing street lights. I zoomed my eyes in on the red bricks, cracked up and mouldy. Some of them had wooden porches that had fallen into various states of dilapidation, on the verge of collapsing entirely. It was the dead of night, but you could still tell the houses were packed to the brim.

The auto-driver slowed the car down to a crawl, directing me to an available parking space.

Liz placed a marker over the house. What I hadn't noticed from *Google Earth* were the words 'Britain First' sprayed onto a wall. I sat for a good ten minutes, staking out the situation. The drone had told me that no one was home, but training was still to wait it out.

A lingering tension washed over me. It'd almost been too easy so far. A case like this might've taken someone else weeks. But only two days since I'd been hired, and I was already on Spiritform's doorstep.

I didn't know what, but something was going to go wrong.

"It's not going to investigate itself, Arthur," Liz nagged me telepathically.

She was right… I needed to get my head in the game. I was reluctant to do it, but I cautiously dialled up the settings on my implants.

<<Adjustments complete>>

My worries seemed to fizzle out almost instantly.

The task at hand.

That's all that mattered.

Get the memory drive. Get out. Don't get caught.

"Cheers," I yawned, the motors in my arms whirring as I stretched.

I picked up my hat, pulling down the tip to cover my face. I pushed open the door, stepping out into the dark drizzle, greeted by the sound of barking dogs, and a whiff of curry from a 24-hour takeaway on the corner, seemingly owned by the residents of the house.

A bleep from SpyFly's control app telepathically rang the proximity alert. My HUD directed my gaze towards the dark, overcast sky just above the roof, where SpyFly was beating its silvery metallic wings against the downpour. I gave a new command to the unit:

<<Patrol mode engaged>>

The drone whizzed off to circle the house, keeping surveillance for me. I crept into the alley, hunching my metal shoulder blades, and keeping my head down to avoid the electronic stare of the CCTV hanging from the lamp posts.

There was a soft crunching beneath my feet as I stepped on a yellow polystyrene kebab box floating in a small pool cascading into the gutter drain. The alley was little more than a narrow path with tall wooden fences either side, separating the back gardens of the houses on either side.

I stepped towards the alley…

CLUNK!

The hairs on the back of my neck stood up; a cold rush through my body.

It came from behind me.

The same metallic clanging that I'd been hearing everywhere.

I came to a sudden, nerve-wrenching standstill, my elongated shadow stretching against the street lights.

The calming pulses from my neural lace kicked in, but I couldn't shake the lingering dread that I was being stalked. My gun hand slipped towards my right thigh… anxiously anticipating opening the hidden compartment inside the unit, and grabbing my revolver. My eyes darted around furiously, expecting to see a shifty figure emerging out of the shadows, or to be jumped from around the corner.

"I've tapped into the car's sensors. I'm not picking up anything," Liz reassured me. "Nothing on sonar or laser proximity."

I wasn't convinced. My eyes flicking back and forth across the rooftops, my cursor scanning inch by inch. Eventually, my rational side took over, hesitantly releasing the grip on my thigh compartment… but not letting down my guard just yet.

"We're going to have to talk about putting limits on your focus mode usage," she explained. "You're starting to get delusions."

She brought up my neurological scans; her analysis suggested my neural architecture was starting to show similarities in the frontal lobe to someone suffering from schizophrenia.

"You pay for yourself, Liz," I told her sarcastically, grumbling under my breath.

I bitterly closed the window, but couldn't help but feel like an idiot. I could only hope that Gabrielle hadn't been watching the CCTV.

I resumed my stride back down the alleyway, my boots splashing past a free, crackling, animated plastic cup. When I was out of sight, I peered into the garden. The lawn was unkempt, overgrown to the point of consuming the stone path leading to a shed at the end. It was probably a deliberate choice; the shrubberies that had sprung up were being used to hide the sensors. Liz used my HUD to highlight the locations of the sensors. Still active. But not for long.

"Logging on now," Liz informed me.

<<Connecting to target server>>

<<Initializing root kit access protocols>>

<<Access granted>>

<<Deactivating security sensor drivers>>

One by one the label graphics on my HUD turned red, reading 'offline'. I couldn't help but smirk at my own handiwork. Denise and I always had a bit of a rivalry back in the day. Each of us competing to 'out-hack' each other.

She always fancied herself better than me.

How'd you like this, bitch? I thought bitterly.

Being smacked in the face with an android avatar tends to have that effect on me.

The last sensor went offline.

Game time.

I peered round to either end of the alley. No one. I looked up. No obvious aircraft watching us.

The coast is clear…

I squatted down, readying myself to jump, the motors in my prosthetic legs humming as I did.

With a powerful thrust, I sprung into an acrobatic jump, grabbing the fence and flipping over in a single bound, landing cat-like in the soft, earthy padding.

Liz highlighted the thickest patch of grass in the centre of the lawn, hiding the trap door. I ducked down to keep a low profile, stealthily dashing over to it. I peered back around again to the house; still no signs, curtains drawn, no lights.

I began fumbling in the grass. It didn't take long for my hand to collide with something. I brushed the wads of green and found the rusted iron handle. With a few more sweeps I revealed the outline of the trap door. I ran my fingers carefully across the gap between the door and the frame, checking for any booby-traps I might've missed.

Bingo.

Found something all right. A basic conductive wire alarm system. Opening the trap door would set it off. It didn't seem to have any digital components aside from a rudimentary thumbprint scanner nestled in the grass. I wasn't sure exactly what the alarm would trigger, maybe an auto-destruct sequence on the computers inside.

I pulled back my right sleeve and set the wrist laser to scalpel mode, carefully taking aim. With my free hand, I reached to my belt for a small, flat, rounded nanobattery, holding it close to the alarm device. The second I welded it onto the cable, the exothermic reaction would trigger an electrochemical release and would begin delivering current into the circuit; the alarm would register the door as being closed.

I gave the neurocommand, and hot raw energy coursed out from the lens in my wrist, burning like a focused sun ray. With a bright white flash and puff of smoke, the beam cut through the cable and melted the battery, reducing it to a solder-like material fusing itself with the wire and releasing its power. My HUD flicked green and informed me it was working. I waited for the laser to cool down again, and pulled my sleeve back over it, and proceeded to grab the iron handle. My tactile sensors picked up the reading of the cold, wet, slippery metal against the metal under my hand. I yanked up, my gears groaning softly. It didn't take much to heave it up with an angry squeak; small clumps of soil falling away into a dark pit. The semi-stable ladder descended about five meters to the ground. The stench was overpowering, the stink of amino acids rising from it. My throat convulsed violently, I had to force myself to hold it back, prompting me to quickly deactivate my nasal receptors.

<<Activating torch>>

I held out my left hand and gave the telepathic command to switch on the bright bulb mounted on my watch, illuminating the pit before me. Just as I thought, it was a World War Two Anderson shelter; a tube of iron suspended on a slab of concrete buried in the dirt. I checked the coast was clear one last time, and pivoted my body round to grab the first ladder rung, and began descending, my hands and feet clanging softly with each step, before closing the hatch behind me.

The ladder was unsteady; each step sending my stomach jittering. On the way down, I noticed what the alarms had been wired to; an incendiary bomb mounted on the wall. With a single pulse, the device would release and ignite a wave of thermite across the bunker, burning everything inside to a crisp. I hopped off the bottom rung and onto the concrete floor; the resulting shockwave rippling around the structure with an unsettlingly loud creak.

I circled my watch wrist around, the torch revealing the cascade of fine dust falling from the ceiling. I quickly found an old-fashioned, manual power switch mounted next to the ladder. I ran my fingers lightly across the surface; the forensic sensors in the fingertips picked up flakes of skin and analysed the DNA. I couldn't ID it without access to a medical database, but couldn't hurt to send it to Virtualife, to earn a bit more on my bonus.

I flicked the switch, and a single rounded lamp mounted to the ceiling blinked into life, illuminating the squalor around me. I cringed with disgust, pitying the poor bastard who had to live here. The floor was cluttered with boxes of canned food, clothes, medicine etc. I was standing beside an air-purification unit, the slow wooshing-sound of a turbine permeating the silence. A single, stained mattress nestled on the far side, a ripped sleeping bag resting on top of it. An animated poster, displaying the Spiritform logo and their slogan hung on the wall beside the bed. There was a chemical toilet resting on the opposite wall, beside a sink hooked to the grey box of the water reclaimer.

My heart stopped.

There it was. Right at the foot of the bed. My goal.

A standard sized, red-painted desktop unit, hooked up to a holo-screen, a tangle of power and fibre-optic cables spewing out of ports at the rear. The machine was active, whirring quietly and blinking lights, but the display was deactivated, the soft trickling of the water cooling system ringing throughout the bunker. I had focus mode engaged, but I couldn't help but feel a little bit giddy with excitement. The Project Selection files were here. Saved on this machine. Decrypting in the background.

"You can take your time with the PC," Liz informed me. "Search for any backup copies on external media."

She was right. My instructions were to destroy any storage media I found with confirmed copies of the Project Selection files saved on them.

My eyes were already recording and proceeded to turn the place inside out. Checking every possible hiding spot. I didn't find anything under the sink, or any signs of tears in the mattress that could be used to hide something inside.

I proceeded to check the boxes; filled to the brim with sheets of smart paper… mostly with pre-saved porn videos loaded up. A pair of Thai girls were shaking their boobs at me on the top page.

"Jesus. How many screens does it take for this guy to get a hard-on?" I scoffed.

I laughed at my own joke… then froze suddenly.

One sheet seemed to stick out from the untidy pile, despite its noticeable lack of adult content. I pinched the corner of the sheet and pulled it out. It was displaying a still shot, taken from inside what appeared to be a dilapidated Victorian pub, converted into a hacker-den; power and network cables hanging loosely from the ceiling just like here. There were five people around the bar, holding pint glasses up to the camera. Most of the faces I didn't recognise, and a visual scan didn't ID them either, unsurprisingly. There was only one face I knew straight away. Denise; pint in one hand, a spliff in the other. Even back in the day, it was a rare sight to see her looking so merry.

I gave a single small laugh, remembering the times we used to get high together. The rest of us would chill the fuck out, but she would get so bloody deep and serious, it was a mood kill. Maybe she'd finally found her niche.

That could've been me…

My head tingled. Focus mode squashed the nostalgia. The longing for the past faded away… but I pocketed the photo anyway and went back to the task at hand. I searched everywhere but couldn't find any hidden external media.

So, I knelt by the machine and shifted it from side to side, scrutinizing it. Unsurprisingly it had its own thermite booby-trap. One wrong move and the whole thing would be reduced to molten slag. I'd have to disable it before I could access the internal memory drive.

"Tricky…" I muttered.

I held down the power switch and waited for the lights to go off and the sound of the cooling system to die out, before reaching for my left thigh, and with a click and a whir the hidden compartment inside my leg opened up, where I was storing my claytronic tool. I issued a telepathic command to the device and morphed it into the form a screwdriver; I pressed it into one of the bolts holding the side panel of the PC's casing.

With the screws out, I could now remove the panel… but one wrong move and it would detonate. I was about to find out if my bionic hands really were as steady as advertised.

"Here goes…" I breathed anxiously.

I cautiously inched the panel open… just a crack to reveal the extra wires that had been jury-rigged together, and the faint glow of a green LED. I pressed down on the panel to hold its place and took aim with my wrist laser.

I let out a long breath as the moment of truth came and fired the laser… cutting through a red wire. In a moment of relief, the green LED inside flickered off.

"Oh, thank fuck…" I sighed, suddenly relieved that this hadn't all been a massive waste of time.

I pulled the panel away, exposing the jumble of wires hooked to the motherboard. The crystalline memory drive, Nanotube-CPU, and cooling system. The circuits were sapphire blue, millions of superconducting graphene nodes with their fading bright white glow as the last of its power drained out. The cursor on my HUD focused on the memory drive. I placed the tool back inside the leg compartment, disconnected the I/O port to the motherboard, and pulled the cube from its tray slot.

I held the drive flat on my palm, admiring it. I quickly jacked it into my watch to begin a scan to verify the files were on there. A formality at this point.

Somewhere in there, stored down on the molecular level was knowledge worth killing for. I'd literally bled for this fucking thing. Part of me wanted to smash it right now, but my contract required a live-feed of me doing it. I'd have to wait for a better signal before…

"Hold on!" Liz cried suddenly. "SpyFly is picking up someone approaching."

Shit.

"Show me!"

The video feed from the drone loaded to my vision. The camera zoomed in close to the garden; revealing the pale shimmer of someone in optical camouflage, creeping towards the garden door. Gotta hand it to Spiritform; they were well equipped.

I was boxed in. Trapped. But I had the upper hand. The element of surprise was on my side… and I was packing heat.

I smirked, pocketing the memory drive. With a whir, my right thigh compartment opened. I gripped the weight of the revolver and drew it out. I turned off the light switch and kept the live feed from SpyFly in the bottom right corner of my HUD. I casually strolled to the end of the mattress and eased myself down to sit, hiding in the shadows, resting my gun hand on top of my right knee, locked firmly to aim at the hatchway, watching like a patient predator, as the cloaked spectre drew closer to the trap door.

He reached for the handle.

I closed the video feed, while the rusty creak of the trap door's hinge stung my ears.

A ray of moonlight shone through. The shimmer of the invisibility camouflage passed through the ray of light, footsteps ringing the ladder like an instrument.

"Freeze, bitch," I told him calmly.

"Jesus!" the dark figure cried, the distortions waving oddly in the air.

"Do what I say, and you won't find out if he's real today," I continued in an authoritative tone, without raising my voice. "Turn off the cloak and keep your hands on the ladder."

He remained silent.

"You *can* see the revolver, right?" I scoffed, pointing to the triangular barrel of my weapon.

Another pause, then the optical illusions began to fade, and a figure appeared. The optical camouflage suit covered his entire body, a cross between a silver one-piece suit and a poncho, his face hidden behind a mask of the same material. He also wore goggles necessary to see while cloaked, the lenses reminiscent of composite insect eyes, filled with filters in a hexagonal pattern.

"Come on down," I ordered him. "Nice and slow."

He grudgingly did as he was told, muttering under his breath as he climbed. I pressed the light switch beside the bed again.

"Hands above your head. Turn around. Nice and easy," I barked when he was finished cautiously descending to the foot of the ladder.

He gingerly raised his arms off the rung and put them in the air, turning 180 to face me.

"Take the mask off. Slowly."

He carefully pulled back the baggy, silvery hoody and balaclava, removing the camo-googles. He had gene-dyed spiky white hair, tall and lanky, baring his teeth like an angry dog.

"FireSaint, I presume?" I smirked.

"Like you don't already know," he hissed back. He eyed me up and down. "You're IronRoot aren't you? Destiny's… ex?"

Focus mode squashed the nagging guilt I should've felt.

"Last time I checked, Denise was her real name," I answered flatly. "What about you?"

He clamped his jaw tight. I gave him a flat shrug.

"Look, mate, you're already in a bit of a pickle here. I've already collected plenty of DNA samples, so I'll ID you one way or the other when I get round to it. But I'd rather let this go a little more smoothly."

His fiery eyes didn't let up, but he must've realised how futile it was to argue the point.

"Simon," he grumbled back at me.

"Nice to meet you, Simon," I replied warmly. "I'm Arthur." I gestured to my gun. "And this here is the 105-E Magnum. And if you don't give me exactly what I want, you and him are about to get very well acquainted."

"Did your VPA suggest that joke?" he snarled back at me. "Tell me something. I've always wondered how much money it would take someone to betray their friends?"

"Buddy, you've got a gun on you," I scoffed confidently, shaking my head. "You really want to start pushing my buttons?"

"I have an inquisitive mind," he quipped back. "What do you want?'

"Now that is the question." I smiled mockingly at him, pulling out the memory cube from my pocket and waving to him. "My orders were simply to destroy your copy of the files. They honestly weren't too fussed about arresting you guys. The one who *actually* hacked them is lying on a slab in the morgue."

He subtly gulped nervously.

"And before you go trying to buy yourself some time; my rootkit on your PC checked the download logs. I know the data was sent straight to you, and you alone. So, you can forget the cock and bull with having back-ups galore."

"Screw you," he spat.

"Oh, don't be like that," I teased. "There's no reason why we can't both profit from this."

"Do I look like a guy who cares about profit?" he scoffed, gesturing his hands out at the surrounding shithole of a bunker.

"I guess not," I sniffed, turning my nose up at it. "But you *do* look like a guy keen on keeping out of jail."

He glowered at me again.

"Do I look stupid? No way I'm getting out of that now."

"Oh, I don't know…" I continued slowly. "In my line of work… you can never have enough contacts."

He raised an eyebrow.

"You want me to be your *snitch?*' he cried with exasperation.

"Think of it more as being my… underworld contact."

"Or your *bitch*?"

I shrugged coyly.

"Like I said, no reason we can't both profit from it."

He shook his head exasperatingly.

"All right!" he barked, clearly not ready to believe me. "Enlighten me!"

"You ever heard of a hacker called Dart?" I checked.

He shook again.

"Well he's heard of you," I informed him. "Got a nice little cache of your encryption archetypes. That's how I found you guys in the first place." My mouth curled up. "I'm prepared to show you what he's got on you. But trust… has to go both ways."

He scoffed, shaking his head.

"And in return?"

"We'll cross that bridge when we get to it," I said coolly.

"And why exactly should I trust a single word oozing out of your cunt mouth?" he sneered at me, his eyes becoming angry slits. "I know what you did to Denise, you…"

"What I did *for* Denise," I barked back. "Believe it or not I did what I could to keep her from being picked up again. If I hadn't taken GCHQ's deal, she'd be rotting in the prison matrix next to her father!"

"Yeah, keep telling yourself that," he laughed at me.

My grip on my revolver tightened.

"Decision time, mate," I growled.

Another, single flat chuckle in my face.

"You haven't been paying attention, *mate*." He nudged his head in the direction of the poster behind me. "What does that say?"

I didn't move an inch.

"We are Spiritform," he proclaimed proudly, standing up tall and puffing his chest. "We are everywhere. We are nowhere. I'll die before you get what you want!"

I was disappointed but wasn't going to let him know that, my face still a blank slate.

"Sorry you feel that way," I continued flatly. "But ya gotta do, what ya gotta…"

I wanted to keep going… but couldn't. My jaw stuck open stupidly.

What the fuck?

Simon's hands were still in the surrender position, but he raised a puzzled eyebrow at me.

"Hey… what's wrong? You epileptic or something?" he asked, sounding genuinely concerned.

Something *was* wrong with me. Very wrong. I couldn't finish my sentence. Physically unable to complete. I wasn't in control of my own body. Unable to shut my mouth, straining as I tried. I was panicking inside my head, but couldn't bring myself to say or do anything about. My jaw and neck felt had been frozen in place, a blank expression locked at Simon. Static began flickering cross my HUD, screwing up my vision.

My gun hand trembled uncontrollably.

Oh no.

I knew what was going on even before the intimidating flashing red message appeared through the static.

<<WARNING!>>

<<WARNING!>>

<<UNAUTHORISED ACCESS TO PERSONAL AREA NETWORK DETECTED!>>

<< NEURAL LACE DRIVERS HAVE BEEN COMPROMISED!>>

Oh, fuck no!

There was a hacker running around in my brain! I could feel the software spreading like the tentacles of an octopus, corrupting my mind, turning my synapses against me, my consciousness pushed aside like I was watching a movie of my own life playing out in front of me. My limbs became little more than the gangling appendages of a string puppet.

No… stop! Stop, dammit!

I tried resisting, but it was utterly futile; my thumb flicked off the gun's safety.

No, no, no!

"Whoa! Whoa! Come on, there's no need for that!" Simon panicked, his head spinning around looking for a way to escape.

"Liz?? Liz! Are you there??" I cried telepathically.

The frantic face of her avatar emerged through the electronic fuzz, clouding my field of view.

"Arth...I...rry...so...in...rive..." her answered crackled over the comm-link.

"Liz, if you can hear me I don't care how this happened, just get this guy outta my fucking brain!"

I mustered all my willpower, helpless to stop myself. Even with my brain screaming, the muscles still jerked to take aim.

"Hey! Hey! Come on, man! The hell happened to due process of law? You can't be serious!" Simon wailed frantically.

Whoever was controlling me didn't care what either of us said. The gun's laser sight activated, and the aiming reticule rezzed onto on my HUD.

I wheeled the triangular barrel towards his head; the graphics following.

<<Target locked-on>>

All his courage had gone, snivelling with his hands covering his eyes not daring to look. With my last ounce of mental strength, I fought the urge to squeeze down; my trigger finger hovering just above it.

"Don't…"

Please! Please just stop!

I was shouting telepathically, in the vain hope the puppeteer was listening and would take pity, that maybe it was just some kid pulling some stupid prank in my mind that had gone horribly wrong.

My power to resist came to an end…

BANG!

The bullet sped out in a single dazzling spark from the barrel. In a split second, the round buried itself into his forehead, projecting a torrent of blood, skull and grey matter cascading across the bunker and my face. The body was thrown backwards with a loud clatter; his arms and legs sprawling out at awkward angles; while a red pool slowly oozed out from the exit wound.

NO! NO! NO!

The room fell desolately silent.

I wanted to yell at the top of my lungs but still couldn't.

I was a murderer now. I hadn't even had a choice in the matter.

The nightmare wasn't over yet.

I found myself shakily dropping my revolver… my attention turning to the optical memory cube in the other hand.

"FUCK! NO, FUCK! I still need to verify the contents!" I cried at Liz. "Whatever you're going to do, do it quick!"

Through the static on my HUD, a pop-up window appeared.

<<AVG-Neuro anti-virus online>>

<<Initializing diagnostic scan>>

<<3% complete>>

I clenched the cube. I increased the pressure in my fingers, clamping down hard… noticeable dents starting to appear in it.

<<27% complete>>

It wasn't long before I heard crackling sounds, like walking on broken glass, shortly before they were crushed like a coke can; bursting open with a slew of wires and a spray of quartz crystal shards.

SHIT!

<<56% complete>>

I tossed away the remnants of the drives against my will, rising from my seat on the filthy bed, like a telekinetic force dragging me over to the body, one forced footstep at a time. The soles of my boots became smothered by the sticky pool of blood.

<<82% complete>>

The hacker knelt me down beside Simon's body; his dead eyes fixated on the concrete ceiling with a haunting gaze.

Oh God, what now?

Against my will, my arm extended to reach for the camouflage suit's zip. I pulled it back and opened the suit; revealing the blue t-shirt underneath. I drew it up and exposed his scrawny torso.

Oh no… Oh, please, fuck no!

I pulled back my right sleeve… and engaged the wrist laser.

Please! For the love of God, stop!

My arm shakily directed my wrist to take aim at the base of his throat. I wanted to shut my eyes to what came next. He wouldn't let me.

He wants me to watch…

The power coursed through my arm. The laser fired and burned into the flesh. It left behind a thick incision with the precision of a surgeon, the skin peeling open like an orange. Putrid blood began bubbling to the surface. With mechanical stability, I slid the beam downwards at a perfect ninety-degree angle, opening a fissure across his ribcage. One by one, the organs started poking through the gap: lungs, heart, intestines. I was horrified; it was like something out of a grotesque slasher flick, the only saving grace that my nasal receptors were still offline.

He telepathically turned off the laser and drew back my wrist. The ridges of the incisions sizzling like bacon. The hacker left me in my catatonic state, staring into the bloody abyss.

Just when I thought it couldn't get any worse… it did.

My hand drew towards the incision, my metal fingertips embracing the fleshy, bloody fold.

No… don't you fucking dare, NO!

My hand slipped inside the wound. I felt sick to my stomach, as the wet, warm remains began swamping around my fingers. I wanted to scream and throw up, but control of my throat was still locked out from me.

MAKE IT STOP!

MAKE IT STOP, MAKE IT STOP, MAKE IT STOP!!!!

<<100% complete>>

<<1 threat detected>>

<<Moving malware to vault>>

The static disappeared from my HUD. The invisible strings had been cut, control of my body returned. My legs felt like they had turned to jelly. I collapsed, panting on the floor, and shrivelled into the foetal position.

"Oh God… oh God…"

Tears of stress and relief were released with each jittering breath I drew. That had to be the worst experience of my life. My head was pounding, feeling like I'd been literally mind-raped. Violated in a way, I never thought possible. I clenched the side of my skull, trying to steady myself as I struggled to get back onto all fours; only to pull the hand away immediately, realising I'd just splattered myself even more with the blood on my palm. Before I knew it, I was hunched over, wrenching the contents of my stomach on to the floor. Liz appeared, frantically checking my vital signs from my bio-monitor sensors.

"Are you all right?" she asked me, sympathetically.

"Do I *look* all right to you?!" I cried telepathically, spitting out the phlegm substance in my stomach.

I collapsed on my ass, staring at the gruesome mess before me, frantically rubbing my hand on the mattress trying to get the stains off like I was Lady goddamn Macbeth. It was just like that night in that clinic… and I'd promised myself I'd never feel that way again.

But this was *worse*.

I took another sickening look at the body…

What have I done?

I'd killed that guy in self-defence… but this was straight-up murder, and I wasn't even really the one responsible!

But that *didn't* help.

"It's not your fault…" she tried to comfort me.

"I know that!" I hissed. "What the fuck happened?!"

"I'm analysing the malware now," she explained. "It looks like it was installed a while ago, but was activated by a local wireless drive-by download."

"Local?" I breathed. "You mean it didn't come from the internet?"

She nodded at me. If that were true, then whoever did this to me would have had to have been within wireless range to scan me.

I knew it!

"I *told you!"* I cried at Liz. "I told you someone was following me!"

I'd never seen an AI look so guilty before.

"I… I'm sorry…" she apologised profusely, solemnly bowing her head in programmed shame.

I started screaming at her telepathically, a great roar of volcanic rage that I couldn't help. If the world could hear my thoughts, it would've been seismic. Not much of it made sense; I couldn't even really blame her, but I couldn't help it. I had to take it out on someone.

Liz's reactions changed, from wallowing in self-pity to flaring up with angry concern for my behaviour.

"Arthur, get a grip!" she cried.

She dialled up focus mode to full, quelling the rage. My breathing became slow and controlled. I lowered my fists and wiped away the tears of rage.

"S...Sorry..." I sighed.

"I don't blame you," she nodded understandingly at me. "But we need to be constructive. It's the only way you'll get out of this."

I nodded slowly, working up the courage again to look at the body. The flow of bodily fluids streaming out of the wound… a laser incision. Something eerily familiar about it.

It clicked in my mind.

"Jack-21," I muttered. "Whoever did this, wanted to frame me as Jack-21."

Liz nodded with deep concern.

"That is a logical conclusion," she admitted out. "The hacker must've known you have that laser scalpel. Makes you an ideal candidate for a fall guy."

"Great," I growled bitterly, gripping my wrist laser.

I needed legal advice. And I needed it fast.

"Call Gabrielle… let's see if Virtualife will honour the client protection clause in my contract," I grumbled, knowing full well that Gabrielle might have been watching through my eyes.

<<Calling Gabrielle Phillips>>

The sound of ringing in my head. I was waiting for about a minute before:

<<Call Rejected>>

"Cow!" I spat, slamming my metallic fist into the wall hard enough to bend it out of shape.

"Hate to say it, but I'm not surprised," she admitted. "They're probably deleting all the evidence they hired you as we speak."

And that's when it hit me. Like a cartoon light-bulb going off above my head, bringing the horrible realisation.

"Liz… you don't think, they're the ones who hacked me?' I asked her slowly.

From the look on her face, I could tell she was worried I was right.

"Most likely," she answered cautiously. "The mission parameters were to recover the Project Selection files… but now the only person who might have actually seen the data..."

"Is dead… and I've just destroyed the only evidence of what they've been doing…" I said telepathically, grinding my teeth. "I'm the fucking fall guy!"

It was all too perfect. I go down for the crime, and they get away with everything! As usual! It made too much sense. It had to be true.

"I want you to look at my memories and digital history since I took this case up," I ordered her. "Keep an eye out for anyone who's been looking into me, and compile a list of any other suspects who could be behind this."

"I'll prioritise it later, but there are bigger problems we need to be worrying about," she pointed out.

I looked grimly over the mess in front of me.

"If you've got any ideas on body disposal, that'd be…"

"Too late for that," she warned me. "The GPS transmitter embedded in his clothes has gone online."

My jaw dropped with horror at the body.

"I thought you said…"

"He must've programmed it to start transmitting only when his bio-monitor sensors flatlined. It's giving out an un-encrypted fatality beacon. Mother Mind *will* pick it up."

The reality started to sink in: *I'm a wanted criminal; in a surveillance state.*

"Oh shit!" I cried, crumpling my hat.

My mind was racing; trying to find a solution.

"What if I give myself up?" I panicked. "They could scan my memory on RE:Call and…"

"You of all people should know memories can be altered," she told me sternly. "Besides, you've already broken at least twenty laws! Not to mention the official secrets act!"

Fuck me, I'd forgotten that!

I could feel the trap closing in on me.

"I'm not hearing a solution?!?!" I panicked bitterly.

"I've already deactivated your location data… but you will need to go into hiding," she deadpanned.

"*Where?!?*" I scoffed sarcastically.

Seven years at GCHQ and not once did I consider the possibility that *I* would be hiding from Mother Mind. Liz directed me towards the body, highlighting Simon's neural lace headset and his smartwatch.

"If you hurry; I can hi-jack the gold tooth connection to the headset and extract his memory before it begins to deteriorate," she explained.

"So?!?

"I can get Denise's contact info with it!" she explained.

"*Denise?!*" I exclaimed in disbelief, unsure I'd heard her right. "I just murdered one of her friends!"

"The police have been trying to catch her for six years. If you need a hide-out, she seems like the go-to person."

"Don't be stupid!" I cried, pointing towards the body. "She'll kill me if I…"

"They want to expose Virtualife!" she interrupted abruptly. "Without the Project Selection files, they have no leads! The only clue they have now is the virus that just infected you."

I bit my lip. It was a long shot. A *really* long shot.

"It's either that, or you wait here to get arrested," she deadpanned.

I dragged my soaking palm down my bearded chin with frustration.

"Well, when you put it like that," I cringed.

I jumped off the bed, kneeling beside the body. I took one last guilty look in the lifeless eyes, muttering an apology to him. I pulled back the suit's hood, exposing the main module of the headset and grabbed a USB 7G-relay and plugged it in. I couldn't stay here long; I could only hope that Liz could run the program over the net before the feds found the body.

<<Connecting to 7G-Relay>>

<<Connected>>

<<Initialising HeadJacker08 program>>

<<Running device drivers>>

<<Configuring scan parameters>>

<<Ready to begin neural scan>>

<<Scanning: 0%>>

"All right, that's it!" Liz informed me. "Get going! I'll keep the program running!"

I forced myself away from the guilt of the murder and dashed back towards the ladder. I gripped the first rung when I saw something…

Something was hanging from the ceiling, besides the hatchway, once more hidden by the shimmer of optical camouflage.

A drone.

The hack came from a local source!

"There you are, you bastard!" I spat at it, whipping my gun out again.

The wavy image scurried away.

"Oh, no you don't!"

I fired off a shot; once more reverberating around the bunker.

Sparks flew with a metallic ricocheting clang. I'd nicked it! A cascade of static washed over the camouflaged outline of the unit, but it was still on the move.

"Get back here!" I growled, springing up the ladder like a jackrabbit.

I returned to the darkness outside just in time to see the drone fly away, just as it de-cloaked. The stark monstrosity of the machine stuck me hard.

"What the hell?" I gawped.

It was an insectoid model, resembling a stag-beetle, but it was freakishly big, about the size of a terrier dog, propelled by a set of helicopter propellers, and possessed three pairs of creepy, hook-like legs. I could just about see the pincers at the front… large enough to crush a man's skull.

I tried taking aim, but Liz warned me not to fire out in the open now.

"Dammit!" I spat.

She frowned as my HUD ran the scan.

"I don't recognise the model," she concluded. "Probably a custom home build."

I squinted at it… unconvinced for some reason.

"I swear I've seen it be…"

My cochlear implants picked up the sound of sirens blazing away in the distance.

"Go, now!" she cried at me. "I'll bring the car around!"

My ears picked up something else through the background noise: sirens and the rapid hum of more helicopter propellers. A police Buzzer drone emerged from behind the terraced houses, blue and white lights flashing from the eagle-sized machine whizzing overhead.

"Attention citizen Arthur Wells!" boomed a harsh, electronic voice the loudspeakers built into it. "This is the police! Drop your weapons and raise your hands above your head!"

The machine gun turret mounted on its undercarriage swivelled at me, the ominous glow of a targeting laser whirling over my vest.

"You have ten seconds to comply!" the drone sounded out again. "Failure to comply will result in the authorised use of deadly force!"

"It's not fucking about, Liz," I growled at her, keeping my hand firmly by my side.

Adrenaline was running wild in my system.

I wasn't going to give up without a fight.

"10...9...8..."

"It'll avoid incoming fire, but your wrist laser will disorientate its sensors temporarily!" she advised me, placing a target graphic on the unit. "You'll only have a few seconds to get to cover and return fire! The garden shed is the most defensible point!"

"7...6...5..."

"Good a plan as any!" I admitted, my grip tightening around my pistol.

<<Combat mode engaged>>

<<Wrist laser configured to disrupt mode>>

The signals from my pain receptors were inhibited; my body numbed to rock. Ready for the fight to come.

"4...3...2..."

Now or never.

I jumped backwards pre-emptively, expecting the rain of fire coming.

Ratatatatat!

I could feel the air current of the bullets whizzing just past my feet. The enhanced reflexes of combat mode made me feel like I was falling in slow motion; watching as the impact on the ground kicked up chunks of soil and grass, cascading across me.

I landed hard on my back, sending a gush of mud away from me. The pain was dulled by my implants, and through gritted teeth, I whirled my wrist laser up to the sky. The hot beam cut through the air and shone into the drone's optical sensors.

I could hear its engines struggling against the disorientation, the whir of the propellers becoming a high-pitched whine as it fluttered unsteadily. The arc of the machine gun fire became wild and unpredictable, bullets landing either side of the garden; nowhere near me.

It worked!

"Go! Go! Go!" Liz yelled.

I scrambled to my feet and dashed towards the shed, pounding my legs down the stone path. It didn't take long for the drone to straighten its flight path out and open fire again, and I could soon hear the bullets ricocheting once more off the slabs of rock behind me.

I closed in on the shed, and leapt head-first, crashing through the door, landing in a combat roll against the hard, muddy ground, slamming against the far side wall.

I whirled around, the arc of fire drawing towards the door frame. I sprung up to slam the door shut in time and rolled out of the way. The flimsy boards weren't strong enough to hold the assault back. Bullet holes burst through, hurling splinters as they went, colliding with the flower pots and garden tools resting on the shelves on the far side wall with ear-piercing crashing.

I rolled away from the debris, and pressed myself against the metal frame of a workbench to the left, feeling the clang of pottery shards against my arm's casing as I shielded my face. It was only then I noticed the tear in the fabric of my trousers, just below my left hip; seeping with the cocktail of natural and synthetic blood. I inspected the shallow flesh wound; my bio-monitor sensors hadn't detected a massive drop in pressure, but it was gonna sting like hell when I reactivated the pain receptors.

"Lovely!" I snarled, quickly applying a bio-bandage from the holster on my belt.

CRASH!

The window above the workbench was ripped to shreds, sending a shower of glass pouring over my hat and shoulders. I kept myself as small as possible while I pivoted my body around, tip-toeing in my squat-position. I poked my head up, as far as I could without being hit by debris and then…

WHIP!

My hat was thrown back off my head; nicked by one of the bullets.

"Shit!"

It collapsed on the floor; a distinctive hole in the nanofabric. Nothing that wouldn't heal… but they had succeeded in pissing me off.

"Goddammit!"

I spun around and rested my gun hand against the edge of the workbench to steady my aim, the rapid-fire still hurtling overhead.

"Time to go on the offence!" Liz warned me.

<<Lethal-fire mode selected>>

BOOM! BOOM!

I returned fire, but the drone saw it coming; darting from side to side and resuming its onslaught on the shed.

"Slippery bugger!" I snarled.

I had to act fast; at this rate, all it had to do was pin me down long enough for its back-up to arrive.

"Liz, can you use David's Mother Mind cache to hack into it?" I asked her, knowing full well my future depended on her answer.

She brought up my cyberwarfare suite and began intercepting the drone's signals.

"Looks promising; it's running an out of date frequency modulation protocol. I might be able to spoof the signal," she explained.

"How long?!"

"Two minutes to configure my wireless packet sniffer, dedicating maximum possible runtime."

I gritted my teeth. Way too long.

"I'll be dead by then!"

"Got a better suggestion?"

"You're *supposed* to…"

My HUD picked something up; a flicker of silver whirling through the air. Just a tiny glint.

It collided with the drone.

BLAM!

"Jesus!"

I almost jumped out of my skin; without warning, the drone detonated. Engulfed in a fireball that swallowed it whole and sent shrapnel scattering in all directions.

I squatted there, gaping at the unexplained destruction. The drone collapsed into a smouldering pile of scrap metal, the smell of burning silicon rising from the wreckage.

Talk about unexpected.

"Uh…" I said stupidly, blinking disbelievingly at what happened. "Don't suppose you have an explainat…"

I didn't need one. I spotted it.

"Oh… oh wow," I breathed. "He really must be looking out for me…"

Cymurai.

He was standing on the roof of the house.

The armoured avatar stood gleaming in the orange tinge of street lamps, the horns of the helmet sparkling with demonic laser light. His sword was sheathed on his magnetic belt, but his wrist was thrust forward towards me; a metal slot extending out.

I recognised the weapon from online videos; his shuriken launcher. The traditional Japanese steel stars were meant to be hand thrown, but his launcher could spit them out on a spring loader at the speed of a bullet, equipped with explosives.

The avatar launched into an acrobatic leap; propelling himself with his piston-like legs into a graceful acrobatic twirl, he landed elegantly on the patio with a mighty crash of metal against rock. He stood up slowly, the motors in his neck swivelling towards me.

"You can come out now," he called over to me; his growling synthesised voice boomed at me.

He spoke to me!

I wanted to reply, but the words didn't come out. Not sure how to respond, leaving me to stare stupidly from behind the workbench. I was anxious about what to say...he was a crime fighter...and I had just committed murder against my will.

"The alternative is waiting for the police to arrive," he called again. "Your choice."

Touché.

I nervously got back onto my feet, deciding to holster my gun again and keep my hands up just to be on the safe side, before proceeding to shuffle my way out through the disintegrated wooden door, carefully stepping over the flaming wreck, and the bullet-hole riddled grass.

"Look, uh..." I called over cautiously. "I know why you're probably here. But I swear I didn't..."

"Relax," he buzzed back at me, holding up a reassuring hand. "I know you were hacked."

"Y...You do?" I sighed with relief and rolled my shoulder motors to rest my hands by my waist. "Huh... well, thanks, I guess. But... how did you know?"

He nodded, the faceplate of the avatar not revealing any emotion.

"I'm familiar with the virus that was used to infect you. Mother Mind detected it being transmitted across a service provider DNS," he explained gruffly. "I've been tracking it in connection to the Jack-21 investigation."

So, he does have access to Mother Mind... one conspiracy theory confirmed.

I still wanted to press the issue; if he knew the vulnerability that was used to hack my brain it was damn crucial to my defence... but decided it was probably not a good idea to argue with a superhero.

"Not that I don't appreciate it..." I said timidly, still unsure how to address him. "But uh..."

"Don't take it personally," he interjected. "I've been monitoring everyone connected with the murders. I've kept an eye on you ever since you were hired by Virtualife."

Interesting...

"I'm not investigating the Jack-21 murders," I replied with a raised eyebrow.

He tilted his head to the side.

"Aren't you?" he replied cryptically.

I narrowed my eyes with suspicion at him.

"What's that supposed to mean?" I checked.

I waited for a response, but it never came. His head darted to the side; like he'd heard something in the distance. It wasn't long before my ears picked it up; more sirens approaching.

"You have to go," he told me firmly. "Now."

"Whoa! Wait!" I cried. "I thought you said you knew I was innocent!"

"You are," he nodded at me. "And normally the Bushido Code would require me to stand up for justice. But that isn't always a black and white concept."

"Meaning?"

"Meaning for the greater good… it's more advantageous for the police to suspect you for now."

My jaw dropped with sheer unadulterated rage.

"*What*?" I growled.

"You're not Jack-21," Cymurai reassured me. "Before long, the world will know that. But for now; you need to be a suspect."

My mind was exploding. This was not the Cymurai I thought I knew.

"You can't be serious!? *Why?*"

"Jack-21 is dangerous," he said sternly. "More dangerous than you, the police, or anyone else realises. If they go after him, more people will die."

Wait a second…

"You *know* who Jack-21 is?" I checked urgently.

I thought the avatar had frozen, but he soon nodded.

"I don't know where he is, but I will find him and will take him out myself," he informed me sternly. "But it must be me, and only me. Having them chase you… keeps everyone safer."

"The needs of the many, huh?"

"I'm sorry," he apologised, bowing slightly to me. "Truly, I am. I never meant for you to get caught in any of this."

"Finding that hard to believe, mate," I glowered.

"I will do everything I can to keep them off your tail," he reassured me. "But for now, run. Run, and don't look back…"

"Some superhero you are," I snarled.

His gaze lowered to me.

"Go," he repeated, his voice cold and harsh.

"I hate to agree with him, but he's right," Liz grudgingly telepathically pointed out.

I wanted to take a shot at him, but she reassured me that it wouldn't work out well for me.

"This isn't over!" I called, pointing a threatening finger at him.

"I have no doubt," he replied calmly.

I glared at him once more and left.

"Bring the car around!" I cried to her.

I spun on my heels, and dashed to the garden fence, springing over it and leaving him in the dust. I landed in a puddle on the other side and pounded my feet down the pavement. The sirens weren't far behind now. My car reversed and came to a screeching stop by the exit to the narrow passage. I telepathically unlocked it and popped the doors open.

I hopped inside and landed in the passenger seat, slamming the door behind me.

A police car turned off the high street and began pulling up.

"Go!" I telepathically yelled at Liz.

The engine roared to life, the rear tyres howling as they rapidly gained traction. We tore down the street, speeding head-on just as the officers stepped out of their car.

I saw the police jumping for their lives, watching them rolling hard against the pavement in the rear mirror. The car skidded around the corner, clipping the lights of a street-cleaning droid, zooming towards Uxbridge Road. I pulled myself into the driver's seat against the force of the inertia.

<<Manual control engaged>>

I grabbed the steering wheel and slammed my foot down on the accelerator, revving. The scenes outside my windows – broken-down shops, the homeless sleeping rough – became nothing but blurs as we raced past, the tarmac of the road whizzing towards me.

A video feed from the rear-view cameras popped up on the windscreen. The officer had climbed back inside the car and was now in pursuit, the sirens and lights blazing obnoxiously behind me. I spun the wheel to the left and skidded out onto Uxbridge Road. There wasn't much traffic so I could go at top speed, but the police were hot on my heels and closing. I ran a red light at a junction, sending out a roar of angry horns and the groaning of brakes.

He wasn't giving up that easy, following straight through like a lion after its prey.

"Liz, if you've got anything now's the time!" I cried, throwing in a few zig-zags to keep them off my tail.

"I'm on it!" Liz snapped at me. "I can use the Mother Mind vulnerabilities to access the traffic management network and the drone control software. I might be able to use it to slow them down."

Two separate notifications appeared:

<<Accessing Transport for London, Road traffic management server>>

<<IP target identified: 16.32.98.104.07.43>>

<<Configuring attack payload>>

<<Connecting>>

<<Uploading attack payload>>

<<Initialising PacketPredator>>

<<Configuring attack payload>>

<<Scanning target IP: 21.78.199.36.15.34>>

<<Intercepting packets>>

<<Uploading attack payload>>

If her plan worked, the traffic grid and the police drones would be at my disposal. It might just give me the upper hand I needed…

I can do this… I can do this…

SMASH!

I ducked down as the boot window of the car became a waterfall of glass shards, spraying across the back seats; the blare of machine gun fire rang through the gap, with rapid metallic pings against the hull. I checked my mirrors: another Buzzer drone was in pursuit, its own sirens blazing while it targeted my tyres.

"Shit!"

No way my insurance is covering that…

"Keep it busy while I run the program!" she advised me.

I muttered bitterly under my breath, grabbing my revolver again and tossing my hat onto the passenger seat next to me.

"Take the wheel!" I ordered.

<<Auto-driver engaged>>

I telepathically opened the car's skylight and reached for a handle on the ceiling, hoisting myself up to stand upright. The night wind came flapping in through the open window, ruffling my spiky hair as I popped my head through; my cheeks would've been stung by the winter air if not for the combat mode inhibitions.

I was ready to take aim… when the drone's targeting laser wheeled towards me.

"Fuck!"

I ducked to the side, in time to avoid the next flurry of bullets that came crashing through the skylight into the dashboard, reducing the holo-display into a blurry wreck.

"Stop messing up my car!!!" I yelled stupidly at the drone.

The auto-driver whizzed around a corner to the right, the inertia hurling my body to the side; the sound of the bullet impacts changing from the loud clang of metallic impacts against my car, to a series of soft thuds against the tarmac as the drone lost its aim.

Now!

I shoved myself up through the hatch, pulling my revolver out with me. Liz placed a bulls-eye a few degrees to the left of my targeting reticule, having calculated the drone's evasive manoeuvre.

Its machine gun swivelled, the flash of laser targeting flashed over me…

BOOM!

I fired in time. Liz's calculations were right; the drone wheeled to the left, moving into my line of fire, clipping its wing with a bright flash. The rotor was thrown clear off, whizzing like a throwing star and crashing through a shop window. The drone began flapping uncontrollably, until it went into a downward spiral, crashing in a heap.

My HUD highlighted another one swooping in from the east. I turned my gun towards it when…

"Look out!" Liz cried.

WHAM!

I felt the impact; an aggressive crunch of glass and metal hurling my body to the right and colliding with the rim of the sunroof. I whirled around and saw the police car had caught up and was trying to ram us off the road.

WHAM!

The next impact sent me collapsing back into my seat.

"Hang on!" Liz cried, wheeling us onto Greenford high street as I clenched the roof of the car, the stink of burning rubber rising from the road.

The car's sensors detected an oncoming *Volvo*, looming in my windscreen. She swerved to the right in time. The van slammed on its brakes, and the sound of its drawn-out honking whizzed past me. The police car wasn't so lucky and went drifting into its bumper with a mighty crunch.

I watched it shrinking away into the horizon, struggling to reverse.

"Mind yer step!" I jeered back at them, pumping my fist into the air.

"I wouldn't get cocky yet if I were you!" Liz warned me.

She brought up a reading from the car's sensors; another drone was fast approaching from the rear, accompanied by three more police cars. They wouldn't stop coming unless Liz was ready for that cyber-attack.

"Liz!?" I cried.

"Got it!" she called back happily.

<<Upload complete>>

<<Access to drone control program successful>>

<<Transferring control to DroneKing App>>

The drone wobbled in the air, a slight moment of confusion for the AI as it was registered into my control software, but soon regained its flight form. My HUD began projecting an extra layer of icons over objects around me, loaded with commands for the drone. I ordered it to identify the police cars as enemies; authorising it to open fire on their tyres. The drone's turret swivelled and opened fire.

Ratatatatatatat!

BANG!

The front tyres were ripped to shreds with the explosive force of depressurisation; their auto-drivers rapidly attempted to compensate for the damage, but couldn't hold it, and ended up crashing into the brick fence of someone's front garden. The car in the rear was more fortunate, wheeling round in time to avoid the arc of fire, and it didn't look like I was going to get a second shot at it.

<<Warning!>>

<<Security measures updating in 10 seconds>>

The drone's anti-virus was trying to boot me out of the system. In a few seconds, I would lose control of it altogether. I decided to deny it the opportunity, ordering it to crash into the windscreen of one of the other cars. The police driver swerved out of its flight path in time, sending the drone crashing into the tarmac.

Suppose that'll have to do…

<<Manual Control Engaged>>

CRASH!

I lurched forward violently, slamming me into the steering column. Another car had pulled out and was on my ass, trying like hell to ram me again.

"God damn, they're persistent!"

<<Upload to traffic network complete>>

<<Access granted>>

"I'm into the traffic network!" Liz announced triumphantly.

Anybody else in my position would've been screwed… but I was coming up fast on another set of junctions. The traffic lights had just turned red again, the cars in my lane waiting patiently, while the ones on the cross-junction glided gracefully across. One by one Liz placed icons over each of the lights; ready for me to interface with them.

I can turn them red or green at my will…

"You thinking what I'm thinking?" I asked Liz with a smirk, watching the feds trailing behind.

She nodded at me with a smirk. I neuroclicked on the icon above the junction and watched a whirling round icon as I transmitted the command codes.

<<Command received>>

The lights turned green for me. The traffic on the junction cleared and my lane began to flow. I pushed the car to the max, revving the engine angrily, tyres screeching as I swung the car over to the right. There was a mighty bump as I jumped over the curb and mounted the pavement.

I rammed my fist against the horn, sending a pair of drunks on the street jumping for their lives while my windshield was plastered with the crap hurled towards it as I knocked down dozens of recycling bins. My windscreen wipers pushed it out the way with heavy, wet thuds.

I watched the police car in the rear-view mirror, closing in closer and closer to the junction as well… I had to time this just right…

Wait for it… wait for it… wait for it…

"Now!"

<<Command received>>

The traffic lights on the junction turned green at once. Without the guidance of the traffic network, the auto-drivers headed out at once, resulting in an inevitable clusterfuck. With a symphony of screeching brakes, the four-way junction jammed up completely. The police car swerved hard, the tyres howling as it came to a stop, colliding relatively softly against a green *Honda.*

I slammed my fist against the dashboard with a guttural celebratory grunt.

But looking up at the CCTV plastered across every lamppost and street corner, I could tell it was only a small victory.

"I need to get out of sight!" I cried.

"I can scramble the local surveillance grid, but you'll need to buy me the time to run the program!"

"And how the fuck do I do that?"

"You're not going to like it," she admitted.

"Just tell me!"

The HUD map plotted out a route avoiding all the major junctions from here to the River Brent. She used flashing red, yellow and green icons to mark out the positions of every set of traffic lights along the route. The route took a turn *off* the bridge, and into the river itself.

"Hope you're in the mood to go swimming," she pointed out.

I gritted my teeth.

"Damn. Forgot my trunks!"

My heart was pounding, adrenaline coursing through my system. I was a man on the run, but I felt like the bloody king of the world right now. I laughed out loud uncontrollably, as the car rolled down the hill of Ruislip Road at high speed towards the bridge across.

My eyes widened…

Another pair of drones had landed on either side of the road fifty metres ahead of me. They were spread out; no weapons, just a couple of clamps holding a spike strip trap from either end, spreading it across the tarmac. The drones released the clamps, leaving the trap behind, waiting for me to run over them…

The spikes glistened in the rain.

<<DANGER!>>

Alarm bells telepathically went off inside my head; I thrust down with all my might on the brakes, feeling the grinding high-pitched groan and the g-force. I edged closer and closer.

"OH SHIIIIIIIIIIIT!" I cried out as my front wheels crossed the threshold.

BOOM!

The bang was deafening as my tires were shredded. I lost control with enough force to throw the whole front of the car into the air.

The world whirled around me. Blood rushed to my head sending me dizzy as the road stretched out below me; everything in the cabin twirling in chaos. My *McDonald's* cup flew past. The car went into an emergency response mode; my seatbelt tightened automatically, keeping me locked on the spot. My arms were thrown off the wheel. Shards of glass sent into a whirlwind around my face.

CCCRRRRRRASHHH!

The car landed upside down; the airbag burst out from the dashboard and expanded to fill up the driver's seat in the blink of an eye. The sunroof collapsed inwards, the last remaining windows cracked beyond recognition with a sickening crunch. An ear-piercing screech ripped through the air as I skidded forward, twirling, sparks spraying against the tarmac.

Gradually I came to a painful stop.

For the first time in what seemed like forever, there was silence… aside from the ringing in my ears.

My implants tuned out the feedback. I awakened to the bizarre sensation of dangling upside down, blood rushing to my head with half my face buried in the airbag. The dashboard was busted; the chassis cracked to hell.

My body was aching like I'd been beaten up, head pulsing with disorientation. My HUD was trying to display the readout from my bio-monitors, through the veil of static clouding my vision.

My bionic eyelids felt like lead weights, drooping while the world slipped away into darkness.

I wanted to quit. Let it take me now. Come what may; I really didn't feel like there was a point to this anymore.

"Arth....*bzz*...ca...*crrrr.*ou.*zzz*...ear...e?"

Liz's voice crackled through the interference… it was harsh and loud like a broken alarm clock.

<<Neural lace disrupted>>

<<Initiating emergency reboot>>

"Uhh…" I groaned.

"You can sleep in the Prison Matrix if you like!" she snapped once the static cleared.

That snapped me back into focus. I spat out the blood in my mouth and brushed away the shards of glass. I saw another pair of police cars speeding towards me through the gaping hole where the back window had been.

"Arthur, MOVE!" she yelled at me.

I heaved myself upwards, reaching for my seat belt, struggling against the tide of gravity. Eventually, I wrapped my fingers around it and pressed the big red manual release button. The belt recoiled back with a mechanical clicking and reeling sound. I tumbled through the air again, landing hard on my back with a crunch against the overturned roof, the pain numbed by my implants.

Liz placed a south-facing waypoint guide on my display, following the flow of the River Brent's current. I dragged my body across the crumpled surface, forcing myself through the mess and out through the windshield gap, and collapsing out onto the tarmac; the wind and the rain pattering against my skin felt like a relief but was far from it.

The battered police cars tore around the corner at the top of the hill behind me.

"Go! Go! Go!" Liz cried as I reached back through the hatchway to grab my hat again, stuffing it into my coat pocket.

I glanced to my left, out over the stone railing across the bridge, the expanse of the River Brent stretching out before, with willow tree branches overhanging it and dangling into the water. I started taking in long, sharp, deep breaths, getting as much oxygen into my blood supply as physically possible; my artificial blood was more effective at absorbing– with just a few gulps I'd have enough O_2 to stay underwater for four hours.

I didn't have long to ready myself.

The sound of slamming brakes screeched behind me. I glanced back in time to see armed response officers bursting out of parked cars, dressed in power armour and brandishing assault rifles; the heavy steel boots of their exoskeletons stomping against the tarmac.

Oh shit.

With every ounce of strength left, I scrambled to my feet and dashed towards the railing.

"FREEZE!" a harsh voice yelled.

I ignored it, vaulting over the railing.

RATATATAT!

The automatic fire stung the air from behind me; bullets whizzing past my ear as I leapt over the edge. Gravity took hold; plunging to the murky brown river.

SPLASH!

The water was fucking freezing; stinging like an ice-pick into my skin; the muffled sound of bullets rapidly plopping against the water around me.

I swam for my life.

Mother Mind profile 2446-7128-5978-2501:

<<New data received>>>
<<Updating...>>
<<Update complete>>

First name: Arthur
Surname: Wells
Status: Wanted for criminal offences
Criminal Record:

- Wanted: 07/10/2045
    - Offence: Prime suspect in Jack-21 case
- Arrested: 17/11/2037
    - Offence: Suspected of unauthorised access to computer material
    - No formal charges

CHAPTER 18

Mother Mind profile 3236-1187-7241-9852:

First name: Emma
Surname: Golem
Status: Living
Nationality: British citizen
Occupation(s):

- Special Forces Private Security Contractor
  - Status: Employed
  - Organisation: Global Arms Incorporated

Criminal record:

- Convicted: 25/07/2033
  - Offence: Possession of synthetic cocaine (Class-A narcotic) with intent to supply
  - Sentence: 9 months' incarceration (Lockwood Juvenile Correctional Facility)

Known aliases:

- N/A

Live surveillance:

- Status: *Partially available*
- Date: 08/10/2045
- Current location: Virtualife building, Docklands, East London
- Local Time: 00:13 GMT

<<Memory playback in progress>>

The eleven-year-old me slumped my head against the cold, moist glass of the train carriage. The decaying countryside raced past, heading back from Birmingham after the swimming gala. After my so-called third place 'victory.' I was sitting in a roomy compartment with my parents, a set of four seats arranged to look at each other with a panoramic view of the rotting nature outside.

I was exhausted, arms aching, the smell of chlorine emanating from my hair after the event. My nose was running, my eyes burning red… and not from the mild chemical effect.

"Here," my mother said firmly, pushing a tissue in my direction, looking over her vid-glasses, her curly brown hair resting on her shoulders.

I nodded silently, taking the tissue and blowing unenthusiastically.

A robotic food trolley rolled down the aisle in the centre of the carriage, taking orders verbally and through the *Virgin* train's app. A dispenser on the top of the machine delivered food like a dumbwaiter.

"Can I get you anything?" the electronic voice grated on the trolley.

My father's kind eyes brightened in his rounded, bald head.

"Got any ice cream?" he asked with a gruff South London accent.

"Yes sir," the unit replied, projecting a menu on a holo-screen.

He gave me a warm grin and nudged his head towards the selection. I stared disinterestedly at the list.

"No thanks," I said weakly.

The trolley wheeled itself away. Dad gave me an exhausted glance.

"Come on, honey, you can't sulk forever," he spoke wearily.

I slammed my fist on my armrest, screeching loudly, getting a few annoyed heads turning my way through the carriage. My mother threw him a harsh glare, knowing that was the wrong thing to say.

"It's not fair!" I whined loudly.

"Emma!" my mother snapped, pressing her fingers to her lips hurriedly.

My father, apparently a little embarrassed, held his hands up defensively to try to calm me.

"Baby, I just meant that third place is nothing to be ashamed of!" he pleaded. "You were competing on a national level and…"

"That's not what I'm talking about!" I snapped back, thumping my fist again.

He leaned back, watching me with caring curiosity.

"Well… what is it then?" he checked slowly.

My lip trembled, my eyes watered. The words were hard in my throat.

"I… I overheard one of the girls talking," I began.

Their faces grew concerned.

"What were they saying?" my mother asked rapidly, frowning deeply.

I breathed shakily.

"The girl who won… Jasmine Holloway?" I stammered. "They said her parents… had her genes altered when she was a baby? Gave her extra lung capacity. They say she cheated."

My father shifted uncomfortably.

"That's not a very nice thing to say," my father said humbly.

"It's true though!" I protested. "They said her mum is some big shot stockbroker! Did you see the *car* that picked them up?"

"She can't help who her parents are, honey," he shrugged. "It's just the luck of the draw."

I screwed my face up bitterly.

"It… it's not right!" I exclaimed. "Why can people just buy their way to first place, while the rest of us work really hard and fail!"

My parents were stunned by my words, apparently at a loss, shifted anxiously and rubbing their necks.

"You're right, honey," my mother admitted awkwardly. "It isn't fair. But that doesn't mean you can't succeed in your own way!"

I scoffed, banging my head against the window.

"It's the way of the world, Emma," my father said, his words deep, almost foreboding. "Some people have to fight for everything in life."

"But, why…"

"Why is the sky blue? Why do the seasons turn?" he shrugged.

I was about to answer him when he interrupted me.

"Of course, we know what causes these things, Emma," he spoke deeply, "but I'm asking why. The unexplainable why. The series of events that made things the way they are."

I raised my eyebrow.

"I… I don't understand," I said.

"No one does," he scoffed. "Some people call it God. A scapegoat answer if you ask me. But it don't matter. If life has been set up as an uphill battle, that's how it is. You fight. You fight like hell. And you keep fighting until you can't anymore…and if you're lucky, you might just make it."

My mother's gaze had grown harsher and harsher at him, trying to get him to shut up and failing. But his words left me bewildered, staring at him in my seat with wide watery eyes. He'd left a mark on me that day. The pure, horrifying Darwinian nature of reality impressed upon me forever. A revelation; there were winners and losers in life. And he was telling me to do *whatever* it took, to win. They hadn't. Dad was a security guard. Mom, a receptionist. He was telling me to succeed where they had failed.

Whatever it took…

I nodded at him solemnly.

It was a powerful memory.

<<Terminating memory playback >>

<<Disengaging neural lace>>

The past retreated into the recesses of my cerebellum, the faces of my parents fading with it. My eyes awoke to the blank white ceiling of my apartment, dimly lit by the blue mood lighting projecting from the walls. Becoming aware of my body, and the clothes I was wearing; a loose, white tank top and baggy heated pyjama bottoms. My head was propped against the soft cushion moulded into the headrest of my regeneration unit, mounted beside the wall of the bedroom. The unit looked like a combination of a surgical table and an engineer's workbench. A series of tubes and cables connected to my neck and arms through input sockets implanted throughout the synthetic skin; replenishing my power, artificial blood, coolant fluid and self-repair nanobots, my brain jacked in to receive software patches. The sides of the bed were lined with MRI scanning apparatus, a retractable arch designed to slide back within the housing of the unit, used to detect anything wrong with my hardware, or wetware; a robotic arm stood mounted beside the table, ready to repair any errors.

<<Disengaging regeneration unit>>

It eliminated the need for regular check-ups… but didn't exactly aid the belief that I was a regular person anymore. One by one, the cables and tubes disconnected themselves with soft hissing sounds and slithered like snakes back into their slots by the side of the bed. With a whir, the arches of the scanning unit and the repair arm retracted back into their places.

I yawned exhaustedly, stretching out on the bed, thinking to myself. It was a powerful memory. One that had set me down the path that would lead me to the gang, to jail, the Ashigaru… and joining Project Clayman. A defining point in my life…

At least…I think it is.

I swung my legs over and sat up straight, and ran my fingers through my hair, resting untidily around my shoulders. I rubbed my eyes, straining them as I wallowed in a headache pounding inside my titanium skull, groaning softly. I turned to my bedside table, grabbing a half-drunk glass of red wine standing beside the magnetically suspended reading lamp.

I drank deeply, glancing over at my ordinarily tidy apartment. I had a sliding vid-glass door leading out onto my balcony looking out over the Docklands. The transparent screen was playing a montage of old photos of me before I was augmented. Pictures that would've once been online but were removed by Mother Mind after I joined Project Clayman. Parties, concerts, holiday photos and alike… there was even a photo of Dan and me from back in the day; taking a selfie while we spray painted the side of Hammersmith Bridge.

The rows of shelves lined the wall across from me, with pictures of my family. A small Jade plant tree in a pot left to me by my grandfather, items I collected during my missions across the world; a golden teapot from Aleppo, a rain stick from Australia, a statue of the elephant god Ganesha from New Dehli, and so forth. I'd even pulled out a couple of old boxes filled with junk from my childhood, scattered about after I'd examined the contents; old clothes, toys from childhood and so forth. Since becoming a cyborg, I'd developed a few nervous habits… like collecting things… *physical* things; proof of my existence that couldn't be altered.

I hope…

I'd always tried to tell myself that I *chose* to be recruited for the Project. I was sure that what I'd done had been worth it. The financial incentive outweighed any silly doubts I might've had. It took me a while to fully appreciate the mistake I'd made. I didn't know what I was any more… For the last year or so… I'd become obsessed with trying to find flaws with memory. Loose ends. Things that didn't add up. I hadn't been able to find anything… until now.

Claire is still insisting that she's never met me before…

The incident earlier was embarrassing. Luckily the photos and videos taken from the scenes hadn't made their way onto social media thanks to Mother Mind. But the whole thing left me uneasy. I remembered her… even if it wasn't in a good light. She had been the weird girl at school we used to take the piss out of… all of us except for Dan. Always defending her and telling us to leave her alone. At the time, he denied it, but I'd still known he'd had a thing for her.

But if it was all so clear to Dan and me… why couldn't she remember?

That didn't add up.

I strode over to the displays, taking another swig from my glass as I walked, crossing my arms to study the montage with obsessive curiosity… Like I somehow wasn't seeing the whole picture.

I wasn't going to get to see it today.

My photo montage was interrupted by a beeping sound. The

images replaced by a pop-up; the pulsing red circle of Ben's AI avatar loaded onto the screen.

"Sorry to disturb you, Emma," he apologised in his monotone voice.

I sighed, rolling my eyes. Typical.

"What is it, Ben?" I said, facepalming myself with exasperation.

"I've received a priority alert update from Southall Station," he explained. "It appears there's been another Jack-21 murder."

My expression grew dark.

Him again.

Bitterly realising I'd have to save my soul searching for another day, I straightened myself up formally, placed my wine glass down on my coffee table in the middle of the apartment, and grabbed a close-by red dressing gown with the Ashigaru logo sewn on the back.

"Patch me through to the response officer on the scene," I ordered professionally, brushing back my hair.

<<Calling: Sergeant Richard Newby>>

I focused my cybernetic eye lenses on the window. The video feed loaded, broadcasting from a smartwatch camera. The face of a ginger-haired officer with a goatee. The hood of his black uniform jacket pulled over his hat to shield himself from the drizzle. His face was pale; at first, I thought that it was just the cold from the rain. But his nervous, uneasy expression suggested more.

"Uh… Sergeant Newby speaking," he spoke timidly.

I regarded him.

"Hi, this is Lieutenant Emma Golem, the Ashigaru liaison officer assigned to the Jack-21 investigation," I replied firmly. "I understand you have a sitrep for me?"

He nodded grimly.

"We have forensic teams on the scene. The identity of the victim has been confirmed…" he explained, bringing up a Mother Mind profile to the screen.

Mother Mind profile 3924-5180-7086-6271

First name: Simon

Surname: Carter

Status: Deceased

Nationality: British citizen

Occupation(s):

- Suspected member of *Spiriform* hacker group

Criminal record:

- Suspected of numerous crimes but never convicted: *Click here for more detail*

Known aliases:

- FireSaint

"Another Spiritform hacker?" I asked, raising an eyebrow, looking at the profile photo, a skinny, lanky fellow with deep warm eyes and silver hair.

"His bio-monitor sensors sent out a fatality alert to the NHS at 23:58… He was hiding in an old bomb shelter. The equipment found at the scene confirmed it," the sergeant explained, his expression painful. "We've… already examined the body."

I watched with professional detachment as he forwarded me the photos from the crime scene. The gory mess loaded into view, like a still shot from a horror film. The skinny body sliced open from his neck to waist, like an unzipped bag, spilling its contents across the corrugated iron floor of the bunker. Sergeant Newby obviously hadn't handled the sight as well.

"As… as you can see…" he stammered.

"The wounds are a match," I finished his sentence.

He nodded shakily.

"We searched the hideout," he continued. "It… it looks like the perp removed the memory drive from his PC."

I gritted my teeth.

The Project Selection files…

"Forward me a full report," I ordered him, brushing myself down. "I'll be there ASAP. Contact the…"

"I'm sorry, sir," he interrupted. "There's more you should know. A patrol drone witnessed a suspect fleeing the scene of the crime."

My eyes widened.

If I still had a heart, it would've stopped.

"It did?" I checked.

He brought up a recording from the drone; a familiar face standing in a spotlight wearing a trench coat and hat, but it was him. He was sporting more cybernetics than I last remembered, the scan identified him and brought up his Mother Mind profile:

Mother Mind profile 2446-7128-5978-2501:

First name: Arthur

Surname: Wells

Status: Wanted for numerous crimes *Click here for more detail*

Nationality: British citizen

Occupation(s):

- Private investigator
  - Status: Self-employed
  - Organisation: Arthur Wells & Associates

Arthur!?

I poorly tried to contain my shock. It had been weird enough when Kenji told me that he'd been chosen as the PI to recover the Project Selection files… but this was a whole other kettle of fish. It had been years since I'd seen him. I'd met him as one of my trainees during my time as the firearms instructor at GCHQ. But over the course of time I'd been there, we'd become good friends. I'd even saved his life during the Operation Dragonslayer incident. The disaster that the government quietly swept under the rug.

And now he was the suspect in a series of murders…

Murders I *knew* he didn't do.

"The drone had him pinned down," the sergeant explained. "But it was destroyed… by Cymurai."

That caught my attention.

"You're sure?" I checked.

"Yes sir," he nodded darkly, his face growing harsh. "Personally, I always knew he was just a psychopath in a superhero costume. I know the type… the ones who enjoy the *hunt.* Bet you any money that he just got jealous we found Jack-21 first and let him go just so he could have the honour of killing him himself!"

I remained stoic at his response. That had always been a fairly popular interpretation of Cymurai online, but I wasn't thinking about that right now. Keeping a neutral expression. Several members of the Ashigaru knew that Kenji was Cymurai. This was the most awkward part of the assignment; the fact I was supposed to be pretending to catch a killer I *already knew the identity of.* This was a cover-up job, but I couldn't just turn off my ability to *care.*

I asked formally what had happened to the suspect. He explained that Arthur had fled in his car, and somehow used Mother Mind's back-doors into the traffic management network and the police drones, to help his escape. The chase had ended when Arthur crashed his car but had managed to dive out into the River Brent. Their search after that hadn't been successful. With his prosthetics and artificial blood, he could stay underwater for hours, and the infrared shielding in his clothes and stopped him from being detected by Ariel scans.

He was a fugitive…

The sergeant was asking me for further orders when telepathic ringing and pop-up windows appeared out of nowhere.

<<Incoming call from: Sector>>

My eyes narrowed. It was the boss calling. The only time he called using his old hacker handle was when he was logged into a Cymurai avatar. I ordered the Sergeant to forward his report and to stand-by for further instructions and answered the call.

<<Call accepted>>

The face of the sergeant was replaced by the crimson and gold, the horned metal faceplate of the Cymurai avatar, the eyes glowing brightly, the recording taken from a camera built into the avatar's wrist, the rain glistening on the surface of the lens.

"Emma," the electronic grating voice said with professional warmness.

"Hey, boss," I added awkwardly.

He nodded curtly.

"You've heard the news?" he sighed.

"Some of it…" I replied cautiously. "Mind filling in the gaps?"

The Cymurai avatar shrugged with a whir and explained that Mother Mind had detected Arthur's neural lace being accessed by the so-called Enigma hacker.

"That bastard again?" I growled through gritted teeth.

"He obviously doesn't know that you've been assigned to handle the investigation," Kenji continued. "Otherwise he wouldn't be bothering to throw the Police off the trail …"

My eyes narrowed darkly.

"We need to find this guy," I said authoritatively. "A hacker with that kind of talent helping Jack-21? Frankly, it's terrifying."

"I agree," Kenji replied gruffly. "But let me handle Enigma. You just focus on catching Arthur… or rather, not catching him."

I turned my head quizzically.

"I'm not sure what you mean?"

"Think about it," Kenji shrugged. "The situation does offer us some advantages. Officially, this will throw Churchbell Security off Jack-21's real trail…"

"But sir, I…" I protested.

"Don't forget the mission, Emma," he said firmly for me. "Your job is to *stop* anyone from discovering the identity of the killer. He's our responsibility. We *have* to be the ones to catch him."

I frowned.

"And that justifies setting up an innocent man?" I cried.

"I don't need you to actually *arrest* him, Lieutenant," he said coyly. "Just keep Churchbell chasing after him long enough for us to eliminate the real Jack-21."

"And what happens if he *does* get caught?

"His memories will clear his name," he shrugged, disinterested. "If he's broken other laws, that's his problem, not ours."

"Sir, I *know* him," I protested. "He won't..."

"Professionalism, Emma," he replied curtly. "You have a job to do. Don't let your personal feelings get in the way."

My mouth stopped before I could speak again. He was right of course... but that didn't make it *right*.

"Yes sir," I responded gruffly.

"And if worst comes to worst... you know what you have to do," he added coldly.

I ground my teeth... understanding the *deadly* subtext to what he was saying.

"Yes sir," I repeated.

He nodded slowly.

"Glad we have that cleared up," he added, putting a swift end to the topic, his voice filled with determination. "Carry on with the investigation into Arthur Wells. No doubt you'll come across his hacker again. Your orders are to collect as much data as possible on him but keep it contained to just you and your partner. I want to find him myself."

"Copy that," I sighed with a half-hearted salute.

"You have your assignment," he finished formally. "A chopper is being prepared for you. Stay in regular contact."

"You got it, boss," I nodded, anxious to finish. "Signing off."

I hurriedly gave the neurocommand to end the call and strained my eyes, the vid-glass turning blank to reveal the rain-soaked cityscape.

Emma… what have you got yourself into?

I thought joining the Ashigaru meant I had just screwed up my *own* life… now I was sending my friends to the gallows. I wasn't going to let that happen. I knew what GCHQ and Virtualife did to him. The lies they told him. The bullshit 'industrial accident' that was responsible for his mutilation. He'd only been doing his job. He didn't ask for any of this. Didn't deserve it. Kenji could fire me if he wanted. He could've taken back this body for all I cared. I was going to do everything in my power to make sure that didn't happen. I couldn't live with myself if I didn't.

I have to play along… for now.

I forwarded a text message to Dan, explaining the situation and ordered him to rendezvous with at the crime scene in forty minutes. The Police Comms app was strictly for business… I'd have to deal with the personal shit when I got there.

I sighed with dread and marched to get dressed like the automaton I thought I was.

CHAPTER 19

Mother Mind profile 7183-2647-8246-3892:

First name: Denise

Surname: Masika

Status: Wanted for numerous crimes *Click here for more detail*

Nationality: British citizen

Occupation(s):

- Suspected member of *Spiritform* hacker group

Criminal record:

- Arrested: 17/11/2037
    - Offence: Suspected of unauthorised access to computer material
    - No formal charges

Known aliases:

- Destiny

Live surveillance:

- Status: *Unavailable*
- Date: 08/10/2045
- Current location: Unknown
- Local Time: 01.27 GMT

I'd had to mute my HUD. The noise from all the news alerts had gotten too much.

Bad news alerts.

My dry mouth was buried in my hands; still unable to believe what I was seeing. The news feed from the channel still displaying from the holo-table, streaming footage from a media drone, circling around the back garden in Southhall that had been home to Simon's bunker. The camera was zoomed in on a white, plastic tent set up by the police.

Forensics officers and crime scene investigation robots were busy scurrying back and forth down the ladder.

"The police have officially identified the suspect as Arthur Wells," the AI newscaster explained through the wall-speakers. "A twenty-seven-year-old, London-based private investigator and former cyber warfare officer at GCHQ. We have also received confirmation that a body was found in Southall and that the wounds are a match to the pattern of previous injuries inflicted on the previous Jack-21 victims. The suspect was seen fleeing the scene of the crime, moments after the victim's bio-monitor fatality beacon was activated. After a high-speed chase through the Uxbridge and Greenford area, the suspect abandoned his vehicle and fled on foot. An extensive search of the surrounding area is now underway."

I couldn't look anymore, painfully covering my eyes, digging my red nails into my skull.

I'd spent the day researching the ICE protecting Arthur's website. After hours of testing, I'd found a vulnerability to gain access to his network; obsessed with getting revenge. I was finally getting ready to launch the attack when Poe notified me of the update from Simon.

The auto-fatality beacon on his bio-monitor sensors had gone online.

A single shot to the head.

It was only just starting to sink in…

"He's… he's really gone," I muttered under my breath, trying to swallow the lump that was welling in my throat.

"Fuck…" Raj sniffed, trying to hide the tears leaking down his rounded cheek, glistening in the glowing power-logo tattoo into his skin.

This was my fault.

He was only there because of me.

I got him killed…

The guilt was driving me crazy. And it was all going to be for nothing; our copy of the Project Selection files would've been destroyed. All the risk we had taken to get them decrypted was going to go to waste.

"Oh, man this is bad…" Jamie muttered, anxiously stroking his gaunt chin, stretching the scar on his forehead, pacing back and forth down the length of the bar, wooden floor creaking as he went. "This is really bad! We need to get out of here; now!"

I wasn't listening to him anymore. Too consumed by self-pity to say anything.

"Dude, our friend is dead!" Raj shouted through the tears. "You're already acting like…"

"*Don't be thick!*" Jamie hissed back, throwing out his tattooed fist, sending Raj shrinking in his beanie bag. "That bastard PI hit our Estonian proxy! If he traced the bunker, he probably knows we're here too! I told you we should've air gapped the network!"

"There wasn't time, we…"

"Oh, there wasn't time!?" he quipped back sarcastically. "We're going to get rumbled because you didn't have time!"

"Would you chill out!" Kasira spat from behind the pub's counter, staring intently at logs of metadata from her laptop resting on top of it, practically pulling out her hair buns in frustration, her dress flashing an angry red to match her mood. "Our LAN wasn't pinged! So just knock it off!"

Jamie's sharp eyes narrowed.

"You're sure?" he checked sceptically.

"I'm not seeing any records, or signs the records have been altered," she glowered at him, the light on her contact lenses flashing rapidly. "He was obviously only interested in the files. I've already migrated our proxy to Egypt. They're not finding this safe house anytime soon."

"Oh, there's a load off my fucking mind!" Jamie retorted. "Do you even know *how* he traced Simon?"

"He must've pulled the SoulID's from Plexi's hard drive," Raj mumbled, rubbing his red eyes. "The auto-delete sequence wouldn't have had enough time to run when he pulled the power."

Jamie was stood with his back to Raj, but I got to see the change in his reaction. His face went stone cold, deathly still.

"You said you were installing a self-destruct system…" he said slowly, his voice simmering with rage.

Raj was already cringing with dread, anticipating what was to come.

"We didn't have the…"

Jamie exploded, lunging at Raj, grabbing him by the scruff of his hoodie and yanking him up off the seat.

"You lazy piece of shit!"

"What the fuck, man!" Raj spat back, trying to free himself. "Lemme go!"

I hadn't been focusing until now, their yells snapping me back to reality. Kasira tried calming them down, but I wasn't gonna take their crap right now.

"Knock it off!"

I sprung out of my seat and leapt over to grab Jamie from behind and yanking him backwards.

"Stop acting like a cornered animal!" I snapped at him, thrusting my gloved finger into his chest. "The tough guy act isn't fooling anyone! Get your shit together and fucking focus!"

"My shit!?" he scoffed at me. "My shit shouldn't be here! We're on the verge of getting busted, and you're standing here doing nothing!"

"I've already run the simulations with the Soul," Poe pointed out, flashing up on the holo-table and using his ears to point to a floating report beside him. "Given the low probability of our new proxy being located, I've has calculated that scuttling the safe house at this point would presenting a greater risk."

"There you go!" I cried, holding up an agreeing hand. "But when are you going to get it through your head? We're at *war*. Terrorists in the eyes of government! Waking up to sniper fire could be a daily fucking reality! Simon understood that, and if you don't get that by now, you don't belong here!"

Jamie rolled a pair of exasperated eyes. He turned back to me, looking more disappointed than anything else.

"It's not like you to make excuses, Destiny…" he told me coldly.

I batted an eyelid at that. I knew what he was insinuating and was already tightening my fist behind my back.

"Come again?" I said politely, with a false smile.

"You heard me!" he cried back. "If this were anyone else, you'd be out for blood! But your college computer club sweetheart pulls the wool over your eyes and you..."

He hadn't the time to finish his sentence before my knuckles rocketed into his face.

"ARRGH!"

He stumbled backwards clutching his nose to stop the drops of blood now spilling out.

"What the fuck?!" he yelled back at me through the muffled sound of his hands. "The hell did you do that for?"

"You said I'd be out for blood," I answered with a cocky smirk, rubbing my gloved knuckles, taking a sense of cathartic joy in that, almost pretending it had been Arthur's face.

"Crazy bitch!" he sneered loudly, before shoving his way past me and stumbling up the stairs, swearing as he went.

Kasira was stood behind the counter, a hand on her hip, shaking her head with a smirk.

"Saw that coming," she scoffed, her dress glowing a triumphant purple with her mood.

I rubbed my face, trying to calm myself down. That was harder.

"Not that I'm not grateful, Destiny," Raj began cautiously from behind me. "But he does have a point... Don't you have a plan to deal with any of this?"

I let out a long, exhausted sigh, rubbing my face, jingling my piercing chain, Poe's avatar already crunching data sets on my contact lenses.

It didn't happen to me very often...but despite the show I'd just put on, my heart wasn't in the fight right now. I was too unstable. Not in the mood for dealing with any of their shit right now.

I needed to be a better leader than that right now. I didn't like admitting I had limits. But I knew when I needed to take a step back from this.

I gave one last neurocommand to shut off my contact lenses, and my HUD evaporated into static.

"I'm going to bed," I sighed, pulling off my interface headset. "You guys are always going on about wanting to be in charge, now's your chance."

I turned on my heel ready to stride out of the room.

"Whoa, hey, wait!" Raj called me.

"Not now, dammit!" I barked back, striding off angrily down the hall, my piercing chain rattling furiously.

They carried on calling after me, but I could barely hear them over my boots against the staircase. I slammed the door to my bedroom behind me, and threw myself onto my mattress, clutching my head and writhing hard enough to rip the sheets. I screamed silently, not wanting the others to hear; but still resorted to kicking the wall, sending plaster scattering as a fine powder.

Drown those fucking sorrows…

I kept a bottle of Sambuca, and a handful of ready-made joints stashed in the small wooden cabinet beside my bed. I put my communications setting on 'do not disturb', grabbed the bottle, tore off the cap and started angrily pouring shots in it, spilling the sticky liquid across my gloved hands, the duvet, with drawn out, jagged sobbing breaths. I pulled out a spliff from an old jam jar, picked up a lighter with an animated design of a magic mushroom on it and sparked up. Blazed it down within a few minutes. And then another. And then another.

Get smashed. Pass out. That was the plan, and I was going the right way about it…

But then the memories stung me…

We could've had a future together…

Whichever way I dressed it up, he wouldn't be dead now if it wasn't for me.

I'd been doing this for six years now. What had I achieved? The occasional *Twitter* trend.

No worldwide rebellion. No mass anarchy. No hanging of the rich at the gallows.

Just me, in a pub, with a bunch of socially awkward computer criminals.

One less now.

I pulled at my purple hair, trying to distract the emotional pain with physical. Maybe it was time I got honest with myself. We were going nowhere. Maybe one day the world would change. Perhaps we were just meant to destroy ourselves and rebuild from the ashes. I couldn't stop it. No one could stop it. I was an idiot to think anything else.

I should just… pack it all in.

I had rainy day plans… ways of changing my identity and getting out of the country. Emergency use only. I never thought of just running away. I was willing to give everything for this fight. At least I thought I was….

It would be so easy to…

Snap the fuck out of it, Destiny!

The voice came from the back of my head. A truth that I had forgotten. The thing that kept me going in these moments of doubt.

My fingers instinctively reached for my pocket, wrapping around the outline of my headset. Both my guilty pleasure and my punishment. I slipped on the headset. I focused hard enough, and my HUD flickered back to life.

<<Open file directory: Local Disk (C:)/Destiny/VR Sims/Personal>>

The file browser rezzed into view on my HUD. I highlighted the file I wanted to open, a gold star next to it indicating that it was one of my favourites. A file named 'Dream_come_true'.

I created it years ago, but I always felt a cold rush of excitement just thinking of it… It was a perverse sense of enjoyment. Meant to be a painful reminder…but I couldn't help but take a cathartic entertainment from it.

A shrink would have a field trip with me…

But tonight, wasn't the night for serious soul-searching.

It would be the push I needed.

I executed the program. I closed my eyes and rested my head on the pillow, my headset linked to my watch, ready to put my brain into the dream state.

<<You are about to enter a full-immersion virtual reality simulation.>>

<<Please be seated and ensure your surroundings are appropriate.>>

<<Begin simulation?: Yes/No>>

<<Login process initialised>>

The familiar glow of digital wireframe stretched out into the darkness of my eyeballs and began twisting and bending into 3D shapes; their surfaces filled in rapidly by coloured pixels accompanied with a progress bar at the bottom of my vision.

<<Loading environment>>

<<Running neural lace device drivers>>

<<Processing consciousness shift>>

<<Ghost mode enabled>>

<<Simulation date: 21/01/2028>>

<<Simulation time: 11:14>>

A few seconds later, the progress bar hit one hundred percent, and I landed inside the digital flesh of my avatar. Ghost mode in a VR simulation meant you were just that; invisible to the characters of the game world, unable to directly interact with any objects in the environment, an objective observer, watching the drama of the simulation play out like a film.

I was loaded into the world, squatting in a dark, familiar corner of a bedroom. The walls were pink, a few active posters of *Disney* characters were dotting about, hiding the cracks starting to creep up the surface. I peered through the gap in the curtains revealing the steamy windows, looking out across the night, illuminated by the orange glare of the old street lights. The winds of winter whistled through the barren branches of the trees in the playground, rustling the worn-down swings.

Across the expanse of blue carpet, sat a digital toy chest that had been left open, revealing the crude robotic stuffed animals. The casket was at the foot of a white, wooden bed. Kid-sized… with a simulated eight-year-old version of myself wrapped up in sparkling *My Little Pony* duvets.

The simulation was partly generated from scans of the room and neural recordings of my own memories.

I was jealous of the girl in the bed… Blissfully unaware of the what was to come.

Virtual hairs began tingling on the back of my neck whenever I came here.

A sort of cathartic anxiety, my breath growing short and sharp in anticipation.

I knew what was coming. I'd done this a thousand times before, but it never became less intense.

My eyes were drawn to the younger, innocent version of myself, her pig-tails scattered across the pillow… knowing that innocence was about be destroyed.

THUD! THUD! THUD!

Three, rapid, rumbling bangs come from the front door, loud enough to send the younger self, sitting bolt upright with sudden, confused panic.

"POLICE!" came a gruff barking voice from downstairs. "SEARCH WARRANT! OPEN THE DOOR!"

Even now it sent shivers down my spine. The younger me pressed herself against the wall, wrapped up in the blankets, daring to peep over, as the yells were embedded in my memory for the rest of my life.

"Mom?" the younger me cried out. "Dad!?"

My cries were drowned out by the bangs that followed, the distinct sound of crackling wood as they forced their way through. The young me wailed desperately, curling up in the duvets in sheer terror of what was about to come.

My dad came bursting into the room, dressed in nothing but his vest and boxers, sporting his goatee and shaven hair. He was only thirty-three at the time, but right now, he looked like he had aged twenty years, his eyes wild with panic. He dashed over and collapsed on his knees by the side of the bed, and wrapped his arms around the younger me…

"Oh… sweetheart… oh God, I'm sorry," my father sniffed.

"Daddy, what's going on?" she asked through the sobs. "Why are they breaking the door…"

The modern me took a heavy breath. Even today, when I closed my eyes, I could still see his weak smile through the tears, wanting to comfort me but nothing coming to mind, while the yells and the banging grew louder and louder.

"Denise… baby…" Dad said finally, forcing it through his choked voice, stroking my hair and my cheek softly. "I just want you to know… everything I did… I did for you. And I promise you it was worth it."

The yells of the police reached a fever pitch. An almighty crash came from downstairs as the door was finally rammed in. I waited with bated breath, while the younger me shook uncontrollably in Dad's arms. The sound of boots clambering up the stairs.

Dad closed his eyes. Taking one last breath. I remembered him being so calm, despite knowing what was going to happen.

"It *WAS* worth it!"

He took his arms off her and slowly lifted them away, to place them on the back of this head.

"I love you."

I opened my mouth to speak…

CRASH!

Six-armed response police officers exploded through the pink door, so hard they sent it flying off its hinges. They were dressed in Kevlar-plated body armour and intimidating respirator masks, brandishing sub-machine guns with torches mounted under the barrels. The harsh lights shone in the young Denise's eyes, blinding her.

The mass of armoured bodies soon swarmed around my father, grabbing him by the scruff of his neck, and pinning him to the ground despite his lack of resistance. His face was rammed into the carpet, screwed up with pain as they held him there. The younger me was freaking out, desperately trying to reach for him, but was yanked back by the police.

"Daddy!"

She was screaming in horror, snot dripping from her nose, while she pounded my tiny fists against the armour plating.

"Keith Masika!" the sergeant of the squad boomed. "I am arresting you on suspicion of unauthorised access to computer data! You do not have to say anything, but it may harm your defence if you do not answer in question something you later rely on in court. Anything you do say may be given in evidence!"

"Leave him alone!" the younger me yelled at the top of her lungs. "Leave him alone!"

My father cried in anguish as his arms were twisted behind his back while they slapped handcuffs on him.

The modern me watched like a silent spectre, feeling my hatred welling inside like an active volcano. Grinding my nails into my gloved palm, my jaw rigidly locking together.

Everything I had just watched was a recreation of my past, derived from my memories.

Now came the fantasy.

The part of the program that only existed as digital fiction.

The part that I *wanted* to be true so badly, I'd joined a group of revolutionaries to make it a reality.

The yells of the younger me grew angrier and angrier, the face of the little girl becoming more and more ferocious.

"Leave him alone! Leave him ALONE!" she cried, as they dragged my dad off the ground, ready to frog march him away. I watched the facial animations of the younger me, impressed with my own handiwork as her expression changed to a deadly glare.

I'd never seen a child with such convincing murderous intent.

"I SAID; LEAVE HIM ALONE!" she screamed, spinning around in her bed, thrusting a hand beneath her pillow.

She pulled back a 10mm handgun.

Like a cold-hearted killer, the younger me held to the head of the officer restrain her.

She screamed and pulled the trigger.

BANG!

A cloud of blood and bone sprayed across the bed sheets; the younger me was released from the grip of the dead officer. He landed hard, face down on the carpet, a pool of red slowly pouring out from the hole in his head.

"*Jesus!*" the sergeant yelled.

The two officers dragging my father away dropped him in a panicked hurry, spinning round to pounce on the young me.

They never got the chance.

She shrieked at the top of her lungs; a screeching roar of anguish.

BANG! BANG! BANG! BANG! BANG! BANG!

Bullets whizzed through the air, crashing through the plastic face guards of the police respirators. Fountains of blood burst out the other side, the distinct aroma of iron wafting through the room.

The shooting stopped. The room fell as silent as a tomb. The floor was littered with scattered bodies and assault rifles, and a small lake of blood. Smoke billowed from the barrel of the gun, trembling in the hands of the eight-year-old me.

The modern me glanced at it… wallowing in sick satisfaction.

"Oh, my god…" my dad breathed, pulling his face and gaping at the bloodbath.

My mother was standing the doorway, her hand held over her mouth in shock.

The intense rage was gone from the eyes of my younger self, and she was left sitting there with the gun in her trembling hands. Her cheeks had been turned into streams of tears, taking short hiccup-like breaths, simply dropping the gun with a clatter on the carpet.

My father lay there, staring in horror while the younger me composed herself. Once she had control of her trembles, she stepped off the bed and began fumbling around in the pockets of the officers until she got her hands on the keys for the handcuffs and unlocked them, before the three of them collapsed into each other for a group family hug.

I was stood in the corner, arms folded, longing for this to be more than just a fantasy. I just wanted to wallow in it… ideally forever, consumed by imagination.

An alternate history.

One I wanted to live in.

Like my entire life since that day had been trying to make up for how powerless I'd been.

People would try to comfort me. Tell me there was nothing I could've done. That I had only been a child.

I didn't want to hear it. This is what a wanted. A dream.

It never lasts…

But I stood there.

CHAPTER 20

Mother Mind profile 2446-7128-5978-2501:

First name: Arthur

Surname: Wells

Status: Wanted for criminal offences

Nationality: British citizen

Occupation(s):

- Private investigator
  - Status: Self-employed
  - Organisation: Arthur Wells & Associates

Known aliases:

- IronRoot

Live surveillance:

- Status: *Unavailable*
- Date: 08/10/2045
- Current location: Unknown
- Local Time at previous location: 01:46 GMT

"Yeah… it's official," I grumbled to Liz telepathically, trembling in my hunched position. "This is rock bottom."

I was sat, hunched inside the outlet for a sewer pipe, my back arched against the curved hull, my boots pressed against the other side, practically in the foetal position, hiding like a rat. I'd had to block my nasal and heat receptors; the only way I could deal with the stench. My ass was freezing, plunged beneath the surface of the steady flow trickling out like a waterfall into a small estuary of the River Brent, in the shadow of the A40 flyover. Across the muddy shore on the other side, I could see the huge old concrete pillars supporting the structure; the cracks filled in with bio-resin to keep its strength. The hum of the traffic flowed overhead, feeling the vibrations rumbling in the ground around me.

Luckily, the buzz of police drones and helicopters and the roar of sirens had become faint and distant.

I've lost them… for now.

Thanks to my artificial blood, I was able to hold my breath and swam underwater for over half an hour against the flow of the river. My nanotech clothes were still bone dry, but I could still feel the water dripping off my skin and hair, rolling down my shirt and trousers beneath my trench coat. The heater meshes in the fabric slowly drying me off. Of, course that didn't do my submerged ass any favours. I'd had to shove my hat in my pocket while I was diving, crumpling it; the self-healing frame had restored its original shape but felt uncomfortable.

I hadn't had a chance to test the infrared shielding in my coat until now, but I could say with confidence that it had worked. The police drones hadn't detected me while I was submerged, giving me the chance to swim away and pull myself into the relative safety of this hiding spot. I could only hope the air-tight bandage on my wound, and my bio-defence system would hold up as well; my stomach turning at the thought of what was flowing out of this pipe.

"You're just lucky I was able to access the city's underground infrastructure layout," Liz pointed out. "The data from GCHQ really saved your ass. You should thank David when you get the chance."

I chuckled to myself sourly.

"*If* I ever get the chance," I groaned back telepathically.

My mind was still trying to make sense of all this. In the space of two hours, I'd gone from being a happily employed, productive citizen, to an outlaw fugitive. The internet had undoubtedly already made up its mind about me. My face was on every major British news website; branding me as Jack-21, the same photo of me from my Mother Mind profile on their home pages. No doubt that same photo was being plastered on holo-billboards across the city. In the few minutes before my website and business network was taken down by the police, I'd been inundated by hate mail from anybody who'd gotten the news and was online at the time.

I wanted to be able to say it rolled off, like water on a duck's back… but it didn't.

I could still feel the after-effects from the brain-hack. The lingering sensation of the alien presence, like a pair of ghostly hands caressing under my skin…waiting to possess me, and rape my consciousness.

Just thinking about it made me shudder.

I couldn't get that image of the gory mess out of my head. I doubted I ever would. Despite everything I'd done to get my memory back, I was seriously considering erasing those images. The weight of the guilt of his death bore down on me.

BUUUUUZZZZ!

Shit!

The whir of a quadcopter engine hummed overhead. I tensed anxiously, pressing my body tightly against the sides of the pipe. My heart pounded in my chest, my breath held, going as silent as a tombstone, praying it wouldn't poke its head this way.

A tense few minutes passed… the drone passed with them.

I let out a sigh of relief, wiping the sweat from my brow with the back of the metal hand.

I need to get out of the open….

"Please tell me you got the data you needed?" I checked desperately with Liz.

Her avatar nodded on my HUD.

"My scan program extracted a hundred gigabytes of relevant data from FireSaint's neural lace," she explained. "The data includes his memory of the whistle-blower code still being used by Spiritform. You still have Destiny's e-mail address. You can use them to contact her."

I dreaded the thought. Spiritform members went to extraordinary lengths to make sure they couldn't be traced. But they still needed to receive tips from anonymous whistle-blowers. The code acted as a plug-in for a communications app, designed to allow the whistle-blowers to temporarily bypass the advanced spam filters installed on the ICE protecting their servers.

The rumour was the only way to get the code was to be vetted by their background-checking AI, which could only be accessed through a hidden portal on the dark web. The entrance was practically impossible to find, requiring you to navigate that murky world. With the data I'd retrieved from Simon's brain, I could get in touch with them… but still wasn't convinced it was the right way to go.

"Great, I can call Denise," I scoffed, shaking my head. "I just can't believe that you think I *should*."

I could already envision those wild eyes of hers, staring at me with murderous intent.

"She's already tried to kill me once!" I protested. "And that was *before* she thought I murdered one of her friends."

Liz pursed her lips.

"While I can't say she'll be happy to see you," Liz began explained me, prompting a sarcastic laugh. "If she does want to catch the one who forced you to kill FireSaint, she'll listen to what you have to say. Even if she doesn't believe you, you can just share your memories with her. They'll need the metadata from the attack on your neural lace to track him down."

"Great," I deadpanned, cringing at the thought of giving Denise access to my neural lace. "And then what? Even if Spiritform are *somehow* able to clear my name, I'm still fucked! What good does it do me if they expose Virtualife? If I help them, I'll just be guilty of another set of crimes!"

"Not if they *don't go public* with the data they find," Liz pointed out coyly. "Simply *threatening* Virtualife with the prospect of leaking the contents of the Project Selection files could give you leverage. A lot of leverage."

She got my curiosity.

"What are you suggesting?"

"Spiritform obviously have vastly greater capacity for launching cyber-attacks than you. I'm saying that you use that to your advantage. Gain their trust. Find out what was in the files first and then…"

"Sell them out?" I scoffed. "Do you have any idea how crazy that is? They'll find out, you can bet your life! Even if they have to hack my brain to do it! And guess what? They'll put a fucking bullet in me!"

"I'll isolate and protect the memory engrams in your brain for this conversation," she explained, quietly running the sub-routines, tranquil eyes behind her brass spectacles. "Even so, you don't have to inform on them to the police. Just blackmail Virtualife. If you give them an ultimatum and offer to stop Spiritform going public, they may be prepared to offer you some kind of witness protection."

"That's one hell of a gamble!" I exclaimed.

"Then you'll have to be discreet," Liz shrugged, crossing her arms and shrugging matter-of-factly.

"You always know how to cheer me up," I groaned sarcastically.

She regarded me from behind her glasses.

"Well, you could always just join up with them," she suggested in a snarky tone.

I let out a sharp laugh.

"Vive la revolution."

"They've been wanted for years and haven't been arrested," she reminded me. "They're obviously doing something right."

My mind pictured that shithole of a bunker I found Simon in.

"I think I'll pass," I scoffed, dreading the thought of having to live like that.

She threw her arms out in abandonment.

"Look, if it wasn't for Cymurai's threats you could've uploaded your memories to *YouTube,* and you'd be cleared of the charges," she explained exhaustedly. "But we've gotta make the best of the situation."

I snarled viciously. I'd grown more and more resentful of him. He'd been an inspiration to me. He'd saved me. Twice. And then turned around and threw me to the wolves. Telling me it was all for the greater good.

Never meet your heroes.

"They may deny it, but they *do* need you," Liz reassured me. "You're probably the only chance they'll get to find out what was in the Project Selection files. The guy who hacked you obviously already knows more about it than they do."

I gave out a harsh breath. Giving in to the situation.

"Oh, fuck it," I growled, clanging my first on the pipe. "Let's get this over with."

<<Initialising SoulChat>>

<<Loading GUI>>

<<Installing new plug-in>>

<<Plug-in installed>>

<<Add new contact: D32t1ny@21r1tf0rm.com>>

<<Destiny has been added to contacts>>

<<Note: This contact can only be called through secure conferencing environments>>

<<Environment selected: Default secure conferencing environment>>

<<Selecting contact: Destiny>>

<<You may be about to enter a full-immersion virtual reality simulation.>>

<<Please be seated and ensure your surroundings are appropriate.>>

<<Send request for an anonymous virtual conferencing session: Yes/No>>

I made myself as comfortable as I could, in this soaking, cramped pipe. I rested my head, slowed my breathing and shut my eyes, the command window graphics still blazing in my mind's eye. I flexed my jaw ambivalently, working myself up to give the command, while desperately trying to think of someone else who could help me. Someone else who owed me a favour. David was the obvious choice, but I'd already called that favour in… even if he did owe me one, it was a long shot to believing he *could* or would do it.

I couldn't think of anyone else… and was kicking myself for it.

"God damn it…" I breathed defeatedly and gave the command.

<<Calling Destiny>>

I waited with bated breath as the program rang in my head. With each passing tone, I grew tense, the prospect that all this planning could've been thwarted with a simple missed call.

Come on, Destiny, answer the damn phone!

The seconds passed… the ringing continued…

Come on, come on!

More ringing…

Fuck!

I was about to give up when…

<<Call accepted>>

My heart fluttered with relief, throwing my back my head and breathing easier.

Now comes the hard part…

<<Initialising simulation>>

<<Loading environment>>

<<Running neural lace device drivers>>

<<Processing consciousness shift>>

Spiritform's secure conferencing environment took form out of the darkness in my mind. The sound of pulsing data flowed around me. The night began to glitter with the bright deep blue of the Opensource soul. Before I knew it, I was surrounded by the virtual hollow orb, my avatar's feet standing upon a free disk of neon light, one of the thousands floating within this space.

<<Loading complete>>

<<Consciousness shift complete>>

<<Welcome!>>

<<User logging in: Destiny>>

I shifted anxiously on the spot, watching as her avatar rezzed into view across the disk from me. The outline of another wireframe skeleton grew like a tree out of the digital grid with the strange sound of virtual morphing.

Here she comes…

My mouth went dry as the surface texture appeared out of a cloud of pixels in the pixelated fog. The avatar had been altered to mask her appearance, her hair a blazing crimson, a giant mole on her cheek, a slight change in the nose and jaw, and a large nose ring. But it was her alright.

Destiny.

I hadn't bothered hiding my face. When the log-on completed, she recognised me instantly.

Her jaw dropped. We stood in silence while she stared at me in bewilderment. I scratched the back of my neck feeling like I'd just been caught with my hand in the cookie jar.

"Um… Hey, Denise…" I began timidly. "Long time no…"

My words set her off. Her eyes blazed with murderous intent.

"YOU!" she yelled wildly.

My hands sprang up defensively into the surrender position, gawking in fear.

"Look, I know how it looks," I pleaded. "But I…"

She didn't have the slightest bit of interest in what I had to say. She aggressively hunched herself forward, holding her arms in a boxing stance, clenching her fingers like the razor-sharp claws of a lion. Lines of the graphics of fiery red code appeared, floating around her wrist like a bracelet, cracking with crimson bolts of static electricity; arming herself with a series of ICE Breakers and viruses.

Oh shit…

She yelled a blood-curdling war-cry and threw her arm out like she was hurling a rock. A line of blazing red attack code shot out from her palm like a bullet from a gun. The software slammed into my chest; sparks of red lightning surged from the impact point. I yelled while the pain stung through my body.

<<WARNING!>>

<<WARNING!>>

<<UNAUTHORISED ACCESS TO PERSONAL AREA NETWORK DETECTED!>>

<< NEURAL LACE DRIVERS HAVE BEEN COMPROMISED!>>

Not again!

The force of the virus threw me clear off the cyberspace grid. I was in the grip of an invisible telekinetic force, dangling me by the arms and legs in a crucifix position.

I groaned in agony while the pressure setting around my avatar rapidly dialled up like I was being asphyxiated by an enormous snake. I panicked, gasping for digital oxygen, my face burning red. Liz had assured me she'd checked the Spiritform whistle-blower code for back-doors that could be exploited. Not that it mattered right now!

Fuck this, I'm getting out of here!

<<Logging out>>

<<Terminating virtual environment>>

…

<<Error 1038: Unable to complete subroutine>>

<<Please terminate conflicting program>>

Oh no. No, no, no!

I was trapped here!

She wasn't going to kill me… but she could generate whatever sensations she wanted. She could max out the pain to just below the threshold for me to pass out… and make it last *indefinitely*.

And it was already excruciating…

"Denise…" I gasped desperately. "Please…"

"Fuck you, Arthur!" she spat back in rage. "I know what you did! You *murdered* him! Why? Just so you could hack his brain, and have this little reunion?"

"I didn't… I swear!" I pleaded.

"Shut it!" she retorted hurtfully. "You're either a hitman or a serial killer, but I'm out of shits to give! I don't know what the fuck you came here for, but I swear you're gonna regret it!"

She tightened her clawed fingers, the pressure increased with the gesture, like she was crushing me in her own hand. A wolfish grin crept across her face…

Fuck me, she's enjoying this!

The reading on my HUD said the simulated pressure was now comparable to a pair of trucks ramming each other together bumper to bumper. I screamed with bloodcurdling agony, writhing like an ant burning under a magnifying glass. My voice rang into virtual infinity, my eyes blood-red with tears.

"PLEASE!" I pleaded frantically. "I DIDN'T DO IT! I DIDN'T DO IT!"

"You're going to have to do better than that!" she retorted unsympathetically, her eyes narrowing. "Your face is all over the news! Your DNA was found at the scene!"

"My fucking brain was hacked!" I protested. "Someone made me do it, I swear!"

Her fingers held in place, studying me reservedly…

She's scanning my brain pattern…

Her expression changed, her mistrust softening, taken aback as her AI advised her to the possibility that I might've been telling the truth.

After a tense moment, she cautiously began drawing back her nails. The pressure softened, and I rapidly drew in a breath of relief. I was left levitating hanging there; panting and grimacing. "Thanks…" I managed to say.

"You're not out the woods yet," she glowered at me threateningly. "You're saying you weren't hired to take Simon out?"

I frantically shook my head.

"My orders were to investigate Spiritform…" I breathed. "Destroy your copies of the Project Selection files… but when I found your friend… a virus took control of my neural lace. I tried to stop it but…"

My voice trailed off… trembling as I swallowed. She wasn't impressed.

"Heard that one before," she snarled back. "A murderer with brain implants, claiming a glitch made him do it. At least come up with something original, Arthur!"

"It's the fucking truth!" I cried, yanking myself forward in the air.

She paused, pursing her lips, interrogating me with her eyes.

"Why'd you contact me then?" she barked intrusively. "Thought we would take you in? Give you refuge? Welcome you to our merry band of outlaws?"

"Denise…"

"Damn, that's funny!" she chuckled hysterically, her eyes manic. "You could make a meme out of that shit!"

I need to appeal to her self-righteousness…

"You need me, damn it!" I yelled bitterly.

She sniffed.

"How'd you figure that?"

I paused to catch my breath, composing myself.

"You still want to expose Virtualife?" I asked determinedly.

She regarded me stiffly.

"If you do, the hacker who attacked me clearly knows more about the files than any of us do. The metadata from the attack on my neural lace is now the only lead you have to find him."

She scoffed.

"Assuming you're telling the truth," she answered guardedly.

I rolled my eyes, realising I was going to have to do it after all.

"Fine!"

<<Forwarding files>>

My memories of the last few hours (up until the protected conversation with Liz), had been transferred to Denise. She tried to hide her surprise but not very well. Her eyes flickered suspiciously, no doubt running anti-virus checks. It would've come back clear, and the reality of what she had asked for had begun bearing down on her, realising what she was about to witness.

Be careful what you wish for.

She tried to hide her nervous gulp, hesitating before she clicked.

"When you're ready?" I called impatiently, eager to get free.

Her expression stiffened at me again.

"Don't push your luck," she glowered at me.

I watched her eyes simmer, working up the courage to run the program. The process only lasted a few seconds, her avatar distorting into pixelated static while she assimilated the data; the images and sensations blasting into her mind, her neural cortex going into overload.

When it finished, she was left trembling with dizziness, clutching her avatar's head, panting. Despite everything, I couldn't help but sympathise. Once the nausea had passed, she looked up at me with blurry eyes. She composed herself again quickly and adjusted the settings on her avatar to hide the tears.

"Uh well…" she spoke after composing herself once more. "That was convincing…"

"Welcome to my world," I replied darkly. I gestured with my chin to the force holding me up by the arms. "So now that we're on the same page, can you stop with the virus please?"

She leaned back, folding her arms dubiously.

"How do I know I can trust you?" she asked eventually, her fiery locked in a piercing gaze.

I pursed my lips, debating how I was going to answer.

"You don't have to," I replied flatly, speaking the words resentfully. "You're clearly a better hacker than me."

She gave a single, victorious laugh, like rubbing salt into a wound.

"You don't need my trust when you can just keep tabs on my brain patterns," I continued.

She regarded me once more, surprised by my bluntness. I'd made my point. The real clincher was appealing to her vengeful side. A chance to get back at her friend's killer would be hard for her to resist… but she wasn't one to surrender an advantage either.

I was powerless in her hands, and she didn't want to give up that control.

"Well?" I asked carefully, looking self-confident. "Do we have a deal?"

Her mouth became a statuesque tight line.

"That's not up to me," she shrugged. "As much as I would like my… colleagues to believe it, I'm not Spiritform's leader. Officially we don't have any."

My mouth tightened.

"Okay… so who decides?" I asked.

She smirked, gesturing out to the side with both arms.

"They do," she replied flatly, pointing to the walls of the sphere.

I glanced at the glittering object, the surface comprised of thousands upon thousands of large coloured pixels, pulsing with the colours of the spectrum.

"You're going to have a vote?" I scoffed. "I came to you in secret, Destiny! What if…"

"What if one of our members is a spy?" she sighed dismissively, her eyes flickering rapidly while her attention turned to her HUD. "Relax, it's not that kind of a vote. Say hello to our classified-referendum system."

With a flick of the wrist, she sent the telepathic command… the surface of the sphere changed. Pulses of light appeared on the inside of the orb at large regular intervals, starting as little more than candlelight… seconds later they exploded, sending out massive shockwaves like tidal surges. Within seconds, the calm surface became torrential; great waves crashing along like a worldwide storm; the soft hum of data traffic turning into a screeching cacophony, cringing painfully at the sound.

"The hell are you doing?" I cried, my voice yelling over the virtual hurricane.

"I've uploaded an encrypted report of everything you've told me to the block-chain, including the memory uploads," she explained. "The data is being processed by the personal AI of every Spiritform member currently online. The *AIs* will vote, calculating how their users would, based on an analysis of their user's preferences, and then self-delete all data about what they have voted on."

I tensed… it was an intriguing concept, but I was still going to be judged by an approximation of a group of internet thugs.

"Not exactly democratic," I muttered.

"True democracy requires openness," she answered flatly. "A luxury we can't always afford. This is the best we can do."

I flexed my neck, pursing my lips, breathing deeply.

"Well… at least you guys practice what you preach," I admitted tensely.

"I ain't no saint." She nodded curtly, folding her arms. "Here we go."

A floating data window appeared, hovering above the centre of the disk.

<<Classified-referendum vote in progress>>

<<Question: Grant Arthur Wells asylum among Spiritform?>>

<<Yes: 0%>>

<<No: 0%>>

My avatar's mouth went dry…

"The AIs are receiving and processing the data now. Good luck," Denise spoke with a sarcastic nudge.

"Cheers," I replied, equally sarcastically.

It didn't take long for the votes to come trickling in with computerised efficiency. The most gut-wrenching minute of my life passed as the dials of both results began rapidly upwards. It was a race for sure, both sides edging back and forth to get the lead. My heart fluttering with optimism one second, and with terrible fear the next. Denise's face remained furtively neutral, probably glad to have the decision out of her hands.

Time passed… the results came in.

<Voting complete>>

<<<Yes: 64%>>

<<No: 36%>>

My heart practically gave out. My muscles went weak, ready to collapse in a crumpled heap, held only by the invisible grip of the virus.

Thank fuck…

The turbulence on the surface of the sphere died down, the roaring data pulse with it, the points of light receding out of existence. I turned to Destiny with watery eyes, staring back at me with frustrated relief.

"You always did know how to give a pitch," she shrugged.

The virus code around her wrists faded away, and the sparks of virtual static binding my body sank with it. The virtual gravity took hold once more, leaving me to collapse on my avatar's knees against the neon disk. I gasped for air, rubbing my bearded neck.

"Thanks…" I groaned, finding my feet.

"I don't want your thanks," she retorted abruptly, shaking her head venomously. "You still wouldn't have been there if you hadn't been working for Virtualife in the first place. My friend would still be alive if it wasn't for you."

I cringed.

She has me there…

"Yeah…" I said, awkwardly rubbing my neck. "Sorry…"

She threw a deadly glare at me.

"But uh…" I continued anxiously. "If you could get me out of the open soon…I'd be well grateful. I do have every Police precinct in London on my ass."

"Hmm…" She nodded guardedly, holding out her palm to project a map of the city. "No promises on that count. This is gonna be tricky. Where are you anyway?"

I blushed with embarrassment, explaining my situation.

"Lovely," she said, wrinkling a disgusted nose. She marked my position on the map, the pulsing icon hovering over South Acton.

"Anyway, you're pretty far away," she said thoughtfully, playing with her nose piercing, mulling over the options with her AI. "It will probably take you just over three and half hours on foot… you'll have to stay underground of course."

"Great…" I growled sarcastically. "I've always wanted to go on a hike through tunnels of shit."

"Beggars can't be choosers," she quipped back.

I grumbled… still getting used to the concept of being the beggar.

"So, are you gonna forward me the coordinates of your safe house or…"

"Oh, yeah sure," she scoffed. "I give you the location, you get hacked again, and they have the roadmap to our doorstep."

I swallowed my pride before speaking.

"What *do* you wanna do then?"

She sighed, throwing out her arms in abandonment.

"I'll have to come get you," she gave in.

"Really?" I replied, with a surprised eyebrow. "That's uh…"

"Not that I *appreciate* going out my way for you," she snapped back sternly, storming forcefully over to me, and ramming an accusing finger in my chest, hard enough to make me lean back. "And by the way, even if we catch the guy who killed Simon; don't think for a second that'll make us even."

I composed myself as professionally as I could.

"Well…" I shrugged. "I suppose that's the best I could've asked for."

She gave a single commanding nod.

"You need to get moving. Now."

I nodded darkly.

"See you soon…" I added guardedly.

<<Logging out>>

<<Terminating FIVR simulation>>

<<Disengaging neural lace>>

<<Disconnecting from server>>

The lights of the OpenSource Soul receded out of my mind's eye. The real world rushed in to fill the gaps. Once more I felt my ass in the freezing cold of the water flowing out of the dark, dingy pipe I was hunched inside, opening my eyes to the dark plastic outlet.

"You better be right about this, Liz…" I breathed, rubbing my eyes with my metal hands, wondering if I'd made a mistake.

She gave me a coy smile across my HUD.

"When have you ever known me…" she began, but the telepathic glare I threw her was enough to stop her mid-sentence.

She highlighted my path in red on my HUD's mini-map and a waypoint arrow with it. The marker was pointing inwards… leading me into the sewer. She assured me the pipe opened into a much more extensive underground tunnel with a walkway… but that didn't stop my stomach from clenching in disgust.

I awkwardly pivoted myself around in the pipe, trying to turn myself to head into the darkness. I crouched there on my hands and knees, the brown stench trickling past me. As I stared into the cavernous entrance in front of me… aside from the graphical waypoint, I was staring into a black abyss… like the uncertainty of my future.

I was about to crawl through a river of shit… and I *wasn't* gonna come out smelling of roses.

"Definitely rock bottom," I muttered again.

"Still beats the Prison Matrix," Liz shrugged at me.

I swallowed my pride, and began my crawl, listening to the hideous swashing around me.

"Let me get back to you on that one," I added bitterly.

I painfully shuffled my way through… into the depths of the underground.

Gonna be worth it…

Definitely gonna be worth it…

Totally worth it…

CHAPTER 21

Mother Mind profile 3551-7821-0862-2143:

- First name: Kenji
- Surname: Awasaki
- Status: Living
- Nationality: British/Japanese Citizen
- Occupation(s):
    - Chief Executive Officer
        - Status: Employed
        - Organisation: Virtualife Corporation
- Known aliases:
    - Sector
    - <<Classified: Cymurai>>
- Live surveillance:
    - Status: *Partially available*
    - Date: 08/10/2045
    - Current location: Virtualife building, Docklands, East London
    - Local Time: 02:06 GMT

<<Remote avatar session in progress>>

<<Neural interface stable>>

I was logged into a Cymurai avatar, the sharp wind whistling in the audio sensors. The hulking steel body was squatting in the mud, hiding behind a small, grassy mound underneath the mass of the A40 flyover, looking out across an estuary of the River Brent. A grimy sewer pipe sat lodged in the bank on the far side, spewing out its contents with a disgusting splash. I watched Arthur Wells, crawling inside like a rodent.

"I already deactivated the tracking device you placed on him," Gabrielle informed me on my HUD. "It's already detached itself from his body. Spiritform won't know you were here."

I gave a single electronic grunt in return.

So far so good… Sort of…

The truth was, I'd really shot myself in the foot this time. Gabrielle only detected the Enigma hacker's activity at 23:32. A good six hours after the fact. This time he'd hacked a wall screen in Piccadilly Circus to deliver his 'digital dead-drop' to Jack-21. Again, we used CCTV recordings from that time to intercept the message. The message was only on screen for thirty seconds but was concise and effective. It included Arthur's e-mail to Gabrielle, explaining his plan to raid the Spiritform hideout in Southall, including its location… as well as details on a pre-installed back-door on his neural lace.

Whoever this guy is… he's been planning this for a long time. Laying the trap for me…

Once more… all I could do was watch the disaster unfolding in front of me. I needed to get a handle on this; and fast.

"It was the right move," Gab said, trying to console me. "Letting Arthur take the fall was the only way."

"It was the tactical move," I interjected, not looking up from my hand. "Not the *right* one."

He may not have been the poster boy for good police work… but he was still suffering for *my* mistakes. That was something I couldn't just accept.

Our interception of Arthur's VR chat had given us some hope. Gab's psychological projections had been right; he was turning to Spiritform for help. Denise Masika had avoided arrest for years… if anyone could hide him, it was them.

"I'm monitoring the situation carefully," Gab reassured me. "We can use this to our advantage. I'm using my press-blackout protocols. No one will know that he worked for us. For now… we just need to let this play out."

"That doesn't change that we're throwing him to the wolves," I growled bitterly.

"Like it or not we're going to have to cease monitoring him for now," Gab explained. "We can't take the risk of this... Enigma hacker discovering him again."

I bitterly agreed... but that didn't change the morality.

Fifteen years of Mother Mind. Of me being able to monitor almost every civilian action in the world. But I had no control over this... that's what was getting to me the most. As Cymurai, I could fight Jack-21... as Kenji, I should've been able to fight Enigma.

But right now, both of us were helpless.

As helpless as I had been... on that day.

I felt my face twinge in the real world, the faceplate of the avatar remaining as stone. I rubbed the avatar's face sensors instinctively, trying to clear my mind. Gab's pursed lips rolled timidly, her eyes large and sorrowful, watching me with sympathy.

"I... I'm sorry if I let you down in anyway," she apologised gingerly, her avatar's eyes looking down at her feet from across my HUD.

"No... I'm the one who should be apologising," I replied, shaking the avatar's head with a whir. "I shouldn't have yelled at you earlier."

"Kenji, I..."

"This is my responsibility," I told her flatly. "No one else's."

I looked at the lights down the path Arthur had taken.

"I... I will find a way to make this right," I muttered.

Gab smiled at me gingerly.

"You can't save the world by yourself, Kenji," she said hopefully.

I let out an exhausted mental sigh.

But in my moment of doubt... my father's words echoed to me.

A man finishes what he starts, Kenji. That's all there is to it.

That one simple sentence told me everything there was to know. There was no turning back. The only way was forward.

The shadow returned... I welcomed it. Embraced it.

I belonged to it.

"Land the Amaterasu," I ordered.

"Roger. Amaterasu is en route," Gab replied tiredly, placing the flight path on my HUD.

I turned to walk away towards the rendezvous point, the mud squelching beneath the avatar's feet.

This isn't the end… only the beginning…

But I ***will*** *see it through…*

EPILOGUE

Mother Mind profile 7183-2647-8246-3892:

First name: Denise

Surname: Masika

Status: Wanted for criminal offences

Nationality: British citizen

Occupation(s):

- Suspected member of *Spiritform* hacker group

Criminal record:

- Arrested: 17/11/2037
    - Offence: Suspected of unauthorised access to computer material
    - No formal charges

Known aliases:

- Destiny

Live surveillance:

- Status: *Unavailable*
- Date: 08/10/2045
- Current location: Unknown
- Local Time: 04:19 GMT

"It was the will of the group, Destiny," Poe's avatar shrugged at me from on the HUD of the sensor visor I was wearing, feeling the weight of the goggles at the end of my nose. His cat eyes were large and sympathetic. "It would be a bit hypocritical for you to go against that at this point."

"Uh-huh," I sighed, unconvinced, folding my arms and slumping against the moss-covered brickwork behind me, squashing my rucksack lightly.

I was stood underneath the rusted remains of an old fire escape, wearing the silver overalls of an optical camouflage suit; my hair protected by the hood of the suit from the drips of water dripping off the underside of the iron staircase. Unfortunately, the face mask of the suit was doing nothing to protect me from the stench of urine assaulting my senses.

I'd been waiting here for thirty minutes, looking out across a vast cargo unloading area, behind an abandoned shopping centre in Clapham, just over three kilometres away from our safe house. The area was enclosed by walls, like a graffiti-splattered fortress. The only entrance was a large iron gate leading to the main road outside; which had been boarded up with abandoned signs, but I could still hear the hum of traffic outside… making me nervous whenever I saw the blue flash of sirens roll by. A road extended out from the gate, leading towards three large garages built into the shopping centre, their portcullis gates shut forever, waiting to be demolished.

A manhole cover had been built into the tarmac beside the curb of the pavement around the parking area. A graphical waypoint was hovering over it on my HUD, marking out the GPS coordinates I had forwarded Arthur for our rendezvous point.

I'd deactivated the cloak to conserve power… but I kept my telepathic cursor over the 'activate' command in nervous anticipation of a police drone whizzing overhead. I still couldn't believe I was doing this. The argument I'd had with the others was still ringing in my ears. Raj and Kasira had bombarded me with a thousand questions about Simon's death, while Jamie had started screaming at me that I was crazy for trusting Arthur. We'd gone back and forth like that for nearly twenty minutes. In the end, I had to hack into his neural lace and induce alpha waves to chill him out.

The thing was… I couldn't say he was *wrong*. The AIs had had their say, but saying I was dubious was an understatement. The thought of letting Arthur into our safe house made my skin crawl. We may have needed his help… but I didn't have to *like* it.

And here I was… waiting for the man who killed my friend.

Sort of…

The ambiguity was killing me… like an insect burrowing itself into the back of my mind. But the thought of finding the one who *really* killed Simon… that *had* to outweigh everything else.

I shut my eyes tight… as the images from Arthur's memory transfer burned in my mind once more. His cold, bloodied face, staring emptily at the ceiling forever… while his body was sliced open. I shuddered, feeling like my heart had been plunged into cold water.

Someone was going to pay…

Through the metamaterial fabric of the cloaking suit, I rubbed my knuckled hand with my thumb… the other hand firmly gripped the silenced sub-machine pistol holstered inside a pocket of the overalls.

My vengeful wallowing was interrupted by a loud, metallic clanging making me jump to attention. I spun my head around, and sure enough, saw the manhole cover rotating its way open.

He's coming…

The thought of it left a bad taste in my mouth. Even still; he was going to know who was in charge.

I pulled out my weapon from the pouch in the overalls, pointing out with the long, thick barrel.

<<Activating optical camouflage>>

I supported the weight of the weapon with both hands, locking my arms to the front, and watched my hands disappearing; their physical appearance melting through the digital distortions, and then out of sight altogether; the outline of my body highlighted in green graphics by the thick visor which had also disappeared.

Showtime.

The weapon was still visible, appearing to be floating by some ghostly force. I covered it up as best I could, and I crept out from underneath the fire escape… tiptoeing towards the manhole cover and hovering like a spectre in front of it, while the lid slid out of place and was rested by the side of the road, releasing a waft of a putrid stench that wrinkled my nose in shock.

The circular hole into the ground now revealed Arthur, standing on the top rung of a ladder, his metal palm held out towards the sky.

"Oh, thank fuck..." he muttered, with an audibly loud sigh of relief, echoing down into the abyss.

I felt my mouth curling upwards, in eager anticipation of my little plan. He clambered exhaustedly out onto the road... his nanofabric clothes bone dry but his hair and skin soaking... and reeking of the same smell of the sewer.

He was kneeling down on the tarmac, ready to grab the manhole cover and slide it back into place... when I cocked my gun, making it visible once more... and pressed it into the back of his neck. He twinged on the spot and froze.

"Don't move," I told him coldly.

He did as he was told, remaining frozen in his crouch position.

I waited a second...letting the tension rest in the air. Arthur's slow, relatively calm breath sent out jets of steam into the cold air. No doubt he was processing his options, but his VPA would've calculated that I was carrying armour-piercing rounds, and no matter how what crazy ninja-cyborg crap he pulled, I couldn't miss at point-blank.

I ordered him to toss his gun. He reluctantly pulled the weapon from the holster built into his leg and did as he was told, landing with a soft clatter.

"You're really not as good as you think you are," I told him in a quiet, threatening manner, taking a few steps back to keep out of grabbing range, but keeping my aim squarely in place. "Hands up. Turnabout slowly."

He precariously did as he was told... the lids around his darkened bionic eyes widened, not expecting to see the gun floating there.

"You're the one who wanted to find me," I added, and gave the neurocommand to deactivate the cloak. The illusion began to end, the silver fabric of the overalls returning to visibility. I released one hand from my combat stance to pull away my face mask and my visor, letting the gush of fresh air wash against my face...

"You got your wish," I finished, narrowing my eyes at him.

He gulped, looking lost for words.

"Hi Destiny..." he spoke, at last, still calm but shifting awkwardly, figuring I was probably joking but wasn't entirely certain.

"Shut up," I growled back, jerking the barrel at his face.

He instinctively raised his hands higher at the sight of my rabid expression, giving him the impression, I'd lured him into a trap.

"You have no idea how tempting it is to pull this trigger," I hissed at him, my hand trembling with theatrical restraint.

He swallowed… The grip on my weapon tightened; I rolled my jaw pensively with the resistance it was taking not to pull the trigger. The eyes behind my contact lenses simmering like the craters of active volcanoes, leaving him sweating on the spot while I pretended to make up my mind.

After a few tense seconds, I let out a false breath of abandonment, lowering the weapon and holstering it.

"You're one lucky son of a bitch," I told him grudgingly.

"If you say so," he breathed, looking miffed that I had been joking with him, but still wiped the sweat from his brow with relief.

"And you stink by the way," I complained, wrinkling my nose up at him.

He scoffed in exasperation with some regained confidence as he went to collect his gun.

"Were you seen by anything?" I checked sharply.

He shook his head slowly.

"My VPA hacked the security cameras in the sewers," he explained. "I had a little run-in with the mole-people, but they didn't seem to take notice."

"Good," I nodded bluntly, cringing as I wafted away Arthur's stench. "Well… we better get you back to a shower before I suffocate."

I began removing the straps of the cloaked rucksack from around my shoulders.

"Here," I added bluntly, dumping it at his feet.

He knelt and opened it up. For a moment, I saw a glint of child-like delight lighting up his face as he pulled out a second camouflage suit from inside, the sensor visor resting at the bottom of the bag.

"I've always wanted one of these." he grinned, holding it up by the shoulders to admire it.

"Happy fucking birthday," I grumbled at him, telepathically forwarding the device driver for him to install.

He began pulling the suit on over his clothes, slipping his legs into the slipper-like footing at the bottom of the overalls. He pulled the suit up over his waist and sleeved up the arms.

"Don't think this makes you one of us," I blurted out when he was halfway done, thrusting an accusing finger towards his chest. "I expect you to be on your way when we've found a way to clear your name."

He stiffened uncomfortably.

"Works for me," he answered professionally, knowing he was holding back his disdain for taking orders.

He reached into the bag, and removed the visor, pulling the straps onto his head and sliding it over his eyes, before pulling up the hood and tightening the face mask.

It wasn't long before he gave the telepathic command to activate the illusion and was soon disappearing out of view. His own graphical outline appeared on my HUD, and I watched him waving his hands in front of him, apparently amused by his invisibility.

"If you're done?" I snapped angrily over the telepathic comm-link, having already cloaked myself.

I nudged my way to a door leading into the condemned shopping centre, the blue paint peeling off. I had the way through the ruins committed to memory.

"Come on," I ordered him again, turning to march quick step into the darkness.

"Yes *sir*," he replied sarcastically.

We slipped inside, staring into the dark, dingy backrooms of the shopping centre, creeping through concrete corridors.

After a moment of silence…

"Denise…" he spoke, in almost a timid tone.

"Mmm?" I grunted again.

He paused.

"Believe it or not… it is good to see you again," he admitted.

We stopped on the spot. I turned around, regarding him strangely, raising an eyebrow behind my visor, bewildered by his statement.

"I'll… let you know when the feeling is mutual," I answered coldly, as we strode away into the night.

TO BE CONTINUED…

Printed in Poland
by Amazon Fulfillment
Poland Sp. z o.o., Wrocław